NAAMAH'S KISS

JACQUELINE CAREY

GRAND CENTRAL
PUBLISHING

NEW YORK   BOSTON

Grand Central Publishing
Hachette Book Group
237 Park Avenue
New York, NY 10017

Visit our Web site at www.HachetteBookGroup.com.

Printed in the United States of America

First Edition: June 2009
10 9 8 7 6 5 4 3 2 1

Grand Central Publishing is a division of Hachette Book Group, Inc.
The Grand Central Publishing name and logo is a trademark of Hachette Book Group, Inc.

Library of Congress Cataloging-in-Publication Data

Carey, Jacqueline, 1964–
Naamah's kiss / Jacqueline Carey.—1st ed.
    p. cm.
    Summary: "After Moirin undergoes the rites of adulthood, she finds divine acceptance . . . on the condition that she fulfill an unknown destiny that lies somewhere beyond the ocean"—Provided by publisher.
    ISBN 978-0-446-19803-5
    I. Title.
    PS3603.A74N33 2009
    813'.6—dc22
                    2008053255

Book design by Charles Sutherland

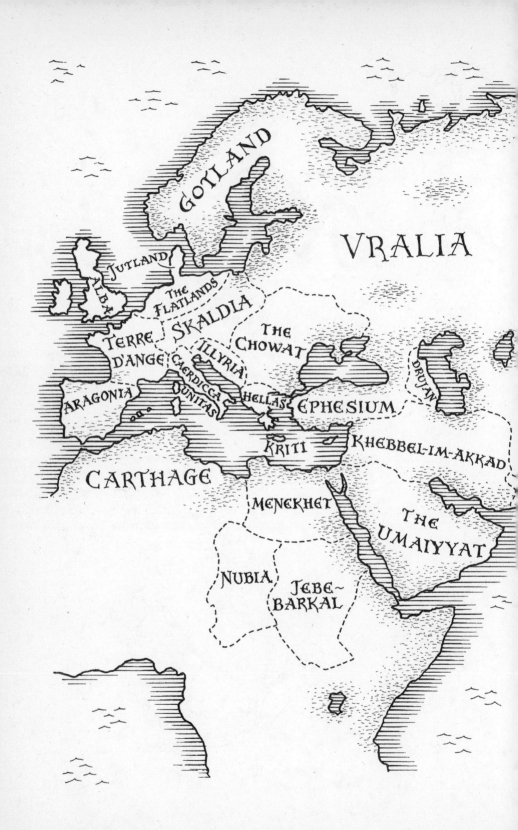

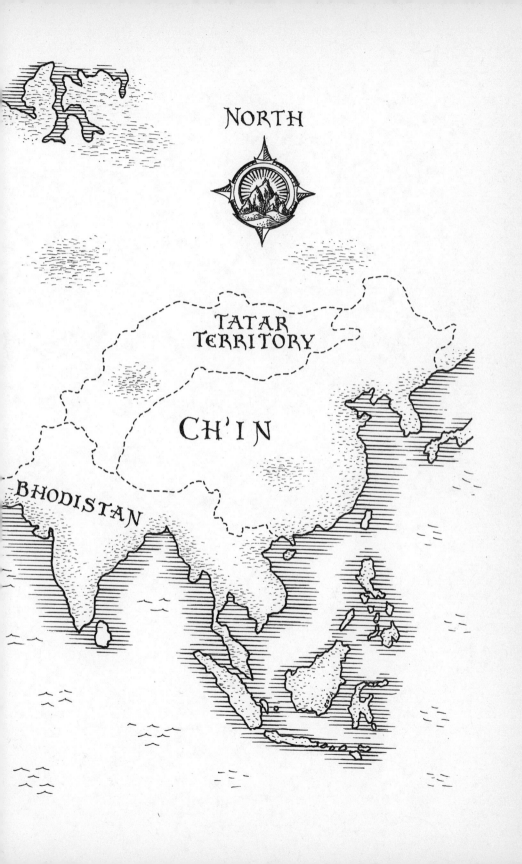

ONE

I was born to the Maghuin Dhonn.

We are the folk of the Brown Bear and the oldest magic in Alba runs in our veins. Once, there were great magicians among us—men and women capable of seeing all the skeins of the future unwind in the great stone circles, capable of taking on the shape of the Maghuin Dhonn Herself.

No more.

It changed long before I was born, when a prince of Terre d'Ange wed a princess of the Cullach Gorrym, the folk of the Black Boar. The greatest magicians among us saw the seeds of our destruction in that union. They acted to avert it; and in the end, they succeeded.

But they did not act wisely, and there was a cost. The Maghuin Dhonn, already viewed with fear and suspicion, were despised in Alba for many long years thereafter. Our great magics deserted us. We turned instead to the small magic of concealment, learning to shroud ourselves and our places in twilight.

It is a simple enough trick. My mother taught it to me when I was some five years of age.

"Close your eyes and think of the time between night and day, Moirin," she said to me. "When the sun's last rays have sunk beyond the horizon, but darkness has not yet fallen. The stars are pale in the sky and the trees are dim around you."

I obeyed.

"Breathe it deep into your chest and hold it," her voice continued. "Then blow it out softly and let it settle around you like a cloak."

I exhaled softly.

"Ha!" My mother's voice was startled and pleased.

I opened my eyes. A glimpse of gentle twilight fled, replaced by bright, hearty sunlight. It made me squint. "I did it?"

"You did. I saw the air sparkle about you. You would have been concealed from any gaze not already upon you." She dropped to her knees and hugged me. "I wasn't sure."

"Why?"

My mother hesitated and stroked my hair. It was as straight and black as her own, but much finer. "You know that our bloodline is not entirely pure?"

I nodded. "We are kin to the kings and queens of Alba and Terre d'Ange, and the lord of the Dalriada, too."

"Like it or not, aye." She smiled wryly. "So. The gifts of the Maghuin Dhonn are not always given to each of us. I'm glad She has chosen you, little one."

I smiled back at her. "So am I. It would be a terrible thing if She didn't, wouldn't it?"

"So it would."

It was some nights afterward that Oengus came for the first time—or at least the first time I remembered. It was his scent that awoke me, a hard, clean scent like fresh-chipped granite and pine, with a musky undertone. Lying in my snug nest of blankets in our cozy cave, I opened my eyes to see my mother rise and go to greet the shadowy figure beyond the threshold.

"Well?" a deep voice asked.

"Moirin can summon the twilight." My mother's voice was tranquil.

"Does she show signs of other gifts?"

"No." There was a faint rustle as she shook her head.

"Have you told her?"

"No!" Her voice sharpened. "She's a child, Oengus. A child of the Maghuin Dhonn. Let her be one for as long as she may. Forever, mayhap. I would be content if nothing more came of it."

"Peace, Fainche." His tone was soothing. "It is just that there are those of us who wonder if She had not some greater purpose, calling you to a stranger." And then his tone changed, teasing. "Or so you claim. Mayhap it was his milky-white skin and green, green eyes that drew you?"

"Hush!" my mother said, but she was laughing.

"Come into the night with me." His voice dropped another octave. "I am here, and you have been too long without the company of men."

"Hush," she said again; but it was different this time. Amused, but different. Something stirred beneath her voice, a current of something dark and rich and heady. It called to something inside of me, something I didn't know how to name.

She glanced over her shoulder at me. I closed my eyes and feigned sleep. She went with him.

I was alone.

I wasn't scared. My mother had left me alone before, and I knew better than to mewl for her return. But I felt strange. There was a fluttering deep in my belly like a dove's wings beating. I called on my *diadh-anam*, the spirit-spark of the Great Bear Herself that dwells in all Her children.

Something else answered.

I had a sense of a lady's presence, bright and laughing. A sense of terrible beauty and piercing desire—though for what, I could not have said. A sense of lips pressed to my brow in a kiss. Words filtered through my thoughts, fond, gentle, and amused.

Not yet. Not for many years.

The fluttering feeling went away.

Comforted, I slept.

In the morning, Oengus was gone and the night's strangeness had passed. My mother was in good spirits. We ventured upstream to forage for arrowhead root, filling my mother's wicker basket to brimming. Splashing happily in the stream's marshy verges, I forgot all about the man in the night and the bright lady's presence. When we returned to our cave, there was an offering.

"Eggs!" my mother said with pleasure. She plucked one from the basket and passed it to me. "Look, Moirin. See how perfect it is."

I cradled it in my palms. It was warm from the sun, brown and faintly freckled. The shell was smooth. I touched the tip of my tongue to it. It tasted chalky and a little acrid. "From Lord Tiernan?"

"I daresay." She smiled. "He's a good man. He keeps to the old ways. We taught the Dalriada to survive in this land and they have never forgotten it. He remembers we are kin, too."

She set the arrowhead root to soak overnight and made a savory pie of eggs and greens that night. When I begged for the story of Lord Tiernan's coronation, she obliged me, tirelessly describing the splendid affair. It wasn't until I was falling asleep that I remembered last night's visitor and my strange vision. I resolved to ask my mother about it in the morning.

But when the morning dawned bright and fair, and my mother promised to teach me to catch trout with my bare hands, I forgot again and did not remember for a long time.

As I grew older, she taught me many things.

Most were simple skills. I grew adept at summoning the twilight—breathing it into me, blowing it softly around me. Thus concealed, I would lie motionless beneath the tendrils of the big willow along the stream, dangling one arm in the water and waiting for a speckled trout to swim into range. I could close my hand around it so gently it didn't even thrash, and lift it into the waiting creel.

I learned to gather greens like purslane, watercress, and dandelion, and roots like arrowhead, burdock, and cattail. I learned which mushrooms were poisonous and which were good to eat. I learned to boil acorns until the bitterness was gone and grind them into meal.

I learned to read weather signs and to track small game. My mother was skilled with a bow. When I was little, she hunted without me, but as I grew bigger and more adept in the ways of stealth and concealment, she took me with her. The first time I saw her kill, it was a hare.

It was a big hare, fat and lazy, crouching in a sunny glade. It began to startle as we emerged from the woods. My mother called the twilight around her, and I did the same. The bright sunlight faded around us, the world turning soft and silvery dim.

"*Hold*," she breathed.

The hare froze. I imagined I could feel its heart beating, a fast, inhuman flicker. Its round, dark eyes gleamed. It saw us, and it saw its death in us.

My mother loosed her bow.

The twang of it startled me out of the twilight. The sunlit world came crashing back. The shot hare leaped, ran a few paces, and fell over onto its side. I swallowed hard. It seemed a much graver thing than catching fish—and somewhat unfair, too.

"Did it . . . *obey* you?" I asked my mother.

She didn't answer right away, beckoning me to accompany her as she went to gather the hare. She laid my hand on its warm fur. I felt a faint movement as the last trace of life went out of it, then a loose stillness.

"In the twilight, we are closer to the world of spirit than flesh," she said soberly. "When we speak, their spirits hear. If their death is upon them, they obey."

"Oh," I whispered.

My mother's eyes were dark and somber. "It is a grave gift and one never to be used lightly. Only to sustain life. We give thanks to stone and sea and all that it encompasses for it, and to the Great Bear Herself. Do you ever use it for sport or any idle cause, it will be stripped from you. Do you understand?"

"I do."

The folk of the Maghuin Dhonn knew the cost of using gifts un-wisely. My mother taught me things beyond woodcraft, cookery, and survival.

She told me stories.

Stories of days gone by, stories of heroes and villains, of great ex-ploits and betrayals. There were stories from the oldest, oldest days when the world was covered with ice and our people left a distant land, following their *diadh-anam*, the guiding spirit of the Great Bear, to Alba. I listened and shivered with awe.

"Have you ever seen Her?" I asked.

She nodded. "Once."

"Where? When?"

She shook her head. "It is a mystery and I cannot speak of it until it is your time. But She is unlike any mortal bear."

There were other stories, too. The story of how the army of Tiberium conquered Alba, bringing stone roads and foreign sicknesses, driving us into the wilderness. How the mighty magician Donnchadh took on the shape of the Maghuin Dhonn Herself and suffered himself to be taken into captivity and tormented for sport, until he tore loose the ties that bound him and slew the Tiberian Governor. Afterward, the disparate folk of Alba united and drove the Tiberians from their soil.

And yet we were despised for it.

"Why?" I asked.

My mother gave me her wry smile. "The man who united the rest of Alba, Cinhil Ru of the Cullach Gorrym, lied. He said the Maghuin Dhonn had sacrificed their *diadh-anam* and gone mad. That the same fate would befall them all unless they set aside their petty quarrels and stood together. And so they did."

"Without us," I said.

"Without us," she agreed. "The world is not always fair, Moirin mine. And yet Alba has never been conquered since, and we are still here."

And then there were the tales of our heritage.

The summer that I was ten years old, my mother took me on a pilgrimage to visit a place made sacred by our history. It was the most exciting thing that had ever happened in my life. We were weeks travelling. She taught me to read the *taisgaidh* markers, the signs indicating the paths we travelled were held freely in trust for all of Alba. No one might bar another's passage nor offer violence on *taisgaidh* land.

Of course, we were prudent and concealed ourselves in twilight when others passed. Still, it gave me a thrill to see other people. My mother identified them for me in a low whisper, willing passersby not to hear her voice. If they heard aught, they glanced around and shrugged, concluding it was merely the wind.

The folk of the Cullach Gorrym looked most like us—slight and dark, with black hair and eyes. But there were others I'd heard about only in stories, the Tarbh Cró and Eidlach Òr and Fhalair Bàn, tall and fair-skinned, with hair that blazed like fire or gleamed like ripe wheat, startling blue, green, or grey eyes.

The first time I saw one, it stirred a memory.

Mayhap it was his milky-white skin and green, green eyes that drew you?

After they had passed and we had released the twilight, I looked at my mother with her warm brown skin. I stretched out my hands and studied them. I was used to thinking of us as almost one person. But my skin was a different hue than hers, honey-colored.

I'd never thought on it.

I closed my eyes and touched my lids. I wondered what color my eyes were. I didn't know.

It may seem strange, but what is obvious to an adult is not always obvious to a child. We led a solitary life. There was me, and there was my mother. Other people were murmurs in the darkness, baskets appearing on the hearth. Tales out of history, tales out of lore. Until I saw my first fair-skinned stranger, it never occurred to me that the tales stopped short.

I had no idea who my father was.

TWO

I kept the question to myself.

 I was a child, but I was old enough to reason. If my mother had not spoken of it, like as not she had cause. If she did not speak of it at Clunderry, I would wait until the moment was right.

Clunderry.

It was the place where things had gone awry and changed forever. It was the place where all had been redeemed.

We arrived in the early evening of Midsummer's Day. Although I know now that it was a simple country estate, the castle and the surrounding village seemed awesome to me. I caught my breath as we emerged from *taisgaidh* land into civilization.

I expected my mother to summon the twilight, but she didn't.

We passed the castle and walked onward. There were balefires burning on the outskirts of the fields. Crops were ripe. I breathed deep, smelling rich, fertile soil. Once again, something new stirred in me.

Roots . . .

Growth . . .

I closed my eyes. Behind my lids, I saw the figure of a man limned in brightness, his head bowed, cupping a seedling in his palm. He raised his head and smiled with infinite gentleness. The scent of apples filled the air.

"Moirin." My mother said my name, calling me back to myself.

I opened my eyes and shivered.

We were approaching the burial mound. A man strode toward us, one hand on the hilt of his sword. He was a warrior of the Cullach Gorrym in the old tradition, elaborate tattoos of blue woad whorling his cheeks and brow. More men waited behind him.

And beyond them, others. My people.

"Lady," the man said curtly. "State your name."

My mother lifted her head to meet his gaze. Sunlight slanted over her high, wide cheekbones. "Fainche," she said calmly. "Daughter of Eithne, daughter of Brianna, daughter of Alais."

He gave a brief bow. "Come in peace and be welcome."

I felt dizzy with the newness of it all. The burial mound loomed. It was a calm place, a tranquil place.

A place of death.

And today, the Maghuin Dhonn watched over it.

"Fainche." A man reached out his hand. "You came."

"I came," she agreed, taking his hand. "Moirin, this is Oengus."

He clapped my shoulder and smiled. The scent of musk and granite and pine surrounded me. "Well met, little one."

Others came then, gazing at me with dark, curious eyes. All of them bore the subtle stamp of the Maghuin Dhonn—a sense of wildness, untamed and dangerous. It should have been reassuring, but it wasn't. They regarded me as though I were *other*, and for the first time, I felt strange and alien to myself.

"Has she shown signs of great promise?" a woman whispered to my mother. My mother shrugged. "Ah." The other woman turned away, disappointed.

"Moirin!" A man with laughing eyes came forward, proffering a short bow sized for a child's draw and a quiver of neatly fletched arrows. "Well met, little niece. I made this for you." He kissed my mother on the cheek. "Greetings, sister. Do you prosper in your hermitage?"

"Aye." She smiled. "Moirin, this is your uncle, Mabon. He has a gift for working with wood."

I had an uncle?

"Thank you," I whispered, clutching the bow and quiver.

He tousled my hair. "Fine as silk." He lowered his voice. "Does she—?" My mother shook her head. "Ah." The same disappointment. "Well, then."

The sound of a harp arose, piercing and poignant and beautiful. I knew of harps only from my mother's tales, but even so, I could sense the mastery in the harpist's touch. He stood apart from everyone else, eyes closed.

"Mother?" I touched her arm. "What is it everyone expects me to be?"

"Hush." She rubbed my back with a soothing motion. "We will speak of it, but not now." She nodded at the burial mound. "Now is for honoring those who lie within and remembering that such a thing should never come to pass again."

I gazed at the green mound.

Our history lay buried there. A princess of the Cullach Gorrym, great with child—the half-D'Angeline child who would have grown to manhood and crushed the Maghuin Dhonn, hunting us down and destroying all our sacred places. And our last two great magicians, Morwen and Berlik, who had slain her and the child in her womb.

They had broken binding oaths to do it.

In the tales, they bore the mark of a magician—eyes as pale as moonlight, unheard of among our kind. My skin prickled, and I wondered again what color my own eyes were.

We stood for a long time while the harp gave voice to a wordless song of knowledge, power, and folly, and terrible sacrifice.

Morwen's folly had been the most grave and her sacrifice the most terrible. By the terms of the oath she broke, her spirit was condemned to wander for ten thousand years without solace.

Morwen . . . Moirin?

I shivered some more.

What a dire night it must have been. No wonder we were still feared in Alba. I was filled with a reverent horror at the choices Morwen and Berlik had made, and pity for the poor princess and the babe that bore the cost of them. Aye, and her husband, too. The D'Angeline prince. Morwen had died here that night, but Berlik had fled, north and ever north, mayhap seeking the land of our distant origin. The D'Angeline prince had tracked him to the snowy ends of the earth and brought back his head.

Dusk was falling.

One last note lingering in the air, then the harp fell silent. An entourage from the castle was approaching across the field. A woman dressed in a fine gown rode at the head of it astride a chestnut horse. The armed men fell in to flank the party. Oengus moved to meet them. He inclined his head in greeting. Her gaze swept over the assembled Maghuin Dhonn. I felt my mother's hands on my shoulders, pulling me close to her. The twilight deepened around us as she summoned it, cloaking me as though I were still a babe.

"Oengus, son of Niall," the finely dressed woman said. "All is well between our people?"

He inclined his head a second time. "By stone and sea and sky and all that they encompass, I swear it, Lady."

This time she inclined her head in response. "Go in peace." She glanced once more over us. "We give greeting to our wild kin."

With that, she took her leave and her entourage went with her. My mother released the twilight and I let out a breath I hadn't known I was holding.

"She's kin?" I asked.

"Aye," my mother said. "A descendant of Alais' and Arwyn's line. There's always one in residence at Clunderry."

"Oh." It meant we shared as kin my great-great-grandmother—Alais the Wise, daughter of the Cruarch of Alba and the Queen of Terre d'Ange. What tenuous place the Maghuin Dhonn held in Alba was due to her. She'd wed one of us—or at least a half-breed. Conor mac Grainne, son of the Lady of the Dalriada and a wandering Maghuin Dhonn harpist. Their eldest, their daughter Arwyn, had gone on to be named the Cruarch Talorcan's heir and ruled Alba in the latter days of her life.

Alais' and Conor's other two daughters had answered the call of their *diadh-anam* and gone back to the wild places we liked best. They had married and mingled with others of our kind.

"Why didn't you want her to see us?" I asked. "Surely we're at peace?"

"Aye." My mother looked around. The Maghuin Dhonn were beginning to drift away in twos and threes. "There's to be a revel, but there's somewhat I wish you to see first. There, we will speak."

We slipped back into the twilight. She led me back toward the castle, then into the woods along a path. In an ancient oak grove, she paused and breathed deeply. I did the same.

It was a sacred place. I could feel the slow pulse of the earth beneath my feet. The oak trees dreamed their slow dreams, roots reaching deep into the earth, remembering year upon year of libations poured in tribute.

A good place.

But we didn't linger. She moved on along the path until we reached the circle of standing stones. This, too, was a sacred place. But it smelled of old blood, and the fine hairs at the nape of my neck stood on end.

"She died here," I whispered. "Morwen."

"Aye."

"Am I named for her?"

My mother hesitated. "Not quite, no. Come."

I let her lead me into the center of the ring. There was a slab of a boulder there, half buried. Here was where the blood-smell came from. My mother sat atop it with thoughtless grace. I stood before her, still clutching the bow and quiver my uncle had given me.

"You know the old ones were able to summon visions from the standing stones?" she asked. I nodded. "Here is where she showed the D'Angeline prince what his son would become. Only when it had come to that. Only when there were no other futures to see. And there were others at first." She was quiet a moment. "In one, Morwen bore the D'Angeline prince a child."

"A daughter," I murmured.

My mother nodded. "She would have been a great magician who brought balance to the struggle and peace to the land. But the prince refused her, and her attempts to bind him failed in misery. That was her great folly." Her mouth quirked. "It seems the gods of Terre d'Ange are particular in matters of love."

"I am named for a child that never was?"

"Aye."

"Why?"

Another silence. She let go my hand to brush fine strands of hair out of my eyes. "Your father was D'Angeline."

I remembered the words Oengus had spoken in the night. "You were called to him?"

"I was."

"Was he a prince?"

She shook her head. "A priest, I think."

"You *think*?"

"Peace, Moirin." Something unfamiliar flickered behind her smile. "It was a revel. Lord Tiernan's coronation. I attended it out of respect. There were many foreign guests in attendance. I asked no questions, only answered the call. The priest felt it, too. I daresay it surprised him."

"A priest of *what*?"

My mother shrugged and spread her hands. "I do not know. I am not versed in the ways of D'Angeline faith."

I took a deep, shaking breath. "Yet you and everyone else expected a great magician to come of one night's dalliance?"

"I did not know," she said simply. "Only that there was some purpose in it. So aye, I named you for a child that might have been. It is not so unusual a name; others have borne it. But it is a name with hope in it."

I swallowed. "And being no great magician, I disappoint."

"No!" Her eyes stretched wide. "Stone and sea, never!"

"Others," I said stubbornly. "I disappoint others."

She sighed. "They dream foolish dreams of glory, even as they remind themselves of ambition's folly." She gestured around at the massive stones standing sentinel in the twilight. "I wanted to bring you here, to tell you here. That whatever you become, that whatever destiny awaits you, no matter how great or how small, you understand in your bones the dangers of knowledge and power, and the toll they may take if used unwisely. Do you?"

I breathed in the scent of old blood and nodded.

Ten thousand years of wandering without solace . . .

I understood.

"Good lass," my mother said softly. "Wise child."

My curiosity wasn't satisfied. "Why did you not wish the Lady of Clunderry to see us?"

"Ah." She touched my cheek. "You bear the stamp of Terre d'Ange on your features, Moirin mine. One of royal blood might question your presence among the Maghuin Dhonn. Our lives are our own. And I am not fond of answering questions."

"Not even mine?" I inquired.

She smiled. "Yours, I tolerate."

"What color are my eyes?"

My mother cupped my face and kissed my brow. "Green," she whispered. "Green as grass, green as the rushes grow."

Before that night, the revel that followed would have been the single greatest experience of my life. The glade in which it was held was spellbound, wrapped in a shroud of twilight that would render it visible as nothing more than a glimmering in the air to anyone without the gifts of the Maghuin Dhonn in their blood. There must have been almost a hundred people there—a great gathering for our folk. There were even a dozen or more children present, some near my age. I should have enjoyed the novelty.

But I felt strange to myself.

My father was a D'Angeline priest.

I was half-D'Angeline.

And I had no idea what that meant—or why, indeed, it should mean anything. Surely there were others.

I searched the memory of my mother's tales. No, never such a pairing. Not between an almost pure-blooded Maghuin Dhonn and a pure-blooded D'Angeline.

So? Why should it matter?

It shouldn't and it didn't—except that my mother had been called to him and he to her, and she had named me for a child that never was. Now the words whispered in the long-ago night and today's disappointed looks made sense. For ten years, the Maghuin Dhonn had hoped I would prove to be a great magician. It made me angry—at them, at my mother. They had no right to place such expectations on me. She had no right to withhold such a great truth from me.

"Pouting, little one?" Oengus stooped to crouch before me.

"No," I lied.

"Ah, she told you." He turned his head to gaze at my mother. A trick of the moonlight through the branches laid shadows like antlers over his tangled hair. "She's a deep one, Fainche."

There was a fire in the center of the glade, burning silvery beneath twilight's cloak. Bare-chested young men were leaping through the flames to the accompaniment of clapping hands and skirling pipes. One swaggered up to my mother and bowed to her, holding out one hand. She shook her head, laughing. Oengus' eyes narrowed.

"Do you love her?" I asked him.

"Aye," he said simply. "I'd have her to wife if she'd let me. But she's solitary and set in her ways." He looked back at me. "Do not judge her harshly. She bears a great love for you and in her own way seeks only to protect you."

It made me feel ungracious. "I will try."

"Good lass." He rose and moved away.

The revel wore on into the small hours of the night. There was music and dancing and an abundance of food—even roasted venison, which we seldom had. There were stone jugs of *uisghe*, a strong spirit begged or bartered from elsewhere, or stolen from tribute-gifts left by other folk. I found a jug with a scant inch left in the bottom and sampled it when no one was looking. It tasted unpleasant, but it blazed a trail into my belly where it simmered nicely, smoothing away the prickly edges of my temper.

I decided I liked it.

The children I'd been too sullen to attempt to befriend began to yawn and crumple, curling up in the grass to sleep beneath the stars. Men and women smiled at one another and went into the darkness together. When Oengus held his hand out to my mother, she gave me an inquiring glance from across the glade.

I shrugged.

She took his hand and went with him.

I should have been weary, but my heart and mind were too full for sleep. I found another jug that sloshed a bit when I shook it and wandered into the night. The charm of concealment had darkened to the deepest purple twilight. Here and there couples were sighing. I found a place on the outskirts of the glade with long grass and sank into it. In the tree above me, an owl hooted softly.

I summoned my own twilight and spotted it. "Hello."

The owl hooted again. It sounded disapproving. The glade was its nightly hunting ground and we were disturbing it.

"I'm sorry." I let my twilight go and sensed a rush of powerful wings as the owl launched itself. "Good hunting."

There was only a little *uisghe* in the jug, but it was late and I was growing tired after all. After I drank it, my head spun. I curled on my side in the tall grass and thought about all the coupling in the glade, all the Midsummer coupling in the tame fields beyond the woods. I knew what men and women did together. I'd seen frogs mating. There was that queer fluttering feeling in my belly again. Combined with the *uisghe*, it made me feel excited and sick.

Not yet, the bright lady whispered in my memory.

I closed my eyes and listened to the grass crackling beneath my ear. I thought about the other one, the one I'd seen in my mind's eye earlier. The man. Bright, though not so bright as the lady. His gentle smile. The seedling cupped in his palm. I opened my eyes and gazed at the grass. There was a tiny, half-opened buttercup nestled amid the long stems, colorless in the fading twilight. I breathed in the remembered scent of sunlight warming the ripe fields, taking it deep into me where it mingled with the warmth of the *uisghe*. There was no sick feeling left, only calm and goodness.

I cupped my hand around the blossom and blew out softly.

The buttercup opened.

Well, well, I thought. Mayhap I wasn't a great shapeshifting magician like those from the days of old, but mayhap I had some small magic that was all my own.

Or was it?

Was it a gift of the Maghuin Dhonn? Or the mysterious, unknown gods of Terre d'Ange?

I wasn't sure I wanted to know.

I murmured a prayer to my *diadh-anam* and sought refuge in sleep, comforted by the rustling grasses.

THREE

It was a blessed relief to return to the solitude of our cave.

I spoke less than was my wont on our long journey home and my mother did not press me. She spoke only of inconsequential things. She taught me to use the short bow that my uncle Mabon had given me, praising my fledgling skills. As we travelled, I got to be quite good with it.

She did not speak of my father and I did not ask.

I did not speak of the buttercup.

Nor did I seek to repeat the attempt, not during our journey. But I paid greater attention to the world around me than I had paid before. Raised from childhood in the wilderness, I had always been attuned to it. Now it seemed that awareness had deepened, as though a sense I'd always possessed had awakened more fully. When I concentrated hard, I heard the songs trees sang to themselves, reaching their leafy crowns toward the sky, sinking their roots deep into the earth with a slow, satisfying slither.

Not *heard*, not exactly. But it was a sense like hearing.

A stand of birch trees grumbled in the shadow of a great spruce. The grasses and scrub of wide-open spaces flourished with a brief, exuberant shout. Wildflowers whispered delicately and perished.

And animals . . .

It was harder because they moved, but I could sense them, too—if I stayed still enough.

Once, a fox-vixen trotted across our path, a grouse hanging from her narrow chops. She saw us and froze, one forepaw raised.

"She's got kits," my mother murmured. "Half-grown, I reckon. Needs to feed them with autumn coming."

I felt relieved that I wasn't alone in my ability to sense such things. "You can tell, too?"

"Aye, of course. And you're growing into your skills if you can." She looked at me sidelong, then addressed the fox conversationally, summoning a flicker of twilight and making a shooing gesture. "Go on, you."

It trotted away fearlessly.

"Do you hear the trees grow?" I asked her. "The grass speak?"

My mother shook her head. "No. Do you?"

I took a deep breath. "I do."

She eyed me. "Well, that's a fine thing, isn't it?"

"Is it?"

My mother smiled. "To be sure, Moirin mine."

"But it's not a gift of the Maghuin Dhonn?" I pressed her.

She walked without answering for a while. "I cannot say for certain. Surely, there have been those among us tied to the sacred places— the springs and groves and the standing stones. But you sense this everywhere?"

"Aye," I murmured. "Not easily, but aye."

She shrugged. "Mayhap it is a gift we have lost."

"Mayhap." I thought of the man with the seedling and said no more.

At the end of our journey, we found our neat, cozy cave had grown foul and smelly and messy with neglect. Mice and other scavengers had gotten into our stores and nibbled holes in our blankets. It took days to set matters in order, sweeping out droppings and spoiled foodstuff, pounding our blankets on rocks in the clean, cold water of the stream and hanging them to dry. It was hard work, but I didn't mind. It was good to be home.

By the end of the first day, we had cleared away the worst of the debris, but a rank odor lingered.

I wrinkled my nose. "Shall I see if there's pennyroyal yet blooming in the meadow?"

"'Tis too late in the day." My mother made a face, too. "And I fear a stench too great for pennyroyal. Do you have a sense we've further unwelcome visitors lurking?"

I shook my head.

"Nor I." She dusted her hands and cast a glance at the sky. "We'll sleep in the open air tonight and have a closer look on the morrow."

As it happened, we didn't have to wait that long. My mother built a merry fire in the firepit while I plucked a grouse I'd shot the day before, much to my considerable pride. We roasted it on a spit and ate it along with handfuls of late-ripening blackberries. As the soft blue light of dusk began to settle over us, I felt warm and content. Insects buzzed in the last summer air. Along the stream, trout were feeding. Tomorrow, I'd catch fish for our supper.

Something in the far reaches of the cave rustled.

My senses sharpened.

There *were* visitors—scores of them. They were so tiny and slept so soundly during the daylight hours that neither of us had sensed them. A vast black cloud of them rushed out of the mouth of the cave, rising into the dusk on flittering wings.

"Bats!" I leapt to my feet, laughing with unexpected delight. The cloud split and streamed around me. Nearly inaudible cries filled the night. I spun around amidst the rising swirl. "Can we keep them?"

"Are you mad, child?" my mother asked, but she was smiling. "No, there's the source of the stench, right enough. We'll let them feed and drive them out in the morning."

"All right." I gazed wistfully after the swarm.

My mother's smile deepened. "Never doubt you're a true child of the Maghuin Dhonn, Moirin mine. From what little I've seen of D'Angelines, none of them would dance amidst a bat-swarm."

I dropped back to the hearth and sat cross-legged in my travel-worn blankets, cupping my chin in both hands. "What was he like?"

"Your father?" She poked at the fire, stirring the embers. A flurry of sparks arose, chasing the feeding bats. "Passing fair to look at. They're a lovely folk, you know."

I felt insulted. "And we're not?"

Her brow furrowed. "'Tis . . . different. There's a keenness to it, a symmetry. Like a well-tempered blade." She smiled wryly. "They certainly think well enough of themselves for it."

"Did my father?"

"No," she said slowly. "He was different. Lovely, aye, but he didn't strike me as one to use it as a weapon." She gave me a quick glance, and for the first time, I saw shyness in her. "Offer it as a gift, more like. Beauty and desire."

"Milky-white skin and green, green eyes," I said.

"Aye."

"What else?" I asked when she said nothing further.

My mother sighed. "What would you have me say, lass? We barely spoke. On the surface he was calm, but desire moved in him like a current, deep and strong. When I looked into his eyes, I felt it." She touched one hand to her chest. "And inside me, the voice of the *diadh-anam* said, *Yes*."

"Do D'Angelines have a *diadh-anam*?"

"No." She shook her head. "I know only a bit. They believe they are descended from their own gods. One was born of earth. The others . . ." She stirred the fire again and watched the sparks rise. "The others came from beyond the stars. One of them called him to me."

"Is it true?"

She shrugged. "Mayhap."

I thought about the bright lady. My memory had faded, but I remembered beauty as keen and deadly as a blade. It drew me and frightened me to think on it now, knowing what I knew. But the man with the seedling had been gentler and different. "Mother? In the morning, there's somewhat I wish to show you."

"All right, my heart."

In the morning, we went to the meadow to gather pennyroyal. It had passed its prime, but it would suffice to dispel the lingering odor of bat droppings once we'd driven them out. My mother cast curious glances in my direction, but asked no questions. In the meadow, I found a plant that would suit my purpose, a dandelion only just beginning to go to seed.

"This," I said. "Watch."

"'Tis an old plant, the greens will be bitter . . ." My mother's voice trailed off as I knelt and cupped my hands around it.

I breathed in sunlight and warmth.

Blew it out.

It was hard—harder than before. And I understood without words that it had been easier before because I'd attempted it at Midsummer, and it had been a smaller thing I'd attempted with the buttercup. The effort made me dizzy. But I held to the sense of rich, fertile brightness and kept blowing steadily until I saw black spots before my eyes. The dandelion blossomed into a sphere of gossamer seeds.

"Stone and sea," my mother whispered.

I took a few deep, gasping breaths. "Whose magic? Ours or theirs?"

"Yours," she said firmly.

"But why? What's it *for*?"

She crouched beside me and blew softly on the dandelion ball. An ordinary breath. The fairy seeds blew away, drifting into the warm air. She watched them go. "Must it be *for* anything?"

"It seems it ought."

She shrugged. "Then no doubt it will be revealed in time."

My mother could be somewhat infuriating. "I saw a vision," I said. "In Clunderry, outside the fields. A man all ringed around in brightness with a seed sprouting from the palm of his hand."

"Oh?"

Very infuriating. "Mother!"

"Peace, Moirin." She laid her hand atop my head. "Mayhap you glimpsed some fertility god worshipped by the Cullach Gorrym. Mayhap it was a sending of one of the gods of Terre d'Ange whose blood runs in your veins. I do not know. It awakened you to certain gifts, which is to the good. But you recall that the purpose of our journey was to be reminded that gifts must be used wisely?"

"Aye," I murmured.

She rose and helped me to my feet. I stood, swaying. "Was this a wise use of power? Exhausting yourself to accomplish what would have occurred naturally in two days' time?"

"I wanted to show you," I said stubbornly.

"And so you have." She kissed my cheek. "Come. We've unwanted visitors to dispel."

I sighed, and went with her.

Four days later, I met Cillian.

I'd been ranging in the pine wood to the southeast of our homesite to gather dry, fragrant pine needles to stuff new pallets for my mother and me. I left off with my basket half full when a light rain began to fall. I didn't mind the rain, but it wouldn't do to gather damp mast. I headed for home with the basket slung over one shoulder and my bow and quiver over the other. Silvery raindrops slid from the needles overhead. Birds twittered in the boughs, telling one another all was well with the world.

If I'd been paying attention, I might have sensed him before I saw him, but I wasn't and didn't. It was plain luck that I came upon him from behind—luck, and the fact that I moved quietly. He was crouching behind an outcropping of stone that overlooked our hearth, peering over the edge. The sight startled me enough that I let my basket fall to the ground with a soft thud.

"Who's there?" He scrambled to his feet and whirled—but I had already summoned the twilight.

A boy.

I guessed he was a couple years older than me. I couldn't see his coloring properly in the dim twilight, but he was fair-skinned. He turned his head from side to side, one hand hovering over the hilt of a dagger.

"Who's there?" he called again.

I unslung my bow and nocked an arrow. "Who asks?"

His eyes widened. "Dagda Mor!" He glanced all around for the source of my voice, but there was nothing to see. He had heard me speak only because I willed it. "Where are you? Will you not show yourself?" When I didn't answer, he stooped carefully and picked up a bulging satchel. "Come, I mean no harm. I'm Cillian mac Tiernan of Innisclan. I've brought an offering." He untied the drawstring and opened the satchel. "See? Fresh peaches."

The peaches smelled ripe and heady and wonderful.

I hesitated.

"You don't want them?" Cillian tugged the drawstring closed. "All right, then. I'll take them away."

"Just leave them and go."

"Ah, no." He shook his head. Even through the gloaming, I could make out the glint of curiosity and bravado that lit his eyes. "Don't the Old Ones love a bargain? Show me your true form. Just a glimpse. I'll take my leave, and the peaches are yours."

I really wanted those peaches.

I let the twilight fade, keeping the arrow trained on him.

"Dagda Mor!" He stared at me. In daylight, his hair was reddish brown. He had grey eyes and a smattering of freckles across the bridge of his nose. "Are you flesh or spirit?"

"Flesh."

"And this is your true form?"

"Aye." I gestured with the arrow. "You may put down the peaches and leave now."

Cillian continued to stare at me. "You're just a little girl!"

I was beginning to get annoyed. "Well, and so?"

A wide grin crossed his face. "You don't imagine you could hurt me with that toy bow and bit of elf-shot, do you?"

"I do."

We regarded one another. "Why do you not vanish?" he asked, curious. "I've had my glimpse, have I not?"

"I can't," I said irritably. "You're looking at me."

"So?"

"It doesn't work that way. You can't hide from an eye that's already on you."

He chuckled. "Then you must have a right great fondness for peaches."

I loosed my bowstring. The arrow thudded into the bulging canvas satchel. Peach nectar oozed around the shaft. I had another arrow nocked before he could react.

"Are you mad?" he shouted, holding the satchel in front of him like a shield. "I come bearing a gift!"

"And spying!"

"Well, you didn't have to show yourself, did you?"

"Apparently I did, if I wanted the bedamned peaches!" I shouted back at him.

"You *shot* the bedamned peaches!" For the space of a few heartbeats, we glared at one another. Then Cillian sighed and lowered the satchel. He took a step backward, raising both hands. "Truce, eh? I spoke you fair. I mean no harm. I wanted only to see what was here."

I lowered my bow. "Why?"

"I was curious." His tone was frank. "All these years and no one's ever had so much as a glimpse. No one imagined there was a child."

My heart thudded. "Do you mean to tell them?"

"Tell them what?" Cillian smiled ruefully. "That I well nigh got shot by a woodsprite with a child's bow?" He looked at my expression and sobered. "Nay, I'll not speak of it if you wish. I'll make you a bargain. Give me your name and I'll give you my silence."

I paused. "Moirin."

"Moirin." He nodded. "My word on it."

I made another gesture with the tip of my arrow. "You should go now."

"All right." He turned, then turned back. I had already breathed a cloak of twilight around me. Cillian blinked. "Moirin?"

I didn't bother to make myself visible. "Aye?"

"May I come again?"

"Why?"

He shrugged. "I like tales of magic. This is the nearest I've come to living in one. I'll bring more peaches," he added when I didn't answer.

I plucked out the arrow that had pierced the satchel and licked the gleaming nectar that coated it. It was thick and sweet, tasting of long hours ripening on the branch and sunshine's promise fulfilled. "These are the last harvest."

"They are?" Cillian sounded startled. "Apples, then. Whatever you like."

"Apples," I agreed. "And honeycakes."

He grinned. "Apples and honeycakes it is."

FOUR

"illian mac Tiernan," my mother mused.

I nodded. "Are you angry?"

"At who?" She bit into a peach. "Him for spying? Or you for showing yourself?"

"Either."

"Neither." She shook her head. "He's a lad; they're full of curiosity and daring at that age. And mayhap I've protected you overmuch. You're old enough to begin making your own choices. I've no fear that Lord Tiernan will meddle in our affairs even if the lad talks. The Dalriada know to leave well enough alone." She took another bite, chewed thoughtfully and swallowed. "It would have been a shame to waste such good peaches."

I was relieved. "You're *not* angry."

"I am not."

"Good," I said. "Because I told him he could come again."

For the first time, I found myself keeping track of the days. Ten passed before Cillian returned. I daresay I would have sensed him this time—I'd not let my awareness lapse as I had before—but there was no need. As though to apologize for his former stealth, he made a racket this time, clattering through the underbrush. Before he was even in sight, he called.

"Moirin?"

My mother and I were mending clothes on the hearth. I glanced at her. She raised one eyebrow in reply.

My choice.

"Aye," I called. "Down here."

Cillian's head appeared over the ridge, then the rest of him. He froze for a moment on seeing both of us, then scrambled down. I was pleased to see he was carrying a satchel even larger than the first one. He reached the hearth and looked uncertainly from one of us to the other and back.

"Lady Fainche?" he inquired, a little breathless.

"And who else would it be?" My mother sounded amused.

He colored and offered a courteous bow. "Forgive me. Well met, my lady. I am Cillian mac Tiernan."

"Well met, Cillian mac Tiernan," she said. "You've a look of your father. Is he well?"

"He is." He proffered the satchel. "Apples and honeycakes. And I thought a wheel of cheese wouldn't go amiss."

She smiled. "You're a thoughtful lad. I'll store these in the back and do you the courtesy of returning your satchel."

Cillian watched her walk into the cave. "Is that her true form?"

"Aye," I said. "Why wouldn't it be?"

"You—" He paused, flushing again.

"I don't look like her," I said softly, understanding. "Is that it?"

"Aye . . . no. Yes and no." He blew out his breath. "You do and you don't. No mind." He glanced around. "This is the whole of it? Your home?"

"You should know," I said. "You spied on it long enough the other day."

His flush deepened. "Dagda Mor! Are you always so rude?"

I blinked. "Am I?"

"Aye!"

"I suppose so, then." I thought about how I might best make amends. "Would you like me to show you how to catch a trout with your bare hands?"

Cillian shrugged. "Why not?"

I showed him first working in ordinary daylight, reckoning it was only fair. It worked that way, too, only it took a lot longer and you had to be almighty patient.

"'Tis no match for a hook and line," he observed when I finally caught one. "Have you not got one? I'll bring one next time."

I shook my head. "No need."

"Don't be daft—"

"Watch." I deposited my fish in the creel and summoned the twilight, conscious of his gaze on me. He made a soft sound. Lying beneath the willow tree, I eased my arm back into the clear water. In the twilight, the swimming trout had a silvery gleam. Almost as soon as the slight ripples I'd created faded, I caught one.

"Magic," Cillian murmured. "Did you make yourself unseen?"

"Aye."

"Yet I could see you. It was only that the air seemed to dazzle about you." He frowned. "Because I was already looking at you, is it?"

"Aye." I wondered if he were a bit slow. "Did I not say so the other day?"

He laughed. "Peace, lass! 'Tis not every day one meets a witchling child. What other magics have you?"

I tied the lid of the creel shut. I didn't wish to speak to him of the man with the seedling. "None."

"No?" he teased. "Can you not summon the wind and catch it in a bag? Can you not charm the birds from the sky?"

"It would be an abuse of the Maghuin Dhonn's gifts to charm a bird for sport," I said with dignity. "And no one can summon the wind."

"They say the Master of the Straits could summon the wind." Cillian leaned back against the willow's trunk and stretched out his legs. "He could cause the seas to rise at his command and call lightning from the sky. But he gave away his book of magic and it's hidden away forever." He gave me a curious glance. "I've heard you speak no spells."

"Spells?" I repeated.

"Incantations. Words of power. Invocations to the gods."

"No." In the twilight, words might have a certain power, but I didn't think that was what he meant. "It's just a gift."

His grey eyes were bright. "Could you teach it to me?"

"I could try," I said dubiously. "But I don't know if it would be right. I'd have to ask my mother."

"Will you?"

"Aye, all right." I trotted back to the hearth and put the question to my mother. Her eyes crinkled with amusement.

"So that's what he's after, is it? Oh aye, let him try till he's blue in the face. He'll take no harm from it."

She was right.

I explained it and demonstrated over and over, but it made no difference. Cillian couldn't get the knack of it because he hadn't the gift. He couldn't raise so much as a glimmer in the air around him. His figure remained stubbornly, solidly visible. After two hours, he stomped around in frustration, kicking at willow roots. I sensed a shiver of distress in my favorite fishing tree as his boots scraped away chunks of bark and laid bare the pale root-flesh beneath.

"Please don't," I murmured. "You're hurting it."

He scowled and knocked on the trunk. "Trees don't feel."

"They do."

He glanced at the sky. "I should be going anyway."

"All right, then." I went to fetch the empty satchel for him. If it was magic he sought to acquire, after today's failure, I didn't think he'd be coming back. The thought made me sad. "Thank you," I said. I tried to think of something else to say that wouldn't be rude. After all, he had brought honeycakes. "It was interesting to meet you."

He slung the satchel over his shoulder. "Is there aught you'd like me to bring next time?" he asked, casting a critical eye over the neatly folded pile of mending on the hearth. "Clothing that's not in rags and tatters?"

I was surprised. "You're coming back?"

Cillian looked hurt. "You'd rather I didn't?"

"No, no!" I smiled. "It would be nice if you did. Thank you." I thought about his offer. I'd no need of fine clothing, but there were other things I liked. "Sausages, mayhap?"

He smiled back at me. "Sausages, it is."

After that, Cillian became a regular visitor. Sometimes eight or ten days would pass between his visits, sometimes only a few. I couldn't teach him magic, but I taught him many things about the woods. Although he hadn't the deeper senses I did, he was still able to pay attention and learn a great deal.

And he, in turn, taught me.

It began the first time I returned to our camp from foraging in the hickory copse to find him already awaiting me. He was sitting cross-legged on the hearth, gazing intently at an object he held in his lap—so intently he didn't hear me approach. I decided to play a trick on him and set down my basket softly, summoning the twilight. Unseen, I crept near and plucked the object from his hands.

Cillian gave a startled yelp.

I giggled.

"Moirin!" He grinned. "Show yourself, woodsprite."

I did. "And what is this object that held you so fascinated?" I inquired, waving it in the air.

"'Tis a tale of the Master of the Straits." He grabbed at it, but I danced out of reach. "I thought you might enjoy it, oh ungrateful one."

"A tale?" I examined the thing. "How is this a tale?"

"It's a *book*, Moirin." Cillian paused. "Not a book of magic, just a tale. Do you, ah, know how to read?"

"Read?" The thing was shaped like a leather-bound box, but it fanned open to reveal myriad square leaves with markings on them.

"You don't, do you?"

I held the *book* to my ear and heard nothing. I smelled it, then touched the tip of my tongue to the finely grained leaves. "I know the words book and read, but I do not know exactly what they mean," I admitted. "How is this a tale?"

He took it from me. "I'll show you." Holding it open, Cillian gazed into it and recited the opening words of a tale. I sat to listen, but he stopped. "Here." He pointed to the markings on the first leaf. "These are the words I spoke. Written here. Each of these is a word."

"No!" I marveled.

"Aye."

"That's a fine magic!"

"It's not—" He paused to consider. "Mayhap it is at that. I never thought on it."

I scooted closer to him. "How do you do it?"

"See these shapes?" Cillian pointed again. "Each one contained unto itself? Those are letters. They represent sounds. You put them together to make words."

"Show me."

He did, drawing on the flat stone of our hearth with the tip of a fire-blackened twig. I marveled over the process, taking to it like a duckling to water. I was so absorbed, I didn't sense my mother returning with her bow over her shoulder and a brace of pigeons dangling from one hand.

"What are you playing at, Moirin mine?" she asked.

"Oh!" I startled. "Cillian is teaching me to *read*."

There was a shadow behind her smile. "Is he, now?"

Cillian got to his feet and bowed. "Not against your wishes, Lady Fainche. Speak, and I will cease."

"You're enjoying yourself?" she asked me.

I nodded vigorously. "Oh, yes."

"So be it." My mother laid a hand on my head. "You have my blessing. But do not trust this new knowledge overmuch. Great truths should be contained in the head and the heart, not consigned to the page. There was a time not long ago when the *ollamhs* railed against the practice."

"The world changes, Lady Fainche," Cillian said diplomatically.

She settled her gaze on him. "So it does. 'Twas your own kinsman founded the Academy at Innisclan, was it not?"

"Aye. Eamonn mac Grainne. Your kinsman too, I believe." He hesitated. "Moirin will prove a swift learner, if I'm any judge. She'd be welcome to study there one day."

My mother looked alarmed.

"'Twould not be for many years," Cillian added hastily. "None younger than fourteen are admitted."

"Fourteen," she sighed.

"I'm not going anywhere," I assured her. "I just want to learn to read, that's all. And Cillian's a fine teacher."

He colored with pleasure. "Am I?"

"You are."

My mother regarded us with an unreadable expression. "Go on with it, then. My blessing is already given."

I'd spoken true; Cillian *was* a good teacher. By the time the woods were ablaze with autumn's bright foliage, I was able to read simple texts on my own, sounding out the words aloud. Once winter came, Cillian wouldn't be able to visit as often, but he had promised to bring me several books on which I might practice, whiling away the long cold months. I had promised in turn to read them to my mother, and I do not think even she was entirely displeased by the prospect.

But when Cillian came next, he came empty-handed and downcast.

"No books?" I was disappointed.

He took a seat at the hearth, looking at my mother out of the corner of his eye. She was sewing a pair of rabbit-skin leggings. Cillian was wary of her, fearing she didn't altogether approve of his presence in our lives. Also, he was still more than half-convinced that she could turn herself into a bear. To be fair, neither of us had disabused him of the notion.

"There's trouble," she guessed.

"Aye." He nodded reluctantly and flushed to the roots of his auburn hair. "My father fears you've ensorceled me."

My mother burst out laughing.

His flush turned an angry hue. "Is it so unthinkable? Bear-witches have done such things before!"

"Not to thirteen-year-old boys," I commented.

Further embarrassed, Cillian looked daggers at me. "It's because I've kept *your* secret, you know!"

"Peace," my mother said soothingly. "Lord Tiernan flatters me. So you've said naught to him of Moirin?"

"I gave my word!" he said indignantly.

"And kept it like a man." She gave a brisk nod. "Has your father forbidden you to visit me further?"

"Aye," Cillian muttered. "I defied him today."

"Hmm."

That sound didn't bode well. "What if I released you from your promise?" I asked Cillian. "Would your father allow you to keep visiting if he knew it was me you came to see?" I turned to my mother. "You said you'd no fear that Lord Tiernan would meddle in our affairs."

She made a noncommittal sound, but Cillian brightened. "You'd do that?" he asked.

"May I?" I asked my mother. I got the raised eyebrow in reply. Again, the choice was mine. "Aye," I said firmly. "I would."

Cillian leapt to his feet. "I'll tell him and see." He paused, giving my mother another sidelong glance. "You, um, haven't, have you? Ensorceled me?"

"I?" Now she looked amused. "No, not I."

FIVE

Cillian returned with good news and bad.

"'Twould make a difference to my father knowing I come to visit Moirin." He handed me a slim leather-bound book. "He sends this as a symbol of his earnest pledge. 'Tis the tale of the trials of Eamonn mac Grainne's courtship of his Skaldic bride," he added. "Fine winter reading. But—"

"Lord Tiernan doubts," my mother said dryly.

"Aye." Cillian nodded. "Lady Fainche, you've not been seen for nigh unto twelve years, neither here nor at Innisclan. And no one had heard any word of a child until now."

"By my choice."

"Which he respects. But if he is to allow me to continue my visits, he wishes to see Moirin with his own eyes."

My mother was very still. "Where?"

"He would welcome you to Innisclan." He pointed at the book I held. "After all, you are kin. Will you not come? You've done him the honor before."

She shivered a little. "Once, for a great occasion. But I do not relish being within stone walls."

"We live in a cave," I commented.

Her eyes flashed. "Walls carved by nature's hand are not the same as those built by men's hands. Are you so eager to learn the difference?"

"No," I murmured, subdued.

"And yet I am not eager to have Tiernan's people come here, trampling around with their great booted feet and disturbing the woods," she mused to herself. Cillian shuffled his feet self-consciously. For a boy of thirteen, they were rather large. She ignored him and studied me with discomforting intensity. "Does it mean so much to you, Moirin mine?"

Although the weight of her gaze made me feel like shuffling myself, I pondered her question and answered with one of my own. "You said we had naught to fear from the Dalriada. Do I shame you in some way that you do not wish Lord Tiernan to see me?"

"Stone and sea, no! Of course not."

"Then why do we not meet him halfway?" I was proud of my solution.

She was, too. She gave a reluctant nod. "Well reasoned. Cillian mac Tiernan, tell your father that Moirin and I will meet him at a place of his choose, halfway between Innisclan and here."

"Aye, my lady!" He was off like a hare.

My mother sighed. "That lad was doomed the minute he laid eyes on you."

I wasn't sure if I was intrigued or offended. "Why ever so?"

She gave me a wry look. "'Tis the way of the world, and men and women in it; aye, and lads and lasses, too. Pray you've a good many years before you learn it."

Not yet, the bright lady whispered. *Not for many years.*

The memory made me shudder.

"I shall," I promised.

Three days later, we rode out to meet the Lord of the Dalriada.

I'd never ridden a horse before. 'Twas Cillian who brought her, a dapple-grey mare, leading her behind his stalwart pony and tethering them both before entering the brambles along the verge of our woods. I'd seen horses, of course, on our journey to Clunderry, but never at close range. The mare was grazing when we emerged from the thicket. She raised her head and gazed at us with lustrous eyes, munching on grass.

"How lovely!" I cried.

Cillian rummaged in his pockets. "I brought you a bit of dried—"

I had slipped into the twilight without thinking. "Hello," I said softly. She bowed her head and let me cup her muzzle, giving a grunting whicker in reply. Her coat shimmered in my vision. I blew into her nostrils. "Hello."

"Moirin?"

"Oh!" I let slip the twilight. "I'm sorry."

He handed me a wizened apple. "I thought you might be frightened of her. Here, hold your palm open."

I fed her the apple. Her lips tickled. "Why would I be frightened?"

"It was a foolish notion," he admitted. "Lady Fainche, do you know how to ride?"

My mother was stroking the mare's shoulder. The mare turned her head to lip my mother's hair. "I expect I'll manage. Your uncle Declan taught me long ago."

Cillian stared. "He did?"

"Mmm. A kindness shown to a distant cousin. You do know we all share a common ancestor in the great Lady Grainne of the Dalriada?" She mounted easily and settled her skirts around her. "Over to yon boulder, my heart," she said to me, guiding the mare with her knees. "You can mount up behind me."

In the exhilaration of the ride, I nearly forgot the purpose of our journey. We veered west, then rode south along a high stony ridge overlooking the sea. I clung to my mother's waist to keep myself from sliding around on the mare's wide back, my skirts hiked up to my knees, bare legs dangling. The wind was off the sea, cool and salt-smelling.

At first we just walked, but once Cillian saw that my mother could indeed ride and I didn't appear likely to fall off, he nudged his pony to a trot from time to time. My mother kept pace with him easily, though she let the knotted reins lie slack around the mare's neck.

"You've a knack for this," Cillian said curiously to her. "Have you ever kept horses of your own?"

"No."

"Why not?"

"Whatever for?" she asked in turn. "What use is a horse in the woods?"

He shrugged. "You could go places."

"So I can on my own two feet without a great maw to feed." My mother leaned over to pat the mare's shoulder. "'Tis not our way to keep animals captive. I reckon they like it no more than I would."

Privately, I thought it would be quite wonderful to have a horse of my own—or mayhap a pony, since my legs were beginning to ache from straddling the mare's girth. And I wouldn't keep it captive, either. It would live free in the meadows and come when I called it, obeying me out of love. We could roam the world and explore it together, free as birds.

I'd never considered such a notion before. It was a new thought.

It gave me a strange feeling—like the fluttering feeling, only higher. A feeling that made me happy and sad all at once. It made me uncomfortable. I pushed the feeling and the thought away together.

And then I saw *them* and forgot about it.

There were six of them waiting for us on the cliffs above the sea—three men and three women, all astride fine horses. The man in front I took to be Lord Tiernan. From what I could see over my mother's shoulder, she was right, Cillian had a look of him, although his father was older and bearded. Sunlight glinted on a gold torc around his neck. All of them wore fine, brightly colored clothing. I glanced down at my shapeless, much-mended brown dress. It was very practical and faded to just the right hue for moving unseen in the woods, but for the first time, I wondered if I ought to have accepted Cillian's offer of clothing and not asked for sausages instead.

Although they had been very good sausages.

"Father!" Cillian said breathlessly. "I've brought them."

The man inclined his head. "Fainche."

"My lord Tiernan." My mother dismounted deftly, sliding one leg over the mare's neck. She helped me down. "This is Moirin, my daughter."

I stood gazing up at them. They sat gazing down at me. Cillian rattled off their names. Far below us, the grey sea crashed on rocks. At last, Lord Tiernan's gaze shifted to my mother. "That child was never sired by one of Alban blood."

"Nor did I claim she was," my mother agreed.

"Who?"

She shrugged. "Since when do the Dalriada concern themselves with the lineage of the Maghuin Dhonn?"

His mouth quirked. "Others might. Or do the wild kin of Alais' line forget whose blood runs in their veins?"

"We do not."

"Poor mite!" one of the women whispered audibly. "Living like a savage."

"What do you expect?" another murmured.

I glanced at my mother's face and saw her eyes take on an ominous glitter. I was angry on her behalf and gave the woman who'd spoken first a glare of my own. She flinched and made a warding gesture.

"Peace." Lord Tiernan held up his hand, silencing them. "Why not bring the child to be raised at Innisclan, Fainche?" he asked in a reasonable tone. "At least during the winter months. Surely it would be an easier living, and if she's an appetite for learning, it would be indulged."

She shook her head. "When Moirin is older, she may choose her own path. For now, she stays with me, and our place is in the wild."

He sighed. "Dagda Mor, you're a stubborn woman." His gaze shifted back to me. "What do *you* will, child?"

I curled my bare toes on the stony ridge. "For Cillian to visit."

Lord Tiernan's expression softened. "So little? All right, then. If the lad wills it, I see no harm in it." He hesitated. "Fainche . . ."

My mother raised her brows coolly. "Aye, my lord?"

Whatever he was going to ask, it withered in the face of her implacable stance. "Stubborn woman," Lord Tiernan repeated. His grey gaze lingered on me. "I reckon the truth will come out in time." He gave his son a brisk nod. "Cillian, so be it. I'll expect you home by supper."

Cillian grinned. "Aye, Father!"

So it was decided.

In the years that followed, Cillian came without fail whenever he could. Not so often in the winter when the snow and cold made travel difficult, but he taught me enough before the first snowfall that I was able to read on my own, and as he had promised, he brought books borrowed from the Academy's considerable library. They were tales of Alban history, Alban heroes. During the long winter nights, I read them aloud to my mother by the light of the little fire that warmed our cave when we couldn't use the wind-scoured hearth, both of us huddled under furs and blankets.

During the day, it was different. Cold as it was, I liked the woods in winter. It was quiet, so quiet! Almost all the world slept. There was only the murmur of pine trees, boughs pillowed white with snow, and the occasional bright crackle of holly. Animals were scarce. One could feel oneself alone in all the world beneath the vast sky, breathing plumes of frost into the bright air. No magic, only being.

At such times, I could not imagine wanting aught else.

But at night there were tales, and I hungered for more.

Spring came, and Cillian came more often. He'd grown over the winter, turning lanky and rawboned.

"Look at you," he teased me. "You're no bigger than a frog!"

"I am!" I said indignantly.

"Hardly!"

My mother watched us indulgently.

It wasn't until early summer of that year that Cillian spoke of my parentage. Ever since our meeting with Lord Tiernan, I'd feared he'd broach the subject, but he'd waited, cunning as a hunter in his own way. We'd been roaming in the woods and were lying on our backs in the sunny meadow, head to head, in comfortable companionship.

"So." Cillian flicked a spray of bluebells with one finger. "Do you know who your father is?"

I sighed.

He rolled onto his belly. "*Do* you?"

I veiled my eyes with my lashes and squinted at the sun. "Not exactly."

"Moirin."

"What do they say?" I asked.

"Will you not look at me?" Cillian's voice was plaintive. I turned over and met his gaze, so close our noses nearly touched. "Little frog." He brushed a dusting of pollen from my hair. "What are you frightened of?"

"I don't know," I said honestly.

"D'Angeline." His voice was steady. "That's what they say, since you're asking after it."

"He was," I murmured.

"Who?"

I shook my head. "A priest. I don't know."

Cillian sat upright. "Well, then, there's a start. A priest, eh? A priest of *what*?"

In my mind, the bright lady smiled gently upon me, warming my heart and setting my stomach to fluttering. "I don't know."

"Do you *want* to know?"

I did and I didn't. "Mayhap."

"All right." Cillian eyed me speculatively. "There are texts in the library on the history and culture of Terre d'Ange. None, I fear, translated into Alban. But I've begun studying D'Angeline and Caerdicci in preparation for entering the Academy. I could try to translate for you if you wished to learn more."

I was confused. "What do you mean?"

"They're not writ in your tongue nor one you would recognize," he said patiently. "I could try to teach you as I learn it."

"Teach me?"

"To speak your father's tongue."

"How so?" I was still baffled. "Are people not the same everywhere? Why should my father's tongue differ from my own?"

"It does," Cillian assured me.

"Stone and sea!" I blew out my breath, exasperated by the very notion of it. "What a piece of confusion. Why would people do such a thing?"

He shrugged. "Would you learn?"

"Aye," I said slowly. "I would."

SIX

"Naamah," I breathed.

"Naamah," Cillian agreed, his finger hovering over the page.

Our gazes met in triumph. It had taken a year for him to gain proficiency in the D'Angeline tongue and teach it to me. A year to find the right text, and for me to draw painstaking details from my recalcitrant mother. She glanced over our shoulders at the illustration of a priest in red robes, bestowing a careless remark on us.

"Oh, aye. That bears a likeness."

Cillian rolled his eyes. I giggled.

Naamah—desire. The bright lady had a name.

I studied the page. I studied all the pages. I mouthed the D'Angeline words to myself. Here was the tale my mother had sketched for me long ago, told in full.

Elua—Blessed Elua. First and foremost of their gods. All the rest had followed him. Fallen from Heaven, fallen from the skies. They gave up their immortal heritage for him. Why? I traced his likeness. Born of the earth, nurtured there. Conceived of the blood of a lone deity's mortal son and the tears of his mortal beloved, essences that mingled in the soil. Claimed by neither earth nor sky, stone nor sea.

He wandered.

The others left Heaven and followed him.

I didn't understand it; I couldn't. It was too strange, too foreign. I couldn't grasp the tales. Were they gods or servants? Was Elua their *diadh-anam*? My mother had said he wasn't. But if not, what was he?

Why did they follow him?

When he hungered, Naamah lay down with strangers to get coin that he might eat. And then they came to Terre d'Ange, where the people welcomed them with open arms. There they stayed and got many children until the lonely god relented and invited Elua and his Companions back to Heaven. But he refused, and went to a different place instead, and all his Companions went with him.

I looked at the illustrations again. One of them showed a priest in brown robes pouring out an offering of grain at the feet of a statue. The statue was of a man holding a seedling in the palm of his hand.

"Anael," I said aloud.

"'Anael, also called the Star of Love and the Good Steward,'" Cillian read. "'He gave unto them many gifts of husbandry, and taught them to grow good things and care for the land.' What's he to do with anything?"

"I don't know," I murmured. I'd never told him about that small bit of magic I could do. "If my father was a priest of Naamah, do you reckon he's descended from her line?"

Cillian shrugged. "Mayhap. After so many years, I imagine the lines are muddled. Why?"

"No reason." I closed the book. "Well. Now we know."

"I could try to find out his name for you," he offered. "I'm sure there's a register of important foreign guests who attended my father's coronation. Mayhap the priest's name is recorded in it."

I glanced at my mother's face. Her expression was unreadable. "No," I said slowly, stroking the cover of the book. "No, it's enough to know this much. Thank you, Cillian."

He smiled. "You're welcome, little frog."

And for a time, it *was* enough. Knowledge, I decided, could be a fearsome thing. I knew who I was: Moirin, daughter of Fainche. I did not wish to become other. And so I locked the name of the bright lady my father served away in my heart along with the name of the man with the seedling whom they called Star of Love and Good Steward, and I prayed instead to the Maghuin Dhonn Herself that I should be one of Her children and no one else's.

In the autumn, Cillian began his formal studies at the Academy and I saw less of him. Still, he came when he could. By spring, he'd grown another three inches and his head was full of all manner of new tales and histories, as well as gossip about the young men and women studying with him.

"You must come when you're of age, Moirin," he wheedled. "It's only two years from now, is it not?"

"One," I said, offended.

"Oh, aye?" He looked surprised. "That's right, I forgot. My sister looked older at thirteen."

It needled me that he should see me as such a child. I was old enough that I could survive in the woods alone. I could read as well as Cillian, and I'd learned D'Angeline as fast as he could teach it to me. But now he was reading works by Caerdicci scholars and learning skills like astronomy and mathematics. Wherever he was going, I was being left behind.

I said as much to my mother.

She gave me her wry look. "Wait."

"For what?"

"You'll see."

Oengus came that summer. He'd come a few times since our pilgrimage to Clunderry. This time, he eyed me critically.

"She's not started her woman's courses?" he asked my mother.

She shook her head. "No. I'd have told you."

I flushed. "Whatever for?"

They exchanged a glance. "It would mean you're eligible to be courted," my mother said. "Time enough and more for that," she added in a firm tone, putting the subject behind us.

That night, she went with Oengus. I lay awake in my nest of blankets, listening to the sounds of the night forest, trying not to think on what they did out there. When I closed my eyes, I saw the bright lady. Naamah, whose gift was desire. She held her hands cupped at her waist, then raised them and smiled at me. *Soon*, she said in a voice like honey, and opened her hands. A shimmering grey dove burst into the air, its fluttering wings echoing the fluttering deep in my belly.

Soon.

Soon came that autumn and winter. My woman's courses didn't start, but my body changed nonetheless.

I grew tall—or at least taller than my mother. At first I was reed-thin with it, but then that changed, too. My breasts and hips swelled. Where once my body had been quick and nimble, it now acquired a lithe, nubile grace.

I felt strange in my skin.

Good, but strange.

A world of sensation abounded. I craved it. I could become absorbed for hours in the softness of a piece of rabbit hide, running the down-soft fur over my cheek. Drawing a comb through my hair. The way my clothing rustled against my skin. The sensual warmth of thawing my hands over the fire after a day afield could make me shiver with pleasure.

"Ah, Moirin mine," my mother murmured, watching me. "You're a beautiful girl."

"Am I?" I asked, startled out of a reverie.

She kissed my brow. "You are."

When Cillian came that spring for the first time in long months, I saw it reflected in another's eyes. I was boiling tender lily buds over the hearth-fire and sensed him coming long before he arrived, a trail of disruption in his wake. He bounded into our campsite on long legs, his voice turned deep and booming.

"Moirin!" he shouted. "Moirin! I'm sorry I've been away so long, but there's the most amazing news—"

I stood. "Oh, aye?"

He blinked. "Moirin?"

In that moment, the balance of power shifted between us forever. I crossed my arms, folding them under my young breasts, and saw his gaze flicker over my body. "And who else might I be?"

"Ahh . . ." Cillian flushed. "You've grown, that's all."

"So I have," I agreed.

"Aye." He stood stupidly, staring.

"What news?" I prompted him.

"Oh!" He started. "Oh, aye." He made a sweeping gesture toward the west. "There's a whole new land that's been discovered across the sea. An Aragonian explorer found it. It's all the talk of the Academy."

"Is it now?"

"It is." Cillian came toward me, dropping the satchel he carried. His hand rose as though of its own accord to touch my face. "Dagda Mor!" he breathed. "Have I been gone so long?"

I leaned away from him. "You have."

"Forgive me?" he begged.

"I might." I ducked and picked up the satchel. "What have you brought me?"

It wasn't much. Stale oatcakes, the dregs of last season's honey, crystallized in the comb. A smoked ham that was nearly rancid. An illustrated history of the Master of the Straits.

"Hmm."

Cillian flushed again. "I'll bring whatever you like next time."

I stepped close to him, until we were nearly nose to nose. "What I *want* is my friend back."

"Moirin." His voice was husky. He clasped my upper arms, his hands strong. It felt good. His dark grey eyes were intent on mine. I'd never noticed how handsome he was. "Have I not always been your friend?"

I shrugged. "When it suited."

"It suits."

He kissed me. His lips were firm, but softer than I expected. Over and over, Cillian kissed my mouth. And then there was his tongue, probing tentatively. At first the invasion startled me, and then I welcomed it. I teased it with my own—teased and retreated, forcing him to delve deeper into my mouth.

Yes, I thought. *This.*

The bright lady agreed, amused.

There was a sound of my mother clearing her throat. She was standing near the hearth, a brace of grouse dangling from one hand.

Cillian sprang backward.

I eyed her.

"So," she said wryly. "Already?"

"We were just—" Cillian began.

"I can see well enough what you were about," my mother said. "Moirin . . ." She sighed. "Grown as you may have done, you're a child in a woman's body yet. Have a care with it, will you not?"

I didn't want to have a care with it and I didn't want to be told I was a child. What I wanted was for Cillian to kiss me again and find out what happened next. But there was a shadow of worry behind my mother's eyes that made me nod reluctantly and keep my peace.

And so I sat plucking grouse while Cillian spoke of the rumors surrounding the new land that had been discovered across the sea; of fabulous cities rising up from lush jungles, folk who dressed themselves all in jade and feathers, and gold beyond telling. It was all very interesting, but I'd rather have been kissing him.

When it came time for him to leave, I walked with him to where his mount was tethered on the outskirts of the woods, feeling my mother's gaze boring into my back. Cillian's stalwart pony had been replaced by a tall chestnut gelding, another sign that he was edging toward manhood.

"He's a beauty." I blew softly into the chestnut's nostrils. He whickered and lowered his head that I might scratch his ears. "Will you teach me to ride him?"

"Moirin." Cillian caught me around my waist. He turned me around and kissed me again. "I'll do aught you wish, my witch-girl," he whispered against my lips. "Only tell me you're not wroth and I'm welcome here."

"Hmm." I pulled back in the circle of his arms. "I *am* wroth. But only because I missed you."

"I'll come again," he promised, pulling me toward him and showering my face with kisses. "I promise."

"Shall I make sure of it?" I teased, tasting my newfound power.

"How?"

I slid my hands into his auburn hair and kissed him in reply, long and deep, pressing my body against his. Cillian groaned into my open mouth. I broke off the kiss and slipped from his arms with a deft twist. The blood was beating hard in my veins and I wanted more as surely as he did—but I knew just as surely that this was *my* gift and I was in control of it.

"Will that do?" I asked innocently.

"Aye," he said in a daze. "That will do it."

SEVEN

My gift.

Desire.

It came to me as easily and naturally as breathing, and once woken, it refused to sleep. I slid into a state of desire as surely as a trout in the stream—only instead of being cool and swift and darting, it was warm and languorous.

Cillian came often that summer. Familiar as he was to me, I learned him in a whole new way. I kissed the corners of his lips and the dimples that formed when they curled in a smile. I bit his earlobes and the sturdy, slender column of his neck until he groaned. I let him put his hands on me, reveling in the feel of them. Where once we had lain for hours in the meadow talking, now we lay and kissed for hours, until I felt my blood had turned to molten gold.

Only the shadow of worry in my mother's eyes kept me in check.

"Dagda Mor!" Cillian pushed himself away from me when I bade him stop. He crouched for a moment, then rose and walked a few steps. I sat up and tugged the loose bodice of my dress back into place, watching him curiously. He glanced over his shoulder and winced at the sight of me. "Do you know what you *do* to me?"

"Aye," I said softly. "You, too."

He spun, fists clenched. "Why make us wait?"

"My mother—"

"Oh, Manannan of the deep take your mother!" Cillian shouted.

I raised my eyebrows.

"I didn't mean it." He flung himself on his knees before me like a penitent, shuddering. "Ah, Moirin! Forgive me."

I touched his cheek. "I do. Of course I do."

But I did wait.

I spoke to my mother about it, asking her why it worried her so.

"You're young," she said shortly.

"How old were you?" I asked.

She was stirring a pot of cattail roots and didn't answer for a long time. When she did, she didn't answer the question I'd asked. "Would you have the truth, my heart?" I nodded and her dark gaze met mine. "It's a powerful calling. I fear losing you to it."

"Cillian?"

My mother shook her head. "The bright lady's gift."

It was my turn to be silent.

"Did you imagine I didn't know?" There was sorrow in her smile. "Ah, I suppose you did. Children are slow to credit their elders. Yet how could I not, when I felt her presence there at your conception? How could I not, when it's hung like a bright shadow over you all your life?" She laid a hand on her breast. "The *diadh-anam* within me says that this is right. That this is as it should be. For reasons I cannot know, the Maghuin Dhonn Herself wills it. But I am a mortal woman and I fear to lose my child. So I have sheltered you from it as best I could. And now that it has found you, I do but beg you to go slowly from me."

My heart ached. "Stone and sea! I'm not going anywhere."

"No?"

"No." I laid my head in her lap. "No."

"Moirin mine." Her fingers stroked my hair. "I pray it's so. Stay a child for a while."

"I will," I promised.

I did.

It was hard, though—so hard! I wanted and wanted and wanted, and Cillian's wanting added to mine, setting my blood to boiling. But I held off through summer and autumn, and then winter came again, necessitating distance between us and cooling our ardor.

I took solace in the cold and the quiet.

Then came spring.

It was a time of greening and new growth, when the soil was damp and fertile. Every plant sent out new shoots, feverish with excitement. Every tree burst into leaf. All my nerves were on edge with it. When Cillian came for the first time that spring, grey eyes hot with yearning and his shoulders grown broad and muscled, there was no question. I didn't even ask what he'd brought in his satchel.

No more waiting.

"Moirin." His voice was hoarse. "Now?"

"Now," I agreed.

In the meadow, he kissed me like he was starving, yanking at my gown with impatient hands. It should have been tender, but it wasn't. We'd waited too long for tender. I didn't care. The feeling of his callused fingertips on my breasts drove me mad. Cillian pushed my thighs apart, fumbling between us. I reached down and took his phallus in my hand. It pulsed against my palm, at once hard and soft to the touch. I fitted the head of it to my nether lips. His hips jerked forward and he groaned, filling me.

Him inside of me—it was like nothing I'd ever felt. For a moment, I almost panicked. His weight pinned me to the ground, pressed the air from my lungs. His chin ground against my neck. His hips moved convulsively. Over and over, Cillian drove into me, and the fullness was overwhelming.

"Slower!" I gasped.

He shuddered and grated out a single word. *"Can't."*

And then, at the end, it changed. Just as his buttocks began to quiver and his back arched, discomfort gave way to pleasure.

"Ah, no!" I clutched his shoulder blades. "Not yet!"

"Sorry!" He spent himself helplessly in me.

We lay quietly for a moment. Cillian's breath was ragged in my ear. I waited until it slowed. "Can we try it again?"

"Aye." He rolled off me and propped himself on one elbow. "Forgive me, will you? That's a winter's worth of wanting you like I've never wanted anything else." He traced a line between my breasts and down my belly. "Gods," he whispered. "There's no one else like you, Moirin. No one in the world."

I smiled. "No?"

His fingers slid between my thighs. "No." He pulled his hand away. Milky seed glistened on his fingertips. "No blood." Cillian frowned. "Was I not the first?"

"You were. Who else would it be?"

"Don't lie to me." There was a note in his voice I'd never heard before. It made me angry.

"Why would I?" I retorted. "I'm a free woman, Cillian. If I chose to take another lover, I would, and it would be no concern of yours. But I'd not lie about it. There's no one else."

Cillian sighed. "I'm sorry! It's only that the thought of anyone else having you puts a knot in my guts."

I thought, choosing my words with care. "You do not *have* me, Cillian mac Tiernan. No one *has* me. I am my own to give. Is that understood between us?"

After a moment, he nodded. "It is."

"Good." I reached for him. "Now let us try this again. Only this time, I want you to go more slowly and not spend so quickly. Is *that* understood?"

He grinned. "Aye, mistress."

The second time was better. I was slick inside with his seed and there was no discomfort. Cillian moved slowly inside me, propped on his arms, watching my face. I felt a quickening deep inside me and found my hips moving to match his rhythm without thinking. Cillian thrust harder and this time I wanted him to. Stone and sea! He was so big and so deep inside me. Faster, now—faster and faster. What my body wanted seemed just out of reach.

And then it wasn't.

Deep, deep ripples of pleasure burst inside me. I abandoned myself to it, grabbing his buttocks, moaning mindlessly. The bright lady opened her hands and an entire flock of doves took flight.

"Oh, gods," Cillian whispered reverently.

When it was over, I felt calm and happy. We lay drowsing in the meadow, limbs entwined. A curious dragonfly came to investigate, hovering above us on gossamer wings. I stretched out one languid arm. It lighted briefly on my forefinger, regarding us with eyes faceted like gems.

Cillian's breath stirred my hair. "Magic?"

"Only the ordinary everyday kind." I watched it take wing.

"Moirin."

I looked at him. "Aye?"

His face was solemn. "Marry me."

I sat upright with a jolt. *"What?"*

"I'm serious." He leaned on his elbows. "I miss you when we're apart—and I daresay you miss me, too. So why ever not?"

I said the first thing that came into my head. "I'm too young."

Cillian gave my naked self a pointed look. "Oh, aye?"

It made me smile reluctantly. "I'm not ready, Cillian. I've not even begun to think about it."

"Surely you don't plan to spend the rest of your days living like a wild thing," he pressed me.

"Why ever not?"

He made an inarticulate sound. "Dagda Mor, girl! You look like something that just stepped out of a fairy tale, and you run around in a dress that might as well serve as a gunny sack with twigs in your hair and no shoes on your feet."

I felt at my hair. "So?"

Cillian tried a different tack. "At least do me a kindness. Promise you'll come to visit Innisclan and meet my family this summer."

"I met your family," I reminded him.

"You stood atop a cliff for five minutes and exchanged a grand total of four words with my father," he said in exasperation. "And it was years ago. Come now." He waved one arm around at the woods. "You've shared every part of your life with me. Is it asking so much of you to let me share a little piece of mine?"

"No," I murmured.

"So you'll come?"

I sighed. "I will."

EIGHT

I expected my mother to speak against the visit to Innisclan, but she
didn't. "You'll pass the night there?" was all she asked.

"Aye," I said. "I promised Cillian I'd stay for supper, and it will be
too late to return afterward." I hesitated. "I won't go if you'd rather I
didn't."

"No, no." She shook her head. "Whatever life you choose for yourself, you need to choose out of knowledge, not ignorance. Go."

So I did.

Cillian wanted to dress me in borrowed finery, but I refused. "Let
them meet me as I am," I said to him. "If they reckon I'm not good
enough to sit at Lord Tiernan's table, no amount of lace and baubles
will change their minds."

He blew out his breath. "Gods, but you're as stubborn as your
mother!"

"And rude, too," I reminded him.

"Aye." He grinned. "But oh, so very, very sweet in other ways."

It was afternoon when we rode into Innisclan, me behind Cillian
on his long-legged gelding. It had been five years since the pilgrimage
to Clunderry, and it felt strange to leave the untamed spaces to which
I was accustomed. Cattle grazed in meadows marked by low stone
fences. Here and there, we saw people who called out greetings to Cillian. When they saw me, they stared, curious. It made my skin prickle
and I fought the urge to summon the twilight and conceal myself from
their prying gazes.

At the top of a rise, we halted and regarded the green hollow below.

"Innisclan," Cillian said in satisfaction.

It was a vast stone hall surrounded by outlying buildings. Cillian pointed out the mill and the smithy and the Academy founded by Eamonn mac Grainne and his Skaldic bride. In an adjacent field, a group of young men played a vigorous game involving sticks and a ball. When we drew near, they hailed him with shouts.

"Cillian, lad!"

"Come, give us a hand!"

And then they saw me and went quiet.

"That's the witch's daughter," someone murmured.

"Aye."

"*I'd* fancy a piece o' that," another voice declared boldly.

There was heat in their eyes. I could feel it on my skin—an itch of a different sort. It set the wings to fluttering in my belly in an unthinking response, but it made me nervous, too. There was no care in their regard, only hunger. I was glad when Cillian shook his head at them and kept riding.

Desire, I thought, could be a dangerous gift.

At the stable, Cillian dismounted and helped me down. The freckled lad to whom he gave the chestnut's reins stared at me with frank awe.

"Witch-girl." Cillian kissed my lips. "Come. Meet my family."

I went with him.

The doors to the hall of Innisclan were tall. Wood, bound with steel. One of Lord Tiernan's men inclined his head to Cillian, doing his best not to stare at me. The tall doors swung open. Despite the brightness of the day, it was dark inside. I hesitated on the lintel, curling my toes on the cool stone. I'd never been inside a man-made dwelling.

"There's naught to harm you here, Moirin," Cillian said softly. "I swear it."

"Moirin!" A young woman hurried toward us, her arms extended. She caught my hands in hers and squeezed them, her eyes bright. "You've come at last."

"This is Aislinn," Cillian said. "My sister the heir."

She hadn't been at the meeting atop the cliff, but I would have known who she was without him telling me. They both had a look of their father.

"Well met." Aislinn kissed me on both cheeks. Still holding my hands in hers, she regarded me. "Dagda Mor! Cillian, she's a vision to be sure, but could you not at least have offered the lass the loan of a decent gown and a pair of shoes?"

"He—" I began.

"I—" he said.

"No mind." Paying our words not the slightest heed, Aislinn tugged me across the threshold. "Come with me. I've things you can borrow."

"I'm fine," I managed.

She gave me a hurt look. "Ah, now! Would you begrudge me the pleasure?"

"Ahhh . . . no?"

"Right you are." Aislinn gave another smart tug on my hands. "Come along, then."

I went with her, casting a helpless glance over my shoulder. Cillian shrugged, equally helpless.

To my eyes, Aislinn's bedchamber was a small, cramped space. The moment she closed the door behind us, I felt stifled and confined. The room had one window and I hovered close to it, breathing fresh air in anxious gulps while she pulled gowns from a chest, holding them up and examining them.

"This ought to suit," she said of a gown of fine-combed green wool. "It will set off your eyes." She glanced up at me. "Are you all right?"

"Aye," I said weakly. "'Tis my first time indoors."

Her eyes widened. *"Ever?"*

I eyed the closed door. "Aye."

Cillian's sister was a quick study. She followed my gaze and hurried to open the door. "Better?"

Something in my chest eased. "Thank you, yes."

"Right, then." She stood in the doorway with her back to me. "I'll stand sentry duty, shall I? You try on that gown."

The gown fit nicely, only a little loose. I smoothed it with both hands, feeling the fineness of the weave, and glanced down at myself to admire the way the fabric clung to my body. Aislinn turned around to regard me with approval.

"Let's do something with your hair, shall we?" Without waiting for my reply, she pointed at a chair. "Sit."

I sat.

When I was little, my mother would comb the tangles from my hair, but it was a painful process and we'd never had a brush. This felt good. I relaxed with pleasure as Aislinn ran the brush through my hair.

She laughed at my expression. "I've a cat that gets that very look when she's being petted."

"Mmm." I noticed that when she smiled, Aislinn had the same dimples that her brother did. I wondered what it would be like to kiss her. Mayhap the thought showed in my face, because she cleared her throat and put down the brush with alacrity, moving behind me.

"I'll just put it in a simple braid."

It didn't feel simple when it was done, braided and coiled and pinned into place. Aislinn picked up a silvery object and handed it to me.

"See how you like it," she said.

The object was a mirror.

I'd never seen a true reflection of my own face before. I studied it. With my hair coiled neatly, it was easy to see. There was the stamp of my mother's blood in the angle of my cheekbones, the shape of my chin. But it was all different, too. And I did have very green eyes.

"Do you like it?" Aislinn asked.

I touched my hair. "Oh, yes. It's lovely."

"Good." She busied herself with finding a pair of velvet slippers that matched the gown. They were narrow and pinched my toes, but I suffered it, reluctant to deny Cillian's sister the pleasure it gave her. Aislinn clapped her hands together. "Perfect!"

When we returned to the main hall, Cillian gaped at me. "Moirin?"

"One and the same," I agreed.

Unexpectedly, he offered me a courtly bow. "And the very picture of beauty thus adorned. Come, will you see the Academy?"

It was large enough to house over a dozen scholars. The students were just settling in to an early supper in the dining hall—young men and a few women, sons and daughters of nearby estates. I recognized several of the young men from the game in the field. While their regard was still avid and curious, this time it was more circumspect. It occurred to me, trying not to hobble in my too-tight slippers, that attire was another form of concealment.

Cillian showed me the library, the pride of the Academy. Running my fingers over the spines of countless volumes, peering at the enticing scrolls in their cubbyholes, I could almost imagine myself studying here. Then he showed me the quarters where the women lodged.

I shuddered.

It was a long, windowless room with a row of narrow beds in it. Just looking at it made me feel trapped and frantic.

"Ah, no," I said feebly. "I think not."

Cillian pulled me away. "You wouldn't have to stay here if we wed," he said in a cunning tone. "We'd stay in the great hall, you and I."

Somehow, I doubted his chamber was any larger than his sister's. "I'll think on it."

"Do."

And then we returned to the hall of Innisclan for our own supper.

Although it seemed very fine to me at the time, I know now that it was a modest affair with only immediate family in attendance. None of the others I'd encountered atop the ridge long ago were present. Only Lord Tiernan and his wife, Caitlin. Aislinn. Cillian.

Me.

When the first course of leek soup was served, I picked up my bowl without thinking and set my lips to the rim. They stared at me in horror. Lady Caitlin actually blanched.

"Like this," Aislinn said gently, demonstrating with her spoon.

"Oh," I murmured, feeling foolish. I wasn't ignorant, I knew what a spoon was. I had a very nice one carved out of horn somewhere. It was just that we did without when it was easier, which was most of the time.

After that, I watched and learned. To be truthful, there were some implements with which I was unfamiliar. *This* utensil went in *that* hand. One did not eat until all the table had been served and Lord Tiernan ate the first bite and nodded, signifying all was well. In between bites, one patted one's lips with the crisp white cloth that had been provided. In between courses, one dipped one's fingers in a bowl of warm water, then wiped them on the self-same white cloth.

The conversation was stilted and awkward. Cillian was no help, turning sullen beneath the weight of his parents' apparent disapproval of me. Aislinn did her best, asking me about my studies and which of the books I'd read was my favorite.

At least the food was very, very good. Especially the stuffed goose.

At Lady Caitlin's behest, talk turned to matters of Innisclan as she prompted Lord Tiernan to relate his efforts to cultivate a transplanted D'Angeline grapevine that had been sent as a gift of the King. It seemed it was failing to thrive.

"Mayhap Moirin might have some insight," she suggested with polite malice. "Have you not been reading about D'Angeline culture, my dear? I seem to recall Cillian asking to borrow some volumes a while ago."

"I hardly think—" Lord Tiernan began.

"Only a little," I interrupted him. "But if you'd like me to have a look at it, I may be able to tell you what's wrong."

My offer was met with a surprised silence.

"It's naught to do with D'Angeline culture. Moirin says plants speak to her," Cillian informed them with a gleam in his eye, their discomfort restoring his spirits.

"Really?" Aislinn looked interested. "What do they say?"

"Not much," I admitted. "It's not words, it's just . . . impressions. You know the way it feels on a bright spring day after a night's rain when all the world is washed fresh and clean, and you can almost hear the trees stretching their branches and the leaves drinking in the sunlight?" Lady Caitlin looked dour, but the others nodded. "It's like that only stronger."

"Fascinating," Lord Tiernan murmured.

And so nothing would do but that after supper, Lord Tiernan sent for the gardener who served as his would-be vintner and we traipsed out into the field to examine the grapevine. In the warm light of the setting sun, the old stock looked hardy enough, but the new growth was paltry, spindly, pallid tendrils barely clinging to the trellis. I stroked it with my fingertips, trying to hear without ears while the aggrieved gardener demonstrated to Lord Tiernan for what was clearly the hundredth time that the soil was rich and black and moist.

Too moist, the roots whimpered, longing for sandier soil.

I wound a pale tendril around one finger, feeling the urge to coax it to grow. "The earth's too rich," I said instead. "This fellow here wants dirt that doesn't hold the moisture so well." I pointed up the ridge. "Do you plant him somewhere higher where the water can drain, I reckon he'll thrive."

The gardener looked indignant. I shrugged. It wasn't my fault if he didn't know his trade as well as he ought.

"Fascinating," Lord Tiernan repeated, stroking his beard. "I may just try it."

"You can't be serious!" his wife said with asperity.

"Why not?" For the first time, he gave me a smile with a hint of warmth in it. "After all, we've tried everything else. And it seems to me that when one is given advice by a beautiful young lady who talks to plants, one ought to heed it."

That didn't sit well with her. Fortunately, the sun was sinking beneath the horizon. When we returned to the hall, I professed myself exhausted and begged their leave to retire for the night. It was true, I was worn out from the unfamiliar strain of being around strangers. Aislinn graciously showed me to a guest-chamber even smaller than any I'd seen. I took off her borrowed dress and folded it carefully, uncoiled and unbraided my hair with an effort, then curled up in a proper bed with clean-smelling linens and tried to sleep.

I couldn't, not for the life of me.

I'd left my door ajar and I could hear the unfamiliar sounds of human activity—boots scuffing, dishes clattering. I tried shutting the door, but then the trapped feeling closed in on me. After what was surely the better part of two hours, I gave up and resolved to slip out unseen and pass the night outdoors.

It was agonizingly difficult to summon the twilight, something that came as second nature to me at home. Somehow it was all different here in this hall built by men's hands with history carved into every stone.

Mine was a gift meant to be used by wild folk in wild places, and I'd suffered myself to be tamed today.

Now that was a fearful thought.

But I made myself be calm and remember, and at last it came. I stole out of the chamber with a profound sense of relief.

The great hall wasn't empty. There was a sentry drowsing in a chair by the doors—and of course, the doors were barred. I paused, realizing that I'd likely wake him if I left, and wondered if it was worthwhile.

And then I realized that Lord Tiernan and Lady Caitlin were sitting in high-backed chairs before the hearth, speaking in low tones.

About me.

". . . don't care if it's rational or not, I don't *like* her!" she was saying. "There's something sly and uncanny about that girl." There was a quiet note of despair in her voice. "Will you tell me you don't see it, too?"

I hoped he would. Uncanny, I'd grant her, but sly seemed unfair. Although given the particular circumstances, I'd be hard put to argue it.

"No," Lord Tiernan said slowly. "No, I do. I'll grant that she's not what I'd choose for a daughter-in-law."

"And yet Cillian's utterly besotted!" The note of despair gave way to hushed fury. "Why ever didn't you put a stop to it?"

He sighed. "I hoped the winter would cool his ardor. Two years ago, it seemed his fancy was passing."

"Two years ago, she was still a stripling child," she said darkly. "Now . . . oh, gods! What does she *want* with him?"

"I don't know," Lord Tiernan murmured.

I curled my toes in an agony of indecision. Part of me yearned to flee, part to retreat. And a third considerable part longed to reveal myself and shout at them that I'd never wanted aught of Cillian but for him to be my friend, and later, lover. It was hardly my fault he was muddling everything up with this talk of marriage.

"Mayhap we could bargain with her," Lady Caitlin mused. "They say the Old Ones like to make bargains, and I suppose she's one of them, whatever else she might be. Do you suppose we might bribe her to leave him alone?"

"With what?" He sounded weary. "They may choose to live like savages, but they're blood royal nonetheless. It's not as though I haven't offered our hospitality over the years. Money?" He shook his head. "They don't lack for it. There's a trust held in keeping for all of the descendants of Alais' line in Bryn Gorrydum, which Fainche knows perfectly well."

I blinked. She did?

"It's Fainche that disappoints me." Now Lord Tiernan sounded bewildered and angry. "Have I not always honored her choices? Why does she send her daughter to bewitch my only son?"

I'd heard enough.

I swept past the drowsing guard and unbarred the great doors, flinging them open, then fled into the warm night.

Behind me, there were cries of alarm.

I ignored them. In the twilight through which I moved, the landscape of Innisclan looked silver-grey and serene. I made my way to the poor, struggling grapevine we'd visited earlier. Now, while there was no one to see, I cupped its tendrils in my hands. Holding an image of dry, arid soil and bright beating sunlight in my mind, I blew softly on it. The tendrils stretched gratefully, reaching for a more secure grip on the trellis.

"Moirin!" Cillian was blundering around the fields, a lantern in one hand. With his other hand, he held up his unbelted breeches. "Moirin! Gods be damned, girl! You sodding little woodsprite! Will you not show yourself?"

When he was almost on me, I did.

"Oh!" He peered at me, then turned and waved the lantern in the direction of unseen pursuers. "It's all right, go back! I've found her!"

I folded my arms. "Sodding little woodsprite?"

"Hush." Cillian set down the lantern and embraced me. Despite everything, it felt good. I couldn't resist running my fingers into his crisp, springing hair. "Too much, was it?"

"Your mother detests me," I informed him. "And your father agrees that I'm sly and uncanny, and he considers *my* mother a disappointment. Oh, and apparently there are further truths she's not yet seen fit to divulge to me."

He ran his thumb over my lower lip. "Aislinn liked you."

"Did she?"

"Aye." Cillian smiled in the starlight. "She said you need to remember that if there's a spoon on the table, it's meant to be used, and that it's not terribly appropriate to look at people's sisters as though you wonder if they might taste good—a sentiment with which I'm in particular agreement. But she liked you."

I felt somewhat mollified. "I liked her, too."

He kissed me. "Give us a chance?"

"I'll try."

NINE

I tried.

For a year, I tried to think of myself as Cillian's potential wife.

The worst part of it was that I *did* love him. Being with Cillian was the simplest thing on earth, familiar and uncomplicated. I loved the way our bodies came together. I loved to look at him in the aftermath of love. His disheveled auburn hair. His limbs and torso, pale and sinewy and freckled. Mine, golden and supple. We could talk for hours entwined that way.

But I didn't want to marry him.

"Why?" my mother asked in her direct way.

I shrugged. "Why did you never wed Oengus?"

She shrugged.

"My father?" I guessed.

"Nooo." She drew the word out. "That was . . ." She sketched a vague gesture. "A gift?"

"So?" I pressed.

"It wasn't the right time," she said firmly. "Oengus, I mean."

"Nor is this," I said. "And his father . . . I think Lord Tiernan might come around in time. But Lady Caitlin despises me. And I simply don't think I'm ready to be any man's wife."

"That's fair."

"Cillian doesn't think so."

"Moirin, my heart . . ." My mother sighed. "I told you long ago, that lad was doomed from the minute he laid eyes on you. He wants you, all of you, all to himself. If you're not willing to give it and accept the same from him, you'd do him a kindness to cut him loose, for he'll never be happy with less."

The thought alarmed me. "And lose him altogether?"

"Likely."

"No." I shook my head. "No, I don't want that."

I tried a different approach with Cillian. I was nearing sixteen and my woman's courses had yet to begin. I knew it troubled my mother, for I was a woman grown in all other ways, and it had begun to worry me, too. When I told Cillian I feared I might be barren, it had the dubious advantage of being true.

He was quiet for a long time. "I should have noticed. But women seldom speak of these things with menfolk."

"They do among the Maghuin Dhonn," I said, remembering Oengus and my mother discussing it.

"Still." Cillian gathered himself with an effort. "It doesn't matter," he said, sounding as though he were trying to convince himself. "I'm not my father's heir. It doesn't."

"It does," I murmured. "You should wed someone who'll be a proper wife to you and a mother to your children. Nothing would have to change between us."

"I don't want a proper wife!" he shouted at me. "I want you!"

I thought that might have changed matters between us, but the next time Cillian returned he was all smiles.

"You're not barren," he informed me.

"Oh?" I raised my brows at him. "Are you a midwife now?"

"No." He settled himself comfortably on the hearth. "But I spoke to a woman who is. And she spoke to another, who spoke to another, who recalled old tales her granddam told her from when the old Master of the Straits was overthrown and D'Angelines first came to Alba." He pulled me onto his lap. "We live in a remote corner of the world. Seems it's common knowledge in Bryn Gorrydum. Like it or not, you're half-D'Angeline, Moirin, and you take after your father's kind. It's different for you. You'll not be fertile until you beseech their goddess Eisheth to unseal the gates of your womb."

"Truly?"

"Truly." Cillian nuzzled my hair. "Elsewise, I'd have gotten you with child ten times over, wouldn't I? And then you'd have to wed me."

I laughed. "Oh aye, like my mother wed my father."

His face darkened.

"Ah, now, don't." I laid my hand across his lips. "If it's true, it's wonderful news. Can you not just let me enjoy it?"

He nodded reluctantly, and we spoke no more of it that day.

That night, I told my mother.

She gazed at me in shock, her lips parted. "Is he certain?"

I'd thought she'd be happier about it. "Aye," I said. "Fairly so. He says it's common knowledge in Bryn Gorrydum. Cillian wouldn't lie," I added, offended on his behalf if that was what she suspected. "Not about this."

"No," she murmured. "No, I suppose not." Her dark gaze was fixed on the distance. "If it's true, it changes things."

A shiver ran the length of my spine. "What things?" She didn't answer. A rare wave of anger swept over me. "Stone and sea, Mother! Is there to be no end to the secrets you keep from me? My parentage, my namesake, the bright lady . . . what of the funds held in trust for Alais' line?" I'd been waiting for the right moment to ask her, but now it just came out along with everything else. "Were you ever going to tell me about *that*?"

She looked startled. "What?"

"A trust in Bryn Gorrydum—" I shook my head impatiently. "No mind. What were you going on about *now*?"

"I forgot about the trust." Her voice was soft. "Forgive me. It's yours to draw on if you wish. I've a signet ring my own mother gave me hidden away somewhere. That's the token. I'll find it if you like."

"Mother."

She stirred the embers of our hearth-fire with a long stick. "Among our people, a year after you enter womanhood, you're to be presented to the Maghuin Dhonn Herself to be accepted as one of Her children."

"Or not?" I asked, chilled.

"Or not." She nodded. "She does not always show Herself."

I was silent for a while. "What happens if She doesn't?"

"Oh." My mother poked at the fire, her head averted. "If She did not, it would be because your heart had changed when you crossed the threshold from child to adult. It happens, sometimes. Your gifts would fade. You would no longer feel welcome among us and would wish to leave." She lifted her head and her eyes were bright with tears. "I swear to you, I've no idea what will happen when you pass through the stone door. I only know I fear it."

"Why?" I whispered. "Do you think She will not have me?"

She was honest. "I don't know."

"Because of the bright lady? Naamah?" I found myself on my feet and pacing. "Or the other one? The Good Steward, Anael? Or is it because of Cillian?"

"Mayhap all." Her voice was steady. "Mayhap none."

I was trembling. "I am *your* daughter! I am one of *Her* children! I asked to be nothing more! If I am not, who *am* I?"

"Yourself."

One word, steady and sure. It drained away my anger. I sank down on the hearth and put my head in my hands.

"Forgive me." My mother's voice floated above me. "Oengus and I . . . When your courses didn't come, we thought it best to wait. And I didn't wish to worry you without cause. I should have told you."

"Yes." I raised my head with an effort. "What happens now?"

"The rite will be arranged." She hesitated. "Unless you've changed your mind and wish to wed the lad."

"Cillian?"

She gave me a ghost of her wry smile. "Is there another?"

"You know there isn't." I ran my hands over my face, remembering how hard it had been to summon the twilight at Innisclan. "No. No, I do not. That was the cost of it all along, was it not? If I were to wed him and become the proper wife his world would make me no matter what he claims, I would suffer myself to be tamed. And I would no longer be a child of the Maghuin Dhonn."

"Aye," my mother murmured. "But as the wife of the only son of the Lord of the Dalriada, you would not be very far lost to me. So I do not speak against it."

"Do you speak for it?" I asked.

She summoned another smile, this one rueful. "No. I would have you follow your heart, Moirin mine."

"Then I would seek the blessing of the Maghuin Dhonn," I said firmly. "Whatever else I may be, whatever foreign gods seek to lay claim to me, I am Her child and yours, first and foremost. Whatever else may follow, all things proceed from that point."

My mother kissed my brow. "May it ever be so."

TEN

When Cillian came next, he was in a rare state.

"There's been a raid!" he informed me, his mood somewhere betwixt jubilant and belligerent. "A Tarbh Cró raiding party wearing the mac Niall's colors. They made off with two dozen head of cattle in broad daylight, taunting us all the while."

"Oh, aye? Listen—"

"They reckon the Dalriada have gone soft," he interrupted me. "Studying at the Academy and all. 'Tis true, my father's men were slow to respond—"

"Cillian—"

"But we mean to go after them!" he finished triumphantly.

I folded my arms. "We?"

He flushed. "Do you not reckon me a proper warrior?"

"I reckon you a lover and a scholar," I said in a soothing tone. "Cillian, don't be daft. Didn't Eamonn mac Grainne and his Skaldic bride found the Academy to give young men wiser and more productive pursuits than cattle-raiding?"

"Aye, but I don't imagine he meant to geld us in the process!" he said sharply. "A man must defend his home and property. Do you not think me capable?"

"I do."

"You don't seem it."

I sighed. "Is it not a matter for the courts?"

Cillian glowered. "Oh, courts be damned. What do you and your wild kin care for courts? It's just a bit of sport, Moirin. Will you begrudge me the chance to prove myself a man?"

"I wasn't aware it was in need of proving," I said pointedly.

"Look . . ." He took a deep breath. "You don't understand. I *have* to do this. As my father's son, I cannot let this insult stand. Arguing about it won't change matters. And I fear I can't linger, either. We ride out before dawn. Will you come back to Innisclan with me? Aislinn says you can wait and worry with her."

I made a face at him. "All right, then. I reckon I'd rather endure your mother's disdain than wait and worry on my own."

Cillian kissed me. "That's my girl!"

Although there was ample time on the ride to Innisclan, I didn't tell him about my mother's revelation as I'd intended before he arrived. His head was filled with details of the raid to come, and I didn't want to distract him. Truth be told, I'd no idea what manner of warrior Cillian was. I knew he was trained to wield a sword, and that on the hurling field where the young men played with sticks and a ball, he was one of the most skilled athletes.

But Alba had been at peace for a long while. The Cruarch, Faolan mab Sibeal, was reckoned a wise and sensible fellow, carrying on the legacy of Alais the Wise, our common ancestor. There hadn't been a major dispute on Alban soil in living memory, only foolish skirmishes like this promised to be, between young men with an excess of high spirits and a shortage of common sense.

I didn't care for it, not one bit.

Cillian, however, was in uncommonly good spirits now that I'd agreed to come. He related with relish the tale of how the D'Angeline prince Imriel de la Courcel had won the respect of the folk of Clunderry by staging a cattle-raid against a neighbor who'd given him insult. I was quiet, remembering the slain princess, the green burial mound, and the stone circle that smelled of ancient blood. At length, Cillian noticed my silence and faltered, recalling the way that tale ended and my people's role in it.

"Forgive me," he said with genuine contrition. "I don't suppose that's a tale the Maghuin Dhonn care to remember."

"We do, actually." I'd never told him about the pilgrimage to Clunderry. When it came to it, I was as bad as my mother for keeping secrets—but it had always seemed a private thing. "Many of us gather at Midsummer to remember it that we should never be guilty of such pride and folly again."

"The Hellenes have a word for it. They call it 'hubris.'" He hesitated. "Were they kin of yours? The magicians?"

I shrugged. "We are nearly all kin to some degree. One day, I suppose there will be too few of us to continue, else we should grow as inbred as your father's hounds."

"All the more reason to wed me," Cillian commented. "New blood."

I glanced down at my arms encircling his waist, the honey-colored hue of my skin. "That, I think, is not one of my worries."

"True," he agreed. "I'll grant you that one."

On the handful of occasions I'd visited Innisclan after that first time, it had always been quiet and peaceful. Today, it was roiling. The playing field was torn up by young men in wicker chariots dashing around, yelling and waving swords.

"Stone and sea!" I stared. "It's a whole army!"

Cillian laughed. "Nowhere near. 'Tis just a raiding party."

In my head, I knew it to be true. The Dalriada hadn't armed in full force since they helped restore Drustan mab Necthana, my own thrice-times-great-grandfather, to the Cruarch's throne—and then crossed the Straits to aid the D'Angelines in beating back the invading Skaldi. Many thousands had fought in that war.

But thousands was only an abstract number. When one is accustomed to solitude, fifty howling lads can seem a great many.

"Go on." Cillian nudged me fondly. "I've got to join this lot. You'll find Aislinn in the great hall."

I dismounted and fled.

I found Aislinn in the laundry, supervising the boiling of linen bed-sheets. "Moirin!" she greeted me warmly. "I'm glad you've come; it means the world to Cillian. Did you try to dissuade him?"

"I did," I admitted.

"So did I, but Father would have none of it." She cast a critical eye over a sheet hung on a rack. "Is that quite dry?"

"Aye, my lady!" a sweating maid gasped.

"Well and good." Aislinn tugged it loose. "Come, you can help me cut bandages. When the damage is tallied, I reckon there will be some sore heads—and likely worse. It will be a point of pride for them to claim they were tended by the hands of a princess of the Dalriada and one of Alais the Wise's own descendants."

"Will it?" I asked.

"It will," she assured me.

It was good to have something to do. We retired to a quiet salon. Aislinn hummed to herself, shears flashing. I did my best to emulate her, sawing away at the clean fabric in an effort to create even strips. We tidied up the loose threads and coiled them into rolls and laid them in a basket. Her mother was nowhere in evidence, for which I was grateful.

"So," she said after a time.

"So?"

Her grey eyes were keen. "Will you wed my brother?"

I flushed. "Please don't ask that of me."

"Do you love him?"

"Yes, of course!" I'd been all right while we were working in silence, but now the stone walls of the salon began to close in on me. It was hot. I tugged at the bodice of my dress—it was the green dress Aislinn had loaned me a year ago, she'd made me a gift of it—and struggled for air. "It's just that I'm not meant to live this kind of life."

"So it seems." Aislinn summoned a maidservant to bring a jug of cool water. I drank gratefully. "Moirin . . . please don't take this amiss. I'm not my mother to imagine that you've enchanted Cillian to some dire purpose. It's quite simple. You're a rare and lovely creature and he dotes on you."

I set down my glass of water. "But."

"But he is the son of the Lord of the Dalriada, not a country peasant without a care in the world beyond the next day's meal. Gods forbid, if something were to befall my father, Cillian would be *my* heir. He cannot run off and live in the woods with you—yet while you string him along, he will not look at any other. If you cannot make a life with him here, I wish you'd make a clean break of it."

"My mother said as much," I murmured.

"Your mother sounds like a wise woman," Aislinn said.

I felt betrayed. "You claimed you were glad I came here."

"And so I am," she said steadily. "Today, because I wished to do you the courtesy of saying these things to your face. On the morrow, for Cillian's sake. I do not ask you to spoil his moment of triumph. But will you think on what I've said?"

Little though I liked it, it was fair. "I will."

She kissed my cheek. "Thank you."

There was a great feast that night, platter after platter emerging from the kitchen. The long table was thronged. *Uisghe* flowed freely, and when the food had been picked over by the ravenous horde, there was music to accompany bloodthirsty songs bawled at the top of the young men's lungs. Lord Tiernan watched it all with an indulgent smile. It was hot and sweltering and awful and I hated every minute of it.

Many of the would-be warriors passed out from drink and began snoring where they lay, Cillian among them. I brushed the auburn hair from his brow and kissed him, preparing to make my escape. I couldn't face the prospect of trying to sleep in the tiny guest-chamber.

"Moirin," he said blearily. "Don't go."

"Only to the stables," I assured him. I'd slept there before. "I'll be here in the morning."

He uttered a faint snore in reply.

The guard on duty let me out without comment. I'd been here a few times by now, and they were accustomed to the witch's daughter's strange ways. Outside, it was cooler by far. I slipped out of the hated pinching slippers and breathed deeply, feeling free and easy in my skin for the first time in many hours.

As always, there was a part of me that longed to flee—but I'd promised Cillian I'd be there. He'd worry if I left, and the worry was a distraction he didn't need. So I made my way to the stables and made myself a bed of loose hay in an empty corner. It was prickly, but fragrant and clean-smelling, and the warm presence of dozens of horses dozing in their stalls was comforting in a way that human presences seldom were.

There, I slept.

I awoke in the dim hours before dawn to considerable commotion and scrambled out of my makeshift nest, dodging horses and men. Despite the night's excesses, the raiding party was assembling.

I found Cillian yawning beside a chariot and conferring with its driver. He gave me a glad, sleepy smile when he saw me, his eyes crinkling and his dimples showing. "There you are. I thought mayhap I dreamed you."

"Ah, no. I promised."

"So you did." He plucked a few stray bits of hay from my hair. "You look a mess. A gorgeous mess. Kiss me for luck?"

I did, pressing myself close to him, ignoring the hoots and envious comments it provoked. "Come back safely, will you?"

"Marry me if I do?" Cillian teased. I didn't answer. He gave my hair a gentle tug, then cupped my chin and kissed me again. He tasted of stale *uisghe*, and underneath it, his own familiar self. "Ah, Moirin! Don't take it so seriously. I told you, it's just a bit of sport. We'll be back before you know it."

"I pray you are," I murmured, shoving him away. "Go on with you."

They went.

They went in a great thunder of hooves, laughing and boasting and shouting to one another. I suppose it was a fine and glorious sight, all of the glossy horses, proud chariots, and long-limbed young men, but it still seemed foolish to me. I came from a dwindling people, and we cannot afford to risk our lives for sport.

It felt strange to be at Innisclan without Cillian's presence. I declined an invitation from Aislinn to pass the hours learning the fine art of embroidery and decided instead to explore the Academy's library. With all the lads away on a raid, it was quiet and empty. I found a history of the Tiberian occupation of Alba and settled in to read it, noting the differences between it and the stories my mother had told me.

I'd been there an hour or so when a fair-haired lad hobbled into the room leaning on a crutch, one leg in a splint—one of the Academy's scholars whose injury had prevented him from taking part in the raid.

"Oh!" He flushed at the sight of me, having taken a while to notice. "Sorry, I didn't see you there."

I smiled. "I'm good at not being seen."

"You're the—" His flush deepened.

"The witch's daughter?" I suggested.

He laughed self-consciously. "My mother would tan my hide for bad manners. Forgive me. I'm Fionn."

"Moirin," I said.

Despite the crutch, Fionn managed a bow. "Well met, my lady."

He selected a text of his own and for a time we read in companionable silence. I caught him stealing glances at me. As the day wore on, sun slanted through the windows, turning his fair hair to spun gilt. It looked as fine and silken as a girl's, and I couldn't help but wonder what it would feel like to run my fingers through it. I tried not to think it, but that only made it worse.

"Will you be studying here?" he asked politely after a while.

"No." I shook my head. "I think not."

"Pity." Fionn smiled. His lips were not as full as Cillian's, but they had a firm, pleasing shape. "You would be a splendid addition."

I wanted him.

The realization jolted me. It was an impersonal desire—I didn't even know the lad. But he was pretty and well spoken, and the urge to exert the power of my gift over him was there. And in that moment, a deeper awareness took root and blossomed in me. It wasn't only Cillian's life I didn't want. It was his possessiveness. My mother had said it. *He wants you, all of you, all to himself.*

She was right.

Aislinn was right.

I sat there dumbstruck at the obviousness and simplicity of it. I had no wish to belong to Cillian and Cillian alone. Mayhap it was the prompting of the goddess my unknown father served, or mayhap it was only that I was sly and fickle after all. Whatever the truth, I could never be the wife he wanted, proper or otherwise. And it wasn't fair to string him along like a trout on a line. I needed to let him go. To set him free to find someone who could love him with her whole heart as he deserved.

"Moirin?" Fionn inquired. "What is it?"

I was staring at him without seeing him. "'Tis naught," I said, collecting myself with an effort. "Forgive me, I was woolgathering." I closed the book I had been reading, rose, and replaced it carefully on the shelf where I'd found it. "My thanks," I said, inclining my head. "You've helped me to discover an important truth."

He stared back at me, nicely shaped lips parted. "I have?"

"Aye." I paused beside him to run a lock of his fair hair through my fingers. It felt as nice as it looked. "Aye, you have."

"Wait!" Fionn called after me as I left, reaching for his crutch, but I ignored him. I felt wretched and scared all at once, but I felt something else, too. As much as my heart ached at the thought of losing Cillian forever, in one guilty corner it soared with a newfound sense of freedom. I would wait. I would pass another night here. I wouldn't spoil his triumph. For one more night, I would be his and his alone.

But on the morrow, I would make an end to it.

"Moirin." Lady Caitlin greeted me sourly in the great hall, carrying a basket laden with the rolled bandages Aislinn and I had made.

"My lady." I gave her a rueful smile. "Have no fear, you'll be rid of me soon enough. I mean to leave your son alone."

She, too, stared. "You do?"

"I do," I said. Just saying it gave me a pang. I steeled myself against it, my eyes stinging. "Only grant him this night's happiness, I beg you. Please believe me when I tell you I take no pleasure in breaking your son's heart."

Her throat worked. "I would like to."

"Then do," I said simply.

Ah, stone and sea! I would that our tale, Cillian's and mine, had ended thusly as I'd written it in my head—hurtful, yet fair.

Would that it had.

It didn't.

The raiding party returned without fanfare, driving two dozen head

of cattle before them. We turned out to meet them. It was a triumph—
it should have been a triumph. But the ebullient young men who had
departed before dawn were quiet and subdued. Even the horses plodded, heads held low and bobbing with weariness and the semblance of
defeat.

One chariot . . .

"No!" I breathed, clutching Aislinn's arm. "Ah, no!"

Even beneath the cloak that covered him, I knew his shape. There
was no part of Cillian I did not know. One arm was outflung, jouncing
with the chariot's jostling, pale and sinewy and freckled. The chariot-
driver looked miserable.

My knees gave way. "No," I whispered.

"Forgive me, my lord, my lady," the miserable chariot-driver was
saying. "I did my best, but—"

His mother wailed.

"—flung loose and trampled . . ."

I ached all over. The words flowed over me, meaningless. Cillian
was dead. I'd spent the day thinking about giving myself to some lad I
didn't know while Cillian was dying.

"Get *out*." A hand knotted itself in my hair, wrenching my head
upward. On my knees, I gazed into the blazing eyes of Lady Caitlin. "All he was trying to do was prove himself to you! And it wasn't
enough, it was never going to be enough! All the while, you meant to
leave him!"

"My lady!" I protested.

She shook me violently. "*Get out!*"

I got to my feet. No one spoke.

"I loved him," I said. "I did."

A few cattle lowed, a plaintive sound. In the chariot, Cillian's body
lay unmoving. I uncovered it, flinching at the sight of his dented skull.
Blood had dried in his auburn hair. I kissed his cold lips. "Good-bye,"
I whispered.

"You should go now," Lord Tiernan said in a stony voice.

It was unfair—and yet it wasn't. I had tried to dissuade Cillian
from taking part in the raid. But I hadn't loved him enough to wed

him. And somehow it seemed to everyone including me that his death was my fault because of it.

Bowing my head, I started walking. When I had gone far enough that I no longer felt their eyes on me, I summoned the twilight and ran, blind and mindless with grief.

It wasn't long before I heard the sound of hoofbeats.

"Moirin!" Aislinn shouted. She passed by me, a shadowy figure on a silvery horse in the twilight—but then she turned and circled back. "Gods be damned, Moirin!" Her voice was raw. "You can't have gotten that far! Show yourself!"

I did.

The horse startled, rearing. Aislinn swore and grabbed at its mane, losing her grip on the rains. For one terrified instant, I thought to see a second scion of Innisclan thrown and trampled. I snatched the loose reins and yanked her mount's head downward.

"Be still!" I shouted at it.

For a miracle, it obeyed. Aislinn took a deep, shaking breath and dismounted. Her face, so like her brother's, was streaked with tears.

"It was their grief talking," she said. "I didn't want those to be the last words spoken to you."

My throat was almost too tight to reply. "You're kind."

"It wasn't your fault." She shook her head. "That stupid, bedamned raid . . . it wasn't your fault."

"I know," I murmured. "And yet."

Aislinn didn't argue with me. She didn't lie and tell me that her mother would regret her harsh words, that I would be welcome to return and share their grief. For that, I was grateful. Instead, she took my hand in hers and squeezed it, fresh tears flowing. "If things had been different . . ." She fell silent a moment, breathing hard and struggling for composure. "I would have been proud to call you my sister."

It was a great kindness and one I didn't deserve. I swallowed against the lump it brought to my throat. "So would I."

There was nothing left to say. Cillian was dead. Aislinn let go my hand and reclaimed her horse's reins. I held its head while she mounted.

In the saddle, she drew a kerchief from her bodice and wiped her eyes. I dragged a forearm over my own, realizing I was weeping without even knowing it.

"Thank you," I managed.

She nodded. "Good-bye, Moirin."

ELEVEN

It was a long way home from Innisclan on foot.

I remember little of the journey. My grief was so vast and unexpected and complicated by guilt that I was numb with it, which was a mercy. Even the urge to flee had passed. I put one foot in front of the other and kept walking. When it grew too dark to see, I summoned the twilight again and continued.

My senses were as dull as though I'd grown dead to the world around me. In the small hours of the night, I tripped over branches and stumbled through brambles. But step by step, I made my way home.

It was beyond late. The fire should have been banked hours ago. But there it was, burning in the pit on the hearth, the flames silvery and eldritch. I let go my cloak of twilight and the fire turned orange and gold and ordinary.

I was so very, very tired.

"Moirin?" My mother lifted her head. She looked haggard. "I felt you coming nigh onto an hour ago. Whatever is it?"

"Cillian—" I couldn't say it.

I didn't have to—she saw it in my face and rose. At the touch of her arms around me, I burst into wrenching sobs. My mother held me close and made soothing, meaningless sounds. When the storm of grief had wrung itself out, I told her how it had happened. And I told her what I'd been doing when it happened, the decision I'd made and the aftermath, my voice dry and flat. She listened without comment.

"Now you feel yourself to blame," she said softly when I had finished.

"Aye," I whispered.

My mother tilted her head. Her eyes caught the firelight and reflected it like a wild animal's. For a moment, I saw her as others did, her features marked by the stamp of the Maghuin Dhonn, uncanny and inexplicably strange. And then it passed and she was only her familiar self.

"It was his time," she said in a gentle tone. "That is all." I opened my mouth to protest, but she shook her head at me. "You could not have saved him, Moirin mine. Not without altering the course of his fate. And what followed may have been worse."

"You can't know that," I said. "Not for sure."

"No," my mother said. "No one can. But if you had gone against the truth of your heart, any promise you made him would have turned to ashes."

We sat together in silence while the fire burned low. At length the sky began to lighten in the east, and here and there a bird twittered. My mother stirred herself and banked the fire's embers.

"We'll take a few hours' sleep," she said. "Time enough to pack and be away by nightfall."

I looked dully at her. "Where?"

"The rite's to be held in the north. We'll be leaving a little early, that's all."

"No." I swallowed. "I can't. I truly can't. Not now."

"You can." My mother gazed steadily at me. "Do you imagine your grief will abate sooner staying *here*?"

I looked around at our tidy campsite. Cillian had taught me my letters on this very hearth, scrawling with a soot-blacked twig. Above us was the ledge where I'd first caught him spying with a satchel full of peaches. There was the willow tree beneath which I'd taught him to catch trout, its roots drinking deep of the stream. There was the path to the meadow in which we'd spent so many hours.

"No," I said. "I suppose not."

She nodded. "We'll be off by noon."

I didn't think I could possibly sleep, but I did, worn out by grief and guilt. When I awoke, the sun was high in the sky and I was wearier than ever—but our meager belongings were packed and my mother was watching me.

"Eat." She handed me a cattail-flour cake. "You'll need your strength."

I didn't want to eat. I didn't want to undertake this journey. I wanted to roll myself in my blankets and go back to sleep. Mayhap if I slept long enough, I would wake to find that my memories had faded. I'd no longer have the vision of Cillian's dented skull vivid before my eyes, the touch of his cold lips lingering on mine.

"There is a glade hidden high in the mountains to the north," my mother said unexpectedly. "It holds a lake and a stone door. On the other side of that door, you may find the Maghuin Dhonn Herself. The door is waiting for you, Moirin. It has waited a year and more."

"You said yourself we'd be leaving early. Can it not wait a few days longer?" I asked plaintively.

"Mayhap. Will you take that chance?" She gestured around. "There is nothing to hold you here. Cillian is lost to you. Mayhap it is a sign. Will you risk losing your *diadh-anam*, too?"

It seemed a cruel threat, but the spark of awareness in my breast pulsed in sudden alarm. I made myself eat a portion of the cake although it was dry and crumbly in my mouth, washing it down with a great deal of water. When I was done, I felt a little bit stronger.

"All right." I got to my feet. "Let us go."

My mother pushed us hard on that first day. We passed from our own small kingdom of wilderness into deeper wilderness. It was hard going and I was already bone-weary from my long trek back from Innisclan. By the time she called a halt to make camp, my muscles were burning from the strain. I dropped my pack and fell asleep where I sat, my head bowed on my knees.

My mother shook me awake. "Eat," she said, pressing a roasted haunch of rabbit into my hand.

The meat was greasy and good. I gnawed and swallowed, my belly rumbling. "When did you go hunting?"

"While you slept."

"It's good." I wiped my lips. "Thank you."

She laid her hand on my brow. "Sleep."

I slept.

How many days we went on that way, I could not say. Most of me was still numb inside. Left to my own devices, I'd have just as soon lay down and slept, not caring if I starved. I'd lost every trick I'd known for living in the wild. I'd grown dense and clumsy with grief. But my mother tended to me and kept me going in her stubborn, patient way.

And bit by bit, I came back to myself.

Cillian was dead.

I was alive.

It was the way of the world. I could hate it and I could rail against it, but I could not change it. I could not change the fact that I'd betrayed him in thought while he lay dying. I could not change the fact that his family, save Aislinn, despised me.

All I could do was live.

"You brought him joy, Moirin," my mother said to me some nights into our journey. "That lad loved tales of magic and enchantment. You, you let him live one."

"He didn't die in one," I reminded her.

"He did, though." She busied herself with plucking a ptarmigan. "In the story he told himself, he did. He died without ever knowing the pain of losing you. He died with his heart unbroken, filled with hope and desire."

"That's a small mercy," I murmured.

She looked up at me. "Aye, it is—but a mercy nonetheless. Remember the joy, Moirin mine."

It was in the foothills of the mountains that we saw our first bear of the journey. I scented it on the wind and felt my dulled senses quicken for the first time in many days. I breathed deep through my nose and opened my mouth to let the air play over my tongue. My mother caught my arm and smiled, pointing.

"Oh!" I said in delight.

I'd seen bears before, but not many—and seldom so close. This one stood on its hind legs, taller than a man, scratching its back against a tall oak tree. Bits of its wiry fur clung to the bark. When it saw us, it dropped to all fours and gave a menacing woof.

"Peace, little brother," my mother said in a soothing tone. Twilight flickered around her, sparkling in the corners of my eyes. "'Tis clear this territory is yours. We do but seek to pass."

The bear grumbled.

"Peace," I added. "We seek the Great Mother Herself."

It gave a mighty snuffle, then gave a low coughing bark and wandered away, shambling through the trees. I watched the vast wilderness swallow it with wonder. The spark of the *diadh-anam* within me sang, happy and glad. "That's a good sign, is it not?"

My mother squeezed my arm. "It is."

For the space of a few minutes, I forgot about Cillian's death—and then the grief came crashing back upon me. I shouldered it and kept going.

Foothills gave way to mountains, and the mountains grew steep. I do not think we travelled so far as we did in our pilgrimage to Clunderry, but the way was harder and our progress was slow. By the time we reached our destination, I was more fit and hardy than I'd ever been in my life.

As for the destination itself, I lack the words to do it justice.

It was the sound of piping that alerted us, high and fluting. At first I took it for birdsong, but no. The melody was too intricate.

A slow smile spread across my mother's face. "I thought we were nearly there."

"Where?" I saw nothing but the mountain slope.

"You'll see."

Soon, I did. A man sat cross-legged on a ledge high above us playing a little silver pipe. He lowered it from his lips and called out to us. "Welcome, little niece! Not so little, I see. Greetings, sister! Can you spot the entrance?"

"I can," my mother said.

My uncle Mabon rose. "Come, then."

He vanished.

I blinked. There was no telltale sparkle of the twilight and I'd been looking at him all the while. Ignoring the phenomenon, my mother made for a great pine tree jutting up from the mountainside. Following as she ducked behind it, I saw that the tree concealed a few promontories like rough steps leading to a dark, narrow crevice.

"Is that it?" My heart raced. "The doorway?"

"Hmm?" My mother glanced over her shoulder. "Ah, no. Only the entrance to the hollow hill."

One by one, we squeezed into the crevice. It was a tight enough space that it made me anxious—but somewhere ahead, I could hear the sound of my uncle's pipe, the sound echoing oddly. I followed my mother as she edged sideways down the dark, narrow passage for longer than I cared to recall.

And then it opened.

I stared, dumbstruck.

It was a cave, but it was like no cave I'd ever seen. For one thing, it was vast. There was light coming from an opening somewhere above, illuminating it. Many of the surfaces were smooth and looked to have been sculpted of milk made solid. Shapes like icicles thrust up from the floor, hung down from the roof. My uncle Mabon stood atop what looked to be a frozen waterfall, playing. The notes of his pipe bounced and echoed from the walls. I wandered in an awed daze. To the right, I could see that there were further passages.

"There is a legend that the mighty Donnchadh carved this place out of the mountain for our people to hide," my mother said behind me. "Me, I suspect it is older, for the stone door stood long before his time."

"It's wonderful," I breathed.

She smiled. "Don't go wandering. Even one of our kind can get lost in here without the gift of stone."

Mabon lowered his pipe. "Any mind, folk are waiting. Come!"

We clambered up the slippery stone waterfall. When I reached the top, my uncle helped me up, then took my shoulders in his hands and gazed at me. "Ah, Moirin child," he murmured. "You may not have proved a great magician, but you're a rare beauty." His dark gaze was soft. "I'm so very sorry about the lad."

My throat tightened. "How did you know?"

He smiled sadly. "We're not all such recluses as your mother. Word of a royal death travels swiftly."

After greeting my mother fondly, Mabon led us farther up and farther inside the mountain. Here and there, shafts of light lit our way. In places, strange crystalline formations grew from the walls, tinted pale blue and gold. There was a gorge where a real waterfall poured into darkness. We crossed the gorge on a narrow, hanging bridge, the underground stream flowing far beneath our feet.

It was beautiful.

And I could not help but think two thoughts. One, that I wished Cillian could have seen it. The other, that this was a place of the Maghuin Dhonn. I didn't need to be told it was a sacred place. I could feel it in every step I took, in the way the air breathed over my skin. And if the Maghuin Dhonn Herself chose not to acknowledge me, I feared this place would be lost to me.

On the journey, wrapped in grief, I hadn't given thought to it.

Now I did, and I was scared.

At last we climbed a smooth shaft into which hand and footholds had been carved. I could sense the presence of people above us and smell wood-smoke. At the top, other hands helped us.

We emerged into a large cavern. It wasn't wondrously sculpted, just ordinary rugged granite, but the scale was impressive. There was a cooking fire in the center beneath an opening to vent the smoke. At the far end, it opened onto sunlight and an expanse of blue sky.

"Moirin." Oengus embraced me. "Welcome."

I inclined my head. "Thank you, my lord Oengus."

A wizened old woman behind him burst into a cackling laugh. "Ah-ha-ha! Lord Oengus, is it? Listen to her, manners fit for a lady of the Dalriada!"

I flushed, hurt and angry and embarrassed.

"Peace, Nemed." Oengus gave her a sharp look. "The lass needs no reminding of her loss."

"Oh, aye." The old woman worked her shriveled lips in a chewing motion. "Forgive me, child. I'm old. I guided your mother through the rite, and her mother before her. Such a pity that one died young."

My mother took a deep breath. "Nemed . . ."

"I mean no harm, daughter of Eithne." She patted my mother's arm. "I was fond of your mother. You'll be blunt-spoken, too, come my age. Now." She tugged my hair with surprising strength. "Bend down and let me have a look at you."

Given no choice, I obeyed.

Nemed peered at me with rheumy eyes, clucking her tongue. "Look at you, caught all betwixt and between!" She sniffed at me. "You'll drive the lads mad, that's for sure. And mayhap a few of the lasses, too."

My mother made a strangled sound.

"Peace, Fainche." The old woman flapped one hand at her, the other still tangled in my hair. "*You* laid down with a D'Angeline. Are you so isolated in your hermitage that you've not heard what manner of mischief *they* get up to?"

"No," she said shortly.

I cleared my throat. My neck was getting stiff.

"Ah, right." Nemed let go my hair with reluctance, letting the length of it run over her crabbed fingers. "But you're here, eh? That's something." She shook her head. "What Herself will make of you, I've no idea."

I swallowed. "I pray She finds me worthy."

"It's not a question of *worthy*." The rheumy eyes were shrewd, but there was compassion in them. "It's a question of whether or not you're one of Her own. Do you believe so, daughter of Fainche?"

"I do," I said.

Nemed patted my hand. "We'll see, won't we?"

Although I had supposed it would be a large gathering like the pilgrimage to Clunderry, there were only two others present—a young woman named Camlan and a young man named Breidh. They were the last two members of the Maghuin Dhonn to have passed through the rite and tradition dictated their presence. Until the moment this was made clear to me, I hadn't realized men went through it, too.

"Of course!" Breidh looked surprised. "How not?"

"I don't know." I felt foolish. "You, ah . . . how is the timing of it reckoned for men?"

Camlan giggled. "A year from the night they first spill their seed unwitting in their sleep." She nudged Breidh. "First but not last, eh?"

He shrugged. "Better our way than yours."

She rolled her eyes. "That's the truth!"

I wanted to feel at ease with them. They were of my people and my own age—and yet I was different. As easy as they were with each other, I could sense that they were uneasy with me.

"Come." Camlan took my arm, doing her best to overcome her discomfort. "Would you see the glade, Moirin?"

"Aye, please."

She led me to the far end of the cavern, Breidh trailing after us. The wide mouth opened onto a ledge that presided over a sharp decline. We were atop the very peak of the mountain. The glade lay below, a green bowl held in the cupped hand of the earth, dotted with pine trees. There was the lake, and there was the stone doorway.

I gazed at it.

It was a simple thing. Two great standing stones, taller than a man's height, with a slab laid across them. Its shadow slanted eastward toward us.

"How . . ." I hesitated. "I don't understand."

"There are worlds and there are worlds," Oengus said in his deep voice. Having joined us unseen, he sat on the ledge, dangling one leg over the drop. "When we call the twilight to us, we take half a step into the spirit world that lies alongside ours, the same and yet different. When you pass through the stone door, you take the whole step."

The younger two nodded, their expressions reverent.

"One day it may be that the folk of the Maghuin Dhonn will pass through it forever," Oengus mused. "Pass into myth and become spirit rather than flesh, haunting the hollow hills and the sacred places of Alba."

"But not today," I said.

He gave himself a shake, and a sideways glinting glance at me. "Not today, no."

We ate well that night. How they had known to expect us, I wasn't sure. I'd never known exactly how my mother kept contact with our people, and I didn't learn it that night, either. But there was a venison stew that had simmered all day, savory with leeks and herbs. "Eat," my mother said. "Tomorrow, you fast." And there was a jug of *uisghe*, and after it had gone around twice, it didn't matter to me how they had known. The warmth in my belly dispelled the memory of Cillian's cold lips.

When we had finished, Mabon played a haunting air on his pipe and we all listened in peaceful silence. Beyond the mouth of the cavern, darkness settled over the glade as though summoned by the sound of his playing. It came to me that this very scene might have taken place a thousand years ago—or five thousand years ago, before mankind thought to record its history.

I was part of a very, very ancient tradition.

The thought made me shiver—both for the wonder of it, and for fear of losing it. I gazed around at the firelit faces of my people and felt a sudden pang of kinship. The spark of the *diadh-anam* inside me blazed wildly.

"That's the spirit." Old Nemed patted my hand again and gave me a dubious look. "Mayhap She'll have you after all."

It wasn't terribly encouraging.

TWELVE

The rite itself was simple.

On the morrow, I fasted. Old Nemed gave me my instructions. When the sun began to set, my eyes would be anointed and she would give me a bowl of mushroom tea to drink. Once I had drunk it, I was to descend alone into the glade and pass through the stone door without looking right or left. Then I was to wait beside the lake until either the Maghuin Dhonn showed Herself to me, or I fell asleep.

Nemed gave me a sharp pinch. "So best you stay awake."

"Ow!" I rubbed my arm. "Is it a test, then? She'll come if I stay awake long enough?"

"She'll show Herself or not as She chooses," she said. "There's no sure way to make it happen." She gave my arm another vicious pinch. "But there is a sure way to fail."

I winced. "Your point is well taken, my lady."

Nemed snorted. "My lady!"

"Nemed . . ." I hesitated. "If I do fail . . . I understand, a little, what will befall me. My gifts will fade, and I'll no longer feel welcome among us. What of this place?" I gestured around. "Will it be forbidden to me?"

"Ah, child," she murmured. "No. You will forget it."

I swallowed. "How so?"

The deep wrinkles around her eyes tightened. "I will pluck the memory from you myself," she said gently. "Such is my gift."

I shivered. "Show me." Nemed gave me a startled look. "I want to see. I want to know how it's done."

She chewed on her lips. "That's not wise."

"I want to know," I said stubbornly. "I want to know what I face, every last bit of it."

Nemed sighed. "Child . . ."

"Show her," my mother said softly. The old woman grumbled. My mother came over to my side and took my right hand in hers. "Here's a good one to choose." She turned my palm upward and stroked a tiny scar in the webbing of my thumb. "Remember how you got this?"

I nodded. "The deadfall." When I was six or seven, I'd tripped and fallen onto the stump of an alder tree that had toppled over. I'd put out my hand to catch myself and driven a splinter through it.

My mother kissed the faint mark and closed my hand over it. "That's not one you'll miss."

After more grumbling, Nemed acquiesced. "You'll have to hold the memory in your thoughts," she said. "It only works if you consent."

"What if I don't?" I asked. "I mean . . . afterward?"

"If you fail?" she asked. I nodded. The gentleness returned to her tone. "If you fail, you'll give your consent willingly. Believe me, child. You'll want the memory of this place gone. They all do."

Her words chilled me more than anything else she'd said thus far. "Just show me."

"So be it." Nemed took my face in her gnarled hands and leaned in so close our noses almost touched. "Hold the memory and offer it freely."

I held it, willing her to take it. I remembered the halting jerk of a root catching my foot as I ran carelessly through the alder grove, and then the sudden shock of pain. Picking myself up from the ground and seeing the splinter run clean through the web of my hand. I remembered the dismay in my mother's voice and her hand clamped around my wrist, holding it immobile as she pulled out the splinter in one agonizing yank.

Nemed inhaled deeply.

Something elusive slithered in the space behind my eyes, slippery as an eel. I felt it spooling out of me and cried aloud at the sense of loss. And then the old woman swallowed and exhaled, blowing softly into the void the thing had left behind. A cool mist filled my thoughts and dissipated.

Nemed released me. "There you are."

"That's all?" I shook myself. "But you didn't do anything."

"Oh, aye?" She smiled dourly and picked up my right hand. "How did you come by yon scar?"

"That?" I glanced at it. "I don't recall. I've had it since I was little." I *did* remember, though; I remembered my mother folding my hand closed over it not two minutes ago, saying it wasn't a memory I'd miss. And it was gone, gone as surely as though it had never existed. My skin prickled. "Stone and sea!" I whispered. "That's a dire magic!"

"Aye." Nemed nodded. "So it is."

"And *that*, I suspect," Oengus said in a disapproving voice, appearing behind the old woman, "is why it works only on the consenting and ought never be used for aught but the most sacred purpose. Little over a hundred years ago, Alba and Terre d'Ange alike were nearly brought to their knees by the use of such magic."

Nemed made a dismissive sound. "That was altogether different and nothing to do with us."

Oengus folded his arms. "Nonetheless."

"Peace, both of you," my mother offered. "Moirin wanted to know and now she does. Mayhap the gift will pass to her one day. After all, it has to pass to someone."

"I'm not *that* old!" Nemed said sharply.

Oengus coughed. "You are, actually."

I let them bicker, rubbing the faint scar and gazing toward the end of the cavern. It seemed impossible that an entire memory was simply *gone*. I thought about the tale Oengus had mentioned. I knew it, of course; it was in one of the histories Cillian had brought me. Magicians from Carthage had stolen away the memories of the Cruarch of Alba and the entire peerage of Terre d'Ange and replaced them with falsehoods, and then stolen the Queen's heir. Terre d'Ange had sunk into madness. It was a terrible and wonderful tale, filled with star-crossed lovers and a demon trapped in a stone. And in the end, the enchantment had been undone and all was restored.

"Can you return it?" I asked Nemed.

She cocked her head. "Eh?"

"A memory," I said. "Can you put it back?"

"No, child." Nemed shook her head. "I can tell you what it was, but I can't restore it to you. I've no gift to hold another's memories to barter and trade, only to take what's offered. Once I've swallowed it, it's gone from you. Gone for good."

"Oh." I rubbed the scar with my opposite thumb. "All right, then."

The remainder of the day passed all too swiftly.

I ate no food, drank only water from a cistern deep within the hollow hill that Camlan and Breidh brought and offered to me in a brimming bucket with a wooden dipper. The water tasted like minerals and stone, but it was cold and good.

All too soon, the bright light at the end of the cavern took on a golden hue. Mabon, watching over the glade, turned to us. "It's time," he said simply.

Nemed beckoned, holding a jar of salve. "Where are the youngest?"

Camlan and Breidh came forward, dipping their fingers in the jar. I closed my eyes and let them smear the salve on my lids. It smelled sharp and stung a little.

"May you see Her true," they said in unison.

I blinked.

"Here." Nemed offered me a steaming bowl. I drank. The mushroom tea was acrid and bitter on my tongue. It warmed my empty belly, but it made me feel a little sick, too. Camlan and Breidh helped me to my feet.

"This way."

I let them guide me to the far end of the cavern. There, the open vista made me dizzy. I struggled to draw breath. The slope fell away at such a steep angle. Beneath me, the glade awaited. Already, the slanting sun threw the stone door's shadow across its green bowl, long and stark. Beyond the door, the lake glinted.

Oengus inclined his head to me.

Mabon played a lilting measure on his pipe and lowered it with a wistful smile.

"Moirin." My mother embraced me, hard and fierce and wholly herself. "I cannot force Her will. Only know that whatever passes, you are *my* daughter and the joy of my life. Now and always and forever."

My throat tightened. "I do."

Her dark gaze was intent. "Do you promise it?"

"I do." I returned her embrace, pressing my cheek to hers. "By stone and sea and sky, and all that it encompasses, I swear it."

She pushed me away. "Go, then."

I went.

It was a long, precarious descent, and my senses were disordered by Nemed's brew. I placed my hands and feet with care. My vision pulsed and throbbed. The rocky scree beneath me seemed at once far and near, the grain of the granite extraordinarily vivid and intriguing. At last, I gained the floor of the bowl. I took a deep breath and looked upward. Six small figures stood silhouetted in the mouth of the cavern. Only one raised its hand.

I saluted my mother in reply, then turned around.

The stone door awaited.

Here in the cupped hand of the glade, it seemed larger. The standing stones loomed, supporting a massive slab of granite. The sun had already sunk below the mountain peak. There were no shadows, only the soft blue dimness of incipient twilight. I crossed to stand before the doorway, looking neither to the left nor the right. The grass was surprisingly lush beneath my bare feet. I gazed through the stone door. Beyond, the lake awaited, its surface placid. Other than that, the glade didn't look any different on the far side of the doorway.

"So," I whispered.

The grass whispered back, murmuring vague protests beneath my feet. The pine trees sighed into the twilight.

I stepped through the doorway.

And everything changed.

I gasped; I couldn't help it. Overhead, the sky reeled, filled with stars. It was dark, but it was bright, too. Here, darkness and light were wedded. Everything was visible, everything stood in stark contrast to itself. Every leaf, every blade of grass. All existed, all were filled with splendid purpose.

There are world and there are worlds.

Oh, stone and sea and sky!

It was beautiful, so beautiful.

I fell to my knees and crawled. The placid lake beckoned. I remembered dimly that I was to wait beside it. Near its shore, I sat and waited.

I waited.

And waited.

Nothing and no one came. The stars wheeled overhead in their slow, stately dance. The strange effects of the mushroom tea on my perceptions faded. My belly cramped with hunger, worse than it ought to after a mere day's fast. I longed to drink from the lake to assuage it, but Nemed hadn't said it was permitted, so I didn't dare. I did my best to ignore the pangs. As the hours wore on, a profound weariness settled into my bones. My head grew heavy and nodded. I caught myself and snapped it upward with a jerk. And then it nodded again. Remembering Nemed's caution, I pinched my own flesh until it hurt.

But She did not come.

"Please," I whispered into the bright darkness. "Oh, please!"

There was no answer. The spark inside me guttered, failing. I was tired and hungry and alone. And I began, slowly and horribly, to understand the thing I could not have grasped before. If I failed here today, tonight, I would be bereft of all I had believed myself to be. Bereft of my people, of all that made me who I was. If that happened . . . ah, stone and sea! The memory of this place would be poison to me. I would give anything to have it gone.

And there were other gods waiting to claim me.

Somewhere, the bright lady smiled.

I gritted my teeth and forced my impossibly heavy head up from my knees. "No! Gods bedamned, I was *Hers* first!"

She came.

I sensed Her before I saw Her—a mighty presence moving across the mountainside. Moving through the forest. The guttering spark inside me blazed once more, driving me to my feet despite my terrible weariness. There was a sliver of a moon overhead that hadn't been there before.

On the far side of the glade, I saw Her emerge.

My heart sang inside me.

Moonlight silvered Her brown fur. She paced across the glade, the ground trembling beneath Her massive paws. I stood, dizzy and wavering, filled with awe and joy. Stone and sea, She was vast! As She rounded the lake, it seemed Her head blotted out the stars. And then Her size changed as She drew nearer, fitting Herself to my scale, only twice the size of an ordinary bear—yet no less wondrous for it.

"You're so beautiful," I breathed, scarce able to speak. "So very beautiful!"

The Maghuin Dhonn Herself lowered Her majestic head toward me. Her eyes were dark and wise, filled with a knowledge older than time. I could have stood forever gazing into them. Her nostrils twitched and I felt Her warm breath on my face.

Hers.

I was Hers.

"Thank you." Tears of joy stung my eyes. "Thank you!" I reached out one hand to touch her moon-silvered fur, unable to resist.

She turned away.

I felt a shock of abandonment. "Wait!" I cried, taking a few stumbling steps. "Please, don't go!" Several yards beyond me, She paused and turned Her head. There was sorrow and regret in Her eyes. "Please!" I begged. "I don't know what this means!" Looking toward the cavern for guidance, I cast a glance over my shoulder and gasped.

The stone doorway stood behind me.

But beyond it lay the sea. It sparkled in the bright sunlight, waves rippling and churning, stretching all the way to the horizon. Overhead, gulls wheeled in the blue sky uttering raucous cries.

I looked back.

The Maghuin Dhonn Herself regarded me with infinite compassion. I took a deep breath, my body trembling. I didn't understand, not really. And yet the spark inside me knew. "I have a very long way to go, don't I?" I asked softly.

She didn't answer.

I wiped my eyes. "May I at least keep this memory?"

Her great head dipped in consent.

"Thank you," I whispered. "I don't know where it is I'm meant to go or what it is I'm meant to do, but I'll try to make You proud."

Brightness shimmered and the expression on Her face changed. It was a look like my mother's embrace, hard and fierce. And it said without words that whatever came to pass, I was Hers, Her joy and Her pride, now and always and forever. My heart too full for words, I nodded in silent acknowledgment. It was a gift of grace I would carry with me always.

She left and did not look back.

I watched Her go, swaying on my feet. The glade was empty. I could feel Her presence moving away. When I could sense it no longer, I turned back to face the stone doorway. It showed nothing but the glade and the mountainside beyond, but I knew that somewhere beyond here lay a sea I was meant to cross.

More than one, mayhap.

I let myself glance around once more. It was beautiful and I longed to stay. Now that I had seen Her, I yearned to follow Her. I would follow Her over the mountains as my ancestors had followed Her across the ice when the world was young, marking neither day nor night in this twilight deeper than any mortal twilight. I would ask nothing more in life than to bask in Her presence.

But it was not to be. Instead, I would carry Her presence with me, never, ever forgetting that I was a child of the Maghuin Dhonn.

The bright spark of Her spirit inside me pulsed with steady life. I pressed one clenched fist to my heart and stepped through the doorway.

THIRTEEN

On the far side of the stone door it was day.

      I blinked in the sudden dazzle of sunlight, shading my eyes. The world wavered and sparkled in my vision. I didn't feel sleepy or hungry, but I was suddenly as weak as a day-old kitten. Dark figures scrambled down the mountainside to assist me.

They didn't ask if I had seen Her.

They knew.

I let them help me back to the cavern. No one spoke, for which I was grateful. I wasn't ready for words yet. When my vision cleared, my mother's face was the first I saw, tears of relief in her eyes. She held a wooden dipper of water to my lips. I drank. It was the best thing I had ever tasted. My mother refilled the dipper, then refilled it again. I drank until my stomach was nearly bursting, then sighed.

"So." Oengus broke the silence. "It seems you are one of us in truth."

I cleared my throat. "Yes and no."

My mother froze, then lowered the dipper very slowly.

"I'm sorry," I said to her, my heart aching. "I wish it were otherwise. She . . . She came to me. But . . ." I told them what had passed. How I had reached for Her and She had turned away from me, then looked back with such sorrow and regret. About the sea in the doorway. As I spoke, my mother rose and walked away. She stood in the mouth of the cavern with her head bowed and her arms wrapped around herself. I faltered and kept going. "Mayhap I was mistaken?" I suggested hopefully when I had finished.

"No." My mother spoke without turning around. "I've always feared this day would come."

"Why?" I asked. "Is there aught more you've not told me?"

"No," she murmured. "Only that I feared losing you."

No one else spoke for a time. Mabon played softly on his pipe.

"Oh, hush that noise, lad!" Nemed said in an irritable tone. She took my hand in a strong grip and squeezed it. "So She gave you no guidance?"

I shook my head. "Do you think I *was* mistaken?" The spark inside me constricted and I winced.

"No," Nemed said ruefully. "I fear you have the right of it, child. Whatever destiny She intends for you, you're meant to find it on your own. And as is the way of such things, I suspect the seeking may be more important than the finding."

"How does one go in search of a destiny?" Breidh asked in bewilderment. "Where would you even begin to look?"

"Across the sea," I said. "That's all I know."

"Aye, but *which* sea?"

My mother gave a choked laugh. I gazed at her rigid back with sorrow. "The one from whence my father came, I imagine," I murmured. "If I am to seek out a destiny, I'd start there and ask *his* gods why they're meddling with a child of the Maghuin Dhonn."

Nemed sucked her teeth. "Aye, that sounds about right."

I was too tired to think anymore. "Mother?"

"Go to the City of Elua," she said in a low voice. "Ask for the temple dedicated to star-crossed lovers. He said it is small but very famous. It was built for his great-grandmother. If he lives, they will know there where to find him."

"Have you always—" I broke off the thought and shook my head. The room reeled a little and I felt myself lurch sideways.

"Stone and sea!" Camlan leapt to her feet in dismay. "You must be starved and weary to the bone."

"It was a long night," I agreed feebly.

She gave me a perplexed look and hurried over to the cook fire.

"Time moves differently beyond the stone door." Nemed stroked my hair. "You were gone three nights and half a day."

I blinked. "I was?"

"You were." She smiled. "Stubborn child."

Camlan brought me a bowl of rabbit stew with wild carrots and onions. I ate slowly, watching Oengus comfort my mother. My uncle Mabon came to sit beside me, his shoulder brushing mine. He smelled familiar, like moss and fresh-peeled birch bark. "Do not worry about your mother," he said softly. "Fainche is strong—too strong, mayhap. And you have been the whole of her life for a long time. Mayhap she will let Oengus lend her some of his strength now."

I chewed and swallowed a bite. "That would be good."

"Aye," he said simply. "It would."

Once I'd eaten, the tide of exhaustion lurking behind my eyes rose and threatened to swallow me. Mabon and Camlan led me to a nest of blankets in a dim corner of the cavern. I wanted to protest, but I hadn't the strength. The moment I lay down, the tide engulfed me.

Behind my closed lids, the memory of Her presence awaited.

"Moirin."

It was my mother's voice.

I forced my eyes open. "Aye?"

She knelt before me, not sad, not angry. Steady, hands resting on her knees. "Wherever you're bound, I'll come with you."

My heart leapt—and the spark within dwindled. My throat tightened. "I don't . . . I don't think it's meant," I whispered.

Tears brightened her eyes. "No?"

"No." I closed my own eyes against the anguish in her face.

Sleep took me.

I woke in the small hours of the night. Casting my senses over the cavern, I found all sleeping but one. I rose, wrapping a blanket around me to ward off the night's chill, and joined my mother where she sat on the ledge of the cavern mouth. We sat together in silence, watching the stars move over the glade and the moon's sliver ascend into the night sky.

"I would have told you if ever you had asked about finding your father," my mother said eventually. "About the temple."

"I know," I said.

She looked at me, her dark gaze searching. "Are you sure?"

I knew what she meant. I took her hand in mine and laid it on my chest so she might feel the spark of the *diadh-anam* beneath it. "I am."

She sighed. "I'll miss you, Moirin mine. So very, very much."

I wanted to cry; I wanted to tell her that I would miss her, too; to tell her I was frightened, that I didn't want to venture across the sea all by myself in search of an unknown destiny. But I didn't want to make her feel worse. Instead, I curled into a ball and laid my head in her lap. "I will always be your daughter," I murmured. "Now and always and forever. But tonight, for one last night, let me be your child."

My mother kissed my temple. "You will always be that, too."

At peace, I slept again.

In the morning, the world seemed a different place—or mayhap it was only that my place in it had changed so greatly. Like it or not, I had a destiny. Camlan and Breidh eyed me with quiet awe, Old Nemed with pity. I wished they wouldn't. I didn't feel particularly well suited to the burden of a destiny. I was a sixteen-year-old girl who'd spent the entirety of her life living alone in the woods with her mother, not some heroine from days of yore.

And yet . . .

I was curious.

I couldn't go home. *Home* had become a place shadowed with sorrow and grief. And even if I could endure the memories of Cillian that were everywhere, I didn't think the spark inside me would let me rest.

The wide world beckoned. I yearned to know why.

After we broke our fast, my mother presented me with a gift, pressing a small, heavy object into my hand. It was a signet ring engraved with two crests—the boar of the Cullach Gorrym and the swan of the D'Angeline royal family.

"The token," I said, remembering. "Alais' line."

She nodded. "You'll need funds if you're to cross the sea. And for other things, I reckon. I don't suppose you can live freely in the City of Elua." When I protested, she folded my hand over it. "Take it, keep it. I've no need of it."

The weight of the ring brought the reality of my situation home to me. "I don't even know where to go with it!"

"I do," Oengus said. "Shall we escort Moirin to Bryn Gorrydum?" he asked my mother.

She looked relieved. "Can we?"

Oengus smiled. "I think we ought."

Mabon played on his pipe. "I'll come," he offered. "A day or two in a city of stone always serves to remind me why I avoid them. Besides, I've a mind to make Moirin a new bow. She's outgrown the last one."

"I was ten," I reminded him. "It was some time ago."

"So it was," he agreed.

Since there seemed little point in delaying, we set out that very day. One by one, we descended the shaft and passed through the wondrous caverns of the hollow hill. Old Nemed grumbled and took forever to cross the hanging bridge over the gorge, clutching the ropes and inching her way across.

I didn't care.

There was a part of me, a large part of me, that longed to stay. In the outermost chamber, I cast a yearning look at the smooth, milky stone walls, the frozen waterfall, trailing my fingertips over the fluid stone.

Go, my *diadh-anam* urged.

I sighed, and went.

Outside it was all ordinary brightness. Nemed seized me in her hard, wiry embrace. "Her blessing on you, child," she muttered. "If it should come to pass that you inherit my gift, use it well."

I returned her embrace. "I'll try."

She gave me a shake. "Do better than *try*!"

I laughed. "Aye, my lady!"

Nemed snorted through her nose. "My lady, is it?"

"It is," I said firmly.

I do not think she was displeased, although she snorted contemptuously a second time. The young ones made their farewells and left with her; and then there were only four of us alone on the mountainside.

Oengus took a deep breath. "On to Bryn Gorrydum?"

I nodded. "On to Bryn Gorrydum."

FOURTEEN

City of stone.

That was what my uncle Mabon had called it—and it was. Cobbled streets, stony and hard beneath our feet. We walked them warily. Passersby gave us curious glances. It wasn't that we looked so altogether different from them. Oengus or Mabon or my mother could almost have passed for one of the folk of the Cullach Gorrym. The physical differences were slight—the angle of their cheekbones, the tilt of their eyes. No, it had more to do with the stamp of wilderness that marked them like a scent.

And of course there was me, looking like none of the folk of Alba.

Oengus led us to the D'Angeline quarter. There, for the first time, I saw my father's people strolling the streets, speaking in their fluting tongue. And they, too, looked like and unlike the rest of the folk of Alba, the fair-skinned tribes. My mother had said it well many years ago. There was a keenness to their beauty, an almost too-perfect symmetry, sharp and deadly as a blade.

I found myself staring at them in fascination. A good number of them stared back, albeit with considerable more subtlety than I managed.

We stopped outside an elegant building with a stone plaque engraved with the words *Bryony Associates*, encircled by a trailing relief of bryony flowers.

"That's it," Oengus announced.

A little bell played a merry tune as we entered. Mabon smiled to himself and played it back on his pipe. A D'Angeline woman with shiny brown hair coiled in a complicated manner hurried into the salon to greet us, stopped short, and stared blankly at us, too startled for subtlety.

It had been a long journey. Now that I thought on it, I realized we all looked unkempt and travel-worn.

"May I—" She cleared her throat. "May I be of assistance?"

"Aye," I said. Mabon had strung the ring on a length of sinew for me since it was too big for my finger. I fished it out of my bodice, pulled it over my head, and handed it to her. She took it in bewilderment. "I've need of money."

She glanced at the ring and turned pale. "Is this what I think it is?"

"As to that I cannot say, for I've no idea what you might think," I said mildly. "But it is a token given to my mother by her mother and her mother's mother before her, back to Alais the Wise."

"Henri!" The woman called out in a stream of D'Angeline so swift and lilting I couldn't make out a word. Cillian had been a good teacher, but I suspected he'd a dreadful accent. A youngish man came at a run. He stared, too. "They've come to make a claim on her highness Alais' historic fund," the woman said in careful Alban. "They come bearing her token."

He blinked. "Truly?"

"So it seems." She turned back to us and inclined her head. "I pray you, forgive our rudeness. I am Caroline nó Bryony and I am at your service. It's only that none of Alais de la Courcel's descendants for whom the trust is marked have surfaced before today, so your appearances comes as somewhat of a surprise." She hesitated, eyeing me. "You're . . . of the Maghuin Dhonn?"

Oengus gave her a bright, feral smile that did nothing to ease her nerves. "We are and she is."

"Moirin is my daughter," my mother said calmly. "Moirin, daughter of Fainche, daughter of Eithne, daughter of Brianna, daughter of Alais."

"Brianna's line, then." Caroline nó Bryony squared her shoulders. "Right. The signet will have to be authenticated, of course. If you'll come with me, Henri will fetch the original imprint of the seal."

We followed her deeper into the building. Feeling the stone walls close around us, I forced myself to breathe slowly and evenly. If I was bound for the City of Elua, I was going to have to become accustomed to being enclosed behind man-made walls.

The room to which she led us was richly appointed. The wooden desk and chairs were polished and gleaming. She took her seat behind the desk and invited me to sit across from her. I stroked the arms of the chair, appreciating the satiny finish. An ornate lamp burned oil that was pure and odorless and gave a remarkably clear flame. There was a carpet on the floor with an intricate pattern like nothing I'd ever seen before. Running my gaze over the pattern was oddly soothing.

"Lovely, isn't it?" Caroline noticed me eyeing it. "It's Akkadian."

"From Khebbel-im-Akkad?" I remembered maps that Cillian and I had pored over. "It must have come a very long way."

"Yes, indeed." She sounded a little surprised. "Ah, good! Here's Henri with the seal."

He carried it on a tray and set it down on her desk with great care. Small wonder, for the wax was ancient and brittle. Caroline nó Bryony produced a fresh sheet of paper and a red wax taper. She lit the taper and let a precise amount of wax drip onto the clean paper. I sat, waiting while it cooled. My mother and Oengus and Mabon stood uneasily near the closed door. I could feel their discomfort. Caroline breathed on the surface of my ring and pressed it firmly into the soft red puddle before giving it back to me.

"Is that a piece of magic?" I inquired. "Blowing on it?"

She gave me a bewildered look. "Magic? No. A trace of moisture helps keep the seal from sticking to the wax."

"Ah," I said.

Her assistant Henri produced a funny little object, a round glass in a handheld frame—like a mirror, only clear. For long moments, Caroline nó Bryony peered through it, comparing the new seal imprint with the old. She looked up and smiled at the curiosity on my face. "No magic here either, only science." She gave me the object to examine. "'Tis but a magnifying glass to let me see the detail more clearly."

I held it to my eye and startled at the sight of her face, looming and blurred. "Stone and sea! So you say. It seems a fine piece of magic to me."

Mabon stirred restlessly. "Does the seal match?"

"It does." She folded her hands on the desk. "So. You have considerable funds at your disposal, Moirin daughter of Fainche. I am here to make them available to you and assist you in any way I might. That was the pledge my predecessors made to Alais de la Courcel. Tell me, what will you? Do you seek to make an entrance into Alban society? I can provide you with letters of authentication to present to the Cruarch."

"No, no." I shook my head. "I am not here to trouble the Cruarch on behalf of his wild kin. I need money, that's all."

Caroline tilted her head. "May I ask what you intend?"

This business of having a destiny was infernally complicated. "I don't know, exactly," I admitted. "I'm bound for Terre d'Ange to start. The City of Elua. Do you know it?"

Henri smirked.

Oengus shot him a look that drove the smirk from his face.

"Henri, leave us, please." Caroline nó Bryony pointed at the door. He went, suppressing a scowl. "So." She refolded her hands, her gaze intent. "You seek funds sufficient to grant you passage to the City of Elua?"

"Aye." I nodded. "And mayhap to dwell there for a time."

"How long?"

I hadn't the faintest idea. "I don't know."

"Elua have mercy!" Unexpectedly, she laughed; but it was a nice laugh with no malice in it. Her brown eyes sparkled, and I suddenly decided I liked her after all. She smiled at me with genuine warmth, enough that it set the doves fluttering in my belly for the first time since Cillian's death. "What did I do to deserve *you* turning up on our doorstep, Moirin of the Maghuin Dhonn?"

I smiled back at her. "I can't imagine."

My mother coughed.

"All right, then." Caroline nó Bryony sobered. "If you're willing to hear it, I'll give you my counsel. Will you all be travelling together?"

I shook my head. "Only me."

She gave me a sharp look and plucked a fresh sheet of paper from a drawer, dipping a pen into an inkwell. "As a young woman travelling on her own, I'd caution you not to carry overmuch in the way of hard coin. A hundred ducats should suffice to book you passage to Terre d'Ange and the City of Elua. For the rest . . ." Her hand moved over the paper, writing in a smooth, steady hand. "I'll issue you a letter of credit. Will that suffice?"

I peered at the number written there. "No doubt."

"Have you the first idea what you're about, Moirin?" Caroline asked.

"No," I said honestly.

She studied me. "Would you like me to arrange for your passage across the Straits?"

"It would be a kindness," I said.

"No." Caroline nó Bryony smiled wryly. "A *kindness* would be to urge you and your kin to retreat to whatever wilderness you came from, for I see the lot of you itching to be gone from this place and I fear the City of Elua will give you no better welcome than Henri did here today. What I am *doing* is my job."

I shrugged. "Nonetheless."

"Nonetheless," she echoed. "So be it."

I left the offices of Bryony Associates with a purse of a hundred gold ducats jingling at my belt and a letter of credit for five thousand more in the City of Elua. It seemed amply fair, given that I'd done nothing to earn it. Bidding us farewell on the doorstep of the building, Caroline paused and pressed my hands between hers.

"Do you have lodging here in Bryn Gorrydum?" she inquired.

"Oh, aye." I smiled. "Oengus says there's a goodly park in the center of the city that's *taisgaidh* land."

Her face went blank. "The park."

"Aye," I said, puzzled.

"Elua have mercy," she said for a second time, half-dismayed and half-amused. "Would that I could hear the gossip you'll provoke. Come tomorrow afternoon, Moirin of the Maghuin Dhonn. I'll see to what arrangements I may."

"My thanks," I said politely.

The park was a little piece of wilderness in the heart of the stone city. We made camp there unmolested. I went hunting with my uncle Mabon and we shot a pair of pigeons apiece. The new bow he'd made me on the journey had a heavier draw and a greater range. It suited me, but I was still getting used to it. We walked back to the campsite in the dusk. He summoned the twilight in slow, rolling waves, letting it trail and dance behind him like a shimmering wake. It reminded me of the music he played on his pipe. I'd never seen the like and tried to emulate it.

"Do you really think you can live among them?" Mabon asked abruptly.

"I mean to try."

He peered at me, his eyes wide-set and glimmering. "They say the entire city is walled by stone. I can't imagine how one could breathe in such a place. And they'll make mock of you for not knowing their ways. That's what she was trying to say."

"I know," I said softly. "But what else am I to do, Mabon?"

He slung one lean arm around my neck and hugged me. "Don't let them."

"I'll try," I promised.

"Don't forget who you are," he warned me.

I shook my head. "Never."

FIFTEEN

On the morrow, we presented ourselves once more at Bryony Associates—or at least I did. Having satisfied themselves yesterday that I was safe enough within, my mother and the others lingered on the doorstep to wait.

"Here is your chit for passage on the *Heart of Gold*," Caroline nó Bryony said in a forthright manner, handing me a scrip. "Departing at dawn two days hence. I can vouch for the captain, Josephe Renniel. I've asked him to keep an eye on you."

I nodded. "My thanks."

"The *Heart of Gold* is a trade ship, but she's equipped to take on passengers as well. She'll head south down the Straits and put in at Bourdes. Your fare guarantees you three meals a day and a private berth." Caroline hesitated. "The latter if you so desire. I note you're not wholly comfortable indoors."

"Not yet," I agreed.

She cleared her throat. "Captain Renniel has been thus advised. Now, you'll have to book passage from Bourdes overland to the City of Elua. I'm not able to arrange it in advance, but there's a stagecoach for hire departing at least once a week. Captain Renniel can assist you in this."

"Stagecoach," I repeated. "Very good."

Caroline handed me a sheaf of papers. "I've drawn up some notes for you, Moirin." She traced them with one elegant finger. "This is the address of Bryony's banking house in the City of Elua, where you may draw on your letter of credit. And these are the names and addresses of reputable lodging-houses in the City of Elua." She gave me a stern look. "You can't live in the park there. You understand that there's no such thing as *taisgaidh* land in Terre d'Ange?"

I did now. "I do."

Her forefinger tapped. "This is a letter of introduction you may present at Court if you so desire, confirming that you're a descendant of House Courcel."

I peered at it. "Ah, that's well thought."

"And *this* . . ." She tapped a different page. "This is the address of the Atelier Favrielle, where a friend of mine is employed." Her mouth curved into a smile. "From their inception onward, they've always enjoyed a unique challenge. I suspect that Benoit might relish that of dressing you."

"Dressing me?" I echoed.

"Child . . ." Caroline sighed. "Yes, dressing you. Oh, Blessed Elua have mercy, you'll present them with a rare challenge, you will." She steepled her fingers. "May I ask *why* you're bound for the City of Elua? Have you kin there?"

I shifted in my chair. "My father, mayhap. It seems he was a Priest of Naamah."

"How in the world—" She caught herself. "No mind. By the look of you, I believe it. Do you know where to find him?"

I shook my head. "Not exactly. He told my mother that there is a temple in the City dedicated to star-crossed lovers. That they will know where to find him. Do you know it?"

"As it happens, I do." Caroline fetched a fresh sheet of paper and wrote in a steady hand, her head bowed. Light from the ornate lamp overhead made her coiled hair shine and picked out a marking I'd not noticed the other day, a cluster of yellow and green bryony indelibly inked on the nape of her neck, curling tendrils disappearing beneath the collar of her gown.

"Are these warrior's markings?" It seemed unlikely, but I couldn't think what else they might be. Curious, I reached out and stroked her tattooed skin with my fingertips, letting them linger. Her skin was very soft and warm.

Her head jerked up in surprise. "I beg your pardon?"

"Warrior's markings," I repeated. "Like the Cullach Gorrym wear."

"Name of Elua, no." Caroline stared at me, mildly disconcerted. Although I had withdrawn my hand, I could feel the bright lady's gift stirring. "It's Bryony House's marque."

"Ah. Like on the doorway."

"No." She shook her head. "Bryony Associates is owned by Bryony House and guaranteed by the Dowayne's treasury, but I assure you, it's altogether different."

"Oh?" I said in an encouraging tone.

"It's a pleasure-house in the Court of Night-Blooming Flowers. I was sworn to Naamah's Service for seven years there."

"You were a priestess?" I asked.

"An adept." Caroline studied me. "Do you know what that means, Moirin?"

"I know Naamah lay down with strangers for coin," I said helpfully. "Is it something to do with that?"

"It is."

"Well, then."

Caroline nó Bryony sighed and put her face in her hands and muttered something in unintelligible D'Angeline. I wanted to touch her skin again, and the fine tendrils of hair loose on the nape of her neck. But it made me think of Cillian telling me that it wasn't appropriate to look at people's sisters as though I wondered if they might taste good, and the sorrow thinking of him evoked made the urge go away, leaving only sadness behind. So I waited quietly until she lifted her head.

"Do you even speak a word of D'Angeline?" she asked me.

I nodded. "*Un peu, oui.* I'm not entirely ignorant, my lady." I smiled sadly. "The Lord of the Dalriada's son taught me."

"The Lord—" Her lips moved soundlessly. "Cillian mac Tiernan. That was you."

It made me uncomfortable to think about such a private grief being a topic of discussion. "What do they say of me?" I asked her.

To her credit, Caroline held my gaze. "That Lord Tiernan's son died ensorceled by a bear-witch's daughter."

"Lord Tiernan's son died on a cattle-raid," I murmured. "To my great and everlasting sorrow. And I am guilty only of not loving him as much as he loved me."

"Is that why you seek to leave?" she asked gently.

"It's one reason I cannot stay." I thought wistfully of the bright-and-dark glade and the compassion and regret in the Maghuin Dhonn's wise, ageless eyes. "But no, my lady. I have passed through the stone doorway and met the Maghuin Dhonn Herself. It seems I have a destiny and I must cross the sea to find it."

Caroline nó Bryony gazed at me with parted lips, then gave herself a shake. "I nearly find myself believing it," she said in a wondering tone. "And not nearly so convinced that the City of Elua will eat you alive." She slid the paper with the address of the temple across her desk. "You'll find the temple in the Tsingani quarter. And do heed my advice and seek out Benoit at the Atelier Favrielle. The D'Angeline peerage may be contemptuous of anyone they think rustic or provincial, but they're mad for novelty. The right attire can mean the difference between the two."

"They sound a shallow folk," I observed.

She began to protest, then smiled with self-deprecating charm. "We can be, yes. Shallow and vain and insular. Also, proud, valorous, and great-hearted. I hope you will find somewhat to love in us."

"I already have," I assured her.

She laughed. "Elua have mercy on the City, Moirin of the Maghuin Dhonn."

Two days later, I set sail for Terre d'Ange.

It was the single most terrifying thing I'd ever done in my young life. Up until the moment came, I hadn't truly contemplated the enormity of what I was doing. There was a part of me still numb from Cillian's death, and another part lulled and reassured by the assistance of Caroline nó Bryony and her confidence in me. But when I saw the *Heart of Gold* bobbing at anchor in the harbor and the wide sea stretching beyond it, it struck me with a vengeance.

Alba was my home. I was born and bred here. All that I knew and loved was here, all that was dear and familiar. And I was about to leave it. My mouth went dry, my limbs went cold and tingling, and I found it hard to breathe.

"Moirin?" My mother searched my face. "You're white as a ghost."

My mother. Stone and sea, how could I leave my mother?

I opened my mouth, but no words came.

"You don't *have* to do this," my mother said fiercely. She turned to Oengus. "She doesn't, does she?"

He bowed his head. "I cannot say."

I thought about staying, leaving this city of stone and its bustling harbor, fleeing to the comfort and solitude of the forest. My heart leapt at the thought; but deep inside me, the spark of my *diadh-anam* guttered. I saw once more the Maghuin Dhonn turn from me with sorrow and regret, the slow, rolling surge of Her gait and the earth trembling beneath Her mighty paws as She walked away, this time forever.

And that loss ached even more than the one I faced.

"I have to go." I forced the words out. "I wish I didn't, but I do. I'm sorry. Please, if you love me, don't speak against this."

"I'll fetch the captain, shall I?" Mabon murmured. I was so grateful to him for understanding, all I could do was nod.

Captain Josephe Renniel was a tall, lean man with pale red-gold hair tied in a braid and wrinkles fanning from the corners of his blue-grey eyes. He managed to survey the four of us with considerable equanimity.

"Lady Moirin, I take it?" He spoke in slow, deliberate D'Angeline and bowed, then offered me his arm. "Will you come aboard?"

I took a deep breath, willing my racing heart to slow. "May I say good-bye to them?"

He nodded gravely. "Of course, my lady."

I hugged Oengus and Mabon. For as little as I'd seen of them throughout my life, it didn't matter. They were my folk, they were kin.

My mother.

Her tears were damp on my skin where her cheek pressed hard against mine. I closed my eyes for a long time. When I opened them and gazed over her shoulder, I saw sympathy in the captain's gaze. My mother squeezed my arms.

"Tell that man that if harm comes to you in his care, I will call down the curse of stone and sea and sky upon him," she said in a low, savage voice. "Until the very earth disdains his touch and every man's hand is against him!"

"Fainche," Oengus murmured.

She gave me a shake, eyes glittering. "Tell him!"

I turned to the captain and inclined my head. "My mother offers her prayers for a safe journey and smooth passage," I said in faltering D'Angeline.

Captain Renniel no longer looked sympathetic. He looked pale. He had understood her tone, if not her words. "I am always grateful for a mother's prayers."

"He promises I will be safe," I said to my mother.

Mollified, she wiped her eyes. "Only come home to me one day, will you, my heart?"

"I will." I paused. "Ah . . . where might that be?"

It made her smile through her tears. "You know, I'm not sure myself. Our cave will be very empty without you. But wherever I'm bound, I'll leave word at Clunderry. They've respect for their wild kin there."

"I'll find you," I promised.

And then there was nothing more to be said. The eastern sky was pink and growing brighter. Captain Renniel offered to have my trunks brought aboard and looked askance at me when I told him I didn't have any, only my bulging satchel and the bow and quiver over my shoulder. Still, he gave me his arm and escorted me up the ramp and onto the ship. D'Angeline sailors watched us with a mixture of curiosity and wariness. The wooden deck moved subtly beneath my feet.

I was no longer on Alban soil.

I swallowed against the surge of terror that thought instilled in me. The captain offered to show me to my berth, but I shook my head. I wanted to keep my mother in sight until the last possible moment. She and Oengus and Mabon looked so wild, lost, and out of place standing there on the quay.

And so he showed me to a place in the rear of the ship where I might stand out of the way, then went about his business. Orders were given. A great rotating device was cranked, raising a mighty chain and a dripping anchor. Sailors scurried around, ignoring me for the moment. Sails were hoisted. The *Heart of Gold* turned its prow toward the open sea. The shore fell away behind us.

My mother raised her hand in farewell.

I raised mine.

The sails filled and grew taut with snapping, rippling sounds. The ship picked up speed, the rolling motion of it growing more pronounced as we made for the open entrance to the harbor. The sun cleared the horizon, sparkling on the waves. Overhead, gulls wheeled with raucous cries. When I could no longer pick out my mother's figure on the shore, I lowered my arm.

I was off to seek my destiny.

SIXTEEN

The first night, I thought I might die of loneliness.

Captain Renniel invited me to dine in his quarters, but I was too heart-sick and the constant motion of the waves made my stomach feel queasy. And too, it wasn't *his* presence I yearned for.

I wanted my mother.

And somehow, I felt it would be worse and more lonely to be alone with a stranger than alone all by myself. So I turned down his invitation. I tried to make myself sleep in the narrow berth I'd been given, but it was impossible. Although the walls were wood and not stone, it was tiny and windowless and cramped, and I felt so stifled my skin crawled. For a mercy, the captain had heeded Caroline nó Bryony's warning and told me where I could sleep on the deck if I wasn't comfortable indoors.

It was chilly at night on the open waters. I wrapped myself in my blanket and leaned against the wall of the forecastle, watching faint clouds scud across the stars. It wasn't just my mother I missed. All my life, I'd been grounded by the earth and surrounded by wilderness. Even in Bryn Gorrydum there had been the park, left to grow untamed, a green presence murmuring on the edge of my awareness, filled with the quick, flickering spirits of the small creatures that dwelled there.

Here there was nothing.

It wasn't true, I suppose. In the daytime there were birds and surely there were fish in the sea. But I couldn't feel them the way I could sense trees and shrubs and flowers, squirrels and deer and foxes.

I'd never felt more bereft and forlorn.

It all seemed very unfair. I'd never asked for a destiny. I wasn't some great magician from days of yore. I had only such modest gifts as were left to the Maghuin Dhonn, and a tiny ability to coax plants to grow.

I couldn't even take solace in bitterness and rail against my fate. Stone and sea, I wanted to! But every time my thoughts wandered in that direction, I remembered the vast sorrow in Her eyes and I knew, sure as the spark within me, that She would not have sent one of Her children across the sea unless it were truly needful.

Why, I couldn't imagine.

So instead I took what meager comfort there was to be found in self-pity. Alone on the open sea on a ship full of strangers from a strange land, I wept myself quietly to sleep.

I woke to early-morning sunlight and a knot of sailors watching me.

They startled when I opened my eyes, jumping backward and whispering amongst themselves. If they hadn't been staring at me, I would have called the twilight, but I was pinned by their gazes. I settled for giving them my mother's best glare.

They jumped back another step, pushing and shoving one another. All but one, a slight, golden-haired lad who couldn't have been more than fourteen. He elbowed his way through the gaggle.

"She's just a girl!" he scoffed. "She won't bite." He squatted a few feet in front of me, his expression less certain than his words. "You won't, will you? You're not going to . . . change?"

"What?" I wasn't sure I understood him.

"Change," he said. "Into a bear."

"Oh." I rubbed my eyes. "No. I think that would be a very foolish thing to do on a ship, don't you?"

He grinned. "Aye, indeed. It's true, though, isn't it? You're a bear-witch?"

"I'm of the folk of the Maghuin Dhonn," I said.

"*I'm* descended from the Chevalier Philippe Dumont," he informed me with considerable self-importance, then looked disappointed when I pled ignorance. "Surely you must know of him! He was the last of Phèdre's Boys. He went with her and Joscelin Verreuil into Vralia to fetch Prince Imriel and the bear-witch's head."

"I know the story," I said softly.

"Damien!" Captain Renniel's voice cracked. The lad leapt up and scurried away, and the rest of the sailors dispersed. "My apologies, my lady." The captain offered a bow. "Pay the lad no heed. Every sailor born within a hundred leagues of Montrève claims descent from Philippe Dumont."

I shrugged off my blanket and stretched my stiff limbs. "Was he very famous?"

"Among sailors, yes." The captain eyed me. "Would you care to break your fast?"

I assessed the state of my belly. It didn't seem to be roiling with aught save hunger. I tried standing. The swaying motion of the ship was more tolerable today. Glancing around, I saw that Alba's shoreline was clean out of sight. There was only the distant shore of Terre d'Ange on our left, looking rocky and inhospitable. My heart ached anew.

Captain Renniel followed my gaze. "That's Kusheth province," he said. "You'll find the landscape more friendly in Siovale province, where we're bound."

"Siovale." I remembered that each of Elua's Companions had staked out a territory of their own, save one. "Shemhazai's folk, aye?"

"Quite right." He nodded. "If you'd care to join me, I'd be happy to tell you aught you might wish to know about Terre d'Ange."

I didn't want to. Trying to understand D'Angeline spoken by those to whom it was their native tongue made my head ache, and I'd sooner be left on my own with a bit of plain bread in a quiet patch of sunlight. But I had a bedamned destiny to find, and Old Nemed had said the seeking might be more important than the finding. Skulking around the ship and wallowing in self-pity wasn't going to help.

So I made myself smile at Captain Renniel. "It would be my pleasure."

By the time we made port in Bourdes two days later, I'd learned a great deal more about the history and culture of Terre d'Ange and the worst of my loneliness had abated. I'd also learned a fair amount about the storied life of the Chevalier Philippe Dumont, courtesy of the boy Damien, who seemed most insistent that I appreciate his famous ancestor.

To be honest, I didn't mind, since he was one of the only sailors who didn't eye me askance and mutter under his breath about bear-witches. Sailors, it seemed, were a superstitious lot. And as it happened, I wasn't wholly unfamiliar with some of the tales he told; it was only that I knew them from the other side of history. Cillian had been particularly fond of the story about how the Dalriada had helped overthrow Maelcon the Usurper to restore Drustan mab Necthana to the Cruarch's throne, then crossed the Straits to help drive an invading Skaldi army out of Terre d'Ange. And then there was a complicated tale of treachery and pirates, the tale of how the Master of the Straits was freed from a curse, and of course, the infamous tale of Berlik and Morwen of the Maghuin Dhonn.

I wasn't entirely clear on the role this Philippe had played, but it seemed he'd been there at nearly every turn, and that was enough for Damien.

"All the good stories are old stories," he said wistfully after finishing one. "Nothing exciting like that happens anymore."

"What about the new land discovered across the western sea?" I suggested. Cillian's tales of cities in the jungle and folk dressed all in feathers and jade had certainly sounded exciting.

Damien scowled. "Terra Nova? King Daniel's content to let others explore it."

"Oh?"

He lowered his voice. "They say there are fortunes to be made, too. But he's not even sent a delegation. The Aragonians are setting up trade in the south, Vralians and Gotlanders and the like in the north. Even your Cruarch's talking about the prospect of establishing permanent trade posts between the two. *We're* doing naught but twiddle our thumbs."

The words boggled me. "Doing *what*?"

He demonstrated. "It's just an expression, my lady. It means we're idle."

"Oh, aye." I thought about it. "Terre d'Ange is a wealthy country in its own right, is it not? Mayhap there's wisdom in being content with what one already has. Would that I'd appreciated it more ere I lost it."

That intrigued him. "What did you lose?"

I gazed at the open sea behind us. "Everything."

"Why?"

I shrugged. "Because the Maghuin Dhonn Herself has chosen a destiny for me. What it is, I've not the slightest idea. Only that I'm meant to seek it."

The lad's blue eyes glowed. "Take me with you!" he breathed. "Don't you see? If the captain will release me, I could swear myself into your service like Philippe Dumont and Phèdre nó Delaunay!"

It seemed unlikely, but I supposed there were worse things than a garrulous young companion if that was what fate willed for me. I consulted my *diadh-anam* and saw in memory the visage of Herself turning away in sorrow and regret. Whatever his ancestry, he was no more meant to accompany me than my mother had been.

"No," I said gently, touching his sun-gilded hair. "I don't think so, Damien. I'm sorry."

He pulled away from me. "It's not fair!"

I watched his retreating back. "No, it's not."

We made harbor at the port of Bourdes, navigating the estuary. A great statue of Shemhazai stood on the bank of the wide river-mouth gazing westward, an open book in one hand. I'm sure it was very fine and impressive, but it wasn't what pleased me the most. I stood in the prow of the *Heart of Gold* and breathed in the scent of soil and green growing things.

Vines.

This was D'Angeline wine country, terraced and tamed. It was rich, though. I could taste the air on my tongue, taste the pride in the burgeoning grape-clusters, a faint silvery sheen on every fruit. I was sorry when we sailed past the outlying islands and the inland fields to put in at harbor and enter the city proper.

Stone and sea, it was *vast*.

Bigger than Bryn Gorrydum, bigger than anything I'd seen.

I tried to find Damien to bid him farewell, but he'd made himself scarce. So instead I accepted Captain Renniel's offer of assistance. He led me through the streets of Bourdes, carrying my satchel while I carried the new bow and quiver Mabon had made me over my shoulder. The streets were wider than in Alba and filled with the clatter of hooves. This, too, made my head ache.

We found the stagecoach post.

"City of Elua?" The man behind the counter glanced up, then gave me a startled second look. "Departs on the morrow, an hour past dawn. The fare's five ducats or twenty silver centimes."

I counted out the money and he gave me a chit.

Captain Renniel escorted me to the adjacent inn and negotiated for a night's stay. After I'd paid in advance, I thanked him, wondering in secret if I might be able to steal out and pass the night in the stables. Appealing as the notion was, I supposed I needed to work harder at being at ease indoors.

"Moirin." He laid his hands on my shoulders. "Are you *sure*?"

I wasn't.

"Aye," I said steadily. "Very sure, my lord captain."

"Elua have mercy." His tone was rueful. "The gods be with you, child—yours and ours. At least I may tell Caroline I've done all I might. She took an odd fancy to you."

"I liked her, too," I said honestly. "Very much. And if you think on it, my lord, please tell Damien farewell for me. Whatever you might think of his tales, he didn't shun me and he made the journey easier to bear."

"I will," he promised.

He went.

I was alone again.

SEVENTEEN

On the morrow, I presented myself at the stagecoach post. An attendant took my chit and slung my bag into the coach, stowing it beneath the seat. The driver, a young man with black hair and darker eyes than I'd seen on any D'Angeline, gave me a courteous nod.

"May I introduce myself to your horses?" I asked him. They were beautiful animals, four matching bays with glossy coats.

The driver looked startled. "If you wish."

I approached the lead pair and blew softly in their nostrils. They lowered their noble heads and lipped at my hair. It tickled, making me laugh for the first time since I'd left home. Their warm presence was familiar and reassuring.

"That's a Tsingani trick. My grandfather taught it to me." The driver squinted at me. "Have you Tsingani blood?"

"No." I stroked the nearest bay's neck. "I know they like to get one's scent, that's all."

"So they do." That was all he offered. We waited a few more minutes to see if any last passengers would arrive, but none did. I was ushered into the stagecoach and the attendant made a show of closing the heavy curtains. As soon as he turned his back, I opened them. The driver flicked his whip and we were off, jolting over the cobbled streets of Bourdes.

Once we were clear of the city, it was better. The horses' hooves didn't make such a clatter without stone walls to bounce the sound back, and the motion of the coach wasn't so different from the swaying of a ship. We travelled along a river at a good clip. I put my head out the window to feel the wind on my face and gazed at the surrounding countryside.

The vineyards stretched forever in endless rows of green. Truly, Terre d'Ange was a rich country. I thought about the modest row of vines Lord Tiernan was cultivating and wondered if they'd bear a good harvest this year. They'd thrived since he'd had them moved as I'd told him to do.

I missed Cillian.

I wondered what he'd have made of this business of a destiny. He'd loved tales of magic and adventure as much as the boy Damien had. I wondered if Cillian would have offered to defy his father and come with me. I wondered if the Maghuin Dhonn Herself would have permitted it.

And in a guilty corner of my heart, I wondered if I would have wanted him to. Here and now, it seemed a wondrous notion and I would have given anything to have his company, but that was only because I was alone and far from home.

I'd never know.

That was the truth of it. I could drive myself mad wondering, but I would never, ever know. So I made myself stop wondering and settled for simply missing him.

The coach halted for the night in a smaller city. At the post station, the driver merely pointed to the inn across the street. I watched with envy as he set about unhitching the horses with a stable-lad's assistance. I'd sooner help him with the horses and spend the night in the stable than pass another night in another small, cramped room. But remembering the stern look Caroline nó Bryony had given me, I sighed and went to seek lodging.

I drew more curious glances here than I had in Bourdes, a port city with a large number of foreigners. At least D'Angelines were a well-mannered folk. They looked, but they didn't stare and didn't intrude. In the common room, I was served a delicious meal of roasted capon flavored with an unfamiliar fragrant, piney herb. When I asked, the woman who had brought my meal told me it was called rosemary.

"Rosemary," I repeated, inhaling deeply to memorize the scent and taste.

The woman gave me an odd look. According to Captain Renniel, D'Angelines took great pride and pleasure in all the finer things in life. Why they should find it strange that someone would visibly savor one of them, I couldn't imagine. At least I was managing to acquit myself well eating with a fork and knife.

After dining, I retired to my rented chamber.

I lasted half the night. I'd spent the entire day confined in the stage-coach. Even with the window, it had been oppressive. Reasoning that it was unfair that I be expected to change all at once, I cloaked myself in twilight and stole out of the inn.

In the stable, the coach-horses were drowsing, rear legs cocked, heads low and nodding. I let go the twilight and stood for a moment, breathing in their warm odor and the scent of hay, feeling more at peace.

Something stirred behind me.

I whirled. In a pile of straw, the driver sat up, naked from the waist upward. He had a blanket beneath him and straw in his tousled black curls. Through a chink in the wall, moonlight silvered his face. It was soft and vulnerable with sleep, unable to hide his feelings. And all of a sudden, desire was a presence in the stable with us—uninvited, yet not wholly unexpected.

"You," he whispered.

"Me," I agreed.

I went to him without thinking. If I'd thought, I'd have hesitated. There was Cillian's death and guilt.

Better not to think.

Cillian was dead, and the stagecoach driver was alive. His lips were warm, not cold. I lay down in the straw and stretched my length against him, running my hands over his ribcage. He rolled me over and kissed me more deeply.

Stone and sea, it felt good.

I was alive too—young and alive. It was different. *He* was different. A different taste, a different scent. And yet it was the same and familiar. The mix of languor and the urgency, the rising tide of desire. I helped the driver remove my green woolen dress, yearning to feel his warm bare skin against mine. When he lowered his head to my breast to suckle, I cupped his head and tangled my fingers in his hair, encouraging him. When his knee nudged between my thighs, I parted them willingly for him.

"Elua!" His hips rose and fell. "I can't stop!"

"Don't," I murmured.

For a long time, he didn't. When he did, I was content. I lay with his weight atop me, stroking his curls. With an effort, he lifted his head, dark eyes glinting. "I could be dismissed from my post for this."

"I won't tell if you don't." I touched his face. "What's your name?"

"Theo."

One of the horses whickered and snorted in its stall, rustling then settling back into sleep. A black cat crouched through a sliver of moonlight, stalking unseen prey. It paused to lift its head and stare at us, green eyes luminous and eerie.

"Kin of yours?" Theo inquired.

I laughed. "Not that I know of."

"It was a jest." He looked at me with frank curiosity. "Lady . . . who are you? *What* are you?"

I yawned. "Not much of a lady for a start. This isn't the sort of thing one's supposed to do, is it? Bed one's coach-driver in a stable?"

Theo smiled. "Not in a stable, no. Is it a secret?"

"No." The thong on which my mother's signet ring was strung had gotten tangled around my neck. I sat up and untwisted it, then shook straw out of my hair. "I'm Moirin." I thought about how Caroline had addressed me. It seemed right. "Moirin of the Maghuin Dhonn."

"Oh!" He stared.

"It's all right," I said wryly. "I'll not be changing into a bear—or a cat. Nor putting any manner of curse or enchantment on you. I was lonely and I couldn't sleep, that's all. I didn't even think to find you here, just the horses."

"The horses like you," Theo said uncertainly, reassuring himself that I couldn't be all that dangerous.

"I like horses." I yawned again. "And I nearly think I could sleep now. Do you mind if I stay?"

"A bear-witch." He wasn't ready to let it go yet. "With D'Angeline blood?"

"Aye." I shrugged into my dress. "Do you mind? I won't even ask to share your blanket. I've one in my pack."

He thought about it, a slow smile spreading over his face. "A bear-witch and me. No. I don't mind."

I fetched my blanket. "Good."

In the morning, I woke to find Theo splashing at the horse trough, scrubbing himself with a rag and a bit of soap. He gave me a shy, wondering smile and offered to share his soap, as well as journeycake and cheese from his own satchel.

"Or I could buy you a meal at the inn," I suggested. "I ate a capon with the most delicious herb there last night. Rosemary. Do you know it?"

He laughed. "Yes, of course. All right, then."

The morning's meal was just as delicious, eggs whipped and baked in a manner Theo told me was called an omelette. There was goats' cheese melted into it and it was scattered with another shredded herb unfamiliar to me. I sniffed at it when the platter was set before me.

"Basil," the serving woman said in response to my inquiring glance.

"Basil," I echoed. She shook her head and walked away.

"I take it the—" Theo lowered his voice. "The Maghuin Dhonn aren't much for cooking."

"Oh, my mother's a right skilled cook," I assured him. "It's only that these are herbs that don't grow wild in Alba—or at least not where we lived."

He looked askance at me. "You lived in the wild?"

"Aye," I said wistfully. "But I'm learning." I took a bite of my omelette. The melted cheese was pungent and so hot it almost scalded my tongue and the *basil* was unfamiliar and delightful. "This helps."

As we dined, I could see Theo grow more at ease in my company, deciding by daylight that mayhap a bear-witch wasn't entirely as fearsome and mysterious as legend would have it—or at least not one so easily pleased by a simple dish of cooked eggs. I felt strange after what had passed between us last night, but not as guilty as I might have thought. Life called to life. Somewhere, the bright lady smiled. Theo seemed a decent enough fellow, and his black hair and dark eyes reminded me of home and family in a nice way. By the time we returned to the post station, I thought mayhap the remainder of the journey might be more tolerable than I'd reckoned.

I was wrong.

There were two new passengers joining us, D'Angeline ladies of middle years. They were overdressed, overcoiffed, and overperfumed, chattering together in voluble tones. My heart sank when I saw them.

"Oh, my!" One of them lifted a magnifying glass on a stick to her eyes and peered at me through it. "Wherever are *you* from, my dear?"

"Alba," I murmured.

"She must be a *half-breed*," the other whispered in the overly audible tones of the hard of hearing.

The first tut-tutted. "Such a pretty thing! So exotic." She fiddled with a lock of my hair and sniffed. "But you simply must do something with your hair, my dear."

I glanced around for Theo, but he was making adjustments to the harness and avoiding my gaze. I sighed. "Aye, my lady," I agreed. "No doubt I must."

In short order we were bundled into the coach.

The ladies—widowed sisters come from visiting a third sister and her family, introduced themselves as Florette d'Aubert and Lydia Postel—insisted on drawing the curtains to cut the wind's chill. They settled into the seat facing me, their stiff, voluminous skirts spreading to crowd the space between us. The scent of their perfume permeated the coach.

"Now." Florette smoothed her skirts. "Moirin, is it?"

"Aye, my lady." I'd given my name as Moirin mac Fainche, reckoning it wiser not to mention the Maghuin Dhonn to these two.

She lifted one finger in admonishment. "Don't say *aye*, dear. Only vulgar common people say *aye*."

"Yes, my lady," I said obediently.

"I can't make out what she's saying!" Lydia complained in a harsh whisper. "Her accent is atrocious!"

I cleared my throat and mimicked Florette's tone. "Yes, my lady!"

"Much better." Florette d'Aubert folded her hands in her lap. "Now," she said firmly. "Tell us all about yourself, dear. Who are your people? How did you come to be born in Alba? How did you come to Terre d'Ange? Where are you bound? Have you kin in the City of Elua?"

I shrugged.

"Don't *shrug*, child!" she said sharply. "It's rude."

"Forgive me," I said in my best polite voice.

Lydia Postel cocked her head. "Eh?"

"Forgive me!" I repeated more loudly. "I'm a stranger here and untutored in your ways. Mayhap you and your sister would do me the kindness of telling me about *your* lives that I might learn from you."

They did.

By the time we paused at midday to water the horses, I'd learned all there was to know and more about the lives of Florette d'Aubert and Lydia Postel. I'd learned that the former had grave misgivings about the manner in which their sister was raising her children, while the latter was a staunch advocate of the old tradition that gave the father the upper hand, though both were childless themselves. I'd learned that Florette's husband had concealed a wagering habit from her and left her with debts she quite resented. And I'd learned that they were perishing of curiosity to hear what the latest gossip was in the City of Elua, where the doings of the Royal Court were paramount.

It seemed King Daniel de la Courcel had remarried after his first wife had died, leaving him with a sole son and heir. The merits of his new bride were a matter of contention.

"Jehanne," Lydia muttered.

"Jehanne," Florette agreed. "The men of House Courcel do *not* choose wisely when they remarry."

The new Queen, they informed me, was young, frivolous, and fickle. She cared nothing for politics, only for parties. She conducted notorious affairs under her long-suffering husband's nose, ruthlessly promoting her favorites at Court.

"What did his majesty expect?" Florette sniffed. "Marrying an adept of the Night Court!"

"I thought it was a sacred calling," I said, puzzled. "Am I mistaken?"

"No, no." She pursed her lips. "Of course there's great honor to be found in Naamah's Service. But it's a question of propriety, dear. If there's a measure of truth to the old tales, even Phèdre nó Delaunay never sought to rise above her station."

"If the old tales are true, I imagine she was too busy saving the world," I offered diplomatically.

They ignored my comment and carried on with a gleeful litany of the Queen's sins. I thought personally that Jehanne de la Courcel sounded rather fun and a good deal more interesting than anyone either of these two had met, but I kept the thought to myself and concentrated on not throwing myself out of the stagecoach.

Much to my dismay, the ladies insisted that I accompany them to dine that evening when we halted at the next waypost. They *tried* to insist that we share a room to conserve our funds, but at that I drew the line.

"I come from a line of very solitary folk," I said firmly and jingled the purse tied around my waist. "Besides, I'm not lacking for coin."

Florette tut-tutted at me. "Put that away, child! Never say such a thing in a public place. It's dangerous—and vulgar, too." She peered at me through her magnifying glass. "A solitary folk? Who did you say your people were again?"

"Oh, no one you would know." I didn't fancy being the subject of their gossip. "Since you and your sister were kind enough to invite me, will you permit me to purchase your supper?"

She hesitated. "Well . . ."

"Of course we will," Lydia said loudly.

They were also kind enough to order several jugs of the inn's best red wine at my expense and lingered long over their cups after extracting the most recent gossip out of the City from the serving girl. It seemed Queen Jehanne remained estranged from her most favorite courtier, Raphael de Mereliot, with whom she had quarrelled some weeks ago. He'd sent her a letter begging forgiveness and sweetened his apology with a bracelet—a pave of canary diamonds, according to rumor. The next day, one of the Queen's ladies-in-waiting was sporting it on her wrist.

"Imagine the gall!" Florette marveled.

"Eh?" I blinked. "I thought you disapproved of her affairs."

"Well, yes, but . . ." She laid a hand on my arm. "You're very young, dear. And, how shall I say it?" She patted my arm. "Unsophisticated. There are discreet and tasteful ways to conduct such matters."

"Why?" I asked. "Elua and his Companions didn't seem to concern themselves thusly."

Lydia hiccupped. "Blessed Elua cared naught for crowns or thrones," she intoned.

Florette gave her a sharp look. "Are you intoxicated?" she hissed. "Oh, Elua have mercy, you are!"

"I'm not," her sister replied with dignity, listing a little in her seat.

I helped Florette d'Aubert maneuver Lydia up the stairs to the chamber they shared, then bade them good night and beat a hasty retreat to my bedchamber. I waited until I heard the sound of snoring through the thin walls before I summoned the twilight and stole out of the inn.

Lamplight spilled through the chinks in the wall of the stable. Inside, I found Theo reading. There was a small jug of wine and two cups beside him.

He lifted his head and smiled at me. "Seeking refuge, are you?"

I smiled back at him. "I am."

"I hoped you might." He rose and lifted the lantern, hanging it carefully on a hook. "Come, then."

I went to him.

EIGHTEEN

hey're not so bad," Theo said drowsily the next morning when I complained about the prospect of another day in Florette and Lydia's company.

"They're insufferable," I informed him.

"Ah, now." He cupped my face and kissed me. "They're ladies of a certain age with naught else to concern themselves in life. In their minds, they're doing you a kindness by correcting your manners and preparing you for life in the City."

"That doesn't make it any more pleasant to bear, and I'm perishing sick of hearing about the Queen." I had a thought. "May I ride with you?"

Theo shook his head. "It's not done, Moirin."

"No?" I brushed the straw from my dress and donned it. "Well then, if it's not *done*, I'll just wait for the next coach. There should be one along in a few days, aye?"

"Oh, fine." He sighed. "Just don't be surprised when the gossip turns to you." He gave me a wry look. "Though I imagine that's bound to happen anyway. You didn't, ah, mention your heritage to them, did you?"

"No. I thought they might take it amiss."

"Doubtless," he agreed.

To be sure, the good sisters took my decision to ride atop the carriage beside Theo amiss. I did it anyway and I was glad. The terrain began to change from cultivated land to a pleasant mountainous wilderness. The valleys were lush and filled with oak and chestnut trees, while the heights had plains covered with fragrant heather and tough, scrubby broom. I breathed deeply, happier than I'd been in days. Theo smiled at my pleasure. In turn, I admired his skill with the coach and the way the muscles of his forearms shifted as he handled the reins.

"Is it hard to do?" I asked.

"It takes some practice," he said. "There's a knack to it. You've got to have a good feel for the horses' mouths."

Much to my delight, he showed me and let me try. Once I'd mastered the complicated technique of holding the reins in my left hand, I thought I could almost manage. I could feel the horses respond to my guidance and I knew instinctively to give them their heads on an upslope and keep them in check going downhill.

"Well done," Theo said approvingly. "Once you learned to use the whip, I daresay you'd make a passing fair driver."

My arm was beginning to ache with the strain. "'Tis hard work." I handed the reins back to him. "Is the whip truly necessary?"

"Only to direct them." He arranged the reins in his hand. "It's not used to punish—"

"*Hold!*"

A pair of men with scarves wrapped around their lower faces stepped out from behind a rocky outcropping ahead of us. One held a loaded crossbow aimed at Theo, who swore softly and drew rein. "I've naught of value, only passengers!" he shouted. Inside the coach, I heard shrill cries of alarm.

"The girl's got a goodly purse. I heard her say so myself." He glanced at his companion and jerked his chin. "Go relieve the biddies of whatever trinkets they carry."

For one brief instant, no one's gaze was on me. I summoned the twilight in a terrified rush of breath. In the gloaming, I saw the first bandit's face turn back toward me, filled with bewilderment at my seeming disappearance.

"What the sodding *hell*?"

I dropped from the carriage, unslinging my bow. I'd kept it with me out of habit, accustomed to shooting for the pot as I travelled. Now I circled around behind him, nocking an arrow.

"I've an arrow aimed between your shoulder blades!" I said fiercely. "Drop your bedamned bow and go!"

The bandit whirled and pulled the trigger on his crossbow, loosing his bolt blindly in the general direction of my voice. It passed so close to me I felt its wind against my cheek. I swore and shot him in the thigh. He cried out involuntarily, dropping his crossbow to clutch at the shaft. I fitted another arrow to my string.

"Next time, I aim higher!" I called.

It was enough. The bandits fled into the hills, the one I'd shot hobbling as fast as he could and leaning on his companion. I waited until they were well out of range, then sighed and lowered my bow, releasing the twilight.

Theo was staring at me. "What . . ." He licked lips gone dry and swallowed hard. "How did you do that? Disappear?"

"It's only a small gift," I said softly. "Meant to conceal us at need from those who mean us harm."

He didn't answer.

I sighed again and went to check on Florette and Lydia. They were pale and fearful, clutching one another. For a mercy, the curtains were drawn and they'd seen nothing of what had transpired.

"What is it?" Lydia asked in a loud, trembling whisper. "Bandits? Are they gone?"

"Aye, my lady," I said. "Gone as gone can be." I showed her my bow. "They thought to rob us with knives. I scared them away."

Florette peered at me. "You?"

"Me," I agreed. "You were quite right to reprimand me for being foolish and boastful last night, my lady. They were after my purse."

She pursed her lips. "I daresay that's a lesson learned the hard way. Be grateful it wasn't worse, dear."

I thought about the breath of wind against my cheek as the bolt passed by me. "Believe me, I am."

When I thought to rejoin Theo in the driver's seat, he wouldn't meet my eyes. "I think it's best you take your place inside."

"Why?" I asked. "You were glad enough of my company before."

He gave me a reluctant sidelong glance. There was still desire in his gaze, but there was fear, too—and the fear was stronger than the desire.

"There's a limit to the amount of strangeness a man can be expected to endure, Moirin. You've just surpassed mine."

I flushed at the unexpected rejection, hurt and embarrassed. "As you will."

The remainder of our journey passed without incident. I suffocated in the coach and endured the cloistered company of Florette and Lydia, who insisted I tell them about the bandit attack in exacting detail. I obliged them by fabricating an account that grew more florid with each telling. They alternated between shivering with horrified relish and chiding me for such risky behavior.

"Those men could have been bent on *heresy*," Lydia said darkly.

"Heresy?" I echoed. I thought I knew the word—thanks to the reading Cillian and I had done, my vocabulary far exceeded my pronunciation—but I was confused.

"Rape and ravishment," Florette clarified. "There are bad men in this world, child. Even here."

"Oh, aye." I nodded. "It's a lucky thing I had my bow, isn't it?"

She gave me a stern look. "Don't say *aye*."

I smiled. "Yes, my lady."

We passed one last night in a small wayfarers' inn, where they served a hearty rabbit stew that reminded me of home. Florette and Lydia pressed me to reveal my plans in the City of Elua and I did my best to deflect their questions with vague generalities.

"At the least, tell us you mean to visit a proper couturiere!" Florette said with asperity. "You're a stunning creature to be sure, but if that dress represents the best of your finery, it looks like you slept in a stable."

I cleared my throat. "Oh, yes. I have a letter of recommendation in my bag."

"For whom?" Lydia demanded.

I tried to recall. "Atelier . . . Fabienne?" I pictured Caroline nó Bryony's smile. "Fabrielle. No, Favrielle."

They blinked in unison, and then Florette patted my hand. "It's good to dream, dear. At least you're setting your sights high. To be sure, you're very striking in a most . . . ah . . . unusual manner. But don't be disappointed if they refuse you. They take on precious few clients."

Lydia eyed me. "They might."

"Not likely." Florette gave a delicate snort. "They turned away her imperious majesty herself for being too demanding."

"Well, as peculiar as she is, our young Moirin's certainly not the demanding type," her sister argued. "And they say Atelier Favrielle does love a challenge."

A less delicate snort. "Our Moirin's that, all right!"

The topic showed all the signs of being one the good ladies could debate for hours. "Well, if they refuse me, I'll simply have to go elsewhere, won't I?" I rose from the table. "If you'll forgive me, it's been a long day."

"I should say so!" Florette exclaimed. "Facing down highwaymen. Who ever heard of such a thing?"

I smiled and kissed her cheek. "Pleasant dreams, my lady."

She flapped her hand at me. "Oh, go on with you, child."

On the following day, we descended from the low mountains and reached the City of Elua a few hours later. Florette and Lydia were sufficiently excited that they consented to have the curtains open once we came within sight of the City's famous white walls.

I had to own, it was splendid. Even at a distance, the Royal Palace loomed, vaster and more elaborate than aught I could have imagined. It could have swallowed up the hall of Innisclan a hundred times. As we drew nearer, the ladies began pointing out all the places of interest.

"That's the Academy of Occult Philosophy founded by Queen Sidonie and Crown Prince Imriel." Lydia indicated an impressive building on the near side of the river.

"Occult philosophy?" I inquired.

She dropped her voice to a loud whisper. "They study *magic.*"

"They most certainly do not," Florette reproved her. "They study the *philosophy* of magic, which is a different matter altogether."

"Why?" I asked. "Do D'Angelines disapprove of magic? Is it vulgar?"

Lydia laughed. "Vulgar! Imagine. No, no, child. As the tale would have it, their royal majesties determined that wisdom enlightens, while power corrupts. Thus, they founded an Academy dedicated to the pursuit of pure knowledge. There are some—"

"Raphael de Mereliot," her sister interjected.

"—there are *some* who hold that they were fearful and overcautious and lobby to have the Academy's mission revised." Lydia gave a wistful smile. "Myself, I fear that if magic exists in the world, D'Angelines have no gift for it."

I wondered if she was jesting. "What of the old tales? Did Prince Imriel not free a demon from a stone?"

"So they say." She lifted one finger. "And yet you'll note, there's no account of a hero or heroine of Terre d'Ange *doing* magic. Only undoing it."

"Undoing whatever harm it wrought," Florette said tartly. "Which is precisely why their majesties in their wisdom chose the course they did; and King Daniel and his grandmother and father before him have sworn to honor their edict."

I nodded. "I see."

"I should hope so!" She gave me a sharp look. "Alban-born as you are, your people should understand it."

Lydia shivered. "Have you ever seen one?"

I wasn't sure what she meant. "One what?"

The loud whisper. "The magicians."

"The Maghuin Dhonn?" I asked.

She hushed me. "It's bad luck to say their name aloud! But yes, the bear-folk."

"I have," I said. "At Midsummer, many of them gather at Clunderry beside the burial mound where Dorelei mab Breidaia lies, with the magician Berlik's head beneath her feet. They gather to pay tribute to their memories and to remember themselves that the like of such folly should never come to pass."

The good ladies stared at me with open mouths. After a moment, Florette closed hers with an audible click. "Your folk are from Clunderry, then?"

"I have kin there," I acknowledged. It wasn't even a lie.

For a mercy, there was enough to see outside the coach that the ladies were soon distracted. We crossed the river on a massive bridge built by Tiberian engineers over a thousand years ago and entered the city proper. My throat tightened as we passed the gatehouse and the white walls closed around us, but I made myself breathe slowly and listen to the litany of Florette and Lydia's description, and the feeling eased.

It *was* beautiful, very beautiful. I marveled at the buildings and temples—and aye, the folk. It didn't seem as noisy or bustling here as it had in Bourdes. The denizens of the City of Elua went about their business at a more leisurely pace, gathering in small knots to chat with friends.

"Home." Lydia sighed with pleasure.

"Home," Florette agreed.

The coach station was on a street near Elua's Square. The moment we descended from the carriage, a handful of young men appeared to offer their services as porters. Me, they regarded uncertainly, but they flirted shamelessly with the ladies. I watched Florette engage in shrewd negotiations with a likely pair.

"Do you know where you're bound, dear?" She cast a disapproving eye over me. I had my satchel over one shoulder and my bow and quiver over the other. "Have you kin here? You never did say, did you? Have you lodgings?"

"You'd be welcome to stay with us for a time," Lydia added.

Florette pursed her lips, then gave a firm nod. "It's no trouble."

I smiled at them both. "You're very kind. But I've lodgings arranged and I've a fancy to stretch my legs and see a bit of the City."

They gave me the address of the townhouse they shared—it belonged to Lydia, Florette having lost hers to her dead husband's creditors—and made me promise to call on them if I'd need of aught.

"You take care of yourself, dear." Lydia patted my cheek. "Remember us!"

"I will," I promised.

As maddening as they'd been, I watched them toddle away with a certain sense of fondness. I turned to find Theo leaning against the stable doorway, watching me.

"You were right," I said. "They weren't so bad."

"They would have felt differently if they knew what you are," he said quietly. "Do you really have lodging arranged?"

I shrugged. "I've an address."

He hesitated. "I'd be pleased to escort you there."

"No," I said slowly. "I think not. You made your choice."

"Forgive me." Theo stepped forward and brushed his lips against my brow in an awkward kiss. He gave me a rueful smile. "Somehow, I suspect I'll tell my grandchildren about this encounter one day, Moirin of the Maghuin Dhonn. Whatever it is you're bound for, I'm sorry I wasn't bold enough to play a greater role in the journey."

"So am I," I said.

Theo bowed, exacting and formal. "Blessed Elua hold and keep you, lady."

"And you." With that, I left.

NINETEEN

I hadn't lied to the ladies; I truly did have a fancy to see the City.

Or more rightly, I had a fancy to see the great oak tree in Elua's Square, scarce glimpsed from the window of the coach. It grew in the very heart of the City and was said to have been planted by Blessed Elua himself.

It was old.

Very old.

The thoughts of trees grow slower and more ponderous with age. This was the oldest I'd ever encountered. Even at a pace away, its thoughts were silent. I stood beneath the vast green canopy and laid my hand on its bark.

"Hello," I said softly.

It was a long time before I felt the tree respond. Slow, so slow! And yet it had a tremendous awareness, greater than any I'd ever encountered. The oak tree remembered centuries. It was only a blink of time ago that Prince Imriel had scrambled into its branches, digging out a hidden gemstone. It remembered when there was no City, only a tiny village in a lush river valley.

It remembered Elua.

It remembered how he had cupped an acorn in the palm of his hand and smiled, turning to one of his Companions. And the Companion had smiled in reply and taken Elua's hands in his and blown softly on the seed.

Anael, the Good Steward.

A little green tail had split the shell of the acorn and wriggled free. Together, Elua and Anael had planted it here.

"So long ago?" I marveled.

So long ago.

I bent my brow against the rough bark. "You've seen so much."

The oak agreed.

And someone stole my purse.

"Oh, gods bedamned!" I felt the tug at my waist as my purse-strings were severed and raised my head in outrage. A wiry youth dashed across the square.

I was angry enough at both myself and him to set out in pursuit. I summoned the twilight without thinking and set out after him at a quick trot, dodging D'Angelines strolling in the square. I might not have known the City, but I was a good tracker and I managed to keep the lad in sight. Sure enough, after turning down a couple of streets, he glanced over his shoulder and slowed down, seeing no one behind him. He smiled and tossed the purse in the air and caught it, clearly satisfied with himself.

I meant to get it back. Although it was not so very much money and I had the letter of credit Caroline nó Bryony had given me, I'd no idea if it would be honored as promptly as my claim in Bryn Gorrydum, where Alais the Wise herself had established the fund. And I'd learned enough on my journey to know that the last thing one wanted to do was start out penniless in the City of Elua. I stole closer, concentrating on the lad. I drew nearer, only a block behind him. I didn't intend to harm him, only to snatch the purse back. It would give him a scare that would serve him right.

I was so intent on my task, I didn't heed the carriage rounding the corner ahead of me.

To be sure, its driver didn't see *me*.

Later, I would learn that it was travelling at a goodly pace, mayhap faster than it should have been in the City. And I would learn that the horses veered, sensing my unseen presence. The carriage struck me nonetheless, knocking me off my feet and onto a hitching post outside a wineshop. The impact jolted me backward and I fell, hitting my head on the street.

Then, I had only the shocking sense of a series of mighty blows and the world whirling around me, going from twilit dimness to dizzying brightness, then darkness.

There were voices in the darkness.

"—came out of nowhere! Swear to Elua, my lord!"

"No, no. Don't move her, Denis."

The darkness retreated, pain surging in its wake. I was lying in the street. My chest was filled with searing pain and it was hard to breathe. A man knelt beside me. He was so beautiful I thought mayhap I was dead or dreaming.

"Lie still." His voice was deep and soothing. "I'm afraid my carriage struck you. Can you breathe?"

Barely. I mouthed the word.

He nodded. His eyes were grey like Cillian's, and utterly unlike Cillian's, intense and stormy. "Slow and shallow. Try to relax. I'm going to feel for injuries."

I closed my eyes and concentrated on easing a meager bit of air in and out of my lungs. He felt me all over, his touch deft and light and expert.

"Can you move your head?" he asked.

I tried. I could, but it set off new waves of agony throbbing at the back of my skull, which in turn made me feel sick. For a moment, I thought I might vomit and choke on my own bile.

"Easy." He placed his fingertips on my temples and peered into my eyes, tawny hair framing his face. "Name of Elua, what *are* you?" he murmured to himself. I couldn't answer and didn't try. "All right, listen. I fear you've dislocated a rib. I'm going to attempt to maneuver it back in place. Can you lie still without struggling?"

I blinked in affirmation.

"Good girl." He turned to someone else. "Denis, come here." He raised my left arm over my head. If I could have screamed, I would have. "I'm sorry," he said in his soothing voice. "I know it hurts. But I promise you, I know what I'm doing. Denis, pull lightly on her arm. Lightly."

Oh, stone and sea, it hurt!

"You're very brave." The tawny-haired man fished my signet ring on its thong from my gown. My eyes widened in alarm. "It's all right, I'm just moving it out of the way. A family heirloom, is it? We'll make sure it's safe." He glanced at it and went still. "Nevil." His voice was tight. "She had a bag. Find it."

"Aye, my lord," a third voice said.

"Right." He turned back to me, then closed his eyes and rubbed the palms of his hands together, murmuring a prayer. When he opened his eyes, they were more intent than ever. "Relax as best you can and keep still."

He put his hands on me.

Warmth radiated from them. It felt like golden sunlight spilling over my skin. Even through the pain, I could feel pleasure in it. He felt along my ribcage, pressing first with his fingertips, then with the heel of one hand, slow and steady.

Something inside me moved.

Of a sudden, the pain in my chest diminished and I could breathe. I took a deep, relieved gasp, then another and another. Air had never tasted so sweet.

The tawny-haired man smiled. "Better?"

I nodded, which was a bad idea. My stomach lurched and a scalding tide of sickness rose in my throat. I turned my head and retched.

"Oh, *hells*!" the man Denis swore. "You owe me a new pair of breeches, Raphael."

"My lord?" The coach-driver's voice, high and strained. "I found her bag. You're going to want to see this, my lord."

"Stay with her, Denis," the tawny-haired man advised. "If you're inclined to chivalry, I'd suggest you put your doublet beneath her head, and I'll stand you the cost of a whole new outfit."

"You're being almighty solicitous of some half-breed street urchin," Denis grumbled, although he obeyed.

The doublet was soft beneath my aching head. I closed my eyes and focused on breathing, fearful I'd vomit a second time. I heard the tawny-haired man—Raphael, the other had called him—utter a startled oath, then confer with his driver in hushed tones. The world went in and out around me. When I opened my eyes, he was leaning over me.

"Moirin?" he asked.

I gave a faint nod.

"Moirin mac Fainche of the Maghuin Dhonn?" His voice was low and steady. "Descended from Alais de la Courcel and Conor mac Grainne?"

"Aye," I whispered.

"Blessed Elua bugger me!" Denis exclaimed. "Are you jesting?"

The man Raphael ignored him. He laid a gentle hand against my cheek, that wonderful warmth still radiating from it. "You've taken a hard blow to the head, my lady, and I'm worried that rib could have punctured a lung. As you've seen, I'm a physician trained in the healing arts. With your permission, I'd like to take you to my home to recuperate. I promise, you'll be treated with the utmost of solicitousness. Is that suitable to you?"

All I wanted was to clutch his hand against me and sleep. "Aye."

He took his hand away. "Good girl."

TWENTY

I woke to sunlight.

I was lying in a strange bed. My head and my ribcage hurt and my memory was hazy. I fought down a surge of panic and made myself breathe slowly. When I'd regained a measure of calm, I levered myself upright.

There was a balcony opposite me, the doors open onto daylight and fresh air. Good. That meant I wasn't trapped. I looked down at myself. I was clad in a long-sleeved shift of the softest white linen I'd ever felt, trimmed in lace as delicate as foam.

My purse.

It was the first memory to surface—the tug at my belt and the fleeing thief. I glanced around in alarm. My head spun and my stomach rebelled. For a mercy, there wasn't much in the latter. I gagged and coughed, but managed not to vomit.

The door opened. "Moirin?"

It was him—the tawny-haired man. Bits and pieces of memory came back to me. The street, the carriage. The marvelous warmth of his hands. He'd taken me home, he and his companion.

"Do you need the pail?" He moved swiftly across the room and picked up a shiny silver pail, holding it under my chin. "Go ahead if you need to be sick; there's no shame in it."

I swallowed. "I'm all right."

"You're sure?"

I nodded and licked my lips. They were very dry. "Thirsty."

"Ah." He smiled and set down the pail. "That's a good sign. Here."

He poured water from a porcelain ewer into a matching cup and handed it to me. "Sip it slowly." I did. It was almost as good as the water I'd drunk after I'd seen the Maghuin Dhonn Herself. The tawny-haired man pulled up a stool with a cushioned seat and sat beside my bed, watching me. "How do you feel?"

A vision of Cillian's dented skull flashed behind my eyes. I felt sick again, the cup shaking in my hands.

"Easy, child." He plucked the cup from my hands. "I'm going to examine you. All right?"

I nodded again.

His name surfaced in my memory: Raphael. It was familiar somehow.

Raphael rubbed his hands together as he'd done the day before. He felt delicately at a tender lump on the back of my skull. Warmth flowed from his touch. He cupped my face and turned my head gently from side to side, peering intently at me. "No bruising to the eye sockets nor blood in the ears." He gave me another smile. It was a very nice smile, brightening his storm-grey eyes. "That's a good sign, too, Moirin mac Fainche. It means you've not cracked your skull. You've a hard head, it seems."

"So I've been told," I murmured.

His hands skimmed my ribs. "Oh, indeed? Well, all's where it ought to be. May I listen to your lungs?"

"Why?" I asked.

"To determine if they're whole and uninjured." He whistled softly. "*That's* the sound we don't want to hear, my lady."

I shrugged. "Go on, then."

Raphael pressed his ear to my breast. "Breathe deep, as deep as you can."

I obeyed, acutely conscious of his nearness. He closed his eyes and listened intently. The sunlight picked out golden glints in his tawny hair. As confused and miserable as I felt, I yearned to run my fingers through it.

He sat upright and grinned. It made him look younger.

"No whistle?" I asked.

"No whistle," he confirmed. "I'll need to examine your urine. Do you think you might manage to use the chamberpot?"

"What?" I wondered if this was some unique breed of D'Angeline perversity.

"To make certain there's no blood in it," Raphael said in clarification. "A hard blow to the midsection such as you sustained may cause damage and bleeding to the organs, my lady. Since I cannot cut you open to see, an analysis of the vital humors is crucial."

I sighed. "All right, then."

"Do you need assistance?" he inquired.

I glowered at him. "No!"

He pulled a decorative chamberpot from beneath my bed and left me with a polite bow and a promise to return. I clambered out of bed with an effort, hiked up the skirt of my shift over my bare legs, and settled myself on the chamberpot.

There, I pissed.

For as much as the rest of me hurt, it felt good. I sighed with pleasure, relieved of a pressure I hadn't recognized. From my vantage point, I could see that while my purse was gone, my satchel rested near the bed, grimy and valuable due to the papers it held. And there, too, was my bow and quiver. All was not lost.

The stream of my piss rattled against the chamberpot. When I finished, I poured fresh water into the nearby basin and washed my hands and face, then I clambered back in bed.

"Moirin?" Raphael called.

"Aye?" I drew the sheets to my chin. I'd never been one for modesty, but I felt weak and vulnerable in this situation.

"Well done." He entered smiling, and to my everlasting chagrin, smelled at the pot, tilting it and studying my humors. "It looks good. Do you think you might be able to take some broth?"

I consulted my belly. The water seemed to have settled it. "I do."

He picked up a bell on a night-stand table and rang it. A manservant appeared in prompt response. When Raphael ordered him to empty the chamberpot and tell the cook to send up a bowl of simple broth, he bowed in assent.

"I don't want to trouble you, my lord," I murmured.

"It's no trouble." He sat back down on the footstool, studying me with those intent grey eyes. "But I must own, I'm curious. Surely, you've D'Angeline blood in you more recent than Alais de la Courcel's era."

"My father," I agreed.

"Truly?" Raphael raised his brows. "However would *that* come about?"

"Is it so hard to believe?" I asked, insulted.

"No, no." He raised his hands. "I didn't mean it thusly. It's only that I thought the Maghuin Dhonn were a . . . let us say a singularly private and solitary folk."

"Say what you mean, my lord," I said with resignation. "Savage and barbaric? Sly and uncanny? Mysterious and dire?"

He touched my cheek. "Mysterious and uncanny, yes. At the moment, you don't appear particularly dire."

It drew a reluctant smile from me. "No?" I prodded the lump on the back of my skull. My hair was matted with dried blood. "To be sure, I'm feeling rather dire."

He laughed.

A maidservant arrived with a tray. She peered around Raphael with wide eyes when he went to take it from her. Despite my protests, he insisted on feeding me himself as though I were a babe too weak to hold a spoon. After the first few bites, my appetite returned and I finished almost the entire bowl. When I was done, I found myself sleepy and yawning. When I apologized to Raphael, he shook his head.

"Sleep's the best healer." He laid one hand on my brow and felt at the pulse in my wrist with the other. "You're young and strong and like to recover. Sleep, and I'll look in on you in a few hours. If you've need of aught, ring the bell and someone will come."

"All right." I settled my aching head against the pillows. As he made to draw away, I caught one of his hands and stroked it. Somewhere beneath the pain and weariness, desire waited, coiled inside me. I saw it reflected in his surprised gaze and smiled. "My lord, for all your kindness, you've not given me your name."

"Raphael," he said softly. "Raphael de Mereliot."

"Stone and sea!" I blinked. "You're the Queen's favorite courtier.

The one who thinks the Academy ought to explore more than the philosophy of magic."

He stared. "How in Blessed Elua's name did you know *that*?"

"Oh, I had a long stagecoach ride." I yawned. "And you're quite the preferred topic of gossip, my lord—you and her majesty."

"Are we, now?" Raphael de Mereliot's tone was dry. He stood and gazed at me, his expression unreadable. "Wait until they get wind of *you*, Moirin mac Fainche."

TWENTY-ONE

I slept for most of my first full day in Raphael de Mereliot's home. By the second day, I felt much better. My ribs ached and the lump on my skull was tender, but the dizziness and nausea had passed and I felt stronger. By midday, Raphael agreed that I might eat solid food and have a bath afterward.

"No vigorous scrubbing!" he warned me. He laid his hands on my ribcage. "You've got to keep still to let the tissues heal and hold the bone in its proper place."

"Aye, my lord," I said innocently. "Would you prefer to scrub me yourself?"

His grey eyes darkened, but he merely shook a finger at me. "Be a good girl and heed your physician's orders."

Stone and sea, that bath was a glorious thing! The tub was a vast marble affair with gilded feet in the shape of leaping fishes. I couldn't begin to imagine how many buckets of water it took to fill it, nor how much wood to heat the water. At the moment, I didn't much care. I only knew it was bliss to sink my aching body into its warmth.

A maidservant too shy to meet my gaze gave me a ball of soap and a soft cloth. The soap smelled of lavender and had the image of a flower impressed on it. It lathered beautifully. I washed myself all over, careful not to make any abrupt movements. When I was done, I soaked the matted blood from my hair and washed that, too. Afterward, the maidservant gave me a robe of thick satin to wear—vivid sea-blue worked with gold in a repeating pattern of two fishes, nose to tail in a circle.

"Better?" Raphael found me back in his guest-chamber, sitting on the footstool and running a comb through my wet hair.

"Oh, aye." I maneuvered the comb around the sore place. "Much. Do you know where my clothes have gone to? My own clothes? They weren't in my satchel."

He perched on the edge of the bed. "You don't care for the robe?"

I glanced down at it. "I do. But—"

"It's the crest of House Mereliot," Raphael informed me. "We're a very old house descended from Eisheth's line."

"Eisheth." I put down the comb. "She brought the healing arts, and . . . music to the folk of Terre d'Ange, aye?"

"Aye," he agreed, mimicking me.

"I know, I know!" I sighed. "Only vulgar common folk say *aye*. My clothes?"

Raphael laughed. "Your clothes, such as they are, have been laundered and are drying. You'll have them back soon. Are you in such a hurry to leave?"

"No," I admitted. "I'd like to feel I *could*, that's all."

He sobered. "Of course you do. I'll have them sent up straightaway. But, Moirin . . ." He hesitated. "You're a descendant of House Courcel. You can't run about the City clad in threadbare rags."

"Yes, my lord," I said dryly. "That, too, has been made abundantly clear to me."

Raphael ignored my tone. "Forgive me for prying, but I noted you'd a letter of commendation for a couturier at Atelier Favrielle in your things. With your permission, I'd be pleased to contact them on your behalf."

"You don't think they would refuse me?" I asked.

"No." His mouth quirked. "I don't."

I cocked my head at him. "Would it please you?"

He gave me a long look that made me shiver inside and answered in a low voice. "To see your beauty clad in a manner befitting it? It would please anyone in their right mind."

I flushed. "Then I thank you for your assistance."

"May I ask what you intend in the City of Elua?" Raphael inquired. "'Tis clear you'd only just arrived. Are you here to seek out your father?"

What was I to tell him? In this elegant, sunlit room, the stone door-way and the Maghuin Dhonn seemed very far away, and talk of a mysterious destiny would sound like a girl's folly. And after all, finding my father was the first step, since I hadn't the faintest idea what else to do. So I simply said, "Yes."

"What's his name?" he asked.

I sighed. "As to that, I cannot say. Only that he is a Priest of Naamah and he attended the coronation of Lord Tiernan of the Dalriada. But he told my mother she might ask after him at the Temple of Naamah here in the City that's dedicated to star-crossed lovers. Do you know it?"

"Oh, yes." Raphael nodded. "And I'll make an inquiry at Court. It ought to be easy enough to find out who was sent as a delegate to the coronation. Like as not, he or she will be able to provide a name. It's unlikely more than one of Naamah's priests was in the entourage."

I thanked him for what felt like the hundredth time. "My lord, why are you going to such trouble?" I added. The words his friend had spoken in the street came back to me. "Surely you don't extend such kindness to every and any half-breed street urchin."

He looked sideways at me. "You heard that? No, no, I don't; although I'd like to think I'd be solicitous of anyone who came to harm through my own fault, or the fault of those in my employ." Raphael frowned. "Although when you're feeling stronger, I'd like to ask you a few questions about the incident."

"Oh, it was entirely my fault," I said hastily. The memory of Theo's rejection was all too fresh in my mind. I didn't want to frighten away this beautiful man whose touch felt like sunlight. "I was careless."

"We'll see." He rose. "I'll see that your clothing is returned to you, then find out what I may learn at Court."

"Thank you," I said for the hundred and first time.

"You're welcome." Raphael hesitated. "I'll own freely, I'm putting myself out in part because you're a descendant of House Courcel and I've reason to wish to be in their good graces. But you intrigue me in your own right. A Priest of Naamah and one of the Maghuin Dhonn . . ." He shook his head. "What a pairing."

"You're not afraid to say it aloud," I observed.

"What's that?"

"Maghuin Dhonn," I said.

"No." He leveled a steady gaze at me. "There's a great deal that I'm not afraid of. And there's a great deal I'd like to discuss with you when you're willing."

I echoed his words back to him. "We'll see."

Raphael de Mereliot ran an efficient household. My clothing arrived very shortly after he left, clean and dry and still warm from being pressed with a hot iron. And, to be honest, quite threadbare. Still, I put on the green gown that Aislinn had given me, which was the best of the lot. I felt less of an invalid in proper attire.

I also felt stifled for the first time since Raphael had brought me here. I opened the door to my bedchamber and toyed with the idea of exploring my surroundings. My head and ribs advised against it. So instead I went onto the balcony. There was a little table and two chairs of some kind of metal filigree and it overlooked an inner courtyard with a lush garden. I closed my eyes and breathed deeply. The air smelled of herbs—some familiar, like comfrey and catmint, some new, like basil and rosemary and lavender. There were others I didn't know. Almost all of the plants were happy and content, although here and there I sensed a discordant note.

Tomorrow, I thought, I would explore.

How long I sat there, I couldn't say. Hours, I suppose. The balcony faced west. I watched the sky turn red and thought about home. I wondered where my mother was and if she was permitting herself to be happy with Oengus.

I hoped so.

I wondered what she would think of Raphael de Mereliot. I wondered what *I* thought of him.

The Queen's favorite courtier.

Her lover, by all accounts. I wondered what the good ladies Florette and Lydia would make of my presence in his home. No doubt they would be beside themselves with scandalous delight. I'd have to visit them.

Sunset turned to dusk. Twilight rose from the garden beneath me, hundreds of herbs and shrubs exhaling wistfully at the passing of the sun. It was profoundly comforting. I drew the essence of the D'Angeline twilight deep into my lungs and breathed it out, letting it surround me like a cloud.

"Moirin?"

Alarmed, I let it go and rose with alacrity.

Raphael stood just beyond the open balcony doors, staring at me with parted lips. "You were . . . sparkling."

"Oh?" I said weakly. "Was I?"

"You were. I called your name at the door," he added. "You didn't answer."

"I was thinking."

He fixed me with his intent gaze. "And sparkling."

I sighed. "It's because you were watching, my lord. And because I was careless once more and didn't hear you or sense your presence. Tame places do that to me. If you hadn't already been watching, you wouldn't have seen me."

"Like Nevil," he said.

"Nevil?" I repeated.

"My driver." Raphael's gaze was unflinching. "He swears the street where we struck you was empty. And I have never, ever known him to lie. He didn't, did he?"

"No," I murmured. "He did not. Tell me, my lord, have I surpassed the limit of strangeness any man might be expected to endure?"

"Not even close, Moirin of the Maghuin Dhonn." With an unexpectedly wolfish grin, Raphael reached me in a few swift strides. He cupped my face in his hands and kissed me, warmth radiating from his hands. It felt glorious. Our tongues and our gifts entangled, healing and desire intertwined in an intricate dance. He lifted his head, grey eyes gleaming. "Ah, Elua! Not even close, my lady. I *like* your strangeness."

I felt dizzy. "Why?"

Raphael stroked the line of my jaw with his thumbs. "Do you feel well enough to dine with me?"

"I do."

He let go my face and extended his arm. "Then come, and let us talk."

TWENTY-TWO

"How is it done?" Raphael asked.

I explained to him how one summoned the twilight, drawing it in and breathing it out. He listened intently.

"Is it a discipline of long practice?" he asked when I had finished.

"No." I shook my head. "It takes a good deal more concentration to do it in a tame place unless there's green, growing life present. Like your garden or Elua's Oak. Do you know, it remembers being planted?" I added. "I've never met a tree so old or with such self-awareness before."

He blinked. "You speak with trees?"

"With that one, aye. Mostly, their thoughts are simpler. Not thoughts, exactly, but awareness."

"And how is *that* done?" Raphael asked.

I shrugged. "I don't know, I just do. It's a small gift, but it's my own. My lord, why are you so curious?"

"Call me Raphael." He gestured to the chef to carve the roast standing beside the table. "Because unlike many in Terre d'Ange, I believe magic is a tool we shouldn't fear to put to good use. But from my studies, I've come to find that the incidence of pure, inherent magic in human beings is exceedingly rare. In most documented cases, it's acquired only by dint of intense study and discipline or great sacrifice. Or both." He poured sauce from a pitcher over the slice of beef the chef had laid on my plate. "The Maghuin Dhonn are a fascinating exception."

Out of the corner of my eye, I saw the chef shudder. "Well, we are a very old people."

Raphael gave me a curious glance. "You think of yourself as one of them?"

"I *am* one of them," I said firmly. "No matter where I am or how far I go, I carry the spark of my *diadh-anam* inside me."

His eyes gleamed in the candlelight. "Are the old stories true? Can you take on the shape of a bear?"

I cut a piece of roast and chewed thoughtfully. "No," I said at last. "The old stories are true, aye. But we lost that gift generations ago, when Berlik broke the oath he swore on behalf of all the Maghuin Dhonn. He was the last to wield it." I put down my fork. "We are also a dwindling folk, my lord Raphael. What magic left to us is small and insignificant, meant to protect and conceal us. I'm sorry to disappoint you."

"On the contrary." He reached out and held one hand several inches above mine. "Can you feel that?"

The air between us vibrated. I nodded.

"Energy." Raphael took his hand away. "It is the essence of all things. It flows through us and around us. With great practice, one can learn to control and manipulate it." He applied himself to his dinner, continuing to talk between bites. "I studied traditional medicine at the Academy in Marsilikos, but in the past year, we've been honored to have a great teacher from Ch'in at the Academy here, Master Lo Feng. It is a wondrous opportunity, for his folk almost never venture this far abroad, and they admit few foreigners to their country. Did you know that the Ch'in have a very different view of the healing arts?"

"No," I said.

"They do." He pointed his fork at me. "And under his tutelage, I've learned there is far more to healing than meets the eyes. After months of practice, I've learned the rudiments of controlling my own energy and using it to help heal others. But *you*—" He shook his head. "What you're capable of, you do without even thinking."

"Aye, but it's not the same thing," I said. "What *I* do is a gift of the Maghuin Dhonn."

Raphael shrugged. "Mayhap it has applications you've never dreamed. We could explore them, you and I." He smiled at me. "Mayhap it was destiny that placed you in that very street at that very moment."

My *diadh-anam* pulsed in my breast as though in agreement. "That," I said, "may be a more real possibility than you know."

He resumed eating. "When you're feeling stronger, I'd love to have you meet him. Master Lo Feng, that is."

"Why not?" I agreed. I'd never met anyone from Ch'in.

"And of course I'll introduce you at Court . . ." Raphael started. "Oh! Name of Elua, I'm an idiot. Your father."

My heart quickened. "You found him?"

He nodded. "I think so, or at least his name. I'm sorry, Moirin. It went clean out of my head when I saw you . . . sparkling." Somewhere in the background, there was a commotion and raised voices. Raphael frowned and beckoned to a manservant standing by with a jug of wine. "Gerard, go see what that is."

Gerard set down his jug and bowed, exiting the dining hall. Raphael watched him go, still frowning.

"My father?" I prompted him.

"One moment," he said absently.

Gerard returned and bent down low, murmuring in his lord's ear. Raphael looked at once grim and oddly satisfied. "I'll speak to him." He dabbed his lips with a linen cloth. "Forgive me," he said to me. "I'll be back straightaway."

Curiosity got the better of me without even trying. I waited all of three heartbeats before following him. As soon as I'd slipped past the watching eyes of the servants in the dining room, I used the memory of Elua's Oak to focus my thoughts, and managed to call the twilight without too much effort. I trailed behind Raphael as he made his way to a large marble foyer I vaguely remembered from my dazed arrival.

There were three D'Angeline men awaiting him clad in some manner of livery. I couldn't make out the color in the twilight, but their doublets bore the emblem of a swan worked in a crest. All of them wore swords.

Their captain inclined his head. "My lord de Mereliot," he said in a curt voice. "Pray tell me your doorman misspoke."

Raphael folded his arms. "He did not."

The captain took a step toward him, one hand hovering above his sword-hilt. I wished I had my bow. "Then I would hear it from your lips, my lord," he said with acid politeness. "So I might assure her majesty there was no mistake. Is it your intention to deny the Queen of Terre d'Ange entry?"

"Is it a crime?" Raphael gave a pointed glance at the captain's sword. "The last I recall, the Queen was not an Empress, and D'Angeline citizens still enjoyed certain rights. Or is there a state of emergency? Are the Skaldi on our doorstep? Does her majesty require refuge?"

The other man's face darkened. "Just answer, damn you!"

"Very well." He executed a crisp bow. "Yes. It is unequivocally my intention to deny the Queen of Terre d'Ange entry to my private domicile. Does that suffice?"

"You play a foolish game, my lord," the captain muttered.

"I?" A muscle along Raphael's jawline twitched. "Jehanne has seen fit to punish me for *three weeks* for missing a single, insignificant engagement. She was angry—well and good. I made my apology, but she didn't see fit to accept it. It *was* a foolish game. She carried it too far and now *I* am angry. You may tell her you heard it from my own lips."

Unexpectedly, the captain sighed. "Oh, fine. She'll be hell to live with."

Raphael smiled. "I know."

The men in livery took their leave. I turned to steal back to the dining hall and found my way blocked by a gauntlet of curious servants who had come to see the confrontation. With a sigh of my own, I turned back to Raphael and let go the twilight. The silvery candle flames turned golden and the foyer took on a warm, pinkish hue. Behind me, a shocked murmur arose. Raphael regarded me.

"Moirin." He didn't sound surprised.

"Aye." I shrugged in apology.

"Sly and uncanny, is it? Ah, well, I suppose I'd have done the same in your shoes." Raphael extended his arm. "Shall we finish our dinner? I believe I was on the verge of imparting some rather important information to you."

I took his arm gratefully, happy that he wasn't angry at me. He rearranged my hand, showing me how to rest my fingertips lightly on his forearm. Members of his household stared and whispered. I could feel the warmth of his breath against my hair, feel the warmth of his body inches from mine. It set the doves to fluttering in my belly.

The Queen's favorite courtier, her lover.

"Do you love her?" I murmured without looking at him.

"Yes," he said in a low voice. I did look up, then, gazing into his storm-grey eyes. Raphael caressed my cheek. "But it doesn't mean she's my destiny, does it? And after all, this *is* Terre d'Ange. I'm not bound to love one and one alone."

There before his entire household, he kissed me again, and this time it was slow and languorous and deliberate. Once again—I could feel the heat and rising energy coiling between us. But when I wound my arms around his neck, Raphael laughed deep in his chest and peeled me off him.

"Ah, no." He settled my hand on his arm. "You've healing to do, my lady. Come."

Over cold meat and mashed tubers, congealed sauce, and a salad of limp greens, he told me that he'd learned that Duc Gautier de Barthelme, who was in fact a descendant of House Courcel, had attended Lord Tiernan's coronation, and that if there was a Priest of Naamah in attendance, it was almost surely Phanuel Demarre, the companion of his youth.

"It's an old custom," Raphael explained. "To assign a priest- or priestess-in-training to a scion of the royal family. Often, lasting friendships are formed."

I toyed with a forkful of tubers. "Do you know where he is?"

He shook his head. "No, but I reckon your mother's right about the Temple. On the morrow, I can—"

"No."

"No?" he echoed.

I stirred my mashed tubers, thinking of the bright lady's smile and the mystery that had called my unknown father to my unlikely mother. "What if he's there? To the best of my knowledge, he's no idea I even exist. I think it's something I ought to do myself."

"As you wish." Raphael inclined his head. "But not yet. I'd rather you gave that rib at least a week to heal."

"A week?" I said in dismay.

He laughed. "Given my druthers, I'd say four, mayhap six. Can you grant me a mere week? If you can, I'll promise you a consultation on the morrow with Benoit Vallon of Atelier Favrielle right here at home. In a week's time, he ought to be able to whip together at least one ensemble befitting you."

My spirits rose. "Truly?"

"Do you consent to my terms?" Raphael countered. "A week's time to rest and recover?" I nodded. "Then yes, truly."

After dinner, he escorted me back to my guest-chamber and bade me good night. He kissed me, but it was a gentle kiss.

"I do feel *much* better," I said without a hint of subtlety.

Raphael shook his head, looking amused. "You won't if you don't take your ease as I ordered." He kissed me again, then turned me around and gave me a tiny shove. "Go on to bed with you."

I glanced over my shoulder. "And in a week's time?"

"We'll see," he promised, and closed the door.

TWENTY-THREE

I fell asleep thinking about Raphael de Mereliot. When I woke up, the first thing I thought about was Raphael de Mereliot.

Stone and sea, I wanted him! And it was a kind of wanting unlike any I'd known before, deeper and harder, an ache I felt in the very marrow of my bones. I remembered my mother saying Cillian was doomed the minute he laid eyes on me. Suddenly, I understood it. I was doomed the minute Raphael laid his hands on me, infusing my battered body with that glorious golden warmth.

And if I hadn't been, that first kiss had sealed it.

My *diadh-anam* agreed. And yet when I thought about the Maghuin Dhonn Herself, all I could see was the sorrow and regret in Her eyes.

"Why?" I murmured aloud, sitting on the balcony. "It's because he loves another, isn't it? And not just any other, but the Queen of Terre d'Ange, who just happens to also be an adept of the Night Court."

There was no reply.

I sighed and rested my brow on the rail of the balcony, gazing at the garden below. The happy plants were sparkling with dew. Raphael de Mereliot, the Queen's lover. Mayhap, my destiny. Why couldn't it have been someone simple and uncomplicated like Theo the coach-driver? I'd spent the whole of my life in a small patch of forest. I suspected a lifetime of learning to catch fish with my bare hands, skin rabbits, and gather burdock root hadn't exactly prepared me for the intrigues of the D'Angeline Court.

There was a knock at the door. "Moirin?"

Already, even muffled, his voice was familiar. "Aye!" I called, rising from my chair. "Come in."

Raphael entered, another man in tow. The newcomer was tall and lanky, but he moved with loose-limbed elegance. When he saw me, he stopped short and narrowed his eyes. "So *this* is what you're hiding, eh?"

"Hiding?" Raphael's tone was nonchalant. "That's an interesting term, Messire Vallon." He winked at me. "May I present my lady Moirin mac Fainche of the Maghuin Dhonn, a descendant of Alais de la Courcel?"

The tall man paled. "Do you jest?"

Raphael smiled. "Not in the least. Moirin, this is Messire Benoit Vallon of Atelier Favrielle."

"Well met, messire," I said politely. He merely nodded in reply, steepled his fingers, and pressed them to his lips, studying me.

"So?" Raphael clapped him on the shoulder. "Will you take the commission?"

"Her majesty would be furious with us," Benoit Vallon said absently.

"Her majesty is already furious with you for refusing her," Raphael informed him. "And with me. Will you take the commission?"

He didn't look away from me. "Yes. Yes, of course."

"Excellent." Raphael smiled at me, grey eyes sparkling like sunlight on the sea. "Then I'll leave you to it, shall I?"

The couturier flapped a hand at him. "By all means, go."

As soon as Raphael had withdrawn, Benoit Vallon prowled around me in a circle, looking without touching. I turned my head and craned my neck, trying to track his progress. "Good bones," he mused aloud. "Youth's dewy freshness . . . How old are you?"

I hazarded a guess. "Sixteen? No, seventeen by now."

"Seventeen." He blew out his breath. "That'll set Jehanne's teeth on edge, bear-witch or no." He lifted a length of my hair in one hand, letting it spill over his fingers. "Fine and glossy and healthy. Has it ever been cut?"

I shook my head.

"We'll trim the ends and celebrate its abundance." Benoit took a step backward. "Strip."

"Strip?" I echoed.

He grimaced, his face saturnine and mobile. "How else do you expect me to appraise you?" I stripped. "Ah." Benoit Vallon nodded in approval. "You've collarbones to die for, my dear."

"I do?" I looked down at myself.

"Oh, yes." He traced them with an impersonal touch. "This hollow? And this? Exquisite. Beauty and allure don't always lie in the *obvious*. Any tuppenny tailor can stitch together a gown to showcase your breasts. It takes an artist to see and highlight the body's more subtle charms." He twirled one finger in the air. "Turn for me."

I rotated obediently.

Benoit studied me with hooded eyes. "Slender and supple . . . I daresay you've led a more active life than most peers, eh?"

"I daresay," I agreed. "Messire Vallon, why did you suggest that Raphael's been hiding me?"

"Mmm." He turned away to rummage in his bag. "Quite apart from the fact that he swore me to secrecy about this visit? And like a fool, I agreed to it. Stand still, I'm going to take your measurements."

I stood without moving while he measured every part of me with a cloth tape. "He's only being discreet for my sake."

"Discreet!" Benoit snorted. "All it took was one witness, child. The entire City of Elua knows that Raphael de Mereliot's carriage struck a young woman in the street, and that he whisked her away to his townhouse, where he's been hiding her ever since." He jotted some numbers on a piece of paper. "*And* he's being almighty close-mouthed about it, *and* it's piqued the Queen's curiosity somewhat fierce." He lifted my left arm and made one final measurement. "Is it true he turned her away yesterday evening?"

"I wouldn't know," I murmured.

"You may put your clothes on." He put away the measuring tape and pulled a case of colored sticks from his bag. "Very good. Now sit for me; I'm going to capture your palette."

I perched on the footstool, my chin in my hands, while Benoit rubbed his colored sticks on the paper.

"See here." He showed me. "Black for your hair, and this warm gold is your skin tone. A shocking jolt of green for the eyes. This will help me choose fabrics that will flatter your coloring. Autumnal hues will suit you best—bronzes, coppers, russets, and greens. Stay away from bright, vivid colors. If you *must* wear color, favor deep jewel tones. Never wear stark white; wear ivory instead. Do you understand?"

"I do," I said.

Benoit wasn't finished. "Now, selecting fabric will be of paramount importance, because I plan to keep my design simple." He gestured at me. "We want to play up that fascinating contrast."

I glanced down at myself again. "Oh?"

"You've got good bones," he said impatiently. "Very elegant lines. At the same time, there's somewhat . . . oh, a bit savage about your face. Wild and exotic. It's a face one might expect to see peering out of an enchanted forest."

"I see."

He gave me a doubtful look. "I'm not so sure of that. But *I* do, and that's what's important. Let me see your hands." He took them in his, examined them, and clucked his tongue in disapproval. "Name of Elua! What have you been doing?"

"Living," I said dryly.

"Your nails are a disgrace and you have *calluses*." Benoit uttered the word as though it disgusted him. He took a deep breath. "Don't worry. We'll have someone tend to your nails before you're seen in public. And I'll have a cream sent over. You're to slather your hands every night and sleep in cotton gloves."

I made a face. "Is that really necessary?"

"If it's your intention to be presented at Court without becoming a laughingstock, yes." Benoit Vallon gave me a shrewd look. "Is it?"

I shrugged. "To be sure, I don't wish to disgrace my lord Raphael."

"My lady." Benoit squeezed my hands, still holding them despite their apparent hideousness. His tone turned serious. "If you'd hear a word of advice, I'd counsel you strongly. Do not think to come between my lord de Mereliot and the Queen. Whatever game they're playing, don't let him make you a pawn in it."

"He's not!" I protested. "He's shown me nothing but kindness."

"It suits his ends," he warned me. "Raphael de Mereliot knows full well that the City's already a-twitter over the secret he's hiding. He's not a bad fellow, but every man has an angel and a devil inside him. You fell into his hands like a gift sent straight from Heaven. He means to use you for all it's worth."

I pulled my hands away. "I don't believe it."

"Believe as you will." Benoit Vallon gathered his things, then gave me a crisp bow. "I'll return in a few days for your first fitting."

That evening, Raphael took me for a stroll in his garden. It was better, so much better, than sitting on the balcony. I took off my shoes and reveled in the feeling of tender grass beneath my bare feet. Raphael smiled indulgently and let me wander. I tasted the air, letting it play over my tongue, and listened for the one discordant note amid the complacent choir.

"This one." I followed the note unerringly to a graceful little tree in a beautiful blue and white pot, its leaves drooping and yellow. "He's unhappy. What is he?"

"A plum tree from Ch'in." Raphael patted the pot. "A gift from Master Lo Feng. The fruit stimulates the bowels. But I'm afraid it's not going to make it through the winter."

I stroked the plum tree's branches, closing my eyes and concentrating. It whimpered through my thoughts, roots coiled in a tight ball.

"It's all right," I whispered. "This is a good place. You'll see." Opening my eyes, I blew softly on it.

The little tree quivered. The tight ball of roots eased a bit, the limp leaves brightening.

"It looks . . . better." Raphael stared at me. "What did you do?"

I was drained. "It's part of my gift. I can't do much, only help a little. He's lonely and drawing into himself."

"Lonely," he echoed.

I tapped the pot. "Take him out of this and plant him. He'll be happier in shared soil, I promise. Raphael, are you using me in your quarrel with the Queen?"

He didn't answer right away.

My heart sank.

"Let us say that I am not unmindful of the impact your appearance at Court will have," Raphael said slowly. "I told you freely, I have reason to wish myself in the good graces of House Courcel."

"The *King's* graces, aye," I observed. "He may look kindly on the kindness you've extended to a wayward descendant of his house. Or mayhap he'll simply be pleased that you're trifling with the affections of someone other than his wife. But by all accounts, Queen Jehanne will *not* look kindly on your actions. So, my lord. Are you using me? If so, what do you hope to accomplish?" My voice shook a little. "Is it your hope that jealousy will drive her back into your arms?"

"Moirin." He leveled that storm-grey gaze at me. "If that was all I wanted, I could have had it last night."

"No." I spread my hands. "Because today I am still a rustic half-breed with calluses on her hands and a threadbare dress, someone to be mocked and dismissed despite any unease my heritage may provoke. In a week's time, with the assistance of Atelier Favrielle, I may become an exotic novelty—the first of the Maghuin Dhonn to be civilized by a D'Angeline."

Raphael winced. "That's unfair."

"Is it?" I asked.

"Yes." He took my shoulders in his hands. That bedamned warmth flowed into me, rousing my own gifts, setting the doves to fluttering and honeyed heat to rising in my loins. I tried to look away from him and couldn't. "I never claimed my intentions were pure. But whatever this is between us, it's real. It's not a game. I want to find out what it is, what it means. Why the gods saw fit to place you in my path. If you don't . . ." Raphael released me and stepped backward with a crisp bow. "I'll gladly see you settled in suitable lodgings and trouble you no more."

"Gladly?" I whispered.

"Gladly?" His beautiful mouth twisted. "Ah, no. That's a figure of speech. Would you hear me say it? Stay. Please, stay."

My *diadh-anam* blazed. The Maghuin Dhonn's eyes had been sad, so sad. "Will you break my heart if I do?"

"I don't know," Raphael admitted.

I sighed. "I'll stay."

TWENTY-FOUR

Gorgeous," Benoit Vallon purred in a silken voice.

I gazed into the full-length mirror. The gown was a shimmering bronze brocade with a subtle pattern of vines. It clasped around my neck in a collar from which two beaded straps descended, leaving my shoulders bare. It fit closely to below my hips, then flared out in pleats lined with bronze silk. My hair was piled atop my head, held in place by a comb with a gilded branch. Benoit had brushed a touch of kohl on my eyelids and carmine on my lips.

No doubt, I looked stunning. "It's beautiful," I agreed.

"Walk across the room for me," he ordered.

The fabric swished and flowed as I walked. Even the brocade slippers fit so well I didn't mind them.

Benoit watched me with a smug look. "See how differently you carry yourself?" he observed. "There's more to clothing than mere adornment. It does more than merely change how the world perceives us. It changes how we perceive ourselves."

I glided back toward the mirror. "So I see."

He laughed. "I'm glad you approve. Now, that's meant for your debut at Court. I've a pair of dresses for ordinary daywear to fit on you."

"May I show Raphael first?" I pleaded.

Benoit shrugged. "As you wish. I suppose my lord de Mereliot should have the honor, since he's footing the cost."

Reaching for the door, I paused. Like an idiot, I'd given no thought to paying the atelier's fee. "What? No. No, I have funds of my own. I've not had a chance to draw on my letter of credit yet."

"That," he said, "is between you and his lordship. But according to him, *he* has commissioned this."

"Let me have a word with him." I didn't want to be any more beholden to Raphael than I was. I walked at a hurried glide down the hall and the great curving staircase, calling for him. One of the shy maidservants was polishing the banister. She'd gotten less wary of me in the past few days, but now she gave me a quick glance, then ducked her head.

"He's in the library, my lady," she murmured. "But—"

"My thanks." I hurried onward.

Outside the library, I heard voices raised in urgent whispers, only slightly less loud than the good lady Lydia when she was trying to be discreet. The door was ajar, but not closed. I could see a sliver of Raphael's profile and his folded arms. I halted and listened.

"—done playing nursemaid!" another man's voice was saying. It was vaguely familiar. "Damn it, Raphael! The Circle can't function without you!"

"They could if they chose," Raphael said in a laconic tone.

"No, they sodding well can't! You're the only one with the focus. And we were close, so close! I felt it!"

The maid's footsteps pattered behind me. "My lady! I tried to tell you!"

Raphael turned his head and spotted me through the gap in the door. In two strides, he flung the door open. "Moirin?"

I sighed. "Aye."

"Name of Elua!" the other breathed. "*That's* our wayward half-breed?"

"It is." There was approval and a considerable amount of heat in Raphael's gaze. "Moirin, do you remember Denis de Toluard? He helped me tend to you and escort you home after you were struck in the street."

"Oh, yes." That was why his voice had sounded familiar. I'd gotten sick on him. "My thanks, my lord. And, um, I'm sorry about your breeches."

Denis de Toluard flushed. He had curly, dark brown hair and blue eyes and I would have thought him very pretty before I met Raphael. He gathered himself, executed a bow, and took my hand to kiss it. I was glad I'd listened to Benoit and used the cream. "I pray you forgive me, my lady. I was ghastly rude in your hour of need."

"Oh?" I raised my brows. "Luckily, wayward half-breeds aren't known for holding grudges."

Denis turned a deeper shade of red.

Raphael grinned. "Is this the gown for the debut? It's splendid." He touched the comb with the gilded branch. "And this is the perfect finishing touch. On anyone else, it would be too much." He turned to Denis. "Mind, you're not to breathe a word of this."

"No, no." The other shook his head. "I'll not ruin your surprise." He gave me an ardent, flustered glance. "You're looking hale as well as beautiful, my lady. Are you quite recovered? Will you be making your debut soon?"

Now him, I could have had by crooking one finger; I knew it as surely as I knew my name. Pity. "Soon, yes," I agreed. "I believe Raphael has an event in mind."

Now Denis turned pale. "You're not!"

"I am," Raphael said calmly. "What better way to celebrate his majesty's natality than to introduce him to long-lost kin?"

His companion made a strangled sound. "Jehanne is going to kill you!"

A muscle twitched in Raphael's jaw. "*Jehanne*," he said with icy precision, "would expect nothing less of me. Don't believe every piece of gossip you hear. You do not know her nearly as well as you think, my friend."

"Do you know," I said to no one in particular, "I would truly have been grateful for a far less complicated destiny, if that's what this is." Both men looked blankly at me. "No mind." I waved my words away. "Raphael, I wanted you to see the gown. But you're not to pay for it. I've a letter of credit."

"I know." He gave me that unexpectedly boyish grin. "I rifled through your belongings, remember?"

"Aye, but—"

"Moirin, let me do this." He toyed with my gown's straps, unobtrusively stroking the skin beneath them. "It helps assuage my conscience for having caused you injury in the first place. Please?"

I couldn't think straight when he touched me. "Oh, fine. Since that's the case, I'm glad you like it."

He kissed me. "Very much. Are you keeping Messire Vallon waiting? I wouldn't advise it."

"All right." I pulled away from him with an effort. "I'll leave you to your mysterious plotting, then, shall I?"

Denis choked.

Raphael merely looked amused. "My dear, if you don't want me to think you sly and uncanny, you've really got to stop eavesdropping." He made a shooing gesture. "Now go! If you earn the enmity of Atelier Favrielle, you'll live to regret it."

I went.

Benoit Vallon was packing his things and looking almighty disgruntled when I returned. It took a good deal of profuse apologizing on my part before he relented and began to unpack them.

"You're young and foreign," he said grudgingly, beginning to help me out of the wonderful bronze gown. "It's his lordship ought to know better."

"He's engaged in mysterious plotting," I informed him.

"Oh?" Benoit's hands went still on the clasp of my collar. "He's a name for meddling in matters he oughtn't," he muttered. "And I don't mean just their majesties' private affairs."

"Magic?" I asked innocently.

He peered into my face. "What would you know of it?" he asked, then thought better of it. "Come to think on it, I'd rather not know." His hands moved briskly, peeling away the gorgeous fabric. "The reputation of your people precedes you."

"Oh?" I stepped out of the gown. "Truth be told, we're quite a peaceable folk."

Benoit folded the gown and snorted.

"'Tis true," I protested. "In the annals of history there is no record of the Maghuin Dhonn going to war, no matter how many times Alba has been invaded. Other follies were committed, yes. Believe me, we are painfully aware of them to this day. But I would ask you not to judge my people based on the actions of one or two of our ancestors."

"You may have a point." He folded away the bronze gown and extended one of fine-spun russet wool worked with intricate trim. "Try this. It's suitable for daywear or even travel, and is based on a very old design created by the atelier's founder, Favrielle nó Eglantine herself."

It flowed gracefully.

"And this." A deep green satin with a heart-shaped neckline. Benoit knelt and tacked a few loose, temporary stitches to improve the fit.

In the mirror, I tilted my head this way and that. "If you're so wary of the Maghuin Dhonn, why did you accept this commission?"

He winced. "Must you keep saying that name aloud?"

"It's not bad luck!" I said in exasperation. "That's just a silly superstition put about a thousand years ago when Cinhil Ru claimed the Maghuin Dhonn had slain their own *diadh-anam*. It was never true. They know better in Alba these days, even if we are not well loved. They've known better since Alais de la Courcel restored the truce between our folk. Even Caroline nó Bryony wasn't afraid to say it, and she's the one commended me to you."

"All right, child!" Benoit raised his hands. "I didn't intend to give offense. And I accepted the commission because the couturieres of Atelier Favrielle relish a challenge more than we fear ought else."

"Even bear-witches?" I asked.

His mouth twisted. "So it seems. Truth be told, you're not a particularly fearful specimen, young and naïve as you are."

I thought about Cillian's death. "Not so naïve, I fear."

Benoit Vallon studied my face. "Not in the ways of life, mayhap, but the D'Angeline Court is another matter. Have you given thought to my advice?"

"I have," I admitted.

He eased the green dress from my shoulders. "But you mean to stay."

"Yes."

"Elua have mercy." Benoit put the dress away. "Are all of the Mag—" He couldn't bring himself to say it. "Are all of your people this stubborn?"

I laughed. "You ought to meet my mother."

He shook his head. "I'll be back in a day's time for the final fitting. You can't say I didn't warn you."

"I won't," I promised.

TWENTY-FIVE

By the eve of my debut, the bronze gown was finished and I had two perfectly suitable dresses for daywear, three pairs of shoes, and a variety of undergarments. My calluses had been softened and smoothed, my nails neatly trimmed and buffed to a shine. The ragged ends of my hair had been trimmed and Benoit had taught me three different ways to style it. There was still some tenderness around my ribs, but the lump at the back of my skull was gone altogether and I hadn't felt sick or disoriented for days.

"I mean to go to the Temple of Naamah today," I informed Raphael at the breakfast table.

He hesitated. "Wouldn't you rather wait until after your debut?"

"No." I slathered a piece of bread with peach preserves. "*You* would rather I wait until after my debut. Mayhap you have lost sight of the fact that I did not come to Terre d'Ange so that you might surprise and dazzle the Court with your exotic protégée. I came to find my father. And wherever he may be, I'd sooner he learned of my existence before the entire City does."

Raphael smiled. "Protégée, is it?"

I shrugged. "Is that not the right word?"

"No, I reckon it's as good as any. Your vocabulary is surprisingly good, and your accent is improving daily."

"Mm-hmm." I took a bite of jam-smeared bread. "And you are changing the subject. I wasn't asking, Raphael. Unless you mean to imprison me, I'm going. With your assistance, I'll go discreetly by carriage. Without it, I'll go on foot."

"No doubt asking directions all the way," he said wryly.

"No doubt," I agreed.

"Oh, fine." Raphael tossed his linen napkin on the table. "I'll take you; of course I'll take you."

"I don't mean to ruin your surprise," I said apologetically. "But this is important to me."

"Of course it is." He hoisted a cup of the bitter Jebean drink called *kavah* toward me in a toast. "I'm a right ass for not acknowledging it, Moirin, and you're not ruining anything."

"No?"

"No." Raphael sipped his *kavah* and stretched out his long legs. "Naamah's priests can keep secrets as well as anyone and better than most." He eyed me. "What do you expect of him?"

"My father?" I had no idea. When I'd set out, I'd hoped my father might be able to point me toward my destiny. Now I suspected it lay in the form of the intriguing, somewhat infuriating, and wholly desirable man across the table from me. "Nothing, I suppose. I want to know him, that's all. What's your father like?"

"Dead," he said briefly.

"Oh." I swallowed. "I'm sorry."

"It's all right, you couldn't have known." Raphael gave me a bleak smile. "I was young when it happened. A boating accident. It took my mother and father both."

"I'm sorry," I repeated. "How old were you?"

"Eleven." He looked away, remembering.

The space behind my eyes tingled with a strange pressure. I saw a freak storm blowing out of nowhere—a great wave, swamping the pleasure-boat as it returned from Eisheth's sacred isle. Cries and shouting, guards thrashing in the water, stripping off their swords and boots. They were rallying to someone. A white hand sinking below the waves. Still, they rallied.

One pair of arms around me, keeping me afloat. A ragged voice in my ear uttering encouragement.

Only one.

"You were there," I whispered. "Your father tried to save you."

"Yes." Raphael rose abruptly and walked away from the table. "He *did* save me. The effort cost him his life. How did you know?"

I rubbed my temples. "I saw it."

He didn't turn around. "More magic?"

"I don't know," I murmured. "There's an old woman, Nemed, among us. She can breathe in your memories and swallow them. Once they're gone, they're lost forever. But only if you let her."

Raphael's back was rigid. "Do you reckon she'd take mine?"

I went to him and wrapped my arms around his waist, pressed my cheek between his shoulder blades. "Who were the guards trying to save?"

"My mother." He drew a long, shuddering breath. "The Lady of Marsilikos. Then, when they lost her, my sister. The heir. Her, they were able to save."

My sister the heir.

The memory of Cillian's voice made me shiver. "The eldest?"

"No." Raphael said softly. "She's younger than me. Eleanore. Nine, when it happened. But Marsilikos was founded by Eisheth herself. From time out of mind, it has been ruled by a Lady. There are no male heirs."

"Oh," I said. "I see."

He turned in my arms, hands rising to take my shoulders in a hard grip. "How did we get here?" His long lashes were damp with tears. "I've never talked to anyone about that day, not even Jehanne. Who are you to draw the very memories from my head?"

"Myself." There was a tremor in my voice. "I don't know, Raphael. It's never happened before. I'm sorry."

"No. No, don't be." He took another deep breath. "It's all right. It's only that it's a bitter memory as well as a hurtful one. If just *one* of the guards had gone to help my father that day . . ." Raphael shook his head. "It's not their fault. They had their orders. Still, I cannot help but wonder."

My heart ached for him. "Of course you can't."

"Well." He let go of my shoulders and dashed one hand across his eyes. "Today should be a joyous one for you, Moirin. I'm sorry to cast an unexpected pall over it."

"You're helping me find my father," I said. "Mayhap we might do it in your own father's memory."

Raphael nodded. "That's a kind thought. Thank you."

In the carriage, he was quiet and withdrawn. I left him to his thoughts, not wanting to trouble him further. Although I would have liked to gaze on the City, I kept the curtains closed and instead pondered the mystery of what had transpired between us, wondering if I were on my way to acquiring Nemed's gift. Raphael's memories had been so clear, so vivid. I could feel the boat pitching on its side and the shock of the cold water, its weight dragging at my sodden clothing. Salt in my mouth, terror and disbelief in my heart.

How did one swallow such a thing?

I had no idea.

Somewhat to my surprise, the Temple of Naamah dedicated to star-crossed lovers was in a humble part of the City. It was a graceful little building of white marble set like a pearl in the midst of inelegant wooden residences. I remarked on it to Raphael.

"Oh, yes." He roused himself. "You don't know the story behind it?"

"No."

"You'll like it." He smiled at me. "I'll tell you on the ride home."

There was a woman in the adjacent building stringing laundry on a ramshackle balcony. She barely spared us a glance.

"This is the Tsingani quarter," Raphael said in my ear as we approached the door to the temple. "They don't gossip outside their own circles."

"Lucky for you," I remarked.

"Moirin." On the doorstep, he halted and gave me a serious look. "You don't have to go through with the plans I've made for you. The debut, I mean. My surprise. You're free to do whatever you like. You don't have to indulge me."

I laid my hand on his chest. "Will it please you?"

Raphael covered my hand with his. "That's not important."

"Strangely, I find that it is." I smiled ruefully. "All right. Will her majesty the Queen shriek and snatch at my hair in a fit of jealous rage?"

He laughed. "No. Most assuredly not."

I squeezed his hand against me. "Then I've naught to fear and I may as well please you, since I'm in your debt."

The door to the temple had a knocker in the shape of a plump dove nestled on a perch. Raphael raised it and rapped sharply. My heart leapt into my throat. I wondered if I would recognize my father if he came to the door. Oengus' long-ago words echoed in my memory. *Milky-white skin and green, green eyes.*

I wondered what I'd say to him.

I wished my mother were here.

"Do you seek sanctuary?" It was a woman clad in crimson robes who opened the door. She had a lovely face that was aging beautifully, honey-gold hair fading with grey. Warm, hazel eyes. "In Naamah's name, be welcome here."

Raphael bowed. "My lady priestess—"

"Oh!" Her hands flew up to press her cheeks. She ignored him and gazed at me, her eyes wide. "You've come a long way, haven't you? All the way from the far side of Alba?"

"I have," I agreed.

"You're Phanuel's daughter. He said you might come one day." The priestess laughed with delight. "Oh, please!" She gave me the kiss of greeting with unabashed warmth. "Come in, come in!"

My head spun. "He knows? You expected me?"

"No and yes." She clasped my hands in hers. "Come inside, won't you? We need to speak." She cast a sidelong glance at Raphael, her eyes sparkling. "You, too, my lord de Mereliot."

He bowed.

Inside the Temple of Naamah, we were served honeycakes and hot tea sweetened with milk and honey. Once proper introductions were made, I learned that the priestess' name was Noémie d'Etoile. To my disappointment, I also learned that my father was not present in the City at this time.

"Where is he?" I asked.

"Wandering," she said. "Phanuel's never been one to stay in one place for any length of time. But he'll be back in a month's time or so." She smiled. "Sooner if he hears word of your appearance." She shook a scolding finger at Raphael. "You've been keeping secrets, my lord."

"Ah, but think what a delightful surprise it will make," he said, unperturbed.

"Is there no way to contact him?" I asked.

Noémie shook her head. "Not when he's wandering afield. He goes where whim takes him. Namarre or L'Agnace, usually."

"L'Agnace," I mused. "Anael's province?"

"Indeed." She nodded. "Phanuel's mother was of Naamah's line, a very old and pure one. But by all accounts, his father was a L'Agnacite farm boy." She misread the look on my face. "There's no shame in it, child. No matter what the peers of the realm would have you believe, the blood of Elua and his Companions runs just as true in farmers and herders and cheese-makers as it does the peerage."

"Betimes more so," Raphael agreed.

"It's not that," I murmured. "It's just that I've seen him, too. Anael, the Good Steward."

"*Seen* him?" His voice sharpened.

"Only in my thoughts," I hastened to add. "Not like—" I cut my words short, not wanting to talk about the Maghuin Dhonn Herself. It was too private. "I saw them first when I was little, before I had names for them. Naamah and Anael. I called her the bright lady. He was the man with the seedling." Noémie was gazing at me with a mixture of wonder and disbelief. I cleared my throat. "You said *was.*"

She blinked. "I beg your pardon?"

"Was," I repeated. "When you spoke of Phanuel's mother and father, you said was. Do I have no surviving grandparents?"

"Ah." Her face softened. "As to his mother, I fear not. She died of a wasting illness some seven or eight years ago. As to his father . . . Phanuel never knew his name. His mother kept no record of it." She touched my arm. "It's not unusual for those of us who serve Naamah to be drawn by whim thusly when the time comes. I haven't felt it myself, but those who have say they feel her hand in it."

"As he was to my mother."

"Yes." Noémie nodded again. "A strange and powerful calling. He always thought a child might result from it."

"Did he say why?" I asked.

"No." She spread her hands. "Only that there must be some purpose in it. That's why we've half expected you all these years."

Raphael eyed me. "Destiny."

"Aye, but *what* and *why*?" I said in frustration. "Stone and sea! This is a confounding business."

"Moirin, would you behold your great-great-grandmother?" Noémie asked unexpectedly. "I don't reckon you'll find any answers, but it might please you nonetheless."

It occurred to me that I knew nothing of D'Angeline burial rites. "She's . . . here?"

"No and yes." She rose, smiling, and took my hand. "Come."

I let Noémie lead me into the temple proper, Raphael trailing behind us. Beneath a modest dome with an opening at its center, a marble effigy of Naamah stood on a marble plinth. Her head was bowed, hair falling to curtain one side of her face. What was visible of her expression was filled with compassion and tenderness. In her cupped hands, she held a pair of doves nestled side by side.

I gazed at her. "I don't understand."

Noémie's hands descended lightly on my shoulders. "Phanuel's great-grandmother, your great-great-grandmother, posed for the likeness. Her name was Amarante, and she was the first royal companion. This temple was built for her."

Raphael was silent.

I looked longer. Sunlight streamed down from the aperture above. The white marble glowed, nearly translucent where it was carved fine. Naamah's effigy regarded her love-birds with infinite gentleness.

My great-great-grandmother.

Shivers ran over my skin. For the first time since I'd set foot on D'Angeline soil, I understood in my bones that I *was* one of them. A child of the Maghuin Dhonn, aye—but D'Angeline, too. Somewhere, my father wandered. He was a descendant of an old line. My great-great-grandmother was real, as real as Alais the Wise. She had existed. She had posed for this sculptor. I had a heritage here that stretched into the past.

"Oh," I said softly. "I see."

"Do you?" Noémie d'Etoile whispered in my ear.

Doves fluttered.

"Yes," I said. "I do."

TWENTY-SIX

On our return journey, the carriage remained curtained and stifling. Raphael sat at apparent ease across from me, telling me the tale of how this particular Temple of Naamah came to be situated in the Tsingani quarter.

It was a charming tale.

I didn't care.

The bright lady's gift, Naamah's gift, was coiling around me and through me, heating my blood. I let it roam freely. When the carriage jolted to a temporary halt, I let it pitch me across the space between us, landing me in his lap.

Raphael's eyes gleamed. "Moirin . . ."

"Shut up," I whispered, sinking my hands into his tawny hair.

I kissed him.

He was a man, and mortal. He kissed me back, his mouth and tongue urgent, his hands hard around my hips, radiating warmth. One hand descended, shoving up my skirts, pushing at my fine new undergarments, moving them out of the way. I fumbled at the buttons on his breeches.

And then . . .

Horses' hooves clopped. I clasped my hand around his erect phallus and fitted it to me with a sigh, pushing downward onto him.

So good.

So deep.

"Nice," I sighed, rocking atop him. The carriage seat squeaked.

"This is *not* what I intended for our first time," Raphael whispered against my mouth.

"I know." I kissed him, then smiled into his eyes. "I couldn't wait."

It should have been tawdry, but it wasn't. My mind was too filled with beauty, with sunlit marble and doves, with the unfolding wonder of discovering who I was. And, too, there was the mystery that had passed between us earlier. When my climax came, it was like slow, rolling waves. I offered up a silent prayer that it would ease the memory of those other waves, cold and killing.

"Elua!" Raphael spent himself inside me with a shudder. He rested his brow against mine. I put one hand on his chest, feeling his racing heartbeat. "Well." He shifted me off his lap with an effort. His tone was teasing, but his expression was relaxed and languid. "You're a singularly determined young woman."

"Aye," I agreed. "Is that wrong?"

"Not in the least." He smiled, and I wanted to kiss him all over again. "But I'd hope we could make a better job of it."

"Oh?" I raised my brows. "Then show me."

Raphael looked at me for a long moment without replying, his grey eyes darkening like stormclouds. It was a look that made me shiver inside. "I mean to," he said at last in a low voice. "Later. And on *my* terms, witch-girl."

My cheeks flushed. "All right."

I thought he meant to take me to bed that night.

I was wrong.

Raphael was gone for a few hours that afternoon on an errand. He returned in the early evening and found me in the garden, trying to recall the names of unfamiliar plants.

"Fennel," he said in answer to my unasked question. "It's good for purging the kidneys of toxins. Also for treating catarrh." He touched the feathery fronds. "The blossoms are yellow and the Tiberians believed it could cure jaundice, but I'm afraid that was mere superstition."

"It smells nice," I said.

"One can eat the bulb. Speaking of which, I believe dinner is ready to be served." He gave me his arm. "Shall we?"

At dinner, Raphael presented me with a pair of emerald eardrops.

"For tomorrow," he said. "You shouldn't make your first appearance at Court without a single jewel adorning you."

"They're beautiful," I said sincerely. "Thank you. You didn't have to do this, truly."

He shrugged. "You're going out of your way to humor me."

Something in his manner gave me pause. "Not so very far out of my way. And you've been more than generous."

"Try them on," he said.

The eardrops had delicate little screws on their backs. I screwed them in place, feeling the weight dragging at my earlobes. It was a strange feeling, but not exactly unpleasant. I gave my head an experimental shake. "Do you like them?"

Raphael nodded. "Very nice."

"Very nice." I echoed his bland compliment. "Raphael, have I offended you? Are you angry with me? Is it because of what happened . . ." I lowered my voice. "Is it because of what happened in the carriage?"

"No." He picked up his knife and fork, then set them down. Picked up his goblet and drank a deep draught of wine. A hovering servant moved to refill it. "Moirin . . . Denis de Toluard told me a tale he heard today. Months' old gossip from Alba. It takes a while to filter through to us here, but what he heard made him prick up his ears. He thought I should know about it."

"Oh?" I felt cold.

"It seems the only son of Lord Tiernan of the Dalriada was ensorceled by a young woman of the Maghuin Dhonn," Raphael said in an even tone. "A very singular young woman to hear the tale. He died because of it."

"Oh, gods bedamned!" I shoved my chair away from the table. "The one had naught to do with the other. Cillian mac Tiernan died in a cattle-raid because he was too proud and stubborn to admit he was more scholar than warrior."

"So you *did* ensorcel him?" he pressed.

"No!" I pushed the heels of my hands against my eyes. *That lad was doomed the minute you laid eyes on him.* "No."

"Moirin."

I dropped my hands. "What?"

"I'll not be toyed with," Raphael said steadily. "You're accustomed to having your way with men, that much is clear. But this is Terre d'Ange, not Alba. If you think to make me your unwitting conquest, think again."

I sighed. "I don't."

"Then stay out of my head." He rose and tossed his napkin on the table. "I don't take kindly to you rummaging through my memories and turning them to your own purposes. And I don't take kindly to your using Naamah's gift to sway me."

"That's not fair!" I protested.

"Isn't it?"

I stood and faced him. "I'm drawn to you, aye. Is it my fault if you feel the same way? And I didn't ask to see your memories any more than I asked to be run down by your carriage, Raphael de Mereliot. You're the one keeps prattling on about destiny. What am I supposed to think? How am I supposed to feel?"

Raphael folded his arms. "Prattling?"

"Aye, prattling!" I was angry. "About destiny and magic and purpose, and how there are oh, so many things you don't fear in the world, myself included! All the while plotting to use me to make your mistress the Queen jealous." I snatched the eardrops from my ears and threw them at his feet. "Don't you dare accuse me of using you for my own ends!"

The eardrops clinked and rolled on the marble floor. It was the only sound in a dining hall that had gone very, very quiet. The servants stood frozen, looking like they wished they could disappear.

Unaccountably, Raphael smiled. "What is it I find so compelling about a woman with a temper?" he asked no one in particular.

My anger drained away, leaving me weary. "Is that what you see?" I asked him, sinking back into my chair. "My lord, may I remind you that I am young and alone and very far from home. You are the nearest thing to a friend I have in this place. If you trust me so little . . ." To my shame, my eyes welled with tears and my throat closed.

"Oh, hells." He knelt on one knee before me. I couldn't meet his eyes. "Moirin, I'm sorry. Look at me, won't you?"

I stole a glance at him.

His expression was serious. "Listen. This is all very sudden and unexpected. What you claim are but small and insignificant gifts are passing strange and wondrous to me. And I'll admit, when I heard Denis' story today, I panicked."

I sniffled. "Shall I leave?"

"No." Raphael picked up the eardrops and pressed them into my hands. "Stay. Wear these tomorrow, and I will escort you with pride. All right?"

I wanted to say no.

I *should* have said no. I should have left; I should have left before. No matter what else he said, not once had Raphael denied using me in his quarrel with the Queen. Ignorant as I was, I had no business dabbling in Court intrigue. But his hands were warm on mine, setting those ridiculous currents of desire swirling in my blood. His grey eyes were earnest and insistent.

And there was the bedamned pulse of the *diadh-anam* inside me.

"All right," I murmured. "I'll stay."

"Good." He flashed a relieved grin at me. "You know, if you promise a third time, it means you can never leave."

I wasn't in a mood for teasing. "I'd as soon not have this conversation a third time."

"Of course." Raphael sobered and took his seat. "Why did you never mention Cillian mac Tiernan to me?"

I picked listlessly at my food. "I don't know. Because it hurts, I suppose."

He rested his chin on one hand. "Did you love him?"

"Aye." My throat and chest tightened again. I pushed my plate away. "Not enough, but aye." I took a deep breath, willing the tightness to ease. "Cillian was my first friend and my first lover, the only one I'd known before I came to Terre d'Ange. I'd known him since I was ten years old. He brought a tribute-gift of peaches and tried to spy on my mother and me." I smiled at the memory. "I caught him at it and we quarrelled. I had my bow with me. I shot the peaches."

Raphael laughed softly. "Whatever for?"

"I don't recall," I admitted. "But it seemed appropriate at the time."

"What was he like?" he asked.

"Oh . . ." I shrugged. "I don't know. He was just himself. I never thought about it. Until Cillian came into my life, it was just my mother and me." I made myself think about it. "Curious. Thoughtful, most of the time. Impatient, sometimes. He was a good teacher, though. He taught me to read. He brought me books to last through the winter. We studied D'Angeline together. It was Cillian who figured out that my father had been a Priest of Naamah . . ."

Once I'd begun talking, the words poured out of me. Cillian's jealousy, my reluctance to wed him. The unexpected horror of his death, and the awful moment when his mother blamed me for it.

"That's why they put it about that you'd ensorceled him?" Raphael asked in a gentle voice.

I nodded. "His sister Aislinn said it was only grief talking. But it was true in a way. I was selfish. I knew I'd never be the proper wife he wanted me to be, his and his alone. If I'd let him go sooner—"

"It wouldn't have changed a blessed thing," he finished for me.

"Mayhap. But it doesn't feel that way." I wiped away a stray tear. "I'm sorry. I didn't mean to ruin your evening."

"Oh, I'd say I made a fair job of that myself," Raphael said wryly. "Please, don't apologize. Talk is healing. It's the unexamined wound that festers."

Like yours, I almost said, remembering that he'd never discussed his parents' deaths with anyone. But I bit my tongue on the thought.

Outside the door to my guest-chamber, he gave me a tender, lingering kiss, tasting of wine and apology. When I leaned against him and put my head on his shoulder, he held me. His arms felt strong and good around me.

"Moirin?" His breath stirred my hair.

"Hmm?"

"Did you happen to fend off a pair of highwaymen with a bow and arrow on your journey to the City?" he asked. I looked up in surprise. Raphael gazed down at me, his eyes glinting with amusement. "There's a tale a pair of dowagers are spreading about a young woman who shared their coach. A very singular green-eyed young woman of mixed heritage. Denis heard it in a wineshop and thought I might like to know."

"Ah." I smiled at him. "Well, I might have. Actually, I might have shot one in the leg from an, um, unseen perspective. But the good ladies didn't know that part because they had the curtains drawn."

"The good ladies?" he repeated.

"They were kind in their own way," I said. "Florette d'Aubert and Lydia Postel. After tomorrow, I ought to pay them a visit. Do you know them?"

"Most assuredly not." Raphael kissed me again, slow and deliberate. "You're really not what one would expect, are you?"

My head spun. "No?"

"No." He let me go and made a bow. "On the morrow?"

"On the morrow," I agreed.

TWENTY-SEVEN

Stone and sea!" I breathed in the palace courtyard.

"It's just a building like any other," Raphael assured me. "Only larger."

"So you say." I gazed at the storied tiers and spires, the expanse of carved marble and granite looming above us. "Only understand that this architecture is as wondrous to me as any gift I might carry in my blood."

He inclined his head. "Fairly spoken."

Guards in the blue livery of House Courcel ushered us through the massive doors. I couldn't repress a shudder upon entering the overwhelming edifice. I'd grown more accustomed to being indoors, but this was far and beyond any man-made structure I'd ever encountered. When the doors closed behind us, my breath came short.

"Are you all right?" Raphael inquired.

I nodded. "One moment." Raphael's footman Jean-Michel was a step behind us, carrying a gift intended for the King—a rare orchid in a blue and white porcelain pot. He halted with a bemused look when I turned to touch the orchid, stroking its delicate purple petals. I breathed in its faint, sweet scent and felt better. "Let's go. I'll be fine."

"If you're not, tell me." Raphael settled my hand on his arm and gave me a serious look. "A gathering of this sort has overwhelmed more experienced souls, Moirin. And remember, you're still recovering from your injuries."

"Oh, those," I said dismissively.

"Yes, those." He squeezed my fingers. "Promise?"

"Yes, my lord physician." I looked up at him under my lashes. "If I survive the evening, are you prepared to pronounce me quite recovered?"

His unreasonably gorgeous mouth quirked. "We'll see."

We proceeded down wide, gleaming marble halls. Servants and guards gave us curious looks. I could hear a whispering tide of gossip trailing in our wake. There was a queue of peers outside the doors to the great hall where the King's fête was being held. I gazed at a dozen backs clad in velvet and satin and brocade, my nerves strung taut. There was a royal herald announcing each set of guests as they were admitted. All too soon, it was our turn. Raphael presented his invitation, printed on thick, creamy paper.

"My lord de Mereliot." The herald inclined his head, then looked at me. A crease formed between his brows. "And your companion?"

"Lady Moirin mac Fainche," Raphael informed him.

The herald repeated it soundlessly, then cleared his throat and announced us.

Heads turned.

We had a clear path to the dais where the King and Queen were seated and exchanging pleasantries with the elderly couple who had preceded us. My nails dug into Raphael's arm as we approached. I could hear the whispers.

"That's the one!"

". . . found her in the street . . ."

". . . half-Cruithne, by the look of her."

I wished the elderly couple ahead of us would never leave. I had begun to think this was a very bad idea and wanted very much to be elsewhere. But, of course, they finished their business with their majesties and moved aside, and I was brought face-to-face with King Daniel and Queen Jehanne.

He was a tall, well-built man of middle years with dark hair, blue eyes, and a bemused smile on his face.

She was exquisite.

It was the sort of beauty my mother had described long ago—a fearful symmetry, keen as a blade. And yet it was delicate and ephemeral, too—as delicate as the petals of an orchid. Her hair was pale gold, so pale it was almost silvery. It was piled atop her head in an intricate coronet, a lone lock left loose to curl along the graceful column of her white throat. Her skin was so fair, it was nearly translucent.

Her eyes . . .

Jehanne de la Courcel's eyes were a light hue of blue-grey, like periwinkle blossoms. They sparkled unexpectedly as her gaze swept up to meet mine, her chin rising as she took stock of me.

"Oh, my." Her voice was sweet and light and teasing. "Are you a rival or a present?"

I flushed.

"Your majesties." Raphael bowed. "Congratulations to his majesty on the occasion of his natality." He beckoned to Jean-Michel, who came forward to present the potted orchid with a bow. "A small token from a rare strain Master Lo Feng and I have been cultivating."

"Yes, my thanks, very nice, I'm sure." King Daniel waved for a servant to take it away. His bemused gaze rested on me. "And you are . . . ? Forgive me, I didn't recognize the name. Mac Fainche? That's Eiran nomenclature, but I fear I don't follow."

"Raphael is having a jest," the Queen said lightly. "Haven't you heard? His carriage struck down some poor lass in the street a week ago and he's taken her into his household to make amends." She snapped open a fan and fluttered it. "Isn't that so?"

"It is," Raphael agreed in a smug tone, deliberately drawing out the moment of revelation. I had a strong urge to kick him in the shins.

"As always, your solicitude is to be commended." Jehanne's fan fluttered. "But it's quite unfair of you to misrepresent the child—and quite inappropriate at a royal fête." She laughed. "*Lady* Moirin? You do the poor girl an unkindness. Not everyone recognizes your sense of humor, my lord."

"Nor when it is absent." Raphael bowed again. "This is no jest. Surely, your majesties would wish me to extend every kindness to a descendant of House Courcel itself."

A gasp ran through the room.

The King glanced at me in inquiry.

"Daughter of Fainche, daughter of Eithne, daughter of Brianna, daughter of Alais," I said to him, executing a passable curtsy. "Of the folk of the Maghuin Dhonn. Well met, your majesty."

He stared.

No one spoke.

It was Jehanne who broke the silence with laughter. It was a bright, infectious sound. "Tell me it's true!" she said to Raphael. Something unspoken passed between them. She shook her head, diamond ear-drops scattering myriad points of light. "A bear-witch? Only you would dare!"

"Oh, it's true." Raphael rocked back on his heels a little, clearly en-joying himself. "Moirin has a signet ring passed down for generations, and a letter of introduction from Bryony Associates authenticating it."

"Moirin can speak for herself," I said with irritation.

"She's here searching for her father," he continued. "It seems he was a Priest of Naamah."

Queen Jehanne arched one perfect brow. "Oh, my."

The news went around the great hall in a whispering susurrus. I felt hot and conspicuous. For a mercy, the King raised one hand, and silence followed.

"Well met, Lady Moirin," he said firmly. "For generations, the ex-istence of descendants of House Courcel among your people has been but a distant rumor. We are pleased and honored by your presence in our Court today."

Relieved, I curtsied again. "Thank you, your majesty. The honor is mine."

"But not the pleasure?" the Queen inquired. Her lovely face was perfectly composed, but there was a note of subtle malice in her voice.

"Jehanne," her husband murmured.

She glanced sidelong at him. Whatever was between them, it was deeper and more complicated than it appeared on the surface. "She seeks to learn the ways of the Court. Shall we not do her the courtesy of hearing her reply?" Without waiting for his answer, she looked back at me with those sparkling eyes. "Well?"

"Pleasure," I echoed. "As to that, it is yet to be determined, your majesty."

Her laughter rang out again. "Well said!" The fluttering fan gestured.

"Go forth and see if you might manage to enjoy yourself." She inclined her head at Raphael, the edge returning to her voice. "I trust that's your purview, my lord."

He smiled at her, showing his teeth. "I'll do my best."

I was grateful to be dismissed. Raphael steered me to an unoccupied corner of the hall near a balcony window.

"You acquitted yourself very well," he said in a low voice. "Wait here. I'll fetch you a glass of wine."

I leaned against the archway onto the balcony. Across the hall, I could see the Queen leaning forward to greet the next set of guests. She had been an adept in the Service of Naamah. Even if the good ladies hadn't told me, I would have known it. Naamah's gift lay over her like a glittering cloak. "Was it everything you'd hoped?"

Raphael followed my gaze. "Yes."

I closed my eyes. "Good."

A few moments passed, not a long time. I let the cool wind from the balcony play over my skin. It felt good.

"My lady . . . Moirin?" an unfamiliar voice said.

I opened my eyes. A young man near my own age stood before me. He had dark, waving hair caught back in a ribbon and deep blue eyes. "Aye?"

He grinned. "You look like you'd rather be well away from this crush. I'm told you're distant kin. Would you care to see the Hall of Portraits? Meet your ancestors, as it were?"

I looked for Raphael and spotted him some distance away. He had two goblets in his hands, but he'd been waylaid by Denis de Toluard and a couple other men, and was deep in animated conversation, gesticulating and spilling wine. "Is that permitted?"

"It is if I say so." The young man's grin spread. "I'm Thierry. Thierry de la Courcel. And anyone who discomfits Jehanne, I'd like to know better."

The good ladies' gossip came back to me. King Daniel had a son and heir born of his first marriage. "You're the Dauphin."

Thierry bowed. "Guilty as charged."

I smiled at him. "I'd love to."

We slipped out of the great hall, followed only by the gazes of a hundred pairs of watching eyes, none of which were Raphael's. Thierry escorted me up a flight of marble stairs and down a corridor. A lone guard attended the door to the Hall of Portraits. He bowed and admitted us without question. Slanting golden light illuminated the portraits that hung the length of the hall.

"Here." Thierry led me to the far end. He pointed. "That's my father as a young man. And there, my mother."

"She has a kind face," I offered.

"She was a kind woman." He touched the frame with lingering gentleness, then moved onward. "My grandmother, Josephine." A striking, sorrow-stricken face. He pointed out portraits of two men alongside her. "This was my grandfather, Gautier. And my great-uncle, Jean-Philippe. The ones who vanished along with their entire fleet and crew."

"Vanished?" I repeated.

He nodded. "Seeking the Master of the Straits' secrets. You know the story of how he hid the pages of the Book of Raziel?"

"I do." It was said the missing pages held the secrets to controlling the very elements themselves.

Thierry sighed. "They say he hid his secrets too well, or at least his accomplices did. Pity. I suspect my father's fear of change and exploration comes from the effects of that ill-fated expedition. Mayhap the Book of Raziel was meant to stay hidden, but it doesn't mean Terre d'Ange cannot explore the world."

I hazarded a guess. "Terra Nova?"

"Would that we could at the least establish a base there . . ." He shook himself. "No mind. I don't mean to burden you."

I moved down the hall, pausing before a portrait of a woman with merry eyes. "And her?"

"Ah." Thierry smiled. "My great-grandmother, Anielle. They call her reign the Years of Joy. Firstborn to the horde, as they called it, although there were only three of them." He went a few paces farther. "Imriel and Sidonie's children."

"The D'Angeline prince," I murmured. "The one who slew the magician Berlik."

He didn't shy away from the comment. "Yes."

They were together in the portrait—the Queen of Terre d'Ange and her Prince Consort. The artist had captured a genuine spark of intimacy between them.

I looked at the next painting. "This must be Alais."

"Indeed."

In Alba, Alais de la Courcel was remembered for her wisdom and her role as an *ollamh*, a learned counselor who served as advisor to the Cruarch Talorcan and brokered peace among the folk of Alba. I never thought of my famous ancestor as a young woman, but she was, here—young and uncertain, her expression wary and tentative. Since I felt much the same way, it was oddly comforting to see. "Her line isn't represented?"

"No." Thierry colored a bit. "Since it parted ways with House Courcel and went on to become wholly Alban, no. But here you can see your . . ." He counted on his fingers. "Great-great-great-grandparents, Drustan mab Necthana and Ysandre de la Courcel."

"Ah." I contemplated the royal couple who had united our countries for the space of their lives and longer. The Cruarch Drustan was wholly of the Cullach Gorrym, black-haired and brown-skinned, with black eyes gazing out from the mask of woad warrior's markings that had largely gone out of fashion by now. Queen Ysandre was D'Angeline through and through, fair-haired and fair-skinned. "They seem an unlikely pair."

"And yet historians agree that it was a love-match." Thierry stole a glance at me. "No more unlikely than your own parents. Is it true?"

"So it seems." I smiled ruefully. "Though I cannot claim it was a love-match, since they didn't even bother to exchange names."

"Does it trouble you?" he asked.

"No." I touched my breast-bone. "My mother says she felt the spark of her *diadh-anam* draw her to him. She would never lie about such a thing, so there must be some purpose in it. I want to know, that's all. My lord Dauphin . . . how am I meant to address you?"

He smiled. "Your highness is the proper form, but I'd take it as a kindness if you'd call me Thierry."

"Thierry, then," I agreed. "Do you suppose her majesty Jehanne is sufficiently discomfited? I suspect we ought to return."

"I suppose." Thierry leaned close to me, touching the bare skin of my back and inhaling. "You smell like . . . wind."

I blinked. "Wind?"

"Wind from a faraway place," he said. "Sunlight on green leaves. Is he your lover?"

"Lord de Mereliot?" I frowned. "I'm not sure."

"No?" Thierry stroked my shoulder. "That's a passing odd thing to be uncertain of, my lady."

"Is it?" I pulled away from him. "If you are asking if he has bedded me, the answer is yes, although there wasn't exactly a bed involved and it was more my idea than his. If you are asking if his intentions toward me involve anything beyond discomfiting Jehanne de la Courcel, I am uncertain, just as I am of yours. Though I should hope that the reasons behind your motives differ."

He laughed and made a courtly bow. "To be sure! Your honesty is refreshing and my motives were mixed, but not impure. Allow me to return the favor, and discomfit Raphael de Mereliot with the sight of you on my arm."

"Not to mention the entire Court," I added.

"Oh, that's already done." Thierry flashed a wicked grin. "Now comes the part where they wonder what we've been up to. Watch the tongues wag when we enter."

That, they most assuredly did.

There was a pause like a collective intake of breath as we entered the hall, Thierry sauntering, one hand laid possessively over my fingers where they rested on his arm. For a moment, there was only the sound of music playing in the background, some intricate and unfamiliar instrument. Then the whispers arose.

I made a face. "Do they have nothing better to do than gossip?"

"No," Thierry said thoughtfully. "Not really."

"Moirin!" Raphael parted the throng and strode toward me, looking genuinely concerned. He saw the Dauphin, checked himself, and bowed. "Your highness, forgive me. I was worried about her."

"I'm fine," I said.

"Why shouldn't she be?" Thierry patted my hand. "Since I found her quite alone and unattended, I escorted Lady Moirin to the Hall of Portraits that she might behold her ancestors. My lord de Mereliot, I must thank you for introducing such a fascinating offshoot of the tree of House Courcel into our lives."

Raphael gave him a thunderous look, then turned his stormy gaze on me, setting the blood to pounding in my veins. "You're sure?"

"Yes!" I said irritably. "You were busy elsewhere."

A woman screamed.

There was a moment of milling confusion. Raphael's head went up like a hound on point, then whipped around, seeking the source of the scream. In the center of the hall, the gentleman of the elderly couple who had preceded us had sunk to his knees, one hand clutching at his doublet. It was his wife who had screamed.

"Your pardon!" Raphael shouted over his shoulder, pushing his way through the crowd.

I shook off Thierry and went after him.

Everyone had gathered to watch in appalled fascination. By the time I squeezed and elbowed my way through, Raphael was kneeling on the floor beside the old gentleman. He'd unbuttoned his doublet and was massaging the man's chest.

He looked up and saw me. "My physician's bag. It's in the carriage. Send Jean-Michel."

I nodded.

The curious onlookers didn't want to let me through. I swore at them, shoving blindly. And then there was an opening, and a pair of slender hands caught my upper arms with unexpected strength.

"What does he need?" Jehanne de la Courcel asked me in a steady tone.

"His bag," I stammered. "In the carriage."

She gave a brusque nod and released me, issuing a string of orders. Guards moved to obey. Forced backward, the crowd thinned. Out of the corner of my eye, I saw Jean-Michel pelting out of the hall.

"*Moirin!*" Raphael's voice rose in a roar.

"Aye!" I flung myself to my knees beside him, bruising myself against the marble floor.

"Help me," he said simply. "His heart is stricken. If it stops, he'll die. Lend me your energy."

The old man gasped for air, his face bluish.

"I don't—" I began.

Raphael's hand closed around my wrist. "Put your hands on mine. Do what you did for the plum tree."

"I'll try," I whispered.

The world shrank to a small circle. There was me, Raphael, and the old man. Raphael rubbed his hands together and said a prayer to Eisheth under his breath. He laid his hands on the old man's slack, pale chest, bowing his head and arranging his hands just so.

I put my hands on his.

I couldn't feel it, not the way I could feel plants. The thing that was wrong, the thing that needed to be fixed or coaxed and cozened. But Raphael could. I breathed in slow and deep. I couldn't summon the twilight and vanish from sight—not here and now with so many eyes watching. But I could still take that half-step into the next world and evoke its charms. That I could lend to Raphael.

I breathed out.

A rill of energy surged from me, leaving me drained—more drained than I'd ever been. Raphael closed his eyes, warmth pulsing from his hands.

The old man took a ragged gulp of air and sat bolt upright. "Elua!"

The crowd cheered.

Jean-Michel appeared with a satchel. Raphael grabbed it from him and rummaged for a small flask labeled in neat handwriting. "Keep still, Lord Luchese," he said briefly. "Moirin, support him from behind." I moved to obey. He uncorked the flask and set it to the man's lips. "It's a distillation of willow bark. It's going to be bitter."

The elderly Lord Luchese drank, grimacing at the taste. I peered over his shoulder, watching healthy color return to his face.

"Is he going to be all right?" his wife asked, her voice quavering.

"Yes." Raphael lowered the flask. "He is."

Lord Luchese summoned a tremulous smile. "I thought for sure my time had come. You're a goddamned miracle worker, de Mereliot."

"No." Raphael lifted his head and gazed intently at me. The crowd murmured around us. "I'm afraid that credit lies elsewhere."

TWENTY-EIGHT

The balance of the evening at the Palace was a brief blur. Overwhelmed and exhausted, I let it wash over me. A litter arrived for Lord Luchese. I leaned against a column, vaguely aware of Raphael issuing further instructions to Luchese's wife, something to do with bed-rest and a tincture of foxglove.

"What just passed here?" Thierry whispered in my ear. "What did you *do*?"

"I don't know." I closed my eyes. "Ask Raphael."

"The air around you . . ." he breathed. "There was a brightness."

I shrugged. "Oh?"

"Prince Thierry!" A light voice, sweetness made sharp. I opened my eyes to see Jehanne de la Courcel. She touched my face, a touch as light as gossamer. I had the strangest urge to lean in to it and rest my cheek against her hand. "Let her be."

"Certainly, *Mother*." Thierry's tone dripped with sarcasm.

Jehanne regarded me. At close range, I could feel Naamah's gifts coiling between us with an unexpected intensity I didn't want to acknowledge. "Are you quite well?"

"No," I said honestly. "I'm very, very tired."

Her lips pursed. "Raphael!"

He was there, bowing. "Your majesty?"

"You've had your fun." Her hand fell away from my cheek. "Now take your young witchling home; she looks near to collapsing. I'll make your apologies to Daniel."

Raphael bowed a second time. "Of course."

As he escorted me toward the door, her voice halted him. "Raphael!" We both turned. Jehanne's face was unreadable. "I'll send for you on the morrow."

He bowed a third time and didn't reply.

In the carriage, he was solicitous, giving me a flask of brandy to sip and chafing my hands between his. Bit by bit, I felt a measure of my strength return.

"Well," I said at length. "That was interesting."

"Interesting!" Raphael gave a short, wondering laugh. "Moirin, that was the singular most astonishing thing I've ever experienced. Did you not feel it?" He lifted his hands before his face and contemplated them, turning them this way and that. "We saved a man from certain death."

"*You* did."

"No." He shook his head. "I meant what I said. I'm a skilled physician, but I can't work miracles. You can. You did. I felt your energy flowing through me. It felt . . ." He fell silent a moment, searching for the right word. "God-like."

"God-like," I murmured.

"Yes." Raphael's hands slid beneath my arms. "Come here."

I let him pull me onto his lap, too tired to protest. Now he kissed me with all the ardor I could have wanted—and I didn't want to respond, but I couldn't help it. Even exhausted, I wanted him so bedamned badly. My body roused to his touch.

"Witchling," Raphael breathed in my ear. His hands slid over my breasts. "I *am* taking you to bed tonight."

"All right," I said helplessly.

He laughed and kissed me some more.

By the time we reached his townhouse, I was dazed with an odd blend of lassitude and desire. In the courtyard, Raphael scooped me off my feet and into his arms. I let him—let him carry me inside and past the whispering servants, up the marble stairs, burying my face against his neck. In his bedchamber, he set me on my feet.

"Moirin." His hands glided over my body, leaving glorious trails of warmth. I shivered. He cupped my face and kissed me deeply. "*My* terms, remember?"

I nodded.

Raphael's terms were sensuous and deliberate. He undressed me piece by piece, his lips lingering on the nape of my neck as he unclasped my gown's collar and unlaced the delicate stays. When I turned in his arms and reached for his doublet to unbutton it, he shook his head at me.

His terms.

"Beautiful," he murmured when I stood naked before him. He reached out and plucked the gilded comb from my hair. My hair fell over my shoulders in a slithering cascade. He laughed softly. "Like a waterfall."

"Raphael . . ." I whispered.

He pressed one finger against my lips, then pointed. "On the bed."

I lay down.

For a long moment, he merely stood and gazed at me, eyes dark with desire. Then, slowly, he undressed. It was absurdly tantalizing. I watched his bare torso emerge as he shed his doublet and shirt. His shoulders were broad. I gazed at the hollow at the base of his throat where his pulse beat visibly and understood what Benoit Vallon from Atelier Favrielle meant about subtle beauties. Raphael shed his breeches and undergarments. The muscles in his flanks flexed, shadowy in the dim lamplight. His phallus was hard and erect, curving toward his flat belly.

Stone and sea, I wanted him.

He untied a thong holding back his tawny hair and shook it loose, smiling sidelong at me. When he joined me on the bed, I reached for him.

"No." Raphael caught my wrists gently, pinning them above my head with one hand. "Slowly. You have a lot to learn, Moirin."

"I do?"

He leaned over me, his hard chest brushing against my erect nipples. Kissed me—slowly. Languorously. His free hand traced the line of my inner thigh. "Yes."

Until that night, I thought myself well versed in the ways of desire. After all, it had come effortlessly to me. But the coach-driver Theo scarce counted and Cillian mac Tiernan was a green lad beside Raphael de Mereliot, who was the Queen's lover. And she was an adept of the Night Court.

He undid me.

From top to bottom, stem to stern. Everywhere he touched me, I ached with pleasure. When he spread my thighs wide and lapped at the slick crease between them, my hips jerked clean off the bed, my fists knotting in his hair.

Raphael lifted his head, eyes gleaming. "Slowly."

"Please!" I whimpered.

He smiled. "In time."

Time . . . what was time? That night, it was measured in the broad, insistent strokes of his tongue, driving me to pinnacles I hadn't known existed. I dissolved beneath it, melting with pleasure.

The bright lady beamed. Oddly, she wore Jehanne's face.

Raphael slithered up the length of my body, bracing himself on his arms, mindful of my healing ribs. He kissed me, tasting of me. He guided my hand to his erect phallus. It throbbed in my fist, beating with a pulse of its own.

I sighed with gratitude. "Now?"

"Now," he agreed. The moment he pushed into me, I came hard—then came hard again as he continued to thrust. In and out, filled and not-filled. It was so good, and yet. Stone and sea, I was tired! It was almost a relief when he shuddered and spent himself in me, his ballocks rising and his buttocks clenching beneath my clutching hands. Almost a relief to feel his softening phallus slipping out of me.

"Ohh . . ." I whispered.

And slept.

I awoke to sunlight and Raphael's absence. It was late morning. The rumpled bed linens glowed white in the bright sun. The room smelled of sex. There was a robe with the House Mereliot crest laid out for me. I rose and donned it, feeling suddenly famished and very much in need of a bath. With an unexpected pang, I found myself missing home. A plunge in the stream and a breakfast of fried trout would be a glorious thing.

Instead, I rang the bell to summon one of Raphael's servants. The maid who answered was a sly-faced creature named Celine, not one of my favorites. She had a habit of smirking at me out of the corner of her eye. This morning was no exception, and when I asked where Raphael was, her smirk widened.

"Why, he's gone to the Palace, my lady," she said with an air of false innocence. "Gone to answer a summons from the Queen."

"I see," I said slowly. I hadn't expected him to refuse Jehanne. Still, it seemed something of an insult to rise from our shared pleasure bed and find him at her beck and call.

"Your bath will be ready shortly." Celine tossed her head. "Will you dine downstairs or shall I have a tray sent up?"

I held her gaze without answering until she flushed and looked away. "A tray will be fine. Have it sent to the guest-chamber, please."

"As you wish," she muttered.

By the time I had bathed and dined, there was still no sign of Raphael. I looked around the sunlit guest-chamber. There was the borrowed robe. There was the clothes press with the gowns commissioned by Raphael. There on the bedside table was a jewelry box he'd given me, in which I'd carefully placed the gilded comb and the emerald eardrops. The only items in the room that were truly mine were the deerskin quiver and yew-wood bow propped unobtrusively in a corner and the disreputable canvas satchel that contained the papers Caroline nó Bryony had given me.

That seemed a long, long time ago.

I hauled the satchel onto the bed and went through its contents. Lodgings, letters of introduction, letters of authentication. From the moment I'd opened my eyes on that street to see Raphael de Mereliot gazing down at me, I'd let all of this fall by the wayside.

"That," I said aloud, "has to change."

"My lady?" A different maid poked her head in the door; Daphne—the shy one who I quite liked.

"Nothing." I smiled at her. "I was talking to myself. Since my lord de Mereliot is occupied elsewhere today, I think I may venture out on my own."

"As you wish." Daphne returned my smile shyly, her deference as genuine as Celine's was false. "But I came to tell you, that you have a visitor."

"I do?"

"Aye." Her eyes widened. "Lianne Tremaine. The King's Poet," she added at my blank look. "She wishes to call on you, if you're receiving."

"Oh." I blinked. "Is there any reason why I wouldn't be?"

"No." She smiled again, ducking her head and dimpling. "That is entirely up to you, my lady. But if you wish to receive her, I'll tell the kitchen to prepare tea and pastries, shall I?"

"Thank you." I nodded, grateful for her discreet guidance, and began stowing away my papers. "I'll be down directly."

It felt passing strange to be entertaining a guest in Raphael's household as though it were my own. It felt passing strange to be entertaining a guest in *any* household when it came to it. To be sure, it was a far cry from sharing the goods Cillian had brought on the hearth of our cave or showing him how to catch trout or blanch acorn meal. Still, I'd grown mindful of the importance of appearances in Terre d'Ange and glided into the salon where the King's Poet waited as though I were the mistress of the household.

The woman awaiting me rose. She was younger than I would have expected someone appointed to the post, with light brown hair and keen golden-brown eyes. Something about the cast of her sharp, pretty features put me in mind of a fox.

"Lianne Tremaine?" I inquired. "The King's Poet?"

"Indeed." A quick smile darted across her face. "Well met, Lady Moirin. I was sorry to miss a chance to speak with you at his majesty's fête."

"Oh?" I said politely, at a loss for anything clever to say.

"Oh, indeed." Her tone had a mocking edge, but I didn't sense any malice in it. "These are good times to be alive, but dull times to be a royal poet. Your arrival and last night's dramatic performance are the most interesting thing to happen in years. I'll own, I'm curious. Was it staged?"

I was bewildered. "Was what staged?"

"The scene with Lord Luchese," Lianne said impatiently.

I stared at her. "Do you jest? No!"

She gave a delicate shrug. "One never knows. I wouldn't put it past

Raphael de Mereliot. He and the Queen have been known to get . . . intricate . . . in their quarrels. Jehanne de la Courcel can compete with almost anything, but a young woman with the ability to bring a man back from death's doorstep . . . ah, that's another matter altogether. He might have staged the entire thing just to unnerve her." She studied my expression and laughed. "The possibility never occurred to you, did it?"

"No," I admitted.

"Such delightful naivete!" Lianne Tremaine sat uninvited. "Well. Now that it has, do you suppose he did?"

"No." I sat opposite her. Quite apart from my own experience, I had the memory of Raphael in the carriage, the wonder in his voice. "I truly don't."

"So it was real." She steepled her fingers. "What did you do and how did you do it?" Put off by her peremptory manner, I didn't answer. Lianne sighed. "I'm being nosy and hectoring, aren't I?"

"Nosy, aye," I agreed. "Hectoring isn't a word I know."

"Bullying."

"Ah." I saw Daphne with a tray of tea and pastries and beckoned for her to set it on the table. "Yes, rather."

"Sorry." This time the King's Poet's smile was wry and charming. "I have an overly inquisitive mind and I can be rude and impatient in the pursuit of knowledge. Let me start over." She lifted the teapot. "May I make amends by pouring?"

"You may," I said.

She poured for both of us, then sipped her tea. "Nice. Raphael always has the best tea, thanks to his connections to that Ch'in philosopher at the Academy."

"Master Lo Feng?" I sniffed my tea. It had a delicate floral aroma. "I thought he was a physician."

"Physician, philosopher, poet, botanist." Lianne shrugged. "It seems the famous Lo Feng is many things. Have you met him?"

I shook my head. "Not yet."

"Imposing fellow." She put down her teacup and regarded me. "All right, I'm starting over. Lady Moirin mac Fainche, pray let me introduce myself. I am Lianne Tremaine, the King's Poet and the youngest ever to hold that post. I'm quite brilliant and a bit prickly. I make a dreadful enemy, but a loyal friend. And unless I miss my guess, you could use one of the latter. You've managed to drop out of nowhere into a rather complicated situation."

"That much is obvious," I said dryly. "Even to me."

Her lips twitched. "So you're not dim-witted, just naïve. Are you in love with him? Raphael?"

My heart rolled over in my chest at the mere question. "I don't know," I said slowly. I didn't know whether or not I could wholly trust her, but it was such a relief to speak to someone about Raphael that I answered honestly. "I've feelings I've never felt before. And I'm drawn to him. Here, in my *diadh-anam*." I tapped my breast. "The spark of the Maghuin Dhonn Herself I carry inside me. There's no word for it in D'Angeline."

"God-soul." Lianne tilted her head, slanting sunlight turning her eyes topaz. "That's how Phèdre nó Delaunay de Montrève translated it."

"Well enough." I nodded. "I don't understand it and I can't explain it. Not yet. Believe me, my lady, I would very much prefer that the man for whom I feel this were *not* the Queen's lover and favorite courtier."

"No doubt," she agreed. "Are you willing to talk to me about magic?"

I sighed. "I'd rather not until I understand it better myself. I have a gift or two, small things as they would be reckoned in the long history of my people. What happened last night . . ." I let the words go. "You mentioned an offer of friendship?"

Lianne grinned. "I said I was a loyal friend. I never claimed to be a tactful one. Very well." She hoisted her teacup. "You're in need of a friend. What would *you* care to talk about?"

"Hmm." I thought about it. "Mayhap whether or not I should seek to make a graceful exit from Raphael's household."

"Do you *want* to leave?" she asked.

"I'm not sure." I picked at a pastry, flaking off bits of golden crust. "Raphael keeps saying he wants me to stay. But I'm not sure it's me he wants or the fact of what I am. Last night . . . I think it aroused him more than I could on my own. And I'm not sure how I feel about that."

I made a face. "Particularly since he informed me that I have a great deal to learn in bed."

The King's Poet sputtered out a mouthful of tea. "He didn't!"

"He did." I sighed again. "Which, while it may be true, in the light of day strikes me as a rather unkind thing to say at the time."

"Rather." Lianne regarded me. "Well then, I suggest you take him at his word."

"How so?"

She flashed her quick, foxy grin. "Name of Elua, girl! Don't let Raphael de Mereliot control your life. You're in Terre d'Ange. You're in the City of Elua. There are hundreds of men and women here sworn to Naamah's Service, any number of whom would be delighted to teach you the full extent of her arts—which is, after all, your rightful heritage. Go to the Night Court and arrange for an assignation and a private Showing."

I blinked. "I can do that?"

"Can and should." Lianne Tremaine rose with alacrity. "Come." She put out her hand. "Let's go right now. We'll take my carriage."

"I meant to go to the banking house today," I temporized. "To draw on my letter of credit. I've no funds of my own until I do."

"We'll stop on the way." She beckoned. "You don't have to schedule the assignation today, but we can still make the appointment. Oh, come on! This will be fun."

It struck me that it would be the first act of my own volition that I'd committed since I chased after the thief who'd stolen my purse. That was the thought that drove me to my feet. "All right," I said recklessly. "Let's do it."

"Excellent!" Lianne squeezed my hand. "Are you familiar with the Houses of the Night Court? Do you know which one you'd choose?"

"Where did the Queen serve?" I asked her.

That got me an amused sidelong glance. "Naïve, but a quick study, eh? Her majesty was an adept of Cereus House, First among the Thirteen. They celebrate the ephemeral nature of beauty."

Jehanne's face and orchid blossoms mingled in my memory. "That's the one."

TWENTY-NINE

Cereus House was lovely.

The Dowayne, which was the title given to the head of each House of the Night Court, received us in an inner courtyard garden. Autumn flowers of marigold, amaryllis, and chrysanthemum bloomed in profusion, vibrant, healthy, and well tended. I breathed in the air with pleasure, tasting their tang.

"Do you like it?" The Dowayne, Neriel nó Cereus, smiled at me. I gauged her to be in her late sixties, tall and slender, with hair gone pure silver. "I heard you had a fondness for the outdoors."

I was startled. "You did?"

Lianne Tremaine sipped a glass of wine. "Lesson the first, Lady Moirin. Gossip travels faster than a thunderclap in the City, and nowhere faster than to the Night Court."

"*To*, yes," the Dowayne agreed. "*From* is another matter. Shall we speak of your desires, my lady?"

I shrugged. "I wish to learn."

She studied me. "Do you think to enter Naamah's Service yourself?" She reached out and touched my arm. "Mixed though your heritage may be, I suspect her gifts are strong in you. They are in your father, you know, and I see a good deal of Phanuel in you."

"You do?" The idea pleased me. "You know him?"

"Oh, yes." The Dowayne smiled again. "Of course. His family has a long history in Naamah's Order." She paused. "But it's too soon for such questions, isn't it? Forgive me. You're not ready to decide; you've only set out on your journey. It would be the privilege of Cereus House to teach you what we may."

I smiled back at her. "I'd like that."

After some discussion, we set a date for two days hence. I signed a contract that spelled out the terms of the assignation and parted with a goodly sum of money. I left lighter of purse, but lighter-hearted. After all, I once again *had* a purse of my own. I was no longer dependent on Raphael de Mereliot for funds or pleasure.

"See?" In the carriage, Lianne regarded me with pleased amusement. "I told you this was a good idea."

"You did," I agreed. "Thank you."

At the townhouse, Raphael was less sanguine.

"Moirin!" he barked at me upon my return, pacing in the foyer. "Where in the seven hells were you?"

"Out," I said briefly.

"Out." He glowered at me. "I had plans for us this afternoon."

"Oh?" I inquired. "You might have bothered to inform me."

Raphael gave me a stormy look, then checked himself. "You're right," he said softly, circling my waist with his arms. "I'm sorry. I was caught up in my own affairs. There's a lad I'd like you to see with me, a young lad." He kissed my neck. "A patient of mine."

I hated the way my knees went weak. "Aye?"

"Aye." His lips curved as though the word were a private jest between us—and mayhap it was. Then he pulled back, his look serious. "It's young Marc de Thibideau. The Comte's youngest and a companion of Prince Thierry. He broke his leg in a hunting accident some weeks ago. His femur. That's the thigh bone. It's set properly, but it's not healing well. I suspect the new bone matter isn't growing as fast as it ought. I thought . . ." He freed one hand and raked it through his tawny locks, disheveling them. "I thought we might try, you and I."

"To coax it?" I asked.

He nodded. "Will you?"

I sighed. "And how *is* her majesty?"

Raphael touched my cheek. "I've made you no false promises, Moirin. Will you come with me tomorrow morning to see the lad?"

"Of course," I murmured.

"Good." He kissed me, then released me. "I'll send word to the Academy. Master Lo Feng has a concoction he says will help, and I'm eager for him to meet you." He paused. "*Out* is a passing vague term. Where did you go? Daphne said you left with the King's Poet."

"To the banking house." I jingled the purse at my waist. "And then to Cereus House. I have an appointment there the day after tomorrow."

It was worth every penny I'd spent to see the look of pure astonishment on Raphael de Mereliot's face. "You do?"

"Oh, yes." I reveled in his disbelief. "The Dowayne was very kind. She's arranging a private Showing with two of their finest adepts that I might witness the full range of Naamah's arts, and then I may take my leisure with either or both as I choose." I raised my brows. "You *did* say I had a lot to learn."

"Blessed Elua bugger me," he muttered. "So I did."

"The Dowayne asked if I thought I might enter Naamah's Service," I added with a certain malice. "She thought I might have the gift for it."

"Moirin." Raphael caught my hands. "Don't rush into anything. Elua knows, I'm the last man to disparage Naamah's Service, but it's not an uncommon calling. What *you* can do . . ." His thumbs rubbed my inner wrists. "It's unique and unprecedented, and we've just begun to explore it. Promise me that you'll give it a chance?"

Now I felt petty. "I will. It's just—"

"I took you for granted." He raised my hands, planting a kiss in each palm. "I shouldn't have done that and I'm sorry for it. Do you accept my apology?"

"I do."

His eyes gleamed. "Do you still mean to keep that appointment?"

I lifted my chin. "Aye, I do."

He laughed. "So be it! The gods also know I've a penchant for stubborn women."

"Oh?" I asked. "Is Jehanne stubborn?"

"Yes." Raphael let go of my hands and regarded me. "I'll make you a bargain. Don't ask me to speak of her, and I'll not speak of you to her. Jealousy doesn't become you, Moirin."

In my heart, I thought it was unfair. After all, *he* was the one to make oblique reference to her and I was more curious than jealous at this point—but there was a warning edge in his voice. I remembered how Cillian's jealousy had pushed me away from him, a memory forever tainted with guilt. I didn't want to cause Raphael to push me away. "All right," I agreed.

He bent down to kiss me. "Good girl."

I hoped Raphael would take me to bed again that night. I thought it would be better between us if I weren't drained and exhausted. But he merely escorted me to the guest-chamber and gave me a chaste kiss good night. Whatever he'd been up to with the Queen, I supposed it had left *him* somewhat drained.

In the morning, we paid a visit on the de Thibideau household.

The Comte de Thibideau greeted us at the door himself, ushering us into the foyer. He was a burly blond man I vaguely recalled seeing at the King's fête.

"Come in, come in!" he said, pumping Raphael's arm. "Ah good, you've got the witch-girl with you. Remarkable thing, that. But if she can help poor Marc, I'll take back everything I've ever said about her folk." He lowered his voice. "That Ch'in fellow's here waiting with his surly lad and some noxious brew. You sure he's all right?"

"Very sure." Raphael extricated himself from the Comte's grip and stepped past him to greet his mentor, clasping his hands together and bowing. "Master Lo Feng, well met."

"Lord Raphael." The Ch'in physician clasped his hands together and inclined his head in greeting. His lilting accent was like nothing I'd ever heard. "It is ever a pleasure."

Raphael bowed again, then turned to indicate me. "Permit me to introduce Lady Moirin mac Fainche to you."

I got a good look at Master Lo Feng and fell in love at first sight. In his own way, he was as elegant as the Dowayne of Cereus House. He wore a robe of black silk worked with a gorgeous square of colorful embroidery in the center. His hair was snow-white and fine as silk, drawn back in a braid and topped with a black hat with a jeweled spire. A narrow, two-pointed beard graced his chin, as fine and silken and white as his hair.

But it was his face that struck me most of all.

Lo Feng had the most serene, gentle, wise face I'd ever seen on another human being. It was written in every wrinkle, in every crease around his dark, tilted eyes. My *diadh-anam* flared within me.

"You're a priest," I said without thinking.

"Some say so." He didn't smile, but the creases around his eyes deepened. "I say I am a humble scholar."

The young man behind him made a faint sound.

"Bao," Lo Feng said in gentle reprove.

The surly lad. I glanced at him. Unlike his master, he wore a plain cotton shirt, baggy breeches, and straw sandals. He carried a staff carelessly over one shoulder, a covered iron pot with a handle dangling from it. He met my eyes with fearless disdain, and I felt a mild shock, reminded of home. Not wholly—and yet. There was something about the planes of his cheeks and the feral glint of his eyes beneath an unkempt shock of black hair that put me in mind of the Maghuin Dhonn.

He looked away.

"Forgive me." I collected myself and bowed as Raphael had done. "Well met, Master Lo Feng."

The self-proclaimed humble scholar returned my bow. "It is an auspicious day, Lady Moirin mac Fainche."

The Comte de Thibideau cleared his throat. "If you gentlefolk are done exchanging pleasantries, I've a young son in a good deal of discomfort."

"Of course," Raphael said smoothly, putting one hand between my shoulders. "Pray, lead the way, your lordship."

Marc de Thibideau was ensconced in a cloistered study on the ground floor, reclining on a couch with his injured, splinted leg propped at an angle. He glanced up sharply as we entered, then eyed me and gave a long, low whistle. "So you're Thierry's witch-girl!"

"Oh, am I?" I asked mildly.

"He'd like to think so." He grinned and struggled to raise himself on his elbows, wincing at the effort. Sweat broke out on his brow, plastering his fair hair. "Sorry. Damned leg."

"Lie still, Marc." Raphael laid a hand on his forehead. "Master Lo Feng? Will you confirm my diagnosis?"

The Ch'in physician nodded, rubbing his hands together. He placed them a few inches above the young lord's thigh. I could sense the energy rippling around him. He moved his hands, letting them hover over Marc de Thibideau in a few places. The pit of his groin, his heart, the space between his eyes. He touched the lad only once, stripping off the thick woolen sock he wore on the foot of his injured leg, manipulating his bare sole with a gentle touch.

"Ow!" The young lord tensed, then relaxed. "Ah."

"Hey, now!" his father cried.

Master Lo Feng ignored him. "You are correct," he said to Raphael. "The break has caused a breach in the flow of his *chi*. As a result, the bone is reluctant to heal." He beckoned. "Bao!"

The surly lad stepped forward, whipping the staff from his shoulder with a flourish. The hanging iron pot rattled down its length and settled onto the floor with unexpected precision. The young man stepped backward, leaning on his staff.

"Bone soup." Master Lo Feng plucked up the pot. "It will help restore the balance of his energies."

"What's in it?" the Comte de Thibideau asked suspiciously, lifting the lid and sniffing at the contents.

"Marrow bones." It was hard to tell, but I thought there was a glimmer of amusement in Lo Feng's eyes. "Seaweed. Deer's antler. Things you do not have a name for. Dang gui and shan yao root. Simmered a long time for goodness."

The Comte sniffed again. "Smells foul."

Master Lo Feng looked serene. "It is healthful."

"De Mereliot?" The Comte cast his dubious gaze on Raphael. "What about the witch-girl? I thought that's what we were about."

"Are you willing to try?" Raphael asked me.

"Say yes." Marc de Thibideau groped for my hand. "Please. I don't want to be a cripple."

"You won't be," I said with more assurance than I felt, then nodded at Raphael. "Aye, my lord. I'm willing."

Like his mentor, Raphael rubbed his hands together. Unlike his mentor, he laid them directly over the break on Marc's thigh, his brows furrowed. "I feel it," he murmured. "Moirin! Lend me your energy."

I tried.

I cast about for the twilight, fumbling. Breathed in and out. I couldn't find it. The room was too tight, too close. There was too much stone around me, too many books and man-made things, too many eyes watching, too many expectations.

"Moirin!" Raphael's voice rose. "Now!"

"Wait!" I turned to the surly lad. Bao. "May I?" I asked him. The staff he leaned on was made of wood. Unfamiliar wood, flexible and segmented, carved with runes and bound with steel bands, but wood nonetheless. I touched it unbidden.

He nodded reluctantly.

It remembered its origin. Groves of slender trees swayed in the sunlight. I breathed in its faint scent and took that half-step into the world beyond.

I breathed it out, my hands settling atop Raphael's. Everything I had, I gave to him to use. Everything.

Warmth surged between us.

"Oh!" Marc de Thibideau's back arched; then he settled. "Oh," he said in a wondering tone. "That's better. So much better."

I sank to my knees, drained. Behind my eyes, I saw only a sparkling darkness. I bowed my head and leaned it against the couch. "Will he heal?"

Raphael beckoned. "Master Lo?"

The two of them examined the young lord together. "His flow is much improved," the Ch'in physician murmured, then said something in his own tongue, an unintelligible stream of strange consonants and rising and falling tones. The surly lad Bao stooped and helped me to my feet, giving me his staff to lean on. I rested my cheek against the wood. "See here," Lo Feng added. He guided my hand to touch the warm skin of Marc's bare foot. "Only minutes before, it was cold."

"I see." I gave Marc's foot a feeble squeeze. "See, my lord? You'll not be a cripple."

He regarded me with awe. "You *are* a miracle worker!"

"No." I shook my head. "But if I was able to help, I'm pleased."

"It is a wondrous gift," Master Lo Feng said softly. "Would you do me the honor of discussing it with me?"

"Aye," I said. "Only not today." Out of the corner of my eye, I could see Bao looking fidgety without his staff. I handed it back to him, wavering a bit.

Raphael caught my elbow. "It wearies her."

"Of course." Lo Feng gave me a bow. "Lady Moirin, perhaps we may arrange a time when you are recovered." For the first time, he smiled. It was a lovely, gentle smile. "I look forward to the pleasure of your company."

I summoned a tired smile in return. "And I yours."

THIRTY

Upon returning to Raphael's townhouse, I went straight to bed and slept clean through until dinner. If Daphne hadn't shaken me awake, I might have slept through dinner, too. I stumbled downstairs to find Raphael in high spirits.

"Here." He plunked a small purse on the table before me.

I hefted it. "What's this?"

"Half of my fee from today." He grinned. "I reckon you more than earned it. I'd give you the whole of it if I thought you'd accept it."

"I wouldn't." I pushed the purse toward him. "And you've already been overly generous."

"Keep it." He pushed it back. "My sense of honor demands it. Besides, you'll need money for a patron-gift tomorrow."

I blinked. "Patron-gift?"

"At Cereus House," Raphael clarified. "It's customary to leave a gift of money or jewelry for your adept. That's how they make their marques. Until they do, they're beholden to their House."

I felt foolish. "Marques?"

"A tattoo of the insignia of their House." He inclined his head and tapped the nape of his neck. "From the base of their spines all the way to here. It's an old custom, somewhat to do with Naamah scoring her lovers' backs with her nails in the throes of passion. You didn't notice Jehanne's?"

"No." I rubbed my eyes. "I didn't notice Jehanne's. How much is it customary to leave?"

"At a minimum, ten percent of the fee." Raphael shrugged. "Beyond that, the sky's the limit. Moirin, are you quite sure you're ready for this?"

"Why ever not?" I picked up the purse. "You've saved me considerable embarrassment. Thank you."

That night, Raphael invited me to his bed. There was a part of me that wanted to decline, still tired and drained and uncertain of his motives. But when he gazed at me with those storm-grey eyes, desire darkening them like thunderclouds, the inexorable answering tide rose in my blood and I couldn't say no.

And it was good.

I clutched his shoulder blades as he moved inside me, his tawny hair falling to curtain my face. I thought about Naamah scoring her lovers' backs and shivered with pleasure.

"Tomorrow," Raphael whispered in my ear, his hips thrusting. His voice was fierce. "You think of *me* inside you."

"I may," I whispered back defiantly. "Or I may not."

He pulled back, propping himself on his arms, leaving only the head of his shaft inside me—and me hovering on the verge of fulfillment. "You will. Say it."

I squirmed.

His eyes darkened further. "Say it!"

"All right! I'll think of you!"

With a grunt, he pushed himself back inside me, filling me and sending me over the edge of the precipice. I convulsed hard around his thick shaft, wrapping my legs around his hips and hating myself for acquiescing. But it pleased him, and he spent himself inside me.

"Raphael?" I murmured. "Tell me. Is it me or my gift that you desire?"

He lifted his head. In the aftermath of pleasure, his beautiful face was boyish and sweet. "Can it not be both?"

"Can it?" I asked, unsure.

He kissed my lips. "Yes, witchling. It can." Raphael eased out of me and rolled onto his back, settling my head on his shoulder. He stroked my hair, kissed the top of my head. "Now sleep."

Too tired to argue, I sighed, and did.

In the morning, he was gone again. I awoke to the rich scent of roasted, brewed *kavah* beans and the maid Daphne watching me uncertainly, a laden tray in her hands.

"Lady Moirin?"

I yawned. "Aye?"

She shifted from foot to foot. "The water for your bath is heating, but I thought you might like to break your fast. His lordship bade me tell you that he will be gone on business at the Academy today, but that he has left the carriage and driver at your disposal. He hopes you will join him for dinner." She ducked her head and gave me a quick, darting glance from beneath her lashes. "Do you really have an appointment at Cereus House?"

"Aye." I pushed myself upright. "I do."

"Lucky them," Daphne said unexpectedly—and flushed. "I'm sorry."

I laughed aloud. "Stone and sea! Please, don't be. You've no idea how much I needed to hear something of the sort."

She smiled, dimpling. "Truly?"

"Truly," I assured her.

Daphne set down the tray with care. "This may please you, too." She withdrew an envelope from the pocket of her apron. "It's an invitation." She lowered her voice, clearly impressed. "From Prince Thierry."

I opened it and read. "So it is. To a hunt."

"Do you ride to the hunt?" Daphne inquired.

I smiled wryly. "It seems I do."

All in all, it put me in a better mood than I might have been in otherwise. Despite what had transpired between us last night, Raphael was being solicitous. I had confirmation of my own desirability. I was perhaps being courted by the Dauphin of Terre d'Ange. So I endured the carriage-ride to Cereus House in good spirits. The Dowayne greeted me with genuine warmth, kissing me on both cheeks.

"I've given you a room that looks onto a courtyard." She put her hands on my shoulders, her gaze oddly troubled. "And . . . I hope the experience pleases you, my lady."

"I'm sure it will," I said.

"I hope so," she repeated.

I followed the servant she assigned me as a guide through a labyrinth of corridors. At last he paused and bowed, indicating a door. I opened it and entered.

"Moirin." In the window seat that looked onto the courtyard, Jehanne de la Courcel raised her head. Sunlight gleamed on the elaborate coils of her pale gilt hair. Her blue-grey eyes sparkled at me. "Lesson the second," she said in her light, sweet voice. "Never trust a poet."

My blood ran cold with anger.

"Do you make mock of me for seeking to learn Naamah's arts?" I asked stiffly. "I had not thought that was the D'Angeline way."

"No!" She rose in one fluid motion. "I'm not here in jest."

"Why, then?" I eyed her. "Is this but some gambit I cannot fathom in the game you and Raphael play with one another?"

"Yes," Jehanne said simply. "And no."

I folded my arms. "Well, I'm not playing."

"Such a glower!" She tilted her head and smiled at me in a disarming manner. "Are you truly that insulted that the Queen of Terre d'Ange wishes to serve as an adept for you? I never did renounce Naamah's Service, you know. It's part of my agreement with Daniel." When I didn't answer, she came closer. "Raphael de Mereliot is a very intelligent, very attractive man. He can be kind and caring, but he can be selfish and ambitious, too. And he *will* control you if you let him."

I could smell her perfume, faint and intoxicating. "And out of the goodness of your heart, you came here to tell me this?"

"No." Jehanne ran one fingertip over my folded forearms in a feather-light caress, watching my skin prickle in response. "The Court's abuzz with talk of you. Raphael expects me to succumb to a jealous fury. If I do, he wins. This . . ." She stroked my cheek with the same exquisite delicacy. "This is my way of changing the game entirely."

With an effort, I pulled away. "Oh, aye! So you might throw it in his face and in the bargain, laugh at my inexperience."

"No." She shook her head. "No, I rather think I'd keep you my delicious little secret. And when Raphael parades you around in all his smug glory, all I'll have to do is think on it and laugh inside. As for your inexperience . . ." She took a step closer to me, eyes sparkling. My heart beat faster. In the sunlight, her fair skin was utterly flawless. "Do you know how long it's been since I let myself indulge in the headlong rush of youth's untutored passion?"

"No," I said softly. This time I didn't pull away.

"Too long." Jehanne kissed my lips, light and sweet as a promise. "Far, far too long, my gorgeous young savage."

I took a deep breath. "This is a very bad idea."

"Mayhap." Her eyes danced. I could feel her gift, Naamah's gift, the bright lady's gift, calling to mine. Desire to desire, simple and pure in the midst of this whole complicated affair. My head spun with images of orchids and doves. I wanted very badly to touch her, to taste her. "If you're going to leave, you'd better do it now."

I didn't.

Instead, I slid one hand around the back of her neck and kissed her. Her lips were very, very soft. They parted beneath mine and Jehanne made a small sound of pleasure deep in her throat.

"Nice," she purred when I stopped. "Very, very nice." She hesitated, then gave me a serious look. "You were promised a Showing and you shall have one. Even the Queen is not allowed to violate the rules of Naamah's Order, and the Dowayne would never have consented to this if I weren't sincere about honoring the terms of your contract."

"Is the Queen of Terre d'Ange allowed to do such things?" I asked.

Jehanne smiled wickedly. "*I* am. You didn't let me finish. With your consent, I'd like to be alone with you first."

"I'd forgotten all about the Showing," I admitted.

She laughed. "Oh, good."

It was altogether different, and altogether lovely. Somewhere in the back of my mind, I had a brief image of my mother looking mildly aghast, but I banished it. This was a different pool of desire, but it was the same element and I moved in it gladly. And I daresay one of the only sights in the world more exquisite than Jehanne clothed was Jehanne naked. Her skin glowed like marble, her silver-gilt hair spilling in unbound coils.

"Raphael's witch." She took my hand and guided it between her thighs so I could feel her, slick and wet with desire. "Do you still think I mean to make mock of you?"

"I want to taste you," I whispered.

Jehanne kissed me, deep and languorous. "Do."

I did.

I did things to her that until now had only been done to me. Her breasts were silken and luscious, tipped with pink nipples. I lost myself in suckling on them, feeling her hands twine in my hair and her breathing quicken. I slid lower, settling between her thighs. She tasted of salt and sweet musk.

"There!" she gasped, reaching down to spread her folds and show me. "Naamah's Pearl!"

I licked and sucked avidly at the swollen pink bud, sliding two fingers deep inside her. Stone and sea, it felt good! In and out, the slow wave of pleasure rising and bursting in hard spasms. I kept going until they stopped, and a little longer.

"Oh, my." Jehanne unknotted her fists from my hair. "Are you *sure* you haven't done that before?"

"Very sure," I said breathlessly.

"Well." She twisted agilely and regarded me, then cupped my face and kissed me hard and deep. "Let's see what I have to teach you, shall we?"

As it transpired, quite a bit.

She demonstrated kisses and caresses, naming each one. Sweet and fluttering—biting and sucking. Gentle as the touch of a butterfly's wing—hard and forceful. It was a veritable banquet of pleasure.

"Enough teaching!" I pleaded at last. "Please!"

"You're sure?" she teased.

"Stone and sea, *yes*!"

Jehanne pushed her fingers into me, curling them and pressing against my inner walls in a way that made me writhe in ecstasy. "I want to watch your face." Her gaze never left mine. It heightened my arousal in a way I couldn't explain. I saw my pleasure reflected in her eyes as I climaxed over and over beneath her impossibly skilled touch. When it was over, she smiled and kissed me. "Thank you. That will be my favorite memory, I think."

"Mine, too."

She laughed and sat up, reaching for an elegant glass pitcher on the bedside table. "Wine? Love-making makes me thirsty."

"Aye, please." Behind the shining, pale fall of her hair, I could see the full scope of her marque for the first time. A vast unfamiliar flower, ivory tinted with the faintest blush of pink, climbed from the base of her spine to blossom across her lovely shoulders. I pushed her hair aside to see where the tip of the uppermost petal touched the nape of her neck. "It's beautiful. How long did it take?"

"Almost two years." Jehanne turned and handed me a wineglass. "I was just shy of my eighteenth year when it was finished."

The wine was delicious and refreshing. "How old are you now?"

Her eyes flickered. "That's a rude question to ask."

"It is?" I lowered my glass. "Why?"

"Cereus House may celebrate beauty's fleeting nature, but that doesn't mean her adepts care for reminders of the fact that their own will wither and fade," she said coolly. "Particularly from the lips of one scarce out of girlhood."

"I'm sorry, I didn't know." I touched her hand. "Don't be angry. I was only curious."

Jehanne pursed her lips. "Twenty-three."

"I think it's safe to say that you're a very, very long way from withering and fading, your majesty," I offered.

It mollified her. "Then satisfy *my* curiosity, Moirin. Why are you here? In Terre d'Ange, I mean."

For some reason, I told her the truth. "I'm supposed to have a destiny. I'm trying to find it."

She smiled a little. "A grave prophecy uttered at birth? Were you born beneath a shooting star?"

"No." I shook my head. "Nothing like that. I saw a vision. Not like in the old stories," I added hastily. "The Maghuin Dhonn haven't sought to scry the future since long before I was born. All I know is that I was meant to cross an ocean. Finding my father was the only thing I could think to do. But now . . ." I fell silent.

Jehanne finished the thought I left unspoken, her tone neutral. "Now you think you've found your destiny in Raphael de Mereliot?"

"I don't know," I murmured. "Only that he's bound up in it."

She sipped her wine, considering her reply. "Please don't think I'm being cruel or vain or seeking to manipulate you when I say this, but so long as I live, Raphael will never give his heart to you."

"Do you love him?" I asked.

"Yes." Her mouth quirked. "Unfortunately."

"And the King?"

"Him, too," Jehanne agreed. She put down her wine and reached out to run a few strands of my hair through her fingers. "Does it seem strange to you? I suppose it must. With Raphael, it's all passion and tumult, but Daniel is the anchor that grounds me."

"Not so very strange," I said. "Not so strange as you being here with me."

"Mmm." The sparkle returned to her eyes. "What if *I'm* your destiny? Did you ever think of that?"

I smiled. "My *diadh-anam* says no. But I wouldn't mind if it were true."

"Your *diadh-anam*," Jehanne repeated. "You're an odd creature to be sure, Moirin mac Fainche." She regarded me. "Is the magic real?"

"Yes."

"Will you show me?"

"Close your eyes." I set down my wineglass and took her hands in mine. I closed my own eyes and breathed in slowly. I could taste the air from the courtyard garden, but it was Jehanne's marque that came to mind. Night-blooming cereus. It was said to have a wondrous, intoxicating scent. I couldn't imagine it was headier than hers. I breathed in the scented twilight of my imagination, exhaled it softly. It settled over both of us like a caress. "There."

"Oh!" Jehanne's voice was soft with awe.

I opened my eyes. All around us, the chamber had grown soft and dim and magical. "You see it?"

Her hands tightened on mine. "I do."

I let it go. "That's my gift as I was taught to use it."

"It's lovely." Jehanne gave me a long, deep look I couldn't interpret, then sighed with regret and withdrew her hands from mine. "And time passes apace, my lovely witchling. Are you ready for your Showing?" She plucked a bell from the table. "I'll send for Etienne. We were often paired when I was an adept here."

"No." I caught her wrist.

"No?"

"I don't want to see you with another," I admitted.

Pleased and delighted, she laughed. "Ah, but I'd be remiss in my duties if I didn't teach you aught of pleasing men. Isn't that what you came for?"

I shrugged. "Be remiss."

Again, Jehanne's eyes danced. "Oh, I have a better idea." She climbed gracefully from the bed and crossed the room to rummage in a cabinet, producing an object and brandishing it. "I'll teach you to perform a *languisement* that will make grown men weep." She read my face. "You've never seen an *aide d'amour*?"

"No." I eyed the large ivory phallus she held, cradling the sculpted ballocks in the palm of her hand. Until this very moment, I hadn't imagined such things existed in the world. "No, I have not."

Jehanne smiled sweetly. "Then I'll be sure to demonstrate all its uses."

THIRTY-ONE

I returned to Raphael's townhouse in a state of dazzled fulfillment.
Jehanne.

I could feel her touch everywhere on my body, her scent clinging to
my skin. It seemed impossible that Raphael wouldn't take one look at
me and know.

"Are *you* going to tell him?" she had asked before I left.

I hadn't thought that far ahead. "I don't know." A flash of my initial
anger returned. "Will it ruin your precious game if I do?"

"No." Jehanne was unperturbed. "But he might take issue with
it and dismiss you from his house. Men don't like being played for
fools." She laughed at my expression. "Moirin, you're looking far too
sultry at the moment to glower effectively. Now come here and kiss me
farewell."

I sighed and obeyed.

She wound her soft arms around my neck, returning my kiss with
ardor. "Don't be too angry with Lianne Tremaine. She hasn't the faintest idea what I did with the information she gave me."

"Was she spying for you?" I asked.

"Oh, yes and no." Jehanne drew a line down my throat with one
fingertip. "She was perishing of curiosity in her own right and our
interests happened to align. Don't make a fuss. All she did was pass on
gossip, for which I rewarded her generously. It's not wise to trust a poet
with one's secrets, but it's not wise to cross them, either," she added.
"One good satire can make you the laughingstock of the entire City."

"Will I wake to find myself that very thing on the morrow?" I asked wryly.

"Are you having regrets?" Jehanne searched my face. The concern in her voice sounded genuine. "Oh, say you aren't, please."

With the last chords of pleasure still echoing through my body, it was hard to refuse her. "Not yet, no."

That satisfied her. "Then you won't, not on my account. One may accuse me of many things, but never violating the tenets of Naamah's Service." She gave me one last kiss, then released me. A wicked smile played around the corners of her lips. "Now go home to Raphael de Mereliot and decide whether or not you mean to tell him that his delightfully uncanny young lover just got very, very thoroughly served by his royal mistress."

Off I went in my daze.

I was hoping Raphael wouldn't be there when I returned, but it was late, twilight falling over the City. I gazed out the window of the carriage, taking comfort in the purple gloaming and wondering if I'd just made one of the most idiotic choices of my life.

It was quite possible.

Not only was Raphael already home, but he heard me return and emerged from his study to greet me.

"Well?" He looked amused.

My face grew hot. "Well?"

He folded his arms and leaned against the door-jamb. "Was it educational?"

"Oh, yes." The hot flush crept down my throat. Despite having used the wash-basin at Cereus House, I could smell my own arousal mingled with the scent of Jehanne's. "Very."

"Good." Raphael smiled lazily. "Mayhap later you'll show me what you learned."

The image of Jehanne with her lips wrapped around the *aide d'amour* flashed behind my eyes. That was before she had shown me its other uses, which had left me pleasantly sore. I cleared my throat. "It's been a long day. Tomorrow, mayhap?"

"All right." He pushed himself away from the doorway and came over to kiss me, holding the back of my head hard when I tried to pull away from him, sure that he would smell her on me. His tongue delved into my mouth. My body, still tuned to the key of desire, responded mindlessly. Raphael cupped one of my breasts and squeezed, his thumb teasing the erect nipple through the cloth of my gown. "You're sure?"

I closed my eyes. "Please. Tomorrow, I promise."

"Did you think of me?" he asked insistently.

"Aye." I took a deep breath, opened my eyes, and lied to him. "I thought of you the whole time."

Raphael let me go. "Good girl. Go freshen yourself; dinner's to be served shortly."

In my borrowed chamber, I sank onto the bed and buried my face in my hands. Stone and sea! I wasn't sure what I was feeling. A complicated knot of pleasure and guilt and confusion lay heavy in the pit of my belly.

"My lady?" There was a knock at the door.

I lifted my head. "Aye?"

Daphne entered with a ewer of fresh water for the basin. "Are you all right?" Her shy, sweet, open face looked worried. "Was it not nice?"

"No." I smiled ruefully. "It was nice."

She looked relieved. "Oh, good." Water splashed into the basin. "All the Houses of the Night Court have their specialties. But they say that Cereus House is the first and oldest and best." Daphne bustled around the chamber, examining the ball of soap to determine whether or not it needed to be replaced and laying out fresh linen towels. She glanced at me and lowered her voice in a conspiratorial manner. "Did you know that Queen Jehanne herself served as an adept at Cereus House?"

"Yes," I said softly. "So I heard."

Daphne's expression took on an unwonted hard edge. "They say her beauty and her wiles cured King Daniel of his grief after his first wife died a few years ago. He wed her out of gratitude and dotes on her yet." Her voice dropped another octave. "Even to this day, his majesty is willing to put up with all manner of her transgressions, including her dalliance with Lord Raphael."

"Oh, aye?" I rubbed my eyes. "Well, from what little I've seen, her majesty can be . . . compelling."

"That's one word for it," Daphne said darkly.

Somehow, I survived that night's dinner. For a mercy, Raphael didn't press me for details of my assignation. He was caught up in some arcane business at the Academy to which he eluded in a vague and offhand manner. Since he was being cryptic, I listened with only half an ear, caught up in my own concerns.

"May I count on your assistance, Moirin?" His eyes were intent. "Your gift may make the difference."

I shook myself. "In what?"

"The project," Raphael said steadily. "Or are you afraid?"

"Of course not." I had no idea what he was talking about. "And of course I'll do my best to aid you. Only I accepted an invitation from his highness Prince Thierry to go hunting tomorrow."

"Oh, yes." Raphael relaxed. "I'll be there as well. We can't make a new attempt for a few more days anyway."

"That's good," I said blankly.

The following day dawned sunny and bright with a hint of crisp autumnal chill in the air. I dressed in one of the riding gowns that Benoit Vallon had designed for me. I should have been excited by the prospect of a day spent outdoors. Instead, the knot in my belly had grown worse.

Poets bedamned; why in the name of stone and sea and sky and all that they encompassed had I trusted Jehanne de la Courcel?

Why hadn't I told Raphael?

At the breakfast table, I tried to tell him. But every time I opened my mouth to speak, a flash of memory came over me, followed by a hot flush. I couldn't get the words out. If he didn't think I'd played him for a fool, he'd think I was a pure blind idiot for giving Jehanne exactly what she wanted. And like as not, he would be right.

"Are you all right, Moirin?" Raphael gave me a curious glance. "You look fevered."

"I'm fine," I managed.

"Let me see." He felt at my forehead and the pulse of my wrist, then bade me stick out my tongue and peered down my throat. "All right, then. Don't overtax yourself today, mind? You're not long out of bedrest." He gave me a wry smile. "And you may have spent a good deal of time in bed yesterday, but I fear it wasn't particularly restful."

Another flush swept over me. "No. No, it was not."

Prince Thierry's invitation bade me to come unmounted and meet him in the courtyard of the royal stables. Raphael rode alongside the carriage on his own hunting steed, a glossy chestnut with powerful hindquarters. I rode in the carriage, sick with apprehension.

One good satire can make you the laughingstock of the City, Jehanne had said. Yesterday I'd taken her warning at face value.

Today I wondered if it had been a taste of things to come.

It wasn't fair. I hadn't done anything Jehanne hadn't done. But she was a highly trained courtesan. I had no doubt she could dissemble in the ways of desire as well and better than any woman. I was a half-breed of the Maghuin Dhonn with no skill whatsoever when it came to hiding my own desires. And I knew, instinctively, that if Jehanne de la Courcel put it about how gullible I'd been and how ardent a role I'd played in my own seduction, I *would* be a laughingstock.

And Raphael would despise me for lying.

I don't know which thought made me sicker.

By the time we reached the royal stables, I was strung tighter than my own bow and half ready to vomit. A footman in Courcel livery helped me from the carriage.

"Lady Moirin!" The Dauphin was standing beside a groom, who was holding the head of a glossy black filly. Thierry beckoned to me, his expression glad and friendly. "Come here, will you?"

I relaxed a measure. "She's lovely." I stroked the filly's neck. "Are you riding her today?"

"No." He grinned, took the reins from the groom, and handed them to me with a courtly bow. "You are. She's a gift."

I stared. "Whatever for?"

"Do I need a reason?" Thierry asked. "A beautiful lady should have a beautiful mount. But as it happens, she's a gift of thanks," he added. "Marc de Thibideau's a good friend and hunting companion. I'm grateful for what you did to aid him."

"It was Raphael's doing," I murmured.

"Raphael had already treated the young man in question with limited success," Raphael offered in a laconic tone from astride his tall chestnut. "Give his highness your thanks."

Unexpected tears stung my eyes. "Thank you, your highness."

"It's nothing." Thierry waved one hand in a dismissive gesture. "You're welcome to stable her here if de Mereliot doesn't have room in his."

"I've room," Raphael said curtly.

I ignored him, captivated by the gentle warmth in the filly's dark eyes. "Does she have a name?"

"D'Antilly's Midnight Blossom," Prince Thierry said cheerfully. I glanced sharply up at him, wondering if it were an oblique reference to my visit to Cereus House. He laughed. "I know, it's a mouthful. What did you say her use-name was?" he asked the groom.

"Blossom, your highness."

The filly pricked her ears.

"A bit pedestrian." Thierry shrugged. "Call her whatever you like, my lady. Her official name's only for the pedigree records."

"Blossom." When I said her name, the filly's head swung back toward me, ears pricked. I smiled. "Blossom's fine. She already knows it." I handed the reins back to the groom, then cupped the filly's velvety muzzle in my hands, blowing softly into her nostrils. She snuffed. For a moment, I was able to forget all my concerns and block out the rest of the world. I could sense her thoughts, curious and unafraid. "Hello, Blossom."

"Do bear-witches speak to animals?" a sweet, light voice inquired.

Jehanne.

I stiffened, then turned slowly. A new contingent of riders had entered the courtyard. Lianne Tremaine, the King's Poet, was among them. I couldn't read the intent on her sharp, curious face. The Queen was mounted on a pretty white mare. At the sight of her, another flush of heat washed over my skin. Her blue-grey eyes sparkled with what could be playfulness or malice. If Jehanne meant to humiliate me, I thought, she would do it now.

"We do," I made myself say. "It doesn't mean they speak back to us."

She laughed. "Fairly said!" Her gaze settled on Raphael. "My lord de Mereliot, since his majesty has pressing business elsewhere and his highness has elected to escort Lady Moirin, mayhap you would do me the kindness of serving as my escort today?"

Raphael bowed in the saddle, his voice both wry and sincere. "Your majesty, nothing would give me greater pleasure."

Jehanne smiled sweetly at him. "Oh, good."

I breathed a silent sigh of relief. It seemed I was reprieved, at least for the moment.

The hunt resembled no form of hunting I'd ever experienced. It took place in a vast meadow—a portion, Thierry informed me, of the royal hunting preserves. There were servants to attend the lords and ladies, servants to set up silk pavilions on the outskirts of the meadows where we would enjoy a luncheon. Servants to handle the sleek coursing hounds in their braces, servants to scout ahead and beat the brush for prey.

The feel of Blossom's soft mouth beneath my reins, her gentle, willing gait beneath me, made me glad. The fresh, crisp air and the melancholy of the autumn grasses we trampled filled me with poignant pleasure.

Still, I was miserable.

Jehanne.

Raphael.

They rode side by side, conversing with heads inclined toward one another in a manner that spoke of long familiarity. Sunlight glinted on her silver-gilt coronet, picked out the bright streaks of gold in his tawny locks. They looked well together. I remembered her hair spread across the pillow, his curtaining my face. I was jealous of them both.

"Tell me you're not going to moon over him all day," Prince Thierry said abruptly to me.

"I'm sorry." I gave him a guilty glance. "Was I?"

"Yes." He rode a handsome bay, his carriage upright. Ahead of us, Raphael leaned close and said somewhat and Jehanne's laughter rose. Thierry's mouth made a hard line. "*She's* in a good mood."

And well she should be, I thought. Aloud, I asked, "Why do you dislike her so?"

He bent a wry look at me. "Aside from the fact that I love and respect my father and Jehanne is a cuckolding bitch?"

"There is that," I admitted. "But is it not the D'Angeline way?"

One of the prince's companions chuckled. "Tell the truth, Thierry. The whole truth."

He flushed. "Go to hell!"

The young man who had spoken nudged his mount and jogged alongside us. He had blue-black hair tied in myriad braids that fell in a cascade. "His highness dissembles," he said affably. "He had designs on Jehanne himself. Only at fifteen, when his father found her the cure for his grief, Thierry was too young to be admitted to the Night Court. Isn't it so?"

Thierry shoved at him. "Goddamned Shahrizai!"

"Love to you, too, cousin." The other blew him a kiss, then winked at me and gave a courtly bow from his saddle. "Lady Moirin, we've not met. I'm Balthasar Shahrizai, and if you should ever wish to sample life's more piquant pleasures, I'd be honored to be your guide."

"Ah . . . thank you," I said uncertainly.

He cocked his head at me. "Do your people practice the art of *algolagnia*?"

"*Algo* . . ." I gave up. "I'm sorry. It's not a word I know."

"It's from the Hellene," Balthasar said. "*Algos*, meaning pain, and *lagnia*, meaning lust." His expression was candid and pleasant. "The art and practice of finding pleasure in pain."

I blinked. "Are you quite serious?"

"Quite." Although his expression didn't change, something predatory surfaced behind his eyes. I could feel his gift coiling around him. It had very sharp edges. "Don't dismiss it until you've tried it, my lady."

"I'll think on it," I said.

Thierry sighed. "Balthasar, go away."

At that moment, one of the beaters flushed a hare. Three of the handlers slipped their hounds from their braces. The hare dashed frantically across the meadow as the dogs gave chase, vying with one another to drive the hare toward their master. A footservant handed Thierry a loaded crossbow, an elegant weapon with decorative pearl inlay.

I unslung my bow from my shoulder and nocked an arrow, but when the hare raced past us, I didn't have the heart to shoot. I could sense its panic.

Thierry's shot went wide and someone else made the kill. "Ah, well." He handed his crossbow back to the servant to be reloaded, then looked at me and laughed. "What in Elua's name is that?"

"What?" I lowered my bow.

He nodded at it. "It's very . . . rustic. Forgive me, I wasn't thinking. I'll see you're given a proper lady's bow."

"Why?" My fingers tightened on the resilient yew-wood. "This is a perfectly good bow. My uncle Mabon made it for me."

"Ah." Thierry sobered. "I see. Were you very close to him?"

"No," I said slowly. "Not exactly." How could I explain how it was among the Maghuin Dhonn? I'd met Mabon only twice—but he was kin. I remembered hunting with him in the park in Bryn Gorrydum where he'd summoned the twilight in rolling waves, making it dance like the tunes he played on his silver pipe. He'd told me not to let the D'Angelines mock me for not knowing their ways. "It reminds me of home."

"Then you must keep it." Thierry leaned over and touched my arm. "I think it's charming. And I promise, I'll not tease you for not knowing how to hunt."

I eyed him. "I know how to hunt."

He smiled indulgently. "Not in the D'Angeline manner."

I bit my tongue on my irritation. It was true. And I didn't much care for the D'Angeline manner of hunting. No one was here because they needed to fill their supper-pot. It was sport, pure and simple. They wagered on the dogs, wagered on one another's prowess. Footmen loaded crossbows for the lords and hunted for spent bolts. The ladies wielded pretty, gilded short bows, mostly conscious of the fact that they made a delightful picture when they drew and took aim in the saddle.

To be sure, Jehanne did.

But the more frantic and terrified the hare, the more difficult the chase, the better the sport was reckoned.

By the time Prince Thierry made his kill on the fourth hare flushed, the sun was high overhead. "I'm blooded!" he called in a good-natured voice. "Shall we pause and enjoy a repast?"

From across the meadow came a chorus of agreement.

The silk pavilions beckoned. As we converged at a brisk trot, I rode beside Thierry and did my best not to moon over the fact that Raphael was saying something even *more* amusing to Jehanne, his head bent toward hers. Her laughter rose in a bright spiral. Even without seeing it,

I could picture the graceful line of her white throat, his engaging smile. Things I had recently kissed.

And then Thierry's horse stepped into a hole and stumbled hard. Thrown from the saddle, he pitched over its head with a shout.

"Elua!"

The bay shied. Beneath me, Blossom shied, too. In a sick flash of memory, I saw Cillian dead on the litter and his dented skull. But there was something else, too. Something other than Thierry's fall was spooking the horses.

I clamped my thighs around the filly, nocking an arrow without thinking. "Hold!"

She shivered and held.

It was a viper. It had been sunning itself on a low, flat rock. Now it coiled, ready to strike, its thick body ochre-red and marked with black. It raised its wedge-shaped head and tasted the air with a forked, black tongue. I breathed in the same air and tasted its fear. Like the hares, it was frightened by this invasion.

Unlike the hares, the viper had recourse.

Amid cries of alarm, Prince Thierry scrambled backward, eyes wide with fear. At his movement, the viper lunged.

"Oh, hell!" I swore and shot.

My arrow pierced the viper clean through. It caught it midlunge, pinning its writhing body to the earth.

The Master of the Hunt came at a dead run, yanking a big knife from a sheath at his belt. With one swift blow, he lopped off the snake's head. Its headless body continued to squirm unnervingly. The huntsman extended his hand to Thierry. "Are you all right, your highness?"

"Yes." The prince rose, his gaze on my face. "Thanks to Moirin."

Others came to take in the scene. Jehanne took one look at the dead viper and went white. She rounded on the huntsman in a perfect fury. "Messire Gabon, this is *unacceptable*. Is it not part of your duties to see that the royal hunting grounds are tended? Were they not combed this morning?"

"Aye, but—"

Her voice dripped poison. "Do you find your duties too onerous? Well, then—"

"Leave off, Jehanne," Thierry interrupted her. "The man can't be expected to account for every stray snake."

It did nothing to abate her anger. "He most assuredly can! You'd make excuses for the wretch when you came within a hair's breadth of dying?"

He scoffed. "As though you wouldn't rejoice to have me out of the way!"

"And leave your father without an heir?" Her delicate nostrils flared. "Your argument would carry more weight if I'd given him one of my own blood. Mayhap it's escaped your notice that I haven't yet?"

"Because you're too vain to disfigure your perfect body!" Thierry shouted at her. "It doesn't mean you wouldn't gladly see me dead!"

"Oh, I'm sure the sainted Moirin would have worked some miracle to bring you back from death's doorstep," Jehanne said in a cold voice. Her gaze moved on to me. What had passed between us only yesterday, whether genuine or false, might never have been. It seemed quite impossible to believe that I had ever seen that beautiful face soft with pleasure. "You shot the viper?"

I nodded. "Aye, your majesty."

She gave me a curt nod. "House Courcel is in your debt. You"—she pointed at the Master of the Hunt—"are dismissed from your post."

The man bowed without comment, his face heavy.

Beneath the silk pavilions, we endured a repast that would have been pleasant under other circumstances. Everyone wanted to hear about how I'd shot the viper midstrike. Thierry, recovered from his scare, told them, laughing, how he'd made fun of my bow and teased me about being unable to hunt. I smiled reluctantly. My rustic, unadorned bow of yew-wood and sinew was passed around and admired.

But the Queen's mood cast a pall over everything. I understood better that day why people spoke of her temper in awed terms. It radiated out of her like a cold fire, withering everything in its path. Raphael danced attendance on her, doing his best to coax her into better spirits to no avail.

There was talk of famous hunting accidents going back into history. It seemed Prince Imriel de la Courcel had saved his cousin the Dauphine from a boar, which had been the start of the realm's most notorious romance of the day. The details of the story were argued and Lianne Tremaine was consulted.

"Half-true," the King's Poet said. "As I recall the tale, her horse bolted, and it was Prince Imriel who went after her. Someone else killed the boar. But that was where it began." She gave Thierry and me one of her quick, foxy smiles. "Mayhap you'll follow in their footsteps and give me a great, epic romance to capture in verse."

Thierry grinned. "Mayhap we will."

"Does your *diadh-anam* say so, Moirin?" Queen Jehanne asked coolly.

I flushed. "My *diadh-anam* is disconcerted by the day's events," I offered, striving for diplomacy.

She looked away. "I see."

It was ridiculous to feel hurt, but I was—by both her frigid manner and Raphael's utter disregard. So I sat and tried to be pleasant while the others teased Prince Thierry for playing the role of the damsel in distress in our budding epic. He endured it cheerfully. I wished I *did* feel my *diadh-anam* quicken for him. I liked him well enough. One might suppose it would be a worthy destiny for one of the Maghuin Dhonn to capture the heart of the heir to Terre d'Ange. It might mean great things for my people. But the spark inside me was quiet.

For a mercy, it was decided that the remainder of the hunt was to be canceled after we dined. Thierry professed himself sore from his fall and suggested an excursion to Balm House.

"The adepts there are among the best masseurs in the world." He smiled at me. "Will you allow me to treat you? It will be my first act of thanks for your saving my life."

Miserable as I was, the idea didn't appeal. I fidgeted with my bow. "Viper bites aren't necessarily fatal, you know."

"They can be." Thierry nudged me. "Say yes."

"Mayhap Moirin has yet to recover from her visit to Cereus House yesterday," Lianne Tremaine drawled. "How *was* your assignation?"

Hot blood scalded my face. "Oh . . ." I glanced involuntarily at Jehanne. A hint of a cruel smile curved her lips. "Fine."

Lianne pressed me. "Oh, come! Who did you have?"

If I could have sunk into the earth, I would have. "Forgive me, but

I'm not accustomed to speaking freely about such matters," I said in desperation. "It's not done among the Maghuin Dhonn."

The King's Poet looked puzzled. "But you're the one told me yourself that—" She caught herself before humiliating me outright by informing the entire hunting party that Raphael de Mereliot had told me I had a lot to learn in bed.

"Oh, leave her be!" Thierry put an arm around my shoulders. "Moirin's been busy saving lives and limbs. I reckon we can give her a few days' grace to accustom herself to D'Angeline ways."

"Visiting Cereus House makes for an ambitious start," Balthasar Shahrizai observed. His vivid blue eyes studied me keenly, the sharp edges of his gift probing. "What made you choose it?"

Once again, my gaze slid toward Jehanne.

"Ah yes, of course." Balthasar smiled and said something in a foreign tongue. The others laughed.

Thierry's face darkened. "Enough," he said shortly. "Let's be off."

As we rode back toward the palace, I asked him what Balthasar had said.

"Nothing of import." He grimaced. "A Caerdicci proverb about two women competing for the same man."

"Oh." At least Balthasar had misunderstood my glance. In a way, he wasn't wrong. I *had* chosen Cereus House because Jehanne had trained there. "Thierry, do you really think she wishes you dead?"

"Jehanne?" He didn't answer right away. "No, I suppose not."

"Then why is she so angry at me for killing the viper?" I asked.

Thierry gave a short laugh. "Moirin, she's not angry at you for saving my life. She's angry because it made you the center of attention. In her world, Jehanne is the sun and the rest of us are but humble planets orbiting around her."

"Oh." It didn't make me feel better. I didn't *want* to be the center of attention. In fact, I didn't have the slightest idea what I wanted anymore. All I knew was that I was a wretched knot of conflicting desires. I wished I'd never gotten caught up in this mess, wished I didn't feel bound to Raphael, wished I'd never let Jehanne seduce me. I wished there was one person in this bedamned realm I could truly trust, so I could at least talk openly with another living soul without finding my confidence betrayed.

I wished my mother were here.

The thought made me so homesick, I nearly wept. I would have given up every gown and bauble Raphael had given me and Thierrry's lovely filly for five minutes of my mother's counsel. The meadow swam in my gaze. With one surreptitious hand, I rubbed my eyes hard enough that I saw red streaks behind my eyelids.

When I opened my eyes, I still saw a splash of red.

On the far side of the meadow, two men were coming toward us, one mounted and one on foot. It was the latter that made the red splash. He was tall and graceful, and he wore robes of crimson silk.

My heart beat faster.

"That's the Duc de Barthelme," Thierry said in a wondering tone. "What's he doing out here with a Priest of Naamah?"

"Looking for me, I hope," I whispered.

Ahead of me, I saw Raphael say something to Jehanne, then check his mount. She glanced back at me, her expression thawing visibly. She drew rein on her pretty white mare and gestured to me.

I rode forward alone.

The priest had hair the color of oak leaves, long and shining. He lifted his head and smiled as I drew near. It was a beautiful smile, calm and serene, like a gift. Everything about him was like a gift. And his eyes were very, very green. As green as grass, as green as rushes.

"Moirin, daughter of Fainche?" he asked.

I nodded.

His beautiful smile deepened. "I believe I'm your father."

THIRTY-TWO

At that moment, nothing in the world could have felt better than my father's embrace.

I didn't plan to throw myself at the man—after all, we were strangers to one another. But he had appeared like an answered prayer, and the look of simple gladness on his face as I dismounted undid me. I flung my arms around his neck. He didn't flinch or falter, only held me in his arms. I buried my face against the shoulder of his robe for a long moment, then gathered myself and pulled away.

I wiped my eyes. "Phanuel Demarre?"

"Indeed." He studied my face with wonder, then gave himself an unselfconscious shake and laughed softly. "I'm sorry. I came as soon as I heard the news. I always wondered, but it's somewhat altogether else to see you in the flesh."

He introduced me to Rogier Courcel, the Duc de Barthelme, who bowed in the saddle.

"Well met, my lady," he said politely.

The rest of the hunting party arrived. Behind the polite exchange of greetings the whispers went around, but there was no malice in them. Both Raphael and Thierry looked genuinely happy for me. Lianne Tremaine wore an odd, absent look as though she were jotting notes in her head lest the scene play out one day in some epic verse.

Even Jehanne was different in my father's presence. "Your daughter's caused quite the stir, Brother Phanuel," she commented.

My father smiled and laid one hand on my shoulder. "So I've heard."

"Surely not the latest." Something in his smile softened her tone. "Not an hour ago, she saved the Dauphin's life."

He glanced at me. "Oh?"

In the oddest way, it reminded me of my mother. "It was only a viper," I said. "They're not always fatal. I'll tell you all about it if you'd like."

"I would," he said solemnly. "I would like to hear every last little detail of your life, Moirin, from your birth to whatever uproar you've been causing. But I don't wish to interrupt." He shrugged and spread his hands with self-deprecating grace. "As I said, I came as soon as I heard."

"Oh, go," Prince Thierry said in his good-natured way. "Balm House can wait. Would you prefer to ride, Brother Phanuel? No doubt we can find a mount to spare."

My father shook his head. "I like to walk."

"Walking's nice," I agreed.

"Well, then, so be it." Thierry gestured for a servant to take my filly's reins. "I'll see her delivered to Lord de Mereliot's stables."

Raphael . . .

I'd promised yesterday that I would show him what I'd learned at Cereus House later today. I gave him a guilty look, but his grey eyes were gentle and warm. No stormclouds.

"This is what you came to find," he reminded me. "Go and enjoy one another's company. My household will be open to you day or night."

I looked shyly at my father.

He tilted his head, sunlight spinning the shining length of his oak-brown hair, and reached out one hand. "Shall we?"

I clasped his hand. "Aye."

We walked.

We talked.

I wanted first to hear the story of my conception. I suppose it might have been strange for some, but my father was a Priest of Naamah and he had no compunctions in discussing such matters. He told me about how he'd first glimpsed my mother at Lord Tiernan's coronation, hovering near the doors of the Hall of Innisclan.

"Such an eldritch little thing she was!" he marveled. "Such dark, wild eyes! I knew right away she must be of the Maghuin Dhonn. No one else mortal could have looked so uncanny in that place."

"Did it scare you?" I asked.

He shook his head. "It drew me."

"Why?"

"I don't know," he said softly. "Only that it did, and that Naamah smiled on it. You've a look of your mother, you know."

I smiled wryly. "Here they say I've a look of you."

"Both," my father acknowledged. "For I knew you in an instant."

It was true. I stole glances at him as we walked through the royal hunting grounds and I told him of my childhood and youth in Alba. After two weeks in the City of Elua, I was far more familiar with my own appearance than I'd ever been in my life. The line of his jaw and throat—I'd inherited those. His full, generous lips, too, although I was quite certain my smile didn't have the same calm beauty. I looked at our clasped hands. Like mine, his fingers were long and tapered. They squeezed mine in warm sympathy when I told him about Cillian.

We paused in a glade where he showed me a spring half-hidden beneath browning ferns. The water was cold and good. My father perched on a low, rocky ledge, his robes spilling around him.

"Is that why you left?" he asked. "Cillian's death?"

I touched the dying fronds with the tip of one finger. Already, the plants were half-asleep, dwindling into their roots. "No. Do you sense plants? What they're feeling?"

"Sense them?" He knit his brows. "How?"

"Like these." The brown fronds rustled when I stroked them. "They're going to sleep for the winter."

"I can *see* that they are," he said. "That's not what you mean, is it?"

"No." I blew a few dry spores from the back of my hand. "I thought mayhap it was a gift of Anael's line. You're of his lineage as well as Naamah's, are you not?"

My father looked surprised. "How did you know?"

"The priestess at the temple told me," I admitted. "But I've seen him in my thoughts, too. When I was little, I called him the man with the seedling."

"Naamah, too?"

I nodded. "The bright lady. The first time I saw her was the first time I remember Oengus coming to visit, and he and my mother went into the woods to make love."

"Oengus?" he inquired, then waved away the question. "No mind, that's not important. Is that why you came, then? Did the gods of Terre d'Ange call to you?"

"No." I shifted restlessly. "It's not that they *didn't*, but . . ." I decided to simply ask. "Do I have a destiny?"

My father blinked. "I imagine so."

"But you don't know what it is?" I pressed.

"It's not given to any of us to know our destinies," he said gently. "Is *that* why you left Alba?"

I sighed. "Aye. There's a sacred rite among my folk where the charge was laid upon me. I want to tell you about it. I do, truly. But I've never spoken of it to anyone save the Maghuin Dhonn."

"Then wait. If and when you're ready, I'm glad to listen." He smiled. "You might tell me of your adventures in the City. Folk are saying you've a miraculous gift for healing and you've stolen Raphael de Mereliot from the Queen."

I made a face. "Did he *look* stolen?"

"Not particularly."

Once I began talking, the story poured out of me. How Raphael's carriage had struck me in the street, how he'd taken me in and cared for me. How my *diadh-anam* had responded to him. How I'd let him use me as a pawn in his quarrel with the Queen; and then how we had combined my gift with his skill to save a man's life at the King's fête.

Even though I could see he had questions, my father listened without comment, letting the torrent flow. He didn't speak until I paused to draw breath.

"A complicated matter," he murmured.

"It gets worse," I said miserably. I told him how the King's Poet had convinced me to schedule an assignation at Cereus House, how I had gone and found Queen Jehanne there waiting for me. "I thought she meant to confront me. Instead . . ." My face grew hot. "Well, she was there for another reason."

My father's green eyes widened. "You didn't."

I nodded.

He looked away, looked fixedly at the ground.

"I'm sorry!" Shame deepened my flush. "I shouldn't be telling you this, should I? It's just that there's no one I can trust. And now I've lied to Raphael about it and he'll hate me when he finds out, and Jehanne's just waiting for the right moment to humiliate me with it." My father couldn't even bring himself to look at me, and I hated myself for disappointing him before we'd even met. "I know it was a foolish thing to do!" I said in a desperate tone. "I'm sorry! It was very, very stupid to let myself be seduced by someone who wishes me ill, no matter how nice she smells!"

His shoulders shook.

A new suspicion dawned. "Are you laughing at me?"

"Not quite." My father lifted his head. His face was red with the effort of suppressing his laughter, and there were tears of helpless mirth in his eyes. "Name of Elua! You've done a remarkable job of getting yourself entangled in a very large mess in a very short time."

I heaved a sigh. "I know."

"All right, all right." He collected himself, dabbing at his eyes with the sleeve of his robe. "The Queen approached you in the role of an adept?" he asked. I nodded. "Then she *won't* use it against you," he said firmly. "She'll let you think she will, but she won't. She can't. Not without being censured by Naamah's Order for dishonoring her vow. And believe me, Jehanne de la Courcel does *not* want that to happen."

It gave me hope. "You're sure?"

"Very sure." My father gave me one of his lovely smiles. "Jehanne takes great pleasure in being the Queen of Terre d'Ange and great pride in being the foremost courtesan of her day. She won't risk losing her status as the latter."

"You're *sure*," I said again.

"Yes." He stroked my hair. "Moirin, you're descended from a long line of priests and priestesses who have served Naamah with honor and distinction. Your great-great-grandmother was the first royal companion. And *her* mother was the first to welcome Phèdre nó Delaunay herself to Naamah's temple. You're not to be ashamed for doing what comes naturally to one of our blood. I won't allow it."

I leaned against him. "No?"

My father kissed my temple. "No."

We sat for a time in companionable silence. I could feel the warmth of his body through the fine silk robes, the steady rise and fall of his ribcage as he breathed. There was nothing more in it. He was my father; I was his daughter. The half-hidden spring burbled at our feet. The oak trees that dotted the landscape blazed with vivid hues of gold and russet and crimson, flaunting their majesty before it was time to surrender to winter's sleep and sink deep into their roots. The dark green pine trees hoarded their needles and gloated.

"The sacred rite I spoke of before is a rite of passage," I said at length. "I underwent it after Cillian was killed. And I saw Her."

He looked at me. "Her?"

I swallowed. "The Maghuin Dhonn Herself."

"You saw a bear?"

"Not just any bear." I wanted him to understand. "*Her.* I passed through the stone doorway and waited. Waited and waited. It was beautiful there. Bright and dark all at once. When She came, She blotted out the stars. Then She shaped Herself to a mortal scale. She gazed on me and breathed on me and acknowledged me as one of Her own. I would have stayed there forever if She'd let me and followed Her to the ends of the earth."

My father's voice was grave. "But she didn't."

"No." I shook my head. "She turned away from me. Stone and sea! Her eyes. She looked so very, very sad. And in the doorway . . ."

"Yes?"

"I saw the sea." I shivered. "Sunlight on the waves, gulls crying. All I knew was that I was meant to go. That I couldn't stay in Alba. And I didn't know where else to go but here. I hoped you might tell me why."

"I wish I could." He was quiet a moment. "You said your . . . *diadh-anam* . . . recognized Raphael de Mereliot. Is he the only one?"

I started to say yes, then remembered. "No. There was one other. Master Lo Feng, the Ch'in physician. He's Raphael's mentor."

"Ch'in, eh?" My father looked startled, but he shrugged. "Well, mayhap Raphael was only the bridge meant to guide you to him."

"Mayhap." I wasn't sure how I liked the idea.

My father looked sidelong at me. "You're not ready to surrender the notion of Raphael de Mereliot, are you?"

"No." I put one hand on my chest. "It *is* a very strong feeling. And it hasn't gone away. We are bound together somehow."

"And Jehanne?"

"Ohhh . . ." My cheeks turned warm. "No, that had nothing to do with my *diadh-anam*."

"That's good." He smiled a little. "At least it makes matters a bit less complicated."

I sighed. "It was still foolish."

My father gazed into the distance. "There's no folly in desire. Jehanne is very beautiful. She may not be an exemplary ruler, but she was always an outstanding courtesan." He smiled again. "And she does smell very nice."

"Mm-hmm." I tried not to remember.

He laughed. "There's a reason for it. They say his majesty had a special fragrance concocted in her honor as a patron-gift when he was courting her. No one else is allowed to wear it and the head of the Perfumers' Guild has sworn to take the formula to his grave."

"Terre d'Ange is a strange place," I mused.

"Says my strange child." My father rose with easy grace, scarlet robes flowing. He gave me his hand and helped me to my feet. "Would that I had better counsel for you, Moirin," he said soberly. "You come from a culture that is foreign to me. I cannot speak to the will of the Maghuin Dhonn, and I've had no practice in being a father. But I am very pleased to find myself one, and honored to have you in my life. Whatever the purpose drew your mother and I together, I hope you find it."

I searched his face. "You're not disappointed in me?"

"Name of Elua, no!" He let go my hand and touched my cheek. His smile curved his lips and lit his eyes. "You're a wonderment."

I had a father.

I liked him very, very much.

THIRTY-THREE

I passed the night in the Temple of Naamah that had been built in honor of my great-great-grandmother.

In the City, I'd seen how my father was loved.

Even folk who didn't know him, loved him.

We walked through the marketplace together. Amid the clamor of vendors hawking their wares, a little silence followed him. Men and women lifted their heads and gazed after him, abandoning their tasks. He gave them his gentle smile like a gift.

They smiled back.

In the Tsingani quarter where the temple was located, the same sallow-faced woman I'd seen on my first visit was once again hanging laundry on her balcony. She gazed down at my father in his red silk robes, her hands going still and her face softening. He lifted his head, smiling at her. For a moment, she was beautiful.

When I glanced at him out of the corner of my eye, I saw his gifts coiling around him, green and gold shimmers in the air, warm and embracing, like a blessing made visible. The heritage of Naamah and Anael.

"Your gifts are lovely," I murmured.

His brows quirked. "You *see* them?"

I nodded.

"Strange child." He kissed my forehead. "Would that I could see through your eyes."

"So do I," I whispered.

At the temple, Noémie d'Etoile welcomed us gladly. We ate and drank and talked until the small hours of the night. There was a young couple seeking refuge there—a sweet young lass and a stalwart lad from a prestigious family in Camlach who opposed their union. Before we dispatched them to their bed, my father gave them good counsel and promised to travel to Camlach to speak to the lad's family on their behalf. Although I understood it was in keeping with his priest's oath, it saddened me to think of his leaving so soon.

"Will you come back?" I asked him in the morning.

"Of course," he said promptly. "Do you think you might manage to avoid further entangling yourself until I do?"

"I can try."

He laughed. "Seek out the Ch'in physician you mentioned. If he's truly linked to whatever destiny awaits you, mayhap he'll have some wisdom to impart."

"I'll do that," I agreed.

I accompanied him as he performed the morning's rite to honor Naamah, pouring out offerings of wine and honey and invoking her aid in removing obstacles from the course of troubled lovers. Noémie watched with approval.

"It's always such a pleasure to have Phanuel here," she said softly. "Do you suppose you might follow in his footsteps and enter Naamah's Service?"

I gazed at the marble effigy's sunlit face, tranquil and beautiful. "As an adept or a priestess?"

"Either path would be open to you," Noémie said. "The path of the adept holds the promise of wealth and prestige. The rewards of the path of priesthood are deeper and more profound."

I thought about the mantle of grace that lay over my father, the smiles of pleasure that trailed in his wake. I thought I understood. But when I tried to envision myself doing the same, my *diadh-anam* flickered with alarm. The majestic face of the Maghuin Dhonn Herself rose before me, and I remembered the vast sense of joy and pride I'd felt when She claimed me as Her own. It could be lost, all lost.

When I blinked, the vision faded, but the feelings lingered.

"No," I said with regret. "That I am Naamah's in part, I do not doubt. I've long felt her presence in my life. But I am first and always a child of the Maghuin Dhonn, and I cannot swear an oath to serve another."

"A pity," Noémie murmured.

"I have a daughter who worships a bear," my father remarked, having finished his offering.

Noémie d'Etoile went pale.

"You would understand if you saw Her," I said. "And I cannot help who I am."

"I like who you are." He smiled at me. "And I do not expect you to forsake your heritage. Only that if the gods of Terre d'Ange speak to you, you listen to them as well. It may be that their will accords with hers."

"I will listen," I promised.

After we broke our fast at the temple, my father escorted me back to Raphael's townhouse. We passed through Elua's Square so I could visit the great oak there. I told my father it remembered being planted by Elua and Anael. He shook his head in wonder, gazing up at the mighty crown of branches. I leaned my cheek against the rough bark and listened with pleasure to the oak tree's slow, ancient thoughts.

And then, all too soon, it was time to say farewell.

I invited my father inside, but he declined. "The sooner I leave, the sooner I'll return."

"I wish you didn't have to go. I'll miss you." Even though I'd known him only a day, it was true. "If Blessed Elua bade his people to love as they will, why do families like that lad's seek to keep lovers apart?"

He smiled wryly. "Because people are human and imperfect. We let matters of status and wealth affect our judgment."

"*You* don't."

"I try." He gave me one last warm embrace. "And if you're your mother's child, I suspect you don't, either. Take care of yourself, and I'll be back in a month's time to see if you've found your destiny."

"All right," I whispered.

I watched my father walk away, his crimson robes swaying gently around him. At the end of the street, he turned and gave me one of his lovely smiles.

Then he was gone.

I sighed and went inside.

Raphael wasn't there, but he'd left word that he hoped I would join him in attending a dinner party that evening hosted by the Comte de Thibideau. One of Prince Thierry's men had delivered the filly Blossom along with a letter congratulating me on reuniting with my father and expressing the hope that I would join him on a delayed excursion to Balm House that afternoon. And Daphne told me that Benoit Vallon had sent a messenger from Atelier Favrielle saying that there were more garments ready to be fitted.

"He said that now that you're well enough to thoroughly disregard his advice, you can present yourself at the atelier." She handed me a package wrapped in pretty paper. "What advice was that?"

"Advice I probably should have heeded." I examined the package. "Who is this from?"

"It's a token of thanks from Cereus House." Daphne looked puzzled. "I've never heard of the like. It must be a new custom."

I unwrapped the package to find a well-worn book titled *Trois Milles Joies*. When I opened the book at random, I was confronted with the image of a man and woman engaged in an act called The Rutting Stag. The faint, unmistakable scent of Jehanne's perfume rose from the pages. Both things sent an unexpected bolt of desire through me. In the back of my mind, I could see her eyes dance with amusement.

"How very thoughtful." I closed the book quickly. "Daphne, I thought I might go to the Academy of Occult Philosophy to seek out Master Lo Feng. Is that inappropriate?"

"I don't see why it would be." She eyed me. "But whatever for?"

"I liked him."

She shivered. "Somewhat about him makes my skin crawl. It's those slanty eyes, I reckon. You don't know what he's thinking."

"Really?" I was surprised. "I thought he was lovely."

Daphne shrugged. "They say the Ch'in eat dogs. They're barbarians."

"Well, I'm not a dog, so I've naught to fear." I didn't feel like arguing with her. "If Raphael returns before me, tell him I'll be pleased to accompany him tonight. And, um . . . do I need to reply to Prince Thierry?"

"Aye, my lady. I'll have paper and ink sent to your chambers." She gave me a disapproving look. "Though you oughtn't turn down an invitation from the Dauphin for no good cause."

"Why?" I asked. "I don't wish to go to Balm House with him."

"But he's the *Dauphin*!"

"Oh, aye," I said wryly. "And his status and wealth should dictate my desires?" Daphne looked hurt, and I immediately felt guilty. My father might have made the same point, but he'd have done it with grace. "I'm sorry." I gave her a quick hug. "I know you mean well."

She sniffed. "Don't forget about Atelier Favrielle."

"I won't."

It was a blessed relief to ride out of the City and across the ancient Tiberian bridge in the open air. Blossom thought so, too. I let my thoughts ease into hers. We got on well together. She was gentle and willing and needed little direction. I let the reins lie slack and guided her with my knees, watching the water of the Aviline River slide past us, laughing when the sun emerged from behind a bank of clouds and Blossom shied and pricked her ears at her own shadow cast in sharp relief on the venerable stones.

"Silly," I said fondly. "It's only your shadow."

The thought seemed to amuse her. Blossom arched her neck and picked up her gait, trampling her own shadow defiantly.

In the courtyard of the Academy, I turned her over to an ostler's care. She looked at me with prick-eared alarm. "It's only for a little while," I assured her, and she relaxed.

The ostler clucked his tongue in a friendly manner. "Smart one, isn't she? You'd almost think she understands you."

I smiled. "Almost, aye. Do you know where I might find Master Lo Feng?"

"That Ch'in fellow?" He jerked his thumb toward the west, his expression hardening. "Try the glass pavilion."

I thanked him and set out in search of it.

The Academy was a sprawling complex with a multitude of passageways and hidden courtyards. Twice, I had to ask passing scholars for directions. They obliged with an air of pleasant distraction. Once I found it, I felt foolish for having had to ask.

The glass pavilion was exactly that: a vast pavilion made wholly of glass. I stood for a moment and gaped at it. I couldn't even begin to imagine how it had been built. The domed roof rose high into the air. The structure that supported it was made of white-washed iron as delicate and intricate as lace. Countless panes of glass glittered in the sunlight.

And behind them, greenery.

It was filled with plants.

At length I found the door and opened it. Warm air wafted out, redolent with moisture and the aroma of green, growing life. I stepped inside and shivered with pleasure. If one had to be indoors, surely this must be the most wondrous place on earth.

A pretty young woman watering an unfamiliar tree glanced up. "May I assist you, my lady?"

"I'm looking for Master Lo Feng."

"Ah." She smiled and pointed. "You'll find him in the bamboo gallery."

"My thanks." I came over to touch the tree's slender, ridged trunk. At the top, fronds like giant ferns radiated outward, brown hairy seeds as large as a child's head clustered beneath them. "Who's this fellow?"

Her smile deepened. "He's a coconut palm."

In its placid thoughts, the tree dreamed of warm breezes murmuring through its fronds. Almost all the plants in the glass pavilion did. I glanced around. "Forgive me, but what does this place have to do with occult philosophy?"

The young woman laughed. "It depends on who you ask, but in my opinion, not much. It was commissioned by Gautier de la Courcel to house the exotic species he brought back from his travels. The Academy seemed as good a place as any."

"Gautier de la Courcel." I remembered Thierry pointing out his portrait and telling me it was his grandfather. "He's the one who vanished?"

"Aye." She sobered. "Searching for the Book of Raziel." She stroked the palm tree's trunk. "He should have stuck to plants." Her bright, curious gaze studied me. "Are you the bear-wit—" She caught herself.

"Moirin," I said wryly. "Of the Maghuin Dhonn."

"I'm sorry, my lady." She colored prettily. "I'm Marie-Thèrese. Welcome."

I thanked her and went on in the direction she'd indicated, deeper into the pavilion, breathing the air with relish. Heat rose from beneath my feet. The panes of glass high above me were opaque with mist. I saw an archway onto a middle section where a grove of tall, slender plants grew on segmented stalks. Their leaves were thin, pointed, and graceful. I felt my *diadh-anam* quicken inside me.

It was somehow familiar.

Master Lo Feng's surly lad lounged in the archway, sitting with one knee drawn up loosely. He looked indolent and bored, but when I approached, his segmented staff swept up to bar my passage. He spared me one glittering black glance from beneath his shock of hair, then looked away, his nostrils flaring.

"You no bother him now," he said with disdain.

Bao. That was his name. Beyond him, I could see Lo Feng seated on a stool in the midst of the grove, wielding a brush on an easel propped before him.

"Will you tell him I'm here?" I asked politely.

He refused to meet my eyes. "You no bother him, D'Angeline girl."

It irked me.

I took a step backward and summoned the twilight. This was a man-made place, but it was a *green* place. My gift came easy. I blew it out, warm and balmy, wrapping myself in tropical dimness. The glass pavilion turned soft and muted and glimmering in my vision, and I had the satisfaction of seeing Bao leap to his feet with a sharp cry and unexpected agility. He lunged forward, his staff sweeping toward my head.

I ducked beneath it and passed through the archway.

"Hahhh!" There was a staccato sound behind me, a breeze passing above me as Bao's entire body arced over my head. He landed in front of me in a crouch, wide- and wild-eyed, his staff spinning expertly in his hands as he straightened and advanced on me. A torrent of incomprehensible Ch'in poured from his lips.

"Stone and sea!" I scrambled backward, losing my grip on the twilight. The world turned sunlit and green. He blinked at my sudden appearance. I glared at him. "What are you trying to do? Kill me?"

He glared back at me. "Yes!"

Master Lo Feng rose. "Bao."

His lean shoulders tensed; then he planted the butt of his staff with an abrupt thrust. They had an exchange in Ch'in. From what I could discern, Master Lo Feng sounded gentle and reproving, and his surly lad defensive. It ended with Bao inclining his head, clearly unhappy. Still, he stepped aside.

"Lady Moirin." Lo Feng clasped his hands together and bowed. The corners of his eyes crinkled. I still thought him lovely. "You honor me."

"I intrude," I said in apology.

"No, no." He beckoned. "Come and see a humble scholar's attempt at art."

I followed him into the bamboo gallery. A scroll of paper was stretched vertically on his easel. In a handful of elegant brushstrokes, he had captured the essence of the tame grove, using only black ink, each stroke filled with purpose. I traced the graceful lines of the bamboo, not quite touching the soft, absorbent paper.

"They yearn to bend and sway," I said.

"Yes," he agreed. "They do."

I pointed to three lines of strange characters. "And this? This is writing in your alphabet?"

"It's a poem." Master Lo Feng said in a tranquil tone.

I searched his face. "Will you tell it to me?"

He inclined his head. "Leaves like green spears seek to pierce the glass dome of Heaven; leaves seek and fail. The air breathes in a quiet hush. Beneath the bamboo, I am melancholy."

"That's very beautiful," I said.

"It is a poor translation," he said modestly. "But I would be honored if you would accept this painting as a gift."

"Ah, no!" I protested. "You're too kind."

"Not at all." After determining that the ink was sufficiently dry, Master Lo Feng took the scroll from its easel and rolled it. He presented it to me with a bow. "The other day, you gave me the gift of wonder. This is a small gift to give in return."

I accepted it. "Thank you. I will treasure it."

"May I ask how you got through the entry past Bao just now?" he inquired. "No one gets past Bao."

Bao, leaning on his staff, muttered darkly.

"Oh." I flushed. "I'm sorry. He did say you weren't to be bothered."

"Bao is rude and overprotective," Master Lo Feng said calmly. "I am not angered. I wish to know."

I told him.

"Hmm." His expression was thoughtful. "You draw *yin* energy from the earth itself in the spirit world. Is this what you used to heal the young man's broken bone the other day?"

"Aye," I said. "Only *I* didn't use it, Raphael did."

"You cannot do it on your own?" he asked.

I shook my head. "Only with plants."

Lo Feng's eyes shone. "Will you show me?"

I glanced around. "Everything here is healthy. I could quicken it. Coax it to flower."

Bao snickered.

"This species flowers but once every hundred years," Master Lo Feng said apologetically. "It is a rare event. Perhaps we should—"

I closed my eyes and breathed in the twilight.

Laid my hand on the nearest stalk and breathed it out.

Coaxing.

Although it was quiet, it felt like a shout. The energy passed through me, passed into the slender stalk, leaving me drained in a pleasant way. It raced upward and downward. Travelled beneath our feet through an intricate series of connected roots and rhizomes. A little breeze sprang up. The spear-shaped leaves rustled.

All at once, the bamboo flowered.

All at once.

I sank to my knees, happy.

"Lady Moirin?" Master Lo Feng stooped before me. Concern was written on his face. Over his shoulder, I could see Bao scowling. Inside my breast, my *diadh-anam* pulsed. "Are you well?"

"Yes." I smiled at him. "Would you take me on as a student?"

His eyes crinkled. "Of what?"

"Whatever you deem fit."

He smiled back at me. "Of course."

THIRTY-FOUR

I will begin by teaching you to breathe," Master Lo Feng said the following day when we met in the Academy's gardens.

I blinked at him. "What?"

"It is the essential process by which we draw energy into ourselves—for you, even more than most. It lies at the heart of your gift. And although this magic of yours is foreign to me, I believe I may help you hone your ability to wield it." He gestured to Bao, who whipped his staff off his shoulder and twirled it. Three mats of woven palm fronds unfurled. Bao arranged them on the grass. Master Lo Feng sat cross-legged on one. "Sit."

I sat.

Bao followed suit, his back upright, his staff across his knees.

"Does he ever let go of that thing?" I asked.

"Do not concern yourself with Bao," Lo Feng said. "Now. The Five Styles of Breathing correspond to the Five Elements. We will begin with the one that is near to your own essence, the Breath of the Pulse of the Earth."

He told me to concentrate on the earth beneath me, to inhale and exhale through the mouth. To draw the breath into the deepest part of my belly, to the very pit of my groin. To listen for the slow pulse of the earth and match the rhythm of my breath to it.

"That's all?" I asked.

"Yes," he said simply. "For now."

For such a simple thing, it was surprisingly difficult. I found myself distracted by passing scholars shaking their heads, by a bell ringing in a tower summoning them to a lecture, by ants crawling on a nearby chrysanthemum.

"You are not going deep enough," Master Lo Feng said in reproof. "Do not focus on the things that live and grow upon the earth's surface. Close your eyes and listen for its pulse."

I closed my eyes and listened.

"You are breathing through your nose."

"Oh." I breathed through my mouth.

"Breathe into your belly, not your chest," he said.

I breathed into my belly, slow and steady. For a time, there was silence. Mayhap it meant I was doing well. I cracked open my eyes and peeked. Master Lo Feng's eyes were closed, his face as serene as a statue's. Bao's eyes were half-lidded, dark, glittering slits watching me. He drew deep, even breaths between parted lips.

"Moirin, do not concern yourself with Bao," Master Lo Feng said without opening his eyes.

"Bao is concerning himself with me," I complained.

"Ignore him."

I tried harder. I closed my eyes again. I thought about the earth beneath me and how deep it went. Deeper than the taproot of Elua's Oak. I listened for its pulse. I drew breath deep into the pit of my belly and breathed it out slowly. I thought about the bright and dark world beyond the stone doorway, and how the tread of the Maghuin Dhonn Herself had made the ground tremble.

A measured tread, slow and stately.

Terrible.

Beautiful.

Like a heartbeat.

When the bell in the tower rang a second time, it seemed faint and distant, summoning me back to myself.

"Oh!" I opened my eyes with an effort, my lids feeling oddly heavy. The shadows cast by plants and shrubs in the garden had moved. A good deal more time than I reckoned had passed.

Master Lo Feng's eyes crinkled. "Well done."

"Was it?"

"Indeed." He struggled to rise. Bao was on his feet in a flash, planting his staff and lending his master a solicitous hand. Master Lo Feng accepted it without a trace of embarrassment. "Old knees," he said ruefully. "Forgive me. Proper breathing will prolong life, but mortal flesh and bone is still mortal."

Bao muttered under his breath in Ch'in.

Master Lo Feng ignored him. "So. You bade me teach you as I saw fit. Will you continue?"

"Is this what you taught Raphael?" I asked.

He shook his head. "No."

"Why?"

"It is not what he wished to learn," he said patiently. "Nor where his gifts lay. Lady Moirin, I ask again: Is it your will to continue?"

I took a deep, experimental breath. My body reverberated with the memory of the Maghuin Dhonn's heavy tread shaking the earth, and the earth's answering pulse. My *diadh-anam* sang inside me. "It is."

He bowed. "Come tomorrow."

I thought Raphael might laugh when I told him that night at dinner that Master Lo Feng was teaching me to breathe, but he didn't.

"Odd as it sounds, there may be merit in it," he said. "I've found it to be true in other matters. As I said before, the Ch'in believe energy flows through the body in specific patterns, concentrating in various points. Under his tutelage, I've learned to sense and manipulate it." He smiled at me. "Greatly more so with your aid. I'm eager to see if that holds true in other endeavors."

"Your secret project?" I guessed.

Raphael nodded. "Make no mistake, Moirin," he said in a somber tone. "This *is* a private matter and you're not to discuss it outside the Circle."

"The Circle?"

"A handful of scholars dedicated to pursuing knowledge. We call ourselves the Circle of Shalomon." He hesitated. "It's naught that's illegal or treasonous, I promise, and we will follow every safeguard and take every precaution. But there are those in the realm who would question the wisdom of our pursuit. Once we've succeeded, it will be different."

I frowned, sopping up meat juices with a piece of bread. "May I ask exactly what it is that you're attempting to do?"

Raphael glanced at the chef standing beside the tray with the roast, the manservant hovering beside him. "You may ask, but I've said as much as discretion permits. I'll divulge no details here. Tomorrow. All right?"

"Oh, I don't know." I eyed him. "What will you give me in exchange for my aid and patience, my lord de Mereliot?"

He smiled. "What did you have in mind?"

"You fell asleep in a rather inconsiderate fashion last night," I pointed out. I'd kept my word and performed the *languisement* Jehanne had taught me. It hadn't made him weep, but it had pleased him greatly. And to be fair, I hadn't followed her instructions to the letter. I wasn't entirely sure she hadn't been teasing about putting my finger in his bottom. She had looked altogether too amused at my reaction to the suggestion. Once I could get past being disconcerted by the lingering scent of her perfume, I'd have to spend some time reading the book on Naamah's arts she had sent me.

"Consider it a tribute," Raphael said.

"Consider this a request," I replied.

He laughed and granted it.

It was nice, the nicest it had been between us that night. Raphael was thorough and considerate, taking his time to please me. I loved the feeling of him inside me, moving in and out, the slow waves of pleasure building. I loved the golden warmth of him. I loved the feeling of his shoulder blades beneath my hands, his hips rocking between my thighs. I matched my breathing to his, Master Lo Feng's lessons somewhere in the back of my mind. I wished it could always be this nice and simple.

Afterward, Raphael slept.

I lay awake for a time, my body sated, but my mind still alert. Raphael sleeping looked younger and more vulnerable. I stroked his tawny, silken hair. "What are you up to, Raphael de Mereliot?" I murmured. "What manner of business best left unsaid before your household?"

He sighed in his sleep and said Jehanne's name.

I fought the urge to tweak his hair. "She's always there between us, isn't she?" I said ruefully. "More than you know. But whatever it is you seek in this mysterious pursuit, it seems only I can give it to you."

He sighed again, wordless.

"Oh, fine." I kissed his cheek. "Sleep."

On the morrow, I had another lesson with Master Lo Feng and the ubiquitous Bao and his ubiquitous staff. I thought the Ch'in physician would teach me another style of breathing, but I was wrong. He merely sat on his mat with his legs folded and bade me practice the Breath of the Pulse of the Earth.

I practiced.

It came easier this time. I got bored, but then the boredom passed. I went deeper into the earth and deeper into my own body, feeling the energy pool and gather in the pit of my groin. There, it sat and radiated, waiting to be tapped. It wasn't a sexual feeling, but almost. I liked it.

"Very good," Lo Feng said when we had finished. The corners of his eyes crinkled in that lovely hint of a smile. "Are you sure there is no Ch'in blood in the People of the Brown Bear?" He glanced at Bao. "Or Tatar, perhaps?"

"No," I admitted. "We came to Alba from far away a long, long time ago when the world was covered with ice. Is Bao a Tatar?"

Bao shot me a scathing look, his fingers tightening on his staff.

"His father was," Master Lo Feng said calmly. "It happened during a raid. Through no fault of his own, Bao is a child of violence."

Bao surged to his feet and stomped away, the butt of his staff stabbing at the grass. A moment later, he stomped back and helped his mentor to his feet, averting his face to hide an expression of rough tenderness.

"Do you ever smile?" I asked him.

"Do you ever stop asking stupid questions?" Bao retorted in heavily accented D'Angeline.

"Yes," I said—and said no more.

His lips twitched.

"You nearly did." I pointed at him. "I saw it. You very nearly smiled."

"Children." Lo Feng's voice silenced us. He shook his elegant head, casting his gaze skyward. "Will you spend your energy wastefully in foolish bickering, or will you conduct yourselves as students of the Way in dignity and discipline?"

I inclined my head. "I'm sorry."

Bao muttered.

Master Lo Feng laid a hand on his shoulder and said something soft and gentle and lengthy in Ch'in. I saw Bao's wiry shoulders hunch and tense, then relax. He propped his staff in the crook of his arm and bowed in the Ch'in manner, hands clasped, an expression of aching yearning on his face as he gazed at his mentor. It wasn't meant to be observed, and I looked away.

"Tomorrow?" Lo Feng inquired.

I nodded. "Tomorrow."

We parted, walking in different directions. I glanced over my shoulder as I made for the Academy stables and caught Bao glancing back at me.

He almost smiled.

Almost.

THIRTY-FIVE

Raphael had arranged for an early dinner that night. After we dined, he called for his carriage and we headed out of the City. When I asked where we were bound, he said it was to a country estate owned by Denis de Toluard's family.

"He comes from a long line of Siovalese peers with a penchant for the scientific arts," he said. "Most were engineers, but his father was fascinated by the occult sciences and studied at the Academy here. He purchased this estate and modified it that he might carry on his studies more extensively."

That told me very little. "I see."

He gave me a quick look. "It's not necessary that you understand what we undertake tonight, Moirin. Only that you lend me your magic."

I folded my arms. "Yes, well, I'd like the chance to try and understand."

"All right." Raphael nodded. "You know that Blessed Elua's Companions were once divine servants of the One God of the Yeshuites? And that they forsook their posts to follow Elua?"

"I do," I said.

"During the time before they passed into the Terre d'Ange-that-lies-beyond, they taught many arts to the folk of Terre d'Ange." He ticked them off on his fingers. "Engineering, architecture, music, healing, pleasure, husbandry, seafaring, warcraft . . . all the gifts we enjoy today. But there are other gifts they did not teach us." He lowered his voice. "And other divine entities who have not served the One God for many thousands of years."

"Why?" I asked.

"They rebelled when he set his son Yeshua ben Yosef above them, lost a battle, and fell from grace," Raphael said. "But they still possess much arcane wisdom. And there is an ancient manual that tells how they may be summoned and compelled to divulge their secrets. King Shalomon of the Habiru wrote it."

I glanced out the window. The sun was setting, gilding the landscape. I thought about watching twilight settle over the burial mound in Clunderry, the grave vigil of remembrance my people undertook there at Midsummer. "The Maghuin Dhonn learned it is not always wise to pursue such things."

"Shall all the world remain ignorant because the Maghuin Dhonn made a mistake a hundred years ago?" Raphael asked in a steady voice.

"No. I don't know." I sighed. "What manner of gifts?"

He leaned forward, bracing his forearms on his knees. "The hidden qualities of herbs and minerals. The ability to speak the tongue of animals. The ability to forge friendship between foes. Does that sound so terrible?"

"No," I admitted.

"One of the greater spirits holds the secret of the commanding the wind and seas," he said in awe. "The very gift the Master of the Straits once wielded!"

"Aye, and hid away for a purpose," I reminded him.

"If he'd meant it to be lost forever, he would have destroyed it," Raphael said. "But mayhap there's another way to find it. Think on it, Moirin!" His eyes shone. "Ever since Gautier and Jean-Philippe de la Courcel vanished seeking the missing pages of the Book of Raziel, Terre d'Ange has been fearful and overcautious. King Daniel ascended the throne at a young age, unready and hesitant. Now he's torn between mourning his first wife and indulging his second. The rest of the world outpaces us, establishing trade with Terra Nova while we indulge in gossip and dalliance. A gift of such magnitude could usher in a new Golden Age."

I frowned, unsure. My *diadh-anam* pulsed inside me as it always did in Raphael's presence, but it offered no guidance. When I thought about the Maghuin Dhonn Herself, Her gaze was level and measured, neither forbidding nor encouraging.

This choice, I had to make myself.

"That's a dream writ large," Raphael said softly. "If we have any success at all, and we've not to date, I imagine it will come on a smaller scale with the lesser spirits. But *do* think on it, Moirin." His voice caught. "Such a gift might have spared my parents. It might save others from meeting the same fate."

I reached out and brushed a stray lock of hair from his brow, remembering the horror of those deaths at sea. "All right. I did promise."

We reached the de Toluard estate in blue dusk. It looked like a pleasant place—a gracious manor house with tall cypress trees surrounding it like sentinels. I breathed in their sharp, piney fragrance, willing them to lend me their proud strength in whatever was to come.

"Lady Moirin." Denis de Toluard gave me the kiss of greeting in the foyer. He looked far more serious than I remembered. Even his curly brown hair looked subdued. "My thanks for consenting to assist us. Come, I'll introduce you to the others."

There were six of them all told, all of them in their mid- to late-twenties. Later, Raphael told me they had all studied together at the Academy of Occult Philosophy. I greeted the first one with a shock of recognition.

"We've met," Lianne Tremaine said in acknowledgment. "Welcome, my lady."

"What further gifts might the youngest King's Poet in the history of Terre d'Ange possibly seek?" I asked, genuinely curious.

She tilted her head, lamplight making her topaz eyes flare. "There are always further thresholds to cross. I seek words of such surpassing beauty that they might melt the hardest heart of stone."

"Oh."

I met the other three. Balric Maitland, a silversmith with broad shoulders and strong, sinewy hands. A quiet, unassuming archivist and language scholar named Claire Fourcay, who cast longing glances in Raphael's direction when she thought no one was watching. The last was another linguist, Orien de Legasse, a pretty, fragile-looking lad whose pale blond hair put me in mind of Jehanne. He wore glass spectacles with gold rims that made his eyes look owlish.

The Circle of Shalomon.

There were no servants present in the parlor. Denis de Toluard poured us cups of a strong, fiery cordial himself.

"To success," he said, raising his cup in toast. "To *knowledge*."

I echoed the toast dutifully and drank.

Raphael's eyes glinted. "The hour's nearly upon us." He laid one hand on my shoulder. "Shall we?"

Claire Fourcay sniffed. "What exactly do you expect her to *do*, my lord de Mereliot?"

"Oh, I don't know." He smiled at me. "But wondrous things seem to occur when Moirin summons her magic. Give her a chance, won't you? We've tried everything else."

She sniffed again. "She makes our numbers wrong."

Raphael ran his hand down my arm and took my hand in his, entwining our fingers. "Consider us one flesh."

"Let's just get on with it," Balric Maitland said curtly.

Denis de Toluard beckoned. "Come."

We followed him to a hidden doorway and traipsed down a set of stone stairs to a lower level. I felt man-made stone closing all around and above me and shivered. Raphael's fingers tightened on mine.

"Breathe," he whispered in my ear.

I breathed.

There was an antechamber that might have been a cellar once. I smelled the faint, lingering odor of root vegetables. Now it was lit by a handful of clear-burning lamps, shadows flickering in the corners. There were shelves with garments of white linen laid ready and waiting, and a standing washbasin in the center of the room. The water smelled of an herb I didn't know.

"Hyssop," Raphael said in response to my inquiring glance.

One by one, the members of the Circle stripped and donned the white linen robes, then washed their hands and faces in the basin. I followed suit. The flagstones were cool and moist beneath my bare feet. The water felt good. And then the silversmith Balric went around, handing out engraved medallions on silver chains.

I examined the design. "What is this?"

"One side bears the Seal of Shalomon; the other, the sigil of Valac." He hung it around my neck, gazing at me with hooded eyes. "One of the lesser spirits. That is who we seek to summon tonight."

"Oh."

Raphael's hand slid beneath my hair. "A modest beginning," he said. "Valac's gift is to reveal things hidden." He smiled at me. "Particularly serpents. I thought it fitting in light of your exploits the other day."

"I see," I offered.

He laughed and kissed me. "Pray that we all do."

We filed into the chamber proper.

It was a vaster space than I would have reckoned from the antechamber. Groin vaults arched, the ceiling soaring. More lamps flickered. I gazed up at the gathering shadows, then down at the floor.

There.

An insignia similar to the Seal of Shalomon engraved into one side of my medallion was engraved on the floor itself. This one contained a circle with a six-pointed star within it. There was a brazier at its center. Words in a language I couldn't read were inscribed along its circumference. Members of the Circle drifted around its perimeter and took up established positions at each point of the star.

"Come." Raphael beckoned, holding out his hand.

I took it.

"Claire?" Denis lifted his head. "Will you speak the first conjuration?"

She did.

Whatever she said, it was in a language wholly unfamiliar to me. The longer she spoke, the more her voice grew in strength. I let it wash over me. The air seemed to pulse and tighten, but nothing happened.

"The second conjuration," Denis prompted her.

She spoke again at length in the strange language; and then again, the third conjuration. The air grew tighter and tighter. In the center of the star, it shimmered. An image formed in my mind of a closed doorway with light streaming around the frame. At one point, Balric Maitland drew a sword and extended it over the brazier, something dangling from its tip. The brazier flared briefly. The light around the doorway in my mind grew stronger.

More words.

"Moirin," Raphael muttered. "Now!"

I took a deep breath, summoned the twilight, and *pushed*.

The doorway in my mind opened and vanished. Crimson light streamed upward from the floor. When it faded, the figure of a beautiful young boy in a white tunic stood in the center of the star.

"Elua!" someone breathed.

The room swam in my vision and only Raphael's hand sliding beneath my elbow kept me on my feet. I'd lost my grip on the twilight. Claire Fourcay, her voice trembling, spoke in a rush of words. The boy's image flickered, then steadied. He made a reply to her in a high, sweet voice.

"It's him," she whispered. "Valac."

"Ask him!" Orien de Legasse's voice was feverish. "Ask him to tell us the charm for revealing hidden things!"

"You speak Habiru as well as I." She was pale. "You ask."

Lamplight flashed off his spectacles as Orien made his inquiry. The boy smiled and replied sweetly, then raised one finger and began to write on the air. Fiery letters in a strange alphabet formed and faded in the wake of his finger.

"Damn it!" Raphael swore. "Lianne, can you commit it to memory?"

"I'm trying!"

I felt dizzy and very much as though I might faint. I breathed the Pulse of the Earth, willing myself to remain upright. Everyone was watching the boy, rapt. With the last of my strength, I summoned the twilight and took refuge in it, hoping to draw strength there. The room turned dim and muted, the fiery golden-orange letters turned to soft silver flame.

The boy turned toward me.

You.

He looked different in the twilight. His eyes were yellow with vertical pupils like a goat's. He wore only a clout of cloth around his loins and his slender chest was bare. Wings as black as raven feathers sprang from his shoulders.

I swallowed hard.

Those inhuman eyes regarded me with curiosity. *What are you?*

"Moirin," I whispered.

His lips stretched in a smile. *What is a* Moirin?

"A child of the Maghuin Dhonn."

Ah. The boy looked past me. *I do not know of this Maghuin Dhonn. But there is a vast presence attendant on you.*

It made my heart hurt. "You see Her? Can you reveal Her to me?"

He shook his head. *She is not mine to command.*

"Oh." I was disappointed. "Well, thank you for telling me nonetheless. It's a comfort."

The boy smiled again, wider this time. His teeth were very white and pointed. *You are welcome. For your courtesy, I will do you a kindness. Be careful, Moirin of the Maghuin Dhonn. We are not all so benevolent.*

"Thank you," I repeated.

Indeed. His goat's eyes were oddly compassionate. *Now go back to your companions.*

He made a sudden violent gesture.

I found myself thrust out of the twilight, stumbling over my own feet. The lamps flared with golden light. The dizziness came crashing back in full force, my knees turning to water. Raphael caught me and steadied me. In the center of the six-pointed star, the boy was an ordinary boy in a white tunic again, except for the fact that he was etching flaming letters on the air. He lowered his hand and said something unintelligible in his sweet, fluting voice. I squinted at his wavering figure.

"What did he say?" Denis de Toluard demanded.

"That the doorway's closing and—"

The world went black.

THIRTY-SIX

onversation swirled around me as I surfaced to awareness.

"—then what's the use of that highly trained memory?" some-one grumbled.

"I'm a poet, not a linguist!" Lianne said in sharp frustration. "Who knew he would write the spell in Habiru?"

Another voice, soothing. "We'll have pen and paper next time to capture it."

"If there *is* a next time." A tart voice. "Will the witch live?"

"Shut up, Claire." There was the sound of skin rasping against skin, palm against palm. One of Raphael's hands rested gently on my brow, the other over my heart. That blessed sunlit warmth sank into my skin and suffused my body. "Moirin? Can you hear me?"

I managed a tiny nod.

"Elua and Eisheth be praised!" he breathed. "I knew it. I knew you could do it!"

With an effort, I opened my eyes. I was lying on a couch in Denis de Toluard's parlor, Raphael kneeling beside it. His face was hovering inches above mine, filled with a mixture of concern and relief.

"Was it worth it?" I asked faintly.

A cacophony of squabbling broke out.

"Yes." Raphael pressed his lips to my brow. "It is a far, far greater beginning than any we've known." His strong arms slid beneath my body. "And *I* am putting *you* to bed. Denis, have you given us my usual chamber?"

"I have."

I let Raphael cradle me in his arms, glad of his strength. My head lolled against his shoulder as he carried me up the stairs. In the guest-chamber, he laid me on the bed and undressed me. His storm-grey eyes gleamed.

"Moirin . . ."

I closed mine. "Now?"

"I love you."

It wasn't true. I *knew* it wasn't true. But I was very tired, very young, and very far from home. And I didn't know what the Maghuin Dhonn Herself wanted of me, only that Her *diadh-anam* beat so strongly in Raphael's presence. So I gave myself to him, let him take me. As he breathed hard and labored above and inside me, charged with un-wonted urgency, I saw flashes beneath my eyelids.

Jehanne.

The spirit Valac, his yellow goat's eyes glinting.

Bao.

It was the last that startled me into coming. Raphael groaned, his chin grinding into the hollow between my throat and shoulder. And that was the last thing I remembered before I slid back into the embrac-ing darkness.

I woke to midday sun. Raphael was dozing in a stuffed chair facing the bed. He startled awake when I pushed myself upright against the pillows. His eyes were bleary and there were shadows under them.

"How do you feel?" he asked.

"Tired." I tried to swallow and found my mouth was horribly dry. "Thirsty." He came over to pour me a cup of water, and I drank grate-fully, putting it down at last with a sigh. "You didn't sleep?"

He shook his head. "I went back downstairs. We were up all night discussing the incident. And I didn't want to disturb you."

"Oh." I rested my head against the pillows.

"Moirin . . ." Raphael sat on the edge of the bed, not quite meeting my eyes. "What I did, pressuring you . . . I'm sorry for it."

"Why did you, then?" I asked.

"I don't know." He sounded miserable. "It's like a fever comes over me and I can't help myself. I'm sorry. I never meant to hurt you."

I rubbed my eyes. "You didn't *hurt* me. It's just . . ." I didn't know what I wanted to say. I pulled my knees up beneath the bedsheets and wrapped my arms around them. "Raphael, he spoke to me."

He looked blank. "Who did?"

I shivered. "Valac."

"Well, he spoke to all of us. But you couldn't have understood. I speak only a bit of Habiru myself. That's why we rely on Claire for the invocations; she's the best—"

"No," I interrupted him. "Not like that. When none of you were looking, I called the twilight again. Only Valac *saw* me. And he didn't need words. He spoke into my thoughts. And he looked different." I took another sip of water. "Very different."

"Different how?" Raphael asked.

I told him.

"Elua!" He looked appalled and intrigued. "What did he say to you?"

"He wondered what I was," I said. "He'd never seen one of the Maghuin Dhonn before. And then he told me to be careful. He said not all of the spirits are as benevolent as he is. Then he did something that thrust me out of the twilight."

Raphael rubbed his chin. "Are you quite sure? You were beyond the point of exhaustion. The mind does play tricks."

I scowled. "Aye, I'm sure!"

"All right, all right!" He put up his hands. "It's only that Valac was there before us the entire time."

I was too tired to summon much of an argument. "Mayhap your there and my there are two different things."

"Mayhap," Raphael agreed. He took my hand in his, tracing circles on my palm. Despite everything, it felt good. His fingertips drifted to the inside of my wrist, testing my pulse. Now he looked directly at me, his grey eyes grave and worried. The concern in them made my heart beat faster. "You do accept my apology?"

I sighed. "I do."

"Good." He raised my hand to his lips, kissed my palm. "The Circle would very much like to make another attempt in a few days' time. No one expected the spirit to write the spell for revealing hidden things in such a fleeting manner. We were ill prepared." Hope replaced the worry in his gaze. "Is it too much to ask?"

"You'd summon Valac again?" I asked. "Not another?"

Raphael nodded. "Only Valac."

I should have said no.

Of course I should have said no.

But it had felt so very, very good to hear Raphael tell me he loved me, even if it was a lie—and there was the pulse of my *diadh-anam* inside me.

"All right," I said. "Yes."

I slept on and off for the entire day. Come morning of the following day, I felt stronger. Raphael summoned his coach and we returned to the City of Elua with promises to return to the manor in three evenings' time. That afternoon, I went to keep my appointment with Master Lo Feng in the gardens of the Academy.

He looked disapproving. He sat on his mat and held a fan, which he wielded with every bit as much skill and elegance as Jehanne de la Courcel. "Yesterday I waited. But you did not come."

I clasped my hand over my fist and bowed to him. "Forgive me, Master. My lord de Mereliot required my services, and I am in his debt."

Lo Feng pointed at me. "You are weak."

I blinked. "Your pardon?"

"Your *chi* ebbs." He clucked his tongue. "You must take better care of yourself, no matter what Raphael de Mereliot believes he requires."

Bao, clutching his staff, muttered under his breath.

I stole a sidelong glance at him and flushed, remembering how his visage had flashed before my eyes at the moment I'd climaxed. He shot me a sour look in reply, and the memory faded. I must have been a little mad to imagine it.

Master Lo Feng rapped my knuckles with his fan. "Would you learn?"

I bowed my head. "I would."

He rapped them again. "Then attend."

I attended.

That day, he taught me the Breath of Ocean's Rolling Waves. I breathed in through my nostrils, breathed deep into the middle pit of my belly. I breathed out through my mouth. I breathed and breathed until I caught the rhythm of it—the slow-building waves gathering in the deep sea, building and building, surging toward the shore. Building and breaking; drawing back and reclaiming their essence, only to rebuild once more. Over and over, the rhythm repeated itself.

I was almost sorry when Master Lo Feng declared an end to the exercise. I felt better than I had since the summoning. Bao helped his mentor to his feet, then busied himself with rolling the mats around his staff.

"Why *does* he always carry that thing?" I asked, curious.

"It is his weapon," Lo Feng said calmly. "In Ch'in, peasants are not allowed to carry blades. Bao is very skilled with a staff."

"Is he your bodyguard?"

"Among other things." He smiled at Bao, who actually smiled back at him. "He assists me with preparing medicines and tonics. He serves as my eyes and ears and my strong right arm. He is quick to learn foreign tongues. Bao is my magpie."

I wondered if Master Lo Feng would ever speak of me with the same warm affection. "I'm sorry I failed you yesterday. I would have sent word if I'd known."

"Mmm." He gave me a contemplative look. "What was this difficult matter you undertook for Raphael de Mereliot? Another healing endeavor?"

"Ah . . ." I'd promised not to speak of it. "In a sense."

Lo Feng thrust his fan into the sleeve of his robe and steepled his fingers. "Raphael has great promise and great skill. I have enjoyed teaching him. But he is young and ambitious. Ambition untempered by caution is like a river in flood. It leaps from its natural channels to forge the shortest course, and it sweeps away all in its path. Do not get swept away, Moirin."

I kissed his cheek impulsively. "I won't. Thank you."

His eyes crinkled. "In our culture, it is inappropriate to demonstrate affection in public thusly. But you are welcome."

The next few days passed without incident. I continued my lessons with Master Lo Feng. I began reading the *Trois Milles Joies*, the book

Queen Jehanne had sent to me, and discovered that she had not, in fact, been teasing in anything she had taught me and that Naamah's arts were even more extensive than I'd reckoned. On an evening when Raphael was closeted with the Queen, I accepted an invitation from Prince Thierry to attend the Hall of Games, where he and a handful of young peers took great pleasure in teaching me the rudiments of piquet and jeu de table. I enjoyed myself and wished once more that my destiny, whatever it was, were less complicated—because every time I thought about the forthcoming attempt at summoning Valac, dread crept over me. It wasn't the spirit himself I feared so much as it was the way the process drained me.

Still, I did it.

On the appointed evening, we returned to the de Toulard estate, where I was greeted with a mixture of gratitude, appreciation, and re-sentment. Claire Fourcay and Orien de Legasse seemed particularly put out.

"They're jealous," Lianne Tremaine informed me.

"Why?" I asked. "This business isn't exactly pleasant for me."

"They've worked harder than anyone else to master the language and the rituals," she said in a pragmatic tone. "It galls them to have to depend on a young, untutored, half-breed bear-witch from the back of nowhere."

Balric Maitland laughed deep in his chest. "Especially a beautiful one."

"But not you?" I asked them.

The silversmith shook his head. "I'm a craftsman," he said simply. "I don't reckon you're after my trade."

"Nor mine," Lianne said.

"I'm not after anyone's trade!" I said in frustration. "I'm not *after* anything."

Lianne smiled her foxy smile. "You're after Raphael de Mereliot."

I gazed across the parlor at him. He was speaking solicitously to Claire Fourcay, soothing her ruffled feelings. Lamplight gleamed on his tawny hair. As though sensing my gaze, he glanced at me and gave me a fleeting wink. As always, my *diadh-anam* quickened. "I suppose."

Denis de Toluard circulated, pouring cordial. "Drink, friends! The hour is nigh. To knowledge!"

"To knowledge!" we all echoed.

Everything was the same. The sense of man-made stone closing around me. The robes, the hyssop-scented water, the medallions. The only difference was that this time the linguists had writing tablets and chalk with them. We entered the chamber and took our places. Raphael took my hand in his, entwining our fingers. His lips brushed my temple in a kiss. I wished it didn't feel so comforting.

"Are you all right?" he whispered.

I nodded.

This time I didn't wait for his guidance. I knew what to expect. I saw the light-streaming doorway in my mind's eye as soon as Claire Fourcay finished speaking the first conjuration. I summoned the twilight, breathed it around me, and *pushed*. A column of crimson light sprang from the flagstones and faded.

Valac.

I held on to the twilight. In the world a mere half-step away, a member of the Circle was speaking to the figure of a pretty boy in a white tunic. I was aware of it in the distance, like the sound of insects droning on a hot summer day. In the world I inhabited, a half-naked boy with raven's wings and goat's eyes grinned at me, baring pointed teeth.

You again.

"Me again," I agreed. The distant droning sounded agitated. "Will you not give them what they want? They'll let us both be if you do."

He shook his head. *I've already done so. Having obeyed the injunction once, I am not compelled to repeat myself.*

"Is this a game to you?" I asked.

His pointed grin widened. *Yes.*

I sighed. "Good to know."

In the world behind me, the droning changed in pitch, sharpening. Someone was speaking harsh, irritated words of ritual dismissal.

Valac laughed soundlessly. *Good-bye, Moirin. And don't be a fool. If they get what they want, they'll only want more. They'll use you up until you're gone.*

He vanished.

It was as though he took the greater part of my strength with him. I crashed back into the mortal world and fell to my knees, my hand slipping from Raphael's grip.

"Moirin?" He knelt beside me.

"Here," I said feebly. "Still here. Raphael . . . I think this is a foolish pursuit. It's a game to them, nothing more. They mean to trick you at every turn."

His eyes darkened. "Well, we'll just have to outwit them, won't we?"

THIRTY-SEVEN

I slept for a full day while the Circle of Shalomon debated and argued. I didn't care what they decided. I wanted only to sleep. During my brief moments of wakefulness, I was glad I'd sent word to Master Lo Feng not to expect me.

"They want to try again," Raphael told me on the carriage-ride home.

I leaned my head against the stiff cushions. "Valac says he's already obeyed their injunction. He's not obliged to repeat himself."

"Not Valac."

I cracked my eyes open. "Who?"

"Marbas," Raphael said softly. "He's another lesser spirit, I promise. But he holds forth the offer of the same gift. The revelation of things hidden. It may be we could complete the spell. And more, too."

"Oh, aye?"

He nodded. "Diseases and their cure."

I studied his grave face. "That would mean a great deal to you, wouldn't it?"

Raphael swallowed hard. "It would."

I closed my eyes again. "Just not soon."

"No." He pulled me into his arms and settled my head on his shoulder. "Not soon. So Valac spoke to you again? He admitted to playing a game with us?"

"Aye," I murmured.

"What else did he say?"

I was silent a moment. "He said if you get what you want, you'll only want more. You'll use me up until I'm gone."

His body stiffened. "That's a damned lie!"

"Is it?"

"Moirin." Raphael shifted me and took me by the shoulders. His grey eyes were stormy and intense. "I swear to you on my parents' graves that I would never allow such a thing to happen. I'm a physician. It would violate my oath and every tenet I hold sacred." His gaze softened. "Not to mention the fact that I'm passing fond of you."

"Oh?" I said. "The other night you said you loved me. But perhaps that was just the fever speaking."

"No." His hands flexed on my shoulders. "Moirin . . . if you want to go no further, I understand. I can see the toll it takes on you. But you're young and resilient and stronger than you know. Who will you choose to trust? Me, or a spirit who's freely admitted to playing tricks on us?" His fingers tightened. "Fate brought us together for a reason. If we can win just one gift, one concession from one of them . . . the cure for just one form of pestilence, mayhap . . . we will have done something great and wonderful."

"And you would be content with that?" I asked. "One gift?"

He hesitated, then nodded reluctantly. "Yes."

"All right."

Raphael let go my shoulders and kissed my brow. "Is it terrible?" he asked gently. "You've seen and spoken to a spirit in his true form. Do they frighten you so very badly?"

"No." My head felt like it weighed a hundred pounds. I laid it back down on his shoulder. "You do."

His voice rose. "Me?"

"You. The Circle." I yawned. "Raphael, you can swear all you like that you'd be content with one gift and you may even mean it, but *they* won't be."

"Well, they'll have to be." His arms came around me again, warm and strong and comforting. "Trust me."

I sighed, and slept.

The summoning had taken more out of me this time—or mayhap it was just that there was less of me from which to take. The next day,

I was still as weak as a day-old kitten, and had to send word to Master
Lo Feng that I wouldn't be able to come. Daphne fed me hot beef broth
and clucked over me.

"Just what is it his lordship puts you up to out there in the countryside?" she asked darkly. "There are rumors, you know."

"Oh?" I asked.

"They say that Denis de Toluard practices alchemy." She saw my
blank look. "He's searching for the formula to turn lesser metals into
gold."

I rubbed my eyes. "Well, if he is, it's naught to do with me." I
doubted the words the moment I uttered them. It wouldn't surprise me
in the least if that was one of the secrets the spirits held out as a taunting promise.

"They say there's all manner of nonsense involved." Daphne lowered her voice. "Virgin's milk and lizards and such."

I laughed. "No lizards—nor any virgins, either, I suspect."

She sniffed. "I mislike it. And now he's got you mucking about
with that Ch'in fellow, too. I wish you'd all have the sense to leave well
enough alone."

I shrugged. "I'd as soon you didn't speak ill of Master Lo Feng. He's
been very kind to me."

Daphne eyed me. "To be sure, you're an odd one yourself, my
lady."

The next day, I felt strong enough to resume my lessons with Master Lo Feng. My heart gave a leap of gladness at the sight of him—and
even of surly Bao leaning on his staff. Daphne might disapprove all she
liked, but the lessons made me happy and I felt a sense of *rightness* in
Lo Feng's presence—even if he gave me a reproving look and chided
me for failing to heed his advice.

"I'm heeding," I said. "I'm here, aren't I? Not washed away."

He merely shook his head. "Today I will teach you the Breath of
Trees Growing. It's soon, but if we wait any longer, we may have to wait
for spring for you to get the proper feel of it."

Bao spread our mats beneath a stand of graceful beech trees, sunlight streaming through their golden canopies.

"Trees breathe," Master Lo Feng said to us. "Standing in one place, they breathe. They breathe in water and sunlight, and they breathe out air. Breathe through your mouth deep into your lungs. As you breathe in energy, be mindful of how your blood carries it from your lungs throughout your body and to your limbs, even as a tree's energy flows upward from its roots and downward from its leaves, carrying it to every part."

This one came easier than the first two. I would have liked to think it was because I was gaining skill, but I suspect it was because I already had an affinity for trees. I sat and listened to the beech trees for a long while before I began, drinking in the sense of how energy flowed through them.

Then I emulated it.

It made me aware of my body in a new way—of my torso echoing the trunk of a tree, my limbs its branches, my fingers and toes its outermost twigs. I breathed inward, aware of the blood circulating to every part. I breathed outward, aware of my lungs expelling air that no longer nourished me.

"The energy of trees and all green, growing things complements our own," Master Lo Feng said in his tranquil voice. "The air that they exhale is depleted of energy they can use, but it is healthful to us. The air that we exhale is depleted of energy we can use, but it is healthful to them. Think about the beauty of this cycle."

I did.

Once again, I was sorry when the lesson ended. Master Lo Feng complimented me and said I'd done well.

"I suspect the Breath of Trees Growing lies nearest to your own natural gifts." He paused. "And I suspect your gifts should be used in the manner that is natural to you, not a manner that suits Raphael de Mereliot's goals."

I fidgeted. "Even if doing so might result in great good?"

He looked troubled. "I am reluctant to disagree. You did a very good thing helping that young man's leg to heal, and Raphael tells me you helped him save a man's life. But I am reluctant to agree. Nothing good comes of going against nature."

"It's only for a little while," I assured him.

Master Lo Feng sighed. "I am an old man and you are something new under the sun. Who am I to advise you?" Bao snorted. His mentor ignored him and waved one hand at me. "Go, and come again tomorrow."

It was two weeks before the Circle of Shalomon met to make another attempt. I had a lesson with Master Lo Feng every day, concentrating on the three Styles of Breathing I had learned thus far and beginning to learn to alternate between them. It would get harder, he said, when I attempted to master and incorporate the last two.

For his part, Raphael alternated, too—alternated between being attentive to me and answering Queen Jehanne's summons.

At least for the first week.

The second was another matter.

I knew that he'd been with her, because I could smell her on him—her perfume and *her*. And I knew that they'd quarrelled because he was storming around the townhouse in a towering fury.

"What is it?" I asked him.

Raphael turned a glowering stare on me. "Nothing that concerns you, Moirin."

"Oh, of course not," I said wryly. "Why ever would it?"

He flung himself onto a couch, blew out his breath, and stared at the ceiling. "She asked me to give you up."

I felt an obscure pang of betrayal. "Why? I mean, why now?"

"Because there are rumors about the Circle and your involvement in it," he said grimly. "Because nothing, no matter how significant, is ever allowed to be more important than Jehanne. She's testing me."

"Does she know about the Circle?" I asked.

Raphael made an ambiguous gesture. "Not exactly. She knows I have certain esoteric interests."

I bit my tongue on a few hundred questions and picked one. "What do you mean to do?"

"What?" He gave me a startled look. "Name of Elua! I'm not letting you go, if that's what you're asking. That's why I said it's nothing to do with you. No, no. We've quarrelled before and we'll quarrel again. Jehanne needs to know I'll not be led around like a bull with a ring in its nose. I'll make it up to her in the usual way." He swung his feet off the couch. "I'm off to the jeweler's to commission a suitable gift."

He sent her a choker of pale blue topaz.

Two days later, I saw it in the Hall of Games, where Prince Thierry was teaching me to throw dice. Jehanne strolled through with an entourage in tow.

I hadn't seen her since the day of the hunting party. And before that . . .

My skin got hot all over again.

"Lady Moirin." The Queen paused beside our table. She held a little silken-haired dog in her arms. It wore a choker of pale blue topaz around its neck, echoing the hue of her eyes. Her gaze rested briefly on me. Whatever it held, it was more complicated than simple jealousy and animosity. "I see you're being corrupted. Do you enjoy games of chance?"

"Oh," I said uncomfortably. "Only a bit, your majesty."

Thierry gave her a brittle smile. "Do you mean to take a turn, Jehanne? If so, put up a stake."

"Why not?" She unlatched her lap-dog's choker and tossed it atop a pile of coins on the table. "Marcel?" She beckoned to one of the courtiers attending her. "Throw for me, will you?"

He threw two sixes and a five.

Neither Thierry nor I came close.

"Bad luck." Jehanne smiled sweetly as her courtier swept up her winnings—and then her smile faded, leaving that complicated something in its wake. "You're looking a bit peaked, Moirin. You oughtn't play games you're bound to lose."

"Can we not—" I began.

She shifted her lap-dog into the crook of one arm and touched my face, her fingertips lingering. "Think on it." I flushed, and Jehanne patted my cheek. "Anon."

Well and so, that was *that* encounter. What it meant, I couldn't say. Only that Jehanne had lost none of her ability to discomfit. Thierry was wroth at her interference, and Raphael was wroth to learn that she'd relegated his gift to a lap-dog's collar and wagered it so carelessly.

Me, I was just discomfited.

At the end of the second week, it was with a mixture of dread and relief that I retraced my steps once more and descended into the subterranean chamber of the de Toluard estate, donning the white robe and silver medallion and taking my place beside Raphael. As much as I feared the toll the night's proceedings would take, I hoped this would put an end to it. One gift, Raphael had promised.

I meant to hold him to it.

In the dim, flickering chamber, Claire Fourcay uttered the first invocation. I saw the doorway, summoned the twilight, and *pushed*.

When the crimson light faded, there was a lion with a black mane in the center of the six-pointed star.

I let the twilight go, curious.

Still a lion, only its mane was tawny. Its jaws were parted as if in a smile. Members of the Circle argued with one another. Orien de Legasse began uttering an injunction in a faltering voice. No one was looking at me.

I shifted back.

Moirin.

"Marbas?" I asked hesitantly. "If so, well met."

The black-maned lion paced the confines of the innermost segment of the star, its tufted tail lashing. *Valac said you were polite.*

I laughed. "I've seldom been accused of it."

To us. The lion sat on its haunches. *What is it you want?*

"Can you not give them one small gift?" I pleaded. "It would make an end to this, or at least my involvement in it."

Unless they can compel me to take human form, I am not compelled to speak in a human tongue. The lion looked smug. *They failed to prepare for that possibility.*

I sighed. "So that's the trick this time, eh?"

Yes. The lion Marbas regarded me with vivid yellow-gold eyes. *However,* you *may ask me. You hear me. You are part of the summoning circle.*

My heart skipped a beat. "Me?"

You.

I shuddered and didn't respond for a moment. I didn't want this responsibility—but I feared it might be wrong to refuse it. "I suppose . . . Raphael would be content with one cure. A cure for a single disease."

It's not so simple. The lion's eyes glowed. *To learn the charm to cure, you must first learn the charm to cause. Leprosy, typhoid, pneumonia, plague . . . I can teach you to invoke and banish any one of these. Would you possess such knowledge? Would you put it into* their *hands?*

I glanced around at the shadowy figures a half a world away. "No," I said at last. "No, I would not."

The lion's jaws parted, revealing enormous teeth and a bright red tongue. *I have another gift to offer to you and you alone. We have studied the Maghuin Dhonn since you summoned Valac. You were once shape-changers. I can teach you that art.*

I drew in a sharp breath.

It tempted me.

With a typical man's self-absorption, Raphael had assumed that whatever destiny brought us together, it would ultimately serve his purposes. But I was a child of the Maghuin Dhonn. My people had expected great things of me, had hoped I would show great promise. Even my name was a badge of hope.

What if *this* was what I was meant to do?

The lion waited patiently, only the tip of its tail twitching.

For the span of a few score of heartbeats, I hungered for the gift it offered. But there was a burial mound in Clunderry where the skull of the last great magician and shape-changer of the Maghuin Dhonn was buried a hundred years ago. He had sworn an oath on behalf of all our people and broken it. The Maghuin Dhonn Herself had taken away this gift. It was Hers and Hers alone to restore.

I bowed my head. "Thank you, but I cannot accept it."

Wise child. For that, I give you a gift unasked. The black-maned lion stretched its jaws wide and roared.

It was a roar without sound—and yet I felt the waves of it beating against my skin. Something settled into my thoughts like a bright to-paz jewel and made a home inside my mind, and I cried aloud at the strangeness of it.

The charm to reveal hidden things. The lion Marbas looked smug again. *Yours and yours alone. The words will be there if you need them.*

"I didn't . . ." I couldn't finish the sentence. Dizziness was beginning to overwhelm me—whether from the prolonged encounter or the charm the spirit had placed in my thoughts, I couldn't say.

I know. The lion showed the tips of its incisors. *You'd better go while there's still some of you left. Tell your comrades not to bother summoning me again. I'm not bound to answer as a man queries I've answered as a beast.*

Marbas roared again and cast me out of the twilight.

THIRTY-EIGHT

I didn't tell Raphael about the gift Marbas had given me.

I couldn't.

For one thing, I was days in recovery this time and lacked the strength to talk. Raphael tended me himself. I woke a few times to see his worried face, then drifted back into sleep. When I finally woke for good, I felt a hollowed out shell of myself. Raphael sprang to my bedside.

"Moirin?"

"Aye." My voice was raspy and frail.

He gave me water and felt at my pulse. His hair hung lank and unwashed, there were dark shadows under his eyes, and he looked nearly as bad as I felt.

That's when the guilt hit me.

I'd been offered the gift he wanted so badly and I had refused it. I'd refused it because it came with a poisonous taint, and I didn't trust the Circle of Shalomon with such deadly knowledge. Not even Raphael.

I couldn't tell him.

"No more." Having satisfied himself that I wasn't about to expire, he gave my hand a firm squeeze. "I've told the Circle that we'll have to continue without you."

A topaz jewel nestled in my thoughts. I took a sip of water. "How do they mean to proceed?"

Raphael stroked my hair. "You needn't concern yourself."

I pushed myself upright and drank more water, clearing the hoarseness from my throat. "Just tell me."

He hesitated. "We're of two minds. Some want to try to summon Marbas again, reckoning it will be easier since he's already been bound once. Claire and Orien are working to perfect the conjuration to force him to take human form. Others among us want to summon the lesser spirit Caim."

"Marbas has already answered you as a beast," I said. "He's not bound to reply a second time as a man."

Raphael nodded. "I suspected as much. So did Lianne. It's much the same trick Valac played. Caim's gift is the speech of birds and beasts and all living creatures." A spark lit his tired eyes. "'Twould be a wondrous gift."

"And one that once mastered would prevent them from tricking you thusly again," I observed.

"Exactly." He refilled my cup with cool water and handed it back to me. "But you're not to take part in it."

"I'm not a child, Raphael." I sipped the water slowly. Relentless guilt gnawed at me. I was keeping too many secrets from him. "Give me one more chance. If I could win but one gift for you, to my way of thinking this would be a passing fine one. The world would be a kinder place for it." I gave him a weary smile. "Although D'Angelines might cease to hunt for sport if they knew their prey's terror."

"That wouldn't be such a bad thing," he murmured. "Moirin . . . you're sure?"

"I am," I said with as much firmness as I could muster.

Raphael knelt beside my bed and lowered his head like a penitent, lashes veiling his eyes. "I should refuse you."

I touched his strong jawline. "But you won't."

His lashes swept up. His gaze was filled with weariness and hope. "One last attempt. After this, no more."

"No more," I agreed.

He kissed me. "I'll tell the Circle."

It was almost a week before I felt strong enough to return to the City and resume my lessons with Master Lo Feng. There had been a cold snap while I was recuperating. The ground was frozen hard and there were only a few brittle brown leaves clinging to the trees. This time we met in a small courtyard at the Academy. Bao had already spread the mats around a small, ornate brazier. Neither of them seemed to feel the cold. I was wearing a fine new cloak that Benoit Vallon had designed for me—thick, luxuriant sable velvet lined with gold silk. I wrapped it around me and shivered.

Master Lo Feng gave me a long, long look, but he didn't reprimand me.

"Sit," he said. "Learn the Breath of Glowing Embers."

I sat, shivering and obedient.

Bao leaned over the brazier and blew softly on the coals. Their hot crimson hearts quickened, turning bright orange. They pulsed beneath a fine coating of ash, colors shifting like fiery jewels.

"The embers breathe in air and breathe out heat," Lo Feng said. "Even as we breathe in cool *yin* energy and exhale hot *yang*. The human heart is your precious ember. Breathe through your mouth into your heart. Feel the energy you inhale stoke it. Feel it pulse within you. Breathe out its heat."

It was hard. I was too cold to concentrate. I gazed at the embers, trying to find the rhythm.

I gazed at Master Lo Feng. His serene face comforted me, but it didn't help.

I gazed at Bao.

Like his mentor, he sat so very still in repose. But his face wasn't serene. He breathed through parted lips, faster than I would have thought by the slight rise and fall of his chest. His face was exhilarated. I knew without being told that fire was the element closest to his nature.

I matched my breathing to his and realized that it resonated with the shifting hues of fire within the coals.

In and out.

Flaring and fading in time with my beating heart.

Bao opened his eyes. "You not cold anymore."

I startled at the sound of his voice—and realized it was true. I wasn't exactly warm, but the cold that had permeated my bones was dispelled.

"Bao." Master Lo Feng delivered the gentle reproof without opening his eyes.

Bao gave me a faint smile and closed his eyes.

I closed mine, too, and breathed.

Somewhere in the days that followed, Raphael and Jehanne made up their quarrel. He didn't tell me about it, but he didn't have to. I knew her scent. I wondered if he'd promised to give me up after all. I wanted to ask him, but every time I thought about it, the topaz jewel of Marbas' gift sparkled in my thoughts, sending a covert pang of guilt through me. I kept quiet. After the next summoning, I would ask him.

There was a fête to celebrate the debut of a new poem by Lianne Tremaine. I accepted an invitation to attend as Prince Thierry's guest, assuming that Raphael would be escorting the Queen. I was wrong, but Raphael dealt graciously with it.

"No mind," he said when I told him. "I'll just be another courtier dancing attendance on her majesty."

"You're not angry?" I wished he would be, just a little.

He laughed and shook his head. "You're a free woman in Terre d'Ange, Moirin. Thierry's a handsome lad and the heir to the throne." And then he kissed me, his tongue probing my mouth, until desire flooded my loins. Raphael lifted his head, eyes gleaming. "Besides, he doesn't make you feel like *that*, does he?"

"You can be cruel," I informed him.

He only laughed again. "You're the one chose to let yourself be courted by the Dauphin."

It felt passing strange to see Lianne declaim her poem. I'd met her as the King's Poet, but I'd come to know her better as a member of the Circle, a white-robed figure engaged in shadowy rituals in a barren stone chamber. Here she wore a gown of bronze silk that suited her coloring and stood before the glittering court in a well-lit salon, speaking in measured tones.

She was very good.

Her speaking voice was pleasant enough, but it was her words that stirred the heart. The conceit of the poem was that it was written in the voice of a long-dead poet, Anafiel Delaunay, mourning his slain lover. Thierry explained to me in a low whisper that these things were all true, that Delaunay had been a famous poet and the beloved of Prince Rolande de la Courcel, one of his own ancestors and mine.

"Rolande was killed in the Battle of Three Princes," he whispered. "And although he mourned him deeply, Anafiel Delaunay—you might know him better as Anafiel de Montrève, the mentor of Phèdre nó Delaunay de Montrève—never did write about his grief."

I nodded and bade him to hush.

It was a terrible, beautiful poem—at once vivid, yet spare and haunting. At first I thought it was brave of Lianne to write from a man's perspective about things she couldn't possibly have experienced—the horror of warfare, the clamor and chaos of the battlefield, the agony of seeing one's beloved cut down before one's eyes. But soon I forgot about the author, caught up rapt in the experience as she gave voice to one man's measureless grief.

There was silence when she finished. Everyone looked to the King and Queen to take a cue from their response. I wiped my eyes, wondering why someone with such a gift would seek even more.

And I wondered, too, what it would be like to love someone so deeply that it felt as though your own heart died with them.

"Magnificent." King Daniel applauded, and we all followed suit. He rose to present Lianne with a token of appreciation, a sapphire pendant on a gold chain. She bowed her head and he placed it around her neck. Jehanne approached and took Lianne's hands in hers, kissed her on both cheeks. I stifled a spasm of envy. Her blue-grey eyes were bright with tears and there wasn't a trace of artifice in her expression.

Afterward, servants circulated with trays of delicacies and wine. My appetite was finally returning after the last summoning. I ate three flaky pastries in quick succession and drank a glass of red wine.

"That was fast," Thierry said with a smile. He took my empty glass. "Where's the fellow with the wine-jug? I'll go find him."

I smiled back at him. "Thank you."

I thought I should congratulate Lianne and tell her how much I liked the poem, but there was a throng of people around her. Near the doorway into the salon, the King and Queen were speaking quietly, their heads close together, guards in House Courcel livery standing a respectful distance behind them.

Curiosity overcame me.

No one was looking. I summoned the twilight and stole near.

"—made you melancholy, didn't it?" Jehanne was saying. She searched his face. "Let me leave with you."

"No, no." Daniel raised her slender white hand to his lips, kissed her palm, and folded her fingers over it. "Stay. Please stay. You know I'm bad company at such times."

She smiled up at him. Tears yet sparkled in her eyes. "Never."

"Liar," he said fondly. "Leave me to my memories, Jehanne. I'll see you anon."

Jehanne pressed his hand to her cheek. "You're sure?"

He withdrew it gently. "I'm sure. Go tend to your errant courtier." A shadow crossed his face. "Do you think you might manage to keep him out of whatever trouble he's courting?"

She sighed. "Elua knows, I'm trying."

"I know." King Daniel kissed her lips, then took his leave. She gazed after him with an expression of such tenderness and sorrow, it made my heart ache for her.

And then she squared her shoulders and turned to sweep back into the salon, so quickly and decisively that the swirling skirt of her gown grazed mine.

I took two hurried strides backward and collided with a servant. A tray of savory tarts clattered to the floor. I winced, letting the twilight slip away.

The manservant gaped, then scrambled to clean up the mess, muttering apologies. Everyone in the room stared.

Jehanne regarded me without speaking.

I closed my eyes. "I'm so very sorry, your majesty."

"Are you?" she asked.

With reluctance, I opened my eyes. Her exquisite face was utterly unreadable. I'd trespassed where I had no business going, and both of us knew it. I answered honestly. "Yes."

"Good." She swept past me.

The denizens of the Court turned their attention elsewhere.

Prince Thierry approached, two glasses of wine in hand, looking good-natured and puzzled. "Where did you go? I couldn't find you. And what in the seven hells was that all about?"

"Ohhh . . ." I took the glass he handed me and drank half of it at a single draught. The wine sang in my veins, making me feel dizzy and lightheaded. I breathed the Breath of Earth's Pulse, centering myself. "Nothing important."

He clinked the rim of his glass to mine. "I'm glad."

I bedded him that night.

I didn't mean to. It was selfish on my part. I knew Thierry had strong feelings for me—stronger than mine for him. It was like Cillian all over again. And yet I *missed* Cillian as much as I mourned him. He had been my friend before he was my lover. And I yearned to want and be wanted in that simple way it had been between us at the beginning.

Thierry gave me that.

He didn't ask until Raphael bade me farewell for the night. He didn't say he'd be spending it with Jehanne in her quarters, but it was clear.

"Take the carriage, Moirin." Raphael touched my cheek before drifting past me. "I'll see you at home anon."

Anon and anon and anon.

Too many anons.

Why should I be jealous? I was there with the Dauphin of my own accord.

"Stay." Thierry's hands were on my shoulders. He kissed me. He tasted of wine and innocence. It didn't set my blood afire, but it was nice. "I'll send someone to dismiss de Mereliot's driver. Stay."

"All right."

Thierry was a skilled lover. I should have expected it; he *was* the heir to Terre d'Ange. And he brought to our bed all the unstinting ardor I could have wished of Raphael, for *I* was its focus. Not my gifts, just me. I performed the *languisement* Jehanne had taught me on him, relishing his groans of pleasure and the hot, irresistible rush of his seed spilling into my mouth. He returned the favor until I begged him to stop.

"You're so beautiful," he whispered as he entered me.

"So are you," I whispered back.

And I wept silent tears, because it was true. He was young and kind and beautiful, and it wasn't enough.

But for one night, I pretended it was.

THIRTY-NINE

Claire Fourcay finished speaking the first conjuration.

I *pushed* and opened the doorway.

Thanks, mayhap, to Master Lo Feng's teaching, I was more aware of myself and the flow of my own energy than I had been. When the crimson light erupted, I understood in my flesh and blood that there was a toll to be paid for keeping the door open. I could feel it ebbing steadily from me.

The extent of its cost would be determined when it closed.

Caim manifested as an ordinary man, olive-skinned and hawk-nosed, a wooden staff held loosely in one hand.

A sigh of relief ran around the Circle.

Orien de Legasse put the first question to him in their unintelligible tongue. Claire Fourcay had chalk poised over her tablet lest he write it in fiery letters.

Instead, the spirit bowed politely and spoke at length.

"Oh, *hell*!" someone swore. "Tell me he didn't just say what I think he said."

"He did," Orien said grimly.

I shifted into the twilight. I'd learn more there.

The spirit greeted me. *Moirin.*

"Aye," I agreed. "You're Caim?"

I am. In the world half a step away from the mortal one, Caim was still mostly human. But antlers like a young buck's rose from his brow, a tangled bird's nest wedged in one fork. His eyes were round and golden like a hunting owl's. They regarded me curiously. *The bear's child does not require this gift. Why have you summoned me?*

I gestured at the shadowy Circle. "For them. What trick did you play them?"

His round, golden eyes flared. *No trick.*

"They're angry."

Yes. Caim looked complacent. *I am teaching them the language of ants. It is composed of scent and touch. When I am finished, I will teach them the language of crickets. You will have collapsed by then and the doorway will have closed, but if it were not, I would proceed to the language of honeybees, which is composed largely of dance. It is quite fascinating.*

I didn't know whether to laugh or weep. "Why? Marbas gave me his gift with a single roar. Surely you could do the same. Would it be such a bad thing for humans to have greater understanding?"

He shook his head. The bird's nest lodged in his antlers wobbled. *You sense the thoughts and feelings of your animal brethren. Your people never lost that bond. This is different. If you were to truly comprehend in its entirety the language of every creature on earth that creeps, crawls, flies, and swims, the cacophony would drive you mad. No mortal could endure it.*

I sighed. "Why offer the gift at all?"

Caim's round eyes glowed. *It is the game.*

Jehanne's words in the Hall of Games came back to me. This was a game I was bound to lose. I bowed to Caim. "Thank you for your honesty."

He returned the bow. A trio of baby thrushes poked their heads out of the bird's nest. *And you for your courtesy.*

I let go the twilight.

A wave of weakness spilled over me. In the center of the six-pointed star, Caim-the-man was still speaking. The members of the Circle all had peculiar looks on their faces. Wavering on my feet, I waited until Caim paused, then tugged Raphael's arm. Raphael looked at me, his nostrils twitching.

"Tell the Circle to dismiss him," I said. "I won't make it past crickets."

He nodded and did so.

Claire Fourcay spoke the words in a sour tone. Caim-the-man

vanished and the doorway closed. I sank to my knees with a sense of blessed relief.

For better or worse, it was over.

It took me a few days to recover. I wasn't quite as drained as I had been after Marbas' summoning—I'd conversed with him the longest— but I had the nagging feeling that each time, there was less of me left to recuperate. Raphael didn't dance attendance on me the way he had last time. After assuring himself that I *would* recover, he returned to the City for two days, coming back to fetch me on the third.

None of the Circle called on me in his absence.

"They're angry, aren't they?" I said when Raphael returned.

He took a deep breath. "They are. Not at you. Elua! It's not your fault. But yes, they're angry. They've been tricked and tricked, again and again. After years of study and effort, all we have to show for it . . ." He wrinkled his nose and rubbed it, an odd look in his eyes. "Thank the gods it's almost winter."

I was confused. "Why?"

Raphael shuddered. "All those scent-trails. Forage, forage, forage. Back to the colony, dig, dig, dig."

I touched his hand. "I'm sorry."

He looked at me sidelong. "Caim spared you, didn't he?"

"Aye."

"I wonder why," he mused.

I shrugged. "They, um, seem to like me."

Raphael uttered a sharp laugh. "They're not human, Moirin. They don't have likes and dislikes as we understand them."

"Why not?" I plucked at the bedsheets. "They're what Elua's Companions once were, aren't they? You'd never say *they* were incapable of loving. Why shouldn't their brethren be capable of at least liking?"

He frowned and gazed into the distance. "Mayhap they were alike long, long ago. But those of the One God's servants who chose to fol-low Blessed Elua did so out of love, and in the process, they became far, far greater than they had been. Those who rebelled and failed did so out of envy and anger, and they are less than they were." He rubbed his nose absently. "At least we know they *can* be compelled."

"Ah, no!" I said in alarm.

"I'm not breaking my promise." Raphael laid his hand over mine. "It's in my thoughts that mayhap this wondrous gift of healing we're able to share was all that destiny ever intended. But the Circle has worked so very hard." His grey eyes were dark and grave. "They're returning to their studies for a time. If they can find a way to outwit one of the spirits, may I tell them you'll at least listen to what they propose?"

"I'll listen," I said. "But they'll be wasting their breath."

"Listening is enough," he assured me.

We returned to the City of Elua, where I discovered that the best gift I could have hoped for awaited me: My father was back. I laughed aloud with delight when I learned that he'd called on the townhouse in our absence, and went straightaway to the Temple of Naamah to see him. I found him kneeling in contemplation before the effigy modeled on my great-great-grandmother, the first royal companion. His face was glad and serene, his scarlet robes were pooled around him, his brown hair a shining fall down his back. I stood in the doorway a moment, just watching him. He had something of Master Lo Feng's gift for stillness. Then he caught sight of me out of the corner of his eye.

"Moirin." He smiled and rose, opening his arms. "Come here."

I hugged him hard. "I'm so glad you're back."

"As am I." My father returned my embrace, then studied me with a faint frown. "Have you been ill?"

I shook my head. "No. Why?"

"You look . . ." He hesitated, touching my cheek with gentle fingers. "Beautiful, of course. But there are shadows beneath your eyes. Has there been trouble?"

"No, no. I wa . . ." I blew out my breath. "I've overexerted myself, that's all. A lack of sleep. It's fine. I'm fine."

"If you say so." He still looked concerned. "What have you been up to?"

I answered with a half-truth. "I've been studying with Master Lo Feng. Do you remember? You told me to seek him out."

"Ah." My father's worried expression eased. "The Ch'in physician, yes. And has he helped you find your destiny?"

"No," I admitted. "But he's teaching me to breathe."

"To breathe," he echoed blankly. "This I must hear."

I glanced up at the oculus of the dome and gauged the position of the sun. In my excitement, I'd forgotten all about my lesson. "I can do better," I said. "Would you like to meet him?"

"Very much so."

It was a wonderful meeting.

A light dusting of early snow had fallen, frosting the barren branches and the evergreen shrubs in the courtyard. The embers in the little brazier glowed cheerfully, sending up curling tendrils of fragrant smoke. We were only a little bit late. Master Lo Feng was there awaiting me, his hands folded in his sleeves. Beside him, Bao leaned idly on his staff.

Not much surprised those two, but I saw their eyes widen at the sight of my father in his crimson robes.

"Master Lo Feng." I bowed in the Ch'in manner. "Forgive my tardiness. This is my father, Brother Phanuel Demarre, only just returned to the City. Father, this is Master Lo Feng and, um . . . Bao."

"Filial duty takes precedence." Lo Feng waved away my apology. He bowed to my father. "It is an honor."

My father clasped hand over fist and returned his bow as gracefully as though he'd been doing it all his life. "Well met, my lord. The honor is mine. I understand you're teaching my daughter to breathe?"

Master Lo Feng's eyes crinkled. "You find it strange?"

My father smiled his lovely smile. "I find it unfamiliar. But I am eager to learn more if you are willing to suffer a novice's presence."

Unexpectedly, my mentor chuckled and stroked his two-pointed beard. "Your path chose you long ago, Brother Phanuel. I do not think this humble scholar has much to teach you. But I would be honored by your presence."

My father inclined his head. "And I grateful for your forbearance."

There were only three mats. After a discussion fraught with insistence and demurral, my father accepted one, thanking Bao for his sacrifice. Bao shrugged and didn't reply, but his face was softer than I'd ever seen it, except for a few unguarded moments when he looked at Master Lo Feng.

I sat cross-legged on my mat, emulating Lo Feng. My father knelt on his, sitting effortlessly on his heels and tucking the folds of his robes beneath his legs. Bao stooped over the brazier and blew on the embers, making them flare to life, then retreated to keep watch over us.

"So." Master Lo Feng tucked his hands into his sleeves. "The Breath of Embers Glowing . . ."

I listened.

I breathed.

Mostly, I stole glances at them. And it seemed to me that day that there were so many kinds of beauty in the world. They were all so very different, these three men from three generations. My father's presence seemed to illuminate it.

When it was over, Master Lo Feng chided me for my inattentiveness, but he did it nicely. And then he asked to have a few private words with my father.

Bao and I withdrew to the far side of the courtyard and stood together in awkward silence. I tried to think of something to say, but between my lingering weariness and sudden happiness, my mind was a blank.

"He's nice," Bao ventured at length in a grudging manner.

I was just pleased that he'd deigned to speak to me. "He is, isn't he? I liked him as soon as I met him."

He frowned. "You never met him before?"

I shook my head. "Only a little while ago. I grew up in Alba with my mother."

"Huh." He leaned on his staff and stared at the two men conversing.

Well, it had been a promising start. "Where did you grow up?"

Bao screwed up his face. "I do not know the word. People who do . . ." Unexpectedly, he tossed his staff high in the air and threw a standing somersault. He caught the staff on its descent, planted the butt, and vaulted into a flip, landing with the staff tucked neatly under one arm. "Like so."

"Stone and sea!" I clapped. "That's wonderful!" He shrugged. "So you were born into a circus family?" I prompted him. "Performers? Acrobats and jugglers?"

"Not born." Bao's face darkened. "Sold."

"Oh." I felt like an idiot. Belatedly, I remembered that Lo Feng had said Bao was a child of violence. "I'm sorry. How old were you?"

"Three." He summoned a fierce, hard smile. "Fifteen when I run away."

"Is that when you met Master Lo Feng?"

"No." Bao eyed me. "Why you ask so many questions?"

"I'm curious."

"Why?"

"I don't know," I said honestly. "I just am."

At that moment, Master Lo Feng called us over. My father smiled and reached out his hand and I took it.

"Strangely, I find all this breathing has given me an appetite," he said. "Moirin, would you join me for an early dinner?"

I smiled back at him. "I'd love to."

We dined at an inn in a part of the City known as Night's Doorstep because it was at the base of the hill where the Houses of the Night Court resided. It encompassed the Tsingani quarter and the inn was owned by a Tsingano. It was called the Cockerel and it had a long and venerable history in the City. The owner was a tall, scowling fellow with an imposing mustache, but he broke into a wide grin at the sight of my father.

"Brother Phanuel!" He beckoned with both hands. "Come, come. Always a table for you."

"Thank you, Stefan." My father laid a hand on my shoulder. "This is my daughter, Moirin."

The Tsingano raised his fist to his mouth and bit his knuckle. "Such a beauty! Not born of any milk-white D'Angeline, either. Was her mother one of ours?"

"I was born to the Maghuin Dhonn," I said.

His eyes widened and he took a step backward. "You're the witch! The one they're all talking about."

"She's my *daughter*," my father said mildly.

"Of course." Stefan didn't quite meet his eyes. "There is a fine dish of stuffed cabbages if you and your daughter are hungry, Brother Phanuel."

"That would be very pleasant, thank you."

Although I would have enjoyed it more if the innkeeper weren't looking askance at me, the food was simple and hearty and good, and we washed it down with tankards of foaming ale.

"So." My father pushed his empty plate away. "Master Lo Feng is concerned about you. He says you've been engaged in some secret business with Raphael de Mereliot that . . . how did he put it? Drains your vital *chi*."

I toyed with my last bite. "I'm fine."

"Moirin."

We may have known each other only a short time, but that was a parent's voice to be sure. I sighed. "I promised not to speak of it. But it's all right. It's over. I won't be doing it anymore."

He leveled a stern green, green gaze at me. "You promise?"

"Yes! I promise."

"Do I need to speak to Lord de Mereliot?"

"No!" I laid one hand on my chest. "I'm trying to follow my *diadhanam*. But whatever it requires, I don't think that was it." Unless it had aught to do with the topaz jewel lodged in my thoughts, anyway.

"All right." My father relaxed. "So everything else passes well? I trust that Jehanne's not bedeviled you beyond bearing since you're still keeping company with de Mereliot. You've managed to avoid further entanglements on that front?"

"Ahh . . ." I remembered seeing a pair of letters addressed to me and stamped with the crest of House Courcel on the receiving tray at the townhouse. I'd hurried out without bothering to open them. "Well. Almost."

He frowned. "What?"

"Prince Thierry has been courting me," I admitted. "I may have, um, encouraged him more than I intended."

My father closed his eyes. "You bedded the Dauphin?"

"Only once!"

His shoulders shook. He wiped one hand over his face and got himself under control. When he opened his eyes, they were bright with a mixture of mirth and rue. "Moirin . . . Elua have mercy!"

"It was only once," I repeated.

My father shook his head. "One thing's for sure. Whatever else you may be, you're Naamah's child and no mistake."

FORTY

My father stayed in the City for a whole month.

It was the nicest time I'd had since I came there. The scholarly members of the Circle had retreated into their arcane research. In the absence of activity, the rumors faded as the gossipmongers of Terre d'Ange moved on to the next topic.

My strength returned, drip by drip.

To be sure, there were setbacks. Raphael concentrated on his work as a physician. A few times, he asked my aid, but only in times of dire need. That, I couldn't begrudge. Together, we saved the life of a woman in childbirth—the young Marquise d'Ilon. She'd begun bleeding heavily during labor.

We staunched the bloodflow, Raphael and I.

There were times when I thought I *did* love him, and that was one of them. When he placed the squalling babe in the grateful young mother's arms and grinned at me through his exhaustion, hair plastered to his brow. He'd attended her while she labored for hours before he sent for me, knowing the toll it would take to aid him.

There were times when I didn't.

There was Jehanne—always Jehanne. The three of us existed in an uneasy truce. The City thrived on discussing it. But it seemed for the moment that she tolerated me and was issuing no ultimatums.

There was Thierry.

He was stubborn and persistent, wooing me with a mix of patience and humor. And he was good company. During those times that Raphael was either attending the Queen or occupied with his duties, I accepted Thierry's invitation to escort me to various functions.

I attended the theater for the first time with him.

I heard my first harpsichord concert.

These were wondrous and magical things to me, and Thierry reveled in sharing them with me. I liked that about him.

I just didn't love him.

But for the most part, I kept up my lessons with Master Lo Feng and I spent as much time as I could with my father.

He liked to walk the City and I liked to walk it with him. I loved seeing that mantle of grace that spread in his wake. He went to the richest and the poorest quarters. It made no difference to him. From time to time, bold strangers, men and women alike, would approach him, fingering the folds of his robes.

"Will you invoke Naamah's blessing for me, Brother?" they would ask.

When he was with me, he always shook his head. "Today, I can give you only my own good wishes."

"What's the difference?" I asked him the first time it happened.

My father smiled at me sidelong.

I understood. "Oh."

I thought a lot about that—the act of love as a benediction, a physical manifestation of divine grace.

It was a lovely notion.

It was a very D'Angeline notion.

And it was something I yearned for. I understood it in the marrow of my bones. It was the source of the infinite brilliance behind the bright lady's smile. And there was passion and compassion and glory and wonder in it. And there was nothing in it that brought sorrow to the magnificent gaze of the Maghuin Dhonn Herself.

One day, I thought, I would know it.

I learned the last of the Five Styles of Breathing—the Breath of Wind's Sigh. For this, Master Lo Feng held the lesson in a bell tower at the Academy. Its arched windows were open to the winter winds. Bao spread our mats on the narrow walkway. A great bronze bell hovered above our heads, the pull-rope dangling into the tower's void.

Gusts flickered through the open tower. It was cold, and I breathed the Breath of Embers Glowing until I was warm enough to concentrate.

"Feel the wind." Master Lo Feng inhaled deeply through his nose. "Draw it into you. Up and up and up." He tapped the space between his eyes. "Here."

I breathed.

Up and up and up.

I felt very sharp and keen, my thoughts focused.

"Let it go."

I let it go.

Another tap. "Take it back."

I took it back.

Like everything Master Lo Feng had taught me, it was the same and different all at once. I breathed in and out. The wintry wind played over my skin, tugged at the folds of my cloak. The space behind my eyes expanded and contracted. I felt weightless and airy, as though I could leap from the tower, take wing and soar.

It was a good month.

It came to an end when another set of troubled lovers came to the temple to ask for aid—a pair of young Azzallese noblemen who had sworn an eternal lovers' oath in defiance of both their families. In turn, their families had disinherited them.

"I don't care about wealth or estates," the older of the two said fiercely, his hand hovering over the hilt of his sword. He had coal-black hair and an imperious manner. "But I'm a scion of House Trevalion. I want my *name* back."

"Armande . . ." the other said soothingly. "Be nice. He's trying to help."

My father spoke to them at length in private and agreed to speak to the families.

I wished he weren't leaving again so soon. "Do you have to go? A little humility might do that prickly fellow good."

He laughed. "Azza's line doesn't humble easily. And yes, I have to go. It's in keeping with my vows and the tradition of this temple."

"Why don't their families want them together?" I asked. "Is it a matter of status?"

"No, but it's a matter of inheritance," he said. "Their families expect them to carry on their bloodlines one day. The oath they've sworn binds them to each other alone until death parts them." He smiled at me. "Young men can be extreme in their passions. Nine times out of ten, it mellows with age. They change their minds when they begin thinking about heirs of their own."

"But not always," I said.

"No," my father agreed. "And if they don't, it means Elua's hand truly joined them. Either way, I'm sure I can convince the families to relent for now."

"I'm sure you can."

He cocked his head at me. "Would you like to come with me?"

My heart leapt—and my *diadh-anam* flickered, dimming. "I can't," I said sadly. "I don't think I'm meant to."

My father shook his head. "You and your destiny."

"It's very inconvenient," I said.

He kissed my forehead. "I'll be back before the Longest Night. Do you think you might manage to stay out of trouble until then?"

"I'll try," I promised.

Things changed once my father was gone. Exactly why, I couldn't have said; it wasn't as though he *did* anything specific to ease life's travails. But his presence was a balm in my life, oil spread over troubled waters. Once he was gone, the stormclouds gathered and the waters roiled.

First, I quarrelled with Thierry.

It was entirely by accident that I overheard him in the Hall of Games, bantering with Marc de Thibideau—whose broken leg was quite well healed—and Balthasar Shahrizai over a dice table. For once, I wasn't eavesdropping. We'd made an appointment. I'd just misgauged the time and arrived early.

"—passel of little witchling babes," Balthasar was saying in a teasing tone. "Do you suppose she'd want to swaddle them in bearskins?"

"Name of Elua, man!" Thierry laughed. They all laughed. "Have you lost your mind? Don't be absurd. I'd never *wed* Moirin."

I froze.

Marc de Thibideau saw me first. A flush of hot blood stained his fair cheeks. He'd begged me not to leave him a cripple, and I hadn't. Balthasar Shahrizai raised his brows and fell silent.

Thierry turned and stammered my name.

"You know," I said to him, "it's not as though I had the slightest interest in wedding you. And yet to find you speaking so dismissively of the notion among your companions hurts nonetheless. I thought we were better friends."

I walked out.

He let me go.

And then there was the Circle of Shalomon.

Denis de Toulard called for a meeting at his country estate. Insofar as such events had gone, this one at least began pleasantly. We had a lengthy and extensive meal with course after course, and a different wine served with each one. Member after member offered toasts to knowledge and their pursuit. Afterward, there was pungent cheese and perry brandy.

"Moirin." Denis leaned forward, his elbows on the table. "Raphael said you promised to hear us out. Will you?"

I glanced at Raphael. "I also said you would be wasting your breath. But I will keep my promise and listen."

Denis nodded at Claire Fourcay. "Go ahead."

Her eyes shone. "Orien and I have dug deep into the archives, and our thought is this: We aimed too low. We've been wasting our time summoning the lesser spirits. Of course they've played childish tricks on us. Of course they've done their best to fob us off with foolish gifts." Her nose twitched and she rubbed it unthinking. "We need to cease wasting time. We need to summon one of the greater spirits."

"Who?" someone asked.

"Focalor," Orien de Legasse announced. "Focalor, who wields power over wind and sea." He inclined his head toward Balric Maitland, his spectacles flashing. "Of course, we'd depend on you to forge a silver chain capable of binding him twice over."

"Of course," the silversmith agreed.

There was a good deal more: arcane arguments backed up by citations of arcane texts as to why *this* time it would succeed, *this* time they had found the means to circumvent any trickery. When it was finished, they all looked at me.

I stood. "I have listened. My answer is no."

"Moirin." Raphael rose, his hands gripping my upper arms. Where he touched me, irresistible warmth suffused my skin. His grey eyes pleaded with me. Memories surfaced behind mine. Cold, cold water dragging at his clothes. A white hand sinking below the waves. A pair of strong arms keeping him afloat. His father's ragged voice at his ear. Raphael's gaze was insistent. "Please?"

I closed my eyes and breathed. *"No."*

He was angry.

They were all angry.

Well and so, I was angry, too. Angry at them for using me, for blaming me when I refused to let myself be used. Angry at myself for agreeing to listen to them in the first place. I should have put my foot down earlier, but I'd been tired and vulnerable.

"I'll take my leave in the morning," I said to Raphael when we returned to the townhouse late that night. "I'll find lodgings elsewhere."

He didn't answer right away. When he did, his voice was low. "Let's not make any decisions tonight. We're both out of sorts. Sleep on it."

It was too late to argue. "We'll talk on the morrow."

Raphael nodded and turned away, then turned back. "I don't want you to go, Moirin."

"You never do. And yet . . ." I shrugged. "We'll talk."

"All right."

The morning brought two things. The first was a letter from Prince Thierry, filled with apologies and self-recrimination. The tone was genuine and heartfelt, unlike his usual cheerful correspondence. Even the very words etched on the page looked as though he'd labored over them. He reminded me that I'd promised to attend a ball that Jehanne was hosting in three days' time and begged me to send word that I'd keep my promise.

I mulled it over and decided to forgive Thierry. He hadn't meant to hurt me. He was young and had responded thoughtlessly to Balthasar Shahrizai's teasing; and I'd already seen how well that one prodded at sore spots. And I hadn't been entirely fair to Thierry myself. At the least, he deserved a second chance.

Besides, he'd promised to teach me to dance, which I very much wished to learn.

So I penned a swift letter accepting his apology and confirming my plans to attend the ball with him. I dispatched one of Raphael's man-servants with it, feeling good about the decision.

Mayhap it was a good day for decisions, I thought.

And mayhap it would have been, were it not for the second thing. I'd risen early. Raphael had only just emerged for his morning cup of *kavah* when an acolyte from the Temple of Eisheth called on the townhouse.

"Tell her I'll see her in a little while," Raphael muttered. "After I've broken my fast."

The servant hesitated. "She's very distraught, my lord."

"How distraught?"

"*Very.*"

"Elua's Balls." Raphael drained his *kavah* and rubbed his hands over his face. "Eisheth's servants aren't readily distressed," he said in reply to my inquiring glance. I was waiting patiently to talk with him. "Send her in."

The acolyte was very young, very pretty, and *very* distraught. She wore the sea-blue robes of Eisheth's Order and her pretty face was flushed and tear-stained. She flung herself on her knees before Raphael and babbled incoherently

"Slow down!" he pleaded. "I can't make out a word."

"Breathe," I said to the girl. "Deep, slow breaths."

She obeyed and managed to gasp out a coherent sentence. "It's her ladyship. She's dying."

Raphael turned pale. "Sister Marianne?"

The girl nodded and looked back and forth between us. "Is it true that Eisheth's granted you the power to work miracles?"

"Someone has." Raphael glanced at me. "Moirin?"

I couldn't refuse. "Let's go."

The young acolyte—whose name was Gemma—had run on foot all the way from Eisheth's temple. Raphael sent for his carriage. While we waited on the front steps, he gently pried the details from Gemma. It seemed the Head Priestess at the Temple of Eisheth had been bitten on the hand by a rat in the granary. The wound turned septic and re-fused to heal despite being drained and poulticed. Now it was poison-ing her very blood.

"You know she might have to lose the arm," Raphael said gently. "I can't promise a miracle and I'm not a chirurgeon."

"I know." The girl swallowed. "It's too late to amputate."

"How high has the red streak climbed?" he asked.

She touched her armpit. "Here, when I left."

Raphael swore violently. "Why did you wait so sodding long?"

Gemma flinched. "Her ladyship . . . she hid it from us. She tended it herself. By the time the fever and chills took over, it was too late. And you . . ." This time she avoided looking in my direction. "There are rumors. The others are fearful."

"Because of me," I said.

She nodded. "They say better a clean death than an unnatural compact with a witch. But I came anyway."

The carriage pulled into the outer courtyard. We scrambled inside and Raphael ordered his driver, Nevil, to make haste for the Temple of Eisheth. In a trice, we were clattering swiftly down the streets of the City.

"What in Blessed Elua's name was the Head Priestess doing chasing rats in the granary?" Raphael asked Gemma.

She laughed through her tears. "She's always been a right scourge. Says they carry disease. She doesn't even trust the cats to do a proper job of it."

He shook his head. "I've known Sister Marianne Prichard since I was a boy," he said to me. "She was the royal chirurgeon of House Mereliot for many years. She took vows in Eisheth's Order after my parents died."

"Oh," I said softly.

"I missed her." Raphael's voice was wistful. "When I came to the City, she was one of the first people I sought out."

We arrived at the Temple of Eisheth in short order and disembarked from the carriage. The building and grounds passed in a blur. Raphael and I hurried after Gemma as she hoisted the skirts of her robes and ran through the temple, down one corridor and another.

Gemma halted and flung open a closed door. "Is she—?"

"Shhh." A priest in sea-blue robes put a finger to his lips. There were half a dozen priests and priestesses clustered around a bed in which a small figure lay. "Trouble her not."

"Sister Marianne?" Raphael called. "It's me."

There was an inaudible whisper in reply, followed by a quiet commotion around the bed. With obvious reluctance, the members of Eisheth's Order bowed their heads and stood aside, looking askance at me.

Raphael beckoned. "Come."

I knew nothing of medicine. Even so, it was obvious to me that the elderly woman in the bed was dying. In her sunken face, her eyes were bright with the awareness of it. She shivered feverishly and convulsively. One arm was skinny, the skin loose and wrinkled on the bone. The other was swollen, the skin taut and streaked with red. It seemed to throb visibly.

"Raphael de Mereliot," she whispered.

He knelt and clasped her good hand. "Why did you hide it?"

She gave a near-soundless wheeze of laughter. "The Head Priestess laid low by a rat? I was embarrassed."

"That was foolish."

"Yes." Her fever-bright gaze drifted onto me. Her withered lips twitched in an attempt at a smile. "So this is your witch. She's quite lovely."

"This is Moirin," Raphael said firmly. "She's here to help you. *We're* here to help you."

Sister Marianne's eyes glazed.

"Ah, no!" I said in alarm.

Raphael rubbed his hands together, generating heat. I could see his gift, Eisheth's gift, coiling around him, rising and ready to encompass mine. I didn't need him to tell me that this would be a more difficult healing than aught we'd attempted. I could see.

We were enclosed in a man-made stone place. I wished we weren't. I closed my eyes and breathed, cycling through the Five Styles of Breathing, drawing energy from every element into every part of me.

His voice cracked. "Moirin, *now*!"

I wasn't ready.

It didn't matter; there was no time left. Raphael laid his hands over Sister Marianne's heart. I laid my hands over his and summoned the twilight, breathing it out.

Energy flowed out of me and into him.

Out of him and into her.

This time I felt it more keenly. It wasn't only one thing like a broken bone or a tear in the wall of a womb. The poison was everywhere. It was in her blood, seeking to stop her heart. He pushed it back and back and back. It pushed back at him, parting like a stream to slither past his touch.

"More," he whispered.

I gave him more.

The elderly priestess groaned. It was a painful sound, but a good sound. An *alive* sound.

The red streaks retreated an inch.

Two inches.

"More!"

Was this destiny? I didn't know. I'd passed through the stone doorway. I'd seen the Maghuin Dhonn Herself and the sorrow in Her eyes. It was bright and dark all at once there. The world sparkled before my eyes. I'd seen an ocean. I'd crossed an ocean. I breathed in and out, trying to hold on to a piece of myself. Somewhere, I could hear Gemma weeping; somewhere, I could hear prayers murmured in awestruck voices.

The red streaks receded. Down her arm, past her elbow.

Raphael's voice was exultant. *"More!"*

More.

The swelling abated. The fever broke. The wound in Sister Marianne's hand burst open and a flood of foul pus drained from it.

Gone.

All gone.

"Gone," I whispered—and fainted.

FORTY-ONE

S ister Marianne lived, and so did I.

There was no more talk that day or the next of my leaving Raphael's household. He took me home and tended me himself. I knew he was grateful.

I was glad we'd saved the priestess' life—and yet. How many such efforts did I have left in me?

Would there come a time when the toll was too high?

I didn't know, and it troubled me.

On the third day, a gift arrived from Prince Thierry—an ebony hair-comb inlaid with three emeralds. The accompanying note said he looked forward to seeing me wear it at the ball that evening.

"Surely you're not still going," Raphael said.

"Why not?" I reclined against the pillows, admiring the comb. "So I'll be good and rested for the next emergency that comes along?"

His eyes darkened. "I'm speaking as a physician."

I put the comb down. "You know, if you were speaking as my lover, I might actually listen. Are you escorting Jehanne tonight or is she attending the King?"

Raphael looked away. "His majesty isn't fond of balls."

"Well, I've never been to one," I said. "And I mean to attend this one."

So I did.

The maid Daphne helped me dress for it, chattering all the while. I wore a gown that Benoit Vallon had designed for me, a slender sheath of forest-green satin that left my shoulders bare. She coiled my hair atop my head, pinning it and securing the comb. I applied a touch of kohl to my eyes and carmine to my lips.

The face that gazed back at me in the mirror looked tired. Beautiful, but tired. My father was right. I looked like I'd been ill.

Mayhap I had been.

Mayhap I still was.

A coach bearing the silver swan insignia of House Courcel came for me shortly after nightfall. A solicitous footservant in Courcel livery helped me into the coach. I rested my head against the cushions thinking, I should be happy. And I wasn't.

At the Palace, I made an effort for Thierry's sake. He hurried over the instant the herald announced me. His lips brushed mine. "I'm so glad you came," he said. "And so glad you decided to forgive me."

I took his arm. "So am I."

And I made an effort for *my* sake. Everything was so very lovely. The hall glowed with warm light. It glinted on the gilded chandeliers; it gleamed on the polished marble floor. It illuminated the faces of the D'Angeline peers in all their finery.

Especially the Queen, with Raphael at her side.

Thierry led me over to greet her. Jehanne was wearing a gown of ivory silk. A coronet of pearls was threaded through her silver-gilt hair and a choker of pale blue topaz winked around her slender throat. Raphael's gift. She looked as beautiful and ethereal as moonlight on new-fallen snow.

I made my greeting and curtsied. "This is all very wonderful. Thank you, your majesty."

"This is a mere trifle." She waved one dismissive hand. "Is it your first?"

"It is."

Jehanne studied me, frowning a little. Another time, her scrutiny would have discomfited me, but I was too weary tonight. "Well. Enjoy yourself."

I curtsied again. "My thanks."

The musicians began to play as Thierry led me away. Everyone watched the Queen, waiting for their cue to take to the dance floor. "That was surprisingly civil," Thierry remarked. "It's all over the City how you saved Sister Marianne's life at the Temple of Eisheth. I'd ex-pected Jehanne to be in a snit over it."

"Oh, well." I shrugged. "Mayhap even her majesty has her limits."

"Mayhap." He sounded doubtful.

We watched Raphael bow and extend his arm to the Queen, escort-ing her onto the dance floor. He wore a dark brown velvet doublet over fawn-colored breeches, an ivory shirt with a ruffled collar, and cuffs that matched the hue of her gown.

They danced very well together.

They looked lovely together.

Thierry bowed to me. "Are you ready for your first lesson, my lady?"

"Yes, please."

On the floor, I did as he told me—one hand clasped in his, the other resting on his waist. I followed his lead, letting him guide my steps with subtle pressure. As I had suspected, I liked dancing very much. I liked the way we swirled and glided over the floor together, each couple in their own private orbit, instinctively avoiding all oth-ers. I thought it must be something like the way the stars and planets moved in their dance, the way everything in the cosmos moved to-gether at once, stately and graceful, never colliding.

Still, it made me a little dizzy.

And more tired.

I danced three times with Thierry, then Marc de Thibideau begged a dance of me. He wasn't nearly as skillful a partner and I tripped over his feet.

"I'm sorry, my lady." He flushed. "It's thanks to you I'm able to dance at all."

"And Raphael," I reminded him.

Marc shook his head. "Without you, he's just another physician."

I thought of the first time Raphael had kissed me, the first time I'd felt my gift intertwine with his. Of Raphael tending to me on the street after his carriage had struck me. Of my aching ribcage and the glorious warmth of his touch dispelling the pain, putting things back in place. "That's not true."

He shrugged. "It's true for me."

There were others, then—too many others. Two or three I didn't know by name. Denis de Toluard, surprising me.

"I thought you were angry at me," I said to him.

His eyes were grave. "I'm hoping you'll reconsider."

Out of the corners of my eyes, I saw trailing flashes of light, candle-flames blurring in my weary vision as Denis spun me into an expert turn. "I won't."

When the song ended, he bowed. "Still. Think on it."

And then Balthasar Shahrizai. He held me close, too close, his hand on my lower back, pressing me to him. I could feel his arousal and tried to pull away. He only pulled me closer.

"Have you no shame?" I asked him.

Balthasar laughed. "You don't know much about House Shahrizai, do you?"

"No," I admitted. "And I'm not sure I'm eager to learn more."

I wished Raphael would claim a dance of me, but he didn't. I was grateful when Thierry reclaimed me, and even more grateful when the music came to a halt. There was a banquet table laid at the far end of the hall. Servants were filing in and out with covered dishes. Jehanne clapped her hands together and proclaimed it time to dine. The musicians resumed playing at softer volume.

The hall spun around me.

"Moirin?" Thierry's hand was beneath my elbow. "Are you all right?"

"Fine." I blinked at him. "I'm fine."

I wasn't fine.

At the banquet table, we were seated across from the Queen and her escort. Of course—Thierry was the Dauphin. He was second in rank to her. The royal chef carved exquisitely thin slices of a roasted beef loin. More servants circulated, pouring wine, serving soup in shallow bowls, dishing out ladles full of mashed tubers and roasted grains, sauteed greens sizzling in fat. Rich sauces were poured. Queen Jehanne gestured—plates were filled.

Beside her, Raphael scowled at me.

"I'm fine, " I said in reply to his unspoken reprimand. I reached for my wineglass, misjudged the distance, and knocked it over. Somewhere inside, I winced.

A red stain spread on the white linen covering the table.

"Elua!" Jehanne sounded irritated. "What ails you?"

I closed my eyes. "Nothing."

"It's not nothing." Raphael rose, his voice crisp. "Your majesty, forgive me. I shouldn't have let Moirin come here tonight. She needs bedrest. I'll escort her home."

Thierry rose, too. "The hell you will, de Mereliot! She'll stay with me."

Back and forth, they argued. With an effort, I cracked my eyes open. All I could see was their arms, braced on the banquet table as they leaned inward and shouted at one another. And Jehanne, looking at once exquisite and annoyed.

I felt homesick.

I wished my father were here.

"I'm sorry, your majesty," I murmured.

"Indeed." Jehanne's gaze flicked from my face to the arguing men and back. Through my haze of exhaustion, I realized it wasn't *me* who was annoying her. Something in her expression hardened as she came to a decision. "I'm going to rescue you now. Any objections?"

I put my head in my hands. "No."

"Good." She beckoned to her Captain of the Guard and issued a few curt instructions. He bowed, turned and relayed them. One of his men departed. Two others moved to take up positions behind Raphael and Thierry, laying hands on their shoulders as Queen Jehanne stood. "Gentlemen."

She didn't raise her voice; she didn't have to. It cut through their quarrel, cool and smooth as a blade. At her guardsmen's unsubtle urging, they took their seats.

"I'm taking Moirin into my custody," she informed them.

Raphael snorted. "You can't just conscript her, Jehanne! Moirin's not even a D'Angeline citizen. You don't have sovereignty over her."

"I'm not conscripting her," she replied calmly. "I'm saving her from herself, since you, my lord, seem intent on killing her by degrees—and you, your highness, are too ineffectual to do anything about it, assuming you've even noticed."

Prince Thierry swore. I hunched my shoulders together.

Raphael half rose. "Jehanne, you don't have the right!"

Her gaze was icy. "She'll come willingly."

He gave a harsh bark of laughter. The other guests watched the drama unfolding with unprecedented delight. "I hate to be the one to destroy your fondest held beliefs, but there *are* people in the world who don't find you irresistible, my lady."

"Are there?" Jehanne seemed to find the notion amusing. "Luckily for her, Moirin isn't one of them." She gestured and her Captain of the Guard came around the table, bowed, and offered me his arm.

"Don't." Raphael glowered across the table at me, his eyes full of stormclouds. "Name of Elua, Moirin! What earthly reason do you have to trust her?"

I looked at Jehanne.

"I kept my word," she reminded me. "*I* never gave you cause for regret."

"You damned, conniving, cuckolding bitch," Thierry said in a low voice. "What did you do?"

I didn't stay to hear the answer or the firestorm of gossip and speculation it was likely to ignite. I turned my head away from Raphael's furious gaze, took the captain's arm, and let him escort me from the hall.

FORTY-TWO

After being examined by the royal chirurgeon, I fell asleep in a luxuriously appointed suite of guest-chambers, and slept like the dead.

I awoke to sunlight and greenery.

Plants.

The bedchamber was full of plants.

For a moment, all I could do was stare, disbelieving my own eyes. There were plants I recognized from the glass pavilion—palm trees and enormous ferns. There were orange and lemon trees breathing a citrus fragrance into the air. There were hastily planted evergreens in large pots complaining at the braziers that warmed the room. It was as though the entire outdoors of some unlikely clime had been transported into the chamber. I laughed aloud for sheer pleasure.

Beyond a giant fern frond, a figure squatting by the door stirred. "You alive, huh?"

I sat up and squinted. *"Bao?"*

"Uh-huh." He rose with careless grace, staff in one hand. "I go get Master Lo."

I looked around. "Am I still in the Palace? What are you doing here?"

Bao shrugged. "Master Lo ask me to stay, I stay."

"How did he know I was here?"

He shrugged again. "You ask for him."

"Oh." I had a vague memory of begging the royal chirurgeon to send word to Master Lo Feng. "How did . . ." I gestured around at the plants.

"Good, huh?" Bao looked smug. "Master Lo's idea. You need wood energy, earth energy. That White Queen, she say bring them all. Fill the room."

I flushed. "Jehanne was here?"

"Uh-huh. Lots of people in and out. You sleep like dead girl. Is it true you and the Queen . . . ?" He made a lewd gesture.

"Um." My face got hotter.

Bao grinned. "I think she like you."

He left to fetch Master Lo Feng. I collapsed back on the pillows, wondering if it were true. One thing was sure, whatever her motives, Jehanne was right. I'd needed someone to save me from myself.

I breathed in the wonderful green-smelling air and dozed for the better part of an hour until Bao returned with Lo Feng.

My mentor shook his elegant head at me. "Foolish girl." He felt my pulse up and down my wrists and made me stick out my tongue for him. When he was finished, he beckoned to Bao, who twirled his staff with a flourish and deposited a silk-wrapped bundle on the bed. "I've prepared a tonic for you." Master Lo Feng untied the bundle to reveal a multitude of sheer muslin pouches filled with dried herbs. "You will steep one pouch in hot water and drink it twice a day. I will speak to the kitchen regarding food that is healthful. Now." He folded his hands into his sleeves. "Will you listen and heed?"

"Yes, my lord," I said humbly.

"Very good." He gave me a sharp nod. "You have a gift, Moirin. But you pay a price for using it. When you draw energy from the earth and give it back to the earth, it is like"—he withdrew one hand from his sleeve and described a rotating circle in the air—"a wheel powered by the stream to grind grain."

I'd seen such a thing. "A waterwheel."

"Even so." Master Lo Feng inclined his head. "The stream's energy makes the millstone turn, but the water is taken and given back. In the end, nothing is lost. All is in accordance with nature."

"I understand."

He raised one finger. "Understand this. The stream is your vital *chi*.

When you draw energy and spend it in a manner unnatural to you, it is as though you spill your water on barren soil instead of returning it to the stream. In time, the streambed will run dry."

I sighed. "I understand, I do."

"You wish to do good," Lo Feng said gently. "And you wish to find your place in the world. Those are very fine desires. And yet desires are encumbrances. It is wise to let go of them. You find yourself in a place of refuge. Rest and be grateful."

"I will," I promised.

He folded hand over fist and bowed. "When you are ready to resume your lessons, Bao and I will be waiting."

I rested in my green-scented chamber filled with plants.

I was grateful.

And for a while, a little while, I let go of the urgent sense of purpose that had driven me across the Straits. I ceased to fret over what the Maghuin Dhonn Herself intended for me. Quiet, efficient servants came in and out at intervals, asking if there was aught I required. My few possessions and increasingly larger wardrobe arrived, transported from Raphael's townhouse. I forced myself not to think about Raphael and how furious he must be. I slept intermittently. I ate the rich and spicy foods Master Lo Feng had ordered the kitchen to make for me. I steeped his muslin pouches and drank his tea. I let myself drift.

Although desire . . .

Well.

I was told that Queen Jehanne had stopped by that first day, but I was sleeping and she left me undisturbed. When she came the second day, I was awake. She stood in the doorway surveying the indoor jungle, then regarding me with an inscrutable look.

I didn't know what to say. "Thank you, your majesty," I managed at last. "This is very, very wonderful."

"You like it?" Jehanne smiled a little. "It suits you. You're looking much improved."

"I'm feeling much improved." I took a deep breath and asked the question foremost in my mind. "Why are you being so kind to me?"

"Oddly enough, I've been asking myself that very question." She dismissed her attendants and bade the guard to see that no one bothered us, closing the door behind him.

"And have you answered it?" I asked.

Jehanne sat uninvited on the end of my bed, curling her legs beneath her gown like a girl. Sunlight filtering through leaves made green shadows on her fair skin. "You know, my motives may not have been admirable, but I had fun with you that day at Cereus House," she said candidly. "It reminded me of younger, more carefree times." She tilted her head. "I was born into the Night Court. Many of us are. Both my parents were adepts of Cereus House."

"I see," I said, although I didn't.

She made a face at me. "Oh, let me talk. Growing up in the Night Court, we learned early. The Dowaynes like to begin training us young. Long before we're allowed to study the arts of the bedchamber, we're trained to be perfect attendants and companions, to serve and entertain. But, of course, we stole into the library to study the sacred texts, we hid in the wings to watch the Showings. By the time formal bedchamber training begins, we knew all there was to know about Naamah's arts, at least in theory. That's true of most adepts."

"But not all?" I inquired.

"No." Jehanne shook her head. Light scintillated from a pair of diamond eardrops adorning her delicate lobes. "Betimes a House will take on a promising young man or woman with no training whatsoever." She smiled. "Some gorgeous unlikely creature from a backwoods hamlet too poor to own a single copy of the *Trois Milles Joies*, with no experience of aught but crude peasant rutting and a hunger to learn more."

I didn't think it was a particularly flattering description, but I bit my tongue on the thought.

She saw it in my face anyway and laughed. "You don't understand, Moirin. As a full-fledged adept, it was part of my job to train them. And that was one of my favorite things in the world to do." She shivered with remembered pleasure. "All that untutored ardor! So eager to please, so ready to be delighted by unimagined pleasures."

I made a noncommittal sound.

"You think I'm mocking you." Jehanne eyed me shrewdly. "I'm not. Innocence fades, you know. And at Cereus House, we're taught to revere the ephemeral nature of beauty. That's why our adepts were sought after for training raw recruits. What they were . . . it was a transient thing. So poignant. We took joy in them as no others could."

"Joy," I echoed softly.

"You made me remember," she said simply. "And then you even showed me a piece of magic when I asked. It seemed such a gentle, lovely thing. Despite everything, I liked being with you. And then I began to watch *you* fade. Far too soon and far too fast. It offended my sensibilities. I tried to make Raphael let you go, and he wouldn't. Aside from making a name as a miracle worker, I don't know what in the seven hells he's been up to with you. Whatever it is, you, apparently, were too besotted to refuse him. So I intervened, and here you are."

My eyes stung. "Jehanne . . ."

"Elua, don't cry!" She sounded cross.

"I'm not." I blinked, rubbed away my tears, and smiled at her. "You should be nice more often. It's very pleasant."

The Queen of Terre d'Ange shrugged one slender shoulder. "Everyone falls a little bit in love with me when I'm nice. It's tiresome."

"I'll try not to add to your burden, your majesty," I offered in a cool tone.

"Oh, please." She glanced sidelong at me. "*You* fell a little bit in love with me the moment you laid eyes on me."

I opened my mouth to deny it, and couldn't.

Her blue-grey eyes danced. "Don't worry, you're far too intriguing to become tiresome. But I should let you rest. Are you wondering if I mean to kiss you before I leave?"

I laughed. "I am *now.*"

"I do." Jehanne suited actions to words. She ducked beneath an overhanging frond of a giant fern and kissed me, gently at first, then with a measure of passion, her tongue darting past my lips. Her intoxicating scent enveloped me.

It felt very, very good.

I kissed her back, slid my arms around her neck. I didn't want her to go. I wanted to see her naked with fern shadows painted on her skin. I wanted to taste her again. "Don't leave," I whispered. "Not yet."

If I'd said such a thing to Raphael, he would have patted my cheek and told me I needed bed-rest. But Jehanne was Naamah's child twice over. She merely gave me one of her sparkling looks. "Well, it's a good thing I told the guard to see we weren't disturbed, isn't it?"

It may not have been a benediction, but it was the nearest thing to it I'd known in love-making. It was slow, languid, and healing. And I knew that whatever else transpired, I would always be a little bit in love with Jehanne, and I would always remember her best as I saw her that day in my sunlit, plant-filled bedchamber, green shadows dappling her fair skin and the pale night-blooming flower of her marque.

"I have to go," she said at last when the shadows were growing long. "I'm dining with Daniel this evening."

"Ohhh." I'd quite forgotten about the King. "What does he, um . . ." I gestured vaguely at the tangled bed linens. "Think of this?"

Jehanne smiled. "His majesty is highly amused."

"Truly?"

She reached for her gown. "Oh, yes. He told me I had to choose between you and Raphael." I stared at her. "I'm very angry at Raphael," she added, stepping gracefully into her gown. "Lace my stays, please?"

I obeyed silently.

"Moirin." Jehanne turned and took my chin in her hand when I'd finished, forcing me to look up at her. "This isn't some ploy in a game, if that's what you're wondering. I haven't told you a single falsehood."

"So what am I?" I gestured again. "What is this?"

She cocked her head. "What do you want it to be? Would you like me to declare you my royal companion? Court witch, mayhap?"

I had to laugh. "I don't know."

"Then don't worry about it." Jehanne kissed me. "As a scion of House Courcel, you're welcome to stay here as long as you like. And you're here under my protection because it pleases me to have you here. Rest. Recover. I'll come see you on the morrow. And when you're stronger, you can return to your lessons with that delightful Ch'in gentleman, and you and I can have a good long talk about exactly what Raphael and his coterie of arcane scholars are up to in the countryside."

The latter, I didn't relish. "You thought Master Lo Feng was delightful?"

"Quite." She twisted her hair into a lover's-haste knot. "He's very modest, but Daniel says in his own country, he's known as the Ninth Immortal."

I hadn't known that. "Who are the other eight?"

Jehanne laughed. "I haven't the faintest idea." She stooped and kissed me again. "You be sure and tell me when you find out."

"I will," I promised. "Jehanne . . . thank you."

She raised her brows. "Why? Do you imagine for an instant I wasn't enjoying myself? I haven't bothered to feign pleasure since I made my marque."

"No." I smiled. "I didn't think that. But I do think you may have saved my life."

"Ah." Jehanne gave me one of her complicated looks, then smiled back at me. "Mayhap I did at that."

With that, my unlikely rescuer departed.

I fell asleep with the scent of her still lingering on my skin.

FORTY-THREE

The hardest part about recovering was facing the Court.

"You're stalling," Jehanne accused me at the end of a week's time. "You're *obviously* feeling well enough."

I sighed. I couldn't deny it, having just demonstrated it at length and with considerable enthusiasm. "Will Raphael be there?"

She shook her head. "He's not been to Court since the night of the ball. He's in a furious sulk." She paused. "Are you ready to talk about him?"

"Nooo." I wound a lock of her hair around my fingers. "Will Thierry be there?"

"It's a state dinner," Jehanne said wryly. "Yes, the Dauphin will be present. But don't worry, the brunt of his anger is directed at me." She sighed, too. "It's my own fault. I shouldn't have dressed him down in public."

"He had strong feelings for you once," I said.

"I know." She pillowed her head on one arm. "I realized it too late. I would have handled it differently if I'd known. I should have treated him as a young man, with respect. Instead, I treated him like a boy who'd lost his mother." One shoulder shrugged. "I was young; I thought it was the proper thing to do. He was insulted, and he resented me for supposing I could take her place."

"Did you?" I asked.

"Never." Jehanne traced the line of my collarbone. "Thierry never understood that his father could let himself love me because I'm nothing like his mother." She smiled sadly. "Nor that she'll always be the one woman I can never compete with. She'll always be first in Daniel's heart."

"That's why Lianne's poem made him so melancholy?" I asked.

She nodded. "And that's why he tolerates my foibles. We're unfaithful to one another in different ways."

"Sad," I murmured.

"Yes, and I'd forgotten you were spying on us that night."

"I wasn't—"

"You were." Jehanne kissed me and bit my lower lip lightly. "Come to dinner, my lovely witchling. People are starting to say I've locked you away in a dungeon."

I glanced around the room filled with sunlight and greenery. "It's a pleasant prison."

"And you're a charming prisoner, but I don't think you're meant to be kept in a cage, Moirin." She untangled her body from mine and slid out of bed. "Besides, I like to parade my conquests."

I eyed her, trying to guess if she was jesting.

I didn't think so.

Jehanne smiled sweetly at me. "Come to dinner."

So I went to dinner.

At the beginning, it was every bit as uncomfortable as I'd feared it would be. I dressed carefully with a maid's assistance. I wore the bronze gown I'd first worn at Court, though not the emerald eardrops Raphael had given me, and surely not the comb that had been Thierry's gift. Jehanne sent her Captain of the Guard to escort me. He was unfailingly polite. Still, the moment we entered the dining hall, there was a little silence, followed by covert stares and murmurs. It was much the same as my first appearance at Court—and altogether different.

Across the hall, Thierry glared daggers at me. His comrades whispered.

I breathed the Breath of Earth's Pulse, slow and deep.

"Lady Moirin." King Daniel clasped my hands and bent to give me the kiss of greeting. "I'm pleased you're feeling better."

I flushed. "Thank you, your majesty."

Jehanne gave me a wicked smile. "Ever so much better, aren't you?"

I scowled at her and she laughed, linking her arm with mine. "Come, sit. Try not to knock over any wineglasses."

And that, it seemed, was that.

I'd been Raphael's witch; now I was the Queen's witch. The speculation was confirmed and the gossip swirled elsewhere. At the far end of the banquet table, a passionate discussion about sending an embassy to Terra Nova broke out.

King Daniel's face darkened.

And I watched Jehanne turn the tide of conversation deftly, charming him, cheering him. Seated uncomfortably across the table from me, Prince Thierry looked disconsolate.

"You'd like to go, wouldn't you?" I asked him. "To Terra Nova."

He glowered at me. "What do you care?"

"I care," I said softly.

"Yes." His tone was stiff. "I'd like to go. I'd like to see Terre d'Ange reclaim its role in the world. I'd like a taste of glory and adventure. Is that so wrong?"

I shook my head. "No, of course not." I lowered my voice. "Listen, Thierry . . . I'm sorry. I never meant to hurt you."

He toyed with the food on his plate. "You look well," he said at length. "Like you did when I first saw you."

"I'm wearing the same gown."

That won a brief smile from him. "I don't mean the gown, Moirin."

I smiled back at him. "I know."

"She's fickle," Thierry warned me. "Fickle and vain and self-absorbed."

I glanced at Jehanne's exquisite profile. "I know that, too."

"Well. As long as you know." He took a bite of roasted capon, chewed and swallowed. "When all's said and done, I'm glad *someone* pried you out of de Mereliot's clutches. I just never expected it to be her."

I laughed. "Nor did I."

After that exchange, things were easier between us. It would be an exaggeration to say the balance of the evening was pleasant, but it was tolerable. There was an awkward moment when the King and Queen retired for the night, bidding us to stay and enjoy their hospitality. Everyone rose and bowed or curtsied at their departure. I hesitated, unsure if I was meant to stay or go. I'd never been a royal companion—if that was what I was—before.

Jehanne saw the uncertainty in my face and murmured something to the King, letting go his arm. He nodded.

I had a sudden fear that she meant to ask me to join them. "Your majesty, I hope you don't expect—"

"Elua, no!" Jehanne glanced at Thierry. "Moirin, you're my guest. Stay as long as you wish. Enjoy yourself." She reached up to cup the back of my neck and kissed me before the entire Court, then whispered in my ear, "Only remember, I don't like to share."

I understood. It was unfair and unreasonable—but mayhap also for my own good. I agreed to it without a second thought. "I'll see you on the morrow?"

She nodded, eyes sparkling. "If you behave."

I watched them depart the dining hall together—the King and Queen of Terre d'Ange, her hand resting in the crook of his arm. My royal mistress and her royal husband, leaving to share the royal bedchamber, the ghost of his lost love between them.

Thierry passed me a flagon of brandy. "Here. It helps."

I sighed, poured, and drank.

It helped.

But despite everything, the days that followed were a good time. I was content to be Jehanne's companion. It was a refuge. Her mercurial moods didn't trouble me. She liked talking to me. I liked to listen to her and I never tired of looking at her. I took a great deal of pleasure in pleasing her; and she took a great deal of delight in introducing me to new pleasures.

"Such a sweet bottom begging to be plumbed." Jehanne's voice, cooing. Already, I hovered on the precipice. Her hands, cupping my buttocks. "You're still a virgin there?"

"Aye," I gasped.

She smiled. "Not for long."

"I don't think—" My back arched and I grabbed at the bedsheets. *"Oh!"*

Jehanne de la Courcel was very, very skilled in Naamah's arts.

In that first month, I saw Raphael only once. I'd resumed my lessons with Master Lo Feng and I encountered Raphael in the halls of the Academy. He was walking and talking with Claire Fourcay.

I had to own, my heart quickened at the sight of him.

He stopped dead, his jaw clenching.

"Raphael," I pleaded. "Can we not be civil with one another?"

He swept past me without a word, Claire hurrying in his wake. None of the members of the Circle were speaking to me save Lianne Tremaine. I didn't care about the others, but Raphael's anger troubled me.

"You feel guilty," Jehanne said later. "That's why you don't want to talk about Raphael de Mereliot and his occult schemes."

I wrapped my arms around my knees. "I promised I wouldn't. It would feel like betraying him twice over."

"He was intent on using you toward his own ends," she observed. "You don't think that's a betrayal of sorts?"

I shrugged. "I consented. And he meant well."

She studied my face. "Do you miss him?"

"Do you?" I countered.

"Some days." Jehanne pulled me against her, sinking her hands into my hair and kissing me until the image of Raphael's face blurred in my memory. "Not today." Her grey-blue eyes gazed intently into mine. "Tell me one thing. Are they likely to succeed in whatever they're attempting?"

"No," I murmured. "Not without me."

She kissed me some more. "Good."

Winter deepened. Snow fell, churned to slush in the streets of the City by horses' hooves and carriage wheels. Preparations began for the Midwinter Masque to take place on the Longest Night. My father had promised to return by then, but there was no word of him.

"You're sure?" I asked Noémie d'Etoile at the Temple of Naamah.

"I'm sure." She patted my hand. "Don't fret, Moirin. It's not unusual for Phanuel to be gone for months at a time. Like as not, he's solving some other lovers' dilemma. Problems needing to be solved have a way of finding him."

"I wish he were here, that's all."

The priestess smiled. "Of course you do. Is everything all right with you otherwise? Does being in the Queen's service suit you?"

"Oddly enough, it does."

Noémie laughed. "Not so odd. It's in your blood, after all. By all accounts, it seems to suit her majesty. They say you're a calming influence."

That I hadn't heard. "They do?"

She nodded. "It's been over a month since she made a chambermaid cry. Thirty-two days and counting. That's a new record. They're taking wagers on how long it will last at Bryony House."

I had to smile. "Folk in this City really need to find new pastimes."

At the Academy, Master Lo Feng praised my progress in the Five Styles of Breathing and began teaching me the rudiments of herbal medicine. To the disappointment of both of us, I didn't have a knack for it. Despite my affinity for the plants themselves, I didn't have a head for the complex formulas he taught me—nor any talent in diagnosing ailments. Thanks to the breathing exercises, I did better at sensing the flow of energy and its blockages, but I didn't have Raphael's gift for manipulating it.

Whatever I was, it wasn't a healer.

At least not of humans.

Plants were another matter. Master Lo Feng was particularly intrigued by the Camaeline snowdrop, a rare white flower that grew in the mountains of Camlach province and blossomed in the snowdrifts there once a year. The flowers were pressed and their essence distilled to make *joie*, a liqueur that was traditionally served on the Longest Night.

"*Very* tonic," Lo Feng said in approval. "And you foolish people have not even begun to explore the properties of the bulb!"

To that end, the King had arranged to have a shipment of living snowdrops collected in the high mountains and delivered to Master Lo Feng. I was there in the courtyard the day they arrived, delicate flowers already drooping in the burlap sack that held them.

I touched one. It sang a frail, fading song to itself.

Master Lo Feng watched me. "His majesty says no one has ever kept one alive. They only grow wild in the mountains."

"They're pining for deep snow and thin air," I told him.

"Bao—"

Bao was already in motion. He thrust his omnipresent staff over his shoulder through a loop of leather and began scooping up snow that had gathered in the corners of the courtyard. I helped. Together, we packed the sack full of snow.

"Better?" Bao asked me.

"Better," I agreed. My *diadh-anam* pulsed in my breast. I knelt gingerly on the cold flagstones and listened to the snowdrops' frail song. I closed my eyes and breathed the Breath of Trees Growing, feeling the energy spread throughout my body and thinking about the cycles of giving and taking that linked all living things. And then I breathed the Breath of Wind's Sigh, drawing air up and up behind my eyes, thinking about the cold, high places where the snowdrops grew.

I summoned the twilight, touched the flowers, and blew on them.

Their song grew stronger and clearer.

And I felt less drained than I ever had exercising my gift. I felt the rightness of it. Master Lo Feng had been right about teaching me to breathe and right in his analogy of the waterwheel. What I had given would be returned to me. I could feel the surety of it in the marrow of my bones. When I opened my eyes, my mentor was smiling his subtle smile.

"Magic," he said serenely. "You could keep them alive all the way to Ch'in."

"Oh." I laughed. "That's a very long way."

"Indeed it is," Master Lo Feng agreed, folding his hands in his sleeves.

I wondered if he were jesting.

I didn't think so.

FORTY-FOUR

I knew the very day that Jehanne took Raphael back.

It was early evening when she breezed into my quarters, planning to give me a careless kiss and a promise of more time on the morrow. I was reading a treatise on the propagation of apple trees by a long-dead duc named Percy de Somerville. She plucked it out of my hands and tossed it aside, sitting on my lap and kissing me.

I'd smelled her on Raphael dozens of times. But I knew his scent, too.

Now I smelled him on her.

"What?" Her eyes widened when I flinched away from her. "What is it?"

"Jehanne." I sighed. "Raphael?"

At first she denied it; and then she got angry and hurled various items about the chamber. A hairbrush, a jewelry box, the copy of the *Trois Milles Joies* that she'd given me, all the pillows on the bed. Her anger broke over the room in waves. I folded my arms and let her rampage.

Then she wept.

And I saw her memories surface behind my eyes. Letters from Raphael, furious letters, pleading letters. She had finally answered one. They'd arranged to meet in secret.

Passion and tumult.

I pushed the images away.

I didn't ask why. I knew. He loved her; she loved him. Both of them had admitted it freely. I let Jehanne cry, her head in my lap, her shoulders shaking. I stroked her hair. When she'd cried herself out, she pulled herself upright and wound her arms around my neck, kissing my face.

I tried to pull away. "Jehanne . . ."

Her arms tightened. "Please?" Her eyes were as bright as stars, lashes wet and spiky with tears. I thought she must be the only woman in the world who could manage to look utterly breathtaking after a crying fit. "I need you. I need you to forgive me."

"Not me," I said gently. "I'm not the one bade you choose between us. It's the King's forgiveness you want."

Jehanne shook her head. "I can't. Not like this. Please?" She kissed my throat. "You *have* to forgive me."

"Why?"

She looked up. "Because you're going to leave me one day, and I hate knowing it. If you want me to forgive you for it, you have to forgive me this."

It didn't make sense, but it didn't have to. It was a truth of the heart and it owed nothing to reason. Jehanne was Naamah's child twice over, and she wasn't lying. No matter how much passion and tumult the day had held, there was a powerful and complicated desire rising in her and I couldn't help but respond to it.

"I *need* you," she said again, impatient.

"I'm here," I murmured.

For once, there was no artistry in the act of love between us. It was fierce, urgent, and raw. There was no smile on the bright lady's face, only a look of deep understanding. Jehanne expended passion like fury, taking violent pleasure in taking me. I gave myself over to it, holding her when she shuddered hard and cried out against me. It wasn't until afterward, when she lay quiet in my arms, that I felt the worst of her terrible need drain away.

"Thank you," she whispered into the crook of my neck, breath warm on my skin. "May I stay with you tonight?"

"Is that wise?" I asked.

"I can't face Daniel yet." She sat up and rubbed her eyes. "Will you tell him I'm here?"

I stared at her. "You want me to get out of bed and go tell his majesty that you're spending the night in my chambers?"

"He'll understand." Jehanne gave me a pleading look. "He likes you."

I shook my head. "I must have lost my wits."

And yet I went.

I found his majesty reviewing papers in the royal study. The guard on duty admitted me without delay. It was a warm, masculine room with friezes of polished wood on the walls and a roaring fire in a great fireplace. I began sweating the moment I entered.

King Daniel, seated at a desk, lifted his head. "Moirin, well met. What is it you wish?"

"Ah . . ." I shifted. "Her majesty asked me to tell you that she'll be passing the night in my quarters."

"I see." He pushed his chair back and rose. "She was with Raphael de Mereliot today, wasn't she?"

I didn't answer.

The King smiled ruefully. "It's all right; you needn't lie for her. Jehanne's not as clever at subterfuge as she thinks. I know full well she was with him." He sighed. "When she chose you over him, I thought mayhap it meant she was ready."

I frowned. "I beg your pardon, your majesty?"

"She didn't tell you?" he asked. "We agreed to certain terms before we wed. Thierry is my heir and I love him dearly, but a monarch with a sole heir is ever fearful. I want Jehanne to bear my children. She begged me to wait. We settled on a period of three years. It ends on the Longest Night. On the first day of the new year, Jehanne will light a candle to Eisheth and beseech her to open the gates of her womb."

"Oh," I whispered.

Daniel clasped his hands behind his back and stared into the fire. "She's afraid."

"Of what?" I remembered Thierry accusing her of being too vain to bear children, but I thought it must be something more.

"Her mother nearly died giving birth to her," Daniel said. "And, too, I suspect Jehanne is afraid of herself." His mouth quirked. "She brought joy into my life when it was empty of all meaning. For that alone, I'm willing to forgive her any betrayal save one: Bearing another man's child."

"Oh," I repeated.

He gave me a wry look. "You can see why I was pleased she chose you over him."

"Aye." I had the urge to comfort him. "Your majesty . . . I do believe the Queen is distraught over her own actions. She wants your forgiveness."

King Daniel's clasped hands tightened. "Yet she confessed to *you*."

"She's afraid to face you," I said. "And she didn't confess. I accused her."

His lips quirked again. "That must have gone over well."

"She threw things," I admitted. "But afterward, she wept and said she wanted your forgiveness." It wasn't exactly true, but I thought it was true enough. And he didn't need to know about the other part.

He gazed at the dancing fire. "You may tell her she has it."

"I will," I promised. "Thank you."

Daniel gave me a sharp look. "Tell her also that I'll be less forgiving after the Longest Night. If she consorts with Raphael de Mereliot while we're trying to get with child, I *will* dissolve our vows and set her aside."

I bowed my head. "Aye, your majesty."

His face softened. "They say you're good for her. I do believe it. Few folk would have had the courage to accuse her, and fewer still to come here to speak to me in person." He cocked his head. "I'm curious. I have men assigned to keep watch over de Mereliot. How did you know Jehanne had been with him?"

"Ohh . . ." I shrugged. "I know his scent."

The King blinked. "His scent."

I nodded.

"Elua have mercy!" He laughed shortly. "My wife and her bearwitch." He waved a dismissive hand at me. "Go, go to her. Take care of her. Tell her I'll see her on the morrow."

I headed for the door, grateful.

"Moirin." King Daniel's voice halted me. I turned. He picked up a sheaf of papers from his desk and let them fall, scattering. "These are petitions," he said. "Petitions from various members of Parliament urging me to send an embassy to Terra Nova. You're an outsider.

Objective. And yet you're a descendant of House Courcel. I know Thierry's spoken to you. What are your thoughts on the matter?"

I hesitated. "I don't know, your majesty. I'm a child of the Maghuin Dhonn. I would have been content to spend my life in a cave if She hadn't willed otherwise. But since you ask, I will say that I think the peers of Terre d'Ange could use a better pastime than wagering on how many days will pass before the Queen makes a chambermaid cry."

He stirred the strewn papers with his fingertips. "Thirty-seven days and counting. Thank you for your honesty." He tilted his head at the door. "Now go."

I went.

In my chamber, I found Jehanne lying on her belly on my bed, still unclad, reading the treatise on apple propagation. She glanced up when I entered. I'd never seen her naked by lamplight before. In the dusky plant shadows, she looked like a creature spun of gossamer and starlight.

"Well?" she asked.

I closed the door softly behind me. "He was having Raphael watched. He knows, Jehanne."

She turned pale—or more pale. "Is he furious?"

"No." I sat on the bed. "He said you have his forgiveness. But he also said to tell you that if you consort with Raphael de Mereliot while you're trying to get with child, he'll set you aside. Why didn't you tell me?"

Jehanne shrugged and didn't answer.

I traced the lines of her marque idly. Her skin was as fine and silken as a child's. "His majesty thinks you're afraid."

"He knows me well," she murmured. "I wish I were stronger. I'm not a very good Queen, am I?"

I drew my finger down the lovely curve of her spine. "You are the scandal and delight of the realm, my lady. Did I ever tell you about the good ladies Florette and Lydia with whom I shared a coach?"

"No." She smiled a little. "Tell me."

I told her the whole tale, how I'd slept in the stables and bedded the coach-driver Theo, how I'd had to listen to the good ladies' eternal gossip as they rehashed every detail of Jehanne's exploits with gleeful relish. How I'd escaped it to ride beside Theo, only to be driven back into the coach to endure further gossip after the bandits attacked us.

Jehanne's eyes widened. "You *shot* a man?"

"Only in the thigh."

She caught my hand and cradled it against her cheek. "You're brave. I wish I were brave like you."

"You're the one who rescued me," I reminded her.

"I did, didn't I?" She kissed my palm. "Mayhap I won't let you leave me, Moirin. Mayhap I'll run away with you instead."

"Oh?" I stroked her hair with my free hand. "Where exactly am I going, anyway?"

"I don't know." Her voice turned cross. "You're the one with a destiny to follow. Ask your stupid *diadh-anam*." Jehanne uncoiled and sat upright in one seamless motion, her unbound hair spilling over her shoulders. "Elua bids us to love as we will. And I do. Why isn't that enough? Why does it have to be so damned complicated?"

I remembered something the good lady Lydia had said in her cups. "We're the ones who make it that way. Blessed Elua cared naught for crowns or thrones."

Jehanne laughed. "Do you know who said that?"

"No," I admitted.

"One of the realm's greatest traitors." She took both my hands in hers. "I don't want to betray Daniel. Help me?"

"I'll try." I squeezed her hands. "Jehanne, my father told me a bit of what it means to be a royal companion. And I'm all wrong for it. It's meant to be someone close enough in age to be a friend to the peer they serve, but older and wiser—or at least more experienced. It's meant to be an acolyte skilled in Naamah's arts. You and I, we have our roles backward."

Her eyes sparkled briefly. "Oh, I've got you well on your way to possessing an adept's skills."

"Well." I smiled. "But he told me, too, why the practice began. At the time, the idea was that the Dauphine should have one person in her life whose loyalty she could trust without question. That, I do believe I could offer you."

Jehanne's expression turned grave. "And are you making me that offer?"

I nodded. "I am."

"You left off part of their thinking," she observed. "The idea that having one loyal confidante would help the Dauphine grow into a wiser, kinder ruler one day." Jehanne raised her brows at me. "Did you really think you had aught to tell one of Naamah's Servants about the history of royal companions?"

I laughed. "No."

"So you'd listen to my deepest fears and desires and keep all my confidences?" she asked. "Tolerate my whims and forgive my weaknesses?"

"I already do," I pointed out to her. "But if you were to trust me to do it and be honest with me, I'd be able to serve you better."

"And in turn, you expect to make me a wiser, kinder ruler," Jehanne said wryly.

I shrugged. "My lady, you *are* a great deal wiser and kinder than you pretend to be. On the eve of embarking on a voyage toward motherhood, there are worse things you could do than demonstrate it."

She regarded me from beneath her lashes, her face unreadable.

"Are you angry?" I asked her. With her mercurial temper, one could never be sure.

"No." Jehanne sank both hands into my hair, leaned forward, and kissed me. "I'm not angry, my beautiful girl." She brushed my lower lip with one fingertip, then kissed me again, deep and lingering. "Not angry at all."

I sighed with relief. "Oh, good."

"Mmm." She toyed with the bodice of my gown. "Moirin, why are you in my bed and still clothed?"

"It's *my* bed," I noted. "And you sent me on an errand that very much required clothing."

Her hands glided over my breasts, cupping and caressing them. "That's the wrong answer to the wrong question."

"What's the right question?" I asked, half-breathless.

Jehanne smiled at me, unlacing the ties of my bodice. "Oh, I don't know. There are so many questions one could ask, aren't there? But I'm quite sure that your answer is *yes*. Don't you think so?"

It struck me that despite her tantrums and tears earlier, I'd managed to get Jehanne in a good mood—and her good moods were infectious. I'd won a measure of trust from her. I could no longer smell Raphael's scent lingering on her skin.

And she was mine for the whole night.

All these things made me happy.

"Oh, yes." I put my arms around her neck and kissed her. "Yes, and yes, and yes!"

FORTY-FIVE

The Longest Night came and went without seeing my father's return.

That was the only shadow that dimmed my enjoyment of the festivities and the weeks leading up to them. Noémie d'Etoile gave me repeated assurances and told me not to worry, and I tried not to.

I kept up my lessons with Master Lo Feng and I tended to his Camaeline snowdrops, keeping their frail song alive.

I had the first test of my service as a royal companion when Jehanne informed me that she wanted to see Raphael again before the Longest Night.

"Just once," she said calmly. "That's all I'm asking. I swear to Elua, just once. I want a chance to tell him why I can't see him again. I want to enjoy the last time knowing it's the last time. At least until . . ." She shrugged. "Who knows how long?"

"Did you discuss it with his majesty?" I asked.

Jehanne shook her head. "I was hoping you would. If you believe me, he's more likely to believe it, too." She searched my face. "You do believe me, don't you?"

I sighed. "I do. I'll speak to him."

Only in Terre d'Ange, I thought, would a man's wife send one lover to ask her husband's permission to bed another lover. But despite my discomfort with the mission, the King didn't seem to find anything odd about it. He invited me to sit in his study and heard me out.

"Do you believe her?" he asked when I'd finished. Jehanne knew her husband well.

"I do," I said. "She's trying very hard to be honest."

King Daniel drummed his fingers on the arm of his chair at length, then gave a curt nod. "Once. And I don't want to see her afterward." He shuddered. "You've got me thinking about his goddamned scent."

So it was arranged.

I thought Jehanne would pass the night with Raphael since their assignation wasn't a secret, but in the small hours before dawn, I was awakened when her guards escorted her to my chambers. I kindled the lamps and admitted her.

"I didn't want to be alone and I didn't know where else to go." There were shadows under her eyes. "Isn't that absurd?"

"No," I said softly. "Raphael . . . ?"

"He didn't want me to stay." Jehanne wrapped her arms around herself, shivering. "He said it hurt too much."

I was silent, remembering the two of them riding together the day of the hunt, heads leaning toward one another, her silver-gilt and him tawny-gold. The bright sunlight gleaming on them in benison. They looked so well together. I'd been jealous of both of them. And I wanted to ask her if it were worth it; but then I remembered too the immense tenderness in her voice when she'd spoken to King Daniel after Lianne Tremaine's poetry recital.

She loved them both.

But she'd wed the King.

I wanted to go to her, but I wasn't sure it was what she wanted. I folded my hands in my lap. "What can I do?"

Jehanne's starry gaze met mine. When she spoke, her voice sounded small and lost. "Hold me?"

I helped her undress and get into bed, and held her. It felt as though I held the whole history of their stormy, turbulent affair in my arms. I breathed in her scent and his, mingled. She shivered against me. I breathed the Breath of Ocean's Rolling Waves, deep and rhythmic. I breathed in tumult and breathed out calm.

Over and over.

And bit by bit, her body eased.

I felt her slide from wakefulness into sleep and kissed the back of her neck. Jehanne made a soft noise in her sleep. I thought about the effigy in the Temple of Naamah for which my great-great-grandmother had posed—the first royal companion. Unfit though I might be on the face of things, I was following in her footsteps and doing it well.

She would be proud, I thought.

My father would be proud.

And my *diadh-anam* was silent. I wished it weren't. I remembered the sorrow and regret in the eyes of the Maghuin Dhonn Herself as She turned away from me. I had a destiny to find and follow.

"Not yet," I whispered. "Please, not yet."

Preparations for the Longest Night continued apace. With Jehanne's blessing, I met with Benoit Vallon of Atelier Favrielle to design my gown for the masqued ball. I'd expected her to take issue with the notion given her standing quarrel with them, but she surprised me.

"I think they're on the verge of relenting," she said. "My forbearance is a gesture of goodwill in keeping with your effort to make a kinder, wiser ruler of me." She smiled and stroked my cheek. "Besides, I've no objection to you looking as stunning as possible now that you're mine, Moirin."

The gown promised to be stunning indeed.

I understood that costumes for the Longest Night were usually intended to depict recognizable mythological or historical figures or themes. Benoit Vallon sniffed and dismissed the idea as pedestrian.

"You're a myth unto yourself, my dear." He made a bracket of his hands, framing my face. "I see ravens taking flight amid the pines, red holly berries against the white snow. A bit savage, a bit elegant. That's what we'll capture."

And somehow, he did. Like his other work, the gown was sophisticated in its simplicity. It was made of a shimmering black silk that clung to my body and left my arms bare, with a narrow, plunging decolletage. In the back, it flowed into a train that swished pleasantly when I walked. There was an ornate headpiece with gilded branches and garnet berries, and a black velvet domino mask that flared into wings. At the first fitting, Benoit kissed his fingertips and proclaimed himself a genius.

At the second fitting he was more subdued, for Jehanne decided to attend.

It made me smile to see the flurry it caused. Atelier Favrielle could refuse to dress the Queen of Terre d'Ange, but they very well couldn't refuse her entry. Benoit and his assistants were harried fitting me into the gown and awaited Jehanne's reaction nervously. She looked at me without speaking for a long, long time.

"Is her majesty pleased?" he asked at last.

Jehanne smiled sweetly at him. "Her majesty is considering dismissing every last one of you to see if the gown comes off as beautifully as it goes on," she said in her most silken purr.

Two of the attendants gave shocked titters. Me, I laughed aloud. Jehanne's gaze flicked back to me and I could see the genuine amusement and affection in it.

Benoit Vallon relaxed visibly and bowed. "Your praise is music to my ears." He hesitated. "Rumor has it that Amélie Sourisse is designing a variant on the traditional Snow Queen theme for her majesty this year?"

"Oh, indeed?" Jehanne raised her brows.

He pursed his lips. "Mayhap next year, her majesty would be interested in discussing something less traditional. More innovative."

Her eyelids flickered and I could feel her mood shift at the implied insult the sought-after offer contained. The temperature in the room seemed to drop. Benoit winced, realizing he'd overstepped.

"My lady." I touched Jehanne's arm.

She glanced at me sidelong, deciding whether or not to accept my silent reminder. The room held its collective breath. She summoned another charming smile. "Thank you, messire. That's very kind."

The room exhaled in collective relief.

Very much to my surprise, I received an offer from Prince Thierry to escort me to the Midwinter Masque on the Longest Night. He sought me out in my chambers to deliver it in person.

"Why?" I asked simply.

Thierry didn't answer right away. He gazed around at the profusion of plants. "This is lovely. I'd heard, but I didn't reckon the extent of it. It might be the nicest thing Jehanne's ever done for anyone."

"It's wonderful," I agreed. "And?"

He smiled wryly. "Do you know, we had a long talk the other day? Jehanne asked to meet with me."

"Did she ask you to offer—"

"No, no." Thierry shook his head. "It was naught to do with you. She told me that she and my father mean to try for children after the Longest Night. She wanted me to know that whatever may come, I'm my father's firstborn and heir, and no child of theirs would ever take my place in the realm or my father's heart. She took blame for the hostility between us, apologized, and said she hoped I'd welcome a sister or brother." He rubbed his chin. "I may have lost my wits, but she seemed quite genuine."

"Thoughts of motherhood may change a person," I murmured.

"It's possible," he agreed. "It's also possible that what everyone's saying is true. For some reason, you calm her. At any rate . . . Moirin, D'Angelines regard seduction as a form of blood-sport. And the Longest Night is a time of especial license. As Jehanne's companion, you're a very desirable target." He flushed. "Not that you aren't in your own right, obviously. But—"

I'd been in Terre d'Ange long enough to understand. "But getting me to betray my loyalty to the Queen would be an almighty conquest."

"Exactly." He nodded. "As your escort, I can fend off the worst of it and see that you're not plagued to death."

"That's undeservedly kind of you," I observed.

"Ah, well . . ." Thierry gave me another wry smile. "When all's said and done, I do like you, Moirin. I like your company. And it would be a pleasure to see the festivities anew through your eyes. So. Do you accept?"

"I do," I said. "With many thanks."

It was a glorious night.

The tradition of the Longest Night was old, older than Terre d'Ange itself. The great hall was polished to a high shine, filled with light and music. Swags of evergreen were draped on every surface and enormous live pine trees in great pots were dotted around the hall, their tops reaching toward the high ceiling, thousands upon thousands cunningly wrought glass icicles hanging from their branches. I inhaled their fresh scent gladly.

"The trees are new," Thierry observed. "It's a nice touch."

The array of costumes on the guests was truly spectacular. We made our way through the glittering throng to greet the King and Queen.

Whatever Benoit Vallon might have thought, Jehanne was a vision in white. The borders of her gown were edged with silver embroidery and she wore a silvery-white cloak trimmed with white ermine, the collar framing her exquisite face. Her fair hair was piled in a coronet and adorned with a sparkling diadem. Beside her, the King wore a matching doublet and breeches of white velvet trimmed in ermine, a simple white domino mask. His dark hair was loose and flowing over his shoulders, a fillet of white gold around his brow. Despite his avowed dislike of balls, he looked happy and relaxed.

They, too, looked well together.

"Moirin!" Jehanne's eyes sparkled at me. "Joy to you on the Longest Night." She gave me a lingering kiss. "Do you like the trees?"

I smiled at her. "I love the trees."

"I thought you would." She glanced at Thierry, who wore simple ash-grey attire—a sleeveless coat over a plain shirt and breeches. But steel vambraces glinted on his wrists and he wore twin daggers at his waist and a sword slung across his back in a harness. "You came as a Cassiline Brother?"

Thierry shrugged. "I'm feeling particularly gallant this evening."

She laughed. "Fairly spoken."

King Daniel gave me a chaste kiss of greeting. "Have you tasted *joie* yet tonight?" he inquired. When I shook my head, he beckoned to a servant with a tray. "You must."

The cordial was served in delicate crystal glasses as thin as eggshells. I breathed in the heady fumes. It was like hearing the frail song of the snowdrops—only it wasn't frail anymore. It was distilled and powerful. We toasted one another and I sipped.

Fire and ice.

It tasted heavenly, and it burned like winter's kiss. I felt it all the way down to my belly, then warming my veins. The lamps seemed to burn brighter and I had the urge to kiss everyone in the hall.

"*Very* tonic," I managed to say.

The King chuckled. "You sound like Master Lo Feng. Have any of his plants survived?"

"Oh, yes." I'd never noticed that his majesty had a very pleasant, melodious voice. Nor that very appealing lines formed around his mouth when he smiled. "I'm keeping them alive for him."

"Moirin has a gift with plants." Jehanne kissed me again. I could taste *joie* on her lips and yearned to taste more of her. "Now go enjoy yourself, my witchling," she whispered in my ear. "Only not too much."

"Aye, my lady," I promised.

To his credit, Thierry was a wonderful escort, as attentive and good-natured as he'd been when I first knew him. He kept his word and fended off the majority of advances made toward me without making any of his own, and I was grateful for it. I hadn't expected to be tempted, but the *joie* burning in my blood and the sense of revelry that pervaded the night made it difficult. Everyone looked so very, very lovely to me.

We danced in an indoor forest, gliding and swirling around the tall pines. I watched King Daniel dance with Jehanne in his arms, her arms around his neck, her adoring gaze raised to his face.

"She makes him happy, doesn't she?" Thierry murmured.

"She does," I agreed.

"I'm trying to accept it." His mouth quirked. "Father says if she bears him a healthy child, he'll let me lead a delegation to Terra Nova."

"Truly?" I glanced up at him. "That's wonderful, isn't it?"

"It is." Thierry kissed me softly, then pulled back. He cleared his throat. "We've become family in a very odd way, haven't we?"

I nodded. "To be sure."

There was a banquet table laden with food. The glittering peers fought for places, but they made way for the Dauphin. Thierry filled a plate for me himself. We sat and ate, then danced until the deep sound of a bronze tocsin being beaten made the air shiver.

Everything went still.

A lone voice cried the hour. We were at the very cusp of the Longest Night of the year. All the lamps were extinguished with ruthless efficiency. I caught my breath at the sudden darkness, breathed in and out, and summoned the twilight without thinking. The hall shimmered in my vision.

I wondered what my mother was doing at that very moment.

I wondered where my father was.

There was a false mountain before which the musicians played. It split apart as they moved away from it. A crone hobbled out, leaning on a twisted staff. Someone pounded on the great doors of the hall; someone flung the doors open wide. A horse-drawn carriage entered, hooves clopping on the marble floors.

A youth in gilded armor leapt from the carriage and pointed a gilded spear at the crone.

She straightened and flung off her mask and rags, revealing herself to be young and beautiful.

I let go the twilight.

All the light of the mortal world returned in a rush of lighted wicks. Folks cheered and the Sun Prince and his Queen departed in their chariot. In their wake came a new influx—adepts of the Night Court. Tumblers and jugglers preceded them, throwing somersaults, green and gold ribbons in their hair. Four strapping young men followed them, carrying a palanquin. They knelt to Jehanne, imploring her to come with them.

"They do this every year," Thierry murmured to me. "The Night Court loves her. She's one of their own."

Jehanne laughed and refused them prettily.

King Daniel whispered to her.

I was attuned to Jehanne; I saw her eyes widen. I watched their hushed exchange. She flung her arms around his neck and covered his face with kisses.

The King beckoned me over. "I thought you might enjoy the chance to see the Night Court in all its decadent splendor. Would you like to accompany the Queen?"

My eyes widened. "Truly?"

He laughed and laid a hand on my shoulder. "Truly. Tonight marks a threshold. There may never be another like it."

I glanced at Thierry. One of the tumblers threw a standing somersault and came up holding an ivory token. "The Dauphin is welcome, of course," he said.

"Elua, no!" Thierry backed away. "Under the circumstances, I think not. I've an idea what transpires in the Night Court on the Longest Night. Moirin, I am pleased to have escorted you tonight, but for better or for worse, Jehanne is my step-mother, and there are limits to what I am willing to witness. Go."

"You're sure?" I felt guilty.

"Entirely." He waved a dismissive hand at me. "Go."

So I went.

We were carried through the Palace on the palanquin and then rode through the streets of the City of Elua in an open carriage drawn by a team of matched horses, two black and two white. Outriders from the Queen's Guard and the Night Court flanked the carriage. The adepts tucked warm fur blankets around us and sang as they rode, voices rising up into the starry sky. Everywhere, the City was ablaze with light. As word ran ahead of us, folk turned out into the streets to see us pass, calling out greetings and blowing kisses, then whispering to one another about the delicious scandal of it all. I thought they would be surprised to learn it had been his majesty's idea.

"How will this fête differ from the one at the Palace?" I asked Jehanne.

"All the adepts of the Night Court will be at Cereus House," she said. "It's the one night a year that they take no patrons and are free to consort with one another in any manner they wish. It's a beautiful sight." She took my hand beneath the furs. "And by the time we arrive, it will be halfway to an orgy."

I eyed her.

"No, I'm not jesting." Jehanne squeezed my hand. "Don't worry, I *do* have a measure of decorum to maintain."

It truly was a beautiful sight. In a realm of folk renowned for their beauty, hundreds of the loveliest were assembled beneath one roof, clad as fauns and sprites, gods and goddesses, demons and angels, warriors and harem girls. Men and women. All were fair-skinned, but there the resemblance ended. Every one of them was lovely in their own way.

None was as beautiful as Jehanne.

They made a path for the palanquin as we entered the great hall, though not a wide one. They pressed close, whispering compliments, stroking the skin of our arms. Naamah's presence was palpable, and I could feel the blood beat harder in my veins.

At the far end of the hall there was a reclining couch on a dais. Our bearers lowered the palanquin and escorted Jehanne onto it. Someone fetched a cushioned stool for me.

I sat and leaned against the couch. "Is this always here for you?"

"No." Jehanne toyed with tendrils of hair coming loose at the nape of my neck. "It's the Dowayne's couch, but the Dowayne has retired for the night. Watch."

I watched.

I watched and drank *joie* brought by attentive adepts in training as the members of the Court of Night-Blooming Flowers danced with one another. I watched as they approached the dais to salute Jehanne, kissing her hands in tribute. She received it with delight, stroking their hair, stroking their faces.

Some kissed me, curious and wondering. I wanted them, I wanted every last one of them. Most of all, I wanted Jehanne.

As the night wore on, the adepts began pairing off in twos and threes. The lamps burned lower. The shadows were filled with writhing sighs. The tributes had tapered off and the *joie* burned in my blood. I glanced at Jehanne, sensing Naamah's gift rising in her in answer to mine.

She looked back at me beneath her lashes. "This damned royal decorum is a nuisance, isn't it?"

"A chamber?" I suggested.

Jehanne shook her head, ruefully amused. "We're far too late. There's not a private place to be found in Cereus House tonight, my lovely. Not even for the Queen of Terre d'Ange."

"There's one." I looked around to make sure no one was watching at the moment, then took her hands. "Close your eyes."

She obeyed.

I found the earth's pulse beneath the sighs and murmurs. I steadied myself and breathed it in. Breathed in Jehanne's scent, the memory of pine trees. Elua's Oak. The tread of the Maghuin Dhonn Herself shaking the earth. A bamboo grove yearning upward beneath the ceiling of a glass heaven.

I breathed out twilight, letting it settle over us both, embracing us. We were alone together in a world half a step away. "Now."

"Oh!" Jehanne whispered, opening her eyes. "I'd forgotten how lovely it was. They can't see us?"

I slid into her arms. "No."

She kissed my throat, placed a line of kisses down the skin laid bare by my plunging decolletage. "Not this?"

I shook my head. "No, my lady."

"This?" Jehanne eased the silk of my gown aside. A jolt of desire shot through me as her warm, wet mouth closed around my nipple and tugged on it with lips and tongue.

My grip on the twilight wavered.

"Ahh . . ." I pulled away from her with an effort. "No. But I need to concentrate."

She smiled. "On what?"

I pushed up her skirts. "You."

Jehanne's smile deepened. "Then do."

I was a far, far more skilled lover than I'd been when Jehanne had first seduced me at Cereus House—and yet no less ardent. I'd wanted her all night. My mask and headpiece got in the way, tangling with her skirts. I took off the mask, disentangled the headpiece and put it aside, shaking my hair loose impatiently. Her fingers slid through my hair, telling me without words to slow down.

I listened.

There are many different ways to perform the *languisement* on a woman. I teased the soft petals of her nether-lips with the tip of my tongue until I felt her fingers tighten in my hair. Then I licked her with quick, delicate strokes like a cat lapping cream. Not until I felt her hips begin to thrust involuntarily did I worship her in earnest, working my tongue as deep inside her as it would go.

It went on for a long time. Lost in Jehanne and the twilight, I took her to the edge many times, until I could sense in the tension of her thighs that once more would be one time too many, and sweet urgency would give way to frustration. I ran my tongue around the swollen bud of Naamah's Pearl, sucked it into my mouth, and took her over the edge.

Jehanne shuddered, hands clenched in my hair, her hips rising to meet my mouth. "Blessed Elua have mercy!"

Afterward, I licked her gently, letting the last spasms subside.

"Moirin." Her fingers stirred in my hair.

I breathed, slow and deep. I was content. I rested my cheek against the soft skin of her thigh. I smiled up at her. "Enough?"

"Mm-hmm." She looked languorous and a bit disheveled. "Not very fair to you, is it?"

I smoothed her skirts back in order, contemplated my headpiece, and decided it was a lost cause. "I don't mind. Not tonight."

"Come here." Jehanne cupped the back of my neck and pulled me toward her, kissing me. She regarded me with one of her unreadable looks, then shook her head. "Sometimes I forget you're exactly what I call you, my witchling. Then you remind me, and I'm forced to confess to a certain awe."

"I'm just me." I looked around the twilit hall. Folk were uncoupling and stirring in various stages of undress. I had a feeling it was later than I thought. "I'd best let it go before someone takes it in their head to sit on the Dowayne's couch."

Jehanne's brows rose. "*That* would have been interesting."

I let the twilight slip away.

Across the hall, an adept in training dropped a tray of empty glasses and stared in shock at our sudden appearance. Heads turned. I watched Jehanne's lips curve in a smile, delighting in the attention. And I thought that despite all her foibles, I did indeed love her quite a bit.

She glanced at me. "Why do you look so solemn?"

"You'd find it tiresome if I told you," I said to her.

Jehanne stroked my hair. "Oh, mayhap not as much as I pretend." A horologist called the hour and she startled. "Elua! That's the call to usher in dawn. Come watch it with me?"

We adjourned amid a gorgeous, tired, satiated throng to Cereus House's rooftop terrace, swept bare of snow for the occasion. The adepts made way to give Jehanne and me a place of honor at the eastern railing. Bare-armed, I shivered in the cold. Jehanne folded me into her ermine-trimmed cloak, and I breathed the Breath of Embers Glowing until I was warmer, watching the dark grey sky.

A streak of gold broke the horizon.

Bells and cheers rang out across the City; the rooftop resounded. The Longest Night was over and light had returned to the world. Beside me, Jehanne was silent.

I wanted to tell her not to be afraid; I wanted to tell her that I loved her. But I didn't know what words would comfort her, so I settled for saying, "I'm here."

"The world becomes a different place for me today, doesn't it?" she mused.

"It does."

Jehanne stole a quick look at me, her face open and vulnerable in the cold light of dawn, her voice low. "What if I'm a dreadful mother, Moirin?"

"You won't be," I promised her.

She sighed and rested her head on my shoulder. "I'm glad you're here."

FORTY-SIX

Later that day, we journeyed to a sanctuary dedicated to Eisheth in the mountains a little over an hour's carriage-ride away.

I was curious about the ceremony. "Does it have to be performed there?"

"No." Jehanne leaned her head against the cushions, eyes closed. "Any temple will suffice. For lack of a temple, a sincere prayer may work. But it's said to be most powerful when performed at the Sanctuary of the Womb, and if I'm going to do this, I'd as soon it were done properly."

"Why is it called the Sanctuary of the Womb?" I asked.

"There's a cavern with a hot spring." She rubbed her temples. "Moirin, will you please not plague me with questions today?"

I fell silent.

"I'm not angry," Jehanne added. "Just tired."

A month ago, she would have snapped at me for annoying her with no hint of an apology. I thought that was good progress.

At the gates of the Sanctuary, her Captain of the Guard rang the bell. A priestess with a broad, pleasant face came in answer. I watched him bow and indicate the royal carriage, watched her nod and indicate an outbuilding where he and his men could wait. There were no men allowed in the Sanctuary.

The priestess smiled as Jehanne descended from the carriage. "Your majesty, we're so very pleased by your decision."

Jehanne inclined her head. "Thank you, Sister."

The priestess glanced at me, her eyes widening. "You must be . . ."

"Moirin," I said. "Of the Maghuin Dhonn."

"My lovely witch." Jehanne summoned the hint of a smile. Tired or no, she did enjoy unsettling people.

"Of course." Eisheth's priestess swallowed. "Well met."

She led us into the Sanctuary. It was a simple, rustic place. In an unadorned chamber, more priestesses in blue robes came to help Jehanne undress. They took down her hair, removed her jewelry. They gave her a long white linen shift to wear. I had an uncomfortable memory of the Circle of Shalomon donning white robes in the summoning antechamber.

It passed when we went back outside. The path to the mouth of the cavern was worn smooth by thousands upon thousands of women's feet. When we entered the cavern itself, I had a sense of homecoming. It wasn't as snug and comforting as the cave in which I'd grown up, nor as spectacular as the hollow hill beyond which lay the stone doorway, but it felt good to me.

We descended a series of well-worn granite stairs. Candles tucked into rocky niches lit the way.

I smelled water and minerals.

There was a crude stone rim around the spring-fed pool—ancient work, Tiberian or older. The milky-white water steamed gently in the cold air. On the far side was an effigy of Eisheth kneeling, her hands cupped. Votive candles flickered around her, flickered in the cavern walls.

Jehanne took a deep breath.

"I'm here, my lady," I murmured.

She nodded.

Two blue-robed priestesses knelt and took the hem of her white shift, raising it. They stripped it from her. Naked, Jehanne shivered. The priestess who had admitted us approached her, a flagon of oil in her hands. Her pleasant face looked grave.

"May Eisheth grant your prayer's wisdom," she said softly, anointing her fingers and touching them to Jehanne's brow. She tipped the flagon, touched Jehanne's breast-bone. "May Eisheth's love fill your heart." Once more, lower. Anointing the junction of her thighs, her nether-lips. Places I'd kissed and caressed only last night. After this, it would all be different. "May Eisheth hear your prayer and fill your womb."

Jehanne shivered harder.

I didn't know if it were fear or the cold air.

The priestess gripped her shoulders. "Immerse yourself in the womb of the earth."

She hesitated, then stepped gracefully over the stone rim and sank into the warm, mineral-rich water—sank and submerged. Her pale hair floated on the surface. Milky water streamed from her as she rose. Wisps of steam rose from her skin. She looked like a young goddess newly minted at some divine forge.

"Well done," the head priestess said gently. She handed Jehanne a thick wax taper. "Now light it at the altar and make your prayer. Place the candle in Eisheth's hands."

Jehanne waded through the thigh-deep water. She bowed her head before the effigy. Her fair skin glimmered in the candle-lit cavern, the beautiful lines of her marque bisected by her wet hair.

She lit the taper. "Blessed Eisheth hear my prayer," she said in a rush, dripping wax into the effigy's cupped hands. She planted the taper firmly in the melted wax. "Open the gates of my womb."

The lit taper held and burned brightly.

Everyone sighed.

It was done.

In the weeks that followed the ceremony, Jehanne withdrew from me. She wasn't cold and distant; I received regular invitations to dinners and other functions, and she made it clear she still considered me her royal companion. But she paid no visits to my bedchamber.

I understood. Whether or not she had committed wholeheartedly to the notion of getting with child, she *had* committed to it, and set about doing it with considerable determination. There was precious little I could do to assist in the process, and I sensed she didn't want the sort of distraction I provided just now. So I kept myself busy. I continued my lessons with Master Lo Feng and tended to his snowdrops. I paid regular visits to the Temple of Naamah to badger Noémie for news of my father, of which there was none.

I visited other temples, hoping to get a better sense of Blessed Elua and his Companions. Some were proud and fierce, like Azza and Camael. Some were a mystery to me, like Kushiel, the administrator of atonement's cruel mercy. Grave, thoughtful Shemhazai appealed to me, and I liked best of all gentle Anael, the Good Steward, and Blessed Elua himself, whose arms were spread wide in benediction.

I accepted various invitations from Prince Thierry with gratitude, nurturing the unlikely familial bond between us.

I borrowed books from the royal library. When the marble walls of the Palace felt too oppressive, I rode Blossom on private excursions into the countryside. I didn't mind the cold air. I practiced the Five Styles of Breathing.

To their everlasting scandal and delight, I paid a visit to the good ladies Florette and Lydia. They plied me with tea and pastries, scolded me for not telling them that I was a scion of House Courcel.

"And a *bear-witch* in the bargain!" Lydia added in a louder tone than she intended.

I smiled into my teacup when they asked me in hushed—well, Florette's was hushed—whispers if *this* or *that* was true of Jehanne and if I ever intended to reconcile with Raphael de Mereliot.

"I've no idea," I said honestly to the latter. "He's quite angry."

"Because *she* crooked her finger at you and you came running." Florette shook her own finger at me. "Naughty girl!"

"That's not true!" Lydia defended me stoutly. "Our Moirin's a good girl."

I let them think what they liked since it pleased them so. Out of an obscure sense of loyalty to Raphael, I didn't wish to tell anyone that he was using me in a self-serving manner that may well have been killing me by degrees. And it only added to Jehanne's reputation to let them believe that she'd stolen me from him so easily. That, I knew she relished.

Whatever the good ladies believed, they both embraced me when I left, tears in their eyes.

Lydia patted my cheek. "Take care of yourself, child."

I did.

Still, for all its potted glory and luxuriant plant growth, my bedchamber was a lonely place during those weeks. And I was forced to admit that there were certain disadvantages to having pledged my loyalty to Jehanne.

When I returned from an excursion to find two of her guards posted outside my quarters, I was very, very glad.

"Her majesty . . . ?" I inquired.

One of the guards winked at me. The other inclined his head. "Her majesty awaits you."

I entered my quarters.

Jehanne, unclothed, reclined in my bed. "I'm perishing weary of wondering if this time, the act of love has got me with child," she said without preamble. "So not a word on the topic, all right?"

I smiled. "As my lady wishes."

It was a blessed release after weeks of celibacy, a state to which I was unaccustomed and unsuited. Jehanne more than repaid the debt of pleasure left standing between us since the Longest Night. Afterward, I lay in a happy daze, trying to guess what topic of discussion might please her.

As it happened, Jehanne had ideas of her own. "Tell me, were you close to your mother?"

I nodded. "Very."

"What's it like?" she asked. "What's *she* like?"

I frowned, thinking. Trying to describe my mother to Jehanne de la Courcel felt like trying to explain the earth to the moon. They were so very far apart. "My mother is . . . my mother. For a long time, she was all I knew. I was ten years old before I understood that we were separate and unalike."

"What else?" Jehanne asked.

"She's very stubborn," I said. "She can be infernally close-mouthed. She likes solitude and wild places."

"Like you."

"Oh . . ." I ran my hand over the graceful curve of her hip. "I'm not so very good with solitude anymore."

Jehanne smiled. "You missed me?"

"I missed you," I admitted.

"Good." She kissed me. "Tell me more."

I thought about it. "There is a ritual all the folk of the Maghuin

Dhonn undergo at adulthood," I said slowly. I'd never spoken about it to Jehanne. "To determine whether or not She accepts us as Her own. Not all are chosen. And I was fearful that She would not claim me, because I was half-D'Angeline." Jehanne listened, her blue-grey eyes grave. "Before I passed through the stone doorway, my mother embraced me," I said. "She told me that whatever happened, I was her daughter and the joy of her life, now and always. She made me promise never to forget it." I shrugged. "That's my mother."

She was silent a moment. "That's lovely."

"I take it it wasn't the same for you," I said softly.

"No." Jehanne shook her head. "Not at all." I waited for her to say more, but she didn't. All she had ever said was that her parents had both been adepts of Cereus House. I knew from Court gossip that her parents were alive and well, that the King had bestowed an estate and minor titles on them as a wedding gift, and that Jehanne had essentially banned them from the Court. "I take it you passed the rite successfully?" she asked at length. "The Maghuin Dhonn accepted you?"

"Aye." I smiled. "That She did."

"Aye, aye, aye." Jehanne tickled my cheek with a lock of my hair, her mood shifting. "Moirin, do you really worship a *bear*?"

"Yes and no." I had to think about this, too. "We don't worship in the way D'Angelines do. But we're *Hers*." I touched my chest. "The spark of Her spirit lives inside us."

She scowled. "I don't want to hear about your cursed *diadh-anam*."

"You asked," I said mildly. "I answered with the only truth I know."

"Oh, fine." Jehanne coiled herself around me and fixed me with an intense gaze. "But for now, you're mine, too, Moirin mac Fainche. And I don't think I'm done with you today. Any objections?"

I laughed and kissed her. "None at all."

FORTY-SEVEN

After those first few weeks, the situation returned to whatever normalcy it had first possessed. Jehanne came to my chambers more often. And bit by bit, she talked more candidly to me.

I learned what I had already known—that her mother nearly died in bearing her. And I learned what I hadn't known—that her mother had ever resented her for it.

"She never wanted children," she murmured. "She did it only to please my father."

"What of your father?" I asked. Fathers were much on my mind.

"Oh, he doted on me." Jehanne gave a wistful smile. "She resented me for that, too. But he doted on her, too. And when it came to taking sides, he always took hers, no matter how unfair it was."

"That's not in his majesty's nature," I observed. I'd seen enough of King Daniel to know he was a very fair-minded man, and a good father to Thierry. Despite his lingering resentment of Jehanne, Thierry adored his father.

"No." She frowned in thought. "It's not, is it?"

"No. And you're not your mother, Jehanne."

She shuddered. "Elua, let's hope not!" She changed the subject. "Any word of your father?"

I shook my head. "None."

Jehanne pursed her lips. "He was bound for Azzalle, wasn't he? Negotiating on behalf of the Trevalion boy and his lover?" I nodded. "It's been too long. I'll ask Daniel to send a scouting party in search of him."

I kissed her effusively. "Thank you!"

King Daniel agreed readily and a scouting party was dispatched. A month later, they returned to report that Brother Phanuel Demarre had indeed negotiated a successful truce between House Trevalion and the d'Argent family and departed months ago for the City of Elua. They'd sought to trace his path to no avail.

I was worried.

And Jehanne was pregnant.

I knew it before anyone else did. Her scent changed. Not the perfume that she wore, the delightful concoction that the head of the Perfumers' Guild had sworn to take to his grave. *Her* scent, the one that underlay it. The one that made it so intoxicating. The first time we were together after it happened, I buried my face in the curve of her neck and breathed in the scent of her bare skin. It was no less intoxicating, only different, like the faint strains of a new note being introduced into a musical symphony.

I lifted my head, eyes sparkling. "Jehanne . . ."

"What?"

I took her hands. "Close your eyes."

In the twilight, I could see it. She shone so brightly there, bright and beautiful, a favorite of the gods. Naamah's kiss on her brow.

And a second spark, faint as a distant promise. Centered below her belly.

I laughed aloud and let the twilight go. "My lady, I could be wrong. I'm no physician. But I do believe you're with child."

"Truly?" Jehanne's expression was torn between dismay and delight.

I nodded. "Truly."

It took the royal chirurgeon another month to confirm it, but she did. The Queen of Terre d'Ange was with child. And quite to her own surprise, Jehanne settled on being pleased at the prospect.

In the early days of spring, once the chirurgeon deemed it safe, the announcement was made and a fête held to celebrate it. I watched Jehanne receive tribute-gifts from the peers of the realm. A brightness clung to her that one could see even in mortal daylight. For once, she was unfailingly gracious and pleasant without uttering a single barb. Even folk who thought they disliked Jehanne fell a little bit in love with her that day, and I don't think she found it one bit tiresome.

A hand descended on my shoulder as I watched her. I glanced up to see King Daniel.

"She's happy," he said softly.

"She is," I agreed. "And you?"

"Elua! Do you jest?" Daniel de la Courcel smiled, appealing lines bracketing his mouth. "I do believe Jehanne was more ready than she knew. Ready to be a mother. Ready, mayhap, to be a different sort of Queen." He glanced down at me. "You've been a good companion to her, Moirin. Thank you."

"I—"

That was all I got out before a commotion broke out near the entrance to the salon. There was a babble of voices and a moment of confusion, then members of the Royal Guard formed a cordon. Hurrying between them in the swirling crimson robes of Naamah's Order was a familiar figure, her face pale and stark.

Noémie d'Etoile.

My heart sank as my worst fears came home to roost.

"Moirin!" She gasped my name and caught my hands. "Your father—"

I wanted to cover my ears. "Is he—?"

"No." Noémie shuddered. "But he's ill, gravely ill. He's lain ill all winter." Tears shone in her warm hazel eyes. "I'm so sorry, child! I was sure it was just Phanuel's usual wandering."

My mind reeled. "How ill?"

"Very." Her hands tightened on mine. "They say you've a gift?"

The salon had gone quiet, watching and listening. On the dais, Jehanne had risen to her feet and was making her way toward us. I couldn't get my thoughts in order. "I . . . no. Not alone."

"Hold," King Daniel said in a deep, firm voice. "Sister, tell the tale from beginning to end."

It braced her. Noémie d'Etoile caught her breath and told her tale. When the snows had melted, another wandering priest of the order had visited a remote hamlet in Namarre, a village so small it hadn't a name, pursuing the rumor of a woodcutter's daughter, a young woman of extraordinary beauty and a possible recruit to Naamah's Service.

He had found her.

She was tending to my father. In the depths of winter, not long before the Longest Night, my father had wandered into the village, fevered and delirious. The woodcutter's family had taken him in. They had hoped he would rally come spring, but instead his condition had worsened.

Now . . .

"Brother Ramiel recognized him," Noémie whispered. "He dispatched the nearest reputable physician, then came straightaway to the temple. Moirin . . . it's an affliction of the lungs. He's having difficulty breathing. Brother Ramiel was not hopeful."

My father, my lovely, gentle father who trailed grace in his wake.

I pressed the heels of my hands against my eyes.

Raphael.

I needed Raphael.

I said the words aloud. "I need Raphael de Mereliot."

And then Jehanne was there, her hands gripping my upper arms with that unexpected strength. "Go to him," she said, soft and urgent. "Beg if you need to. Raphael *owes* you. Remind him. Tell him I'll beg, too." Her gaze was steady. "Do whatever is needful."

I went, stumbling, accompanied by an escort of guards dispatched by the King.

At Raphael's townhouse, the maid Daphne answered my knock. She regarded me with open hostility. "What do *you* want?"

I stood shivering on the doorstep. "I need to speak to Raphael, Daphne. Is he here?" She didn't answer. "Please? It's very urgent. Will you at least tell him I'm here?"

"Wait here." She closed the door in my face.

I waited.

For long moments, I thought he meant to turn me away. I wrapped my cloak tight around me, trying to quell my shivering. I couldn't concentrate well enough to breathe properly. I wouldn't leave, though. If Raphael refused to see me, I'd damn well lay on his doorstep until he relented.

But at length Raphael came to the door, his eyes bloodshot, the smell of alcohol on him. He regarded me and my guards with profound distaste. "To what do I owe the honor of a visit from the royal bedwarmer?"

"May I speak to you?" I asked humbly. "It's about my father. He's very ill."

His jaw tightened. With a curt nod, he beckoned me inside. "You and you alone. The guards stay outside."

In the marble foyer, I poured out my tale. Raphael listened with folded arms. I finished by pleading for his aid.

"You *humiliated* me, Moirin," he said when I was done, slow and deliberate. "You made me the laughingstock of the City. And now you beg me to ride posthaste all the way to Namarre to assist you?"

"I do." I dropped to my knees. "Raphael, please! I did a great many services for you, too. I helped you save the life of someone dear to you. Can you not find it in your heart to do the same for me?"

"In exchange for what?" His tone was neutral.

I swallowed. "What do you wish?"

A cruel edge crept into his voice. "Would you forsake Jehanne?"

I thought of her steady gaze. *Do whatever is needful,* she had said. I bowed my head, my heart aching at the thought of betraying her. "Is that your price?"

"No." Raphael grabbed my chin and forced it upward. "You were always more use to me out of bed than in it, Moirin. My price is this: When we are finished in Namarre, you will assist the Circle with one last summoning. You will swear to do this and to speak to no one of our bargain. Do you agree?"

I hesitated, then nodded. "I agree."

He let go my chin. "Swear it. Swear it by the oath of your people, the oath the magician Berlik swore."

I took a deep breath. "I swear by stone and sea and sky, and all that they encompass, that I will assist the Circle with one last summoning and speak to no one of our bargain. I swear it by the sacred troth that binds me to my *diadh-anam*."

"Good." Raphael shouted for his footman Jean-Michel, who came at a run. "Pack a pair of saddlebags and see that my medical kit's in order," he said brusquely. "I'm riding to Namarre."

FORTY-EIGHT

With Brother Ramiel for a guide and an escort of four royal guardsmen and a footman, Raphael de Mereliot and I rode to Namarre.

It was a horribly uncomfortable journey.

For the first few days, Raphael didn't deign to speak to me. Brother Ramiel made some effort to soothe the troubled waters between us, but he didn't have my father's gift and Raphael's determined silence soon quelled him. I'd come to be friendly with a number of the Queen's guards, but these were the King's men and strangers to me.

We pushed the horses as hard as we dared, and I was grateful for the times when a swift pace made conversation impossible. When we slowed to a walk, the silence was deafening.

All around us, the world was awakening from winter's sleep, the last snows melting, trees beginning to bud. Any other time, I would have taken joy in it. Now all that burgeoning life seemed a cruel reminder that I didn't know if we'd find my father alive or dead.

On the fourth day, Raphael's shell of silence cracked.

"I don't understand it," he announced out of nowhere. "You have a *gift*, Moirin. A gift no one else in the world possesses. Gods! You have the potential to do great things." He turned his frustrated gaze on me. "Why in the name of Blessed buggering Elua would you give it up to become Jehanne's lap-dog?"

The others kneed their mounts and jogged a discreet distance ahead of us.

"I didn't," I said softly. "Raphael, whatever gift I possess, it was never what you wanted it to be. It's not endless. *I'm* not endless. Using it as I was on your behalf was killing me slowly."

His nostrils flared. "And yet you're willing to use it on your father's behalf."

"Aye," I said. "Call me selfish if you will. I only just met him. I don't want to lose him."

"How nice for you to be given that choice," Raphael said bitterly.

I closed my eyes, remembering. The cold water, the uplifting arms, the ragged voice. "I'm sorry."

He lowered his voice. "One success in the Circle's endeavor could save a thousand fathers' lives."

"So you say." I felt weary.

"Oh, the prospects are real." Raphael rubbed his nose. "I've proof of it. The goddamned ants are coming out of hibernation."

I wanted to say that it was a trick, that the spirits they summoned were ancient and clever, and it was always going to be a trick. But in the back of my mind, I heard the black-maned lion Marbas' soundless roar, and the topaz gem he had placed in my thoughts winked. The charm to reveal hidden things, a gift unasked for. So I kept my thoughts to myself and said only, "I gave you my oath. I'll do as you wish."

"Good."

"Raphael . . ." I wished there were some way I could reach him. "Why does it matter so much? Why do you want it so badly?"

He didn't answer for a moment. "If you have to ask, you'll never understand."

"I might if you told me," I said.

Raphael glanced at me, then looked away, his mouth hardening. "Practice your lap-dog skills elsewhere, Queen's confidante. I told you once before to stay out of my head. I'm telling you again."

"It might be good for you to speak of it," I murmured.

"Gods!" He raised his gaze skyward. "Why in Blessed Elua's name did destiny place you in my path if not for somewhat truly worthwhile? It makes no sense!"

My *diadh-anam* pulsed inside me, faint but insistent. "I'd like to know that myself."

"Well, you'll not find the answer in Jehanne's bed," he said in a cruel tone.

"Did you?" I asked pointedly. Raphael looked back at me, eyes darkening with anger. I held his gaze. I had as much right to be angry as he did.

In the end, he broke off his gaze. "This isn't conducive to healing. Better we not talk than quarrel, Moirin."

"All right."

The uncomfortable silence returned. We lodged at wayside inns. In the common rooms, the guards spoke quietly among themselves. Brother Ramiel told me tales of my father, trying to raise my spirits. Raphael was silent, attended by his manservant.

Two days later, under Brother Ramiel's guidance, we turned off the main road onto a narrow dirt track. It was near dusk when we reached the nameless hamlet. Folk turned out to gape at our fine attire and the guards in their livery of Courcel blue, pointing the way to the woodcutter's cabin.

It sat on the verge of the Senescine Forest, a humble building of expertly hewn logs. There was a chill in the air and smoke curled from the chimney. My heart thundered in my chest.

Before Brother Ramiel could knock, a woman opened the door. She was work-worn but lovely, tears in her eyes. "You're here! Elua be thanked!"

"He lives?" I forced the words out.

She hesitated. "His breath yet clouds a mirror."

Raphael was already in motion, dismounting and unlashing the bag that carried his medical supplies. He met my eyes and there was no hostility in his gaze, only a healer's intense concentration. "Come with me."

The cabin was small and cramped, warmed only by a cooking stove. The woodcutter bowed as we entered. A slender figure kneeling beside a cot on the far side of the stove rose, golden hair glowing in the dim light. A mirror flashed in her hand.

On the cot lay my father.

He looked like a newly dead corpse, frail and bloodless. His skin was translucent and the beautiful bones of his face were too prominent, the hollows of his eyes sunken. He was utterly motionless, not even his chest rising and falling. An involuntary keening sound burst from my throat.

"Moirin." Raphael caught my wrist. "Be strong."

I nodded.

Raphael borrowed the girl's mirror and knelt, holding it to my father's lips. After an eternity, it clouded faintly. "How long has he been this way?"

"Two days, messire." Her voice was low and steady despite the threat of tears in it. "I done give him all the medicaments and poultices that the physician the good Brother Ramiel sent gave us, but he only done worsened and worsened."

"You did very well," he said soothingly. "The infection in his lungs had taken too deep a grip."

I waited in an agony of suspense while Raphael examined my father, taking his pulses and listening to his chest, rubbing his hands together and hovering them over his body. The woodcutter's daughter eyed me with wonder.

"You're his daughter," she said in awe. "The Queen's witch."

"Aye."

"I never seen anyone like you," she said simply. "He kept asking for his daughter. Seemed to give him comfort when I tended to him. Can't think how he'd mistake us."

I spared her a glance. She was truly a rustic beauty, golden-haired and blue-eyed, clad in a homespun gown. "You tended to him with a daughter's loving care. I daresay that was what he sensed, and I'm grateful for it."

She flushed. "I done my best."

"Moirin." Raphael lifted his tawny head, his expression grave. "There's no time to waste. Are you ready?"

Panic washed through me. I pushed it away and sank to my knees beside him. I forced myself to cycle through the Five Styles of Breathing, drawing energy from the earth below me, the memory of the ocean, the trees around us, the embers glowing in the stove, and the very air itself.

Raphael rubbed his hands together, his gift rising and calling to mine. He splayed his hands over my father's chest.

"Now!"

I placed my hands over his and summoned the twilight, breathing it out.

I poured my energy into Raphael.

More.

More.

More.

We were three entities and we were one, conjoined. The water-wheel of my spirit's energy turned. I spilled into Raphael; he spilled into my father. Pushing, pushing at the thick congestion that clogged his lungs. Coaxing at the spark of life that lingered. The wheel turned and turned. I emptied myself heedlessly, turn after turn of the wheel. Golden warmth spilled from Raphael's hands. In a distant part of myself, I wondered what would happen when the stream ran dry. The stone doorway beckoned.

My father woke and coughed.

Raphael pushed harder, his brow beaded with sweat, damp hair hanging in his eyes. I poured the last of myself I had to give into him.

My father coughed again, wet and rattling. He rolled onto one side and the woodcutter's daughter was there holding a bowl to his lips, catching the endless flow of thick, ropy greenish yellow sputum that he coughed from his lungs, dispelling the vile infection. On and on it went until at last there was no more. With an effort, he opened his eyes. *"Moirin?"*

I smiled at him. "Aye."

And then I slid sideways into darkness.

FORTY-NINE

I lived and so did my father, although we were some days recovering. The woodcutter and his wife and daughter were more gracious hosts than anyone could have asked for. They made up a second cot for me near the stove, all three of them retreating to make their bed in the cabin's loft. Later, I learned that the hamlet came together to give lodging to Raphael and his manservant, Brother Ramiel, and the members of the King's Guard who escorted us.

Mostly, I slept.

When I awoke, I was glad. My father was alive.

He was thin and pale, but he had no fever and his lungs were clear, only a dry, hoarse cough remaining. Raphael came twice a day to examine him.

"Eat and sleep," he advised. "Regain your strength." His gaze settled on me, rueful and compassionate. "Both of you."

Slowly, slowly, the dry streambed refilled to a trickle.

The first day I was able to take to my feet, Raphael came to bid us farewell. "Your father's healing well," he said. "There's nothing more I can do for him. I reckon he'll be strong enough to travel in a few days. Your guards have procured a carriage. Just see that he doesn't exert himself and he's kept warm."

"I will," I promised. "Thank you."

Raphael hesitated. "Will you come outside a moment?" I followed him. It felt good to breathe the damp, fertile air. "Moirin . . ." He took my hand. "I'm sorry things went so badly awry between us."

"So am I," I said softly. "I never meant—"

"I know. I know you didn't. As for your oath . . ."

Hope flared inside me. "Aye?"

He squeezed my hand. "Take as much time as you need to recover. I won't press you and I'll say naught to the Circle until you're ready. I'll await your word. All right?"

And hope guttered and died. "All right," I said with regret. "I'll send word when I'm ready."

He gave a brisk nod. "My thanks." With that Raphael de Mereliot took his leave. I watched him swing himself astride his horse, weak sunlight picking out the strands of gold in his hair, his long limbs moving with easy grace. He gave me a parting wave, then kneed his mount.

I went back inside, where I found my father awake. "De Mereliot's gone?" he asked.

"Aye," I murmured.

He reached out to pat the adjacent cot. "Come, sit. You're not steady on your feet." His green eyes regarded me, large and vivid in his pale, gaunt face. "Moirin, unless I'm mistaken, I've heard you referred to as the Queen's companion in the last few days. Or are my wits more feveraddled than I know?"

I sighed. "Nooo . . ."

My father raised his brows. "We *are* speaking of Jehanne and not some other member of House Courcel?" I nodded. He laughed, then stifled a cough. "Well, that explains the coolness on de Mereliot's part. How in Blessed Elua's name did that come about? When I left, you were fretting over having bedded the Dauphin."

I glanced at the woodcutter's daughter, whose name was Sophie. She was scrubbing dishes in a tub on the other side of the stove, listening with avid fascination. I was reluctant to divulge the whole truth before her and I didn't want to lie. "Ohh . . . 'tis a long story. I'll tell you on the journey home."

"Is it true her majesty done had a magic bower built for you, my lady?" Sophie wanted to know. "Where it's always summer?"

I smiled at her eagerness. "True enough."

My father regarded me and shook his head in disbelief. "You're an unpredictable one to be sure, my strange child."

Several days later, we bade farewell to the woodcutter and his family. I thanked them a hundred times over for their generosity and promised to send a purse when I returned to the City. They refused, saying Brother Ramiel had already given them an ample reward on behalf of Naamah's Order.

"We're not greedy folk, my lady," said the woodcutter, Luc. He had a sweet, tired smile. "Was reward enough to see Brother Phanuel restored to life."

Sophie gave me a shy embrace in parting. "Mayhap I'll see you in the City one day, Lady Moirin," she said. "I'm thinking on Brother Ramiel's offer to enter Naamah's Service."

"You would do her honor," I assured her.

She blushed prettily, eyes aglow. "Aye?"

"Aye, indeed," I said wryly.

Despite the lingering sense of weariness that plagued me, the return journey was far, far more pleasant than the outbound one had been. I told my father the true story of how I had come to be Jehanne's companion, leaving out only those parts that concerned the Circle of Shalomon. He listened and understood in a way no one else could have.

"When we do a kindness for another, we grow in ways we cannot fathom," he murmured when I had finished. "I suspect that may be true for her majesty. And I suspect in turn that it is true for you as well, Moirin. You gave Jehanne a gift she didn't know she badly needed."

"Well." I smiled. "The role isn't without its rewards."

"Doubtless." My father regarded me gravely. "Your tale confirms my fears. You shouldn't have put yourself at such risk to save me."

"How could I not try?" I asked simply.

"How could I live with myself if you'd perished in the effort?" he countered. "Promise me you'll not do it again."

I shook my head. "That's not a promise I can make. Can you promise me you'll not take ill again?"

His generous mouth quirked. "I'll do my best."

We reached the City without incident, arriving in the early evening. I tried to convince my father to take lodgings at the Palace, where I was sure he would be welcome, but he refused, insisting that the peace and calm of the temple would do him good. In turn, he invited me to stay at the temple, an offer I declined.

"Jehanne will be missing me," I said. "She may even admit to it. How could I pass up such an opportunity?"

My father laughed and kissed my brow. "Go, then. Come see me on the morrow."

At the Palace, I was received with a certain measure of relief. A servant was dispatched to notify her majesty of my return. I retreated to my enchanted bower and sent for a bath to be drawn. My quarters had been kept warm in my absence, not quite warm enough for the likes of the tropical plants and too warm for the evergreens. I listened to their voiceless songs while I waited, promising to tend to them when I felt stronger.

When my bath was ready, I luxuriated in it, my first proper bath since I'd left the City. A year ago, I'd have been content with a quick wash in a cold stream. A year ago, Cillian had been alive and nagging me to wed him. I thought about the strange course my life had taken between then and now. From cave to palace, from the unsuitable would-be bride of the Lord of the Dalriada's son to the Queen of Terre d'Ange's valued companion.

Strange, indeed.

Following my drifting thoughts, I drifted asleep in the warm water. When the maid returned with a freshly heated bucket and plucked the sponge from my limp hand, I didn't protest, lingering in the darkness behind my closed eyes. She began bathing the back of my neck with uncommon tenderness, warm water cascading over my shoulders.

I opened my eyes and smiled at Jehanne. She was sitting on the stool beside the tub, dressed in state regalia, sponge in hand.

"You're back." Her eyes sparkled at me. "I had to see for myself that you were more or less intact."

"More or less," I agreed, delighting in the incongruous sight of her playing the maidservant.

"Your father?"

"He's recovering at the temple," I said. "The babe?"

Jehanne splayed her free hand over her belly, which evinced a very slight hint of roundness. "Progressing well, I'm told." She flashed an impish smile at me. "Would you like to examine the progress for yourself, or shall I leave you in peace to recuperate?"

The bright tendrils of her gift, Naamah's gift, encompassed me, embracing and strengthening me. The blood beat harder in my veins. I sat upright in the bath, water sloshing. "Stay," I said, reaching for her. "Please, stay."

It was nice, so nice.

And best of all, Jehanne didn't leave afterward. We lay naked and entangled in bedsheets damp with bathwater and smelling of lavender and love-making. I was tired and drained, but in a good way, languid and happy, gladly undone by her immeasurable arts and charms. When I asked if I should summon a maid to help her dress, Jehanne shook her head sleepily.

"I told Daniel I meant to pass the night here if you were willing," she said in a drowsy tone. "I've missed you."

I tightened my arms around her. "That's nice to hear."

"Mmm." She planted a gentle kiss beneath my right ear. "And it cost me nothing to say it. Imagine that."

I laughed. "I missed you, too, my lady."

"So I noticed." Jehanne squirmed out of my embrace and propped herself on one arm, studying me. "This healing took quite a toll, didn't it?"

"Aye," I murmured. "It did."

She kissed my lips, soft and lingering. "I'll not speak against it, my witchling. I bade you go, and I envy you your affection for your father. He seems a kind and lovely man. So far as I know, all the world loves Brother Phanuel." Jehanne settled back to twine herself around me once more, her limbs warm and soft, her head coming to rest on my shoulder. "I'm just glad you're safely home. And I'm so very glad Raphael agreed to give his aid unstinting," she added in a low, sleep-rich voice. "It pleases me to be able to think better of him."

My heart ached.

"I'm glad, too," I whispered, wishing it were true.

The days that followed should have been pleasant ones. My father was home and healing. My strength continued to return. Spring was bursting across the land. Jehanne continued to be sweet-tempered, which put everyone around her in good spirits. I resumed my lessons with Master Lo Feng, who praised me for my sense of filial duty rather than chiding me. While his snowdrop bulbs had sunk into dormancy, there was a spark of life in them I continued to nurture.

But my oath to Raphael cast a pall over everything.

I wished, very badly, that there were someone I could speak to about it—but I couldn't. I'd sworn not to speak of it. I'd sworn by stone and sea and sky, and on my *diadh-anam* itself. If I broke my oath, I broke faith with the Maghuin Dhonn Herself. My *diadh-anam* would gutter and die inside me, my gifts would fade. And I would never know what destiny She had intended for me.

So I kept my silence.

I practiced the Five Styles of Breathing, learning to better focus my energies. As I grew more adept, Master Lo Feng gave me verses to contemplate as I breathed. I began to develop the first tenuous inklings of a grasp on the discipline he called the Way, which allowed one to live in harmony with spirit and nature. I was grateful for his wisdom and teaching, grateful for my progress. And all too aware that each day brought me closer to the day I would have to fulfill my oath to Raphael.

A part of me yearned to delay it as long as possible, but a greater part wanted it over and done with. At the end of a month's time, I reckoned I was as fit as I'd been before my father's illness. I went to Raphael's townhouse to speak with him.

This time, he received me graciously, serving me tea and pastries in the parlor. It felt passing strange to be a guest in the house where I'd lived as his consort. I wished for the thousandth time that my *diadh-anam* didn't flicker in his presence, that the sight of him didn't quicken my blood. Raphael dismissed his servants and closed the parlor doors.

"You look well, Moirin," he said to me. "Are you up to the task at hand?"

I took a deep breath. "Raphael . . . I've come to beg you to release me from my oath. Please, don't do this thing. Nothing good will come of it."

He set down his teacup. "You're frightened."

"I am," I said honestly. "Frightened for myself and frightened for *you*. It's unwise to seek to force the world into the shape of your desires. It's unhealthy to harbor such terrible ambition."

Raphael looked away. "You've had a surfeit of Master Lo Feng's philosophy."

I tried a different tack. "Jehanne believes you aided me out of the goodness of your heart," I told him. "It pleased her so much to think so. You could make it true."

A muscle in his jaw twitched. "Does it please her so greatly that she will forsake Daniel for me? I think not. She's bearing his child. She's made her choice. Why should I care what Jehanne de la Courcel thinks of me?"

"Because you do," I said.

He gave a short, harsh laugh, running his hands over his face. "Elua help me, it's true. But not enough, Moirin. Not when she feeds me crumbs and spreads a feast for others. Once, I would have done anything for her. Not now."

Sensing the depth of his misery, I was silent. I'd been thrust between them from the beginning, first on one's side, then the other's. I'd let Raphael use me as a pawn in their game, knowing that he loved her. And I remembered all too well how Jehanne had come to my quarters, lost and shivering, and asked me to hold her after Raphael had bade her go rather than stay the night. She loved him. But she *had* made her choice between the anchor and the storm—and I'd helped her. I had a seat at her banquet table.

This was not an argument I was going to win.

"So." Raphael cleared his throat, dismissing the topic. "Let me assure you that the Circle will take every precaution. And let's arrange a sign, you and I. I'm not a monster, Moirin. I promise, I'll not trade your life for this endeavor. We do but make an attempt. If you're starting to feel faint, squeeze my hand hard and I'll bid Claire to speak the words of dismissal. All right?"

"As you will," I murmured. "When?"

He rose gracefully. "I'll need to consult with the others. The timing of this will be different. Focalor is one of the greater spirits, a grand duke of the fallen. He's to be summoned between the hours of sunrise and noon. I'll send word."

With a heavy heart, I inclined my head. "I'll await it."

It came on the morrow in the form of a letter.

Come to the townhouse at dawn, two days hence.

FIFTY

On the appointed day, I awoke in the dim hours before dawn. My room, my enchanted bower. It seemed very precious to me. I kindled a lamp and dressed beneath the shadows of a hundred plants, breathing in their scent.

I thought about the task at hand and wondered what trick Focalor would play.

It was always going to be a trick.

I thought about the oath I had sworn—and tricks. And I swore softly to myself, wrenching open the drawer of the desk in my outer chamber and rummaging for paper and ink. I'd sworn not to *speak* of my bargain with Raphael.

I hadn't sworn not to write of it.

There was no time left to think. Acting in desperation, I scrawled a swift note to Jehanne, telling her where I was bound and why. I kissed it and sealed it, praying she'd have a better idea of what to do about it than I did—or at least the sense to consult with someone who did, like King Daniel. On my way out of the Palace, I hunted down one of her guards and gave it to him.

He eyed me warily, holding the sealed letter as though it were a serpent. "You'd have me *wake* her majesty at this hour?"

"I would," I said. "Have I ever asked any guardsman for aught?"

The guard sighed. "Never, my lady."

I nodded. "Then you know it's important."

In the royal stables, a sleepy ostler saddled Blossom and led her out for me. The gentle filly Thierry had given me was game for the adventure, ears pricked. I rode her through the empty streets of the City to Raphael's townhouse, praying I'd find him lagging. Every moment of delay would hasten my missive.

But no, Raphael de Mereliot was awake and ready, his horse saddled and waiting in the courtyard. "Best to make haste," he said. "I'll send for the carriage later if it's needed. The rest of the Circle assembled last night."

We made haste—too much haste. The grey air was damp and moist, smelling of fertile soil and new growth, a hovering mist turning golden as the sun rose. Raphael's chestnut horse snorted and stretched its legs. Blossom followed suit, her reaching hooves eating up the road as they vied with one another. The white walls of the City of Elua fell away behind us. I kept glancing backward in the saddle, hoping for signs of pursuit.

There weren't any.

Altogether too soon, we arrived at the de Toluard country estate, the gracious manor house flanked by tall cypress trees. It was like a bad dream revisited. I let Raphael lead me inside. None of the Circle pretended to affection, nor did I. Still, the ritual was observed, the cordial poured.

"*To knowledge,*" Denis de Toluard said in a hard voice, lifting the glass to his lips and tossing back its contents.

The others echoed the toast and drank.

I emptied my glass on the floor.

Raphael's hand closed on my elbow, hard and painful. "Moirin, that is not helpful!" he hissed in my ear.

I shrugged. "Go to hell. You forced this bargain on me, Raphael. You made me buy my father's life with it. I'll keep my oath, but I don't have to wish you well in this. I think you're fools for attempting it."

The members of the Circle stared at me with hatred and resentment. I stared back at them with my mother's best unblinking glower until they looked away.

It was as dark as ever in the underground chamber, all traces of sunlight banished. I went through the familiar movements of preparation as slowly as I dared, donning the white linen robe and washing my face and hands in the hyssop-scented basin. My mind was miles away.

I shouldn't have trusted my letter to the guard. I should have awakened Jehanne myself, but I'd feared I'd violate the terms of my oath if I had to speak to her. Or mayhap I should have dispatched the letter to someone else—to my father, or to King Daniel himself. Thierry—Thierry would have heeded me. Or Master Lo Feng, mayhap. He was so calm and wise, surely he would have known what to do.

But it was too late.

"Lady Moirin." The silversmith Balric addressed me in a dispassionate voice, holding out a silver medallion engraved with a new sigil. "We're waiting."

I took the sigil and hung it around my neck, shivering.

There was one change to the ritual. In the great chamber, Balric produced an enormous silver chain from a leather satchel. Each link was etched with tiny, precise sigils. He wound the chain twice around the center of the six-pointed star, securing the ends with a silver lock.

"That will hold him," Orien de Legasse said in satisfaction. "Well wrought, smith."

Raphael imprisoned my hand in his, holding it hard. "Are we ready?" he asked the room at large. There were nods and murmurs of assent. "Then let us begin."

In a steady voice, Claire Fourcay began to speak the first conjuration in the Habiru tongue. The familiar sense of pressure filled the air. I gave a silent prayer to the Maghuin Dhonn Herself and abandoned hope to concentrate on the task at hand. Claire's voice echoed in the chamber. The torches flickered. The pressure intensified until my head was ringing with it.

In the center of the star, the air shimmered. I fought to steady my breathing, fought to remember my lessons.

A doorway, limned in pulsing flames.

It was vast, vaster than before. The top of it reached for the vaulted ceilings and there seemed to be no bottom. I pulled away involuntarily, not wanting to know what lay behind it, but Raphael's grip on my hand brought me up short.

"You gave your oath," he reminded me in a low voice.

"So I did." I gritted my teeth, a blaze of fury running through me.

I hated him, hated every last one of them. They wanted what I was capable of doing for them—well and so. Let them have it. "So be it."

I summoned the twilight and *pushed*—hard, harder than I'd ever pushed before.

The doorway flared and a wild wind whipped through the chamber. I let go the twilight. Someone cried aloud. Claire's voice faltered, then took up a new invocation. A vast bank of stormclouds boiled through the doorway, the sense of a great presence encompassed in it. Thunder rolled and lightning forked in the clouds. Claire uttered ringing syllable after syllable. Balric's silver chain rose to encircle the roiling cloud bank, rattling wildly, forcing the presence within to take form and manifest.

The wind died.

A tall man stood in the center of the star, a silver chain wrapped twice around his bare chest and pinning his arms to his sides, so tight the links strained. Immense wings striated like an eagle's sprang from his shoulder blades, free of the chains. Incandescent blue-white sparks flashed in his eyes and a terrible, terrible brightness hung about him.

Everyone was very quiet.

I shifted into the twilight. He looked the same, only brighter. It hurt my eyes to look at him. He glanced sidelong at me and smiled. I shifted back.

Claire Fourcay said something in a tentative tone.

"You may address me in your native tongue," the tall man said pleasantly. "I am Focalor, Grand Duke of the Fallen, not some lesser spirit to play at foolish pranks and pretend to less knowledge than I possess."

Most of the members of the Circle relaxed. I didn't. My fury vanished, giving way to a rising sense of alarm. This spirit was far, far more powerful than any we had summoned before. I could feel my strength ebbing steadily and I could sense the malice in him. I squeezed Raphael's hand hard, remembering the promise he'd made me. "Bid her dismiss him," I said urgently. "Now!"

He hesitated. "So soon?"

"Moirin, *shut up!*" Lianne Tremaine hissed. "Claire, don't listen to the spirit! It's just another trick. Give the proper invocation and demand his gift!"

Ignoring them, I tried to close the doorway myself.

It didn't work.

Focalor's wings spread open wide with a crack of thunder, shedding droplets of bright light. He was blocking the way, absorbing my efforts. The chains around his torso strained. He beat his wings once and the thunder cracked again. A sense of menace rose from him like steam.

"Claire!" Raphael shouted. "Dismiss him!"

"Too late!" Focalor's voice broke in waves against the walls of the chamber. Lightning flashed in his eyes. With a sharp crack, the chain that bound him burst and fell uselessly to the flagstones. "Ahh." He rolled his shoulders and shuddered with pleasure, smiling beneficently around at the Circle. Everyone stood frozen. I stood, weak and helpless, no more able to move than if my feet had taken root in stone. "You." He pointed at Claire Fourcay. "You mispronounced two words in the spell of binding. And you." He pointed at Balric Maitland, clucking his tongue. "A single drop of solder obscured the sigil on the seventeenth link of your chain."

Balric flushed and muttered under his breath.

"Poor silversmith." Focalor stepped lightly out of the coils of his broken chains, out of the center of the six-pointed star. He towered over the smith, lifting his chin with one hand. "Lucky for you, you're here out of love for your craft." He moved away. "Let us determine who else among you can claim such purity of heart, for you and you alone will enjoy the protection of your Elua and my apostate brethren." Blue-white sparks flickered in his eyes. "As for the rest of you, your gods cannot save you from yourselves."

Orien de Legasse fainted dead away before Focalor's regard. The spirit chuckled. "Silly little scholar," he said in affectionate tone. "Be glad your love for the arcane arts surpasses your gift for them this day."

Focalor paused before Lianne Tremaine, stroking her cheek with one wingtip. She shivered violently, but held his gaze with a measure of defiance. "Ah, poet," Focalor said with false sympathy. "You yearned for great tales and a greater gift to tell them. Be content to survive this one."

He moved on to Denis de Toluard, who squeezed his eyes closed briefly. "All knowledge is worth having," Focalor quoted. "Isn't that what you say, Shemhazai's scion?" He chuckled. "You have learned today that you are foolish. I hope you find it worth the price."

Four reprieves had been granted.

Three of us were left.

I felt Focalor's regard settle on me. He crossed the flagstones, lifting one hand to caress my face. His touch was at once insubstantial and palpable, crackling against my skin. "So this is the bear's child," he said. "Curious." He touched my brow. "I see Marbas' gift here. Have you found a use for it?"

"No," I murmured. "What is it *you* seek, my lord?"

"Clever child." Focalor smiled at me. It was a smile like a well-honed blade, like the cutting edge of a storm. It was filled with impersonal malice, and there was death and mayhem in it. Tossing seas and staved hulls, an ocean of sinking limbs beneath a raging sky, filled with the sheer joy of destruction. "After so many centuries, need you ask? I seek to take flesh and live in the mortal world."

"I see." I wavered on my feet, the room darkening in my eyes. I gathered my failing energies, thinking it would be a very, very bad thing if Focalor's wishes were to come to pass. I couldn't close the door—but I could cause it to be closed. "Sorry to deny you."

I poured myself into him, emptying every drop I could.

The Grand Duke of the Fallen cried out and thrust away from me, his wings beating in alarm and shedding drops of brightness. I felt my *diadh-anam* gutter inside me as I sank to my knees. Raphael's arms came around me, golden warmth spilling into me.

"Don't," I whispered. "Stone and sea! For once, listen to me."

For once, he did. Raphael let me go. I slumped onto my side, resting my cheek against the chilled flagstones. The doorway I'd opened began to flicker and fade. In its place, the promise of the stone doorway loomed. On the far side, the Maghuin Dhonn Herself awaited me. In the privacy of my thoughts, I begged forgiveness of those I loved. I apologized for failing them. And then I smiled, at peace with the notion of death.

I'd made so many, many bad decisions. This was not one of them.

"No!" Focalor raged. "No, no, no!"

"Yes," I breathed faintly.

"*No.*" The doorway I'd opened had not yet closed. We were neither here nor there, caught between mortal and spirit worlds. Thunder rattled the vaulted ceiling. "This isn't over yet." The spirit Focalor strode across the floor. With insubstantial hands and the force of his will, he wrenched Claire Fourcay's head upright. Her eyes grew huge and her face paled. "Jealousy and yearning does not true love make," he said brusquely. "I would speak at greater length if there were time. Your motives are tainted."

Through slitted eyes, I watched Focalor cover her lips with his and inhale sharply.

She fell, limp and lifeless.

He strode back across the chamber. Knelt, clasped the back of my neck, and clamped his mouth over mine. Raphael pushed ineffectually at him.

I tried to struggle, tried to die.

I couldn't.

He breathed, Focalor breathed into me. He forced Claire Fourcay's life force into my lungs. It was alien and unwelcome—but it was mortal and vital. I coughed, gagging on it, feeling it unfurl inside me and infuse my limbs.

The stone doorway faded.

The other remained.

Focalor let me go and rose. I knelt, retching, trying to expel the energy he'd forced into me. "Let it be, little bear-witch," he said in his pleasant tone. "You'll live. Long enough, at any rate." He turned to Raphael, clucking his tongue with mock dismay. "You should have cleaved to the gifts of healing, physician. The purity of that love, I might have believed."

Raphael pulled me to my feet and thrust me behind him. "Let Moirin go, my lord," he said in a ragged voice. "She wanted nothing to do with this. She's here for love of her father, nothing more. Her motive is the purest of them all."

"How can you think I mean her harm?" The spirit's eyes widened in a parody of innocence, lightning flickering in their depths. "Why, I saved her life when she tried to spend it. *You* brought her here, physician. *You* found her a useful tool. I do but complete the task to which you set her. I'll make you nigh unto a god." He smiled his knife-blade smile. "Although I fear there won't be much of *you* left to enjoy it."

Thunder rumbled.

Focalor held Raphael effortlessly, putting his mouth over his and exhaling, pouring his own essence into Raphael's body.

I tried to grapple with him to no avail. As long as the doorway stood open, we were not wholly in the mortal world and he had strength without substance. The cords on Raphael's neck stood out and his chest heaved as he struggled helplessly against the invasion, unable to breathe, his eyes terrified. Focalor's manifestation grew transparent as his essence filled Raphael. I wept in frustration and horror.

Somewhere, a door crashed, mortal and ordinary.

The spirit hesitated, his form growing more opaque.

And then there were panicked voices shouting in D'Angeline, another voice shouting wordlessly, and yet another speaking a foreign tongue in a calm, sonorous tone. A lean figure swept into the chamber like a whirlwind, spinning in circles, twirling a staff so swiftly it was a blur in his hands. Sparks shot from the ends of the staff, bursting with loud cracking sounds like an ember, only louder and brighter.

"Bao!" I cried.

"Stupid girl!" he yelled, driving Focalor toward the center of the star. "Get the stupid man away!"

I yanked Raphael backward. He took a deep, gasping breath and began coughing and retching, bracing his hands on his knees.

Bao's staff had ceased to shoot sparks. Bits of charred string and paper hung from the ends. Focalor eyed him as he spun it, then took a step forward.

And then Master Lo Feng was there, chanting serenely, holding a small, round mirror in his hands. Focalor averted his gaze from the mirror, held at bay.

"Stupid girl!" Bao retreated and cuffed my head. "Close the door!"

I winced. "I can't!"

"Then you die!"

"Bao is correct," Master Lo Feng said calmly. "You opened this doorway, Moirin. Now that the demon-spirit is unbound, only you can close it. If you do not, you will spend your essence and perish, and the spirit will linger, trapped and capable of much mischief."

"She can't." Focalor raised his head and gave me a smile full of malice. "There were great magicians born to your people once, weren't there? No more. What can you do on your own? Play peekaboo in the dusk? Sing to plants?"

I didn't answer.

He laughed. "You're good for nothing by yourself! You're a useful tool for other hands to wield. Save lives? I think not. You couldn't even open this doorway without the aid of a handful of inept scholars." Members of the King's Guard spilled into the chamber, hugging the walls, swords drawn. I wondered what they saw. Focalor sidled closer to me, avoiding Master Lo Feng's mirror. He loomed over me, bending his face close to mine, his spread wings casting me in shadow. A scent like the aftermath of a lightning strike hung in the chamber. "You're the half-breed offspring of a dwindling folk, nothing more."

He was vast.

But I had seen vaster. I had seen the Maghuin Dhonn Herself blotting out the stars. I had felt Her tread shake the earth. She had accepted me as Her own. I was Her child. I clung to that memory, and I felt Her presence embrace me, settling over me like a mantle. I was angry. She, too, was angry at his words. I drew strength from it.

I pointed at the doorway. "And you are nothing more than a god's discarded servant. *Go.*"

The foundations of the manor house trembled. Thunder rolled and rattled. I breathed the Breath of Earth's Pulse and said it again, pushing with all the strength I had—mine, and poor Claire Fourcay's, and the anger of the Maghuin Dhonn Herself.

"*Go!*"

It came out as a guttural roar. And he went, Focalor went, retreating and banished. Step by step, he retreated, grimacing with rage. I felt the last of Claire Fourcay's fading life force drain out of me and pushed harder, drawing on my own dwindling reserves. The doorway sucked

Focalor into itself, and I closed it with one last tremendous push. Its outline flared and vanished.

Done.

I sighed.

Bao rested one hand on my shoulder. "Not bad, stupid girl."

I leaned wearily against him. "Thank you."

FIFTY-ONE

The mood in the chamber was subdued, to say the least.

The surviving members of the Circle avoided meeting one another's eyes—and most especially, they avoided my gaze. Orien de Legasse buried his face in his hands and wept. Balric Maitland turned his face to the wall and said nothing. Lianne Tremaine and Denis de Toluard clasped one another's hands, but didn't look at each other.

Raphael sat on the flagstones, Claire Fourcay's head in his lap, his head bowed over her lifeless figure.

The King's guardsmen glanced at one another, helpless and confused.

"I'm sorry," I said to Master Lo Feng. "I'm so sorry. I couldn't find a way to tell you."

He folded his hands into his sleeves. "Be grateful your Queen was wise enough to do so."

King Daniel entered the chamber, his face taut with fury. His guardsmen stood at attention. He was imposing in his anger. He spoke to Denis de Toluard in a low voice, and then to Lianne Tremaine. I saw the latter wince, then incline her head in acceptance. I suspected the youngest King's Poet in history had been stripped of her title.

He stood before Raphael. When he spoke, his voice was wintry. "De Mereliot."

Raphael shifted Claire's body with tender care and rose. "We broke no laws, your majesty," he said in a dull tone.

The King regarded him with contempt. "I have no words for you."

And then he came to me.

"I'm sorry," I whispered, repeating myself. I was weary beyond telling. Only Bao's strong hand under my elbow kept me upright. "So sorry, your majesty. I failed you, I failed my lady. I failed everyone."

"Not in the end, child," he said with a gentleness I didn't deserve. "Come, let's get you home. Jehanne's sick with worry."

Home.

Home sounded like a wonderful notion. Once it had been a cave, warm and snug and safe. Now it was a bower at the Palace. All I wanted to do was fall into bed beneath the overhanging ferns and sleep for days, then awake to apologize a thousand times and find absolution in Jehanne's arms.

But I had to confront Raphael.

To his credit, he met my gaze without flinching. And I found that like the King, I had no words for him. Instead, I stooped and touched Claire Fourcay's cheek. Her skin was still warm. Her motives may have been tainted, but at least I could understand them. I'd been just as foolish. I should never have let Raphael use me in the first place. Once upon a time, I'd wanted so much for him to care for me.

"Moirin." His voice was hoarse. "Lest it need saying, I release you from your oath of silence. And—"

I straightened and found a word worth saying. "Good-bye."

Raphael nodded and said nothing more.

He stayed behind when we left. All the members of the Circle stayed. And although a large part of me hoped I never saw any of them again, I couldn't help but glance behind one last time as we left the chamber. Raphael was watching me. For a second, I thought I saw a faint spark of lightning in his grey eyes; then I blinked and it was gone, leaving only guilt and abiding sorrow in its place.

I shuddered.

Never in my life had I been so glad to see the sky. I breathed deeply with no particular art, just filling my lungs with clean air. After what had transpired, it seemed like it should have been the dead of night, but it was still morning.

"Can you ride?" King Daniel asked me gently. "I'll commandeer a carriage if you're not strong enough."

"I'll manage." I swallowed. "You shouldn't be so kind to me, your majesty. I'm as guilty as any of them."

He was silent a moment. "Raphael de Mereliot spoke the truth," he said at length. "You broke no laws. And it is in my thoughts that mayhap if I had not governed so cautiously, if I had given my people somewhat greater to strive for and dream about, these few would not have been driven to such lengths in search of glory."

"Mayhap," I murmured.

"One is never given to know such things," he mused. "Such is the burden of rule. But I do hold you less to blame, Moirin. For all your uncanny ways, you're young and inexperienced. De Mereliot forced your hand cruelly; and even so, you found a way around your oath. Still, I heard him release you from it, and I expect you to give a full accounting of this business, holding back nothing and protecting no one, least of all Raphael de Mereliot. They may have broken no laws, but this is a matter that must be exposed. Will you do so?"

I nodded fervently. "With all my heart!"

It was a somber ride back toward the City. The guardsmen spoke in hushed whispers of what they had witnessed. King Daniel conversed in low tones with Master Lo Feng. I concentrated on remaining upright in the saddle, grateful for Blossom's smooth gait and mindful that I was only conscious, let alone alive, by virtue of Claire Fourcay's unwilling sacrifice and the grace of the Maghuin Dhonn Herself.

Bao stuck close to my side, ready to catch me if I toppled, muttering under his breath about my stupidity. For once, I couldn't begrudge him.

"How did you know what to do?" I asked him. "How did you make sparks and thunder come from your staff?"

He shrugged. "Everyone know you use *pao* to drive away demons. You no have *pao* here?"

"No," I said. "I don't think so."

Bao showed me the charred bits of paper dangling from the end of his staff. "String of *pao*. Only fire-powder and paper. No magic. Mirrors good, too. Demon can't look at they own face." He raised his eyebrows at me. "You lucky we in time. That demon-spirit, he get into Lion Mane, maybe nothing make him go. Big trouble then."

I was confused. "Lion Mane?"

"The stupid man," he clarified.

"Raphael."

"Uh-huh." He nodded. "Master Lo right. You lucky the White Queen smart enough to send for him." He snorted. "Ten time smarter than you, anyway. If she don't . . ." He drew his thumb across his throat. "I think you and lot of people get dead."

"I know," I said quietly. "Believe me, I do."

Bao regarded me. "You did good. Strong." Unexpectedly, he grinned. "You see the face on that demon-spirit when you shout and make the ground shake? Big surprise."

It made me smile a little. "Very big surprise. For me, too."

"Uh-huh." He looked away. "Huh. Rider coming."

I glanced down the road to see a guardsman in Courcel livery approaching at a good clip. King Daniel raised his hand to call a halt. We waited. The guardsman approached and drew rein, his lathered mount prancing sideways.

"Your majesty!" he called in an urgent voice. "There's a rather large delegation coming! And begging your pardon, they were quite insistent."

The King frowned in perplexity. "I expected no such thing. What delegation? Are they hostile or friendly? Who are they and from whence do they come?"

"From Ch'in." The guard pointed at Master Lo Feng, who sat serenely upright in the saddle. "They're looking for *him*."

I glanced at Bao. He shook his head. "Very big surprise."

"Well," King Daniel said mildly, looking sidelong at Master Lo Feng. "That's never happened before. Let's see what they want, shall we?"

A short time later, we rounded a curve in the road and came upon the delegation. I sucked in my breath at the sight of them. There were at least fifty mounted warriors riding in a tight formation, all with the golden-brown skin and dark, tilted eyes of the Ch'in. They wore armor plated like scales and adorned with gilt and pointed helmets, curved swords at their sides. I was accustomed to Bao and Master Lo Feng, but such a large party of their countrymen looked strange and out of place here. The King's guardsmen regarded them uneasily, hands hovering over their sword-hilts.

"Lo Feng Tzu?" the leader inquired.

Master Lo inclined his head. *"Shi."*

In unison, every last warrior dismounted and bowed. Head still lowered, the leader poured out a torrent of Ch'in, bowing again to Master Lo and then to King Daniel.

"General Tsieh apologizes for disturbing you, your majesty," Master Lo translated. "He comes on a very urgent errand."

"Name of Elua!" The King looked dumbstruck. "How urgent can it be? How many months have they been on the road?"

There was another exchange.

"Many months at sea," Master Lo said. "They came by one of the greatships and only rode from your city of Marsilikos." Even he looked impressed. "None has ever travelled so far before. Truly, they carried wind in a bag."

"What do they want?" the King inquired.

Master Lo Feng spoke to the general and listened to his lengthy reply, his face growing ever more grave. My chest grew tight and I felt a strange pressure and ringing in my ears. The sense of the Maghuin Dhonn's presence was back and the spark of my *diadh-anam* was quickening inside me. All too well, I remembered the sea shining through the stone doorway and the infinite compassion in Her eyes. And I remembered what I had said to Her.

I have a very long way to go, don't I?

"No," I whispered. "Not yet, please!"

"How you know what they say?" Bao asked irritably. "I can't even hear!"

I shivered. "I don't."

General Tsieh stopped speaking. He and Master Lo exchanged bows; then Master Lo turned in the saddle and bowed to King Daniel. "The Emperor's daughter is very ill. I am summoned home to tend to her."

The King hesitated. "You're free to go as you please, of course. We are grateful for the wisdom you've shared. But forgive me . . . if they were many months at sea, surely it will be far too late for you to be of assistance."

"No," Master Lo Feng said with regret. "I fear it is no mortal illness. If she has not been slain, she lives. Bao and I will leave on the morrow." He conferred with the general again. The latter shook his head violently several times, glancing in my direction. Master Lo shrugged and folded his hands in his sleeves, looking calm and implacable. The general sighed and gave an abrupt bow in acquiescence.

I wanted to look away and couldn't.

"Moirin, my student." Master Lo's gaze settled on me. "If you are willing, I would very much like you to accompany us."

My *diadh-anam* blazed wildly in my breast. My ears rang with a sound like trumpets, the sound of destiny calling me.

I was tired, so tired.

I wanted to say no. I wanted to stay; I wanted my bed and my bower. I didn't want to cross untold oceans and venture to a stranger land than this one. I wanted the refuge I'd found as the Queen's royal companion, to continue to smooth the sharp edges of Jehanne's prickly temper and delight in her abundant passions. I wanted to spend time with my father, so recently found and so nearly lost to me. I closed my eyes and prayed to the gods of Terre d'Ange I knew best, begging them to let me stay—but Naamah turned her bright face away. Anael bowed his head over his cupped hands, showing me a bulb with a single shoot, a Camaeline snowdrop.

Their will accorded with Hers.

I was meant to go.

I rubbed my stinging eyes. "Aye, Master Lo. I'll go."

FIFTY-TWO

The worst part was telling Jehanne.

She knew something was amiss. She was there to receive us at the Palace, Prince Thierry at her side, unexpectedly attentive, her entourage around her. She kissed her royal husband with glad relief, and me no less gladly, her lips lingering on mine.

"My poor girl," she murmured in my ear. "You should have written me sooner. I'd have made him release you."

I shivered. "I didn't think of it."

Jehanne pulled away from me. "It *is* over, isn't it? This business with Raphael?"

"Aye," I said miserably. "But—"

A shadow crossed her face. She put two fingers over my lips. "Whatever it is, don't speak of it now. Tell me later. Alone."

Tired though I was, I kept my word and met with King Daniel. In the privacy of his study, I told him everything I knew about the Circle of Shalomon, every detail of the summonings we had attempted. He listened gravely, asking questions and taking notes, then dismissed me when I was finished at last.

"Moirin." He called me back as I went to leave. "I heard your answer to Master Lo Feng. Is there aught I can say to change your mind?"

I touched my chest. "Can you silence my destiny?"

"Would that I could." He studied me. "You're sure?"

I nodded. "Would that I weren't. I don't want to leave, your majesty. But I'm very, very sure."

The King sighed. "Blessed Elua hold and keep you. Go."

When I returned to my quarters, I found Jehanne there waiting for me. And alone in the bower she'd had created for me, I told her.

Jehanne slapped me hard across the face, hard enough to wrench my head sideways. And then she crumpled to the floor at my feet, weeping as though her heart were breaking.

I felt as though mine were.

"I'm sorry!" I cradled her head in my lap, wrapping my arms around her. I felt awful and there was nothing I could say to make it better, no words of comfort I could speak. All I could do was hold her until the worst of the storm had passed. "I'm so very sorry. Jehanne, I don't want to leave you. I don't."

She sniffled. "But you are."

"Yes," I said softly.

She grew still and quiet in my arms. "I knew. I always knew you would. I just didn't think it would be so soon, Moirin."

"Neither did I."

A fresh bout of weeping shook her. "I thought you'd stay at least until the child was born!"

I closed my eyes, hot tears leaking beneath my lids. "So did I. I'm *sorry!*"

"I know," Jehanne murmured when she could talk again. She gave a sad, lost laugh. "At least as an adept of Cereus House, I'm taught to revere the transient nature of beauty. This was a fleeting and precious thing."

I stroked her hair. "You'll take another companion now that you know it suits you."

"Oh, please!" It was a relief to hear a cross edge to her voice. "Will you insult my intelligence? Surely it hasn't escaped your notice that there *isn't* anyone else like you in the world."

"No." I kissed her tear-damp cheek. "But you don't need a half-breed Maghuin Dhonn witch to serve as your companion. You just need someone you like well enough to trust." I smiled despite my aching heart. "Some gorgeous young creature from the backwoods with a generous soul, a good deal of patience, and buckets of untutored ardor." At that, Jehanne smiled a little, too. "You'd like the lass who tended my father," I told her. "The woodcutter's daughter, Sophie. Kind and sweet, very beautiful, and very, very untutored."

"Oh?" She peered up at me.

"Aye." A sharp pang of jealousy shot through me at the thought of the woodcutter's daughter in Jehanne's arms. "You needn't look *that* interested."

"I'm not." She sat upright. "Oh, Moirin! It's not that easy to trust anew."

"You gave me your trust willingly enough," I reminded her.

Jehanne took my hand, twining her fingers with mine. "There was already a bond of trust between us. You took a considerable leap of faith when you let me rescue you. It made it easier to return the favor." She paused and searched my face, her blue-grey eyes earnest and vulnerable and as bright as stars. "Do you love me at least a little bit?"

I couldn't help it; I laughed. And I wept, too. "Do you truly have to ask? Yes, Jehanne, a thousand times, yes. You're absurdly beautiful, utterly infuriating, and inexplicably charming, and I love you far, far more than you deserve."

"Good." She put her arms around my neck, smiling at me through her tears. "Tell me more, please."

I did.

I pulled her close and kissed her over and over, and I told her everything I loved about her—decent and indecent.

And this, too, felt like a benediction.

Naamah had turned her face away when I begged her to let me stay. Now that I had accepted my fate, she turned it back to me for a fleeting moment in time.

To us.

Whatever else was true, Naamah's blessing was on this union. Desire rose like a tide in my blood, driving out weariness and hunger, overriding sorrow, holding even destiny at bay. An answering passion rose in Jehanne—Naamah's gift, rising in a golden spiral, entwining with mine. At some point, I helped her rise from the floor, tugging her hand and urging her into bed, unlacing her stays and stripping off her gown and underclothes. Beneath the hanging fronds, Jehanne kissed me fervently, her tongue urgent in my mouth.

"This," I whispered. "This, and this, and this, I love."

This was her breasts, grown larger with the babe in her womb, a faint tracery of blue veins showing beneath her translucent skin. I suckled at her breasts, drawing on her rose-pink nipples, never wanting to stop.

This was the sweet juncture of her thighs, between which I was happy to lose myself, coaxing creamy nectar from her cleft. I licked and drank deep of her. Jehanne clung to me, abandoning her arts for raw passion. I reveled in her hands clutching my head, tangling in my hair.

"This!" she said fiercely, tugging me upward. "Yes!"

That, too.

I let her do what she wished, let her take me and have me, surrendering to her insistent fingers probing inside me, her lips and tongue lashing me to new heights, until I arched my back and came so very, very hard for her. And it was good—stone and sea, so good! I wished it would never, ever end.

But it did.

"Moirin." Her voice was low. "I have to go."

I struggled to sit upright. "Please, my lady! I don't want to be alone. Can you not stay this last one night with me?"

"No." Jehanne gazed at me, a world of sorrow in her blue-grey eyes. "Raphael was right about one thing."

"What?" I asked.

She kissed me. "It hurts too much to stay."

I helped her wash and dress, then watched her go. I wanted to beg her to stay, but I didn't. Jehanne had been fair. She hadn't begged me not to leave her. Unlikely as it seemed, she'd given me her trust and her passion and her aid unstintingly. I didn't have any right to make this more difficult for her.

Still, it hurt.

When the door closed behind her, I felt alone and bereft. It was almost a mercy when the profound weariness that Naamah's blessing had driven away came crashing back upon me. I thought briefly that I should send for a dinner tray, but I was too tired to eat. And I thought with a twinge of guilt that I should have gone to see my father instead of spending long hours wallowing in pleasure, but I pushed the thought away. He would understand better than anyone else. I would see him on the morrow. I damned well wasn't leaving without saying farewell to him. The Emperor's daughter in faraway Ch'in had waited many long months. She could wait a few more hours.

I wished I could see my mother, too.

The thought brought tears to my eyes and made me feel sorry for myself. I blew out the lamps, curled up in my lonely bed, and wept myself to sleep.

In the morning, it all seemed unreal. Only a day ago, I'd been preparing to fulfill my oath to Raphael, penning a desperate letter to Jehanne. The misbegotten summoning of Focalor, Claire Fourcay's death, my near-death . . . events of such magnitude should have cast a shadow over my life for a long, long time. Instead, my world had been turned upside down.

And unreal as it seemed, there was proof awaiting in the form of a message from Master Lo Feng bidding me to join them at the City's southern gate at noon. I sent a polite reply saying I would be there as soon as possible and began to get my affairs in order.

There wasn't that much to be done. Jehanne had given the Palace staff orders to assist me in any way I required. I recruited a maidservant to find traveling trunks and pack my clothing. There wasn't much else. A few pieces of jewelry, including my mother's signet ring. Some cosmetics. My bow and quiver, my letters of introduction from Bryony Associates in Bryn Gorrydum.

That seemed a long time ago.

I'd arrived in the City of Elua with little else, a ragtag creature from the backwoods of Alba with a small gift for magic and a purse quickly stolen. I was leaving as the Queen's royal companion and . . . what?

Master Lo Feng's student?

A budding magician of a greater magnitude than I knew?

Or just a useful tool?

I didn't know; and truth be told, I was too exhausted to wonder. I forced myself to keep moving. I went to the banking house and withdrew a portion of the remaining funds from my letter of credit, reckoning I might need them.

And then I went to the Temple of Naamah.

My father was waiting for me. He already knew. I should have guessed it, knowing the way the City thrived on gossip. The King's guards had heard me give my answer to Master Lo Feng. They'd kept their silence for a while; I daresay no one wanted to be the one to break the news to Jehanne. But once I'd told her myself, tongues had begun to wag.

"Ah, Moirin, child." My father held me and let me cry on his shoulder, tears dampening his crimson robe. I'd done the same thing when first I'd met him, overwhelmed by conflicting desires, tangled relationships, and my own folly, alone and friendless in a strange land, distraught by Jehanne's unkind toying. Even though he was a stranger to me, I'd taken comfort in his embrace.

It was a piece of irony that I wept now because he was dear to me, and Jehanne was dear to me, and I didn't want to leave.

My father lifted my chin and asked me the same question the King had asked. "You're sure?"

I got myself under control. "Aye."

He kissed my brow. "Naamah's blessing on you, love. I'll pray for your safety every day and hope for your return." He paused. "You *will* return?"

"I don't know." My voice was small. "I don't even know why I'm going. I only know I have to."

My father shook his head. "They say the gods use their chosen hard. I fear 'tis no less true of your Maghuin Dhonn than any other."

"It's all of them," I murmured. "Naamah and Anael, too."

He cupped my face and kissed my brow a second time. "Then you must be very dear to them to place such faith in you," he said firmly. "Whatever your destiny and wherever you're bound, I've no doubt you'll make me wondrous proud, my very strange daughter."

It made me feel immeasurably better.

"Thank you." I hugged him hard. "I'm so glad I found you!"

"So am I." My father rested his cheek against my hair, then let me go. "You're bound to leave today? Is there time to explain this tale of summoning dire spirits to me?"

"A little." I wiped my eyes. "Not much. Will you do me a kindness and send word to my mother in care of Clunderry Castle in Alba, telling her where I've gone and why? It may reach her."

"Of course." He hesitated again. "What shall I say? What is it that calls you? Your . . . *diadh-anam,* is it?"

It leapt inside me like a flame.

"Aye," I said sadly. "That's exactly right."

FIFTY-THREE

Whether I liked it or not, I was sent off with fanfare.

"It's not necessary," I said to Jehanne, who had organized a royal escort to the southern gate of the City. "Truly, it's not."

"It is." Her extraordinary beauty couldn't mask her grief. There were faint violet shadows smudged beneath her eyes. Still, she held her chin high, daring me to defy her. "You're leaving a maelstrom in your wake. I'll not have it said that you were banished for your role in yesterday's doings. And Daniel agrees. So don't argue."

I didn't.

I rode beside them, the King and Queen of Terre d'Ange. My father rode behind me, Prince Thierry at his side. An entourage of guards surrounded us. And the folk of the City turned out to watch, cheering and throwing petals, reveling in the spectacle without caring why, slowing our progress.

We were late. On the far side of the gate, the Ch'in party was waiting, patient and impassive, Bao and Master Lo Feng among them, waiting.

I swallowed hard, dismounted, and said my good-byes.

To Thierry, a better friend to me than I had been to him. He embraced me hard, then turned away to hide his eyes.

To King Daniel, who had been nothing but kind to me.

My father, my lovely father.

Jehanne.

"How, my lady?" I asked her. "How do you find beauty in something that hurts so much?"

"Ah." She touched my cheek. "Because it will always be this, Moirin. I'll always be young and beautiful in your memory, and you in mine. You'll always be the beautiful witch-girl that I saved from herself and claimed for my own." Her eyes were bright with tears. "You'll never grow up and forsake me for another, never be tempted to betray me. And I'll never grow fickle and restless and seek to replace you." Jehanne wound her arms around my neck, kissing me. "It will always be this, and this, and this."

The crowds cheered.

My eyes burned. "Do *you* love me at least a little?"

"Need you ask?"

I nodded.

Her arms tightened around my neck. "Yes, my beautiful girl. Even though you break my heart. I love you far, far more than you deserve."

And then there was nothing left to say but good-bye, so I said it. Jehanne took my hand and put something in it, a small, hard object in a silk pouch. She curled my fingers, closing my hand over it.

"So you don't forget me," she said.

Despite everything, I laughed. "My lady, I think that would be quite impossible."

She kissed me one last time. "Good."

I mounted Blossom and rode slowly through the gate. At a word from Master Lo Feng, guards transferred two trunks of my clothing and my battered satchel onto a waiting supply wagon, Bao supervising. Master Lo Feng looked at my mournful face with compassion.

"Moirin, you need not do this thing for my sake," he said gently. "If you wish to stay, stay."

I took a deep breath. "Thank you, Master, but I think I'm meant to go. Forgive me. I don't mean to disgrace you."

"You are no disgrace." He gave a faint smile. "Although I believe General Tsieh and his men are finding Terre d'Ange very peculiar in this moment. None of them ever envisioned a land in which the Queen is allowed a concubine."

I'd grown more D'Angeline than I knew, for it had ceased to seem strange to me long ago. But glancing around, I saw that the general's men were blushing and avoiding looking at me. "Is that why they don't want me here?"

"No." Master Lo's expression turned somber. "Outsiders are not welcome in the Celestial Empire. But do not concern yourself. Their hearts will change in time. We have a very long journey before us."

"I know." Although the prospect daunted me, I made myself face it. I tucked the object Jehanne had given me away in my purse. "Bao?"

Bao looked up with a questioning glance.

I nodded at the bow and quiver lashed to my satchel. "Will you hand those to me, please?"

He shrugged and obeyed. "You think we get attack by bandit? All these men?"

"No." I slung the quiver over my shoulder and tested the bowstring. It wanted tending and the skin of my fingertips had grown soft and easily abraded where once it was callused. *I* had grown soft, pampered and coddled in luxury. "But I think I need to remember that I'm Moirin mac Fainche of the Maghuin Dhonn."

Bao shrugged again and swung himself into the saddle. "You say so."

General Tsieh asked a question; Master Lo replied. The general gave an order and our party began to move forward, horses' hooves clattering, wagon-wheels creaking.

We were going.

I glanced behind me only once. The royal party was still standing in the open gate, watching us go. Jehanne stood close to King Daniel, taking shelter beneath his arm. She had one hand pressed to her belly. I wished I could have stayed long enough to see her child born. Her face looked very pale. My father raised one hand in salute, his crimson robes flickering around him.

I waved once in reply, then turned to face forward.

We rode in silence until the white walls of the City of Elua were only a wan smear in the distance; then Master Lo Feng spoke without preamble.

"Empty yourself of everything," he said. "Let your mind rest at peace. Ten thousand things rise and fall while the self watches. They grow and flourish and return to the source. Returning to the source is stillness, which is the way of nature. The way of nature is unchanging. Practice your breathing and think upon this, Moirin."

My heart and mind were too full. "I don't think I can, Master. Not today."

Bao snorted.

"Today more than ever." Master Lo Feng was unperturbed. "Breathe, and let go. Watch."

I did my best.

At first I just breathed. I breathed the Breath of Earth's Pulse until I felt it deep in my body, felt it echoed in the slow, staccato beats of Blossom's hooves beneath me. I breathed Ocean's Rolling Waves into the pit of my belly, in through my nostrils and out through my mouth. I remembered Jehanne's mouth on me, my back arching, waves of pleasure surging through my flesh. I tried to let go of the memory.

Ten thousand things rise and fall.

I watched.

I breathed the Breath of Trees Growing, and thought about how all things returned to the source. This air I breathed deep into my lungs fed my body and limbs, fed the blood circulating in them. This air I expelled, the trees and plants drank.

I listened to their songs.

I listened to the faint, scintillant song of the Camaeline snowdrop bulbs nestled in pots in Master Lo's transport wagons, awaiting my care.

The cycle was eternal.

The cycle was unchanging.

I found a point of stillness I didn't want to leave.

"Enough." Master Lo Feng leaned over in the saddle to touch my arm. We were approaching a town and it was late, later than I would have guessed. The sun was dwindling on the horizon. "Fire and Air can wait. You are a good student, Moirin."

"For a stupid girl," Bao added.

"Bao!" Master Lo chided him in Ch'in; Bao retorted in aggrieved tones. I wavered in the saddle, wanting only to sleep now. We entered the town and accommodations were arranged. Our escort would camp on the outskirts, while I was to have a room of my own at the inn, as were Master Lo Feng and Bao.

We ate lamb stew spiced with mint in the common room together. It was very good and I was hungrier than I knew. The serving lass kept stealing curious glances at us. To be sure, we made a peculiar trio.

"Why she stare?" Bao complained. "I grow two heads?"

"Maybe she likes you," I suggested wearily.

"You think?" He looked interested.

"No," I said. "I think she stares because she's never seen anything quite like the three of us before."

His face darkened. "You think no stupid D'Angeline girl can like me?"

"No!" I sighed. "I didn't mean it like that. Actually . . ." A memory flashed behind my eyes, and I felt myself flush. I'd pictured Bao's face when Raphael made love to me the night of the first summoning largely against my wishes. Of course, I'd pictured Jehanne's too—and the spirit Valac's. But Bao's had been the last. "Ah . . . it might help if you'd stop referring to us as stupid girls."

Bao looked smug. "Why you turn red? *You* like me?"

"Not at the moment," I muttered.

He laughed. "Uh-huh! I save your life. Big hero. You wait, you fall in love. Forget all about the White Queen."

"Aren't you some sort of monk in training?" I asked. "I thought you took a vow of celibacy."

"Vow of what?"

"No . . ." Unsure of his vocabulary, I made a lewd gesture he'd used long ago.

"No!" Bao's eyes widened. "Where you get that idea? I am Master Lo's magpie. No monk."

"Oh." I felt foolish.

"Stu—"

"Bao." Master Lo Feng raised one finger. "In meditation, go deep into the heart. In dealing with others, be gentle and kind. In speech, be true."

"Yes, Master." He accepted the reprimand. "D'Angeline people too proud for they own good," he said eventually. "They think they better

than everyone. They not see Master Lo is great man. I think is stupid. Maybe you not so much that way. You make some stupid choices,
though, and say some stupid things. But maybe you not so stupid,
really."

"You're too kind," I commented.

He shrugged. "True or not?"

"True," I said ruefully. "But if you'd care to be gentle and kind, I'd
thank you for not making me think this was one of my more stupid
choices." I extended my hand across the table to him. "Can we not
agree to be friends for the duration of this journey?"

"Friends." Bao echoed the word, looking dubious.

I nodded.

"All right, sure." Bao clasped my hand, his grip strong, sinewy, and
callused. He frowned briefly at our clasped hands, then looked unexpectedly cheerful, grinning at me. "Until you fall crazy in love with me,
not-so-stupid girl."

I laughed. "We'll see."

It lightened my heart a little, and Master Lo Feng seemed to approve. But alone in my bedchamber, I felt the weight and enormity of
the decision I'd made come back to rest on my shoulders. My chamber
was stark and barren. For the first time in a long while, I felt restless
and confined behind walls of man-made stone.

I missed my enchanted bower.

I missed Jehanne.

I fished her gift out of my purse and opened the silk pouch to find
a small, stoppered bottle of cut crystal. I laughed softly to myself and
pulled out the stopper. The scent of Jehanne's intoxicating perfume
filled the air. It wasn't the same as when she wore it—but it was still
nice, so nice.

I tilted the bottle and wetted one fingertip, then touched it to the
hollow of my throat. There, the scent breathed outward, whispering of
night-blooming flowers and a pale, delicate marque limned on pale skin.
I stoppered the bottle carefully and returned it to its pouch, tucking it
back into my purse before I disrobed and lay down for the night.

At peace, I slept.

FIFTY-FOUR

Some days later, we reached Marsilikos.

It was a large, sprawling harbor city dominated by a palace with a golden dome, so big it loomed almost like a second sun. I have to own, I gaped at it. None of the Ch'in folk seemed overly impressed. When we drew in sight of the harbor, I saw why.

The Ch'in ship was enormous. It dwarfed all the other ships in the harbor, at least three times larger than the second largest. It had five masts adorned with vivid red sails shaped unlike any other ship's sails, and towered several stories high, the sides of its upper deck adorned with ornate scrollwork. My mouth fell open at the sight of it.

"Careful," Bao said. "You catch flies."

I closed my mouth. "Master Lo . . . I mean no disrespect. But all this just to fetch you home?"

"Emperor Zhu loves his daughter very much." He looked troubled. "Too much, perhaps. He would spare no effort to save her life."

I'd been too caught up in my own concerns to give much thought to the Emperor's daughter. "But you said it wasn't a mortal illness."

"No." He hesitated. "The matter is complicated. I would speak of it later unless it may change your thoughts on accompanying us. I wish to be fair."

I shook my head. "No."

"Later, then."

We proceeded to the quay. At least I wasn't alone; there were D'Angelines and trader-folk of other nations gathered to stare at the greatship, still a novelty after many days. They stared at us, too, and I heard murmurs among the D'Angelines. A few covert fingers pointed and I heard my name whispered. We'd made good time, but we hadn't outpaced gossip.

If there were any question about it, it was confirmed by the arrival of the harbor-master, striding down the dock with a handful of armed guards. His gaze went straight to me. "Moirin mac Fainche?"

"Aye." I wondered what in the world he wanted.

There was nothing friendly in his expression. "Her grace the Duchese de Mereliot wishes an audience with you. Yon floating castle's going nowhere until she gets it."

The Lady of Marsilikos.

Raphael's sister.

I'd managed to avoid thinking about that fact, having avoided thinking about Raphael altogether.

"This lady look for a concubine, too?" Bao asked insolently.

"No," I murmured. "She's Raphael de Mereliot's sister. I think I'd best see what she wants. I don't want to cause any trouble here."

Bao conferred with Master Lo Feng. "I go with you."

I eyed the guards. "All right."

It felt reassuring to have Bao at my side as we accompanied the harbor-master to the palace. The guards regarded him with disdain, but I'd seen him whip his staff around with lightning speed, driving back Focalor without a trace of fear. If there *was* trouble, I had a feeling Master Lo's magpie was a handy person to have around.

The palace steward escorted us into a beautifully appointed salon. A young woman awaited us in a high-backed chair, surrounded by peers and attendants, none of whom looked friendly. She sat very upright, arms stiff along the chair-arms. I would have known her anywhere as Raphael's sister. Her hair was darker than his, but she had the same storm-grey eyes, the same lips, the same jawline sculpted by a more delicate hand.

Right now, those eyes were staring at me and filled with contempt.

"So you're Moirin," she said in a venomous tone. "I wanted to see the bitch that ruined my brother."

"Your stupid brother ruin his own damn self, lady," Bao retorted.

Her gaze shifted to him. "What is *this* and why is it speaking?"

I sighed. "Bao, will you keep a civil tongue for once? My lady . . ." I dredged her name out of memory. "My lady Eleanore, I'm sorry about what passed between your brother and I, but I'll not accept sole blame for it."

Eleanore de Mereliot's voice rose. "You made him a laughingstock! And now nigh onto a traitor!"

I stood my ground. "How well do you know your brother, my lady?"

"He's my *brother*!"

"Aye," I nodded. "And he is a beautiful, compelling man who possesses great gifts and harbors terrifying ambitions. I don't know why. I asked him to speak of it, and he refused." Tired of gossip and distortion, I held her gaze and spoke the truth that was in my heart, hoping she might hear it and understand. "I suspect it has something to do with the loss of your parents and the lingering sense of helplessness it left in him. And mayhap with this." I gestured around. "Always knowing that you were the heir to Marsilikos, while he, the firstborn, was expendable."

She was silent.

"Mayhap it has to do with his love for Queen Jehanne," I added. "And her choosing his majesty over him, despite loving Raphael, too. I don't know. All I know is that nothing he's ever wanted has been his in full, and it's left a void in him." I smiled wistfully. "I would have filled it if I could have. I thought he was my destiny. In the beginning, I would have given him my heart. But that's not what he wanted."

"And so you betrayed him for it?" Eleanore's gaze remained hard. "Chose to humiliate him publicly?"

"Your damn brother almost kill her!" Bao interjected.

I wanted to clamp my hand over his mouth; but he was right, and I was growing angry. "Being with your brother *was* killing me, my lady. Do you think I lie? A woman is dead because of Raphael's ambitions! I watched her die before my eyes! Do you think *I* forced him into sorcery? I didn't want any bedamned part of it!" I was shouting. "I did it at first because I was too stupid and besotted to say no to him, and I did it at the end because it was the only way he'd agree to help save my father's life!"

The Lady of Marsilikos blanched. "Raphael wouldn't do such a thing!"

"But he did," I said grimly. "Lady Eleanore, I'm sorry, but that's the truth. And I have nothing further to say on the topic of your brother. Am I free to go?"

She looked away and gave a brief nod. "Mayhap there is truth to what you say," she said in a bitter voice. "Even so, I would to Elua that he'd never met you, for you brought out the worst in him."

"I know." Now I just felt weary. "I wish it had been otherwise."

Raphael's sister looked back at me. "Get out of my sight."

Gawking at the exchange, the guards were slow to clear our path to the door. Bao spun his staff so fast it was a blur, one end coming to an abrupt halt a scant inch from the nearest guard's chin. The guard flushed with anger and reached for his sword-hilt, then thought better of it and stepped back.

"Smart man." Bao's voice was as smooth as silk. I didn't know whether I wanted to hug him or thump him. Both, mayhap.

We rode back to the harbor together. There was no escort this time, for which I was grateful.

"Thank you for coming with me," I said to Bao. "I wouldn't have liked to face that alone."

He nodded. "She mad because she love her brother. Still, not fair to you. I not like the way they treat you." He glanced at me. "Feel pretty good to yell, huh?"

"Aye." I hadn't realized it, but he was right. I carried a great deal of unspoken anger toward Raphael. "Still, not fair to her, either. She didn't know the truth—or, at least, didn't want to believe it."

Bao shrugged. "Life is not fair."

There was something else troubling me that I hadn't spoken of. "Bao . . . do you think we drove the spirit wholly out of him?"

He was silent a moment. "Why?"

"I don't know. When I looked back at Raphael at the end, the last glimpse I had of him, it seemed like there was something there." I touched my breast, where my *diadh-anam* had never ceased to quicken for him. "Whatever's between us, I'm not sure it's over."

Bao snorted. "You think he follow you over the ocean?"

I didn't. "No."

"Better hope it over. Lion Mane no good for you. That demon-spirit . . ." He shook his head. "Ask Master Lo. Maybe he know, maybe not. Is a foreign demon. Not the same as demon-spirit at home like the one got into the Emperor's daughter."

I reined Blossom to a halt. *"What?"*

Bao looked guilty. "Master Lo, he want to tell you his own self."

I felt lightheaded. "Is that why he asked me to come? Does he expect me to banish it into the spirit world like I did Focalor? Does he expect me to *survive* this time?"

"No!" He flushed. "Master Lo ask you to come because you his student. He meant to teach you. All the signs say so."

"What signs?" I asked.

Bao leaned over in the saddle and tapped my breast-bone. "You feel it here?"

"Aye," I admitted.

"That the only sign you need."

"Is that how it was for you?" I was curious. "How did you come to be Master Lo's . . . magpie?"

He regarded me through half-lidded eyes. "You ask a lot of question. One day, I tell you. Not today."

"All right. I'll wait." I didn't know why I was so curious, except that Bao was the nearest thing I had to a comrade in this venture and he was an enigma to me. If he disliked me half as much as he pretended at times, I was in for a miserable journey—but I didn't think that he did.

I knew that Master Lo Feng had chosen in his latter years to wander the world in search of further wisdom and worthy pupils to impart it to. I knew that he'd chosen Terre d'Ange as a destination because he was curious about tales of an entire folk descended from a wandering god and his divine Companions, and the land in which Blessed Elua had chosen to settle.

Why Bao had chosen to accompany him, I hadn't the faintest idea.

When we returned to the quay, the harbor-master's second in command gave us grudging approval to board the immense Ch'in ship. I whispered reassuring things in my filly Blossom's ears, soothing her with my thoughts until her hide stopped shuddering and she suffered herself to be led aboard, disappearing into the belly of the hold.

Stone and sea, the ship was huge!

And I felt lost boarding it. Everything that was familiar fell away behind me. I was surrounded by Ch'in soldiers and sailors chattering in their own tongue, eyeing me with a mixture of curiosity and disapproval.

We were given rooms on the next-to-upper deck. Master Lo Feng's was large and sumptuous; mine and Bao's smaller quarters adjoined it on either side. The wood was rich and glossy and smelled very nice, mixed with the tang of sea air. Left alone in my chamber, I breathed in deeply and tried to fight a rising sense of panic.

"Here." Bao appeared, lugging a heavy pot in his arms. Snowdrops, the bulbs dormant but alive beneath burlap wrappings. He set it on the floor. "Master Lo say they better with you; you feel better."

I listened to their faint song.

Better.

Keeping them alive gave me a purpose. As for the rest, I would have to learn and adjust. I nodded at the bed. I recognized the raised pallet's purpose, but not the odd, low, scooped wooden structure at the far end. "My thanks. Bao . . . what is that?"

He stared at me. "A bed?"

I pointed. "That?"

"For rest your head." He clasped his hands behind his neck. "Like so."

"Oh."

"You want I show you?"

"Nooo . . ." I wasn't ready for the sight of Bao in my bed. "You reckon *that* a pillow?"

"Uh-huh." He nodded. "We sail now. You want to see?"

"Aye, I suppose."

Sailors were swarming all over the main deck. Somewhere below, incredibly long oars protruded from oar-holes and began to churn the water, turning the ponderous vessel. Bao led me to the stern of the ship on the uppermost deck. We watched the harbor of Marsilikos appear before us as the massive ship turned.

"They use oar only in the harbor," Bao told me. "Only wind and water moving at sea." He lowered his voice. "They not open the bag of wind here where foreigners can see."

"Bag of . . ." I gave him a startled look. "I thought that was just a turn of phrase. You mean there actually *is* a bag of wind?"

He nodded. "Long time ago the Emperor marry the wind god's daughter. Thousand years ago. Almost empty now, maybe. Better to save."

"Oh." I didn't know what else to say. I gripped the railing and watched the harbor slowly fall away behind us as the ship's mighty sails filled and it got under way, moving at a stately pace past smaller vessels. Bao stood beside me, silent for once, leaning on his staff. Terre d'Ange, the land that had adopted me in unexpected ways, dwindled in my vision until the golden dome of the Palace of Marsilikos was only a bright glint on the horizon.

I turned to face the open sea.

I was leaving a mess of intrigue, ambition, and betrayal behind me, as well as love and trust and acceptance I'd never imagined finding. My father. Jehanne. I was venturing farther into the unknown, farther from my home and my people. My mother. And I still hadn't the faintest idea what it all meant.

But my *diadh-anam* burned strongly in my breast and I felt the Maghuin Dhonn's approval; and too, I felt the presence of Naamah's blessing on me, and to a lesser degree, Anael's.

I was venturing into the unknown, but I carried my gods within me.

"Well," I said aloud. "Here we go."

FIFTY-FIVE

We were at sea for a very, very long time.

For the first few days, I felt strange to myself. Truly, the ship was more like a floating city than a ship—based, to be sure, on my very limited experience with ships. I was surprised to learn there were other women aboard.

"Companion for the soldier," Bao explained. "All noble sons who agree to come search for Master Lo."

"Oh," I said for the thousandth time.

The women tittered behind their hands when they saw me and wanted nothing more to do with me—not that I could have spoken to them if they had. The men, soldiers and sailors alike, eyed me askance. I didn't know if it was because I was reputed to be a witch, or the Queen's concubine, or simply because I was foreign.

"All three," Bao explained. "Mostly . . ." He reconsidered. "No. All three." He regarded me with indolent curiosity. "What you do in bed, anyway? Two women together. Yin-yin." He banged closed fists together. "Makes no sense."

I scowled at him. "Nothing that concerns you."

He shrugged. "Fine."

Everything was strange.

The food was strange, laced with strange spices. Not bad, but strange. I ate what was brought to me, fumbling with the lacquered wooden sticks the Ch'in used for eating utensils. The bed with its wooden pillow was strange. The pillow made my neck ache. I tried to use it only once. After that, I slept with my head cushioned on my arms.

For a mercy, there was Master Lo Feng.

There was a small terrace extending beyond his quarters in the next-to-highest deck and it was there that we met for lessons, Bao spreading straw mats on the wooden planking with his usual alacrity. We sat cross-legged on them.

"Happiness is rooted in misery," Master Lo Feng said in his tranquil voice, his wrinkled eyelids closed. "Misery lurks beneath happiness. Who knows what the future holds?"

I didn't.

I breathed the Five Styles and thought about his words as I cycled through them. Like all the verses he gave me to contemplate, it was deceptively simple. I was beginning to get a better sense of the philosophy of the Way; a sense of how all things were in flux and yet all things were in balance, and one thing gave way to another thing. All things arose from the Way and all things returned to it. But today I couldn't find that point of stillness. I couldn't ponder the future without a very large question plaguing me. "Master Lo?"

"Yes?"

"What ails the Emperor's daughter?"

He opened his eyes. "I have been waiting for you to ask. Are you ready to hear?"

I nodded. "Aye."

Master Lo Feng folded his hands into his sleeves. "Xue Hu was born to Emperor Zhu's Third Concubine. Although he tried for many years with the Empress and many concubines, she is his only child. As I told you, he loves her very much. Although his councilors advised him to adopt a male heir, the Emperor refused to do so. Against their wishes, he named Xue Hu his heir."

"Her name mean Snow Tiger," Bao added helpfully.

"So it does." Master Lo gazed into the distance. "And it suited her. She was a beautiful, fearless child. Emperor Zhu was determined that she should inherit the Celestial Throne. He raised her as he would a warrior son. When I last saw her, she could ride and shoot and wield a sword as well as any boy her age."

Bao nudged me. "Maybe *she* like to take a concubine."

I ignored him. "What happened?"

Master Lo's gaze returned. "Before I left, a marriage was arranged for her to the son and heir of a feudal lord in the south. All agreed it was a good match and would bring greater peace to the Celestial Empire." He sighed. "According to General Tsieh, the marriage took place as planned eight months ago. That day, the Empire celebrated. That night, Xue Hu went mad and tore her bridegroom limb from limb in the bridal chamber."

My mouth fell open. I closed it before Bao could mock me. "Truly?"

"I fear so." His gaze was somber. "A demon-spirit took possession of her. Every effort was made to drive it out."

"*Pao* and mirrors?"

Master Lo Feng smiled sadly. "Oh, yes. And many more. Lord Jiang, the bridegroom's father, lent his own great physician to the effort, Li Xiu."

"Black Sleeve," Bao murmured. "Not only physician. Sorcerer. Not so nice."

My mentor nodded with a troubled look. "But he knows much of the spirit world and much of alchemy. When Black Sleeve's efforts failed, Lord Jiang called for Snow Tiger's execution, threatening rebellion in the southern provinces if she were not put to death to avenge his son's murder. That is when Emperor Zhu sent for me. That is all I know."

I exhaled. "Do you reckon she lives?"

"I hope it may be so," Master Lo said. "General Tsieh says the Emperor had a special chamber with iron bars built to hold her." His brow furrowed. "The madness comes upon her when she beholds her reflection, even in another's eyes. When it comes, she knows only unnatural strength and rage. Snow Tiger suffers herself to be blindfolded willingly and grieves over her deed. Blind, she knows herself."

"Oh," I whispered.

It was a terrible tale. My heart went out to the young woman at the center of it and the young bridegroom slain. Stone and sea! "How, Master?" I asked. "How and why? Did she court such a fate like Raphael?"

His shoulders lifted in a faint shrug. "I cannot think the child I knew would do such a thing. And yet I cannot say. Perhaps it is a jealous ghost that haunts her. The Empress ever resented Snow Tiger, and she died some years ago." He looked unwontedly perplexed. "And yet how could Black Sleeve miss such a thing?"

"Lord Jiang's sorcerer no friend to her," Bao muttered.

"There is goodness and wisdom in him," Master Lo Feng admonished him. "Never say there is not. It is present in all of us."

Bao inclined his head, but his eyes glittered.

"Enough." Master Lo struggled to rise, his knees creaking. Bao was on his feet in a flash, helping his mentor upright, tender and solicitous.

"You rest now, Master," he murmured.

"Yes," Master Lo agreed, leaning on Bao. His gaze rested on me. "So. Now you know what we face, Moirin."

"Aye."

I sat in contemplation for an untold period of time. The ship's decks rose and fell, riding the swelling waves. I breathed the Breath of Ocean's Rolling Waves into the pit of my belly and out through my mouth, trying not to think. Bao returned to join me, sitting cross-legged on the mats. He closed his eyes and breathed the Breath of Embers Glowing. In and out we breathed, complementing one another. His knee brushed mine in a companionable manner.

"Snow Tiger," I said.

"Uh-huh." His face was tranquil. "I do not think she is meant to live behind bars."

I didn't think so, either. "So we do . . . ?"

Bao opened his eyes. "We do what we need to. We do whatever Master Lo say."

"You said if the spirit Focalor had taken possession of Raphael, it might have been impossible to drive him out," I reminded him. "How is this different?"

He shrugged. "Not a foreign spirit. I don't know. You ask too many questions!"

"I'm just trying to understand," I said reasonably. "Which reminds me . . . Bao, do you think you could teach me to speak Ch'in?"

"Which one?"

I blinked. "What do you mean which one?"

Bao looked smug. "Many different language in the Celestial Empire. Which one you want to learn?"

"Whichever is most common." That, I thought, would resolve the matter.

"Different in different places."

"Whatever you speak!" I said in frustration. "Whatever Master Lo speaks! Whatever they speak where we're going!"

"Master Lo speak seven different language from Ch'in. Me, only three." Bao took pity on me. "All right, all right! Stop look like you going to spit! I teach you Shuntian official language. All the scholars speak it."

"Thank you." I was mollified.

Learning Ch'in—or at least the official tongue of Shuntian, which I learned was the capitol city where the Emperor's court resided—was a good deal more difficult than I anticipated. One of the first things Bao told me was that I regularly mispronounced his name in a manner that meant anything from womb to cooking pan to rain shower. He said it for me four different ways, with four different intonations. I could *hear* the difference, but I struggled to emulate it, let alone retain it.

"What does it mean *your* way?" I asked after half an hour's worth of repeating the same syllable. "Your name?"

He was silent a moment. "Treasure," he said reluctantly. "Is a common baby-name for a boy."

"Oh." I waited.

"My mother call me Bao." His mouth quirked. "Only thing I keep from those day."

"Before they sold you to the circus," I said softly.

Bao nodded. "When I born after the Tatar raid, they wait to see. Maybe I look like my father or my mother." He shook his head. "I look like the Tatar who"—he made the lewd gesture—"my mother. She want to keep me," he added, his back stiff and upright, shoulders squared. "But it is too great shame for my father. She cry when the contract is stamped and the circus take me, tell me I always her treasure. I remember."

It was an old hurt and a deep one, and I very much wanted to put my arms around him—but his posture warned me not to.

"My mother said something much the same to me, once," I said instead. "And I will never forget it."

"Did she send you away?" he asked. "Across the sea?"

"No." It was my turn to be quiet. "No, it was the Maghuin Dhonn Herself who sent me. The Great Bear my people follow."

Bao understood. "She who make the earth shake when you shout that day."

I nodded. "Aye."

"Why?"

I gazed past him at the unbroken horizon. Sunlight sparkled on the endless rippling waves. Sea, and sea, and sea. Somewhere on the far side of it waited a young woman blindfolded behind iron bars, a young woman who had torn her bridegroom apart limb from limb. What it had to do with me, I couldn't begin to guess. "I would by all that's sacred that I knew. But I reckon I'll find out one day."

He smiled a little. "I think so, too."

FIFTY-SIX

Slowly, slowly, I learned to speak Ch'in.

For a mercy, the strange intonations were the worst of it. Once I developed a rudimentary grasp of them and began calling Bao "treasure" more often than I did "cooking pan," it got easier. The structure of the grammar was actually simpler in some ways than Alban or D'Angeline, without a multitude of conjugations to master.

"That how I learn to speak different language while we travel," Bao explained. "Make it simple like Ch'in language. Master Lo, he study D'Angeline until it perfect. I learn just enough of the others."

"What others?" I asked.

He shrugged. "Tatar, Akkadian, Ephesian, some Bhodistani . . . many." I was impressed. Bao eyed me shrewdly. "Smarter than you think, huh?"

"To be sure," I agreed.

I learned other things on our journey, too. I learned that Master Lo Feng had served three emperors and claimed to be a hundred and seventy years old.

"That's not possible!" I said in shock.

Master Lo's eyelids crinkled. "There is a reason why my old knees creak," he said tranquilly. "Practice your breathing and contemplate the Way."

During our language lessons, Bao told me more in hushed tones. "Master Lo, he do alchemy once like Black Sleeve. Try to make elixir of immortality." He shook his head. "One day he see is all false. Only the Way is true."

"Is that when you met him?" I asked.

"No." His voice was curt. "That happen much, much later."

As our greatship sailed farther south into warmer climes, I learned that thanks to Bao's acrobatic training, he could juggle, bend his back into a perfect circle, walk on his hands as easily as his feet, and balance with ease on the narrowest of railings, bare toes gripping the wood, traversing it effortlessly, heedless of the drop below. I learned too that Bao had a deep-seated restless streak that was belied by his discipline in practicing the Five Styles of Breathing.

When Bao got restless, he picked fights.

One sunny afternoon, I watched it happen. For the first time since I'd known him, Bao was jittery and ill at ease, unable to concentrate on our meditative exercises. I watched him make his apology to Master Lo Feng, kneeling on the sun-warmed planks, bowing and gesturing to the deck below us where the soldiers were wont to spar with one another. I watched Master Lo Feng nod and lay one elegant, long-fingered hand on Bao's head in benediction.

It seemed there was a standing wager at stake. Bao approached a group of soldiers on the main deck and spoke to them, then waited calmly, leaning on his staff while they laughed and argued among themselves. Coins were proffered; he shook his head and said somewhat in reply. In a little while, two Ch'in women clad in bright silk garments emerged from their quarters, and further discussion ensued, soldiers gesturing back and forth. Standing on the upper deck, I couldn't hear the details, but in the end, Bao gave a broad grin and nodded vigorous agreement.

The women leaned their heads together, whispered and giggled. Neither of them seemed displeased at being wagered. I felt an unexpected pang of jealousy.

Master Lo sighed.

"Do you disapprove, Master?" I asked him.

He was silent a moment. "No. It is Bao's nature to fight. He has his own demons to conquer."

"Aye?" I prompted. "His family?"

He glanced at me. "If he wishes you to know more, he will speak of it."

I watched Bao fight two soldiers that day. He was good. He was beyond good. I watched him shuck his loose-fitting shirt and caught my breath. His drawstring trousers clung to his narrow hips, and sunlight glistened on his golden-brown skin. Lean muscles surged beneath it in a complicated play of light and shadow. His dark eyes glittered above his high, wide cheekbones. Stone and sea! He was *beautiful*.

How had I not seen it?

His face was at once fierce and happy, oddly calm. He moved with careless grace, sandal-clad feet skipping over the deck. The staff was a blur in his hands, darting in and out, striking with both ends. His opponents fell, rolling, clutching their heads, swords dropping from their hands. The other soldiers roared with laughter, mocking them.

Bao bowed, tucking his staff into the crook of his arm.

I watched him go with the women to their quarters, his arms around their waists. He glanced up once to see if I was watching, and I looked away. Master Lo Feng regarded me.

I shrugged. "He's very skilled."

Master Lo nodded. "Yes."

Two days later, Bao brought me a pillow—a real one made of silk and stuffed with soft materials. I was so delighted, I hugged it to me.

"For this, I could kiss you," I said. "Where did you get it?"

He looked smug. "One of the women make for me. I make them feel sorry for you. They curious now. Ask all kind of questions what you like."

"What did you tell them?" I asked wryly.

Bao laughed. "I tell them to meet you they own damn self if they want to know. You want to?"

"Aye," I agreed. "I'd like that."

After weeks of relative isolation, it was a pleasure to be in the company of my own gender. Mei and Suyin, the two women that Bao had bedded, received me with wary curiosity that gave way to giggling warmth at my futile efforts to communicate.

"Different tongue," Bao informed me in D'Angeline. "They from the country, they no speak Shuntian. Also, you sound like a duck quacking."

"Oh." I was discouraged.

The bolder of the two girls leaned close, studying my face. She tilted her head and peered intently at my eyes, reaching out to brush my eyelashes and eyebrows with one fingertip. Uncertain, I held still and let her. She shivered with horrified delight, then addressed Bao in her own dialect.

"She never see jade eyes," he said to me. "She ask if it a witch-sign."

"No, of course not." I frowned. "They were docked in Marsilikos for days. Surely they saw other D'Angelines."

He shook his head. "Not close. They stay on the ship."

I stared at him. "After six months at sea, travelling all that way, they never left the ship? Are you jesting?"

"No." Another head-shake. "They here for the soldiers." He grinned. "Mostly." The women conferred, then the bold one—Suyin, I thought—addressed Bao again. Whatever she said made him chuckle. "She say you almost beautiful for a foreigner," he told me. "If you like, she can help. She shave you eyebrows and show you how to paint them like a willow leaf. Lend you cream to make your skin white. Make you beautiful like a Ch'in woman."

I glanced at Suyin, who smiled and bobbed her head, gesturing helpfully at her white-painted face etched with eyebrows as fine and narrow as the blade of a willow leaf. It had a certain haunting charm, but it wasn't a look I was eager to embrace. "Ahhh . . ."

"What?" Bao asked me, his eyes glinting. "You not want to look like a bald egg with a face painted on it?"

I flushed. "Not especially, no."

He laughed. "I thank her for you anyway."

Nonetheless, the meeting marked a threshold of sorts. I left it pleased by the warmth that the women had shown me—and they seemed to find me less alarming. I practiced the Ch'in that Bao taught me daily and began to pick up an odd word of different dialects here and there. I kept mainly to my cabin and our deck, but the soldiers and sailors I encountered appeared more comfortable in my presence. They came to consult with Master Lo Feng on matters of health and he treated many of them for ailments and minor injuries. I tended to his snow-drop bulbs, coaxing along their faint song.

We sailed.

And sailed.

My ability to speak the Shuntian tongue improved. My mastery of the Five Styles increased. Betimes I visited with Suyin and Mei and a few of the other women, communicating with gestures and broken phrases when Bao wasn't on hand to interpret. Mostly, he was. The women enjoyed his company, and I gathered from their demeanor that his prowess with a staff had other implications. I gathered, too, that Bao had a reputation of his own that owed naught to being Master Lo's magpie; but on that topic, he remained close-mouthed.

I had to own, it intrigued me. Ever since the day I'd first seen him fight, I'd looked at him differently. But despite having teased me earlier about falling in love with him, on the ship, he treated me with a friendly diffidence that began to irk me.

If it hadn't been for Master Lo Feng's tonic, that might not have changed.

By my reckoning, we'd been almost three months at sea when Master Lo asked us to sample a decoction he had rendered from the dried and powdered bulb of a Camaeline snowdrop. Bao and I were sitting on our straw mats on the sun-warmed deck, anticipating a lesson in the Five Styles.

"You are skilled enough to practice this discipline on your own," he said in his serene manner, pouring liquid from a flask into tiny porcelain cups and extending them to us. "All ways lead to the Way. Now drink."

Bao drank without question and set down his empty cup.

I took a sip.

At first, it was bitter, with none of the headiness of the *joie* I'd tasted on the Longest Night. But the taste changed in my mouth. It unfurled inside me, turning to something deep and rich, at once earthy and sharp-edged.

I gasped, and drank the rest.

"*Very* tonic." Master Lo's eyes twinkled. "Good for stimulating the blood. I will leave now. Tell me if you experience increased vigor."

Beyond the ship's ornate railings, the changeless sea rolled past us, waves peaking and sparkling in the sunlight. The air was warm, and yet I tasted mountain air. High places, cold places. The bulbs buried in a pot in my cabin sang. My skin prickled, drinking in the sunlight and craving more. Touch, sensation. The golden spiral of Naamah's gift rose from my core, awoken from slumber. All at once I felt hot and cold, my heart expanding within my breast, beating hard and fierce. "Bao . . ."

His eyelids flickered. "Uh-huh?"

I *wanted*. Stone and sea, I wanted! "Do you feel it?"

He sat like a cross-legged statue. "Yes. Lucky for you, I have great strength of will."

I straddled his lap. "Lucky for us both, I don't."

I could feel the want in him. I could feel it pressed against me, taut and straining. I lowered my head and brushed his lips with mine. Not a kiss, not quite. "Why don't you like me?"

His breathing came hard. "I do."

I shook my head. "You don't show it."

"Moirin." It was the first time in memory he'd called me by name. His hands landed on my hips, flexing. His fingertips dug into my buttocks, warring with his urges. I pressed myself harder against him. "This is nothing. This is medicine. This is Master Lo's art, nothing more."

I rubbed myself against him. "I don't care."

"*I* do."

"*Why?*" I glared down at Bao.

"I don't know!" he shouted at me. "Because you're a goddamn witch! Because there are strange forces working here and I want to live through this! All I want is to be a not-so-bad person! Because there are goddamn gods and spirits hovering over you! And a destiny! A goddamn destiny that might swallow me whole! You don't know me! You don't even know if *you* like me! And if you're not going to fall—"

I shut his mouth with a kiss.

It was a very good kiss. I'd learned more than a few things in Jehanne's bed. I wanted Bao to relent, and he did. His lips softened and parted to admit my tongue, letting it war and dance with his. Hard and deep, I kissed him, tasting fire and heated metal in his essence. It was like breathing in a forge, overheated and intoxicating. We complemented one another. And after a long, thorough kiss, I lifted my head. "Aye?"

". . . in love," Bao mumbled.

"I might." I traced the outer curve of his ear with the tip of my tongue, then spiraled inward, teasing and tantalizing. "You never know."

He made an inarticulate noise, grabbed my head, and returned my kiss.

More fire.

More hot metal.

I nearly purred when Bao lifted me, it felt so good. I'd been celibate too long. I wrapped my legs around his waist, nuzzled his neck.

"Good?" he asked in my cabin.

"Good," I agreed.

And it was good, stone and sea! So good. The vast ship rocked beneath me; Bao rocked and thrust above me, propped on arms corded with lean muscle, his eyes half-lidded and his expression intense, at once distant and present. His phallus filled me and his hips rose and fell, buttocks flexing, joining me at the exact right spot, the exact right angle. I spread my legs wider, arched my back and welcomed him deeper and deeper inside me, my hips rising to meet him again and again, ankles locked around his hips. My blood pounded in my veins, urged onward by the snowdrop bulb's decoction, until I climaxed hard beneath him, nails digging helplessly into his skin.

"Oh, the hell with destiny!" I gasped.

Bao laughed deep in his chest.

On and on it went. In my little cabin, we made love a half a dozen times in a half a dozen different ways, all of them good, until we were both gleaming with sweat and thoroughly wrung out. I could feel the presence of Naamah smiling on me, her smile filled with grace. The bright lady was content.

So was I.

"Do you think he knew?" I asked, my head resting on Bao's thigh, near his lolling phallus. I traced its veined length with one fingertip, feeling it twitch under my touch, unsure if I had the energy to see if I could awaken it one more time. "Master Lo, I mean."

He gave me a look. "Of course. Don't you?"

"Aye." I met his gaze. "So . . . why?" Bao shrugged. I took a firm grip on his phallus and tugged. "Why?"

He yelped. I let go.

"All right, all right!" Bao sighed. "That I cannot tell you. But I will tell you something else if you like. You want to know how I became Master Lo's magpie?"

"Mm-hmm."

He folded his arms behind his head, leaning against the pillow. "In the circus, there were stick-fighters. By day, they perform like a dance. All part of the show. At night they take wagers and fight with towns-people, make better money. Sometimes there are good fighters in the village and they lose. Only one man, Brother Lei, he never lose no matter what. His name, it means thunder." He shrugged again. "I wanted to learn stick-fighting. I ask Brother Thunder to teach me."

I propped my chin on my hands. "Why?"

"Those fighters, everyone look up to them. They do what they like. An acrobat, it's not such a good life. Not so much respect. I wanted to be a fighter. Maybe it is in my blood, I think. I wanted it like a starving man wants food." Bao smiled wryly. "Also I was in love with Brother Thunder's daughter, Lin. I was thirteen and stupid. So I ask and he say, 'You be my peach-bottom boy, I teach you.'"

"Peach-bottom . . . ?"

Bao gave me a sidelong glance. "Uh-huh. Brother Thunder, he say if ever I beat him fair, no more—" He supplied the lewd gesture.

I swallowed. "How long?"

"Two years." His expression was cynical. "I beat him fair. Then I ask Lin to run away with me." He shook his head. "But she was angry at me for destroying her father's reputation. People made fun of him for losing to a boy."

"Did she know about the—?" I gestured.

"No." His face softened. "Lin, she loved her father. I couldn't tell her. Too much shame for everyone."

I didn't know what to say.

"So." Bao blew out his breath and flexed his hands together. Muscles in his upper arms tensed and rippled. "I ran away alone to Shuntian.

There, I fight for myself. I give myself a new name. At first everyone wants to fight me because I'm young. But I keep winning more than losing, getting better and better. There was this gang. One by one, I beat them all. It took years, but I was patient. Then one day, I beat the leader. The next day, I *was* the leader."

"What sort of gang?" I asked.

He shrugged. "Usual kind. We made merchants and people give us money to protect them whether they need it or not. Beat up their rivals for money. That sort of thing. Pretty good living for a peasant-boy sold to the circus."

"Oh."

The cynical look returned. "Not so sure you like me now, huh?"

"I don't know," I said honestly. "But I'm listening."

Bao looked away. "So maybe five, six years go by. Good years, I think. Anything I want. Wine, women. Whatever I like. I don't even have to fight so much. Everyone, they know I'm good. Nobody want to challenge me. One day, Master Lo, he comes to this place, the square in Shuntian where the stick-fighters meet. He says he looks for a companion for this long journey to the land of angels. Someone clever to help him in all things, someone bold who did not fear danger. Someone humble and willing to learn about the Way."

My *diadh-anam* flared in memory. "And you knew!"

He shook his head. "I laughed. Everyone laughed. In Shuntian we said the great Master Lo Feng has lost his mind. Why else would he ask a bunch of no-good thugs for help?"

"Oh."

"Uh-huh." He nodded. "Two days later, this boy comes to me. Some peasant-boy from the country. He asks me to teach him to fight. Young—not so young as I was, but young. Fourteen, fifteen. Still like a willow. He wants to learn from the best." Bao pursed his lips. "I made him the same offer Brother Thunder made me."

I sat up and shivered, withdrawing instinctively.

"I don't know why," Bao mused. "Only he reminds me of me. That stupid boy who wanted to be a stick-fighter so bad he was willing to do anything to learn. And I wanted to punish him for it."

A long silence stretched between us. "Did you?" I asked at last.

"No." He gazed into the past. "The boy took off his clothes. Now he looks like a plucked chicken, shivering."

I saw the memory surface in his thoughts. A naked boy, trembling, the narrow blades of his shoulders hunched in fear. And Bao . . .

"You walked away," I said softly. "You walked away from all of it."

It didn't seem to surprise him. "Yes. For some reason, all I could think of was Master Lo Feng's offer. Maybe he knew what he was doing after all. Maybe it was meant for me. I was clever and bold, but I had forgotten how to be humble, and I never had any teacher who was kind and wise. I wanted to be someone different. So I walked away from that boy, from that gang, from that city. I took my best staff. Nothing else. I even left behind the name I had given myself. I took back the baby-name my mother called me."

I said it aloud. "Bao."

The light in the cabin had grown dim. His eyes glittered. "Now you know. You ask why Master Lo seeks to join us together with his medicine. I don't know. Maybe he thinks you will hate me if you learn the truth first."

"No." I shook my head. "No, I don't think so. I think mayhap he knew you needed to speak of this, and I needed . . ." I flushed. "Well."

Bao laughed.

I smiled. "You walked away. How can I hate you for somewhat you didn't do? As for the rest . . ." I shrugged. "You did what you set out to do. You're not that person anymore." I thought a moment. "Did you ever hear the tale of the stolen D'Angeline prince?"

"No."

So I told him the story of Prince Imriel de la Courcel, who was stolen by slave-traders as a boy and subjected to unimaginable horrors in distant Drujan before being rescued by two of the realm's greatest heroes. I told him how Prince Imriel wrote openly in his memoirs of struggling to be a good person despite the memories that haunted him; and how he had grown up to become a great hero in his own right, saving Terre d'Ange from an insidious peril.

Bao listened intently. "I know some of that story," he said when I'd finished. "There was Ch'in women in that place. Drujan."

I'd forgotten. "Aye, that's one of the things that piqued Master Lo's curiosity about Terre d'Ange, wasn't it?"

"Uh-huh." He nodded, thoughtful.

I rubbed my eyes, fighting a yawn. It was late and I was tired; I had a vague memory of someone knocking politely on the door hours ago with an offer of dinner. Now it was almost pitch-black in the cabin.

"Sleep," Bao said immediately. "I'll go."

"Stay if you like," I offered.

He hesitated, then climbed out of bed and fumbled for his clothing. "No. You need to think about what I told you. I was not like the prince in your story, Moirin. What I did, I chose for myself. And what I chose to make of myself was nothing more than an ordinary thug."

"Not so ordinary," I said sleepily. "At least you were a prince of thugs. Bao, are you really afraid I have a destiny that's going to swallow you whole?"

"Uh-huh." An unexpected grin glinted in his shadowy face. "Only now I think maybe it's worth it."

FIFTY-SEVEN

In the bright light of day the next morning, both Bao and I were afflicted by the self-consciousness that can accompany a sudden shift from familiarity into intimacy. He flushed when I emerged from my cabin, busying himself with boiling a kettle of water on our small brazier. I watched his strong, sinewy hands as he poured the water for Master Lo's tea, remembering how good they'd felt on my breasts.

"Ah!" Master Lo sipped his tea with pleasure. "So?"

Bao and I glanced at one another. He cleared his throat. "Ah . . . very tonic, Master."

"*Very* tonic," I agreed. "Master Lo . . . why? You told me once that it was best to let go of desire."

"So I did." He regarded me. "I believe I underestimated its force in your nature. Your desire for Raphael de Mereliot led you into folly; and yet if I understand what I observed, your desire for Queen Jehanne led her to a greater peace and wisdom. It may be that the gods of Terre d'Ange have their own ways of guiding their children to harmony."

"All ways lead to the Way," I said, remembering what he'd said yesterday.

Master Lo inclined his head. "Even so."

"What about me?" Bao asked.

His mentor eyed him tranquilly. "It would have happened sooner or later, but you have a stubborn and contrary streak, my magpie. I thought you needed a push."

Bao gave him a skeptical look. "Hmm."

"Is anyone complaining?" Master Lo inquired. "Because the sounds

I heard for many hours do not suggest a pair of healthy young people with anything to complain about."

This time, I flushed.

Bao grinned at me. "No," he said. "You?"

I shook my head. "No."

"Good." Master Lo blew on his tea and took another delicate sip. "Then let us practice the Five Styles. After yesterday's excesses, perhaps a little discipline and guidance would not go amiss after all."

It was hard to concentrate. I was too aware of my body, indolent with lingering pleasure after a long drought. I peeked under my lashes, studying Bao's calm face with its high, wide cheekbones, wondering again how it was I hadn't noticed he was beautiful. He could be so calm, so still, and yet there was somewhat wild and untamed at his core that appealed to me. I thought about what he'd told me last night. Of his own will, he had walked away from his former life and had chosen a path of humility, but it had done naught to diminish the fierce pride within him.

That, I thought, was very interesting.

"Moirin." Master Lo chided me with a word.

I closed my eyes.

After a moment, Master Lo sighed. "Bao."

I opened my eyes to see Bao contemplating me under half-closed eyelids.

"I fear I have unleashed the whirlwind," Master Lo said with rueful good humor. "Go. Enjoy one another. I shall paint, and we will attempt this again on the morrow."

If anything, it was better today. There wasn't the driving urgency that Master Lo's tonic had imparted, but I'd always had ardor to spare and Bao certainly wasn't lacking. With his acrobat's body and his disciplined will, he was a very, very good lover, as skilled and inventive as any D'Angeline.

"Who taught you Naamah's arts?" I asked him afterward, wondering if it would draw forth any further dark revelations.

"Married ladies." He smiled lazily at me. "Rich wives bored with their husbands. I make them feel dangerous and exciting. And I like knowing a lowly peasant-boy makes them squeal with pleasure."

"Charming," I commented.

"You asked." He shrugged and picked up the little crystal bottle beside my bed, toying idly with the stopper. "Like you said, I'm not that person anymore."

I sat up quickly and touched his hand. "Don't, please. It was a gift."

Bao set the bottle down carefully. "From the White Queen?" he asked. I nodded. "Do you miss her?"

"Aye," I said softly. "I suspect a part of me always will."

"What about *him*?"

"Raphael?" I shook my head. "No. No, what was between us went so bad. I don't know, mayhap it never was good. I try not to think about him. And when I do . . ." I shuddered, remembering the Circle, the spirit Focalor, Claire Fourcay's death, the subtle flicker of lightning I thought I'd glimpsed in Raphael's eyes when it was over. "There's a part of me fears it's not finished between us, Bao. Even though I'm halfway around the world from him. And whatever's left to be played out, it's going to be bad."

His face darkened. "I wanted to split his head open for what he did to you. I wish I had."

"You're jealous!"

"Maybe." He gave me one of his sidelong looks. "Of him, anyway."

I was curious. "Why not Jehanne?"

Bao laughed. "Might as well be jealous of the moon for shining as be jealous of that one," he offered in a philosophical tone. "No, Lion Mane, that was different. He had a gift. Even Master Lo thought so." He spread his hands, gazing at them. "Healing hands. It would have been enough for me. Not him, not after you came."

"I know." I laced my fingers with Bao's. "*I* like your hands."

"Fighter's hands."

"Lover's hands, too." I kissed his hardened palms. "Did you love any of them at least a little bit? Your rich wives?"

"No." He was silent a moment. "There was a girl, though. Not Lin. Another girl, when I was older. In Shuntian, a merchant's daughter. Her *amah* used to bring me messages. Once we met in secret. I climbed a wall into her family's garden. She swore she loved me. I thought I did.

We made promises to one another." He lifted one shoulder in a half-shrug. "Didn't happen. She married another merchant's son."

"You're a hopeless romantic!" The revelation delighted me. "Despite everything, you are! I'm sorry. But it's true, isn't it?"

He scowled. "I *was*."

I showered his face with kisses. "You still are. Are you in love with me?"

"No!" Bao held me off, laughing. "Not yet, you crazy witch-girl. Are you?"

"No," I admitted. "But I'm warming to the notion." A thought struck me. "Bao . . . do you suppose Master Lo Feng has ever been in love?"

I thought he would say yes or no, but instead Bao looked thoughtful. "I don't know," he said at length. "Whether you believe it or not, Master Lo has been alive longer than anyone's memory. There is a rumor that he had a wife, once. And a rumor that he loved her very much." Both shoulders lifted and fell. "If it is true, he never speaks of it."

"Not even to his magpie?" I asked.

His hands slid up my arms, calluses making me shiver. "No," Bao whispered against my lips, kissing me. "Not even to his magpie."

I breathed in the scent of red-hot metal and kissed him in return, feeling a little dizzy. "Oh, well."

Bao shifted me expertly, pulling me atop him. "Want to try falling in love again?"

I wriggled. "Gods, yes!"

It was a long journey and our efforts were prodigious; and yet we spoke of love more in jest than not. Despite his teasing and his comfortable demeanor in the bedchamber, there was a part of Bao that remained guarded. I daresay the same was true of me. I was at ease in Bao's company in a way I hadn't been with anyone since Cillian; and yet the realization of that truth evoked sorrow. I'd loved Cillian, but not enough. And I'd scarce given myself a chance to grieve for him before flinging myself at Raphael de Mereliot, convinced he was my destiny.

Raphael . . .

I'd been a useful tool to him, nothing more. It was true, and it was galling to acknowledge. He'd used my desire to his own ends. I'd let my yearning for destiny and his healing hands blind me to the truth. Raphael had never really cared for me, never wanted *me*. Only what I could do for him.

And then there was Jehanne. Against all odds, there was Jehanne, my unlikeliest of rescuers.

I daresay she was right; if I had stayed, matters between us would have changed sooner or later. She was fickle and vain and everything her critics claimed. And I wouldn't have been content forever with a seat at a banquet table where I was never more than a guest. In the end, it wouldn't have been enough.

And yet . . .

It had ended too soon.

Betimes I watched the waves swell and break around the ship, bright foam sparkling on their crests, and thought of Jehanne. Tasting the salt-spray on my lips and wondering if she'd driven any chambermaids to tears since I left. Wondering at the tides ebbing and flowing in her body, wondering at the rising swell of her belly. Counting the days and weeks and months on my fingers and thinking, *Not yet*.

I wished I were there.

I'm here. I'd said that to her when she was frightened. And I'd meant it. I'd meant to stay as long as she needed me. Instead, I'd left her as she'd always known I would. Jehanne had forgiven me for it. She'd forgiven me before it happened. For all her foibles, despite the mercurial temperament that made me smile, she had a vast and passionate heart. And she had loved me. No matter what else happened, that would always be true.

I missed her.

So Bao and I danced and sparred and bedded one another, Master Lo's magpie and his witch, both of us nursing our bruised and scarred hearts.

We sailed through calm seas.

We rounded the tip of a continent and sailed through battering storms and rough seas, where I thought I might die. And when we did, when the ship the size of a city was dwarfed by the pitching waves it rode, its hull and ribs threatening to crack beneath the massive pressure, I was grateful for Bao's strong arms around my waist.

"What happens?" I gasped. "What happens to you if you die?"

He tightened his arms. "No one's dying today."

"But *what*?"

"Our spirits go to the city of Fengdu," Bao said in my ear. "Where the Yama Kings sit in judgment. First we are presented to the God of Places, who reviews a record of all our deeds. After forty-nine days, we are sent to the courts of the Yama Kings. Each of the Yama Kings judges our different sins and sentences us to punishment. For example, gossips and liars are sent to the Chamber of Ripping Tongues. Merchants who cheat their customers are forced to climb the Mountain of Knives with bare hands."

I shivered. "This isn't helping."

"You asked," he reminded me. "After we have suffered all our punishments, we go before the tenth Yama King, who is in charge of the Wheel of Souls. This Yama King decides what form we deserve in our next life, a prince or a beggar or a lowly animal. There we drink the Broth of Oblivion and fall from the Bridge of Pain into the River of Rebirth to begin our journey anew."

"Does it ever end?" I asked. "Must everyone suffer? Is there no place for mercy and forgiveness?"

"For some," Bao said. "Only a very few, who have led lives without sin. They go to paradise to feast with the gods." He shrugged. "Also there is the Maiden of Gentle Aspect. If a person's good deeds outweigh the bad, she may take him from the God of Places and lead him straight to the tenth Yama King to be reborn."

"No punishment?"

"No punishment," he confirmed. "I am not looking forward to the punishment. But I told you, no one is dying today."

The ship pitched alarmingly. "You're sure?"

"Ahh . . . no." Bao braced himself around me. "What about your people? Where do you go?"

I leaned my head against his shoulder. "We pass through the stone doorway to join the Maghuin Dhonn Herself in the world beyond this one."

"That's all?"

"Aye." The memory calmed me. "It's enough."

"Everyone?" He sounded skeptical.

I shook my head. "No. No, the bad ones, they wander lost for a time that they might ponder their wrongs. And oath-breakers . . ." I fell silent, remembering Clunderry. The green mound in the field and the standing stones in the blood-soaked wood. Morwen, my ancestral almost-namesake, had died there. She had sworn an oath and broken it deliberately, offering herself as a sacrifice. Her spirit would be forsaken for ten thousand years, spurned at every turn. I touched my chest where the spark of the Maghuin Dhonn Herself burned within me. The thought of losing it was unbearable. "It's longer for them."

Bao was dismissive. "Doesn't sound so bad."

"No?" I twisted in his arms. "It's a different kind of hell, Bao. And I would rather have my tongue ripped out than my *diadh-anam*."

To that, he had no reply.

My cabin door crashed open. I yelped. A flash of lightning showed Master Lo Feng in silhouette.

"My pupils." Despite the raging wind tugging at his beard and whipping his robes around him, he sounded as tranquil as ever. "You may find this instructive. Come and behold the storm."

"Master Lo!" Bao protested.

Our mentor beckoned. "Come."

We went.

Stone and sea! It was terrible and it was awesome. We stood atop our deck, clinging to the carved railing. The waves surged around us, lightning forking overhead amid the dark, roiling clouds. I stared, agape, as our ship climbed up the slope of a wave the size of a mountain, teetered on the precipice, then plunged into the trough.

"The sea is like the Way!" Master Lo called above the cacophony. "Ten thousand things arise from it!" He released the railing, clasping his hands together. "Surrender and be at peace with it. Let go of your fear and breathe."

I closed my eyes and drew shallow breaths, my chest tight with fear, salt-spray lashing my face. I didn't dare let go of the slick railing. The ship crashed into the bottom of the trough, timbers groaning. Sailors' shouts pierced the din faintly, distant as bird cries. Water sluiced across the deck.

Bao angled himself behind me, bracing me once more. "I'm here," he murmured in a low voice.

The familiar words made my heart ache. I had left Jehanne because my *diadh-anam* had sent me here. The least I could do was try to understand why.

I let go of the railing and rode the plunging ship.

When Master Lo spoke of the Way, I understood only bits and pieces of his meaning. What was the Way? It was the force and essence behind all things, the one thing that gave birth to ten thousand things even as the sea gives birth to clouds and rain and rivers and lakes. And it was far, far too vast for me to grasp.

So I thought instead of the Maghuin Dhonn Herself, who had led my ancestors south when the world was frozen. Her mighty tread, Her head blotting out the stars. On uninhabited Alba, Her immense paw sank into the soil for the first time, Her fearsome claws digging furrows in the earth. A freshwater spring rose bubbling around it.

In that moment, my people came to be what we were. And from that moment, our long history arose.

I thought about Naamah, lying down with a stranger for the first time—the bright lady surrendering herself to earn coin that Blessed Elua might eat. What had wandering half-mortal Elua known of love and desire and sacrifice before that moment? Nothing. Somewhere in that moment, the seed of the nation and the people of Terre d'Ange was engendered.

And a thousand years later, a Priest of Naamah laid down on the soil of Alba with a woman of the Maghuin Dhonn, and *I* was engendered.

Now I was here.

It felt like a revelation too large to encompass. I let it go. I let myself stop trying and breathed the Breath of Ocean's Rolling Waves, yielding to the moment. I was content to understand that the Way was as much bigger than my destiny as the ocean was our ship. Like the ship, my destiny would yield to it or break and be swallowed.

The knowledge gave me a strange sense of peace. Although I was soaked to the skin and my wind-whipped hair was lashing around my head, I was no longer afraid.

We stayed on the deck until the storm abated. Slowly, slowly, the waves dwindled from mountains to hills, from hills to hummocks. Lightning ceased splitting the heavens, thunder ceased to boom. The pelting rain diminished to a shower, then stopped altogether. The glowering bank of clouds broke apart, revealing a patch of blue sky.

"So." Master Lo Feng wrung out his soaked sleeves, then folded his hands into them. "Did you find it instructive, my pupils?"

Bao grumbled and banged the side of his head with his hand, trying to dislodge water from one ear. "Yes, Master."

I thought about my answer. I wanted to put my almost-revelation into words, but it was still too big and my understanding too imperfect. "Aye, Master Lo," I said at last. "I believe I did."

My mentor inclined his head. "Like the unborn chick scratching at the shell, you perceive the beginning of wisdom."

I sighed. "Just the beginning?"

Master Lo smiled. "It is a very good beginning."

FIFTY-EIGHT

We sailed and sailed.

We sailed through an endless, narrow strait with green, fertile land on either side of it, land so close it made me yearn for earth beneath my feet and the scent of growing things. I nearly wept when it fell away behind us. We entered a new sea, turned north and set our course for the still-distant coast of Ch'in.

The more I learned about Ch'in, the more I learned I had to learn. I'd only begun to grasp the tenets of the Way and recognize the names and titles of myriad gods tangled up in Ch'in lore when I discovered that many folk followed a different path altogether.

Suyin gasped with shock when she discovered my ignorance. "You not know Sakyamuni? The Enlightened One?"

"No," I admitted.

She turned to Bao and conversed with him in her native dialect too quickly for me to follow. He protested; acrimony ensued.

"Come." Suyin grabbed my hand, leading me deeper into the women's quarters. "You meet him now."

She led me to a tiny chamber in which a beautiful bronze figurine sat cross-legged on a shrine, eyes closed, a peaceful smile on his face. The chamber was hazy with incense. Suyin lit another stick and placed it in the brazier, kneeling on a cushion before the shrine and pressing her brow to the ground.

"He was a prince in Bhodistan," Bao informed me. "He sat under a tree and meditated until one day . . ." He made an expansive gesture.

"He understood everything all at once. That's why he is the Enlightened One."

"Everything at once?" After my brush with revelation, it sounded overwhelming.

"Uh-huh." He nodded. "His teaching is called Dharma."

I gazed at the Enlightened One's face. Although it was youthful, the serenity in it reminded me of Master Lo. "How is it different from the Way?"

"Celibate monks." Bao grinned when I shot him a skeptical look. "It's true!" He thought a moment. "There are other differences. Masters of Dharma do not practice medicine like Master Lo—or alchemy," he added.

"Like Black Sleeve," I said, remembering.

He nodded. "In Dharma there are many more teachings, many more schools. They practice breathing meditation, but not like the Five Styles." Bao pursed his lips. "To follow the Way is to seek to live in harmony and balance with the world. To follow Dharma is to seek to be free of the world."

Suyin rose and spoke to Bao, pointing at a smaller figurine, a bronze woman standing gracefully beside the Enlightened One.

"That is Guanyin," he said to me. "She Who Hears Our Prayers. She is one who found enlightenment, but came back to help the suffering."

Suyin held out a stick of incense. "Now you make prayer."

I hesitated, then shook my head. "I'm sorry. I can't pray to a god I've only just met." Bao chuckled. Suyin thrust the incense at me and said somewhat insistent and aggrieved in her dialect. I put my hands behind my back, refusing her offer. "I'm sorry, but I can't! Bao, tell her I'm sorry."

He spoke soothingly to her. In time she relented and accepted my refusal, though it was clear it troubled her.

Later, I talked to Bao about it.

"Was that wrong?" I asked. "Did I offend her?"

"No," he said slowly. "Scared her a little, maybe. She can't understand why you wouldn't offer a prayer. I explained that you are a very

strange barbarian girl who worships a bear, and that she must give you
time."

"It's just . . ." I shrugged. "I don't know. I've been trying so hard
to learn and understand, when I don't even know why I'm here in the
first place. It was a shock to discover there are still so many big things
I *don't* know. Big things right here on this bedamned ship, right under
my nose."

"I know." Bao gave me a sympathetic look. "I'm a peasant-boy a
long way from home, remember?"

"Aye, but you're going home," I reminded him.

He ran a few strands of my hair through his fingers. "You'll like it
there. Look how well you speak the Shuntian tongue already. Better
than I ever learned yours."

"Aye, because I've had naught else to do but practice for weeks on
end!"

Bao laughed. "You'll see."

"When?"

"Soon," he promised. "We will sail into Guangzhou harbor, and
then Imperial barges will take us up the Grand Canal to Shuntian.
We will help Master Lo to drive out the demon inside the beautiful
Princess Snow Tiger. Lord Jiang will relent, all will be forgiven, and the
Emperor will shower us with rewards." He smiled smugly. "And then at
last you will realize you're in love with me, and we will marry and have
many fat, happy babies like in your D'Angeline hero's story."

I eyed Bao doubtfully. He didn't have an ounce of fat to spare, and
I couldn't imagine our children would either. "Fat babies, eh?"

"Round as dumplings," he said cheerfully. "You'll see."

I sighed. "Well, I hope you're right about the first part."

He was right about one thing, at any rate. After being at sea for so
long that my previous life had begun to seem like a half-remembered
dream, the end of our journey was in sight. We reached the coast of
Ch'in and began inching our way farther north.

Days passed.

Weeks.

The day I heard a sailor cry out from the observation platform in
the tall center mast, I scarce dared credit it. But the cry was taken up

and echoed by a hundred other tongues, the ship's crew and myriad passengers bursting into a babble of excitement.

"Guangzhou! Guangzhou!"

"Truly?" I whispered to Master Lo Feng. "We'll make landfall today?"

He nodded. "Truly."

Guangzhou was situated at the mouth of a great river delta. With ponderous grace, the enormous ship entered the delta and made for the harbor. I saw clusters of buildings and the green haze of willow trees. Soon, we would leave the sea behind us. I clutched the railing of our deck and forced myself to breathe the Breath of Earth's Pulse, slow and deep, containing my excitement.

"Uh-oh," Bao muttered.

Master Lo stroked his beard. "Hmm."

Half a dozen ships were heading for us at an alarming pace, oars churning the waves. Flags fluttering from their masts bore the emblem of a white dragon coiled on a blue background. I glanced up at the Imperial flag we flew. It was similar, but the flag was yellow, the dragon a vivid scarlet.

My heart sank. "Those aren't Imperial ships, are they?"

"No," Master Lo said soberly. "They are flying Lord Jiang's banner. I fear the war has begun."

The largest of the ships came alongside us, the others ranging behind it in a semicircle. All were filled with Ch'in soldiers. The big ship carried a strange cargo on its deck, immense bronze tubes pointed upward at us, hollow mouths gaping ominously. I didn't know what it meant, but my blood ran cold.

"I think we shall wish to hear this," Master Lo said.

We descended to the main deck. General Tsieh beckoned us over to the railing. "Jiang's men," he said grimly to Master Lo. "I think they mean to demand our surrender. Would you have me stand and fight?"

There were six ships to our one, but Lord Jiang's warships were only a fraction of our size. Counting in my head, I thought the numbers of soldiers must be nearly even; and surely with our height advantage, our archers could rain arrows down upon them. But Master Lo didn't answer, gazing at the deck of the warship below us, his gaze fixed on one man in particular. Not a soldier—a tall, elegant man in crimson robes.

"Black Sleeve," Bao murmured to me.

"Can we flee?" Master Lo asked quietly.

The general shook his head. "We're too big and the delta is too small. They would be on us in the time it took to turn. But—"

On the other ship, a portly man in ornate armor raised cupped hands to his mouth. "Esteemed General Tsieh!" he called. "I am Admiral Wen Chao. In the name of Lord Jiang, I humbly request that you surrender this Imperial greatship and its cargo!"

There was an acrid smell in the air. It stung my nostrils, evoking a distant memory that seemed out of place. Bao in the Circle of Shalomon's chamber, his staff spitting sparks.

"In the name of his Imperial Majesty, Son of Heaven and ruler of the Celestial Empire, I must humbly refuse!" the general retorted.

The admiral bowed politely. "Then I regret to inform you that your ship will be destroyed by the Divine Thunder!" he shouted in reply. "And all survivors will be put to the sword!"

Black Sleeve leaned over and spoke to him. Despite my rising fear, I couldn't help but wonder why he was called Black Sleeve when his robes were as crimson as a Priest of Naamah's.

"Except for the Venerable Master Lo Feng!" the admiral amended his threat.

Master Lo gazed without blinking at Lord Jiang's physician. A sorcerer and alchemist, a fellow adept of the Way. Mayhap his pupil, once.

Black Sleeve bowed to him with grace and regret.

"General Tsieh." Master Lo spoke under his breath, never shifting his gaze. "If we cannot turn, we must make for the canal itself. It is time to open a bag of wind."

"We won't get far," the general warned him. "The canal wasn't built to handle greatships. The first bridge will put a halt to us."

The acrid smell grew stronger. Smoke drifted across the water.

"I believe we're about to experience the alternative," Master Lo said. "General, if you value my counsel, give the order."

General Tsieh hesitated.

On the warship, Admiral Wen Chao raised his voice once more. "This is merely a warning!"

Soldiers clustered around one of the bronze tubes, raising its angle of elevation. Sparks flared, and then . . .

Ah, gods! The tube belched fire and there was a sound like a thunderclap, the loudest thunderclap I'd ever heard. An object moving too fast to be seen was spat out of the tube, crashing into the top of the tall center mast and bursting into flame. The mighty ship shuddered at the impact, soldiers and sailors alike crying out in fear. Sparks and bits of slivered wood rained down on us. Bao, cursing, wielded his staff like a demon, warding off the falling debris, protecting Master Lo and me from the worst of it.

Everywhere, shouting. High-pitched shrieks from the women's quarters. And in the midst of it, General Tsieh's voice raised to a roar.

"Fetch the Thousand-Cloud Bag!"

Men raced everywhere; sailors with buckets putting out fires, soldiers obeying the general's order. Another bronze tube belched fire, another clap of Divine Thunder rattled my bones. Another object hurtled through the air, taking out the top of another mast before splashing into the sea beyond us, steam hissing at the impact.

More scorched debris fell from the skies.

Two of our sails now slumped in tattered despair beneath their shattered topmasts. But on the rear deck, General Tsieh's men were working feverishly to unfold a vast expanse of embroidered silk.

"Lord Jiang wishes to be merciful!" his admiral bawled over the din. "Cease your efforts and *surrender*!"

Fold upon fold of the bag was opened. Each one was comprised of squares of silk embroidered with clouds, exquisite clouds. Fluffy clouds, wispy clouds, menacing clouds, wrought in shades of white, silver, grey, and sun-shot gold on a sky-blue field. Wholly unfolded, the Thousand-Cloud Bag covered the entire aft of the main deck, laying slack and empty over its expanse. A knotted silk cord pulled its mouth firmly closed.

Across the water that divided them, Master Lo and Black Sleeve gazed silently at one another.

"Now!" General Tsieh shouted. "Loose the wind!"

Feverish fingers worked at the tightly knotted silk cords. Slowly, slowly, the mouth of the Thousand-Cloud Bag opened.

Without thinking, I breathed the Breath of Wind's Sigh, drew it high up into me and breathed it into the space between my eyes. Remembering the cold winter winds blowing through the bell tower where Master Lo had taught it to me. It could only help.

And it seemed the world breathed with me, taking a deep, indrawn breath like an endless sigh. The bag rose and billowed, taking in air, towering over the main deck.

I breathed in.

I breathed out.

When it happened, it happened all at once. Another bronze tube barked fire and coughed thunder. The Thousand-Cloud Bag exhaled, filling the massive sails of the Imperial greatship—or at least the three of five yet intact.

It was enough.

The Imperial greatship leapt forward, surging past Lord Jiang's warships. Past the projected missile, which fell harmlessly into the sea, another gout of steam arising. Across the harbor, into the narrow confines of the Great Canal.

Away.

I spared a glance behind us and saw the dwindling figure of Black Sleeve unlock his gaze from Master Lo and settle on me. Belatedly, his brows formed a furrow, perplexed at my existence.

"Too late," I whispered.

We rode before the wind, leaving him behind.

FIFTY-NINE

It was a terrifying and exhilarating journey.

The Thousand-Cloud Bag billowed and blew. We hurtled past the buildings of Guangzhou with their tip-tilted roofs. In peacetime, I daresay we would have wreaked havoc, crashing into lesser vessels and sinking them with our sheer bulk and momentum, but for a mercy, the Grand Canal was largely deserted.

Buildings gave way to countryside. The canal spilled us into a larger river lined with willow trees. Beyond the trees, peasants working in the fields lifted their heads to stare in wonder as the Imperial greatship rushed past them, its upper decks towering over the trees.

In the end, it wasn't a bridge that put a halt to our flight. After the better part of two hours, the Thousand-Cloud Bag blew itself empty, settling with a sigh on the aftdeck, its many embroidered squares flat and slack once more.

Bereft of wind, the greatship drifted to a halt.

"It's a fighting head start," General Tsieh said philosophically before raising his voice to give a new order. "Unload the ship!"

A scene of pandemonium ensued. Soldiers and sailors alike worked frantically to unload the greatship. A vast plank was lowered to the shore. Suyin and Mei and several dozen other women emerged, white-faced with fear beneath their cosmetics. Food stores, cargo, and personal belongings were unloaded. Horses were led from the hold on unsteady legs, blinking in the sunlight.

I led Blossom out myself. I'd visited her many times during our journey, walking her up and down the narrow exercise corridor in the belly of the greatship, and she was the only horse among them to look calm and alert. She listened to me with pricked ears as I spoke softly to her, soothing her thoughts with my mind.

Peasants gathered to watch. Several of General Tsieh's men interrogated them. They seemed friendly, nodding and pointing toward the north.

"Good news." The general strode over to us. "We're only a hundred *li* or so from the border of Qilu Province. That's as far as Lord Jiang's grasp extends. If we push the horses as hard as we dare, we ought to make it."

Master Lo frowned. "There are no mounts for the women and sailors."

The general shrugged. "Those without will have to make due. With all we'll be forced to leave behind, they can bribe the peasants to hide them."

"My bulbs!" Master Lo said in alarm.

General Tsieh cast an acerbic eye over the massive pot that Bao had lugged ashore. "I'm sorry, Venerable One. But yes, if you do not wish to be captured by Lord Jiang's men, your bulbs must stay." He jerked his chin at the two trunks of my clothing. "Those, too."

I sighed. There were gowns I'd not seen since we left Terre d'Ange in there, the finest creations of Atelier Favrielle, sumptuous, elegant gowns that were wholly impractical for travel. "Master Lo, I've an idea. Bao, lend me a hand."

I emptied out my battered canvas satchel. There wasn't much I truly needed to keep. I put the thong with my mother's signet ring around my neck and tucked the crystal bottle of Jehanne's perfume into the purse at my belt. With Bao's aid, I transferred the bulk of the snowdrop bulbs into my satchel.

The fragile bulbs protested faintly.

Sleep. I blew softly over the soil. *Deeper and deeper. Sleep.*

"We must go!" the general called impatiently. "Time to ride!"

"Suyin!" I beckoned to her. She hurried over with the graceful, mincing gait Ch'in women favored, gazing at me with wide, fearful eyes. "There are some items of value in these trunks. Gowns . . . or at least the fabric, mayhap." I couldn't picture her in one of Benoit Vallon's immodest creations. "Eardrops, jeweled combs, a headpiece. Share them among the women. Use them as best you may."

She looked blankly at me. I'd reverted to speaking D'Angeline without thinking.

Bao translated.

Suyin bowed three times in rapid succession, speaking quickly to me in her native dialect.

"She says thank you and she will pray for you! They will all pray for you!" Bao flung himself effortlessly astride his mount despite being burdened with many of the rest of Master Lo's bags of medicines and possessions. He glanced behind us. There was a faint smear of dust rising on the southern horizon. Lord Jiang's forces were in pursuit. "Moirin, we must go. *Now.*"

"All right, all right!" I slung the satchel over one shoulder, my bow and quiver over the other, and hoisted myself into the saddle. "I'm ready!"

General Tsieh gave the order. "Ride!"

A hundred *li* was not a great distance—a little over ten leagues if I understood correctly. A strong, fit mount could easily cover that distance in a day.

But we were not riding strong, fit mounts.

Weakened by long months at sea and unsteady on dry land as any of us, the horses stumbled and staggered through the tall fields of wheat. I couldn't help but wince at their struggles, any more than I could help wincing at the swathe we cut, trampling the late-winter grain ready for harvest.

It was better once we gained the road and sure footing—but not for long. The toll the journey had taken on our mounts was too great. One by one, they began to founder. General Tsieh called for a halt to determine which ones had the strength to continue. There were only a score, Blossom among them.

Thirty men would stay behind to guard our passage. I watched them string and test their bows, preparing to make a stand.

"So many lives spent to save one woman," I murmured to Master Lo. "Is it worth it?"

He looked troubled. "I cannot say, Moirin. But I fear there are greater stakes here that justify their sacrifice. What Black Sleeve has done . . ." He fell silent.

"The Divine Thunder?" I asked.

"Sorcery," Bao said darkly.

"Not sorcery." Master Lo's voice was filled with sorrow. "Only alchemy and engineering. The possibility to use fire-powder to create such a terrible weapon has existed for many, many years. It is a secret that many of us have kept for a long time, and for many years, I have feared that someone would discover it. Now it seems it has happened. But I never thought it would be him."

"Was he your pupil?" I asked.

"No." He said no more. I raised my brows at Bao, who shook his head, knowing no more than I did.

And then General Tsieh gave the order, and we were off once more.

We rode through the day and into darkness, coaxing and pleading with our mounts. A little while after nightfall, we saw the faint sparks of lanterns on the road behind us. The sacrifice of thirty men may have delayed them, but our pursuers were drawing nearer.

"Moirin." Master Lo spoke for the first time in hours. "If we are caught, use your gifts to escape unseen. Bao, go with her. Black Sleeve will see that I come to no harm. I cannot guarantee the same for you."

"Aye, Master." I felt heartsick at the prospect, and too weary to argue. Bao merely nodded, looking as sick as I felt.

We dismounted to lead our staggering horses up a long mountain pass. My thighs were quivering with exhaustion after hours in the saddle. The satchel over my shoulder seemed to weigh a thousand pounds. The sparks behind us were drawing closer. I put my head down and trudged, praying that my *diadh-anam* hadn't led me halfway around the world to abandon me. All the gods knew, I wouldn't be the first of the Maghuin Dhonn to misunderstand Her intent and pay the price for it.

At the crest of the mountain, shouting.

I lifted my heavy head. Bao pointed wordlessly.

There was a walled city in the valley below, dimly visible in the starlight, lamps burning in its watchtowers.

"Ride!" General Tsieh shouted. *"Ride!"*

I scrambled gracelessly back into the saddle. Sensing our urgency, the horses found one last burst of panicked strength as we plunged down the mountain slope. Feeling Blossom's lungs and valiant heart labor, I prayed for her forgiveness.

Behind us, more shouting. Our enemy was in hot pursuit.

Had it been daytime, I daresay we wouldn't have made it. They began loosing arrows at us when we reached level ground. Two soldiers slumped and went down, crying out in pain; then, an order counter-manding the attack.

"They can't see," Bao said breathlessly beside me. "Don't want to hit Master Lo."

"Lucky for him!" I gasped.

"Lucky for us all!"

General Tsieh was shouting at the watchtowers as our ragtag party drew near. "Emperor's men! We're Emperor's men! If this city is still under the Mandate of Heaven, open the cursed gates!"

More torches flared atop the walls. Men yelled, ran and scrambled atop the walls.

Slowly, slowly, the massive gates swung open.

We swept past them—only to find ourselves trapped in a high-walled courtyard, the inner gates yet closed. Hot on our heels, Lord Jiang's men surged inside after us.

My heart sank.

"Disappear!" Bao was yelling at me. "Disappear!"

Blossom checked and wheeled at the closed inner gate. I lurched in the saddle, the heavy satchel falling from my shoulder. One of Lord Jiang's soldiers was bearing down on me, a fierce grimace on his face. "I can't!"

Bao grunted, wielding his staff. The butt end of it caught Jiang's man under the chin, knocking him from his horse. "Heh." Bao grinned; and then his mount collapsed beneath him, pinning him under its bulk.

Another soldier on horseback came at me, leering, a raised cudgel in one hand. He meant to capture, not kill.

Cold anger came over me.

Spoils of war—that's what Master Lo had meant to imply. That's what I would be considered if I were captured. That's the fate that may have already befallen Suyin and Mei and the other women from the ship.

I couldn't summon the twilight, not with the soldier's gaze on me. But in that moment, I didn't want to.

My hands moved smoothly and precisely. I unslung the bow from my shoulder, the yew-wood bow my uncle Mabon had made for me. I was Moirin mac Fainche of the Maghuin Dhonn, and I'd been shooting for the pot since I was ten years old. With unerring speed, I drew an arrow from my quiver, fitting it to the string. I pulled the string taut against my cheek, and loosed it.

The soldier clutched his chest and looked at me in surprise before reeling over backward in the saddle.

I smiled grimly and nocked another arrow. "Who's next?"

As if to echo my question, a volley of arrows fell from above. There were archers atop the high walls behind us, shooting into the courtyard, driving Lord Jiang's forces back toward the outer gates. Some fled, some stayed and fought, no longer caring who they killed.

The outer gates crashed shut, trapping those who stayed.

Bao was on his feet, cursing a blue streak, putting himself between Master Lo and me and Jiang's men, his staff a blur, battering away arrows in midflight. I don't know how many times he saved our lives that night.

And then it was over.

Ten of our men were dead. Three dozen or more of Lord Jiang's soldiers had been slain. I dismounted on shaky legs and stooped to pick up my fallen satchel, settling its weight on my shoulder. Blossom gave a weary whicker and nuzzled my hair.

"Is this victory?" I asked Bao.

He leaned on his staff, looking unspeakably tired. "Don't know."

I looked up. "Master Lo?"

Slumped in the saddle, he roused himself. "No. Victory . . . no. A brief reprieve in what promises to be a long battle."

The inner gates of the courtyard opened with a crash. Torchlight spilled into the square, silhouetting a stocky fellow who beamed at us, flanked by a hundred men in armor. The Imperial flag waved above them.

"Forgive me, esteemed friends!" he cried cheerfully. "We had to be certain you were who you claimed to be." He clasped his hands together and bowed, low and deep. "I am Governor Po. Welcome to Ludong City."

SIXTY

We spent the night in Ludong.

Governor Po had a warm-hearted wife and seven lively daughters delighted to be awakened by the excitement of our arrival, and I found myself whisked away in their company. Despite the lateness of the hour, they took me to a bathing chamber, the daughters crowding around to watch and assist as I washed away salt-spray, sweat, and grime, feeling truly clean for the first time in long months.

"Tell us about the barbarian lands!" one of the middle daughters pleaded.

"Tell us of Master Lo Feng!" begged one with a scholar's dreamy gaze.

"No, no!" The eldest daughter giggled. "Tell us about his handsome ruffian apprentice!"

Tired as I was, it made me smile. "You think he's handsome?"

Amid much more giggling, all but one of the older girls agreed that Bao was handsome; the scholarly daughter proclaimed with a sniff that he had Tatar eyes and looked ill-mannered. And then Madame Po, vexed at their chatter, scolded them for wearying me and drove them from the chamber.

"Poor child," she said sympathetically, folding me into a clean cotton robe. "So far from home! You should not be travelling alone with men, even a man such as Master Lo Feng."

"There were other women on the ship," I said, wondering if Suyin and Mei and the others had escaped unharmed. I hoped so.

Madame Po made a clucking sound and shook her head. "Unsuitable women. Have you no parents? What must they think!"

"Oh." I smiled sadly. "'Tis a complicated matter, my lady. But if my mother were here, she would thank you for showing her daughter kindness," I added, an unexpected swell of longing tightening my throat.

"Poor child," Madame Po repeated in a murmur, combing out the tangles in my wet, wind-whipped hair. I swallowed against the lump in my throat, hearing the universal love of mothers for their daughters in her gentle tone. "Poor little jade-eyed girl."

I wondered if I'd ever see *my* mother again, hear her call me *Moirin mine* in that same tone.

I hoped so, very, very much.

Afterward, a servant roused from the kitchen brought me a bowl of noodles in broth studded with bits of spiced pork. Suddenly ravenous, I forced myself to eat at a measured pace while the two eldest daughters rummaged through their clothes-presses in an effort to find garments that might fit me. I'd escaped with nothing but the dress on my back, which was much the worse for wear. Luckily for me, the girls took after their sturdily built father.

"You have *very* long legs!" Second Daughter said in an aggrieved tone, holding up a pair of loose trousers that fell well above my ankles. "Do all barbarian women have such long legs?"

"No," I said. "My father is tall."

She cocked her head at me. "What does your father do?"

"Ahh . . . he's a priest."

"What kind of priest?"

I flushed at the thought of trying to explain Naamah's Service to a curious fourteen-year-old Ch'in girl. "The kind that solves other people's problems," I said. "Especially troubled lovers."

Her eyes widened. "What kind of problems?"

"Enough." Madame Po intervened, taking the trousers from her. "I'll have Seamstress sew a border on these. That will suit very well." She clapped her hands briskly. "Now, back to bed, girls!"

I passed that night in First Daughter's bed while she shared her second sister's. Another time, it would have troubled me to sleep indoors in a strange, man-made building surrounded by strangers. Not tonight. I was glad of it, even as I was glad of the high stone walls surrounding Ludong City. The girls' innocence, the sound of their deep, untroubled breathing served as a buffer between me and the ugliness I'd witnessed earlier.

The soldier I'd killed . . .

Each time I neared the verge of sleep, his surprised face loomed in my memory, his hands clutching the arrow blossoming from his chest. In the heat of the moment, all I'd felt was grim satisfaction. Now it haunted me.

I had killed a man.

Well and so, he had deserved it. If I hadn't killed him, I would be chattel—or dead. I repeated the thought to myself over and over, taking comfort in the soft breathing of Governor and Madame Po's daughters, until weariness claimed me and I slept.

In the morning, we departed for Shuntian.

I hated to leave so soon. I could have stayed for days, enveloped in Madame Po's maternal concern, distracted by the curiosity and chatter of her lively daughters, protected by the high stone walls that would have once made me so uneasy.

But my *diadh-anam* flared at the sight of Bao and Master Lo; and there was another man's daughter awaiting us. The Emperor's warrior daughter, blindfolded and caged behind iron bars.

Demon-possessed Snow Tiger, who had torn her bridegroom apart with her bare hands.

Bao grinned upon seeing me in borrowed clothes. I wore a long jacket of peach silk trimmed with brocade over a pair of ivory trousers with a similar border hemmed in haste. "You look good. Almost like a Ch'in girl now."

I eyed him. "And you look like a peasant still. Will you wear that to greet the Emperor?"

He shrugged, hard, lean shoulders moving gracefully beneath the homespun cotton of his shirt. "It shows humility."

"Does it?" I had my doubts about Bao and humility, no matter how hard he strove for it.

Bao narrowed his eyes at me. "Do you want to say good-bye to your horse, witch-girl who sometimes talks to animals? She is not fit to ride yet. None of our mounts are."

That softened me. "Aye, I do."

Governor Po's daughters trailed me into their father's stable, where I said my farewells to Blossom. The filly leaned her head wearily over the stall door, apologies in her eyes. I rubbed the base of her ears, sensing the deep, trembling exhaustion in her.

Peace. I breathed the thought at her. *Rest.*

Blowing out her breath through flared nostrils, Blossom agreed.

"She was a gift from a royal prince," I said somberly to the Governor's daughters. "The Dauphin of Terre d'Ange himself." They gazed back at me, wide-eyed. "On the very day he gave her to me, I saved his life. She was bred to carry royalty, and she is a very, very long way from home. If I may return for her, I will. But if I cannot, will you see that she is treated gently? If you do, she will bear you each in turn with a good and true heart."

They nodded in fervent agreement, falling in love with Blossom the way of girls and horses the world over.

I bowed in the Ch'in fashion, hand over fist. "My thanks."

And then we were off, off once more.

I will not chronicle the whole of our journey to Shuntian. It is enough to say that it was swift and uneventful. We rode mounts borrowed from Governor Po. Lord Jiang had secured his hold in the south. North of Ludong City, the Emperor's rule was yet law.

We traversed flat, fertile lands along the rivers where peasants plowed the earth, guiding placid water buffalo with fearsome-looking horns.

We scaled mountains with pockets of snow nestled in their hollows.

In the mountains, I saw for the first time the Great Wall that the Ch'in folk had been building since time out of mind to keep the Tatar menace at bay. And I must own, even though I glimpsed it at a distance, the scope of it made me shudder.

It wasn't beautiful like the architecture of the City of Elua.

But it was so, so very *vast*.

It went on for leagues and leagues, crawling over the spine of the mountains, winding and climbing, tall watchtowers spiking toward the sky. I couldn't even begin to imagine how many men had given their lives in the process of building it.

"Many," Bao said softly in answer to my unspoken thought. "They say it is the largest graveyard in the world."

I met his gaze. "Your blood-father came from beyond the wall. Do you ever wonder about him?"

He shrugged. "No."

At other times, we spoke in hushed whispers of Black Sleeve and the Divine Thunder, wondering if a weapon so terrible could bring down the Great Wall itself. Bao was of the opinion it could.

"Lord Jiang, he does not have enough yet," he said darkly. "Not enough to challenge the Emperor's army. But every day, he is making more. One day he will have enough."

"Why would he do it?" I lowered my voice further. "Black Sleeve, I mean. And why is he called *Black Sleeve*?"

"For the first part, no one knows except maybe Master Lo," Bao said. "And he is not saying. They call him Black Sleeve because he carries poisoned darts in his sleeves," he added. "One day in the mountains seven bandits attacked him." He made a sweeping gesture with one arm. "He killed all seven just like that."

"Oh." I stole a glance at Master Lo Feng sitting upright in the saddle, wondering for the hundredth time at the relationship between them. "Not someone I'd care to cross."

"You already have," Bao pointed out.

I remembered the alchemist frowning at me in puzzlement and shivered. "True."

It was midday when we finally arrived at Shuntian and passed through the massive outer gates. It was a city so large it dwarfed my notion of cities. Stone and sea! There were so many people! They made way for us in the streets, staring after us with open curiosity. Whispers followed us, filled with speculation and hope.

"Lo Feng!"

"Lo Feng has returned!"

Master Lo ignored the whispers, as serene as ever; and yet I thought his face looked careworn. Bao ignored them too, but he carried his head high, eyes glittering as he returned to the city where he had once been the prince of thugs, the city where he had left his former self behind.

For my part, I kept my eyes lowered, trying to draw as little attention as possible.

It worked for a time.

General Tsieh and his men escorted us to a city within a city—the Celestial City, a city of crimson walls and yellow tiled roofs, walled and moated within a city of walls and moats. We dismounted outside its gates, subjecting ourselves to the scrutiny of guards in full armor. Their commander recoiled and shook his head when he came to me.

"No foreigners," he said firmly. "It is not permitted for barbarian eyes to gaze upon the Son of Heaven."

Master Lo folded his hands in his sleeves. "She is my pupil."

"It is not permitted!"

My mentor inclined his head. "Then we will go."

The general sighed. He, too, had travelled a very, very long way to reach this moment, and I felt sorry for him.

"Master . . ." I began.

He silenced me with a look. "Your gods placed you in my care and brought you here, Moirin. I do not know how your destiny accords with mine. I only know that it does. Will you heed it or not?"

My *diadh-anam* sang.

I sighed, too. "Aye, Master Lo."

The commander glowered underneath his bushy brows. Messengers ran to and fro, conferring. In the end, we were all admitted to the Celestial City, passing through the inner gates and stepping over the tall lintel.

"Meant to keep demons out," Bao informed me. "Don't step on it! Nothing but bad luck if you do."

"It didn't do such a good job, did it?" I muttered.

He shrugged. "Maybe not."

Inside the inner gates, there was another courtyard, a vast expanse filled with guards and attendants. And then another moat with five bridges traversing a narrow river. We crossed a bridge and passed through yet another gate, stepping carefully over the high lintel.

Another courtyard, this one housing a pavilion.

And the Son of Heaven.

So the Ch'in reckon their Emperor, and there is a special obeisance accorded him, performed on hands and knees. Despite his purported hundred and seventy years, Master Lo performed it gracefully, kneeling before the throne and touching his brow to the ground three times. Along with Bao and the general and his men, I followed suit, sinking to my knees and humbling myself.

"Old friend." Emperor Zhu's voice was heavy. I peered at him beneath my lashes. A man, only a man. Tall for his folk, with a warrior's mien, but a sorrowful, defeated aspect. He wore robes of yellow silk, embroidered with scarlet dragons. It looked well on him. Coiled dragons rode the columns that surrounded his throne, their claws reaching for the skies. A flat-topped crown sat atop the Emperor's head, dripping with strings of beaded gems. "My old, old friend. You have come at last."

Master Lo rose and straightened. When he spoke, his voice was infinitely gentle. "Yes, Celestial Majesty. You sent for me. I am here."

I felt the Emperor's gaze descend on me, weigh me, and dismiss me. "Will you see her?" he asked Master Lo. "Will you see my daughter?"

Master Lo bowed. "I will."

SIXTY-ONE

Snow Tiger.

    Xue Hu, in Ch'in.

My skin prickled as we made our way through the endless labyrinth of the Celestial City, trailing a long line of attendants, two of them carrying a tall standing mirror that Master Lo had requested, veiled in silk. There was some question as to whether or not Bao was to be admitted to the women's quarters, where men were not allowed, but once more Master Lo insisted and prevailed.

"What about them?" I asked in confusion, indicating the attendants.

"Them?" Bao glanced. "They have been cut."

"Cut?" I echoed.

He made a slicing motion toward his groin. "Not full men anymore. Serving in the palace is one path toward power," he said thoughtfully. "Not one I would choose."

I swallowed hard. "Gods, no!"

At last we entered a small inner courtyard where gnarled trees grew amid curious limestone rocks. It was a pretty place—or at least it would have been if it were not partitioned by a wall of iron bars, the cage extending into the living quarters beyond.

"Noble Daughter!" The Emperor's voice cracked as he summoned her. He cleared his throat and collected himself. "Master Lo Feng has come to see you!"

She emerged.

Beside me, Bao drew in a long, hissing breath.

Hearing tales of the daughter raised as a prince, I had expected a more imposing figure—but no. Snow Tiger was as delicate as a flower, slender as a reed, and half a head shorter than me. Her natural beauty was what the women on the greatship sought to emulate with their cosmetics and painted brows.

And yet . . .

She wore crimson robes embroidered with exotic birds. A sash of crimson silk was bound around her eyes, the ends trailing down her back. Despite it, she walked across her enclosed courtyard with deliberate, sure-footed grace, her spine as straight as a spear, her carriage proud and unbowed. And I did not doubt, not for one heartbeat, that she was a warrior.

"Truly?" Her voice was low. "After so long, he is here?"

Emperor Zhu's strong hands gripped the iron bars that divided them. "Truly, Noble Daughter."

My *diadh-anam* flickered and flared. I felt dizzy. I shook my head, trying to clear it, while Master Lo examined her through the bars. He felt the pulses in her wrists, studied her tongue, listened to the sound of her breathing. She bore it patiently, doubtless having been through the like a hundred times before.

With Bao's assistance, he lit a taper of incense that gave off prodigious amounts of fragrant smoke, waving it around her. The smoke writhed and coiled in intricate patterns.

Coiled like . . . what?

"Forgive me, Noble Princess." Master Lo's voice sounded genuinely apologetic. "I must ask you to remove the blindfold." He nodded at the attendants. "Unveil the mirror."

Snow Tiger bowed her head in acquiescence, hands rising to undo the knot. "Step away from the bars, please. You must be sure your people are safe."

"Do as her highness bids," he agreed. "Step away."

I meant to—gods know, I did! And yet I didn't. Instead, I stood rooted to the spot and summoned the twilight without thinking, breathing it in deep. As the crimson blindfold fluttered to the ground and Snow Tiger opened her eyes, I flung the twilight around both of us.

And a half-step into the world beyond, I *saw.*

I caught my breath.

Her head turned, unerring. Something not human looked out from her eyes, looked out and *saw* itself reflected in mine. She was not alone in her body. Silver-white brightness coiled and uncoiled throughout her being.

You see me.

The voice in my thoughts crashed and echoed like mountains falling.

"I see you," I murmured in awe.

You see me! It thundered, male and triumphant. *You see me! I see myself in you!*

"What is it?" The Ch'in princess stood very straight and still, her dark gaze with unspeakable brightness behind it fixed on my face. "You are a foreigner. Why are you here? What have you done? Who *are* you?"

Somewhere, half a world away, alarm was rising. I concentrated on breathing, tuning out the frantic mortal voices.

"Moirin," I said firmly. "I am Moirin mac Fainche of the Maghuin Dhonn, my lady. And I bid you to look." In the gloaming light, I reached through the bars and turned her chin toward the full-length mirror that Master Lo had ordered brought. "Look and see."

There was no lovely Ch'in princess reflected there. There was only the infinite coils of a dragon, twining and untwining, pearlescent white scales gleaming in the depths of the mirror. As I watched, it raised its bearded, long-jowled head with joy.

You see me!

"I see it," Snow Tiger breathed. She put one slender arm through the bars, her splayed fingertips touching the mirror. "Oh! I thought it would be hideous. But it's beautiful, so beautiful."

I didn't know . . .

The memory not my own surfaced. Desire, shuddering pleasure; an awakening onto dawning horror. Blindness. Thrashing panic, soft flesh tearing in the pursuit of unattainable freedom. And blood—gods! So much blood.

I felt sick.

"The dragon awoke inside you while you were making love with your bridegroom," I whispered. "He didn't know. He was only trying to free himself."

Her throat worked. "How? How did this happen?"

I shook my head. "I don't know." The sounds of alarm were growing. My grip on the twilight wavered. "My lady, we'd best go back."

STAY!

I winced at the volume of the dragon's voice in my head. Desire and panic, twined together, roiled through me. Snow Tiger caught my hand, nearly crushing it in an inhumanly strong grip. I forced myself to breathe through the pain. "I'm here," I said to the immortal being behind her eyes. "Be gentle. It's all right. I'm not really going away. It's only blindness, only for a little while. Can you endure it?"

For you, I will try.

The princess nodded in agreement, her grip loosening.

I eased my hand away and stooped to pick up her scarf. "Cover your eyes."

When I loosed the twilight, the world crashed down upon us, filled with chaos and shouting. Hands grabbed my arms, yanking me away from the cage. Bao yelled, his staff whirling as he attacked my assailants.

The dragon . . .

LET HER GO!

The furious roar in my head didn't quite drown out Snow Tiger's high, fierce cry. Driven by the dragon's fury, she dropped the scarf in her hands and flung herself forward, hitting the iron bars with terrible force. The bars screeched and bent. She caught sight of the mirror and froze, then flung herself forward again, howling. With the twilight banished, the dragon could no longer see his reflection, and it maddened him further, the enormity of his rage driving the princess like a goad.

"Cover the mirror!" I shouted. "Cover the bedamned mirror!"

Bao dashed to obey, a wary eye on the princess. Once the mirror was covered, she made a great effort to wrestle herself under control, squeezing her eyes shut and tying the scarf in place.

Attendants seized me again, forcing me to my knees. The Emperor drew a long, curved sword. "You bring a barbarian witch to torment my daughter, old friend?" he asked Master Lo, his voice filled with grief and menace. "What manner of betrayal is this?"

"Father!" Snow Tiger called. "Let her go!"

"Hush, child," he said over his shoulder. "You don't know yourself."

"It is not so!" she said in frustration. "Noble Father, I beg you, spare the foreign woman and let her speak."

Master Lo's face was pale, but composed. He folded his hands in his sleeves. "I urge you to heed your daughter's plea, Celestial Majesty. My pupil's people have a gift for magic and her destiny has led her to this place. If you wish to hear what she has to say, I suggest you let her keep her head. Your daughter's fate may depend on it."

Emperor Zhu hesitated, knuckles white on his sword-hilt. Out of the corner of my eye, I saw Bao sidling closer, trying to decide if saving my life was worth assaulting the Son of Heaven. I shook my head at him, sure it would be his death sentence if he did.

"Let her up." The Emperor sheathed his blade brusquely and nodded at me. "Speak."

I rose unsteadily, only now beginning to tremble. I breathed the Breath of Earth's Pulse until I could speak. "It's not a demon. It's a dragon." I pointed to the embroidered crimson figures swirling on his robes. "Like that, only white. Like the dragon on Lord Jiang's standard," I added. "It's trapped inside her. I don't know how or why, but it is."

Master Lo paled further, an involuntary sound escaping from him. That shocked me as much as anything that had transpired.

"It's true." Snow Tiger clutched the iron bars hard enough to make them creak in protest, but her blindfold was in place and she maintained control. "Father, I *saw* it."

"Sorcery," Emperor Zhu said grimly.

"No, old friend." Master Lo's voice was faint, but steady. It grew stronger as he spoke. "I fear she speaks the truth."

A memory that made no sense surfaced in his thoughts. A toddler, plump and merry as any of Bao's imaginary babies, playing with a shimmering pearl the size of a ball. I blinked and frowned, not comprehending.

Master Lo met my gaze for a long, grave moment, then turned to Snow Tiger. "Noble Princess, someone gave you a drink the night of your wedding, did they not?"

"You did, Master," she said in perplexity. "That is, I drank the tonic that you gave to Lord Jiang's physician to hold in keeping for my wedding night." Beneath the blindfold, her cheeks turned faintly pink. I could hazard a guess at the tonic's intended effect.

My mentor nodded. "And you had no cause not to trust Lord Jiang's own physician. It tasted of vinegar, did it not?"

"Yes. Why?"

He took a few steps, turning away from all of us. "It is well known that a dragon hides the essence of his spirit in a great pearl," he said in a low tone. "As it is well known that a pearl dissolves in vinegar. When I was a young man, I did many foolish things in the pursuit of ambition. One of these things was to lull a dragon to sleep and steal his pearl."

Two things came together in my mind.

"Oh, gods!" I blurted out the words without thinking. It made sense. The child. The pearl. "Lord Jiang's physician, Black Sleeve. He's your *son*."

Master Lo bowed his head. "Yes."

SIXTY-TWO

A moment of silence followed Master Lo's revelation.

Emperor Zhu broke it by swearing, crashing his fist into his other hand. "So, old friend. Leaving aside the matter of Black Sleeve's paternity, how do we get the dragon *out* of my most treasured daughter?"

HOME!

I winced at the sudden joyous thunder of the dragon's voice in my thoughts and echoed the word. "Home."

Bao gave me a curious look. Master Lo inclined his head. "My pupil is correct. Snow Tiger must journey to White Jade Mountain, where the dragon resides. Only in the lake where the snow-capped peak is reflected can she disgorge the pearl."

Home . . .

It was a more wistful tone. In my head, I saw a dizzying aerial image of a white mountain-top reflected in the pristine waters far, far below. "You *see* yourself," I murmured. "That's why it's important to you. It's part of what you are. That's why it maddens you to see and not be seen, not to see yourself reflected."

Yes, the dragon agreed. *It is better not to see at all.*

"Are you talking to it?" Bao asked me suspiciously.

"Aye."

He shook his head. "You get stranger and stranger every day."

The Emperor was pacing, yellow robes swirling. Helpless attendants trailed in his wake. Behind the bars, Snow Tiger stood with her head tilted, concentrating on listening. "White Jade Mountain is deep within Lord Jiang's territory," the Emperor mused. "But surely he will call off this war once he knows what Black Sleeve has done, and that it is no demon my daughter houses." He gave a decisive nod, beckoning to an attendant. "I will send word to him at once."

"Unless . . ." Master Lo said softly.

"What?" Emperor Zhu turned on him.

"Unless he already knows, Celestial Majesty." My mentor met the Emperor's gaze fearlessly. "We do not know that Black Sleeve acted without Lord Jiang's blessing."

The Emperor recoiled. "You suggest that Jiang Quan would sacrifice his own son?"

"He has three sons, Celestial Majesty." Master Lo lowered his head in deference. "It would be a terrible thing to do. And yet . . ." He gestured at Snow Tiger. "What befell your daughter gave him cause to challenge the Mandate of Heaven."

"Also, he tried very hard to stop us from coming here," Bao added. "I do not think he wishes the Noble Princess to be saved."

My skin still prickled, and there was a strange pressure rising in the courtyard that had nothing to do with the issues being debated. *Come,* the dragon crooned in my thoughts. *Here, now.* I glanced over at Snow Tiger and took a few steps toward her, compelled by the force of it. Her body was rigid, hands still locked on the bars. The pulse in the hollow of her throat beat visibly.

"What are you doing to her?" I whispered fiercely. "Why?"

". . . simply cannot believe . . ." the Emperor's voice trailed away in the ringing that filled my head.

I am making amends, the dragon said simply. *I understand now. I caused her mate to be killed. I have chosen you to replace him.*

A short, horrified laugh escaped me. "You can't!"

You see me. There is no one else.

Snow Tiger's tense, blindfolded face swung my way. "Can you make it stop?"

It wasn't hurting her. It was untwining the strands of horror and desire, trying to separate them and spin something pure and bright and joyous out of it, a rising spiral of yearning born out of the dregs of panic and terror. Now that it had found a way to communicate with her through me, it was trying to make up for the terrible loss it had caused her. But it was too much, too powerful—a dragon's understanding of desire, filled with thunder and lightning.

And she was fighting it.

"Stop," I said to the dragon. "You have to stop! She's only human!"

I cannot. There was regret in its tone—and truth. *I have chosen you. Once a dragon's mating is begun, nothing under Heaven can halt it.*

". . . if you are wrong, Celestial Majesty, we tip our hands," Master Lo was saying. "Is it not better to preserve an element of surprise?"

"Is it not worth the effort to avert a war?" Emperor Zhu shook his head. "No, no, old friend. We will bargain in good faith. Have you not always bade me to seek the most harmonious path?" He clapped his hands together briskly. "Now! I will have a missive to Lord Jiang prepared. You shall be fed and lodged as heroes!"

NO!

"Let me stay." The words fell out of my mouth. I drew a deep breath, shuddering all over. "Forgive me, Celestial Majesty. But let me stay."

"Noble Daughter?" The Emperor sounded doubtful.

She was silent a moment. "The dragon within wishes it so."

Master Lo folded in his sleeves and bowed. "My pupil Moirin is of royal blood from two lands, Celestial Majesty. She has attended a queen before."

I wondered if he had any idea.

Bao made a choked noise.

He knew.

And yet I could not choose otherwise. I stood to one side as a tall court eunuch with an impressive chain of office came forward to unlock the princess' cage. Snow Tiger retreated to the doorway of her living quarters, a slight and still figure glowing in the fading light, the crimson scarf bound over her eyes.

I entered her cage.

The iron gate clanged shut behind me. I was alone with the princess and the dragon.

On the far side of the bars, Master Lo regarded me with a worried gaze. But it was Bao who came forward, strong, brown fingers lacing around the bars.

"You're sure?" he asked. I nodded, unable to speak. "Stupid girl." He breathed the words in the tongue he had taught me himself, one hand reaching through the bars to caress my cheek. "Try not to get killed."

Tears stung my eyes. "I'll try."

And then they left, and we were truly alone. Unsure what to do, I followed the princess as she turned and entered her quarters, keeping a respectful distance behind her.

It was growing dark inside her rooms. I busied myself by lighting a dusty taper from a smoldering brazier, then kindling the lamps with their red silk lanterns. They cast a warm glow that should have been comforting.

It wasn't.

Snow Tiger paced like a caged . . . well, like a tiger. The air around her quivered with fury and urgency. The spiral of desire was rising— higher and higher, tighter and tighter. "You cannot make it stop?"

I shook my head, forgetting she couldn't see. "He says he cannot. I do not think he lies, my lady."

"Of course he doesn't lie!" She whirled on me. "He's a dragon!" Not knowing what to say, I was silent. She wrapped her arms around herself as though to keep herself from shivering apart under the rising pressure. With a visible effort, she forced herself to speak evenly. "Forgive me. Your magic. What is it? What does it do?"

I made a helpless gesture. "It's . . . difficult to explain. My people, the Maghuin Dhonn, we were great magicians once. We could see many paths into the future. We could take the shape of the Great Bear Herself. No longer. This gift is all that is left to us." I shrugged. "When I was younger, I was told it was a way to conceal ourselves, to hide. Now I think it is something more. It is a way of taking half a step into the spirit world beyond. Strange things happen there."

Her arms tightened. "You took me into the spirit world?"

"Halfway."

"I see."

"We call it summoning the twilight." I breathed the Breath of Trees Growing, remembering green Alba where my mother had first taught me, and found a calm point within myself. I called the twilight and breathed it out softly, wrapping it around the entire room. The world glimmered, the glow of the red lanterns turning silvery.

Yes! Come, here, now!

Snow Tiger's head snapped up. She was breathing hard and fast, fingers gripping her arms so hard I thought they would leave bruises. Still, her will didn't waver. "It is not safe for you to be here. I should not have let you stay."

"Mayhap." Swallowing hard, I crossed the room and untied her blindfold. "But I fear it is already too late for me to leave, my lady."

The dragon roared in exultation. I saw it reflected in her eyes, as it saw itself in mine. Her hands dropped to her sides, fists trembling. She lifted her chin.

"I want . . ." she said in a low voice. "I *need* . . ."

"I know," I whispered.

And then her hands were at my head, pulling it down sharply, and her mouth was on mine, fierce and urgent. A dragon's desire, spun out of panic. I was caught in its coils, and it was strong enough to kill me. I struggled against it, struggled against the terrifying leap of blood in my veins, struggled to draw breath. The pressure of her fingertips was so strong it felt like my skull would burst. In a distant part of my mind, I wondered if anyone had ever been kissed to death before.

Gentle! I flung out the thought like a desperate lifeline. *Be gentle!*

It was not gentle.

It eased enough to spare my life, but it was not gentle, and I have no words to describe it. There was no place in this coupling for tenderness or artistry. It was like the great storm at sea, savage and powerful, terrible and beautiful. Her hands tore at my robes and hers—to no avail, I tried to slow her, tried in vain to find a measure of gentleness that the dragon's unleashed desire superseded. Gods, she was strong! Unnaturally strong, dragon-ridden. Her whole body shuddered when I slid my hand between her thighs, slid two fingers deep inside her. Slender limbs, dragon-strong, coiled around me.

Yes! That is what I awoke to. That is the gift I restore!

Not exactly, I thought—but close enough. And riding above us like the storm above the sea was a dragon's memory of mating, filled with clouds and rain and thunder, gleaming coils intertwining, flashing in the bursts of lightning.

Snow Tiger cried out loud, pressing against me so hard I thought my wrist would break or my ribs shatter.

And then it was over.

The dragon sighed, content. The storm had passed, leaving only a few clouds drifting over the moon, the seas calm below.

The princess released me and pulled away, withdrawing into herself. She sat cross-legged at the foot of the bed, gazing through the open doorway at the twilit garden beyond, her slender back fiercely upright. I stayed where I was, wishing I had the faintest idea what to do or say.

"Thank you." Her tone was unreadable.

I inclined my head, unseen. "My lady."

"Dragons mate in the skies, don't they?" she mused. "It was fearful, yet lovely."

"You saw it?"

"Yes." Her shoulders moved. "Through you, I think. You and the magic you summon. Tell me again, what is your name, Master Lo's pupil?"

"Moirin."

Her head turned slightly, revealing her delicate profile. "Moirin. It is late, and you should go. I cannot know what harm I might do in my sleep. I will summon an attendant to release you."

The dragon stirred. *I would never harm you.*

"He said—"

"I heard. I am learning to hear in this twilight of yours. Still, I would prefer that you go."

I wondered if it were for my sake or hers. "As you wish, my lady. I will have to release the twilight."

"Ah, of course." Snow Tiger rose in one impossibly fluid gesture, then stood still a moment, looking around the room. "The world is beautiful, isn't it? I'd almost forgotten." She stooped and picked up the fallen blindfold.

"My lady, wait, please." I climbed out of her bed, my body aching as though I'd fallen down a mountainside. I opened a clothes-press and found a sleeping-robe, unfolding it for her.

"A wise thought," she said dryly.

"It's not that." I gathered my torn, scattered clothing. Snow Tiger waited with patience while I dressed, the scarf dangling from one hand. The dragon reflected in her eyes roiled slowly, peacefully, dreaming of clouds and rain. "You did not choose what happened here tonight," I said, taking care with my words. "Therefore, I do not know if Naamah's blessing may be upon it, though desire be sacred to her. But my gods sent me here, and I consented to this. Let us pray that it is blessing enough, my lady. And I promise, if I may serve you and the dragon within you in any other way, I will."

She touched my lips—gently. Very gently. "Moirin."

"Aye?"

"You should go." Snow Tiger tied the blindfold deftly over her eyes. "Banish the magic."

I'd held it for longer than I'd done since leaving Terre d'Ange, longer than I could remember. Now I let it go, and the world came rushing back, the silk lanterns glowing red once more. Moving with unerring precision, she picked up a small hammer from a table by the door and struck the dull, tarnished gong that stood there.

In the darkened garden, a lantern came bobbing. A key turned in the cage's lock.

I was dismissed.

SIXTY-THREE

I t's not what you think," I said to Bao. "Or at least not in the way you think it."

"The royal concubine has found a new princess to serve," he said in a smooth tone. His relief at finding me bruised and aching, but otherwise unharmed, had been short-lived. "She owes no explanations to the peasant-boy."

"You know," I commented. "Wrong though it may be, I cannot help but be delighted by your jealousy." His mouth twitched, repressing a faint smile. "It's misplaced, though. *She* didn't want me there. The dragon did. As soon as it released her, she sent me away. I think she was glad to see me go," I added.

"What did you expect?" Bao asked. "This is not Terre d'Ange, Moirin. The Emperor's enemies say he challenged the Mandate of Heaven when he chose to raise his daughter as his heir. Do you think Snow Tiger does not wonder about it herself?" He shrugged. "The dragon she swallowed drove her to tear her husband from limb to limb. Now it has driven her to bed a foreign woman, a complete stranger, against all custom, in violation of her own will. Did you expect her to be grateful for it?"

I sighed. "No, of course not. It's just . . ."

"Come here." He slid his arms around me. I pressed my face against the column of his throat, comforted by the considerable, but mortal, strength of his embrace. "I do not think you can understand how unsettling it was for the princess to be at the mercy of such a need. You are a foreigner. She is the daughter of the Emperor of Ch'in. Despite everything, her life has been a sheltered and privileged one in many ways. Allow time to pass before you look for her to be at ease with you."

"It was unsettling for *me*, too," I observed.

His arms tightened around me. "Was it terrible?"

I nodded, then shook my head. "Terrible, but beautiful, too. Like the storm. I . . . *we* . . . saw what it is like when dragons mate."

Bao's warm breath stirred my hair. "I cannot compete with dragons, Moirin."

"Oh . . ." I lifted my head and kissed him. It felt familiar and very, very good. "I wouldn't be so sure."

He smiled. "Strange girl."

"You do love me, don't you?" I challenged him. "You were willing to assault the Son of Heaven himself on my behalf."

"Maybe." He lowered his head to return my kiss. "Maybe not. Let us settle the matter of the princess and the dragon first. Because among other things, I do not think I would care to rouse a dragon's jealousy."

I remembered the way Snow Tiger had flung herself at the bars when the Emperor's eunuchs had seized me. "Good point."

It was a time of waiting. An Imperial delegation had been sent to negotiate with Lord Jiang. The crowded streets of Shuntian were filled with rumor and speculation. Master Lo was quiet and withdrawn. Although the Emperor had offered to host us like heroes, Master Lo had chosen to take modest lodgings in the city. In the courtyard, we repotted the Camaeline snowdrop bulbs that had travelled so far, storing them in the coolest, shadiest corner.

"They live yet?" he asked me.

"Aye." Their song was fainter than ever, fading. I stroked the soil with my fingertips. "They'll not survive if they're not planted in a high, cold place ere winter comes. What do you mean to do with them, Master?"

"It is my hope that we might transport them to White Jade Mountain," he said soberly. "Though I fear for our chances."

Bao and I exchanged a glance. It was the first time Master Lo had spoken of it since our arrival. "You do not think Lord Jiang will relent?" he asked.

"I fear not." His tone did not encourage further inquiry on the topic.

I brushed dirt from my hands. "What will you do with the bulbs, then? Brew more tonic?"

"Perhaps." He gazed into the distance. "When I discovered their properties, it was my thought that they might provide a cure for an old friend's ailment. The situation was not so complicated then."

I blinked, confused.

Bao's eyes widened. "Emperor Zhu is *impotent*?"

Master Lo gave him a sharp look. "It is worth your life to speak those words where other ears might hear, my magpie."

"You said he tried many times, with many women, to get a male heir," I reminded him.

He smiled sadly. "I did not specify the manner in which he failed. Snow Tiger's mother was the only woman to rouse him. I suspect that is why she was poisoned when the princess was yet a babe."

"Stone and sea!" I shook my head. "This tale grows sadder with every turn."

"Yes." Master Lo's gaze returned to the distance. "And I fear it is far from over."

Although I didn't think she would wish to see me again, Snow Tiger sent for me two days after dismissing me. Once again, I entered the red walls of the Celestial City, surrounded by an escort of royal attendants and armed eunuchs. And once again, her cage was unlocked to admit me.

You!

Despite everything, the leap of joy in the dragon's voice made me smile.

Beneath her blindfold, the princess was not smiling. "The dragon within is restless," she said in a formal tone. "I believe it wishes to *see*." She gestured to the tall mirror, still veiled in silk, now placed within her quarters. "I said aloud that I would send for you if it promises not to . . ." Her voice faltered. "To do what it did before. Without your magic, I cannot be sure it understands."

"Do you?" I asked the dragon.

Yes. Its tone was wistful. *I give my promise. I wished only to give her a worthy mate and the pleasure I took from her.*

"I know," I said. "But you cannot restore her husband, and she did not wish that pleasure returned thusly. It is not your place to choose a mate for her. You must never do it again."

His tone brightened. *Even if she asks it of me?*

"Ah . . ." I eyed Snow Tiger. "That will not happen."

It might!

"It won't."

"Are you *arguing* with it?" the princess asked with a trace of impatience.

"A little," I admitted. "But it's all right, my lady. He gives his promise."

Her tense shoulders relaxed a fraction. "Then summon your magic, please."

I did.

Daylight turned to dusk, settling all around us. Either it was growing easier or I was growing stronger. The seemingly endless length of silver-white brightness that roiled throughout Snow Tiger's being, turning over and over itself, turned faster, glad and excited.

Yes! Now!

I uncovered the mirror as she lowered the blindfold. Her face softened, almost childlike with pleasure. Then again, she *was* young. No older than me, mayhap younger. It was easy to forget. I watched her watch the dragon's pearlescent coils in the mirror's depths, filled with a terrible sympathy. The dragon's happiness and contentment at seeing itself reflected ran through my thoughts like a song, and I knew she heard it, too. It was a song without beginning or end, a song of snow-capped mountains and clouds and reflections, solitude and contemplation.

"It's so peaceful there," Snow Tiger murmured.

Yes.

I don't know how many hours I spent there. Many. She sent for me every other day while we awaited Lord Jiang's reply; and every day, it was the same. The dragon greeted me with delight.

The princess seemed to do her best to ignore my presence.

Mindful of Bao's warning, I bore it well the first two times. I was comfortable with silence and solitude, having experienced a great deal of it in my childhood. My mother and I could go for long hours without speaking to one another, doing whatever needed to be done together with no words required. I sat still and quiet and practiced the Five Styles of Breathing. I understood that I was a necessary imposition that the princess was within her rights to resent, especially given what had passed between us earlier.

And yet . . .

"You know, I did not choose this, either," I said on the third visit. "I consented to it. There is a difference."

Snow Tiger's dark, dragon-reflecting gaze flicked over to me, then away.

"I didn't want to leave home in the first place, but at least I found a piece of happiness in Terre d'Ange," I continued, suddenly and unexpectedly determined to make her hear me. "Unnatural though you may find it, I was content to serve as the Queen's companion. I was respected and appreciated. And it wasn't only about the arts of the bedchamber, it was about being loyal and listening. Jehanne was with child when I left, and she was frightened. No doubt that seems weak and foolish to you, because gods know you must be impossibly brave to have survived this past year without going mad, but Jehanne was brave in different ways."

Now the princess was staring at me incredulously, but I couldn't stop myself.

"In matters of love and desire, she was fearless." The words spilled out of me. "Jehanne never apologized for loving two different men, or for loving me, either. She insisted on holding a farewell progress to make sure all of the City knew I was leaving with honor, and she was very beautiful and smelled nicer than anyone I've ever known." My voice rose. "And I've not even begun to touch on my father, who I'd only just found, nearly lost, and liked very much! I know that's naught to what you've endured, but I didn't choose this. And . . . and I am *not* just an inconvenient necessity or a useful tool for other hands to wield. I am a person with thoughts and feelings of my own."

Snow Tiger stared at me a moment longer. "Are you finished?"

It occurred to me that I could probably lose my head for speaking to the Emperor's daughter thusly. "I am."

"I am sorry for your loss," she said in her formal tone. "Although

I do not pretend to understand exactly what you were talking about, clearly you are grieving, and I am adding to your burden." She squared her slender shoulders. "This, I do understand. I killed my bridegroom, a man I may well have grown to love, with my bare hands."

"I know," I murmured.

"I thought it was the work of a demon-spirit within me," the princess said in a clear, precise voice. "As did everyone. And I reviled my own weakness that I should fall prey to such a creature. So did almost everyone around me." She ticked them off, one finger at a time. "Servants who once fawned on me are grateful to be excused from attending me. Warriors who swore to follow me unto death shun me. My tutors . . ."

Her voice trailed away.

"Aye?"

She gathered herself. "Swordmaster Wu has gone into exile of his own accord. Master Guo, who taught me calligraphy and poetry, filled his sleeves with stones and waded into a lake. He is dead now."

My heart ached. "I'm sorry, my lady."

Her shoulders lifted and fell. "For over a year, every day I thought of taking my own life in shame. Every day. Two things stayed my hand, over and over. One is the knowledge of the grief it would cause my father. The other is the fear that if I took my own life, the demon that inhabits me would be free to prey upon another." Her face shone with unexpected hope. "Ah, but . . . things are different now. Would it free the dragon if I were to die?"

No. The dragon was succinct, offering nothing further.

"He says it would not," I said softly.

"I heard." The momentary brightness faded. Snow Tiger folded her hands in her lap and gazed at me, delicate frown-lines etched between her brows. "So. All these long months, I have struggled to cling to my sanity, holding on to the faint thread of hope that Master Lo Feng's return offered. You, I did not expect. For a second time, my world has been turned on its head. Although it is very much a change for the better, there is a great deal that I do not understand. I cannot fathom why Black Sleeve would do such a thing. I cannot imagine how Lord Jiang would sacrifice his own son to such a terrible fate. In these precious hours of peace your magic affords me, I am struggling to make sense of it all. I am sorry if you find me remote."

I smiled wryly. "Given the circumstances, I cannot exactly blame you for it. It is an awkward way to begin an acquaintance."

"Yes." Snow Tiger flushed, but she didn't look away. "It is not that I am ungrateful. But it is . . . awkward, yes." She cocked her head. "Why *are* you here?"

"Oh . . ." I sighed. "Because my *diadh-anam* sent me." She gestured for me to continue, and I explained it as best I could, although it was always difficult to convey to anyone not of the Maghuin Dhonn. Even the other folk of Alba do not carry their *diadh-anams* inside them as we do.

"Strange," the princess mused when I had finished. "Why would your bear-goddess send you so very far away to aid me?"

I cleared my throat. "With all respect, my lady, I believe there is more at stake than the fate of you and your dragon. There is a war pending. Black Sleeve has created weapons, terrible weapons, weapons that Master Lo and others have prayed no one would ever discover. Weapons that spit fire and roar like thunder, hurling deadly projectiles with greater force than any catapult. Had we not opened the Thousand-Cloud Bag and fled, they would have sunk our greatship with ease. If he is not stopped, I think . . . I think the world will suffer greatly for it."

Quick as a flash, Snow Tiger moved. Dragon-strong hands gripped my shoulders as she stooped before me. "You think there is some purpose in all of this," she breathed. "Some greater purpose."

"I do." I gazed at her lovely face, lit anew with fierce hope. "I'd lose my wits if I didn't."

"I did not know about the weapons." She released me and rose to pace the room. "I suspect my father concealed the truth from me, fearing it was more than I could bear. He blames himself. He does not want me to do the same."

"Nor should you," I murmured. "You are innocent; and the dragon, too."

Yes.

For the first time, the princess looked at me, truly looked at me, as though she was pleased by my presence. She inclined her head with grace. "I owe you a great debt, Moirin of the Maghuin Dhonn."

"Not so very great," I said. "Not yet. We are a long way from succeeding, my lady."

"Still, you have given me hope, and that is a powerful gift." Snow Tiger touched the mirror's surface, gazing at the dragon's undulating coils. "We are grateful for it."

Yes.

"Thank you," I said simply to both of them. "And, ah . . . I hope you will forgive me for speaking out of turn earlier."

"I do." She turned back toward me, looking uncommonly young once more, an unexpected look of girlish curiosity on her face. "You spoke of love and desire. What of the handsome young man with the irritable aspect? Master Lo Feng's apprentice? I caught a glimpse of him fighting my father's guards, and I heard him speak to you later. He seemed to have a great care for your safety, and you for his concern."

"Bao?" I flushed.

"Is that his name? Yes."

"Oh . . ." I shrugged. "I don't know. Neither of us do. We enjoy one another. Betimes I think it is only circumstance that flung us together. And yet . . . I am beginning to find it hard to imagine his absence."

Snow Tiger smiled, sinking to sit cross-legged with fluid elegance, keeping one eye on the mirror. "Perhaps you are more like this queen of whom you spoke than you know. Quick to love and desire, fearless with your heart."

"Mayhap," I murmured.

"I am also a person with feelings," she remarked. "And if you are to be my inconvenient necessity, then I am fortunate that you are capable of great loyalty as well as great passion, no matter how strange."

In the mirror, the dragon's shimmering coils twisted and flowed, turning over and over, an endless intertwining. We both watched it, more at ease in one another's presence than we had been.

"My father is a great man," Snow Tiger said presently. "But doubt has made him fearful, and he is reluctant to further risk the Mandate of Heaven. Depending on the outcome of his delegation to Lord Jiang, I may have to defy him and seek a way to White Jade Mountain."

I roused myself. "I know."

"That goes against all I have been taught."

"I know," I repeated.

She glanced at me. "I cannot do it alone, and your magic is the only thing that calms the dragon. May I count on your aid?"

"I meant what I said the other night, my lady," I replied. "If I may serve you in any way, I will."

The princess inclined her head. "Thank you."

We sat in silence awhile longer, breathing in the twilight, until the dragon's coiling and uncoiling slowed and it drifted like clouds in the mirror, dreaming once more, its opalescent eyes lidded.

"She must have been very wise and gracious to inspire such loyalty," Snow Tiger commented. "This foreign queen you served."

I laughed. "No. No, she was capricious, vain, and fickle. But she could be kind and generous, too. And when she was in a sweet temper, it was as though the sun shone and all the birds in the sky sang at once."

"I see."

There were thoughts and memories unfurling in her mind, doubts and questions. Musings on what might have been had she been raised differently, had her own mother survived. But she did not voice them, and I held my tongue and kept my knowledge to myself, breathing quietly while the dragon drifted and dreamed.

In a little while, Snow Tiger dismissed me.

At least this time, I did not think she was glad to be rid of me.

SIXTY-FOUR

Lord Jiang refused.

"He claims it is a trick." The Emperor paced in his council chamber, as restless as his daughter in anger. Dozens of councilors huddled on their knees, their heads bowed. I knelt behind Master Lo, keeping my eyes lowered. "A trick! As though I would resort to such subterfuge." He fetched up before my mentor. "Can you prove it otherwise, old friend?"

"Not beyond a shadow of doubt, Celestial Majesty." Master Lo's voice was heavy. "The way the incense smoke coiled around the Noble Princess indicates the dragon's presence. But I cannot prove its existence."

Bao nudged me.

"I can try, Master," I offered. "Your teaching has made me stronger. I can summon the twilight and *show* them the dragon in the mirror."

"Smoke and mirrors." Emperor Zhu waved a dismissive hand. "No, no. They will not believe it. Especially not when foreign sorcery is involved."

Master Lo inclined his head. "Then we must find a way to convey the Noble Princess to White Jade Mountain ourselves."

The Emperor stiffened. "And provoke a civil war?"

"It is coming whether you provoke it or not, old friend," Master Lo Feng said softly. "Forgive me, but my son has ensured that it is so, and I believe he has done so with Jiang Quan's knowledge and consent. If you hesitate, you lose what advantage is left to you."

"No." Emperor Zhu shook his head. Beads of gemstones dangling from his flat yellow crown swung and rattled. There were harsh lines of sorrow and grief etched in his face. "No, no, no. I will not do this thing. I will not plunge the Celestial Empire into war." He took a deep breath, his chest rising and swelling. "If I have lost the Mandate of Heaven, if I must surrender the throne, I will."

No!

"Peace," I whispered to the distant dragon.

It settled reluctantly.

"And the Noble Princess?" Master Lo murmured.

The Emperor looked away. "I grieve, old friend. I have grieved from the moment it happened. But I do not have the right to further offend Heaven on my daughter's behalf." He spared a glance in my direction. "Your jade-eyed witch soothes the dragon. Let her continue to do so."

I waited for someone else to implore the Emperor to take action, to convince him that he had not lost the Mandate of Heaven.

No one spoke.

They had not heard the dragon's thoughts, they had not seen its endless pearl-bright coils reflected in the mirror. Only Master Lo Feng's foreign witch and the possessed princess claimed to have done so. But they *had* seen the nuptial bedchamber drenched in blood, the dismembered corpse of Lord Jiang's son—or if they'd not seen it with their own eyes, they'd heard it described in horror a thousand times over.

Not a man among them would challenge the Emperor.

The decision was made.

Once dismissed, we backed out of the Imperial presence and returned to our quarters in silence. I thought of my promise to Snow Tiger and wondered how in the name of all the gods to broach the topic.

Bao did it for me. "So." He fetched a jar of rice wine from our humble kitchen and brought it into the courtyard. Master Lo glanced at him in surprise. "There is a time to drink strong spirits, Master," he said, pouring three cups. "This is one of them. Now, how are we going to save the princess and the dragon?"

I choked on the sip I was taking.

"You had other plans?" Bao turned his dark, ironic gaze on me. I shook my head. "No, I didn't think so."

"I promised to aid her if it came to this," I admitted.

"She would defy her own father?" Master Lo sounded appalled.

"It's not just her, Master," Bao observed. "There is the dragon, too. It is a celestial being, an immortal. It cannot stay a prisoner inside her. That is against all nature." He cocked his head. "Why did you give the pearl to Black Sleeve, anyway?"

Master Lo Feng picked up his cup, turning it around and around in his elegant, long-fingered hands. "He was called Yaozu then," he said softly. "That was the name his mother and I gave him when he came of age. When he was a babe, she called him Tadpole. The dragon's pearl was his favorite toy." In one swift gesture, he downed the rice wine in his cup.

Bao refilled his cup without a word.

Master Lo coughed, eyes watering. "I believe you are right about the time for strong spirits, my magpie." He took another drink. "Yaozu blames me for his mother's death. We parted bitterly. I gave him the pearl in the hope that it would remind him of happier times."

"How . . ." I hesitated. "How did she die, Master?"

"She died of old age," he said simply. "Peacefully, in her sleep. My Mingzhu never had the patience to practice the Five Styles of Breathing. She was like a hummingbird, restless and bright." He smiled with sorrow. "Unalike as we were, I loved her very much. Yaozu believed I failed her when I turned away from alchemy and the quest for the elixir of immortality. He begged me to return to it. When I refused, he begged me to teach him. I refused." He drained what was left in his cup. "He never accepted it. Now at last it seems he has found a way to punish me for it, and to punish the world along with me."

"Which is why we must stop him," Bao said pragmatically. "And the first step is to get the princess to White Jade Mountain and free the dragon."

"What's the second step?" I asked.

His eyes glinted. "I am hoping one is all we need. After all, it is a very difficult one. It will reveal the extent of Black Sleeve's betrayal. And you seemed to find the dragon . . . impressive."

I shivered. "Oh, it is."

Both of us looked at Master Lo.

"How can we possibly spirit the princess from the Celestial City itself . . ." Master Lo halted. The sorrow etching his features seemed to ease a measure. "Of course. Moirin's gift."

I nodded. "I do not know how long I can hold the twilight nor how many I can hold within it. To be sure, not enough to conceal us all the way to White Jade Mountain, no longer than a single day at best. But I can hold it long enough to get Snow Tiger out of the Celestial City unseen." A problem occurred to me. "There is the matter of the cage."

"Can you pick locks?" Bao asked hopefully.

"No."

"I could disguise myself as a eunuch," he mused. "Thump her jailor-attendant over the head and steal the key."

Master Lo raised one hand. "We pace ahead of ourselves, children. If we are to attempt this thing, we must be certain the Noble Princess and the dragon desire it alike. And we three alone do not suffice. There must be other guards to accompany us."

Bao gave him a skeptical look. "No disrespect, Master, but I think the Noble Princess can take care of herself."

"Not at the risk of revealing her identity. It will be necessary to travel in disguise." He inclined his head toward Bao. "And I mean no disrespect to your skills, my magpie, but they would be spread too thin. We must have others. Loyal others."

Bao grumbled.

"Mayhap Snow Tiger can help," I suggested. "She said there were warriors loyal to her once. If she is willing to take such a desperate step, surely she has other allies."

"Ask her," my mentor said.

I did.

When Snow Tiger sent for me the next day, she had already heard the news. She was as focused and contained as she could be under the circumstances, although the dragon within her was anxious and restless.

You will help? You WILL help?

"I will help," I assured it. "Look into the mirror and be at peace for a moment. The Noble Princess and I need to speak."

It sighed and obeyed.

Beneath the shimmering veil of twilight, we waited until the dragon was calm, soothed by the hypnotic coiling and uncoiling of its reflection.

Snow Tiger raised her brows in inquiry. "What passes?"

I gazed at her slight, regal figure. Despite her luxurious, embroidered crimson robes, she looked like a weapon, a slender dagger, bright and deadly. "My lady, I must ask this formally. Master Lo Feng's honor demands nothing less. Your father, the Son of Heaven, has resolved that he will not wage war against Lord Jiang. On the day that Jiang Quan's forces assail Shuntian, he will cede the throne and the Mandate of Heaven."

Her shoulders tensed. "Yes. I know."

"Is it your will to defy him?" I asked. "Is it your desire that we find a way to convey you to White Jade Mountain?"

Yes!

"Yes." Snow Tiger's gaze flicked to the mirror, then me. "I would defy my father. It is my will and our desire, Moirin of the Maghuin Dhonn." She took a deep breath. "It is a difficult thing for me to confess. How many times must I say it?"

"I only needed to hear it once more," I assured her. "Master Lo insists that you must have a guard. Are there none left who are loyal to you?"

"No." Her head turned, showing her delicate profile. "None."

I tried not to show my disappointment. "Then we will find others."

Her head swung back to me. "Where?"

"Oh . . ." I shrugged. "Somewhere. Anyway, we must settle the problem of the cage also. I must find a way to free you from it, and obtaining the key will be a tricky matter."

The princess laughed humorlessly. "*This* cage?"

"Aye."

"Come." She rose with that unnerving, boneless grace and crossed the twilit courtyard. I trailed in her wake. Slim fingers grasped the iron bars and pulled.

The bars bent, opening a gap large enough for both of us to pass through.

I gaped.

"The cage is for show," Snow Tiger said to me. "It helps ease my mind, and the minds of those who attend me, although they do not know it. But there is no cage that can contain the dragon, save the cage of my mortal flesh."

Iron screeched as she straightened the bars.

I swallowed hard. "Duly noted, my lady. That eliminates one obstacle."

"Good." Her expression softened briefly. "I'm sorry. It is a hard task I've laid upon you. I wish I had more to offer."

"We will find a way," I assured her with a confidence I didn't feel.

On the heels of my assignation with the princess and the dragon, I reported to Bao and Master Lo Feng. Like me, they were awed at the demonstration of her strength; and like me, they were disappointed to find that the princess had no other allies save us.

"She *must* have a guard!" Master Lo fretted. "Honor and common sense alike demands it!"

Bao was silent a moment. "I can get us men."

"Where?" I asked.

He jerked his chin in the direction of Shuntian's city center. "There are men out there who were loyal to *me* once. All I need to do is challenge their new leader and take over once more."

"Thugs and bullies?" Master Lo asked in horror. "How can you possibly think to trust them?"

Bao laughed. "You trusted me, Master."

"On my own behalf, yes," he observed. "Forgive my candor, but on first acquaintance, I would not have trusted you with the Emperor's daughter, my magpie. And what would happen if you were to lose your challenge?"

"I won't lose," Bao said simply. "And I will treat only with those willing to swear the Thieves' Oath."

"You were a thief, too?" I asked.

He shrugged. "Untrustworthy men must have some way of trusting one another. That is why the Thieves' Oath was created, and it is the one oath none of them will break. To do so involves many, many years of hideous torment in the courts of the Yama Kings," he added. "I can describe it to you if you like."

I shuddered, remembering the Chamber of Ripping Tongues. "Thank you, no."

We went around and around with the matter, but in the end, there were no better options. As highly regarded as he was, Master Lo had spent much of his life in relative solitude. And he was a man of honor—he knew no one he could trust with such an unthinkable breach of propriety.

"They would think I have lost my wits," he mused. "And perhaps I have."

On the following morning, Bao was in surprisingly good spirits as he prepared to set out for the park where the stick-fighters dallied.

"You're not concerned that you'll be tempted to slip back into your old ways?" I asked him.

He shook his head. "We are on a quest to save a princess and a dragon, Moirin. Today I fight for noble reasons." He fiddled with his staff. "Just because these men lead unsavory lives, do not assume they are all bad. Some are, some are not. Many come from harsh childhoods like me. No one has ever offered them something good to fight for."

I was skeptical. "These are the same men who mocked Master Lo when he came seeking a travelling companion?"

"Some," Bao admitted. "It has been years. But Master Lo is not a beautiful princess in need of heroes to rescue her."

"You're counting on there being a hopeless romantic or two in the lot."

He grinned. "Uh-huh."

I eyed him. "I'm going with you."

Bao argued against it, but he didn't argue hard or long, and I thought that despite his bravado, he would be glad to have me there. I fetched my bow and quiver and went with him.

Although the mood in Shuntian was restless and uncertain, people were going about their daily lives. The park was a pleasant place, open for all the folk of the city to enjoy. We passed a square filled with young women practicing a graceful dance with long scarlet ribbons that swirled and trailed in the air, reminding me of the dragon's coils. We passed long pavilions where old men sat and played games with porcelain tiles or polished stones. Our passage drew a few curious glances, but as long as I kept my eyes averted, no one stared.

We heard the clash of stick-fighters sparring before we reached the square they considered their own. There were over twenty of them, laughing and shouting, some engaging in mock duels, others lounging on benches. They were a colorful lot, flaunting their ill-gotten wealth in bright clothing.

At the edge of the square, Bao planted his staff and stood, waiting. Beside him, I unslung my bow, holding it loosely.

A tall fellow with an even taller hat was the first to spot us. "Hey, peasant-boy!" he called. "You come to pick a fight?"

"Uh-huh."

"You've come to the right—" The tall stick-fighter paled. *"Shangun?"*

"Lightning Stick?" I murmured.

Bao gave me a sidelong glance. "I was young and foolish, all right?" He jerked his chin at the tall fellow. "Gaomen! Who leads you these days?"

It had gotten very quiet in the square. All sparring ceased. The men lounging on benches got to their feet, staves in hand, all save one handsome, strapping young fellow. They were staring at Bao—and they were staring at me, which meant I couldn't summon the twilight. I tightened my grip on my bow, calculating how quickly I could draw and nock an arrow.

"Well?" Bao faced the twenty-odd members of his former gang. "Who leads you these days?"

"You've come to challenge?" asked a burly fellow with a sloping chin.

"Tortoise." Bao smiled a little, and I eased my grip on my bow. "Yes." He made a gesture with his staff. "Do I need to prove myself to the new blood? Or do you concede my right to challenge your leader?"

The stick-fighters exchanged murmurs.

The young man yet lounging on the bench rose. The others parted and made way for him. "I will accept the challenge."

Bao inclined his head. "You lead here?"

"You don't know me?" The young man planted his staff and gripped it with white-knuckled intensity, staring at Bao. Alone among the stick-fighters, he hadn't the slightest interest in me.

"Ah . . . no."

"I was the boy you didn't deem worthy of teaching, Shangun," he said grimly. "I was the boy you humiliated and abandoned. But I found other teachers, and I learned until I bested them all. Now I lead in your place." With one deft move, he whipped his staff to a horizontal position. "And I am more than ready to accept your challenge."

Bao looked blankly at him. "You're that boy? And you're *angry* because I didn't bugger your ass?"

The others snickered.

Their leader flushed. "You promised to teach me!" Now he did look at me with a hot, appraising gaze. "I am willing to put my leadership at stake. What will you risk, Shangun? Will you risk the foreign woman? Will you give her to me if I defeat you?"

"You think you're man enough to handle a sorceress?" Bao shook his head. "Boy, she would shrivel your manhood with one glance."

The men regarded me uneasily. I raised my brows and did my best to look capable of executing his threat.

The young man's flush deepened. "We'll see. Are you ready to run away again, or will you stand and fight me?"

Bao shrugged. "I came to fight."

SIXTY-FIVE

The young man attacked without a word of warning, quick as a snake, one end of his staff lashing out at Bao's head.

Bao was quicker, his staff rising to catch it. "Heh."

With that the fight began in earnest. Everyone, me included, scrambled to clear a space for them.

It was brutal and beautiful, like some strange, violent dance. They wielded their staves with two hands, the ends moving so fast it was hard to see. Back and forth across the square they went, bamboo clattering on bamboo. At first glance, I thought mayhap they were evenly matched.

And then Bao planted his staff and vaulted over the younger man's head, just as he'd done to me long ago in the glass pavilion. His opponent spun, but Bao was already in motion. He leapt backward onto the low railing surrounding the square and balanced there with careless grace. The other man swore, lashing out at his legs. Bao hopped just high enough to avoid his blows, sandal-clad feet landing with deft precision. His staff whirled in his hands, tapping his opponent on both shoulders.

A couple of the stick-fighters cheered, others groaned. And one struck Bao hard across the back of his knees from behind.

It was the tall man with the tall hat. Bao yelled and toppled forward, turning his fall into a somersault. He came up with his staff in his hands and eyes blazing, his battle-grin giving way to genuine anger.

I loosed the arrow I'd nocked without thinking. It plucked the embroidered hat from the tall man's head and thunked into a pillar of the distant pavilion behind him, the hat dangling from the shaft. "The next man to interfere gets an arrow in his chest!"

Bao's grin returned. "I told you so," he said cheerfully to the boy he'd refused to teach. "She's dangerous."

The other merely grunted, fighting for survival.

After that it didn't last long. The young leader was good; Bao was better. Somehow he got inside the lad's guard, hooked his ankle with one sandaled foot, and shoved hard with his staff, sending him sprawling to the flagstones. Bao reversed his staff, holding it poised to jab at the other's heart. "Do you concede?"

The lad closed his eyes.

Bao poked him none too gently. "Huh?"

"Yes, Shangun," he murmured. "Yes, all right!"

"Good." Bao planted his staff and extended one hand. After a moment, the lad took it. Bao hauled him to his feet. "You're pretty good. Must have found good teachers. What do you call yourself?"

"Ten Tigers Dai," the other said stiffly.

"Tigers, huh? That's a good omen." Bao patted him on the back, then turned to survey the others. "So. Who's willing to swear loyalty to me on the Thieves' Oath?"

The burly fellow he'd called Tortoise stepped forward, raising one meaty hand. "Me, boss!"

As it transpired, six others agreed, Ten Tigers Dai among them. The tall man with the hat declined.

We retired to a nearby teahouse, where the hostess' eyes lit up at the sight of Bao, although she clasped her hands and bowed formally. "Shangun! We had rumors of your return. I am pleased to find them true. Will you have your old room?"

"Yes, please," he agreed, kissing her cheek and making her giggle and blush. "You are as lovely as ever, Liling."

I raised my brows at him.

"What?" He smiled. "Don't worry, you've no cause for jealousy. No other woman in the world would have shot a man's hat off his head in my defense. I like it when you lose your temper."

I shook my head. "And you call me strange."

Our motley band was ushered into a private room upstairs, where we were served tea and an array of steamed dumplings with a spicy dipping sauce, as well as tiny fish fried up hot and crispy. Once we were alone and the door firmly closed, the seven men swore loyalty to Bao on the Thieves' Oath, replete with gory details that would result from breaking it. He listened to them with eyes half-lidded.

"They speak the truth?" he asked me in D'Angeline.

I shrugged. "How should I know? I've no gift to determine whether or not a man speaks the truth."

"I will tell them you do," he informed me.

He did, and one man paled and left, trembling. It occurred to me that Bao had a considerable gift for theater. The men who remained hung on his words, perishing with curiosity, and none more than Ten Tigers Dai.

"So." Sitting cross-legged, Bao laid his staff across his lap and steepled his fingers. "You have heard the gossip. You have heard the stories. I am here to tell you the truth. Black Sleeve is a traitor. Lord Jiang is a traitor. The Son of Heaven has been tricked. He has *not* lost the Mandate of Heaven. His Noble Daughter has been tricked. It is *not* a demon that possesses her." He paused to let them murmur and speculate, his eyes glinting. "She houses a dragon's spirit within her flesh. And we mean to free them both by conveying her to White Jade Mountain, where the dragon is meant to reside. Men, I offer you an opportunity. Will you be petty thugs and villains all the days of your lives, or will you be heroes and claim a place in an epic tale? May I count upon your aid?"

They roared in agreement.

"Hopeless romantics," I murmured.

"Uh-huh." Bao nudged me. "A lot like you, eh?"

I smiled. "Mayhap."

It took some days to formulate a plan. There were three men willing to participate to the fullest, to risk the wrath of Heaven in escorting the princess to the mountain. Slope-jawed Tortoise, steady and none too bright; and his boon companion Kang, a clever wiry fellow with a narrow, pock-marked face.

And Ten Tigers Dai.

There were three others reluctant to commit to the journey, but willing to give their aid—and that was enough.

Piece by piece, we put together a plan. Our unlikely allies assisted us, gathering the necessary implements of our disguises and making arrangements.

"Are you certain we can trust them?" Snow Tiger mused when I told her of our evolving plan. "These thieves and ruffians?"

"I trust Bao," I said, surprised to find the words true. "And we have little choice."

I trust you.

I smiled at the dragon in the mirror, touching the smooth surface in which its opalescent gaze was reflected. "I will try to be worthy of it."

Snow Tiger was tense, her posture rigid. "The disguise that Master Lo Feng proposes may be a blasphemous one. Those who follow the Path of Dharma will be sorely offended, and perhaps the gods, too."

"Not by you," I assured her. "It is only the men who will take on the guise of travelling monks."

"Still—"

NO. The dragon's coils lashed, curling and uncurling. Its horned and whiskered head surfaced to regard us, its luminous gaze intent and grave. *There is no blasphemy here. There is only need. The balance must be restored.*

"I understand," we said in unison.

"And I will need my sword," Snow Tiger added. "Especially since we will be travelling with ruffians. We must retrieve it before I leave the Celestial City."

I sighed. "Aye, my lady."

"Moirin." She caught my wrist in that unnaturally strong grip, her eyes searching mine. "Forgive me. I question the method, but not the purpose. I will leave a letter for my father detailing my purpose. It is my belief that once we are committed, once I am gone, my father will shake off his doubts and rise to the occasion. He will commit his armies. The Son of Heaven will rise to Lord Jiang's challenge and seek to thwart him."

"I hope you're right," I said. "Because if he delays, Lord Jiang will have enough weapons to conquer all of Ch'in. And once he does so, why should he stop there? Why not conquer the world?"

The dragon reflected in her pupils coiled uneasily. "You voice my fears," Snow Tiger said soberly. "How soon may we go?"

"Send for me in two days."

She nodded. "I shall spend the time composing my letter."

If anyone had suspected what we were about, we'd never have gotten away with it. And twilight or no, if Snow Tiger had not been dragon-possessed, I'd have had no chance of spiriting her out of the Celestial City. Of course, it also wouldn't have been necessary; but if it had been, it would have been impossible. She would have been surrounded by attendants at all time. But she had banished her retinue after her husband's death, and no one had argued against it. The princess in the cage had no attendants save those who came and went as quickly as possible to bring her meals and fresh attire or empty the chamberpot.

And no one suspected us. It was simply too unthinkable. Children did not defy their parents, and ordinary folk did not plot against the Son of Heaven's edict.

Even so, I did not expect it to be easy. Snow Tiger was insistent that we retrieve her sword, and I could not find my way alone through the endless labyrinth of halls and chambers that comprised the Celestial City.

And then there was the outer city, teeming with people. The twilight would conceal us, but it wouldn't remove us from the physical world altogether.

We would have to be very, very careful.

Early in the morning on the appointed day, I bade farewell to Bao and Master Lo. They would depart Shuntian before me and leave a false trail for any pursuers to follow before doubling back in disguise to await us at the designated meeting place, an empty farmstead some leagues southwest of the city.

With great regret, Master Lo Feng had resolved to sacrifice all but three of his Camaeline snowdrops, hanging them to dry in the court-yard we would be abandoning. The remaining three were nestled in a small, tight-lidded porcelain jar. I stored it carefully in the bottom of my satchel.

Bao was unhappy, dark eyes worried. "I do not like leaving you, Moirin."

"I know." I tied my satchel closed. "Nor do I like being left. But Master Lo is well known, and you to be his pupil. You're the ones they'll follow. No one else can leave the trail."

"And I fear no one else can take Moirin's role in this, my magpie," Master Lo added. He had regained his customary serenity, though it was more strained and careworn than before. "We have set this thing in motion. Now we must let ourselves flow with the events as they unfold."

Bao sighed and kissed me, cupping my face in his hands. "Try not to get yourself killed."

My eyes stung. "You, too."

They left.

A few hours later, Snow Tiger's eunuchs came with a palanquin to fetch me. They looked askance at my battered satchel and yew-wood bow, but offered no comment. I was the foreign witch who soothed the dragon, and the Son of Heaven himself had ordered it so. My barbarian ways were a strangeness to be tolerated.

I found the princess wound tighter than a child's top, pacing her encaged quarters. "All is in readiness?" she inquired abruptly.

"Yes." I set down my satchel. "Peace, my lady. Attendants come and go. You must not be seen to be restless in my presence."

She shuddered to a halt, wrapping her arms around herself. "*He* is restless."

I didn't need her to tell me. I could sense the dragon's eagerness, its essence spiraling and cavorting throughout her being. In its excitement at the prospect of home and freedom, its thoughts were an inchoate jumble, vibrant and joyous, with a deluge of images and single spoken refrain.

Home, home, home, home!

"Aye." I smiled at its happiness. "But it is a long and dangerous journey, treasured friend, and nothing is certain. You can help best by remaining calm that the Noble Princess may do the same."

It quieted.

"Thank you." Snow Tiger unwrapped her arms. "Although it wards off his madness, the blindfold is no longer as effective as it was. Ever since you came, I sense his thoughts and presence more clearly. Each day, it grows."

"I'm sorry, my lady."

She shook her head. "Do not be. It is better this way. Better to know it is a being of such beauty and majesty that dwells within me, and not a demon. It is only that he is so very powerful, and he does not know his strength."

I am trying. Insofar as a dragon's voice could sound small, his did.

"He says——"

The princess smiled. "I heard. We are learning, I think, he and I. Will you call your magic, please?"

I did.

While the dragon drifted and dreamed in the mirror, we waited. As was our wont, I released the twilight and Snow Tiger donned her blindfold when a servant came with the midday meal, placing it fearfully on the table and hurrying out, the iron bars clanging shut behind her, a key turning in the lock. I breathed slow and deep and called the twilight back. A musician sat in the courtyard, playing a haunting, plangent melody with a bow on a two-stringed instrument that was unfamiliar to me, notes shimmering in the gloaming light. The Emperor had sought many ways to ensure that his daughter's life was not without pleasure.

Snow Tiger listened, not touching her food. "I hate that I am doing this."

My heart ached for her; and yet I did not think this was the time for kindness and comfort. "You needn't do it. But if it is your will to choose otherwise, tell me now. If it is not, my lady, I suggest you eat. We cannot afford weakness."

She inclined her head and picked up her chopsticks. "As you say."

After we had dispatched our meal of steamed fish in a ginger sauce with rice and crisp slices of lotus root, the servant returned to take away our dishes. Snow Tiger tied her blindfold in place and I banished the twilight. The musician bowed and took her leave.

"Now?" The princess' voice was fierce.

The dragon cavorted in joy. *Now?*

"Now," I agreed, summoning my magic.

It came in a rush, dusk descending for the third time that day. I would need to hold it for a very, very long time. Mindful of the fact, I breathed the Breath of Earth's Pulse, grounding myself.

"Come." Driven by the dragon's excitement, Snow Tiger surged to her feet and extended one hand. "Moirin, now!"

"I am here," I said softly, letting her tug me upright.

In the courtyard, the iron bars of her cage bent and screeched beneath the pressure she exerted on them. I winced, knowing the sound was audible in the physical world. Still, no one came. We slipped through the bars, and then the princess straightened them with no visible effort.

"Your letter—" I began.

"It will be found." She caught my hand once more. "Come! We seek the Armory of Distinguished Blades."

Those are not hours I would wish to relive. The Maghuin Dhonn are a solitary folk. So we have been time out of mind; and my gifts were meant to serve a solitary existence in the wild woods and hills of Alba.

Not this.

Not this cloistered labyrinth of humanity, filled with people hurrying to and fro. Servants, attendants, councilors. Time and time again, I was forced to flatten my back against the crimson walls and let the world surge past us. For the first time in many months, I found myself breathing hard at being confined in a man-made space. Only the discipline of Master Lo's teaching let me keep a grip on the twilight.

"Here!" Snow Tiger darted past a pair of guards into the chamber beyond.

I hurried after her. "My lady, please! Go slowly and do not leave me behind."

She nodded briefly, scanning the room. There were swords in elaborate scabbards displayed on a multitude of tables, each one with an etched stone tablet beside it. One sword was more slender, more delicately wrought than the others, with gilded filigree on the small round guard and a tassel on the hilt.

That was the one the princess seized. She withdrew it a few inches from the scabbard of lacquered wood, gazing at the blade. Shimmering coils were reflected in the steel.

My anxiety was rising. "My lady, we must go."

"Yes." Snow Tiger shoved the blade home. "Follow me."

It felt as though it took hours longer to navigate a path out of the

Celestial City, although I daresay it was less. We eased our way around corners, dashed through brief openings in busy doorways. My heart was pounding the entire time. Again and again, I nearly lost my focus in the midst of a close encounter. When at last we gained the vast outer courtyard, I could have wept with relief.

We had to wait for a procession to exit. I tried to use the time to calm myself, cycling through the Five Styles, but I was growing drained. Not the way I was when I let Raphael channel my gift, not the kind of drained that caused my life force to ebb, but drained nonetheless. I wished I hadn't agreed to help the princess retrieve her sword. I could feel the twilight beginning to waver, hints of color seeping into my dim, shadowy dusk.

"What is it?" Snow Tiger asked in alarm.

"I'm weakening," I murmured. "My lady . . . if they do not open the gates soon, we may have to turn back."

No! The dragon's voice surged in volume, then softened. *I can help.*

The princess shot me an indecipherable glance, but she moved without hesitating, putting one hand on the back of my neck and pulling my head down to kiss me.

I panicked at the first touch of the dragon's energy slithering between my lips, into my mouth, deep inside me. It was too like what the spirit Focalor had done, breathing poor Claire Fourcay's stolen life force into me. I would have pulled away if I could, but Snow Tiger's grip on my neck was as strong as iron. She kissed me relentlessly, and the dragon sent such a surge of fondness and affection into my thoughts that I ceased to struggle and found myself responding instead.

It was like . . . stone and sea! Like my first taste of *joie* multiplied a thousandfold. The dragon's essence was wild and joyous, moonlight over clouds, snow-covered peaks reflected in deep water. Its silvery brightness coiled in my belly, infused my limbs. And it was being gentle, so very gentle, but it was still so unimaginably vast, it made my head spin.

The princess released me abruptly.

I gasped, catching my breath.

Better?

"Aye." I gazed around in wonder. With no conscious effort on my

part, the twilight had deepened. All at once, everything was brighter
and darker, almost as it had been on the far side of the stone door. The
memory made my heart yearn with longing. "Oh!"

"Moirin." Snow Tiger pointed at a formation of soldiers marching
across the square, led by a man on a horse. "Pay heed. They will be
opening the gates soon."

"I see, my lady. I am ready." I was filled with inhuman strength
and energy, so much I could barely contain it, my *diadh-anam* singing
inside me. I couldn't imagine how the princess lived with it day after
day without bursting out of her skin.

And I couldn't imagine how she had ever mistaken it for aught
other than somewhat glorious and majestic.

It was different when I was afraid, the dragon offered. *Very, very
different.*

Snow Tiger glanced at me, then away, still unreadable. I wondered whether I ought to thank her or apologize to her. Once again, I
hadn't the faintest idea. Not even D'Angelines had a protocol for such
circumstances.

She did not find it as distasteful as she pretends. Unlikely as it seemed,
the dragon's tone was smug. *You are very beautiful, and you have an agile
tongue for a human.*

Her back stiffened.

I cleared my throat. "Well, then. Let us fall in behind them, shall
we?"

The massive gates swung open to allow the phalanx of soldiers to
depart. Unseen in the brilliant twilight, the princess and the dragon
and I slipped through the gates in their wake.

The gates closed behind us.

We were free of the Celestial City.

SIXTY-SIX

Snow Tiger and I made our way to the marketplace.

It should have been every bit as terrifying as our escape from the Celestial City, but the dragon's essence yet blazed in my veins, rendering me fearless. This time, I led the way, slipping and twisting through the crowded streets of Shuntian, dodging passersby, feeling stronger and quicker than I ever had in my life.

It was a good feeling.

It ebbed, though. And I felt bereft and drained once more when it did.

I am sorry, the dragon murmured. *I did what I could.*

"You did enough," I assured him.

"Do you know," the princess remarked in a deceptively casual tone. "If the two of you are intent on carrying on this very strange romance, I would rather it be done through someone else's person."

Despite everything, I laughed.

She spared me a glance, rueful humor in her dragon-reflecting eyes. "Are they here? Your ruffians?"

"There." I pointed at a modest single-horse carriage laden with such fabrics and goods as a countrywoman of means might purchase in the markets of Shuntian. Tortoise, Kang, and Ten Tigers Dai were lounging alongside it looking bored.

We hurried across the square, and I leaned in close, willing my voice to carry beyond the twilight. "Tortoise. We're here."

He jumped. "Lady Moirin?"

"Aye, and the Noble Princess," I said softly. All three of them glanced around at the empty air before them, a bit wild-eyed. I sighed. "Remember the plan?"

It took a moment, but they gathered themselves, huddling to block the carriage from view while I plucked out a green silk robe of modest quality for the princess to wrap around her crimson finery and wide-brimmed conical hats with veils for both of us—mine sheer, hers dense and opaque.

"Will it suffice?" I asked the dragon.

For now.

Snow Tiger twisted the crimson scarf in her fingers. "I would feel more certain with the blindfold," she said in a low voice.

"We cannot have a blindfolded young woman seen leaving the city," I reminded her. "And I am losing strength again. Unless you wish to—"

"No." She raised one hand to forestall me. "No, it is a long journey. I must learn to accustom myself to this. It is well. Release your magic and let us depart."

I let the twilight go with regret and relief. Color returned in a rush to the sky above, the broad backs of the stick-fighters shielding us from view. Ten Tigers Dai peeked over his shoulder and turned beet-red at the sight of the veiled princess.

"Noble Princess?" he whispered.

She inclined her head.

"No, no, no!" I paled to see Tortoise and Kang turn with awestruck faces, all three of them preparing to kneel without thinking. "From this moment onward, it is only Lady Chan Song and her maid. You may give her a respectful bow, but you do not kneel to her!"

"Forgive us," Ten Tigers Dai stammered, still red-faced. "It is only . . . it is only that . . . that . . ."

"It is only that we will be late if we do not leave," I said firmly, ushering Snow Tiger into the carriage. "And my lady very much wishes to be home before nightfall. So." I climbed into the carriage beside her. "Let us go."

Kang leapt into the driver's perch and took up the reins, and Tortoise and Dai settled into positions on either side of the carriage.

With that, we were off.

No one looked twice at us as we proceeded through the bustling streets of Shuntian. We were a wholly unremarkable sight. Still, I didn't relax until the guards at the southern gates of the city waved us through with barely a cursory glance.

The road opened before us. Beside me, Snow Tiger shivered—and I realized that for all her courage and strength of will, she was still a young woman leaving behind everything she had known, abandoning all her filial duties to leave home in the company of strangers.

I took her hand in mine, squeezing it gently. She startled, her veiled head swinging in my direction, but she didn't pull away. "My lady, I know how you feel," I said gently. "I have done this twice. The first night on the ship that took me from Alba's shores, I was so scared and lonely that I wept myself to sleep. I think perhaps you are one of the strongest, bravest people I have ever met. But it is all right to be afraid."

The dragon crooned in my thoughts, urging me to offer greater comfort, but I did not think she would accept more than this.

After a moment, the princess squeezed my hand in return. "Thank you."

It was a journey of several hours, but for a mercy, it was a dull one. For the first part of it, Snow Tiger was quiet and withdrawn. I left her in peace, content to gaze out the latticed window at the passing countryside, listening to the sighs of late harvest wheat growing in the fields. I was happy to be out of the city, happy to have the scent of soil and growing things to breathe.

In an hour or so, the princess returned from wherever her thoughts had taken her. "Tell me, Moirin of the Maghuin Dhonn. What is the punishment among your people for defying the Son of Heaven?"

"We have no Emperor," I said.

She made an impatient gesture. "Your king, your ruler."

I shook my head. "The Maghuin Dhonn have no ruler."

Beneath the hem of her veil, Snow Tiger's mouth fell open. "How do you live?" she asked in astonishment. "How?"

"Oh . . ." I shrugged. "We are a solitary folk, preferring to live in the wilderness. If there is a thing to be decided, it will be discussed by the oldest and wisest among us. But I do not think that there have been any great decisions made in my lifetime," I added. "We made a very bad choice a long time ago, and the Maghuin Dhonn Herself punished us for it."

She stirred. "The gifts you spoke of . . . that night. The ability to see the paths of the future, to change shape. Is that how you lost them?"

"Aye, my lady."

"It must have been a very bad choice."

I thought of the green burial mound in Clunderry, the ring of standing stones in the forest. "It was. Would you hear the tale?" She nodded, so I told her the story of the D'Angeline prince and his Alban bride, binding magics, oaths made and broken, the babe who would have grown up to destroy us slain in the womb.

Snow Tiger listened without a word, exhaling softly when I finished. "It is a terrible tale," she mused. "And yet the magicians redeemed themselves in the end. The sacrifices they made saved their people."

I nodded. "That is why we remember them in grief and sorrow, and honor the bitter lesson that their history teaches us."

"Then I will try to do the same." She cocked her head. "Master Lo Feng said you were descended from the royal blood of two lands. How can that be when your mother's people have no ruler?"

"Alba has a ruler." I smiled. "It's just that the Maghuin Dhonn don't exactly acknowledge the Cruarch's sovereignty over us. And since the time of Alais the Wise, the Cruarchs of Alba have been content to leave us alone."

"Then it is your father who is of royal blood?" The princess sounded perplexed. "The father you discovered in Terre d'Ange? I do recall you shouting at me about him."

I flushed, embarrassed at the memory. "No, no. My father is a Priest of Naamah."

She leaned back against the seat. "I am very confused."

"I'm sorry, my lady."

Snow Tiger dismissed my apology with a gesture. "You may as well explain it to me. We have a long journey, and . . ." She paused, her voice taking on a wistful tone. "Despite your peculiar accent, I find I like hearing your stories. No one has told me a story since I was a very small girl."

And so I told her tales for the remainder of the day's journey, spinning out the complicated history of my ancestry, the tale of my parents'
unlikely encounter, my search to find my father in the City of Elua—
although I left out the more uncanny details of my complicated relationship with Raphael de Mereliot and I did not explain how I came to
be Queen Jehanne's companion.

Still, it was enough.

She listened to it all with a sense of mortified wonder. "Are they *all*
so licentious? D'Angelines?"

"They do not reckon it so." I rubbed my face beneath the veil, having talked myself hoarse. "Nor do I. Blessed Elua bade them to love, and
they . . . we . . . do. I have felt Naamah's blessing upon me. I do believe
there is divine purpose in it, my lady." Before she could reply, the carriage came to a halt. I peered out the window. It was dusk, true dusk,
and we were in the rustic courtyard of the abandoned farmstead.

Tortoise rapped on the carriage door, his homely face appearing
in the window, expression uncertain. "Noble . . . ah, Lady Chan? We
have arrived."

"Yes, thank you," I said to him. "Give us a moment."

Two more figures emerged from the farmstead's main lodging, bearing paper lanterns that cast a warm glow—two of Bao's stick-fighters
who would not accompany us on the rest of the journey, but allies and
hopeless romantics nonetheless.

"Is she here?" one called. "Is the Noble Princess here?"

"She's here!" Ten Tigers Dai called in eager reply.

"They should see me as I am," Snow Tiger said decisively, untying
the sash on the oversized green robe and shrugging out of it. "It is the
daughter of the Son of Heaven they have agreed to aid, not this Lady
Chan Song. Is it safe here?"

I peered out the window again. "I think so, yes."

She set aside the veiled hat, closing her eyes tight and tying her
crimson scarf over them. "Then let me meet my unlikely heroes."

They cheered boisterously when she exited the carriage—cheered,
and then fell silent and knelt in awe. I did not blame them. Slender and
upright, crimson-robed and blindfolded, her scabbard clenched in her
right fist, the princess was a picture from a story.

I hoped it would be a happy story.

I watched the men's rapt faces as they fell in love with her, one by one.

"Gentlemen." The princess inclined her head to them, the trailing ends of her blindfold swaying. "I am in your debt," she said simply. "And all I can say is thank you."

They cheered again.

"Moirin." She reached out with her free hand. "Forgive me, but the terrain is unfamiliar."

I settled her hand on my sleeve. "I am here."

SIXTY-SEVEN

Bao and Master Lo were late in arriving.

It was an anxious, uncomfortable time. Everyone was restless and uneasy. The stick-fighters remained awestruck by Snow Tiger's presence, rendered tongue-tied and uncertain, stumbling over themselves.

Despite her regal demeanor, the princess was nervous. I daresay the men couldn't tell, but I'd come to know her well enough that I could; and too, I could sense the restlessness it engendered in the dragon.

Soon? he asked me for the tenth time.

"Soon," I assured him, hoping it was true. What in the name of all the gods we would do if Master Lo and Bao didn't arrive, I couldn't say. The prospect filled me with quiet dread. I did my best to contain it, but as the hours wore onward, I was hard-pressed to maintain a semblance of calm. When at last the door opened to admit them, a cry of relief escaped me.

Beneath the broad brim of a woven straw hat, Bao's eyes gleamed. "Did you think we would not come?"

"I was afraid," I admitted.

He slid one arm around my waist, stroking my hair with his other hand. I pressed my face against his neck, inhaling the faint forge and metal scent of his skin. "I would not let that happen, Moirin."

It was as close as Bao had ever come to a declaration of love. My heart leapt unexpectedly and I glanced up at him. He gave me a faint, wry smile I very much wanted to kiss.

"He does not like that." The princess' voice was stiff. I turned to see her on her feet, her blindfolded face turned toward us. The dragon roiled unhappily inside her. "Not at all."

"Noble Princess—" Bao released me and began to kneel.

"No." She put out one hand. "Do not address me so. I ask only that you restrain yourselves." A little shudder ran though her. "I do not mean to impose on you, but it will make it easier for all of us if you do not disturb him."

"They shall, my lady." Master Lo Feng removed the rough-spun garment he wore over his scholar's robes. He gave Bao and me a warning glance, then swept the room with it to include the other fighters. "All of them shall. We leave this place as monks on the Path of Dharma, sworn to celibacy. From this moment forward, you will view no woman as an object of desire, but as treasured sisters to revere. Is that clear?"

The men mumbled agreement, a couple of them blushing to hear such words spoken in the presence of the princess.

The dragon settled.

"Very good." Master Lo folded his hands in his sleeves. "It is late. I fear we were unavoidably delayed, but all is well."

"The innkeeper's wife had many ailments she wished to discuss with Master Lo," Bao murmured to me. "Many, many ailments. It was a long time before we were able to escape her attention and don our disguises."

"Is my father searching for me?" Snow Tiger asked hesitantly.

"His men follow the trail Bao and I laid for them," Master Lo confirmed. "In the morning, I suspect they will broaden their search. If you would heed my counsel, my lady, I suggest all of us take a few hours of sleep and depart before dawn."

She nodded. "So be it."

The farmstead was a simple, rustic place with only one bedchamber. The princess and I retired to it. Bao appointed himself to guard the door, dozing before it, staff held loosely in his hands. I made myself a pallet of blankets on the floor at the foot of the bed, waiting and watching out of the corner of my eye as the princess paced the room, paused, then tugged decisively at the sash of her crimson robes, undoing jeweled buttons.

"My lady, would you like me to assist—"

"No." Her tone was curt. "I have long since grown accustomed to attending to my own needs."

"I am here to serve you," I said diplomatically. "For whatever reason your gods and mine decree."

"I know." Her voice softened. The bed creaked as she climbed into it, pulling the linens to her chin. "Forgive me. You meant it as a kindness. I do not mean to seem ungrateful. It's just that this is all so very, very strange to me. I find it hard to imagine myself doing such a thing. And yet here I am."

"I know," I echoed. If she had been anyone else, I would have gone to her, offered the simple comfort of a warm, living presence. But she was a princess of Ch'in and the daughter of the Son of Heaven, and I'd already pressed my limit today by taking her hand in the carriage. Instead, I curled up in my bed of blankets, willing sleep to come.

"Have you concluded that you love him?" Her voice drifted down from the darkness above me.

"Bao?"

"Who else?" There was a hint of amusement in it. "You may answer. The dragon sleeps."

"Oh . . ." I sighed into the night, reliving that unexpected moment that had made my heart leap with joy. "Mayhap. I don't know. More, I think, than I reckoned. If I do, it's nothing like the tales I've heard led me to expect."

She sighed, too. "I suspect nothing ever is."

"Your husband," I said softly, daring a different kind of intimacy. "You spoke of him as someone you might have learned to love. Was that not as you expected?"

For a long moment, Snow Tiger was silent, and I thought mayhap I had overstepped my bounds. "I expected my father to choose a warrior," she said at length, her voice almost inaudible. "Jiang Jian was a scholar and a poet, happier with an ink-brush in his hand than a sword. We met several times with attendants present before we wed. To my surprise, I liked him very much. He was kind, polite, and respectful. We spoke of our favorite poems. His intellect challenged me. His passion pleased and inspired me."

"Was he handsome?" I asked. It was a shallow question, but I did not think it would displease her.

"Yes," she whispered in the darkness. "He had the kindest, gentlest eyes, like one who has lived many lives. Perhaps Master Lo Feng looked thusly as a young man. I think . . . I think that because Jiang Jian had a gentle spirit, my father thought him weak. A husband I could control. And . . . perhaps that is also why his own father valued him so lightly. But I did not find him weak. Not at all. I thought he had a keen mind and a calm, quiet strength of his own. And on our wedding night, before what happened . . ." She was silent for another long moment. "I think we would have been well matched in many ways."

The spectre of her memory arose—the blood-soaked bed, torn flesh, and dismembered limbs. I swallowed hard. "I'm so very sorry."

"I know." Snow Tiger stirred. "Moirin, I do not think I can speak of this any longer."

"Aye, my lady," I murmured. "Forgive me for troubling your thoughts. It is late. Let us try to sleep."

Despite everything, we did.

I awoke in the small hours of the morning to a faint scratching at the door and opened it to find Bao looking oddly apologetic, a pair of shears in his hand. In the primary chamber of the farmstead, the transformation of the men of our company into Dharma monks had begun. Already, they had donned the loose, undyed jackets and trousers of a travelling order. Now they turned their attention to their hair. I saw Ten Tigers Dai wince with visible dismay as his braid of glossy black hair was severed at a single chop.

"It's Master Lo," Bao said sheepishly. "I couldn't bring myself to do it. Will you?"

I glanced at our mentor. "Master?"

He sat serenely in his coarse, homespun clothing. "Bao is being foolish. Appearance is no measure of a man. I would be pleased if you would do the honors, Moirin."

"Aye, Master." It did feel like a kind of sacrilege. I knelt behind him, taking his tidy braid of silver-white hair in one hand, the shears in the other. Swallowing hard, I snipped it off.

Master Lo chuckled. "I feel strangely liberated."

I cut his hair as close as I could with the shears, trimmed away his elegant white beard, averting my gaze as I did so. He bore it patiently. Bao handed me a jar of salve and a keen-edged razor with a lacquered handle. Carefully and fearfully, I shaved Master Lo's head and chin until he was as bald as an egg.

When it was done, he looked immeasurably different. The same gentle wisdom shone in his dark eyes, but at a glance, I would never have recognized him.

"My turn." Bao sat cross-legged before me.

I ran one hand over his thick, unruly mane, relishing the crisp texture of it. "Why do you wear it short?" I asked, curious. "Is it another piece of your supposed humility?"

He shook his head. "Better for fighting. You can grab a man by his braid, yank him down. It's stupid for a fighter to have long hair."

I set to work with the shears. "I see. Well, you'll have none at all soon enough." Bao shrugged, and I nearly cut him. "Hold still!"

By the time I had finished shaving Bao's head, the princess had awakened and emerged from the bedchamber of her own accord, clad in the modest green robes of Lady Chan Song, a strip of plain linen bound over her eyes. Her spine was taut and her head turned from side to side, blindly seeking. "Moirin?"

I stood. "Here, my lady. We do but complete the transformation of your escort into monks on the Path of Dharma, shaven heads and all."

She eased, favoring me with a rare smile. "How do they look?"

I smiled in reply. "Surprisingly handsome."

At least in Bao's case, it was true. He had a nicely shaped skull, neat ears pinned close to his head. The absence of hair set off his high, wide cheekbones and his sculpted jawline. If some of the others were not so fortunate, I held my tongue.

"Master Lo Feng." Snow Tiger inclined her head in his general direction. "Is there an altar as I requested?"

"Yes, of course, my lady." Master Lo rose smoothly, guiding her. A small, gilded statue of Sakyamuni had been placed in a niche in the wall, an even smaller statue of the goddess Guanyin beside him. "Would you offer a prayer?"

"I would."

With his assistance, the princess lit a taper of incense and placed it in the brazier. Unaided, she knelt and bowed three times, pressing her brow to the floorboards, hands palm-upward in graceful supplication.

A shiver ran over my skin.

One by one, the others followed. The stick-fighters, Bao, Master Lo, all knelt without reservation. I was the last.

I knelt, gazing upward.

The statues looked inward.

"Forgive me," I whispered in Alban, in my mother tongue. "I am a stranger here, and foreign to your worship. I am a child of the Maghuin Dhonn. But I am doing the best that I may to aid those in need. I beg you to have compassion and guide us on this journey."

There was no answer.

They hear you, the dragon murmured.

"Aye?"

His presence coiled around me, warm and embracing. *Always,* he whispered. *The gods do not always answer, but they are always listening.*

SIXTY-EIGHT

We set out on the road ere dawn.

It was damp and chilly, the eastern sky a dull grey. Snow Tiger and I rode in the rustic carriage, Kang once more in the driver's perch. Master Lo and the others walked on either side of the carriage, ghostly figures in the predawn darkness. The fighters' staves had been adorned with banners from the fictitious House of Chan. Beyond that, they carried only begging bowls.

Beside me, the princess shivered.

"Are you cold, my lady?" I tucked a woolen blanket more firmly around her.

"No." Her voice was low. "It is only that I mislike leaving thusly." She bowed her head, fidgeting with the sword she held across her lap. "It is dishonorable."

I thought about my reply. "Those men have staked their honor on this venture, my lady." I nodded out the window at Tortoise and Dai. "Honor most of them never knew they possessed. Bao gave them a chance to be heroes and they seized it. You cannot see it, but their eyes shine when they look at you. For the first time in their lives, they attempt something noble and good. They are on a mission to rescue a princess and a dragon. Would you strip that honor from them?"

Her fingers drummed on the lacquered scabbard. She angled her veiled head in my direction. "You do know that were circumstances otherwise, I could have you beaten for speaking to me thusly?" she inquired in a mild tone.

I smiled, sensing no genuine malice in her threat. "Were circumstances otherwise, I would not be here," I said calmly. "Which I think you know full well. And that does not make my words any less true."

One corner of her mouth lifted. "Fairly spoken, my necessary inconvenience. I will seek to be worthy of the honor yonder thugs accord me, as well as the venerable Lo Feng and his apprentice."

"Good." I hesitated, lowering my voice. "My lady . . . is it true that Master Lo is a hundred and seventy years old?"

Snow Tiger shook her head. "I cannot say. But my father has known him since he was a boy, and he says Lo Feng was ancient even then."

"I wonder how old Black Sleeve is," I mused. "He had to have been born a very long time ago if his mother died of old age."

"True." She shuddered. "For all that I have pondered the matter, I cannot grasp why a man would do such a thing. Why would he set such terrible events in motion?"

"I don't know," I said slowly, thinking of Raphael de Mereliot. "Some losses cut deep and the wound never heals. He must have loved his mother very much to blame his father for her death. And ambition can be a dreadful force, warping all it touches."

"Like Lord Jiang."

"Yes."

The princess was silent and I held my tongue, knowing she was thinking once more of her wedding night. I had no words to assuage the memory of that blood-soaked horror. "I must believe as you do that there is a greater purpose in this," she said presently. "You are right, to believe elsewise is to invite madness." Her slender fingers caressed the scabbard in her lap. "But there is vengeance, too. I must confess, it would please me very greatly to send Lord Jiang Quan to his death for sacrificing his son to such a fate. Black Sleeve, too."

I didn't doubt her; nor could I blame her. Still, something in her implacable tone made my blood run cold, reminding me that she *had* torn a man apart with her bare hands.

The dragon stirred. *I would never harm you.*

"I frightened you." Snow Tiger turned her veiled face toward me. "Forgive me, I didn't mean to. Tell me . . . tell me something pleasant. Tell me . . ." She paused, rethinking her choice. "Perhaps it would be best not to speak of your fondness for Master Lo Feng's apprentice."

I eyed her. "I think that's wise, my lady."

Beneath the edge of her veil, she smiled. "Tell me more about your licentious D'Angelines. Tell me about this Queen you served. You said she was very beautiful?"

"Oh, aye." I smiled, too. "You might not think so. It is a different kind of beauty than one finds in Ch'in."

"Like you?"

"No." I shook my head. "Jehanne was fair, very fair. Not only her skin, which was as white as milk, but her hair, too. It was the palest hue of gold I'd ever seen. Strong-willed as she was, she looked so very fragile and lovely. And her eyes were blue-grey, like . . . There is a flower, but I don't know its name in your tongue. Only . . . only it wasn't the color, it was the way they shone when she was glad. Like stars."

"Enough to make all the birds in the sky sing at once?" She sounded amused.

I flushed. "You did ask, my lady. I take no comfort in being mocked. Strange though it may seem to you, I did love her very much. And in her own way, my lady Jehanne showed me great kindness."

"I did not intend mockery." Her head tilted, considering. "Nor have I shown you much kindness, have I?"

"Not always," I murmured. "But you have more pressing matters at hand."

"Yes." Snow Tiger paused. Behind her veil, it seemed as though she were frowning in thought. "That does not make it just. I think . . . I think perhaps you are doing your best to be a friend to me, Moirin. If I do not always accept it with grace, it is because I have never had a friend before," she said simply. "Servants, tutors, companions at arms, yes. Never a friend."

My eyes stung. There was no trace of self-pity in her words, but there was an unspoken ache of loneliness. "I will try to be a worthy one if you let me, my lady."

Whatever the princess meant to say was drowned out by the sound of approaching hoofbeats, riders coming hard and swift on the road behind us. Her hand closed on my upper arm, fingertips digging in hard enough to bruise.

I glanced out the window.

Riders—Imperial riders.

Two of them raced past our company, not even deigning to give it a second glance. They were not looking for monks. The third hesitated, drawing rein. His impatient mount danced, the Imperial banner affixed to the back of his saddle fluttering. I took a deep breath, yearning to summon the twilight. Suddenly, our meager disguises seemed foolish and inadequate. All he had to do was bid us lift our veils. My green eyes and the half-D'Angeline cast of my features would give me away in an instant, and Snow Tiger . . . ah, gods. I could sense the dragon within her beginning to panic at the prospect. I feared it would end in blood, a great deal of it.

It seemed impossible that he would not suspect us.

And yet he didn't.

The rider's gaze skated over us, quickly dismissing the contents of the carriage. Two veiled country women in modest attire, one clutching the other. It was quite simply beyond his ability to imagine that the daughter of the Son of Heaven would ever lower herself to travel thusly.

"Honored Brother!" he shouted at Master Lo. "Have you heard the news? His Celestial Majesty's daughter has vanished. Have you seen aught to report?"

"I have not." Master Lo raised his begging bowl with serene composure. "Alms for a pilgrim's blessing?"

Coins rattled into his bowl. "Wish us luck!"

Master Lo bowed. "Of course."

The rider heeled his mount and raced onward. The dragon's alarm ceased to rise. Snow Tiger released her death-grip on my arm. I rubbed it, wincing. "He looked right past us, didn't he?" she marveled. "We were right here, and he looked right past us!"

"So he did," I agreed, dizzy with relief.

"How very curious," she said thoughtfully. "I was not entirely convinced this plan of yours would work. But not expecting to see me thus, the courier was quite thoroughly incapable of doing so. It is a lesson to remember. If I am ever to serve . . ." Her voice trailed off.

"Has Ch'in ever been ruled by a woman?" I asked.

"Oh, yes." It brought her faint smile back. "Yes—and no. There have been a number of powerful women who have risen to rule in deed, if not in name. But until my father, no Emperor has ever dared appoint a female child his heir."

"It is a brave and honorable thing his Celestial Majesty does," I offered.

The princess' head tilted into her considering pose. "There is one benefit to your frequent insolence," she commented. "When you tell me something I wish to hear, I have no doubt that you are speaking your mind in truth. Perhaps that is a hallmark of friendship I must learn to value."

I laughed.

Snow Tiger leaned against the backrest of the carriage, and I had the sense that she had closed her eyes behind her thick veil. "Tell me another story, Moirin. Tell me tales of your shapeshifting bear folk and your scandalous D'Angelines."

Clearing my throat, I obliged.

In hushed tones, I told her tales my mother had told me when I was a child, tales of how the Maghuin Dhonn crossed the world when it was covered with ice, claiming fair Alba for our own. I told her how we had welcomed and taught the folk that had arrived after us, and how they had repaid our kindness with tribute, until the Tiberians came with hard steel, stone roads, and foreign diseases. I told her the tale of the mighty magician Donnchadh, who had taken on the shape of the Great Bear Herself and suffered himself to be tormented for sport at the hands of invaders, until he burst loose his chains in the arena and climbed the stands to slay the Tiberian governor.

She liked that story.

I told her the most glorious and scandalous tale of Terre d'Ange that I knew, the tale of Phèdre nó Delaunay de Montrève, the courtesan-spy who rose from obscurity to save her nation from invasion and insurrection, and the warrior-priest Joscelin Verreuil who was her companion.

Morning wore into day while I spoke, and day into early evening. Three more times, Imperial couriers passed us by, dashing to and fro on the road. None of them paid us any heed. By the time we halted for the night, I'd talked myself hoarse once more, and I'd ceased to flinch at the sight of the Emperor's insignia.

Bao poked his head in the window. "We're going to make camp. Is that all right, my lady?"

The princess inclined her head. "It is."

"Moirin?" His voice softened. "Is all well?"

I raised my veil and smiled at him, resisting the urge to rub his stubbled scalp. "Aye. And with you?"

He grinned. "Ten Tigers Dai is complaining of blisters, being unaccustomed to walking for any length of time, especially in sandals. Tortoise's belly is growling with hunger because he is unaccustomed to going without food for more than two hours. Both of them are angry that Kang is skilled at driving the carriage. Master Lo and I are fine." He raised his begging bowl, jingling it. His dark eyes gleamed beneath strongly etched brows. "Got some alms, too. Pretty good plan, huh?"

"Pretty good," I agreed. We smiled foolishly at one another until the dragon rumbled in my thoughts and the princess stirred uneasily. I raised my eyebrows at him and jerked my chin in a significant manner, and Bao withdrew in haste.

"He's a *bit* like a warrior-priest, I suppose," Snow Tiger said dubiously. "At least in guise."

Tired, I stifled a yawn. "Only in guise, my lady. In other ways, Bao is quite impossible. I have no idea why I like him so."

"And yet you do," she observed.

"True."

With permission from a nearby farmstead, we made camp under a stand of pine trees. The farmer's wife, shy and blushing, brought a tray of steamed dumplings out to us. I watched Master Lo charm her effortlessly while Bao instructed the others in the manner of setting up the cunningly crafted tent of oiled silk and bamboo we'd brought to shelter the princess. The men would sleep in the open like the humble monks they pretended to be.

I heard the farmer's wife inquire tentatively after the purpose of our journey and tensed as Master Lo began to explain that the Lady Chan Song was on a pilgrimage to offer prayers to a very famous effigy of Guanyin in the south—Guanyin of a Thousand Eyes, who had appeared to Lady Chan in a dream and promised to cure the blindness that afflicted her. We had concocted the tale to justify our general destination and explain the impenetrable veil the princess wore, but hearing it told to a stranger for the first time, it sounded a feeble lie to my ears.

But once again, my fear was mislaid. The farmer's wife merely nodded in understanding. Casting a sympathetic glance in Snow Tiger's direction, she whispered a promise to pray for her. With that, she left us.

Despite the initial success of our venture, it was a relief to be away from prying eyes. I removed my hat and veil, breathing deeply of the pine-scented air and listening to their vibrant, healthy thoughts. The princess removed her hat, too, tying the blindfold she preferred in place. Master Lo sat in quiet contemplation while the younger men argued over the best way to prepare our meal.

"I have cooked for Master Lo ten thousand times!" Bao's tone was aggrieved. "I know how he likes his meals!"

"It is not only Master Lo Feng we cook for tonight, Shangun," Tortoise said in a placating manner. "You use too much ginger root, too much garlic. It is too much yang for the Noble . . . for Lady Chan. My father was a cook. I know."

"He's right, Shangun," Ten Tigers Dai said mildly. "Less garlic, more bean curd."

I stole a glance at Snow Tiger and found her smiling. "Do I hear your hardened thugs quarrelling over the best way to prepare my dinner?" she inquired.

"You do, my lady."

"How very strange my life has become." For the first time, she sounded more bemused than disturbed by the notion.

Whether or not the balance of yin and yang in the resulting dish of noodles and broth was a harmonious one, I couldn't have said, but it was good. It made me laugh to see the hungry stick-fighters looking surreptitiously at the princess, waiting for her approval before eating. To her credit, she was gracious with them. Bit by bit, they began to ease in her presence.

Afterward, they indulged in a bout of sparring. It seemed strange to me that monks travelling a path toward enlightenment would engage in such a violent practice, but Master Lo assured me that it was not uncommon.

"It is a useful method for focusing mind and body and spirit." His eyes twinkled. "I think you do not come from a meditative folk, Moirin."

"Not in the way you have taught me," I agreed. "And yet . . ." I thought about my childhood, filled with endless days of solitude and wilderness, and the simple pleasure it had brought me. "The Maghuin Dhonn live very close to nature, Master. In a way, it is a kind of meditation unto itself."

Master Lo inclined his head. "I do not speak against your truth. Many of the greatest sages of the Way have found wisdom and enlightenment in returning to a lifestyle your people never left."

Listening to the sounds of staves clattering, the princess fingered her sheathed blade and looked wistful. "Would that I could take part in their practice."

"Can you fight without eyes to see?" Master Lo asked. She nodded. "Then why not?" He glanced around. "Dusk comes soon. Beyond this copse, the trees block the view from the farmhouse. The roads and fields are empty. There is no one to see."

Her blindfolded face turned toward him. "Are you certain?"

"Of course." He raised his voice. "Bao! I have a task for you, my magpie!" He waited while Bao left off coaching Dai and came over. "The princess wishes to spar."

Bao pursed his lips, glancing at her. "Is that wise, my lady?"

Her hands shifted on the scabbard, gripping it as though it were a short staff. "I will not draw steel." A bright edge crept into her voice. "Are you afraid?"

He began to scoff, turning it into a circumspect cough instead. "On the one hand, I am concerned that the glorious and celestial entity whose spirit is housed within you does not wish me well." His tone took on a smooth answering edge. "And on the other hand, if the dragon restrains himself, I fear I might injure you, since your sight is compromised."

Snow Tiger *did* scoff. It seemed insolence in fighters was a thing to be tolerated. "As for the latter, I assure you, there is no need to fear. As to the former . . . Moirin? Will you speak to the dragon?"

I sighed. "You're not to harm Bao. Let her highness fight her own fight. This is only for sport, for play. Do you understand?"

Yes. The dragon sounded offended. *I am not foolish. I know he is an ally. It is only that I do not like the way he looks at you. She needs you much more than he does.*

Whether or not the princess heard him, I declined to translate the last part. "He says he understands."

With dusk beginning to fall over the recently harvested field, Snow Tiger paced off a rectangle on the far side of the pine trees, marking the corners with a thrust of her scabbard. "These are the dimensions of my living quarters," she said to Bao. "I know them well. Remain within them and I promise there will be no question of compromise."

He bowed, bringing his staff to a horizontal position. "As my lady wishes."

I'd caught a glimpse of the potential grace and beauty inherent in the sport when Bao fought Dai.

This was on another level altogether.

To be sure, they were unevenly matched. With her dragon-possessed strength, the princess could have shattered Bao's longer staff with a single full-force blow. But nor had she reckoned on his acrobatic skill. Quick and precise though she was, he could easily have taken greater advantage than he did of her sightlessness.

Back and forth they went, weapons a blur, the resulting clatter faster and more staccato than I'd ever heard. Within seconds, Bao's battle-grin had emerged. He pressed her hard, vaulting effortlessly over her and letting her know with an impudent tap he *could* strike her from behind if he wanted. Snow Tiger didn't smile, but her expression took on a fierce brightness that echoed his. Her green robes flared as she whirled and spun, glowing an unearthly emerald in the fading sun. She pressed him, too. When they locked staff and scabbard, she pushed hard enough to let him know she could break it.

The other stick-fighters gathered to watch in awe.

In an odd way, I was jealous, reminded of the feeling I'd had watching Raphael and Jehanne together after I'd bedded them both. At the same time, it made me happy to see them both so glad.

My life, too, was passing strange.

By mutual accord, they left off, both breathing hard. Snow Tiger inclined her blindfolded head to Bao. "You are skilled indeed. Thank you."

He bowed. "It was an honor, my lady."

SIXTY-NINE

Thus began the pattern of our days on the road.

Imperial couriers raced to and fro, passing us coming and going. Betimes they stopped to make inquiries of Master Lo or one of the others; betimes they passed us without a flicker of interest. Impossibly and consistently, they paid not the slightest heed to the veiled Lady Chan Song and her veiled maidservant. Merchants and other travellers paused to exchange gossip, and betimes offer alms in exchange for blessings.

None of them were interested in Lady Chan and her maid, either.

During the day, I endured the carriage and did my best to entertain the princess with tales. Our company begged and bartered for food, making camp on the outskirts of friendly farmsteads. In the evenings, the stick-fighters honed their skills, the blindfolded princess sparring among them.

They warmed to her.

It wasn't that their sense of awe at her presence among us was diminished, but it thawed considerably, turning into a complex mix that encompassed admiration, pride, and a possessive protectiveness.

Of me, they remained wary.

Betimes, it frustrated me. *"Why?"* I demanded of Bao. I gestured at the princess, who was talking with a tongue-tied but delighted Ten Tigers Dai. "Truly, am *I* more unnerving than *her*?"

"Yes." His hand slid down my spine to settle in the small of my back, pulling me to him, my hips pressing against his. It felt good. I acceded willingly, gazing up at his face. "Moirin, if we succeed, the princess and the dragon will be parted. He will be free in all his celestial glory. She will be human once more—the daughter of the Son of Heaven, yes, but a woman of Ch'in nonetheless." His lips brushed mine, defying the customary prohibition against such public displays. "You will still be you. A witch, and a foreigner."

"Which doesn't seem to bother *you*," I commented.

"I may have exaggerated your perils," Bao admitted. "But it is better for your safety that the others remain fearful of your reputation." His eyes glinted with amusement. "Are you angry?"

"Yes." I kissed him. "No. Maybe."

The dragon rumbled.

Master Lo Feng cleared his throat.

With reluctance, Bao let me go. "When this is over—"

"When it is over we will talk," I said firmly. "About this and fat babies and many other things. Assuming we live through it."

"There is always that," he agreed. "And hopefully we will do much more than talk."

A week into our journey, the mood of the Imperial couriers who hurtled past us on the road changed. No longer did they pause to ask questions, and a new pennant flew from the standards affixed to their saddles beneath the Imperial insignia: a crimson banner.

The first time one passed, a wave of cries trailed in its wake. Beside me, the princess tensed. "What is it?"

I shook my head. "I've no idea, my lady."

"War!" Bao's face appeared in the window, exultant. "His Celestial Majesty's riders are flying the red banner of war!"

"He's done it," Snow Tiger breathed. A ripple of relief ran through her; for a moment, she buried her veiled face in her hands. "Ah, gods be thanked! Mayhap there is a greater purpose in this."

"It must have been a powerful letter you left for him," I said.

"Yes."

I thought she would say more, but she didn't, not then. Not until later, long after we had made camp for the night, long after the simple supper and sparring, when she and I had retired to our tent of oiled silk. I was nearly asleep when her voice floated in the darkness, hushed and disembodied.

"I said many things in the letter I wrote," the princess whispered. "I begged my father to put his faith in his bravery and wisdom, not his doubts. I assured him that he had *not* lost the Mandate of Heaven, that he could lose it only through inaction. I told him that this was the battle he was born to fight, the battle of a lifetime, ten lifetimes. And . . ."

"Aye?" I propped myself on one arm.

"I said that *I* would fight it if he did not," she murmured. "That once the dragon and I were freed from the curse Black Sleeve laid upon us, I would raise an army to confront Lord Jiang and his vile sorcerer. And that if my Noble Father had failed to stand by me, I would consider myself an orphan and the rightful heir to the Mandate of Heaven."

I caught my breath, aware of exactly how grave an offense this was for a dutiful Ch'in princess. "A dire threat, my lady."

"Yes." A rueful note crept into her voice. "But a necessary one. They tell me my mother was unafraid to cross him at times, and he loved her better for it. It seems there is a certain fondness for insolence in our lineage."

I reached out one hand in the darkness between our pallets. "I'm sorry. I cannot imagine how difficult it was for you to do such a thing."

She squeezed my hand in gratitude, then let go. "Thank you. If you would do me a kindness, I would ask you never to speak of it to anyone."

"Of course," I promised readily. "Your trust honors me."

"It is strange," Snow Tiger mused. "What you once shouted at me is true. There is great value in having a loyal listening ear into which to whisper one's troubles. Perhaps I begin to understand your D'Angeline customs better. Perhaps I am not so different from your Queen as I thought."

The dragon stirred, a hopeful thought beginning to form. *If you are not so different—*

"Nor so alike, either," the princess added hastily. "It is friendship of which I speak, nothing more."

I smiled in the darkness, knowing she couldn't see me. "I do not think people are so different, my lady. It is only that in Terre d'Ange, the expression of desire in all its forms is sacred, so long as it is offered freely. They worship aspects of pleasure some peoples deny or reckon unsuitable. But they are not the only nation to celebrate the act of love." I paused. "Do not the Ch'in have manuals on the arts of the bedchamber? Bao told me as much."

"Oh, yes." Her voice turned wistful. "If my mother had lived, she would have presented me with such a book before my wedding night. None of my father's other wives saw fit to do a mother's duty."

"A pity." Although it was on the tip of my tongue to offer her whatever instruction she might desire, I managed to swallow the words. I did not want to spoil the moment. "From what you told me before, it sounds as though you and Jiang Jian would have managed without it."

"Yes." She was silent a moment. "But I would find it difficult to trust myself in such a way again. At least of my own will."

The dragon didn't speak, but the tenor of its thoughts was chastened.

"One day you will find a way, my lady," I assured her. "I do not doubt it."

Whether or not Snow Tiger believed me, I could not say; but she had begun to allow herself to trust me and accept my friendship. It was enough.

Now all the gossip that passed along the road was of war. Rumor ran rampant from every quarter. Imperial troops were said to be on the march, recalled from duty elsewhere. It was said that they meant to sail into Guangzho and strike at the heart of Lord Jiang's forces; it was speculated that Lord Jiang would move his army to the outskirts of Ludong and begin by taking that city.

Then it changed. Then it was rumored that Lord Jiang's army was withdrawing to the south, that the mere threat of war with the Imperial army had them in retreat.

I didn't believe it.

Nor did Master Lo. "They will have heard the rumors, too, my lady," he said to the princess. "Including the tale of your disappearance."

Her head tilted. "So?"

We were arrayed around a makeshift map etched in the loose soil of yet another harvested field. Master Lo's elegant hands sculpted a mountain in the southern provinces. "My son is not a fool. It may be that he and Jiang Quan have crafted enough of their terrible weapons to defeat any army your Noble Father raises. I cannot say. And yet there remains one battle they dare not lose." He guided her hand to the mounded soil. "White Jade Mountain."

Home! The dragon's voice soared.

Kneeling, the princess was very still, listening.

"My son and Lord Jiang know we are coming, my lady," Master Lo said gently. "They know that I am here, and that we have puzzled out the nature of their deed. Although I counseled against it, your father tipped our hand. If we succeed in freeing you from this curse, it does not matter how many battles they win, how many weapons they possess, how many men they command. We will set loose a dragon in all its glory. If we succeed, the truth will be known, and ten thousand times a thousand hands will be raised against them. No one will take up arms against you. No one will man their terrible weapons. That loss, they cannot afford. Therefore, they will make a stand where it matters most."

"Here." Despite her blindfold, Snow Tiger's hand moved unerringly, drawing a line in the dirt. "In the pastures surrounding White Jade Mountain."

He bowed his shaven head. "Even so."

Her head returned to its considering pose. "Can we hope to outpace either army?"

Glances were exchanged, heads shaken.

"No," I said aloud for her benefit. "It seems we cannot, my lady."

Home, the dragon repeated, a poignant ache in his voice. *Oh, home!* I yearned to comfort him. Her. Them. I couldn't help it.

"Home." The princess echoed the word. Her hand clenched into a fist. "So be it." She inclined her head, neat and precise. "Thank you, Venerable One. If your words be true, and I do not doubt their wisdom, it seems your son has chosen the battlefield." Her smile was tight and hard. "Let us bring the battle to them."

SEVENTY

We took to the river.

For my part, it was a relief, a blessed relief.

Our carriage was a less stifling affair than D'Angeline carriages, but it was still an uncomfortable way to travel. I preferred being in the open air, not jounced and battered along the road.

In a large fishing village, Bao and Dai scoured the waterfront until they found an entrepreneurial merchant willing to trade a boat called a *sampan* for the horse and carriage. It was a good-sized boat for its kind, long and low, with a midsection covered by an awning of tightly woven fronds.

Still, it was small enough that it dipped noticeably under each person's weight as we stepped aboard. I got the princess settled comfortably under the awning, then eyed Bao as he took up a post at the long rudder pole. Suddenly, the boat seemed more precarious and the current swifter. "Are you sure you know how to steer this?"

He grinned at me. "Of course. I am Master Lo Feng's magpie. I can do whatever he requires."

"Right now, he finds it needful that his magpie be more discreet, Younger Brother," Master Lo said mildly.

Bao sighed, chastened. "Yes, Honored Brother."

Once we were under way, any fears vanished. For all his boastful streak, Bao never boasted in vain; he was skilled at the rudder. He swung the boat into the center of the river, letting the swift current take us. When Kang took to the oars, the little boat moved at an even livelier pace, much faster than we'd been travelling in the carriage, constrained by the foot-speed of our unlikely attendants. The scent of the river and the chilly breeze against my face made me smile, happier than I had been since our journey began.

The dragon was happy, too.

"He likes being on water," Snow Tiger commented.

Yes. I wish I could see, he added.

"So do I," she murmured, touching her thick veil. "So do I."

I glanced around. No one was watching, and the awning concealed us from the casual view of outsiders. "Why not?" I hadn't summoned the twilight since we'd left Shuntian. Given the effectiveness of our simple disguises, it hadn't been necessary. The princess had not asked it of me; nor had the dragon, eager to be helpful. It hadn't occurred to me that both must be longing for it in different ways. I took a deep breath and called the twilight, wrapping it around both of us. The sky dimmed, the river turned silvery, the green slopes leading down to it turned a soft heather-grey.

Ten Tigers Dai let out a sudden shout of alarm. "Where—"

"Here," I murmured, letting him hear me. "It's all right, be quiet. The lady and the dragon wish to see, and I am helping them."

He stared through me, pale with fear. "Ah . . . all right."

The princess removed her hat and veil, her dragon-reflecting eyes meeting mine. "It *is* all right, Dai. I promise. Tell the others."

He eased. "As you say, my lady."

The river? Please?

"Yes." Beneath the awning, Snow Tiger leaned over the edge of the narrow boat, gazing at the moving waters. The dragon sighed with pleasure. She beckoned to me. Kneeling beside her, I watched the reflection of dragon's pearlescent coils undulate with the flowing current alongside our boat, eeling through the reeds.

His happiness was like a song, a caroling chorus of gratitude running through it. *Thank you, thank you, thank you!*

"Of course," I said softly. "I am sorry I did not offer before. You have only to ask, treasured friend."

The princess dipped her fingertips into the water, letting them trail just below the surface. The dragon's reflection rippled and wavered. I sensed his delighted reaction, like an immensely vast and impossibly glorious dog having his belly rubbed.

"Despite everything, I will miss him," she said in a low voice. "Now that I know what he is. Now that I *know* him. Does that shock you?"

I shook my head. "I will miss him, too."

"It is not the same."

"No, of course not." All too well, I remembered that quicksilver energy surging through my veins in the Celestial City when the dragon had poured a measure of his essence into me through her kiss. Like a storm in my blood, wild and joyous. "No, it is not, my lady. And yet I will miss him nonetheless."

"And he, you." She withdrew her hand from the water, letting it rest briefly on my shoulder. "Betimes I wonder, Moirin of the Maghuin Dhonn. Bear-worshipping witch, child of desire. The unlikely confluence of deities that begot you flung you into the world to work their will without guidance. Tell me, where does it end? With this greater purpose you perceive? Are you a minor character in my tale, or am I a lesser figure in yours?"

"I don't know, my lady," I murmured. "I suppose it depends on who is telling the tale."

The princess contemplated me. The dragon's doubly reflected image swam in her black pupils, coiling and uncoiling endlessly. "I suppose it does."

Since it made the stick-fighters nervous, I didn't hold the twilight long, only long enough to soothe the dragon. The men whispered and murmured at our reappearance. Bao smirked at them. I wondered what further lies he'd told them about me. I wondered, too, whether he'd done it to protect me, or simply to aggrandize his own reputation.

Both, likely.

Although it should have bothered me, it didn't. Now that I knew him, Bao's cheerful arrogance, so at odds with the humility he tried to cultivate, couldn't disguise the fact that he was loyal and fearless, not to mention a hopeless romantic at heart.

What the future held for us, the gods alone knew.

I watched the river unfurl like a ribbon before our boat, green and unending, and thought about what the princess had said. It was not entirely true that the unlikely confluence of deities who begot me had given me no guidance. My *diadh-anam* flickered steadily within me, a divine compass telling me that I was where I was meant to be, no matter how very, very far from home.

Of course, I'd been sure it was telling me I was meant to be with Raphael, too.

It had seemed so right. The unlikely collision of our meeting, his unhesitating acceptance of me, the way our gifts intertwined. Stone and sea, I'd been *so* sure! And I'd been so, so very wrong. The destiny that the Maghuin Dhonn Herself laid on me, Naamah's gift, Anael's gift, Master Lo's teaching . . .

I didn't understand what it all meant.

Patience. The dragon's voice rumbled through my thoughts, tinged with a profound fondness and amusement only an immortal creature could muster. *You are very young. Live. Learn. Love.*

Startled out of my reverie, I smiled. "I am trying."

He poured an immense surge of affection into me. *You are doing well. Remember, the journey is more important than the destination.*

"Old Nemed said the same thing," I said aloud.

Yes. You would do well to remember the wise-woman when the time comes.

"What do you mean?" My voice rose. "What do you *know*?" The dragon fell silent, his thoughts turning misty and vague as they did when he dreamed and drifted. With the exception of the veiled princess, everyone on the boat stared at me. I cleared my throat. "Ah . . . forgive me. It is only that the dragon said something unexpected, and now he will not tell me what it means."

"It may be that he cannot," Master Lo said philosophically. "He is a celestial being, Moirin. Like sages, they speak in riddles."

"Why?" I demanded. "It's very irritating!"

His eyes twinkled. "Sages do so to instruct, to prod the lazy mind into thought. I suspect dragons have their own rules."

Yes. The dragon surfaced to agree. *Such as forgiving the follies that budding sages committed in their youth.*

That, I declined to translate.

"Speaking of lazy minds . . ." Master Lo glanced around the boat. "Many sages claim the journey and the destination are one and the same. Perhaps, with the Lady Chan's gracious permission, we might use this time to examine Sakyamuni's teachings and the search for enlightenment undertaken by those on the Path of Dharma, and how it compares to the path of those following the Way?" He stroked his shorn chin. "It seems fitting."

Snow Tiger inclined her head. "Of course, Venerable One."

SEVENTY-ONE

I learned a great deal during our time on the river. Most of all, I learned that I was unsuited for following the Path of Dharma.

"These are the Four Noble Truths taught by Sakyamuni, the Enlightened One," Master Lo said in his tranquil voice. "To live is to suffer. The origin of suffering is desire. It is possible to cease suffering. To do so one must walk the Path of Dharma, shedding all mortal attachments."

I squirmed.

He bent his gaze on me. "You disagree, Moirin?"

"It is not what you taught me, Master," I said, temporizing. "You said all ways lead to the Way."

"So I did." He folded his hands in his lap. "And this is one way among many. I do not claim to be what I pretend in guise, and yet I have some knowledge of the matter. Are you so wise that you will reject it at a glance? Or will you listen and hear?"

I sighed. "I will listen, of course."

I liked the tale of the Bhodistani prince whose father had kept him so sheltered that for many long years, he did not know that such things as sickness, age, and death existed. At the same time, I thought he took the revelation overly hard. Surely, I thought, not all of life was suffering.

"You find it hard to grasp because you are a foreigner," the princess observed.

I eyed her, uncertain whether or not she was teasing me. "Mayhap it is because I love the world and many people and things in it, my lady."

Master Lo raised one finger. "Ah, but what if the followers of the Enlightened One are right, and the world is but an illusion? Then your love is equally illusory, and the attachments you form to illusions prevent you from perceiving the truth."

Betimes he made my head ache.

But I liked listening to him, and it was a relief to be spared the sole burden of entertaining the princess. The young men talked endlessly while they took turns at the oars, mulling over the ideas Master Lo fed them. Not Bao, who had long been his pupil, but the others. I could almost hear their brains stretching. No one had ever spoken to them as though they were worth teaching before.

I thought, too—although some of my thoughts I kept to myself. I thought a great deal about desire, being constrained not to express any for the first time in my young life. I found it surprisingly difficult. It wasn't a question of celibacy; even if our guises and the dragon's jealousy hadn't made that necessary, our quarters on the boat rendered it a moot point. It frustrated me to have my fledgling relationship with Bao forced into an impasse where neither of us could speak openly of our feelings, but I could accept it for the duration of our quest. What bothered me most was being denied almost the whole spectrum of physical affection.

That, I hated.

I yearned for it, yearned to touch and be touched with an ache that was no less real than thirst or hunger.

I thought about Naamah, the bright lady.

Jehanne had told me that each House of the Night Court held that Naamah had given herself as she did for different reasons. Now, with naught to do but listen and think and watch the river flow, I thought mayhap it was simply in her nature. She *was* desire. She could no more keep from giving herself over to it, whether it was the carnal desire to take a lover or the innocent desire to caress a child's soft cheek, than the sun could stop from shining or the rain from falling.

And if Master Lo was right and all ways led to the Way, the path of desire was as valid as any other.

One day, I said so.

It made the stick-fighters snicker self-consciously, although Bao didn't. The princess turned her head away slightly, as though to suggest the topic was of no interest to her. Master Lo was intrigued.

"How so?" he inquired.

I fidgeted, uncertain how to articulate my half-formed thoughts. "There is an element of surrender in it, Master. Of giving oneself over to a greater force. If it is done with the kind of mindfulness you describe in the practice of the Path of Dharma, if it is done with love and compassion . . . well, then. On the greatship, you said perhaps the gods of Terre d'Ange were capable of using desire to lead their children to wisdom and harmony. Might it not also lead to a greater form of enlightenment?"

To my surprise, he understood. "You speak of one such as your father."

"Yes, exactly!"

"Indeed." Master Lo nodded. "Having met one who treads it, I think we may infer that such a path exists." He studied me. "Do you think it is yours to follow?"

I flushed. "I don't know. I am only thinking about it because of your teaching, and because of . . . other things I am thinking about."

"I am pleased to find any pupil of mine thinking." He glanced at the princess, her expression unreadable behind the veil. "Though perhaps it would be best if we confined our discussion to the topic of more traditional paths. Although one might argue it is the least of my worries, I do not think his Celestial Majesty would be pleased to find this conversation taking place in his daughter's presence amid such mixed company."

As the days wore onward, we began to see more traffic on the river. Ships flying the Imperial banner—not greatships, but very large ships—carrying hundreds and hundreds of soldiers passed us, making the princess and the dragon restless.

"Our progress is too slow," she fretted.

"You knew we could not outpace them," Master Lo reminded her. "Do you wish to take the risk of revealing yourself and seeking their escort?"

She hesitated, then shook her head. "No. No, I dare not."

"Then we continue."

We passed into territory nominally under the control of Lord Jiang's forces, now abandoned as they withdrew to make their stand at White Jade Mountain. Many of the towns had been plundered for supplies and left lawless. The Emperor's well-stocked ships sailed serenely past. Carrying as few stores as we did, we didn't have that luxury. When we put ashore, it grew harder and harder to buy food, let alone beg for it.

The farther we went, the worse it got.

We tried to shelter the princess from the knowledge, but it was impossible. Although she and I stayed prudently close to the boat whenever we moored at a village, guarded by at least two of the stick-fighters, Snow Tiger was keenly observant. Even without sight, she could hear the rising tenor of anger the farther south we travelled, voices in the marketplaces taking on a hard, desperate edge.

It troubled her.

In one town, a riot broke out. We beat a hasty retreat, begging bowls and food-sacks empty. Back on the river, the princess was silent and withdrawn.

"What you are witnessing is the face of war a great ruler seldom sees, my lady," Master Lo Feng said to her. Her veiled face turned his way, listening. "No matter how righteous the cause, no matter who wins, the commonfolk suffer. Without plenty, the wealthy lack compassion for the poor, hoarding without sharing. Without law, the strong bully the weak, stealing by force. People will go hungry. Some will starve. Men and women will be forced to choose between feeding their parents and their children."

"You did not counsel against this war," she said in a low voice.

Master Lo inclined his head. "Only because I believed it too late to be averted. If there had been a better way, I would have counseled it. Since you are here, I would have you understand what war truly entails. It is a lesson few rulers are given to grasp."

"I think it is also a reason that followers of the Path of Dharma believe that to live is to suffer," Ten Tigers Dai murmured unexpectedly. "For many of us, it is—or at least it has been."

The others, including Bao, nodded.

The princess' back straightened as she squared her shoulders firmly. "Then it is a lesson I will take to heart."

Gods know, it was true. Two days later, we moored overnight at a village reputed to have a functioning market. Tortoise and Kang rose before dawn to stake out a place in the square, awaiting the arrival of the farmers with goods to sell. The rest of us lingered near the boat.

I was eying fish swimming in the shallow edges of the river, thinking that I could easily summon the twilight and catch a few given a discreet opportunity, when Tortoise and Kang came hurrying back with half-filled sacks over their shoulders.

"Another riot!" Tortoise called out, huffing as he ran. Complicated emotions flitted over his homely face. "They're taking everything. Stick-fighters, wouldn't you know?"

Bao swore in a distinctly un-monkish fashion and began untying the mooring line. "Time to go!"

"No." Snow Tiger fingered her sword. "We will confront them."

He gaped at her. "Are you crazy?"

She tilted her veiled head. "Are you afraid?"

"Heh." His battle-grin appeared. He dropped the rope and seized his staff. "No."

Ten Tigers Dai whooped.

"Noble Princess—" Master Lo began.

It was too late; not even his calm wisdom could dissuade her. And the dragon within her was exuberant, happy with any course of action. In a daze, I watched her set out for the square, swift and unerring despite her inability to see, flanked by Bao and Dai; then I shook myself and swore, scrambling aboard the boat to retrieve my bow and quiver.

The boat, loosed from its mooring, began to drift.

"Oh, gods bedamned!" I caught the line in one hand and splashed through the shallows, towing it back to shore, holding my bow high with the other hand so as not to wet the string. "Tortoise! Tie it up! Kang, come on!"

We ran.

It was mayhem in the market square; mayhem with a small, slender figure in green robes and a veiled hat at the center of it. On either side of the princess, Bao and Dai leapt and whirled and fought, staves a blur. A dozen stick-fighters were arrayed against them—and losing.

Everywhere else, folk cowered. Farmers come to sell rice and chickens and cabbages huddled over their wares. Folk come to buy or barter retreated to cringe along the outskirts of the square.

Kang plunged into the fray, battling a path to our allies, assaulting their assailants from behind. I followed in his wake, bow in hand and arrow nocked, identifying targets should it be needful. But by the time we reached the princess, it was over.

The beaten stick-fighters groaned.

Snow Tiger stood very still before the farmers, listening to the murmurs arise. We arrayed ourselves around her; but it was *her* at whom the commonfolk stared.

And me.

I realized my hat had blown off along the way, revealing my half-D'Angeline features and green eyes. They knew. They knew who we were.

I kept an arrow nocked.

"My people." Snow Tiger's voice was crisp. "We are in a time of war. This is a hardship you suffer. Lord Jiang claims to command here, but he has left you bereft. In the name of my father, his Imperial Majesty, the Son of Heaven, I bid you to endure this hardship with kindness and compassion. I bid you to aid one another. Let the wealthy have charity for the poor. Let the strong have mercy on the weak. And I promise, if we are victorious, such a time shall never come again." Holding her sword at eye level, she unsheathed the weapon that had remained in its scabbard during the entire fight. Naked steel flashed in the sunlight. "This, I swear to you on my blade. Will you heed me?"

In awed silence, they knelt to her—every man, woman, and child in the square, kneeling and pressing their brows to the ground.

"Well," I said to no one in particular. "*This* complicates matters."

SEVENTY-TWO

We cannot stay on the river much longer," Master Lo said ruefully. "There is one thing that flies swifter than any hawk, and that is rumor."

"I did but act on the lesson you taught me," the princess murmured. "Perhaps I misunderstood?"

He sighed. "No, my lady. You understood it all too well. But in dangerous times, noble impulse must be tempered with caution."

She accepted the rebuke with a graceful nod. "What is your counsel?"

Master Lo stroked his chin. "We must strike out over land. The monastery temple that houses Guanyin of a Thousand Eyes and many other famous carvings is not far from here. If he is still alive, the abbot is a man I knew well, once. It is one reason I chose to invoke the place as our destination. He will conceal our trail from any seekers."

Snow Tiger tilted her head. "Then let us go there."

It sounded simple.

It wasn't.

The Ch'in folk do build temples in their cities, many of them. But the ones they love best, the ones that are most sacred to them, they build in the highest, most remote places one can find.

This was such a one.

The following morning, in a towering gorge where the cliffs rose sheer around us, Master Lo pointed to a tiny landing. Bao steered the boat expertly toward it. There, we climbed out of the unsteady vessel and unloaded our meager possessions.

Tortoise eyed the narrow track that stitched its way up the steep cliff face and sighed with profound misgivings. *"There?"*

"Uh-huh." Bao tossed him a half-empty sack of rice, then cut the boat loose to drift. "Master Lo and the lady say climb, we climb."

We climbed.

How far, I could not say. I had no head for reckoning distances, save in terms of the time it took to traverse them. It took us a day to climb the face of the cliff. But the distance was the least of it. It was the growing height and the precariousness of the path that made the journey a terrifying one.

At the halfway point, my legs began to tremble. Below us, the green ribbon of the river dwindled and shrank. I dared not look down lest the drop make me dizzy.

Be strong, the dragon whispered in my thoughts. *I will not let anything harm you.*

Once, my foot slipped. Pebbles bounced and scrabbled down the face of the cliff. Unbalanced, I teetered. The princess' hand shot out to close around my wrist, hard enough to leave a bracelet of bruises, anchoring me.

I will not let anything harm you, the dragon repeated.

I swallowed hard and breathed the Breath of Earth's Pulse, finding my center of balance. "Thank you."

She nodded.

Bit by bit, we labored up the cliff face. At the top, I would have been content to fling myself to the earth and rest forever; and I daresay some of the others would, too, especially Tortoise.

But no.

Master Lo Feng pointed. "There is the path to the monastery."

I stared, too awestruck for words. The steep path led to a gorge lined with the most colossal carvings I'd ever seen, enormous effigies of Sakyamuni and his followers and myriad other deities carved into the living rock of the mountain. Even at a distance, I could tell they were at least ten times life size.

"How . . ." Words failed me. "How . . . Who did this, Master?"

"It is the work of many, many hands over the span of centuries," he said calmly. "Followers of the Way, followers of the Path of Dharma. Come, let us see if my old friend Abbot Hong remains with us."

As we made our way down, I couldn't stop staring. The scale of the carvings was just so immense, the labor required so unimaginably vast. Serene faces taller than I was gazed tranquilly into the gorge. It was a relief to me to see that Bao and the others seemed no less impressed than I was, goggling at the looming figures and exclaiming at the imposing sight in hushed tones.

"I should like to see it," the princess said wistfully. The dragon echoed the thought.

"You shall," I promised. "Only I do not think now is a good time."

"No."

Luck favored us. Master Lo's old friend the abbot was alive and well. Fetched by a pair of very startled acolytes, he hobbled out to meet us, leaning on a gnarled cane. The abbot took the measure of our company in a single keen glance. Although he was bent and wizened with age, beneath his wrinkled lids his eyes sparkled with inner joy and a lively wit. Even if I had not known, I would have guessed in a heartbeat that he and Master Lo were friends of long standing and considerable mutual respect.

"Lo Feng Tzu," Abbot Hong said in a thin, reedy voice. "You have been gone a very long time. Where is your braid and your beard? I scarce know you!"

Master Lo smiled and bowed. "I have borrowed your guise, old friend, and brought you a dilemma."

"So you have, so you have." The abbot inclined his bent back in the direction of the veiled princess. "Even here, I have heard rumors of your disappearance. Be welcome, Noble Princess."

She bowed in return. "Thank you, Revered Brother."

In the plain, rustic chambers of a building with tip-tilted roofs perched atop the gorge, we shared our food, dined, and took counsel with Abbot Hong. For being the head of a monastery in such a remote place, he was surprisingly well-informed about the doings of both Lord Jiang's forces and the Imperial army, warning us that while the Imperial army was gathering in mass, Lord Jiang had left scattered companies of men behind to hunt for us.

Tired as I was, I let the conversation wash over me. Knowing nothing of the terrain, I let them make their plans. Acolytes on the Path of
Dharma came and went in simple brown robes, bringing full dishes,
carrying away empty ones. Some of them looked askance at us; some
didn't.

"Forgive me, old friend." The abbot's voice was apologetic. "But
I must ask before I pledge myself to speak untruths on your behalf.
Rumor held the princess was demon-plagued. This business of a
dragon . . . Are you very, very sure?"

Snow Tiger's shoulders tightened.

I roused.

"Yes." Master Lo's voice was firm. "I am. I violated the sanctity of
White Jade Mountain and stole the dragon's pearl. I cannot undo the
folly of my youth, but I recognize its handiwork."

"But you have not *seen* it . . . ?" the abbot persisted.

Now, please, the dragon whispered. *Now. You must show them.*

I breathed the Breath of Trees Growing, breathed it in, breathed
it out. It was easy here. The ancient trees that grew on the mountainside aided me. I summoned the twilight. No one was looking at me. I
breathed it in, taking it deep inside me, and breathed it out, flinging it
like a cloak around the princess and me, bathing us both in dusk.

Someone uttered a short, startled cry.

"Come, my lady." I rose and extended my hand. She took it. "Master Lo, will you please ask the abbot to follow?"

I led her along the paths of the gorge. Master Lo and the abbot and
the others trailed behind us, curious and uncertain. Somewhere, there
was the sound of chanting, steady and sonorous. The sun was setting,
bathing the immense carvings with their serene faces in golden light.
Removing her veiled hat, Snow Tiger gazed at them in awe.

"Here." I tugged her into a recessed grotto, where the gilded figure
of Guanyin resided. Her inward-looking face was filled with compassion. She sat cross-legged and held a thousand arms upraised, a seeing
eye embedded in each gilded palm.

In every palm, the dragon was reflected.

Oh . . . he sighed. *Oh!*

The others crowded behind us. I breathed slowly and deeply through the cycle of the Five Styles, reaching deeper into the twilight. This was a holy place, sanctified by centuries of prayer. I spun the cloak into a net, cast it over the entire grotto.

They saw.

A thousand pearlescent dragons coiled and uncoiled in a thousand gilded palms, in every gilded curve, beautiful and celestial and unmistakable. There was a soft sound, the sudden intake of every watcher's breath.

I was too tired to hold the twilight for long, even in this place. I warned the princess, and she donned her hat. The dragon murmured in disappointment as I released the twilight. Everyone blinked as the golden light of the setting sun returned in a rush and the images of the dragon's reflection vanished.

"I see." Abbot Hong bowed to me. "A doubting man might claim that this is merely an illusion worked by barbarian magic. I am not a doubting man. If the gods allowed you to work falsehood in this place, I have spent my life in vain."

All I wanted to do was lie down and sleep, but I bowed in return. "Thank you, Revered Brother."

The abbot turned to Master Lo. "I will aid you in any way I can."

SEVENTY-THREE

I passed the night sleeping on a mat in a humble cell, waking to the sound of chanting. It would not be an unpleasant way to live, spending one's life in prayer and contemplation, surrounded by such beauty. I thought about the three Camaeline snowdrop bulbs nestled in a jar at the bottom of my satchel, and wondered if they would thrive here in the mountains. It seemed a fitting place for them.

No, the dragon said. *It is not high enough, not cold enough. You will plant them in the snows of White Jade Mountain, and I will watch over them always, remembering you.*

There was a poignant note in his tone that made my heart ache. "I pray you're right, treasured friend."

So do I. His tone brightened. *Today is a good day for hope!*

I smiled. "So it is."

Indeed, it felt like it. There wasn't much the abbot could do to aid us, but what aid he could give, he gave unstintingly. Our meager stores had been replenished, and we were armed with knowledge of several companies of Lord Jiang's men laying in wait for us. After the princess had revealed herself in the marketplace, that knowledge was more valuable than gold. We had the abbot's promise not to reveal our passage. The sun was shining and I was well rested.

It was a good day for hope.

After we broke our fast, the abbot himself and a score of his monks escorted us down the gorge. At every step of the way, I marveled at the continuous carvings. On one plateau, there was an effigy of Sakyamuni reclining that was so immense, it dwarfed all the others.

Bao laughed at my enthusiasm. "Maybe you'll decide to follow the Path of Dharma after all, huh?"

"Oh, I haven't abandoned the notion of the Path of Desire," I assured him.

"Good to know." He caressed the back of my neck. "I'm looking forward to our changing guises, so I no longer have to pretend to be a celibate monk. It is difficult thinking of you as—" He froze.

"What?"

"There." Bao pointed. Ahead of us, a swaying bridge spanned the gorge. On the far side, the descending path continued around a curve. "Men's shadows, moving." His voice sharpened. "Stop! Everyone stop!"

We halted.

It didn't take long for them to reveal themselves. Ten warriors and one anxious-looking young monk came around the curve. One of the warriors carried Lord Jiang's standard, the white dragon coiling on a background of blue.

The rest carried bows, arrows nocked and aimed.

"No!" Abbot Hong cried out in anguish, spreading his hands as though to ward off an attack. "Oh, my son, what have you done? No, no, no! This is all a misunderstanding. You must not do this thing."

"Tell that to young lord Jiang Jian, torn apart on his wedding night," one of Jiang's men said grimly. He gestured with the tip of his arrow. "Move aside, Revered Brother. We do not want to spill blood in this place, especially yours."

"I will not," the abbot said with calm dignity. As one, his acolytes spread out before us, forming a wall of robed, shaven figures.

"What is it?" the princess asked in a low voice. "Who, and how many? What arms?"

"Jiang's men." I felt sick. "One of the monks betrayed us. He must . . . he must have left before we showed the dragon to the abbot."

"Ten men," Bao added grimly, hands flexing on his staff. "Swords and bows. They were lying in ambush. They have arrows trained on us, my lady."

"Are we trapped?"

I glanced up the path behind us. Our only avenue of retreat would leave us utterly exposed. "Aye."

The dragon keened in alarm, panic and fury beginning to rise.

"*Move!*" the leader of Jiang's men shouted, gesturing violently. "I mean business, Brother! I do not want to shed your blood, but I will. Stand aside and give us the demon-princess!"

The abbot didn't budge. "Please, listen. Through no fault of your own, you have been deceived. You have—"

Without a word, the leader loosed his bow with a sharp twang. The monk standing to the right of Abbot Hong clutched his side and crumpled, a bloodstained arrowhead protruding from his robes. None of the others so much as flinched. On the far side of the gorge, the young monk who had betrayed us covered his face with his hands, his fingers trembling. The leader nocked another arrow.

"*Enough!*" Snow Tiger's voice echoed off the mountainside, high and fierce. She pushed effortlessly past the line of monks. "I killed Jiang Jian. It is me that you want, is it not?" She gestured behind her. "All of them, they are innocent. This is a sacred place. If I come willingly, will you promise to spill no further blood here?"

The leader hesitated. "I will."

"He lies," Bao muttered.

I thought so, too. "My lady, please!" I whispered urgently. "Do not listen, do not trust him—"

"Hush." She turned back to me, put her hand over my lips. "The time for caution is past. This may be hardest of all on you, my necessary inconvenience. I have no choice but to unleash the dragon. You will have to reach him, call him back from the abyss of madness. Can you do that for us?"

My eyes stung. "I will try."

"Good." She turned to Abbot Hong and bowed, hand over fist. "Revered Brother, I beg your forgiveness for what I am about to do here."

He bowed in reply. "You did not bring this on yourself in this lifetime, Noble Princess. I forgive you."

With obvious reluctance, the abbot and the monks stood aside to make way for her. Master Lo Feng, his face unwontedly pale, bent to attend to the injured monk.

Beside me, Bao quivered with fury. I could sense the other stick-fighters doing the same.

At the near end of the bridge, Snow Tiger untied the sash that bound her robes and freed her sheathed sword. She held it up for display, then stooped and laid it gently on the ground. Lord Jiang's leader grunted and beckoned with his arrow tip.

Hatted and veiled, she stepped onto the bridge.

It swayed under her slight weight. Her hands reached out to grasp the thick rope cables. Step by step, her head bowed, the princess traversed the gorge.

I held my breath.

Ah, gods! She didn't look dangerous—she didn't look dangerous at all. Despite knowing who she was and what she had done, the leader of Lord Jiang's men smiled with relief and lowered his bow, sure of his victory. His men followed suit, chuckling a little. Showing them her empty hands, the princess raised her veil and gazed into the leader's eyes.

And the dragon went mad.

It couldn't help it—*couldn't* help it. It owed nothing to logic. It was a celestial being that beheld its reflection; that was its nature. Without its reflection, the dragon was undone and severed from itself. It was already in a state of near-panic. Seeing its absence reflected in the man's pupils, fear and madness came upon it. It roared like a storm in my mind, its unleashed fury pouring through the princess, filling her with its preternatural strength. Snow Tiger seized the arrow from the bow that Lord Jiang's leader held, plunging it into his throat in one deft jab. Arterial blood sprayed the beautiful carvings as she yanked it free, whirling on her next victim, casting her veiled hat aside.

"Go!" Bao chanted, suiting actions to words and launching himself toward the bridge. "Go, go, go!"

Jiang's men were plunged into chaos, forced to fight at close quarters. Two of them had the presence of mind to peel away, taking aim at the oncoming stick-fighters. Bao planted his staff and vaulted; the others zigged and zagged behind him, trying to make themselves difficult targets. I snatched an arrow from my quiver, willing my hands not to tremble. The yew-wood bow my uncle Mabon had made for me sang, and one of the archers went down, the haft of my arrow protruding from the socket of his left eye.

I swallowed against a violent surge of nausea and nocked another arrow, but it was too late. The battle was too confused, too chaotic.

And there at the center, a slender figure in green, only this time, her robes were streaked with blood. She had an arrow in each hand now, spinning and striking, wielding them as gracefully as a dancer, dealing out death with every blow.

It was intense and brutal, and quickly over—at least for Lord Jiang's men.

Not for the dragon.

Kang was down, injured. Tortoise knelt beside him. Bao and Dai stood protectively before them, staves still in a defensive pose. Behind them all, the young monk cowered against the cliff wall.

Mindless with the full force of the dragon's fury, the princess turned on them.

"Oh gods," I whispered, and began to run.

"Moirin, no!" Bao shouted, doing his best to hold her at bay. But she was right, I had to try. No one else could reach the dragon. And I couldn't summon the twilight, not with so many eyes on me.

I reached them just as she seized the end of Bao's staff and shoved, sending him hurtling backward. His head struck the carved rock with a sickening thud, and she began to turn toward Ten Tigers Dai.

I flung myself between them.

Her eyes met mine in the blood-streaked mask of her face. They were stretched wide and glittering, filled with an inhuman fury, and I no longer had the slightest question in my mind about why everyone had believed a demon possessed her.

In an act of sheer faith, I squeezed my eyes shut and reached out to the maelstrom of rage within her. "You promised!" I cried, willing him to hear. Blindly, I reached out with one hand, covering her eyes. "You promised you would never harm me!"

I could feel her quivering beneath my touch, quivering like an overtight bowstring ready to snap.

But it didn't.

"I am here," I said softly—to her, to the dragon. "Peace. Be gentle."

Bit by bit, the storm of the dragon's fury lessened. I sensed it recognize me, sensed it know itself once more. I felt that terrible, terrible tension drain from Snow Tiger's body in a profound shudder as the dragon released her.

"Thank you." Her voice was faint.

Yes. Thank you.

I nodded, daring to open my eyes. All around us, there was carnage. Beneath my hand, her blood-streaked face was only a girl's, grave and lovely. Filled with fear, I swallowed against another surge of nausea. "You're welcome. Now let us find you a blindfold, my lady. Let us see how badly Kang is injured and if Bao's head is as hard as I pray it is."

She shuddered again, a different shudder. "I pray so, too."

SEVENTY-FOUR

As it transpired, Bao's head was very hard.

"I'm fine!" he said in an aggrieved tone when Master Lo ordered him confined to a day's bed-rest. "I can travel."

I poked his chest, hard. There were no words sufficient to express my profound relief at finding him alive. "You're *not* fine. And no one is travelling today."

He eyed me. "Stupid girl. Always flinging yourself into danger. You could have gotten yourself killed, you know. Moirin, are you *crying*?"

"Aye, a little. So?" I rubbed my stinging eyes, then leaned down to give Bao a long, lingering kiss, not caring if it defied custom or roused the dragon's ire. "You were in more danger than I was, stupid boy," I murmured against his lips. "And we may count ourselves very, very lucky that none of us were killed."

Lying on his back, Bao lifted one hand to tug gently at my hair, winding it around his fingers. "I hate seeing you in danger," he whispered in reply. "But you have a point. I am glad to be alive to argue with you."

It was true. On the whole, we had been fortunate in unfortunate circumstances. No vital organs had been pierced in the monk shot by Lord Jiang's archer, and Master Lo gauged that he would make a full recovery in time. Kang had sustained a deep sword-cut on his right thigh. It was severe enough that he would not be continuing onward, but Master Lo judged that so long as it did not take septic, Kang too, would recover. Bao had a nasty lump on the back of his skull, and an irascible attitude.

I was relieved and glad.

Glad for him, glad for me.

And glad, perhaps most of all, for the princess and the dragon. She had taken this risk deliberately. If she had hurt him badly, she would have a hard time forgiving herself.

In the aftermath of battle, she was quiet and withdrawn. Once I left Bao's side, I managed to get her into the bathing hut. Moving stiffly and painfully, she didn't protest when I helped her out of her blood-soaked robes.

"Are you injured?" There was so much blood on her, I couldn't tell if any of it was hers. "You should have said something! My lady, please don't punish yourself."

"I'm not injured." She sank into the tub. Sponge in hand, I eyed her doubtfully. "I hurt. Everywhere." She leaned her head against the rim of the tub. Even her hair was clotted with blood. "Mortal flesh was never meant to channel that much force."

I felt like an idiot. I'd not considered the physical toll such inhuman exertion would exact on her. "Of course." I dipped the sponge and squeezed it over her skin, beginning the long process of washing away the blood. "I'll ask Master Lo for a tonic for the pain."

The fact that she didn't argue against it gave me an idea of just how badly it hurt.

I am sorry.

"Do not be." The princess pressed her hands over her blindfolded face. There was blood under her nails, too. "You cannot control it. And if it were not for you, we would all be dead. I am grateful."

It took a while, but I got her washed and dressed in clean robes, then went to find Master Lo. He and Abbot Hong were interviewing Brother Liu, the young monk who had betrayed us. I waited until they had finished, torn between anger at the monk's impetuous deed and sympathy for his genuine remorse.

Master Lo looked as weary as I'd ever seen him when he emerged. "Moirin. How is her highness?"

"In pain." I told him of her suffering.

He nodded. "I'll prepare willow-bark tea for her." He sighed, running a hand over his white-stubbled scalp. "It may be that there is a windfall in these unfortunate events. The young brother reports that Lord Jiang's men tethered their mounts and made camp at the base of the mountain. Abbot Hong is sending acolytes to secure it. So." He glanced down the path of the gorge, where robed monks were quietly gathering the dead and scrubbing blood from the beautiful carved walls. "We will have horses. And we will have new guises if we can stomach them."

I swallowed. "You mean for us to dress in the dead men's garb?"

His expression turned gentle. "Not you, nor her highness. But yes. Bao and I and the others will appear to be Lord Jiang's men, escorting you as our prisoners. It will allow us to travel far more swiftly and freely."

"I see." I was glad I wouldn't have to wear the clothing of a man I'd seen violently slain.

Master Lo put one hand on my shoulder. "Despite Bao's chiding, what you did today was very brave, Moirin. It is clear that the dragon's regard for you is not based on your gifts alone. You have a valiant heart."

"Oh . . ." I flushed at his praise. "Thank you, Master."

He gave me a weary smile. "I wanted you to know that it did not go unnoticed. I am fortunate to have such a pupil, and the princess to have such a . . ." He paused, at a loss for the proper term.

"She calls me her necessary inconvenience," I offered.

"Does she?" His smile deepened briefly, less weary, more genuine. "Well, her Noble Highness is fortunate to have you."

In the middle of the night, when Snow Tiger's restlessness woke me, I thought of his words. I lay on my narrow mat listening to her toss and turn, then rise to sit with her head bowed against her knees, shivering violently.

I pitched my voice softly into the darkness. "Would you like more willow-bark tea, my lady?"

"No. I'm sorry. I didn't mean to wake you." Her head lifted, turning in my direction. "Go to sleep."

Instead, I rose and did what I had wanted to do many times when fear troubled her in the night. I went to her, knelt behind her, and put my arms around her. The princess stiffened, but only for an instant, and she didn't pull away. Slowly, slowly, her tense figure relaxed into my embrace. Remembering the night Jehanne had come to me for comfort after her last assignation with Raphael, I held her and breathed the Breath of Ocean's Rolling Waves, deep and rhythmic and soothing, until her breathing slowed to match mine unwittingly.

"It's the blood," she murmured at length. "All that blood."

I had seen the memory of her wedding night. "I know."

After a time, I shifted to a more comfortable position. Snow Tiger lay curled against me, my arm over her slender waist, the fingers of one hand interlaced with mine. With one arm flung over her, I felt her exhausted, aching body loosen gradually into sleep.

Comforted by the contact, I slept, too.

In the morning, I woke before her. I extricated myself gently, knowing that daylight hours were different from night hours. Despite the blindfold, the princess looked sweet and peaceful in sleep, her features almost as delicate as a child's. I thought about cleaning the blood from beneath her fingernails in the bath yesterday and shook my head, wondering at how very, very far from home I'd come, and how very strange the journey.

To be sure, no D'Angeline had ever served as a royal companion in such a violent, bloody manner.

She needs you, the dragon said sleepily. I *need you.*

"I know." Knowing I wouldn't have the chance to do it when she was awake, I stooped to kiss her cheek. "And I am here."

This time, our descent into the gorge was uneventful. Abbot Hong and his acolytes had ensured that the path was clear.

I felt bad at leaving Kang behind; I daresay we all did. But he had lost enough blood to render him weak and pale, and his wounded thigh rendered him unfit for travel. He gazed at the blindfolded princess from his sickbed, his narrow, pock-marked features transfigured by awe into something beautiful.

"You won't forget me, will you?" he begged. "Promise you won't forget me!"

She knelt beside his mat, clasping his hands in hers. "Noble companion, I swear I will never forget you."

He sighed, happy.

I caught Bao's eye. He looked rapt, hopeless romantic that he was. Seeing my gaze on him, he coughed and flushed, trying to hide it.

"Stupid boy," I said fondly, sliding my arms around his neck. "You've a lump the size of a goose-egg on the back of your skull, and you look a little sickly. Are you sure you're fit for travel?"

"Uh-huh." His hands descended to my buttocks. "Want me to prove it?"

I did, actually.

Snow Tiger stiffened and the dragon rumbled. I loosed Bao. "Later, yes."

He eyed the princess. "Yes. Later."

SEVENTY-FIVE

We found the camp as promised. After travelling so simply, it was a luxury to have mounts to spare, pack-horses, and ample supplies. It was strange, though, to see the men in fish-scaled armor, their shaved heads hidden under pointed helmets. I'd grown accustomed to seeing them as monks.

Snow Tiger bade farewell to Abbot Hong and his acolytes, thanking them for their aid and apologizing for the trouble we had brought upon them.

"The fault is not yours," he said kindly. "And it was one of my own who brought the trouble to our doorstep. I have seen a dragon reflected in the hands of Guanyin herself. It is a thing to remember. For the sake of the Celestial Empire, I will pray for your success, Noble Princess."

She bowed. "And I for your health, Revered Brother."

His bright gaze shifted to me, so youthful in that wizened face. "Master Lo's most unusual pupil. You seemed taken with this place. If ever you have the chance to return, I would be pleased to speak with you, and to learn more of your people, too." His reedy voice took on a puzzled tone. "Is it true you worship a *bear*?"

I smiled. "Yes. But She is not any mortal bear. If I have the chance, I would be honored to speak with you, Revered Brother."

As soon as our farewells were said, we set out.

One unforeseen difficulty arose immediately; neither Tortoise nor Ten Tigers Dai had ever been astride a horse. Neither of them looked anything remotely like warriors, sliding and jouncing, clutching des-

perately at their saddles. Despite his aching head, Bao laughed until
tears came to his eyes.

"It is not funny, Shangun!" Dai's face was red with anger and hu-
miliation. "You were nothing but a peasant-boy once, too! If you had
not been wandering the world with Master Lo, when would you have
learned to ride a horse?"

"My cursed rapist of a father was a Tatar," Bao said with far better humor than the statement deserved. "If nothing else, I come from
horse-riding stock. I am quite certain I did not bounce in the saddle
like a sack of cabbages my first time."

Dai gritted his teeth. "You need not mock me. I swallowed a great
deal of pride to serve under you on this quest."

Tortoise merely grunted, concentrating too hard to quarrel.

"I suggest that you ignore Master Lo's rude apprentice," the princess
said mildly. Everyone fell silent, chastened. A faint smile curved her
lips. "Perhaps the blow to the head has addled his wits. And I suggest
that we have a brief lesson in horsemanship, since it is inconceivable
that *I* would have been taken prisoner by men who ride like sacks of
cabbage. The first thing you must learn is to grip the horse's barrel with
your thighs."

They listened and learned.

I watched them practice riding at a walk, then a trot, then a canter,
stroking my mount's withers as it seized the chance to graze. Snow
Tiger was a good teacher, patient and firm, borrowing Bao's eyes to
gauge their progress. I could imagine her as a child, her delicate face
set and grave, absorbing hours of instruction, drilling on foot and on
horseback, learning to handle all manner of edged weapons, while I
had been wandering the Alban wilderness with my mother, learning
to summon the twilight, harvest greens, and catch fish with my bare
hands.

Strange, indeed.

By the time we passed through the first village, Tortoise and Dai
had grown comfortable enough in the saddle that their inexpert seats
didn't give us away. Although the village was little more than a humble
collection of farmsteads, it was the first test of our new guises and I
tensed as we passed through and folk in the fields lifted their heads

to stare at the small party of Lord Jiang's soldiers with the blindfolded princess and me in their midst.

"Is it true?" an elderly woman called to them. "Have you captured the daughter of the Son of Heaven?"

"It's true, Old Mother!" Bao called back to her. "The demon-princess herself, and the foreign witch, too! We're escorting them to Lord Jiang!"

There were murmurs in our wake, but they didn't sound doubtful. I relaxed.

I shouldn't have.

We made camp that night some distance beyond the village. Instead of sparring against their staves, Snow Tiger instructed the stick-fighters in the proper handling of their newly acquired swords, a different skill altogether.

"It has no reach," Bao complained. "A good stick-fighter can beat a swordsman any day."

"You need to at least *look* capable," the princess said in a calm tone.

He acquiesced, grumbling.

We retired when dusk began to fall, the men drawing straws to determine the order of standing guard, since that would be expected in a company of soldiers escorting prisoners. Tortoise drew first watch. The others were grateful to have a tent and blankets to share—even, I daresay, Master Lo.

Although she hadn't evinced signs of pain during the day, once Snow Tiger and I had retired to our own tent, her movements stiffened. Once again, she didn't protest when I helped her disrobe, only winced.

"It is still very painful?" I asked, keeping my voice low so that Tortoise, posted outside, would not hear. I suspected she'd been concealing the extent of the pain from them. "You should have told me, my lady."

She shrugged. "It will pass."

I spread my hand gently over the bare skin of her right shoulder blade, letting it rest there a moment. I wished I had Raphael's healing touch, the ability to spread that glorious warmth like balm. Or that I had studied with the famed masseurs of Balm House, who were said to be able to soothe away any ache. I had no gift or skills to offer her.

That's not true, the dragon said. *There is pleasure in your touch, even the simplest.*

The princess tilted her head slightly. "I will not miss having the privacy of my thoughts invaded," she remarked.

It made me feel better. I smiled and slid her sleeping-robe over her shoulders, and did not say what I was thinking, which was that I would miss being privy to them.

She touched my arm. "Thank you. I owe you a great deal, not least for your kindness. Do not think I am not mindful of it."

I inclined my head. "Thank you, my lady. I am grateful to know that I am not entirely an inconvenience to you, albeit a necessary one."

There was a rare note of affection in her voice. "I think you know full well that you are not, Moirin of the Maghuin Dhonn. I suspect it is my honor to consider you a friend."

I fell asleep happy because of it.

I awoke to shouting and torchlight, shadows cast by struggling figures darkening the oiled silk walls of our tent.

"What is it?" Snow Tiger was on her feet in the opened tent-flap before I'd fully awakened, sword in hand. Her blindfolded face turned to and fro, frustrated by her inability to see. "Are we under attack? Who? How many?"

I stumbled past her into the night, rubbing my sleep-filled eyes, and beheld the sight of Tortoise fighting for his life to hold off half a dozen men and youths armed with torches, cudgels, and farm implements. The other tent had collapsed under the attack of at least a dozen more. Bao had planted himself to guard Master Lo, cursing like a demon, his staff a blur. Ten Tigers Dai was fighting like a madman. Their assailants were shouting fiercely in a dialect I didn't understand, but here and there, I heard Snow Tiger's name. "Ah, gods!"

The princess thrust me behind her with one protective sweep of her arm. The dragon keened in rising alarm and anger. *"What?"*

"Farmers!" I caught her arm, holding her back. "Country folk! My lady, don't harm them! I think they've come to rescue you!"

She froze. "No."

"Aye!"

"Stop!" Her voice rose. "Stop, now!"

They were too immersed in fighting to hear. Helpless to stop it, I watched a boy with a sickle clutched in his hand go down under the butt end of Bao's staff.

Lend her your gift, the dragon said softly. *Lend* me *your gift. Make a gateway.* It showed me a picture in its thoughts.

I didn't dare pause to think, to wonder. I called the twilight, but instead of breathing it out, I poured it into Snow Tiger, my hands still clutching her arm, feeling my energies ebb.

She shone.

It was the way I saw her in the twilight with the dragon's silver-bright celestial energy coiling all around her and through her, only it was here on mortal soil in the ordinary darkness of night. Stone and sea! Barefoot and blindfolded, in a sleeping-robe of plain cotton, a naked blade of steel in her hand, she *shone.*

The fighting straggled to a halt.

The fighters gaped.

"My people." She didn't have to raise her voice. "On behalf of the Son of Heaven, I thank you so much for your valor and loyalty. But these men are friends." She gestured. "Do you imagine his Celestial Majesty's daughter so easily captured? We travel in guise. We travel not to surrender to Lord Jiang Quan, but to oppose him." She spread her arms, effortlessly freeing herself from my grip. Silvery brightness coiled around her. "We travel to thwart an army and free a dragon! Will you fight us or aid us?"

To the sound of cheers, I sank to my knees and let the twilight go.

It was enough.

"Stupid girl," Bao muttered, stooping beside me and flinging my arm over his shoulders. He helped me to my feet. "Your doing?"

I leaned against him, grateful for his presence. "Only a little. Master Lo?"

"He's fine."

We watched the farmers kneel and offer fealty to the princess. Tortoise limped over to join us, groaning at the effort. Ten Tigers Dai escorted Master Lo to do the same, unexpectedly solicitous. We stood together in the torchlight, watching the princess accept the farmers' oaths of loyalty with grace and dignity. Even without my gift opening a gateway, something about her shone.

"Well," Master Lo said presently. "It seems we are leading an insurrection against the insurrection."

"Uh-huh." Bao's arm tightened around me. "It does."

SEVENTY-SIX

We couldn't get rid of the farmers.

They wanted to accompany us, wanted to fight on Snow Tiger's behalf. I couldn't fault them for the sentiment, but it was a mixed blessing. With their presence, our progress was slowed and our guise in tatters.

"It is in tatters anyway," Master Lo Feng said to the princess. "Already, word spreads. You set this in motion when you revealed yourself in the marketplace, your highness. If you would have my counsel, I would say, heed the wisdom of the ancients. Yield, and overcome."

"Let us determine which ones have any fighting potential, my lady," Bao said on a more pragmatic note. "We have weapons and mounts to spare. We can outfit a few. The rest will have to fend for themselves and keep up as best they may."

So it was decided.

I didn't expect any of the folk not chosen to ride with us to keep up, but to my amazement, some of them did, at least for a time. They were a lean, impoverished lot, but they had hearts like lions. They trotted alongside us with mattocks and scythes in hand. And when the pace grew too grueling, they faded into the countryside, carrying word of our presence to folk they trusted, country folk like themselves.

More came to replace them.

More men, young men armed with cudgels and farming tools, fire in their eyes. Old grandmothers toting sacks of rice hidden in their stores, giving them freely to feed our unlikely army. Folk of all ages carrying news of the armies' movements.

By day, the princess received them all with grace.

At night, alone in the tent we shared, she allowed herself to express her fears and doubts, pacing restlessly.

"So *many*!" There was a note of despair in her voice. "So young, so poor, so untrained. Merciful gods, Moirin! How am I to protect them all?"

"They don't expect you to, my lady," I said softly. "They expect to protect *you*. Because you are the daughter of the Son of Heaven, and that is the way the world is meant to be." I thought of telling her the story of the great D'Angeline Queen Ysandre, whose folk had helped her quell an insurrection; but I held my tongue. In that tale, the insurgent army had believed their queen dead. Once they got sight of her, they surrendered with scarce a blow struck.

I did not think that would happen here, not unless we succeeded in freeing the dragon. The commonfolk were one thing, but Lord Jiang's men were another. They had the very real, very gruesome death of young lord Jiang Jian to avenge. If they had not been willing to listen to Abbot Hong in all his wisdom, they would not be swayed by a foreign witch's gifts.

And Lord Jiang's army stood between us and White Jade Mountain.

Rumor held that both armies had massed in an uneasy standoff. Lord Jiang's forces surrounded the base of the mountain, with a handful of companies posted in the pastures in the foothills to hold the high ground. There were fewer of them, but many peasants reported seeing them transporting weapons such as we had seen, bronze tubes mounted on ox-drawn carts. The Imperial army had made camp in the fields some distance away, and the Son of Heaven himself was in command.

Neither army, it seemed, was eager to make the first move.

"My father is waiting for me," Snow Tiger murmured. "Even now, doubt plagues him. If we do not arrive soon, his resolve may weaken."

"Why does Lord Jiang hold his hand?" I wondered aloud.

"Because he does not know where I am," she said grimly. "If we succeed in freeing the dragon, it will overturn their plans at a single stroke. Until he is sure of my whereabouts, it is more important to guard the mountain and its passes than to rush into battle. Once he is sure, he and Black Sleeve will not hesitate." Her shoulders tightened. "And that prospect grows more likely with each day that passes."

I tried to console her. "But your father's army stands between Jiang's forces and everything else. In choosing to guard the mountain, they have isolated themselves."

"True." She pressed the heels of her hands against her blindfolded eyes. "But Lord Jiang had other hunting parties searching for us," she reminded me. "And we have not had word of them for days. Even now, I fear that they be carrying news of my whereabouts to him."

"Your father's army would not let them pass, my lady," I assured her with a conviction I didn't feel. "Surely, they will have sentries posted."

The princess sighed. "I pray you are right."

As it transpired, I was.

And that was not a good thing.

If it hadn't been for our impromptu network of spies, we would have ridden straight into the ambush. Of course, if it hadn't been for our ragtag army of peasants and the gossip they spread, there would not have been an ambush in the first place. And as Master Lo had observed, if the princess had not revealed herself in the marketplace of the fishing village, none of this would have been set into motion. But it was also true that if he had not piqued her sense of honor and duty, she would not have done so.

It didn't matter, not really. What mattered was that we learned that there was an ambush awaiting us.

"Three *li*!" The boy who had brought the news was doubled over and gasping for air, hands braced on the threadbare knees of his coarse pants. "Lord Jiang's hunting parties! In the pass!"

Snow Tiger nodded at Bao, bidding him to speak for her. He knew what questions she would ask.

"You are very bold to run so far, so fast, Little Brother," he said with uncommon gentleness. "How many men are there? What weapons do they carry? Can you tell us the lay of the land?"

With an effort, the boy straightened. His dark gaze slid from the blindfolded princess to Bao and back. "Are you her general?" he asked in awe.

Ten Tigers Dai snorted.

"I am what passes for it, yes." Bao scowled at Dai. "So, Little Brother. Speak, and leave out no detail. Tell us what you may."

By the boy's best count, there were at least forty soldiers awaiting us in the low mountain pass ahead, all mounted, all armed with bows and swords. At this point, we had at least fifty men in our motley army, but only ten bows, not including mine, and the princess was the only trained archer among the fighters.

"Is there a way around the pass?" Bao inquired.

The boy shook his head helplessly. "Not one that will not bring you within sight of them, General. They picked their spot well."

The princess steepled her fingers, bowed her head, and touched them to her brow. "We must find a way to distract them. I need to think."

A memory came to me unbidden—the highwayman on the journey to the City of Elua. I had summoned the twilight and shot him in the thigh. "My lady . . ." I swallowed, recalling another memory. My mother's voice, a hare frozen in the twilight, seeing its death. *It is a grave gift and one never to be used lightly.* Surely this was a grave matter. "My lady, I could bring you to fall upon them unseen."

Her blindfolded head lifted. "What you suggest is dishonorable."

"Mayhap, but—"

"No." Her voice was gentle but firm. "Even if it were not, it is too dangerous. Halfway into the spirit world is not far enough to protect you from the arrows of forty desperate men, Moirin, and you are the one person I dare not risk." Her head turned in the direction of distant Snow Jade Mountain. "I fear your gifts will be needed before the end."

A handful of farmers were whispering with the boy. One of them came forward, his expression tentative. "Noble Princess?"

She turned to him. "Yes?"

"There may be a way." He nodded to the nearer mountains. "The boy says Naxi folk live in the hills. They've no loyalty to Lord Jiang; he's tried to outlaw their customs. It might be that a couple of us could get through, looking no threat. Naxi folk hunt with slings. If they were to attack Jiang's men from above . . . is that what you mean by a distraction?"

Her face lit with fierce hope. "Very much so. What is your name?"

He flushed with pleasure. "Chen Cao, Noble Princess."

She nodded. "Chen Cao. I will remember this. Go with the boy, and see if you can find the Naxi and sway them to our cause."

He bowed three times in quick succession. "Yes, Noble Princess! I will not disappoint you, I promise!"

The wait was agonizing. At Snow Tiger's order, we moved our company as close as we dared approach without being detected. She made the mounted men check their arms and gear thoroughly, lest Jiang's men grow weary of waiting and decide to investigate. When it was done, she beckoned to me. We rode some distance from the others.

"I will have to unloose him again," she said softly. "Even with the aid of Naxi slings, we are no match for forty archers. I must get among them at close range, and . . ." She didn't voice the thought. We both knew. "If you summon your magic, for yourself alone, before I lower the blindfold, do you think it might help?"

I felt sick. "Mayhap."

Yes. The dragon's voice was sure. *If she is in the twilight world, she can see me. I will know.*

"Then will you do so the moment I give the order to ride?" the princess asked.

"Of course, my lady."

The sun crawled slowly across the sky. We waited and waited. How many hours, I could not say. I worried about the farmers, simple tools clutched in their hands. I worried about Bao and the stick-fighters, none of them trained to fight in the saddle. I worried about the princess, sure to take the gravest risk on herself. I worried about the dragon, wondering what would become of him if she were slain.

I would end, he said matter-of-factly.

"Oh," I whispered, and worried more.

At last, there came the sound of shouting in the distance. I'd never heard the sound of men surprised by an unexpected attack, but it was unmistakable.

"Now!" the princess cried.

Her mount pricked its ears and surged forward. With fierce cries, the other riders followed her, the unmounted fighters pelting after them on foot. Beside Master Lo, I struggled to breathe the Breath of

Earth's Pulse, fought to find a calm place within myself and summon the twilight.

It came hard.

I felt the unreasoning wave of panic that slammed into the dragon when Snow Tiger lowered her blindfold, the spiraling rage that followed; and I felt him fight it with sinking despair. It gave me strength to find what I needed. I breathed in the twilight, breathed it out, and wrapped it around myself.

The world turned dusky and lovely. I *saw* him, that silvery brightness coiling through the small mounted figure on the road ahead. I felt his fury and madness abate.

You see me.

"I do." With a shock of alarm, I realized that if I didn't follow, I would lose sight of him. I nudged my mount and gave him his head. "Master Lo! I have to go after them!"

Ah, gods . . .

It was a sight I'd rather not have seen. I fought to breathe calmly, fought to maintain my grip on the twilight. The princess raced far ahead of the others, a small lone figure, her lead increasing with every stride. Of course. It was her plan; it had always been her plan. She wanted to protect them. Only Bao came close to keeping pace with her, trailing a distant second. Although he rode well, her slight weight lent her horse greater speed. Tortoise and Dai pounded after them, jouncing in the saddle. And after them came all the rest, on horse and on foot, untrained, passionate, and so terribly, terribly vulnerable.

"Maghuin Dhonn protect them all," I whispered, tears in my eyes.

Lord Jiang's men had had their backs turned, shooting into the foothills at the unlikely assailants raining rocks upon them. Now they turned back.

Bows sang.

Snow Tiger crouched low in the saddle beneath the rain of arrows, her cheek pressed to her mount's neck. In response to her reins, he snaked this way and that, legs reaching and hooves drumming, making a difficult target. Through the dragon, I sensed her mix of exultance and horror.

At twenty paces away, her mount went down with a horrible squeal, struck by several arrows. Pitched from the saddle, the princess rolled in a deliberate fall, coming up with her sword in hand, steel gleaming. Among Jiang's men, she began to fight with grace and brutal precision, dancing her awful dance, robes swirling.

In the twilight, it was beautiful.

Somehow, that made it worse.

I made myself watch, made myself hold tight to the twilight, to the sense of the dragon's presence. His essence sang in her veins, sang through her, filled her with dreadful strength. Where those lovely, shimmering coils that only I could see passed, death followed.

One, two, three, four . . .

And then Bao was there, his mount plunging and wheeling. Despite his lack of training, he fought well from the saddle. Between the two of them, they halved the odds, and halved them again.

Yelling and shouting, the others converged. Hands clutching farm implements rose and fell. Lord Jiang's men fought and died.

It is over.

I rode forward through the twilight, picking my way past corpses. Snow Tiger's naked face turned to me, the dragon reflected in her eyes. Once again, her robes were drenched with gore. Her body quivered with the aftermath of unspeakable energies. She had a cut on one cheek and the blood on her sword gleamed darkly in the gloaming. "Did I—?"

"Yes, my lady." I glanced over the battlefield. Forty men dead, none of them ours. Bao slumped in the saddle, his staff held loosely in his hands. Tortoise and Dai flanked him, looking equally tired. The farmers looked dazed by their victory. I dismounted. "You protected them." With gentle hands, I raised the blindfold she had tugged down. She closed her eyes, obedient to my touch. "You protected them all."

I settled the blindfold in place.

"All?" she repeated. "All?"

"Aye." Before I released the twilight, I found a spot on her brow that was not blood-spattered and pressed my lips to it. "All."

SEVENTY-SEVEN

After the battle, the mood was sober and awed.

Snow Tiger refused Master Lo's attention, bidding him tend to the other injured fighters first. I went to assure myself that Bao was unharmed. Although his staff was scarred and splintered in places, his skin was intact. He summoned a weary grin for me. "I almost kept up with a dragon. Pretty good, huh?"

"A hero in truth," I said honestly. Taking his hand, I raised it to my lips and kissed his bruised knuckles. "You fought a valiant fight."

He glanced over at the princess. She was alone, slowly cleaning the blood from her blade with a clean cloth. A crowd hovered in her vicinity, but none dared approach. "She meant to do it, didn't she? Outpace us all?"

"Aye."

Bao shook his head. "Stupid princess," he murmured. "Risking her life for a bunch of stubborn peasants."

"So says my stubborn peasant-boy," I observed.

"Uh-huh." His expression was somber. "Moirin, as much as I like having you beside me, the peasant-boy thinks the royal concubine should attend her noble mistress. She should not be alone at such a time."

I went to her, listening to the farmers whispering. If there had been any lingering doubts in their minds, they had been erased this day. The Granddaughter of Heaven had done the impossible, and she had done it to protect them.

She looked very lonely.

Her head lifted at my approach, her blood-streaked face brightening a little beneath the blindfold. "Moirin?"

It occurred to me that I was the only person to have felt the touch of her dragon-possessed strength and lived. For that alone, I thought, she was glad of my presence. "Aye, my lady," I said softly. "I am here."

We made camp on the outskirts of the battlefield. The Naxi folk came down from the mountains, slings in hand, shy and deferential—yet proud, too. Snow Tiger received them with her customary grace, thanking them generously for their aid. She promised to see that they would be allowed to keep their traditions. They bowed in awe and retreated back into the hills. It wasn't until they had gone that she let me tend to her, washing away the gore as best I could with a bucket and sponge.

She winced when I cleaned the cut on her cheek.

"I'm sorry," I murmured.

"No, it's just . . ." Her voice was wistful. "Do you suppose it will leave a scar?"

"I don't know, my lady," I said. "I hope not." My heart ached for her. Beneath everything, she was still just a young woman, subject to any girl's foibles and vanity. I busied myself setting a kettle on the brazier to brew willow-bark tea, knowing every fiber of her body would be hurting. "Tell me, these Naxi people. They're shepherd folk, aye? What are these customs that they hold so dear?"

It sufficed to distract her. I listened with half an ear as the princess explained that the Naxi practiced a form of marriage and matrilineal inheritance not accepted elsewhere in Ch'in, reminding me of the quarrels that had nearly torn apart Alba. I got her into clean robes and set the others, stiffening with gore, to soak in a bucket.

Master Lo Feng came to tend to her cut cheek, smearing it with unguent. She did not ask him if it would leave a scar.

When darkness fell, I didn't wait for the night terrors to come. In our shared tent, I laid my blankets close beside hers. I felt her sigh with reluctant pleasure when I put my arm around her in the darkness, the tight-strung bow of her body loosening against me. Without a word spoken, her hand sought mine.

"Sleep," I whispered. "Sleep without dreams, my lady. You have earned it. You protected them all."

She slept.

I did, too.

Somewhere, the bright lady smiled quietly.

Three days later, we came upon an Imperial watch-post.

Our network of country spies alerted us to their presence. Wanting to avoid any misunderstanding, we sent a handful of farmers ahead to notify the Imperial forces of our approach.

I daresay they doubted it anyway, for they waited to receive us in full armor, bows drawn and arrows nocked. Bao reported this to the princess in a low murmur. She listened, then held up one hand.

"I bid all of you to wait here," she said in a clear, carrying voice. "Let me ride forward alone to greet my Noble Father's men."

I held my breath and watched, my fingers itching for my own bow. Beside me, Bao clutched his staff so hard his knuckles were white. Despite my best efforts, Snow Tiger bore little resemblance to the re-splendent figure I had first encountered clad in embroidered robes, adorned with jewels, a crimson sash binding her eyes. Her modest robes were worn and frayed, blotched with faded brown stains I hadn't been able to remove. Her blindfold was a grimy strip of undyed cotton, and her hair was bound in a simple braid. Still, her regal carriage was unmistakable.

At least, I hoped so.

Waiting out of bowshot, none of us could hear what words were exchanged. When I saw the Emperor's men go to their knees, I re-leased the breath I was holding. I heard dozens of others do the same, a sound like a soft wind sighing through a wheat field. Snow Tiger turned in the saddle and beckoned to us. As we approached, the Im-perial soldiers stared at our motley party with disbelief and dismay, appalled to find the daughter of the Son of Heaven in such disrepu-table company.

"Give these people every respect," the princess said, sensing their silent disapproval. "They have served the Celestial Throne with great loyalty and honor."

Rising to the occasion, the captain offered a deep bow. "On behalf of the Imperial army, I offer my gratitude."

All around me, weather-beaten faces glowed.

She will be a great ruler one day, the dragon offered. *If we live.*

I shivered. "I think so, too."

While the princess, Master Lo, and our stick-fighters took counsel with the captain of the watch-guard, I occupied myself with grooming my mount, a long-legged bay gelding who was grateful for the attention. A few of the farmers drifted nearby as though they might offer to perform the chore for me, but no one did. I didn't mind—I was glad to have something to do—but it served to remind me that I too was very much alone in the midst of many.

You have me. The dragon's tone darkened. *And that insolent warrior is very fond of you.*

It made me smile. "Thank you, treasured friend. It is good to remember."

You will always find love on your path. Hers will be a lonelier one.

"I know," I said softly. "I am doing my best to make it less so."

Yes.

After the counsel session ended, we learned that the Imperial army's camp was a mere half day's ride away. It had been decided that we would set out in the late afternoon that we might arrive under cover of darkness. The captain and half his men would escort us, leaving a handful behind to safeguard our passage.

With gentle adamancy, Snow Tiger dismissed the farmers.

They didn't want to go. They knelt and stretched out their arms to her, protesting and pleading, but this time, she would not be swayed.

"No," she said firmly. "You have done me a great service for which I will ever be grateful. Here, it ends. We must travel swiftly and unencumbered. Go. Go home, and pray to the gods for our success."

There was more wailing and pleading, but at last they went, urged none too subtly by Captain Li Shen and his men. I watched the princess' shoulders ease in relief as the country folk departed. They had aided us, aye, but it was one less burden for her to carry.

And soon . . .

Home! the dragon caroled.

I tried not to think about the army that waited between us and White Jade Mountain, and the terrible weapons they wielded. The booming roar of the Divine Thunder echoed in my memory. "Aye," I agreed. "Home."

SEVENTY-EIGHT

An hour into our journey toward the Imperial army, White Jade
Mountain came into view.

It was beautiful, so beautiful.

I would have thought so anyway, but my awareness of the dragon's
yearning made it all the more poignant. The mountain loomed in the
distance, impossibly tall, its snow-capped peak rising high above a
mantle of dark green spruce forest.

"Oh," I whispered, drawing rein involuntarily. "Oh! It's lovely."

Yes.

"Where is the lake, treasured friend?" I asked him. "The reflecting
lake where you hid your pearl?"

Snow Tiger tilted her head in my direction, listening.

High in the mountains. The dragon sounded apologetic. *Very high.*
You will have to climb very far.

I glanced at the princess. "Then we will."

By the time sunset gilded the snowy peak, we could make out a
vast sprawl of tiny figures arrayed on the slopes of the mountain and
around its base. From a distance, they seemed no more consequential
than a colony of ants.

The nearer we drew, the more it changed.

Men, so many men. There were tens of thousands of them. When
dusk fell, we saw the fires they kindled. Cook fires, watch fires. Thousands spilling down the mountainside, circling around its enormous
base. Thousands more on the flat fields where the Emperor's army
awaited us.

Opposite them, bronze tubes mounted on wheels glinted in the fading light, death lurking in their metal gullets. The weapons looked small in the distance, but my skin prickled at the sight and I found myself shivering in the saddle, remembering the devastating power they had unleashed.

"Moirin." Bao pulled alongside me, his expression worried. "Are you all right?"

"Aye," I murmured, unsure if it were true.

Dusk turned to darkness. We lit lanterns and kept riding. The light from all the fires ahead of us illuminated the night sky.

"So many," Snow Tiger said in dismay. "So *many*!"

A few hundred yards from the outskirts of the Imperial camp, we paused to wait while Captain Li and several of his men rode onward to bring the news of the princess' arrival to the Emperor. Our plan was to bring her into the camp without causing a stir that the enemy would notice.

We succeeded, barely.

Captain Li returned to fetch us, accompanied by our old companion General Tsieh and a detachment of Imperial guards. On the greatship, I'd reckoned the general a stoic fellow, but tears shone in his eyes as he gazed on the princess in her stained, threadbare robes. He bowed low in the saddle, hand over fist.

"Noble Highness," he said in a hoarse voice. "It is so very, very good to see you."

"Honored General." She inclined her head. "The pleasure is mine. Had you not undertaken so long and dire a voyage on my behalf, I would not be here before you today. I am grateful for it."

"It was an honor to do so." The general straightened, clearing his throat. "If you would do me a further honor, it would be my privilege to escort you into your father's presence. I assure you, the men have been ordered not to respond to your arrival. His Celestial Majesty is most anxious to see you."

Beneath her blindfold, the princess' face softened. "And I him."

The soldiers of the Imperial army were trained and disciplined. True to their orders, they kept quiet as we entered the camp. No one cheered, no one bowed or knelt. But they stared at her in the firelight as we rode past, and even in the silence, one could *feel* their reaction. A ripple ran through their ranks, as though the pelt of some unimaginably vast animal had shuddered. The soldiers stared at the princess, they stared at all of us. At Master Lo, at Bao and Tortoise and Ten Tigers Dai, their staves strapped across their backs, faces stern. At me, the foreign witch.

And I understood that whatever else happened, we had just ridden into legend.

A shiver ran down my spine.

The Emperor's tent was in the center of the camp, a vast pavilion of yellow silk. Flanked by guards, he stood before it, cutting a splendid and imposing figure in gilded armor. There was a terrible hunger in his gaze as he watched his daughter approach, her hands sure on the reins despite the blindfold.

At ten paces away, Snow Tiger gestured for us to wait. My throat grew tight as she dismounted and approached on foot, then knelt gracefully before her father and pressed her brow to the earth. "Noble Father and Most Celestial Majesty," she whispered. "I humbly beg you to forgive your most disobedient daughter."

"Is it . . ." Emperor Zhu's voice trembled. "Is it true?"

"Yes, Father." She lifted her head. "I am here."

With shaking hands, he helped her to her feet, gazing at her face. "Oh, my child." He touched the sword cut on her cheek with infinite tenderness. "You are forgiven. A thousand, thousand times over, you are forgiven."

I swallowed and blinked away tears.

The Emperor glanced over at us. "And you, my old friend," he said to Master Lo Feng, his voice rough with emotion. "You are forgiven, too. You and your stick-wielding ruffians and your jade-eyed witch. For bringing my daughter safely here, you are forgiven."

Master Lo bowed deeply. "For that, I am profoundly grateful, Celestial Majesty, as are we all. We did not undertake such disobedience lightly. But I fear this is no ending, only a new beginning."

"Yes." Emperor Zhu's hand tightened on his daughter's slender shoulder. He frowned at it, only just now realizing that it was the first time since her wedding night that he had dared to touch her—or that she had allowed herself to be touched by him. "White Jade Mountain will not be easily gained. Jiang's men are guarding the passes."

"Then we have a strategy to plan," Snow Tiger said quietly. "Do we not?"

"Yes." The Emperor gave a brusque nod, removing his hand from her shoulder. "Yes, we do."

Well into the small hours of the night, we laid our plans, poring over maps in the Emperor's luxurious silk pavilion. There were no good options, but there was one bad one.

General Tsieh traced the route for us with a fingertip. "If you circle to the south, the approach to White Jade Mountain is guarded by the Stone Forest," he said. "It is a maze of limestone. Although they will have posted sentries, there is no way Jiang Quan's men can guard it effectively." He gave me a wary glance, months upon his ship having rendered me no less strange to him. "If the foreign witch possesses the gift of concealment you claim, it is your best chance for slipping through unseen."

"Her name is Moirin," the princess remarked. "Moirin mac Fainche of the Maghuin Dhonn. And she is descended from royalty."

He inclined his head. "Lady Moirin, then. My apologies."

I studied the map, eyes bleary for lack of sleep. "I can only do it for a while. Can we get there unseen?"

"No." His voice was heavy. "I fear not."

Details, details. For long hours, they debated details. What route to take, how many men to accompany us. How the Imperial army might give cover to our movements. I was tired enough that my head swam. At some point, Bao positioned himself behind me, angling his shoulder so that I might lean against him, letting myself relax against the strength of his corded muscles and breathing in the familiar hot metal scent of his skin.

The dragon grumbled.

"Be *quiet*," I said, sleepy and irritable. "Am I not deserving of comfort?"

Yes. His voice was small. *I am sorry.*

Everyone stared.

"The dragon speaks to Moirin," Snow Tiger said. "Be very, very grateful that he listens, too."

They didn't understand. How could they? I didn't blame them. It was a strange and peculiar intimacy that bound us together, the princess and the dragon and I. But I was grateful to her for giving voice to it.

In the end, it was decided that a small company had a better chance of gaining the Stone Forest on the southern slopes of White Jade Mountain than a large one. In the morning, the Imperial army would stretch its southern flank to ward our progress, and we would set out behind their ranks to circle the mountain, our escape route guarded by an elite squadron of Imperial archers.

I roused myself. "Would it not be better to travel at night?"

"The terrain is too harsh to travel without the benefit of torches or lanterns, and there are sentries watching our every move," General Tsieh said soberly. "I fear this is a risk we must take at the outset."

"You can see in the dark when you call your magic, can you not?" Snow Tiger asked me. I nodded. She cocked her head. "Perhaps it is best if the two of us go alone under the cover of darkness."

"I do not think that is wise," Master Lo Feng said in a gentle tone. "Moirin's strength is not boundless, nor is her control over her magic perfect. One slip, and you would be exposed and vulnerable in open terrain."

I held my tongue, knowing he was right. My *diadh-anam* flickered in agreement, warning me of my own mortal limitations.

"But in the darkness—" the princess began.

"No." The Emperor raised one hand, silencing her. His voice was adamant. "I will not allow it. There is only so much trust I am willing to place in the magic of one weary foreign sorceress. Noble Daughter, you will go by day with your worthy companions and a squadron of Imperial archers to defend your passage, or you will not go at all."

She bowed her head in acquiescence. "As you bid."

The matter settled, General Tsieh began rolling up his maps. I stifled a yawn, longing for sleep.

"Venerable Master Lo Feng." The princess hesitated. "You have served the Celestial Empire with dignity and honor in a difficult time. Now we have come to a task that requires a warrior's skill, not that of a sage and physician. War is upon us. I would ask you to remain here, where you might do the greatest good."

"I would be grateful for your aid, old friend," the Emperor added softly. "Truly."

Master Lo bowed his head. White stubble on his scalp glinted in the lamplight. There were deep creases in his cheeks that I didn't remember seeing before. "Then I shall abide by your wishes, Celestial Majesty, and pray that my pupils do me honor in my stead."

"We will, Master Lo," Bao assured him, nudging me with his elbow. "We will make you proud, I promise." Tortoise and Dai murmured agreement, echoing Bao, nodding their heads fervently.

I straightened my back. "Aye, Master! I promise, too. We will make you proud."

His dark eyes shone with tears. "Ah, children! You already have."

SEVENTY-NINE

In the light of day, our task seemed even more daunting.

We were given the swiftest horses to ride and a squadron of five hundred elite archers to protect us, men trained to shoot from the saddle at a full gallop. Speed would be essential. Once we were exposed, Lord Jiang's men would try to cut us off. I would summon the twilight to conceal Snow Tiger and myself as long as possible, but I couldn't hide five hundred men, and we needed their protection. As soon as we began to move, Jiang's men would know somewhat was afoot. All we could do was try to outflank them.

All throughout the camp, soldiers donned their gear, checked their quivers, and honed their swords. We waited, nerves strung taut. Soldiers assembled in tidy ranks beneath their banners, awaiting orders. On the far side of the meadow that separated us from the enemy, riders dashed back and forth.

They suspected war was upon them.

Struggling to keep my teeth from chattering with anxiety, I forced myself to breathe through the Five Cycles. It helped, a little. I watched the princess bid her father farewell. I couldn't see her face, but the look on his made my heart break.

"Is it customary for the Emperor himself to ride into battle?" I asked Bao, seeking to distract myself.

"No," he said somberly. "Usually it is a general who leads. But Emperor Zhu has always been a warrior. And I think he looks to prove beyond a doubt that he has not lost the Mandate of Heaven."

And then, all too soon, it was time.

The Son of Heaven in his gilded armor mounted a snow-white charger, looking more splendid than ever. He raised one hand and gave an order. His banner dipped and swayed, conveying it. Other banners took up the order, passing it on. The Imperial army began to move, thinning and spreading its ranks toward the south.

Snow Tiger rode back to us, her face pale beneath the blindfold.

"Now, my lady?" I asked.

She nodded. "Please."

The men had been given their orders. They averted their eyes as I summoned the twilight and wrapped the two of us in it. In the velvety dusk, the scene was surreal. Snow Tiger lowered her blindfold, eyes meeting mine. The dragon's reflection coiled uneasily in her dark pupils.

"Stay with me, treasured friend," I murmured.

Yes. I will try.

There were soft gasps at our disappearance. Bao swung his head in my general direction. "Moirin?"

"I am here," I said to him. "We are both here."

He muttered under his breath, then gave the order to move out.

Accompanied by the five hundred archers who would do their best to guard our avenue of escape, we rode slowly behind the Imperial lines. The ranks were too densely packed to see aught of the enemies' movements, but word trickled through the ranks. Lord Jiang's outnumbered army was not advancing. Instead, they were repositioning their bronze weapons in response to the Imperial army's shift.

Whether that was good or bad, I didn't know.

We reached the outskirts of the army's massed ranks, now spread dangerously thin. What came next would be a desperate sprint across a battlefield toward the river two *li* to the south. If we reached it, our archers would make a stand there.

"Moirin?" Bao asked. "Are we ready?"

I glanced at the princess. She gave a terse nod, then remembered he could hear her if she willed it. "Yes. Give the order, please."

Bao drew a deep breath and loosed it in a shout. "Ride! *Ride!*"

We clapped heels to our mounts' flanks and burst out of concealment, racing across the open meadow.

The Divine Thunder boomed in answer, its deep cough echoing off the peaks of White Jade Mountain.

The Imperial archers were meant to serve as a shield between us and the enemy; but no mortal flesh could stand against the missiles spat out by the Divine Thunder. I saw a man borne down only a few yards away, his horse rendered an obscene carcass of torn flesh. I veered in horror, losing my grasp on the twilight. The gleaming dark carnage before me turned the vivid red of blood.

Again and again, the Divine Thunder boomed.

Everywhere, screaming.

And the dragon was loose.

I felt its madness and fury rise, spiraling to heights that dwarfed aught that had gone before, so terrible it disoriented me. As though the gifts of my ancestors had been restored, I saw a glimpse of a dreadful future unspooling, a future written in metal and smoke and blood, a future in which all the sacred places of the earth had been violated, and there were no longer dragons or bear-witches in the world.

NO!

The dragon's roar made my head spin. I shook it, trying to clear it.

The princess had turned her mount, and ah, gods! She was riding *toward* the battle, toward the terrible weapons, ready to destroy them all, a naked sword in her hand and a captive dragon's blind fury in her eyes.

"You can't!" I heeled my mount and checked her progress. "My lady, you can't! There are too many! And I cannot hold the twilight! *Close your eyes!*"

She hesitated.

Ahead of me, I saw Bao turn back; but Tortoise was closer. He jounced in the saddle as he hurried to aid me, his homely face terrified but determined. A hero after all, no matter how unlikely. And then the Divine Thunder coughed, a hot, acrid wind passed overhead, and Tortoise was no longer there. His remains smoldered in a crater.

"Please, my lady," I said in a choked voice. "Please, please, please listen to me and close your eyes. My friend, please let her hear me!"

Something human surfaced in her gaze. "I cannot ride blind in this chaos."

I held out one arm. "Then I will be your eyes. Ride behind me."

Screwing her eyes shut tight, Snow Tiger grasped my arm. In a single, deft move, she sheathed her blade and swung herself out of the saddle, settling herself astride behind me. I sensed a measure of the dragon's fury abate as she raised her blindfold.

"Flee!" I flung the command like an arrow into my mount's thoughts and gave him his head.

How long did it take us to outrun the range of the Divine Thunder? Two minutes? Three? All I know is that it felt like an eternity. There was a taste like copper in my mouth. My heart was hammering in my chest and my breath came in wheezing gasps. All around us, deadly projectiles fell from the sky. There was nothing that could stand against them, no weapons that could fight them. Smoke drifted across the sky. The ground shook and trembled. Men and horses died. Craters dotted the earth, torn limbs were scattered across it, blood soaked it.

It was more horrifying than anything I could have imagined.

Anything.

At last there was a pause in the booming assault. Daring to peer over my shoulder past the princess, I caught a frenetic glimpse between racing archers. Jiang's army was mustering a squadron to give chase. They were repositioning the fearsome bronze weapons to hold the Imperial army at bay.

"Moirin!" Bao shouted at me, his dark eyes glittering with rage and grief. "We have to gain the river! Don't slow down!"

I nodded my understanding, and didn't look back again. I rode and rode, Snow Tiger's arms wrapped tight around my waist.

Not until we reached the river did I pause. It was a wide, swift river and tricky to ford. Our horses picked their way with care, the water rising belly-deep at times. I stroked my chestnut's lathered neck, whispering praise. The archers remained on the near side, gathering to make their stand. I wondered how many, if any, would survive. It was a sickening feeling.

And on the battlefield, the Divine Thunder was crashing again.

"Noble Highness!" Dai was splashing across the river, leading the princess' mount behind his own. Although his face was rigid with horror, he had kept his wits about him. "Here!"

I drew rein until he came alongside us.

"Dai." There was relief in Snow Tiger's voice. She slipped deftly from the back of my saddle into hers. "Thank you. Is everyone . . . no, of course not. I saw men die." She bowed her head. "How many? Who?"

"Scores of your father's men," I murmured. "And Tortoise."

"Ah, no!"

"Yes," Bao said grimly. "And if we do not make haste, their sacrifices will be in vain."

The princess turned her head in the direction of the battlefield, and although she could not see now, she had seen enough in the twilight to guess at the carnage. The Imperial army would retreat if it could, but not until we were safely away—or confirmed dead. The backs of the Imperial archers formed a living shield between us and Jiang's men. Her hands tightened on the reins. "Then we will ride as though every demon in hell were chasing us," she said in a hard, clear voice. "And put an end to this madness."

Yes, the dragon agreed fiercely. *Yes!*"

I thought of the future I had seen unwinding on the battlefield. Even if we succeeded, I was not sure it could be averted. I understood better the terrible choices my ancestors among the Maghuin Dhonn had made in their efforts to alter the future. If it were within my means to do the same, I would be tempted to try.

But I had no choices here, only a very slender thread of hope.

The princess gave the order.

We rode.

EIGHTY

It was like a familiar nightmare.

Riding and riding in an endless, desperate flight. A valiant horse laboring beneath me. Men left behind to guard our passage, men sure to die. Eventually, the sound of pursuit in the distance.

But these were good horses, excellent horses, the best and swiftest in the Imperial army, and though the chestnut I rode was no more gallant than my Blossom, he was fit and hardy, in the peak of condition. All of them were. They had not shied at the Divine Thunder. Now they carried us willingly at a breakneck pace over the harsh terrain.

Bit by bit, we extended our lead.

When we could no longer see or hear our pursuers, Bao consulted with the princess and called for a slower pace. Our mounts plodded steadily, heads low, breathing hard through blown nostrils.

We could still hear the Divine Thunder booming in the distance. I tried unsuccessfully not to think about the toll it was taking.

It is fire that impels it? the dragon asked. *This killing man-made thunder?*

"Aye," I said wearily.

Then I will end it once I am free. His voice was still fierce. *I will drown their evil weapons in rain. I will call down lightning to strike them dead. Every single one of them.*

"No." Snow Tiger straightened in the saddle. "No, my friend. That you must not do. It is enough to silence their thunder. Lord Jiang and Black Sleeve will pay for this atrocity, but the men they command are innocents misled. If we succeed, we must show them mercy."

Why? The dragon's tone darkened.

"Because it is the correct thing to do," she murmured. "Because they believe they are fighting to avenge the death of a man I killed with my bare hands. And they are not wrong about the reason, only the cause."

I felt him acquiesce without words, and sighed with relief. The princess' blindfolded head turned in my direction, sharing my thoughts.

All throughout the day, we walked and trotted and cantered the horses, pressing as hard as we dared without foundering them. We rounded the base of the mountain range, keeping eyes and ears alert for pursuit, increasing our pace when needed. The distant snow-covered peak that was our destination seemed to rotate with our progress, showing us a different face.

General Tsieh had reckoned we could gain the Stone Forest in a hard day's ride, but by the time the light began to fade, I was beginning to doubt. Bao and Ten Tigers Dai argued in low tones about whether or not to press on in darkness and risk missing the Stone Forest altogether.

"If we had lanterns, we could see in the dark," Dai said bitterly. "Tortoise wanted to bring lanterns."

"If we carried lanterns, we might as well announce our presence to any waiting sentries." There was a raw edge to Bao's voice. "Do you imagine I grieve for Tortoise any less than you? He was the first to swear loyalty to me."

Dai's eyes blazed. "And look where it got him!" The princess flinched at the words. Dai looked mortified.

"Stop, both of you." I knew it was only exhaustion and frayed nerves that made them quarrel. "Think. If I call the twilight, I can see—" I stopped, staring into the distance. "A campfire."

"That won't—" Bao began.

"No." I pointed. A tiny spark of flame lit the dusk. "There's a campfire ahead of us." Inspiration struck me. "My friend, you know this terrain," I said to the dragon, holding an image of our location in my thoughts. "Are we near the Stone Forest?"

Yes, he said promptly. *Very near.*

"That's the entrance to the approach, then," Bao mused. "And those will be Lord Jiang's sentries." He and Dai exchanged a glance.

"Only a few," I reminded him. "General Tsieh said there would be others hidden in the maze."

"Uh-huh." Bao plucked his staff loose from the straps that tied it across his back, whipping it over his shoulder. His teeth shone whitely in the dusk as he flashed his battle-grin, harder and fiercer than usual. "And maybe we can slip past them. But these are the ones guarding the entrance. And Dai and I can approach them unsuspected, seeming to be their fellows. Noble Princess, I beg you to let us deal with them. You and the dragon dare not risk yourselves unnecessarily. Not now, with so much at stake."

"Others will come, drawn by the commotion," Snow Tiger warned him.

"Perhaps," he said simply. "If they do, it will make it easier for you and Moirin and her magic to evade them. We will hold them off for you as long as we can. Perhaps they will never know you were there."

Dai nodded.

"No. No, no, no." Realizing they were speaking of sacrificing themselves, I shivered. "There must be another way. Let me think. If we wait . . . can we afford to wait? If we wait for full darkness, the others waiting on the mountain will be forced to fumble their way blind, or announce their presence with lanterns and torches. I can summon the twilight and lead you past them."

I can guide you if I am allowed to see, the dragon added.

"So be it," the princess murmured.

We waited.

I hated every nerve-racking minute of it. Waiting and waiting, while dusk deepened to velvety darkness. Listening, ears pricked, for sounds of pursuit. Staring at the distant campfire, trying to count the flickering shadows of the figures around it.

No less than four, no more than six.

"Oh, you should have posted more sentries, Lord Jiang-buggering-Quan," Bao crooned, stroking his staff lovingly. "You should have been more clever, Master Lo's no-good, ambitious son. And now you will pay."

"For Tortoise," Dai added.

"For Tortoise," Bao agreed.

Snow Tiger was silent. I knew her well enough to know that the slaughter of innocent, misguided men troubled her. And I knew her well enough to know that she had gauged the necessity of this moment and consented to it; and that knowing it must be done, she would rather take the burden of it on herself. But Bao was right, the stakes were too high. She dared not risk herself unless it was absolutely necessary.

Once the darkness was absolute, Bao jerked his chin at Dai. The two of them rode forward, clad in battered armor borrowed from dead men who had served Lord Jiang. The princess and I trailed behind them at a discreet distance.

Jiang's sentries sprang to their feet at the sound of unexpected hoof-beats in the night, nocking arrows. They relaxed and lowered their weapons as Bao and Dai rode into the circle of their campfire's light and dismounted.

"Hey, brothers!" one called. "Well met. What news from the battlefront?"

"For you, my brother? Death." With casual grace, Bao whipped one end of his staff at the soldier's head. There was a dull thudding crack, like a melon being split open upon rocks. The soldier slumped bone-lessly to the ground.

It went fast.

They were good, Bao and Dai, and they were angry. They fought well and swiftly and hard, taking down all six sentries. I didn't blame them. I, too, grieved for Tortoise, who had always seemed too humble and kind for the lifestyle he had chosen. Homely Tortoise, first to swear loyalty, first to embrace the impossible romance of our quest. In his honor, I made myself watch Bao and Dai avenge his death. Jiang Quan's men got out a few shouts of warning, but not many.

Answering shouts came from the mountainside above them, and scrambling sounds.

The princess leaned over in the saddle and touched my arm. "Now, Moirin. We must go."

"Aye, my lady." I wiped my eyes with my sleeve and nudged my mount hard with my heels. He leapt forward willingly. We rode into the circle of firelight where six men lay dead, and two living ones leaned on their staves, breathing hard.

I dismounted and turned my horse loose, knotting the reins around his muscled neck. "Run free, brave heart," I whispered to him. "Where we go, you cannot carry us."

He whickered softly, chestnut ears pricked.

I slapped his flank. "Go!"

He went; they all went, hoofbeats scattered in the darkness.

"So." I turned my gaze to the mountainside. The entrance to the Stone Forest loomed above us like a gateway, like an immense dolmen. This was a place where water had eaten away all the soft parts of rock. What remained, endured. It was truly an immense maze. Here and there, sparks of torchlight were moving on the steep slopes, briefly glimpsed and swiftly hidden. I breathed deeply and summoned the twilight, folding it like a cloak around the princess and myself. The night took on a silvery sheen. "Lead on, my lady."

Snow Tiger lowered her blindfold that the dragon might look out of her eyes. "This way."

If the waiting had been agonizing, the climb was a thousand times worse. In my eagerness to prevent any unnecessary sacrifices, I'd overlooked the one glaring flaw in my plan, which was that Bao and Dai couldn't see to follow us. When I took Bao's hand to guide him, he shuddered violently and nearly pulled away.

"I'm sorry!" he whispered. "It's like being touched by a ghost."

Although his hand felt warm and solid to me, I remembered how it had felt when the spirit Focalor had touched me, at once tangible and unsubstantial, strange flickers of energy crackling against my skin. I hadn't liked it either, but I saw no choice here. "Well, you'll have to endure it."

Thus did we pass beneath the stone doorway and enter the labyrinth, the invisible leading the blind. I followed Snow Tiger's shimmering figure, coiled all around with the dragon's gleaming life force, leading Bao by the hand. Dai followed hard on his heels, one hand on Bao's shoulder.

Torches descended toward us, bright as falling stars in the twilight. A handful of men gained the base of the mountain and discovered our handiwork. Others wandered lost in the darkness, shouting to one another in confusion.

The dragon led us in a twisting, circuitous route to avoid them. Were it not for his guidance, we would surely have gotten lost ourselves. Time and time again, we paused and huddled on the far side of a great stone obelisk while one of Lord Jiang's soldiers scrambled and huffed past us. Bao and Dai hunkered in the deepest shadows, holding their breath. I forced myself to breathe slowly and deeply, holding the twilight firmly in my grasp.

At least we were outdoors.

It helped; it helped a great deal. Gods knew, I was scared. My nerves were strung as taut as a bowstring. But it was a rational fear based on very real danger, not the unreasoning panic that threatened me when I was trapped in man-made spaces. Living rock surrounded me. Above us, I could sense the drowsing thoughts of spruce trees in the darkness.

And the Stone Forest was beautiful. We wound our way around intricate limestone formations, top-heavy towers, rugged archways. There must have been underground streams, for here and there we crossed natural bridges over pools of clear, placid water that reflected the dragon's pearly coils.

So near, he whispered in longing. *So near!*

Near to a dragon; far to a human. We climbed, huddled, and hid, climbed and climbed. My legs began to ache and tremble with the effort; and I'd gotten precious little sleep for the past two days. My grip on the twilight wavered precariously.

"Moirin." The princess' voice was gentle. "Without your magic, we are all blind. Can you continue?"

She needs my help.

Her dragon-reflecting eyes met mine. I nodded wordlessly, too tired to apologize. But she only smiled faintly, gave her head a rueful shake, slid one hand around the back of my neck, and kissed me with surprising tenderness.

This time I was expecting the unnerving rush of the dragon's energy pouring into me, but even so, it made me gasp. It was so vast and wild, so unspeakably glorious. He poured as much energy as he could spare and all his immense affection into me, and I drank it in deeply, feeling my blood sing and my limbs tingle, my *diadh-anam* blazing within me.

"Moirin," Bao whispered, squeezing my unseen hand. "Is there a reason we have stopped?"

"Ahh . . ." I took a deep breath, trying to contain the sudden surge of exuberance. The princess looked quietly amused. "Aye, there was. But we can continue now."

Knowing it would not last, I did my best to hoard the dragon's energy. It was hard. Once again, the twilight had deepened and brightened, reminding me of the profound beauty of the world on the far side of the stone doorway. Our pace seemed frustratingly slow. I wanted to run, to race through the labyrinth. I wanted to sing; I wanted to fly.

Yes, the dragon agreed. *That is how it is.*

Instead we kept to our careful, crawling pace, navigating the endless maze. I made myself cycle through the Five Styles of Breathing, grateful for Master Lo's teaching. I thought about Snow Tiger, who had lived in this heightened state for days upon days, since first I had shown the dragon his reflection in the mirror and calmed his terror. I felt grief at the slow trickling loss of the dragon's energy ebbing from me, and wondered at the depth of the bereavement the princess would feel when he was gone.

Already, I pitied her.

Stay with her, the dragon said softly. *At least for a while. You are the only one who knows what it was like.*

I glanced at her slender back. "If she wills it. But in the end, I must follow my *diadh-anam.*"

Yes, he agreed. *Still, there is time for grace.*

An hour passed without any sightings of Jiang's soldiers. It seemed we had passed the last of them in the darkness, climbing and hiding endlessly upward in our torturous, circling route as they hurried down the mountainside in pursuit of us. We could still see the starlight sparks of torches moving below us, but they were not eager to ascend in the night. It was far, far too easy to get lost amidst this deadly beauty.

The air grew thinner, and our lungs labored.

Dawn came, changing the quality of the twilight—light made dark, rather than darkness made bright. With it came the end of the Stone Forest, marked by a narrow pass that led to an even steeper ascent, at the top of which White Jade Mountain loomed.

The pass was the last, best place to stage a defense and it should have been guarded, but it wasn't. Our gambit had drawn away its guards, and now they were somewhere below us. In the daylight, they would attempt a return.

"Shangun Bao," the princess addressed him. "It is my thought that this is a good place to make a stand to guard our passage. Is it yours?"

Bao eyed the pass. "Uh-huh. Together, Dai and I could hold it for a long time."

"Forever," Dai agreed, his brows quirking as he spoke to the seemingly empty air. "For as long as you need, Noble Princess."

Her face tilted toward the snow-covered mountain peak. The dragon caroled in happiness. Despite the half-healed sword cut on one cheek, her face looked peaceful and lovely. "Then I will continue alone from here."

"My lady," I protested. "You can't!"

She met my gaze fearlessly in the twilight. "Yes, I can. Once I turn my back to you, I do not think there is anything left between here and there to madden him. Nothing to reflect his absence. At last, I can see with my own eyes. And I can travel more swiftly alone. You have travelled far enough and more, Moirin mac Fainche. You have been a friend to me. Let me be one in turn. Stay, hide yourself, and let our noble companions guard you. Let me make an end to this."

NO! the dragon roared.

My *diadh-anam* flared in agreement.

I winced, letting go of Bao's hand and clutching my head. "You need me," I gasped through the pain. "Or the dragon does. Did you not hear him? I don't know how. And I don't know why. I do not mean to be a burden. I only know I need to go with you. Please, my lady, I am begging you. Do not deny me."

Snow Tiger looked uncertain. "I heard, yes. But the dragon is ever reluctant to be sundered from your presence." She took a deep breath. "You're sure? *All* of you? For it would ease my heart to know you were safe."

Yes, the dragon murmured with sorrow. *I am sure.*

The Maghuin Dhonn Herself paced through my thoughts with ponderous grace and unspeakable presence, looking at me with Her grave, grave, sorrowful eyes. Once again, I felt Her warm breath on my brow. Beyond the stone doorway, oceans glittered, so many oceans. She had claimed me for Her own. She had laid a destiny upon me. And I had not travelled so very, very far to fail Her. I gritted my teeth against the pain and choked out my reply. "Yes, my lady. Very, very sure."

The princess bowed her head, consulting with her own gods. "My necessary inconvenience," she murmured. "If you say it is so, I believe. And dragons do not lie. I have come too far to doubt." She lifted her head. "So be it. Come with me."

Grateful, I went.

EIGHTY-ONE

Before the princess and I set out for White Jade Mountain, I released the twilight and said good-bye to Bao and Ten Tigers Dai, unsure whether or not I would see them again.

Dai was easy.

"There is a thing you should know," I said to him, clearing my throat. It was not my place to say it, but I felt it needed to be said nonetheless. "Bao . . . that is, Shangun, as you call him. He did not refuse to teach you because he thought you were unworthy. He, um . . . he realized that if you paid the price he demanded, he would have become the thing he despised. That is why he fled."

The two men exchanged a glance.

"I know," Dai said gently. "I have known that for some time. Maybe I always knew it."

"Oh." I felt foolish.

"Moirin . . ." Bao wrapped his arms around me. I clung to him, burying my face against his throat, inhaling the hot metal and forge scent of his skin and ignoring the dragon's displeasure. "Just . . . don't die, huh?"

I laughed through tears. "That's all?"

"Yes." He let me go with reluctance, putting his hands on my shoulders, fingertips flexing hard and digging into my flesh as he gazed down at me. "Afterward, we will talk. Because there *will* be an afterward."

He said it with such conviction, I believed him. "Stupid boy." Wiping my eyes, I offered him the same parting words he had given me more than once. "Try not to get yourself killed," I said, adding confession to it. "I do love you, you know."

Bao gave me a crooked smile, his dark eyes gleaming. "I know."

It was so very like him, I couldn't decide whether I wanted to kiss him or throttle him; and it was the only response I could have endured without feeling as though my heart were breaking. So I kissed him once, soft and lingering, then pulled away with an effort. Collecting myself, I turned toward the princess. "Are you ready, my lady?"

"Yes." Blindfolded once more, Snow Tiger bowed to Dai and Bao. "Noble companions, I could not have asked for better or more valiant escorts. May all the gods keep you safe until we meet again."

They bowed in reply, too overcome for words.

With that we took our leave. I glanced back only once to find Bao watching me. He raised one hand in a last farewell, and I lifted mine in answer.

It hurt to leave him.

And the princess was right, she would have travelled more swiftly without me. Although she didn't give voice to her impatience, I could sense it. I forced away my weariness, channeling the last of the dragon's dwindling energy into my tired, aching limbs, trying to set the fastest pace I could. Bao and Dai would shout if there were pursuers approaching. Until then, we had agreed I needn't summon the twilight, hoarding my strength for the climb itself.

The thin air grew thinner. I breathed the Breath of Wind's Sigh, drawing the cold, thin air into the space behind my eyes, imagining myself a creature of the airy mountain heights.

Like me, the dragon offered.

"Yes." I frowned in thought. "Do you know why I must come on this journey, treasured friend? You told me something once. You told me to remember the wise-woman when the time comes. Is that it?"

No. He said nothing more.

I sighed. "Dragons and sages."

"It's no use getting impatient with him," Snow Tiger murmured. "I suspect if the dragon were to say too much, it would upset the balance of nature."

Yes, the dragon agreed. *There are rules. But . . . there is another thing you must remember soon.*

An image flashed through his thoughts, a glimpse as quick and slippery as a salmon's leap, vanishing as quickly in the depths. All I caught was the fleeting impression of a lashing tail and a distant roar.

As if in echo, the Divine Thunder began to boom on the distant battlefield once more. Snow Tiger pressed the heels of her hands against her blindfolded eyes.

"At least it means your father's army is not defeated," I said softly.

"True." She shuddered. "It also means they were not able to retreat. Ah, gods! This battle should not have been fought on open ground. They should have been behind thick walls. And I am the one who chose the battlefield."

"No," I said firmly. "Black Sleeve and Lord Jiang chose the battlefield. When every wall was pounded to rubble and there was nowhere left to hide, it would have come to this in the end. It would never have been otherwise."

"Perhaps." The princess turned her face toward White Jade Mountain. "Let us make haste."

After that, we spoke no more, saving our breath for the climb.

It was not so steep as the climb up the cliffs to the monastery, but it was infinitely longer. Hours passed, and the snow-covered peak seemed to grow no nearer. If Bao and Dai had failed to hold the pass, if there was pursuit coming on the trail behind us, we would have no way of knowing.

Upward and upward, we climbed.

I grew faint and dizzy with exhaustion, gasping for breath. But when Snow Tiger asked quietly once more if she might go ahead without me, my *diadh-anam* flared in alarm, and I shook my head in silent refusal.

She took the lead, feeling her way blind over the rough semblance of a path more swiftly than I could with eyes to see. She clambered effortlessly up steep inclines, reaching a hand back to haul me ungently after her. I accepted her aid gratefully.

Far, far below us and to the north, the Divine Thunder coughed and boomed. And with every thundering crack that split the sky, I knew there was a cost in carnage, more corpses littering the battlefield, torn and rent beyond recognition.

I prayed.

I prayed to the Maghuin Dhonn Herself, I prayed to Naamah and Blessed Elua and Anael the Good Steward, and the thousand-fold gods of Ch'in, the older ones whose names I did not know, and Sakyamuni the Enlightened One, and Guanyin, She Who Hears Our Prayers.

In the oldest, oldest prayer of my people, I prayed to stone and sea and sky, and all that they encompassed.

Moirin.

I was startled at the touch of the dragon's voice in my thoughts, half imagining I'd been addressed by a god. I didn't recall the dragon calling me by name before. "Aye?"

I need to see. I think we are nearly there.

I glanced up at the snow-covered peak looming above us. It was still very, very far away. "But—"

"We seek the reflecting lake, not the mountaintop itself," Snow Tiger reminded me, sounding hopeful for the first time in many days. "No human has ever scaled the heights of White Jade Mountain. Ah, gods!" An edge of dismay crept into her voice. "The *reflecting* lake."

"At the very end, he would have seen his absence and gone mad," I murmured. "That's why I had to come."

She put her hand on my shoulder. "Do you have the strength to summon your magic?"

"I will find it."

I sat cross-legged on the mountainside and breathed the Five Styles. I called upon memories that lent me strength. My enigmatic mother who loved me with all her fierce, taciturn pride. My kin among the Maghuin Dhonn. My gentle D'Angeline priest of a father, who trailed grace in his wake. Others I had loved. My lost Cillian, still my first and best friend. My lady Jehanne, her star-bright eyes sparkling at me with unstinting affection. Master Lo Feng in all his kind, generous wisdom. My peasant-boy Bao, whose infuriating rudeness could no longer hide the vastness of his impossibly romantic heart.

The dragon.

The princess, too.

And stone and sea and sky, and all that they encompassed.

I loved them. I loved them all. I drew strength from it, finding a place within myself where I could spin it into magic. I breathed the twilight deep into my lungs, exhaled it gently around us.

Snow Tiger sighed with relief, and lowered her blindfold. "This way."

Weary beyond weariness, yet strangely exalted, I followed her darting figure through the forest of spruce pines that dotted the mountainside. Now that they were awake, they sang fine songs to themselves, those vibrant spruces. The three long-neglected Camaeline snowdrop bulbs at the bottom of my satchel roused to answer with a thin, feeble chorus.

HERE! the dragon roared. *HOME!*

Ahead of me, I saw the princess check herself violently, recoiling as the spruce forest opened onto a new vista.

I hurried to join her.

We had gained the lake. True to the dragon's vision, it reflected the snow-capped peak of White Jade Mountain in its depths. The water was very pure and clear and still. In the unaltered daylight, it would have been a translucent shade of green. The reflected mountain barely wavered on the surface of the waters, suggesting a placid, enduring eternity. Even in the twilight, it was a beautiful sight, a sight I could have gazed at for a thousand years.

And it lay in a valley far, far below us. There was no path to descend, only a sharp overhang, the sheer drop from which the princess had recoiled.

Snow Tiger glanced at me, the dragon reflected in her eyes. "I will have to jump," she said calmly. "Tell my father—"

I interrupted her. "You can't swim, can you?"

She didn't answer.

"I can." I held out my hand to her, trying to ignore the vertiginous drop before us. "I grew up in a cave alongside a river. I can swim. My lady, I have not come so far to help you die. Are we not friends? If you must jump, then I must jump with you."

She took my hand.

We jumped.

And fell, and fell.

EIGHTY-TWO

H ow long does it take to die?

As long as it took us to fall—or at least, that was what it felt like. I lived and died an entire life in that fall.

Until we hit the water.

The impact and the utter shock of the cold mountain water was so vast, so unimaginable, that for the span of a few heartbeats, I didn't know if I were alive or dead, didn't know if I were broken or whole.

Cold, so cold.

I felt the breath burning in my lungs and opened my eyes. I was underwater in a glimmering green world. The princess was sinking slowly opposite me, trails of bubbles rising from the air trapped in her robes. Her wide, terrified gaze met mine.

I had lost the twilight, and there was no dragon reflected in her pupils.

She opened her mouth, and nothing emerged.

Only in the lake where the snow-capped peak is reflected can she disgorge the pearl. That was what Master Lo Feng had said. But he hadn't said *how,* and none of us had thought to ask. We had been so concerned with the multitude of obstacles that lay in our path, we hadn't thought about what would happen once we reached our destination. If I had thought about it at all, I had supposed that the dragon's essence would simply spill out of her, returning to its natural habitat.

But that was not happening, and the dragon's panic was rising. I grabbed Snow Tiger's robes with both hands and kicked strongly with my legs, intending to propel us to the surface. In the grip of the drag-on's madness, she fought me off.

I hadn't thought about that, either.

If only I could *breathe,* I thought in despair, I could concentrate. But the water was so, so very cold. It was leaching my life and my wits away with every heartbeat. The weight of my sodden robes dragged at me. If I abandoned the princess and made for the surface, I would be abandoning her forever. I caught one of her arms with both hands and tried again.

Again, she struggled wildly, her braid lashing around her head in the water like . . .

Like . . .

An image flashed before my eyes. A black-maned lion with yellow-gold eyes pacing in the innermost circle of an etched star, its tufted tail lashing. A hint the dragon had given me in a fleeting glimpse.

The spirit Marbas, summoned by the Circle of Shalomon.

It had offered me a gift, the gift of shape-changing, the gift the Maghuin Dhonn had lost before I was born. And although I hungered for it, I had refused.

Wise child, it had said. *For that, I give you a gift unasked.*

And then . . . ah, gods! My chest ached and my lungs burned. More than anything, I wanted to breathe. But I remembered, I made myself remember, I remembered that the black-maned lion had opened its fearsome jaws and roared without sound, and some-thing like a bright topaz jewel, as yellow-gold as the lion's eyes, had made a home inside my mind, and I had cried aloud at the strange-ness of it, at being given this unexpected gift that Raphael and his companions so coveted.

The charm to reveal hidden things, the lion Marbas had said to me. *Yours and yours alone. The words will be there if you need them.*

What was the dragon's spirit if not a hidden thing? Hidden first within a pearl, hidden twice within the princess.

The topaz jewel nestled in my thoughts sparked to life, dazzling. I reached for it and found myself speaking unfamiliar words in an un-familiar tongue. A series of round, shimmering bubbles rose from my lips, ascending through the green water as I spent the precious air in my lungs to speak the charm.

The dragon roared in my thoughts, an exultant, triumphant roar wilder and louder than any lion's. The water around us shivered.

Snow Tiger's lips parted helplessly. Her face was transfixed and rapt as translucent brightness spilled out of her mouth—at first a trickle, then a rushing stream. It came and came endlessly, pouring out of her, taking immense shape in the depths of the jade-green water.

Coils, familiar coils, elegant and twining. Legs with pearly claws.

A noble, long-jowled, whiskered face.

I caught a glimpse of my own reflection in one enormous eye; and then the lake erupted around us.

We shot upward like corks. My head broke the surface of the churning water. I took a deep, gasping breath of air. Kicking my legs to keep afloat, I reached out blindly and grabbed a fistful of the princess' robes, hauling her toward me, treading water and turning her face toward the sky.

"Lady, don't fight me!" I gasped.

She made a ragged sound of assent.

The lake erupted again. In the once-placid depths, a wave like a giant hand gathered beneath us, lifting us and carrying us toward the shore. I kicked my legs frantically and kept a tight grip on Snow Tiger, my icy fingers frozen in the folds of her robe, trying not to let either of us drown.

The wave cast us ashore on a rocky ledge. Beginning to shiver violently with the profound effects of the cold, I dragged the princess to safety.

The dragon was not finished.

The dragon was only beginning.

The wave retreated, gathered again. It tossed up a gift, two gifts. My satchel and my bow and quiver, forgotten in the fall.

I retrieved them weakly.

And then there was a stillness, a gathering stillness. Shivering, I breathed the Breath of Embers Glowing, wrapping my arms around the princess to share what little warmth I could conjure with her.

I had a sense of the dragon's essence coiling and coiling unto itself in the depths of the reflecting lake. Forming a ball—an enormous pearl—and descending slowly through the green waters, settling gently onto the lake's floor, coming to rest in the place from which it had been stolen by a younger Master Lo Feng.

HOME, the dragon thundered. *I am here and awake and I am HOME!*

The entire valley shuddered.

The shudder began in the lake, stirring its waters. It rippled up the cliff from which we had leapt. It rippled up the snow-covered flanks of White Jade Mountain, all the way to the peak.

The peak stirred, coming alive.

The dragon raised his immense head from its resting place. His coils unwound from the peak, sun-gilded snow turning to pearlescent scales. Mighty claws were extracted from the snow-covered rock. I stared in awe, too awestruck to feel the cold, to feel the ache of the jarring impact of the fall in my body. In my arms, Snow Tiger had gone utterly still with the same wonder.

"HOME!"

With a deafening, joyous cry, the dragon launched himself into the blue sky, his coils gleaming in the sunlight, casting a vast, moving shadow over the mountain below. And all at once, I was laughing and crying and babbling, because it was the most beautiful, glorious thing I had ever seen.

"Moirin, Moirin!" The princess was shouting at me, tears streaking her face. "Listen!"

I was bewildered. "To what?"

"Nothing!" Her tear-bright eyes shone. "The Divine Thunder! It's gone quiet!"

I gazed at the dragon spiraling overhead. "They can see him from the battlefield."

She laughed. "I imagine they can see him from Shuntian! Come, we've got to find a way out of here." I dragged myself to my feet. Snow Tiger rose, stumbling. She caught herself and swayed, the dragon's loss hitting her for the first time.

I put out one hand to steady her. "Are you all right, my lady? We very nearly drowned, not to mention the fall."

"Yes." She bowed her head a moment. "Just sore and aching, and . . . weak." She held out her hands, gazing at them. "I had forgotten what it was like to feel human. So very vulnerable, so very weak."

"I know," I said softly. "Perhaps . . . perhaps we might rest and wait for rescue. If my satchel is not soaked through, I may be able to kindle a fire."

Do not fear, the dragon said in my thoughts. *I will come for you.* Startled, I glanced skyward. High overhead, the dragon was heading for us like a gleaming arrow.

"You still hear him," Snow Tiger murmured.

"Aye, I do."

She gave a short, broken laugh. "A year ago, I could never have imagined it would hurt so much to be free of him."

"I know," I said again.

And then the dragon in all his glory descended, settling over the landscape as gently as an enormous cloud. The wonder of his presence drove away all sorrow, at least for the moment. His vast, whiskered head dipped to the princess.

"Noble Highness," the dragon said in a low rumble. "Granddaughter of Heaven. I beg your forgiveness for the pain I have caused you. I thank you for the gift of my freedom and your extraordinary valor. There are no words fit to praise your courage. If there were, I would speak them." One massive foreleg shifted forward, rotating to offer a cage of glistening claws. "Please allow me to carry you both to safety."

In silence, Snow Tiger raised one hand to the dragon's face, caressing the pearly scales. His body shifted again, almost imperceptibly, curling around her with great tenderness. She leaned her brow against the hinge of his jaw, letting herself relax against him. His opalescent eyes closed briefly.

What they had truly shared, no one could know.

Not even me.

"Thank you." Her back straightened. "Your generosity is appreciated, Celestial One. I am grateful to accept."

The princess stepped into the cupped palm of the dragon's claw and held out her hand to me. Her eyes met mine—mortal, grave, and dark.

I gathered my things and took her hand, climbing into the dragon's palm. Glistening claws clicked shut around us.

The dragon launched himself skyward.

EIGHTY-THREE

It was like . . .

Ah, stone and sea! It was like nothing anyone else in the annals of history had ever known.

The ground fell away beneath us.

We were airborne.

Snow Tiger and I clung to the thick columns of the dragon's claws, peering out between them.

His energy surged through us. It was not the same as it had been when he was trapped within her. It was more distant and secondary, a mere affect of physical nearness. But it warmed and strengthened me, and drove the shivers from my bones; and I think for her, too.

We soared above the mountain.

"There!" I shouted, pointing. Two figures in a narrow pass clogged with dead men's bodies jumped up and down, waving to us. "It's Bao! Bao and Dai! Can we not rescue them, too? Please?"

Grumbling deep in his chest, the dragon descended.

Bao and Ten Tigers Dai scrambled aboard his outstretched claw, eyes stretched wide with wonder.

The dragon launched himself again.

I eyed Bao, reassuring myself that he was still in one piece. Although his staff was broken into two pieces, Bao appeared to be intact. "Are you all right?"

"Uh-huh." He gazed in awe at the receding ground. "Moirin . . . we are riding in a dragon's hand."

I laughed aloud for the sheer joy of it. "I know!"

Dai stole shy glances at the princess, almost as awed by the sight of her bare face as he was by the dragon.

The journey that had taken us two days on horseback and foot was a matter of minutes' work for the dragon. He glided effortlessly through the sky, and wind streamed through the protective cage of his claw. I should have been frightened, but I was exhilarated instead. I daresay all of us were.

At least until we reached the battlefield.

From such a height, nothing looked real. It looked like a child's game of toy soldiers and horses one might find spread out across the floor of a nursery, littered with broken pieces. But I knew all too well that each of those broken toys had once been a living, breathing being, and that the red smears on them were blood, not paint.

All the fighting had stopped. Men who had been locked in mortal combat only moments ago stood side by side, gazing at the sky and the impossible glory of the celestial creature soaring above them. The bronze tubes gleamed silently in the sunlight.

The dragon roared, the sound echoing off the distant peak. Below us, soldiers dropped to their knees.

I am going to call the rain. He sounded apologetic. *You will get wet again. But they need to know Heaven is displeased.*

"He is calling the rain," I said to the others. "And we are getting wetter."

The clouds gathered first around the peak of White Jade Mountain, water rising from the snow, from the hidden lake. White wisps rose and gathered, thickened to billows, then began to darken, blotting out the sun.

The dragon roared again, calling them.

A long, rolling peal of thunder answered him, growing louder and louder, crashing over the battlefield in a mighty crescendo. I caught a glimpse of men clapping their hands over their ears in pain, it was so loud. There would be no doubt in the minds of any who had fought that day at White Jade Mountain. They had heard a thunder that was truly divine.

And then the storm was upon us, and I saw no more.

It was terrifying, but it was beautiful, too. We were *inside* the dark,

ominous rain-swollen clouds, a thousand times thicker than the dens-
est fog. Here and there, lightning flickered. The clouds unleashed a
torrent of rain, sending it sheeting down onto Lord Jiang's side of the
battlefield, drowning their campfires behind the lines of battle, drowning the bronze weapons and their deadly fire-powder. Rain lashed us,
too, but the dragon held us clutched gently beneath his immense chest,
sheltering us from the worst of it. He swam joyously through the clouds,
twisting and twining, sinuous coils shining like moonlight in the midst
of the maelstrom.

How long it lasted, I couldn't say.

Long enough to satisfy the dragon. His chest swelled above us as
he drew a deep breath, stretched out his neck, and blew through his
nostrils, blowing the clouds away. They dispersed obediently.

The skies cleared and the sun returned.

The dragon flew in a lowering spiral, signaling his intent to land.
Below us there was shouting as men ran to clear a space on the battlefield, retreating to their respective sides, taking the dead and wounded
with them.

A gilded figure rode beneath the Imperial standard, giving orders.
Although he rode a different horse, it was clearly the Emperor. "There,"
Snow Tiger breathed with relief. "My father."

"I will take you to him," the dragon rumbled aloud.

For such a vast creature, the gentleness he was capable of was a mar-
vel. I never would have guessed it when his spirit was trapped within
the princess; but then, mortal flesh was never meant to contain such
force, a force as wild and huge as mountains and thunderstorms.

Gently, gently, he sank to the rain-soaked battlefield, landing on
three clawed legs, the fourth claw upturned, but still closed. His shimmering silver-white head turned once in the direction of Jiang's army,
enormous jaws parting to loose a warning roar. Soldiers scrambled
backward in further retreat, laying down what arms they yet held.

The dragon's head swung toward the Emperor, dipping briefly in
acknowledgment. "Son of Heaven."

Emperor Zhu bowed deeply in the saddle. At close range, his gilded
armor was scratched and dented, splashed with drying blood. There
were deep lines etching his face, and his voice trembled with hope and

fear and exhaustion. "Most Revered and Celestial One, we are honored by your presence."

The dragon's long, elegant jowls curved in a smile. "And I am honored to restore your Noble Daughter."

He unfurled his claw.

Snow Tiger stepped down from his palm. She was soaked and bedraggled, clad in worn, blood-stained robes of dubious quality, a sword cut marring the delicate perfection of her face. But her carriage was proud and upright, and her eyes were open and shining, able to look upon the world without fear for the first time in long, long months, and in that instant she was without a doubt the most regal thing I had ever seen.

The Emperor made a wordless sound, his voice catching in his throat.

I don't know who began the cheer. It seemed to arise spontaneously from a thousand throats at once—ten thousand throats, a hundred thousand.

It went on and on, rolling like thunder. And I realized it was not only the soldiers of the Imperial army who were cheering. Lord Jiang's men were roaring, too, shouting and laughing and crying, glorying in their own defeat.

I glanced at Bao and Dai.

They were battered and weary and rapt, tears making streaks on their dirty faces. I laughed, unable to help it, my own voice breaking. "Hopeless romantics!"

"You're crying, too," Bao observed.

"Aye." I touched my eyelashes, and my fingertips came away wet with tears. I had come so very, very far from home. And for the first time since the Maghuin Dhonn Herself had turned Her face away from me with love and sorrow and regret, for the first time since I had glimpsed the ocean beyond the stone doorway and sensed the long and difficult destiny awaiting me, it seemed to me that despite whatever mistakes I had made along the way, the journey had been worthwhile. "So I am."

EIGHTY-FOUR

In the aftermath of battle, things were less simple.

Thousands of men were dead, thousands more were wounded. We found Master Lo Feng toiling in the physicians' tents behind the Imperial battle lines, bone-weary and haggard. Tired as he was, Bao set himself to aiding Master Lo, transforming himself from a warrior to a physician's apprentice in the blink of an eye, fetching herbs and liniments and decoctions, holding down injured soldiers who needed bones set and wounds sewn.

"Guard her highness," he said tersely to Dai. Dai nodded, needing no instruction. He had appointed himself Snow Tiger's shadow. Where the princess went, Ten Tigers Dai was behind her, staff in hand.

I stayed to help with the wounded. Although I wasn't as skilled an assistant as Bao, and neither of us had a gift for healing, I knew enough of Master Lo's trade to help. It was grueling, gory, horrible work, and if I never saw the like of such destruction of human flesh again, it would be too soon.

From time to time, Master Lo bade me to sit with men too grievously injured to live. I thought at first that they would not like having the foreign witch keep them company in the hour of their death, but I was wrong.

Along with the princess, Bao, and Dai, I had descended from the sky in a dragon's claw.

I had helped stop the war.

And if I had come too late for them, they bore me no grudge. My green eyes and half-D'Angeline features didn't matter. I was a lucky talisman in the midst of horror, a glimpse of hope to take into the courts of the Yama Kings to face judgment in the afterlife. I was a living presence, offering whatever simple comfort I might.

Somewhere in the small hours of the night, I fell asleep holding the hand of a young man whose chest had been crushed by one of the Divine Thunder's projectiles. It was a wonder that he lived at all, drawing shallow, wet, laboring breaths that were terrible to hear. I held his hand and sang Alban cradle songs to him, and woke to find his fingers stiff and cold in mine and Dai shaking my shoulder.

"Her highness sent me to find you," he said. "You need to rest, and I do not think she wishes to be alone."

Too tired to protest, I stumbled after him. Master Lo was still awake, gliding like a spectre through the tents. Bao was propped in a corner and napping, his back against a tent-pole, the two halves of his broken staff across his knees.

Campfires and lanterns dotted the campsite. Everywhere, exhausted men slept. The dragon had departed to the distant peaks of White Jade Mountain. Although he had promised me that he would return, I felt his absence.

A respectable tent had been found for the princess. Dai led me to it, then took up a post outside the opening.

Inside the tent, a handful of sumptuous appointments gleaming, including a copper basin filled with water warm enough to steam. I met Snow Tiger's gaze. She was clean and scrubbed, dressed in clean sleeping-robes of rich, embroidered silk. She should have looked more like the daughter of the Son of Heaven, but she didn't. She looked very young and vulnerable and lost, and it was a loss no one else in the world could understand.

She drew a breath to speak, then shook her head, wordless.

"I know," I said softly. "It's all right. I understand." Keenly aware of how very filthy and tired and sore I was, I undressed and bathed with difficulty. "What news is there of the surrender, my lady?"

"Jiang Quan's generals have all surrendered without condition." She sounded as weary as I felt. "Lord Jiang and Black Sleeve escaped into the mountains. They are still missing, but their own men are hunting them."

I eased my aching body into a clean sleeping-robe. "That's good."

"Yes." Her voice hardened. "Once they are found, *their* fate is sealed."

My eyes felt gritty. I rubbed them, mindful that I had not slept for days. "What of the thousands of men they misled into battle? Surely your father will be merciful."

The princess hesitated. "To most, yes."

"He seeks to make an example of some?"

"No." She shook her head. "Black Sleeve may have perfected the formula for the fire-powder, but he did not create the weapons of the Divine Thunder on his own. He taught the formula to dozens of lesser alchemists. Hundreds, maybe thousands, labored on the design and production of the tubes. Hundreds more were taught to arm and wield them on the battlefield." In the soft, crimson glow of the lanterns, her face looked haunted. "My father is a strong man, strong enough to obey the will of Heaven. He does not seek this knowledge for himself. But there is only one way to keep it from the hands of others, and that is to put every man possessing some piece of it to death."

"Oh," I whispered, my blood running cold.

"Yes." Snow Tiger sighed. "And I can see no argument against it. It is a difficult choice only the Son of Heaven can make."

It seemed to me that there *was* some argument, some way that no one had conceived, but whatever it was, I was too exhausted to think of it.

"Let us sleep, my lady." I blew out the lanterns, one by one, until only dim light from the campfires outside filtered through the tent's walls. "Sleep is a great healer and restorer. Perhaps in the morning, all will be clear."

"Perhaps."

The dragon's absence yawned like a chasm between us. Knowing the princess would never ask, I went to her bed unbidden, settling my arm around her and pulling her into the curve of my body.

"I feel so empty, Moirin," she whispered into the darkness. "Although we have won a great victory, I cannot rejoice. So many dead! And I miss him. Deep inside me, I ache at his loss. I cannot say it to anyone else. But I do."

Already falling asleep, I kissed the nape of her neck. "I know. I miss him, too."

She found my hand and squeezed it. "I know."

Alas, morning did not bring clarity.

Morning brought news of the capture of Lord Jiang Quan and Master Lo Feng's son Lo Yaozu, better known as the alchemist Black Sleeve.

Long before their arrival, our camp buzzed with the news; both camps, in truth, the two having been combined into a sprawling one. And I daresay the soldiers who had fought under Lord Jiang's standard were more bloodthirsty than those who had fought beneath the standard of the Imperial dragon, for they had been lied to and misled, profoundly betrayed, their loyalties twisted and used against them. On the heels of their surrender, Emperor Zhu had been quick to ensure the true story of Lord Jiang and Black Sleeve's treachery was made known, and the news had spread like wildfire throughout the former enemy camp.

After the dragon's appearance yesterday, not a man among them doubted it.

We saw them approaching in the distance, two men on horses, surrounded by several dozen of their former retainers armed with bows and arrows, their dirty faces grinning with triumph.

Emperor Zhu had issued an order that no one was to harm them, and no one did. The crowd of soldiers parted ranks. Not a few of them hissed and spat onto the ground as they passed, but no one raised a hand against Jiang Quan and Black Sleeve.

And we were there to see it. The Emperor and his daughter had given us a place of honor at their side—me, Bao and Dai, and Master Lo Feng.

Him, I worried about.

Stone and sea, it was his *son* who was the architect of this horror. That plump, laughing toddler I had seen in his memories, the joyful babe playing with a shimmering pearl the size of a ball, had been his son. A man, now, bitter and angry.

For many, many years. No one but Master Lo knew how many.

They came, riding slowly.

Far away in the blue skies, the peak of White Jade Mountain erupted in splendor. I felt the dragon coming and smiled to myself. Gods, he was glorious! His glistening coils decorated the sky as he arrowed toward us, growing larger and larger the nearer he drew, a hundred thousand shouting throats heralding his arrival. He descended softly, drifting downward like a gentle avalanche to settle onto the former battlefield, his gleaming claws digging into the earth, his opalescent eyes regarding the proceedings, all-seeing and impassive.

Heaven's emissary had arrived.

Lord Jiang Quan was a broken man. I don't know what else I had expected. Once, he had been a strong and stalwart fellow, a brave, ambitious leader. But he had taken a terrible gamble and lost. He dismounted before the Imperial presence, his head bowed, shoulders slumping.

"Jiang Quan." Emperor Zhu's voice was clear and deadly. "You stand accused of rebelling against the Mandate of Heaven. You stand accused of sacrificing your own eldest son to your ambitions. Do you deny it?"

Lord Jiang shook his head, defeat etched on his broad features. "No."

The dragon rumbled deep in his chest.

"Noble Daughter, do you wish to take this on yourself?" Although a company of Imperial archers stood at the ready, the Emperor turned to the princess, offering her the right of vengeance she had once craved. I was glad when after a moment's hesitation, she refused it with a slight shake of her head. She had enough blood on her hands, and I cared for her, more than I had ever reckoned. The Son of Heaven nodded, raising one hand and lowering it. "So be it. Let us make an end."

Imperial bows rose and sang.

I don't know how many arrows pierced the stalwart figure of Lord Jiang Quan, the enemy I barely knew. A dozen? Two dozen?

Enough. He fell without a sound, his body bristling with arrows.

Black Sleeve was different.

Clad in crimson robes, he sat upright in the saddle. However old he was, he looked no older than fifty or sixty years, a younger version of his father. His long, elegant face was rigid with disdain, dark eyes blazing with fury in it, his gaze locked on his father's. Master Lo returned it without flinching, returned it with grief and compassion. The alchemist made no move to dismount until the Emperor gestured, and several of his guards stepped forward to prod the captive with spears.

"Lo Yaozu, known as Black Sleeve." This time, there was sorrow in Emperor Zhu's voice. "You stand accused of conspiring against the Mandate of Heaven and inciting rebellion. You stand accused of exploiting one of the Celestial Beings to defile the reputation of the Imperial heir. Do you deny it?"

Head held high, Black Sleeve made no reply until the dragon arched its long, shimmering white neck and uttered another menacing rumble. At that, the alchemist paled, though he held his ground. "I make no denial."

"*Why?* The word slipped from Master Lo's lips, filled with anguish. He bowed rapidly three times toward the Emperor. "Forgive me, Celestial Majesty. I cannot help but ask."

The Emperor nodded. "And I would hear Lo Yaozu's answer. Why?" He gestured at Lord Jiang's motionless, bristling body. "Jiang Quan's ambitions, I understand. He sought the Throne of Heaven for himself. What did you seek and why?"

A spasm of emotion crossed Black Sleeve's face, curling his upper lip. His gaze settled on us, one by one.

I shivered at the pain and venom in it.

"Look at them, Honored Father," he said with contempt. "You would not lift a finger to aid your beloved wife, my beloved mother, when she lay dying; and yet you crossed oceans and mountains to aid this abomination of an heir to the Throne of Heaven, this girl masquerading as a warrior."

Snow Tiger's head snapped up, eyes blazing, her sword singing free of its sheath.

Black Sleeve ignored her. "And them." He jerked his chin at Bao and me. "You would not consent to teach your own son. Do you not see what promise I held? I might have saved my mother if you had consented to teach me. Look at the pupils you chose instead. A common peasant—some Tatar's bastard by the look of him—and a sorcerous barbarian, neither with the wits to master the ancient arts." The pain of an old, old wound trembled in his voice. "Are you proud, Father? Are you proud?"

"No," Master Lo Feng said quietly. "I am not proud of the youthful folly that led me to steal a dragon's pearl. I am not proud of the youthful ambition that led me to seek to overturn the order of nature. Most of all, I am not proud of my failure to convey the wisdom of my maturity to my son. For that and what my failure has wrought, I grieve most deeply. Oh, Yaozu! Do you not understand that your mother died as she wished, at peace and in harmony with the world?"

The alchemist turned away, averting his head as though to avoid his father's words.

Master Lo's voice continued, gentle and sad and remorseless. "It is true. And yes, my son, I *am* proud of seeking to aid her Noble Highness, a warrior in truth, violated by your deed. I am proud to play a role in undoing the folly of my youth."

The dragon made an approving sound.

"And I am proud of my pupils, so very proud." Master Lo glanced at us, love and kindness shining through his deep, deep sorrow. "What I have been privileged to teach them, they have learned very well indeed."

"Have they?" Black Sleeve's voice quivered with rage. "Then let us see how well you have taught them, Father."

He turned in a graceful arc and flung out one hand, the sleeve of his crimson robe flaring.

Why is he called Black Sleeve?

In the blink of an eye, a handful of poisoned darts sped toward us. I heard the dragon's helpless roar of fury. Beside me, Snow Tiger was already in motion, her sword angled, avoiding Dai's efforts to protect her; but she no longer possessed the dragon's immortal strength and speed. Skilled as she was, she was no longer the quickest person there.

Bao was.

With a fierce cry, he flung himself between us and the alchemist's darts, whirling like a dervish, one half of his broken staff in each hand. The deadly little darts thudded into the battered bamboo.

All but one.

If Bao's staff hadn't been broken, he might have done it. He was that quick, that deft, and that good. But there was a gap between the broken halves, a gap that he filled with his own body. The dart caught him in the throat, in the sculpted curve beneath his jaw where I liked to press my face and breathe in the scent of his skin. There, the haft of the dart jutted forth. Such a tiny thing.

He took a step toward us, his face apologetic. "Moirin . . ." he said—and crumpled.

With a look of sick determination, Black Sleeve began another graceful turn, the other sleeve of his crimson robe swinging toward us. Half-blind with tears, I reached for my bow, knowing it was already too late.

A streak of silver shot past me, followed by the belated echo of Imperial bowstrings thrumming.

The arrows found their target, but Snow Tiger's sword found it first. She had thrown it with furious and immaculate skill. I knew it by the gilded filigree on the round guard, the golden silk tassel dangling from its hilt.

Black Sleeve sank to his knees, wrapping his hands around the hilt that protruded from his chest. He looked down at it, uncomprehending. He might have been a hundred years old, a hundred and fifty. But in that moment, his face was a wounded boy's.

"Father." He raised his face toward Master Lo Feng, his gaze bewildered. A trickle of blood spilled from one corner of his mouth. "I'm sorry."

My mentor made a choked sound.

His son fell over sideways, eyes fixed and motionless.

I ran for Bao, flinging myself on my knees beside him.

EIGHTY-FIVE

Late, too late.

Black Sleeve's poison was fast-acting.

I plucked the dart from Bao's throat, bent my head, and tried to suck the poison from his skin. I sucked and spat, my lips turning numb and tingling.

"Moirin, no!" a voice behind me said. I ignored it.

Bao's eyelids fluttered. It seemed he couldn't move his limbs. His unfocused gaze met mine, and he tried to smile. "Should have told you—"

Nothing.

The words died on his lips.

My *diadh-anam* faltered in my breast, the spark of it guttering low in despair. Ah, gods! Like a fool, I had always assumed it was Master Lo for whom it had flared—my teacher, my mentor. They had always been together. Even after I had come to desire and care for Bao in all his insolent pride, to love him, I had never realized it had been him all along.

I was an idiot.

"No." I shook my head in denial. I shook Bao where he lay, shook his limp, lifeless shoulders. "No, no, no, no! You stupid boy, you can't be dead!"

His head lolled, lids half-parted.

Dead.

Master Lo Feng sank to his knees beside me. He felt at the pulses in Bao's wrists and throat. Felt, and felt again, seeking any sign of life, and finding none. His grave eyes told me the news I did not want to hear.

"An antidote," I pleaded. "There must be one!"

"No." The word fell like a stone.

I bowed my head. I was vaguely aware of Master Lo rising and walking away from me, his hands folded in his sleeves. Vaguely aware of hands pulling at me. Vaguely aware of other hands batting them away, the princess' voice, high and fierce.

"Let her be!"

I was grateful for it. I laid my head on Bao's still chest, pressing my cheek against his cooling flesh and closing my eyes.

"Moirin." It was Master Lo's voice, deep and commanding. He had returned. I opened my eyes, unsure how much time had passed. "Oh, child!" He sighed. "Today I have seen the son of my heart slain by the son of my blood. Today I realize I have lived too long. If you are willing, there may be a way. Will you share your magic? I have never asked this of you, but today I do. Are you willing to give a part of yourself that my magpie might live?"

"Anything!" I gasped.

He knelt beside Bao's body, his head bowed in silent prayer as he cycled through the Five Styles of Breathing, then rubbed his palms together, conjuring energy. "Then let us attempt this."

I knelt opposite him.

There was power in that place. There was the sacred energy of White Jade Mountain, its pristine reflecting pool and untouched snow, the mountain's peak thrusting toward Heaven, its vibrant mantle of spruce, all present here in the dragon himself.

And there was dark power, too—the blood of thousands of men and horses spilled in unnecessary sacrifice, soaking into the earth.

I breathed it in, all of it. I fed it to the guttering spark of my *diadh-anam*. Master Lo waited patiently, his dark eyes somber. When I was ready, I nodded.

"Whatever happens, know that I spoke the truth," Master Lo murmured. "I am proud of you, my last and unlikeliest pupil."

"Thank you, Master," I whispered.

He laid his hands on Bao's chest. "Now." I put my hands atop his and called the magic, making a gateway of myself.

It came in a rush more powerful than ever before, spilling through me—bright and dark, twined together in a braided torrent, taking a part of me with it. I breathed it out, breathed it into Master Lo Feng. On and on, the rushing torrent poured. Master Lo's hands grew warmer beneath mine, warmer and warmer, almost too hot to touch, but I didn't pull away. I let the magic flow through me, draining me, until spots of glittering darkness danced before my eyes and I began to fade.

The stone doorway beckoned.

And there was a part of my fading self that yearned for it, yearned to pass through it. The dragon's cry echoed in my mind. *Home.* On the far side of death, home and the Maghuin Dhonn Herself awaited me.

Ah, gods! It was a peaceful thought. I was tired, so tired. Tired of blood, death, fighting, jealousy, ambition, and cruelty, tired of being a stranger far from home. And after all, I hadn't failed. I had found my destiny and fulfilled it.

No, the dragon said in my thoughts. *It is not finished.*

Master Lo Feng took a deep breath, a breath so deep it seemed he breathed all the Five Styles at once, his entire body expanding with it. Through failing eyes, I saw him smile his wise, gentle smile one last time.

He released his breath.

My *diadh-anam* flared to life—flared and doubled. I felt it blaze like a beacon inside my chest . . .

. . . and inside Bao.

Bao loosed a shout, his body jerking to life. He scrambled wildly to his feet, clutching his chest and staring at me. "What have you done? *What have you done?*"

"I don't know!" I cried. My vision had cleared, but I was too weak to move. "Master Lo—"

"Master Lo!" Bao crouched beside him. "Ah! No!"

Master Lo Feng's eyes were closed. The hint of a peaceful smile yet curved his lips. But there was no breath in his lungs, no life in his body.

He was gone.

"Take it back!" Bao's eyes were wild and staring-wide, white around the irises. "Moirin, undo it! Take it back!"

"I can't!" I said in agony. "*He* did it! I didn't know, Bao! I didn't know!"

Baring his teeth in fury, he lunged at me, shaking my shoulders. "*Take it back!*"

"I *can't!*"

The dragon roared a deafening warning. Hands pulled Bao away, more hands helped me to my feet, helped me to stand. I wavered, Dai's hand beneath my elbow keeping me upright. Bao glared at me, breathing hard, his chest heaving. He had the two halves of his staff clutched in his hands once more, and he looked ready to fight. Either my vision was not wholly clear or a faint, dark shimmer hung around him. The princess positioned herself between us, keeping a wary eye on Bao.

Emperor Zhu cleared his throat. "Stand down, young hero," he said quietly. He was the ruler of the Celestial Empire of Ch'in, and the Son of Heaven. Bao lowered his gaze a fraction. Everyone else stood gazing in fascination at the unfolding drama. The Emperor stroked his chin, choosing his words with care. "I have known your master since before you were born, and he was old when I was a child. Today I heard Lo Feng Tzu say that he had lived too long, to see the son of his heart slain by the son of his blood."

Bao glanced at him, his brow furrowed in pain.

"He never told you, did he?" The Emperor smiled sadly. "Perhaps sometimes even the wisest among us become too caught up in duty and honor to say the words that matter most. Your master chose his end. I, too, am a doting father. I knew what Lo Feng Tzu intended when he spoke those words. No one else did. Do not blame them. I chose to respect your master's sacrifice. I suggest you do the same."

"It's not . . ." Bao's voice broke. "It's not that easy, Celestial Majesty. You see, I was dead, and—"

"And now you are not."

"No." Bao touched his chest, where half of my *diadh-anam* burned bright as a flame inside him, calling to me. His eyes met mine. "Now I am not."

He bowed three times to the Emperor, bowed three times to his daughter. He bowed to me, low and lingering, and there was a farewell in it.

My heart constricted. "Where are you going?"

"I don't know."

EIGHTY-SIX

It was the glimpse of the stone doorway that made me remember.

I awoke from a deep sleep, gasping. The memory was clear, so clear, even if the jumble of remembered voices that accompanied it wasn't.

You would do well to remember the wise-woman when the time comes.

Mayhap the gift will pass to her one day. After all, it has to pass to someone.

Old Nemed, chewing her lips.

I had a scar on my right hand, a tiny scar on the web of skin between my thumb and forefinger. I didn't remember how I'd gotten it. That was important.

Memories.

After I had passed through the stone doorway, I had begun to see vivid glimpses of others' memories. Raphael's memory of his parents' death. The blood-drenched horror of Snow Tiger's wedding night. Bao's memory of the naked, shivering boy who had grown up to become Ten Tigers Dai. Master Lo's poignant memory of a happy toddler playing with the dragon's pearl.

Those memories had not been offered freely, and I had done nothing more than bear witness to them. But if they *had* been offered for the taking . . .

A profound, wordless sense of understanding blossomed within me. I thought mayhap I knew how Old Nemed wielded her gift.

Across the room, the princess stirred in her berth. "Moirin?" Her voice was drowsy. "What is it?"

I shook myself more fully alert, remembering where I was, and why. We were in a very pleasant home vacated for Imperial usage by the governor of the village nearest the battlefield. It was three days since Bao's death and rebirth, and he had not yet returned. I knew where he was—or at least the direction he'd gone. I could point it out unerringly, anchored by the lodestone of my *diadh-anam*.

He had not gone far.

But that was not important to anyone in the Celestial Empire of Ch'in but me. What *was* important was that on the morrow, every soldier in Lord Jiang Quan's army with any knowledge of the workings of the Divine Thunder was sentenced to be executed.

Unless . . .

I rose from my bed, pacing restlessly. "There may be a way, my lady. A *better* way, a way the people would embrace. If I can do it." I shivered. "I am not sure. I am not sure I have the gift, or the strength and courage to wield it."

Snow Tiger sat upright. "Tell me."

I slipped a silk outer robe over my sleeping clothes. "I need to walk. I need to think, and I can't think indoors."

She rose without comment to accompany me, shaking her head in silent refusal at a sleepy maidservant who came in to see if we needed aught.

Outside, it was quiet and still. I breathed in the night air and the scent of trees, trying to focus my thoughts as we strolled along the garden path that bordered the decorative lake. There was a full moon high overhead, bright enough that both the moon and the distant peak of White Jade Mountain were reflected in the still water. We crossed a bridge that led to a tiny little pavilion in the center of the lake, built just for the purpose of contemplating the moon and the mountain's reflection.

I told Snow Tiger about Old Nemed and what she had done, and what the dragon had said to me.

She was silent for a long moment. "That seems a dangerous gift."

"I know."

"And yet if they were given the chance to offer up their memories freely, to be rewarded instead of punished . . . yes. It would be better, much better." The princess looked at the bright silvery disc of the moon's reflection wavering on the water. "Those who seek to flee and hide would come forward willingly, especially the alchemists and engineers who possess the most dangerous knowledge." She glanced at me. "You truly think you can do this thing?"

"I don't know," I murmured. "I see the possibility of it in a way I never did before."

She turned to face me. "Then let us try."

"Now?" I felt anxious and unready.

"There is very little time, Moirin," she said gently. "We must know if it is possible and can be proved. Tell me what to do."

I rubbed the tiny scar on my hand. "You need to choose a memory, hold it in your thoughts, and offer it to me. And . . . I do not know how to prove it, my lady. If it works, you will have no memory of it, and no way of knowing I speak the truth."

"True." Snow Tiger thought a moment. "I do not believe you would lie, but there should be proof. Let us send for paper and ink. I will write down the memory I have chosen. You cannot read, can you?"

"Not Ch'in characters, no," I admitted, adding, "I can read perfectly well in my own language."

She smiled a little. "I did not mean to offend you. But if you are able to tell me what I have written, a memory I cannot recall recorded in my own hand, I will know beyond doubt that it is true."

We returned to wake the drowsy maid and send her for paper and ink. Snow Tiger sat at the writing table, wetted her brush on the inkstone, and gazed at the blank scroll, hesitating. I had a good idea what she was thinking.

"It can be any memory you choose, my lady," I said softly. "One you would be glad to be rid of."

"It is tempting." Her voice was wistful. "But to deny such memories is to dishonor the dead. I will not do it." She dipped her brush again and wrote on the scroll, characters flowing with strong, graceful lines. "There."

I glanced around the room. "Can we go back outside? It will be easier for me."

"Yes, of course."

Watched by the curious maid, we returned to the edge of the lake. I breathed the Breath of Trees Growing, centering my thoughts. Snow Tiger waited with a calm patience that reminded me of Master Lo, waiting for me to prepare myself. I pushed the thought away, concentrating. "I will need to touch you."

"At least you are warning me this time," she said wryly.

It made me laugh, and eased my tension, which I daresay she intended. I cupped her face in my hands. She raised it trustingly to me, the silver moon reflected in her eyes, a reminder of the dragon's coils. I leaned close, so close our noses almost touched. "Hold the memory in your thoughts, and offer it freely."

She did.

I sensed the memory unfurl in her thoughts, a happy memory of her sword tutor praising her for disarming him for the first time, and the warm glow she felt at the first kind words he had spoken to her.

"Oh, my lady!" I said in dismay. "Why did you choose such a nice memory?"

"So that I would know there was no part of me that willed it gone," she said in a steady tone.

I wanted to shake her for her relentless nobility, to tell her to go back and write down a different memory, some trivial childhood mishap. But it was late, I was ready, and unlikely to convince her anyway.

So instead I called the magic and made myself a gateway. I took the memory she offered, inhaling it into myself in one deep breath. It slithered like an eel through my thoughts; and then I swallowed, and it was gone, gone into the spirit world.

I breathed a cool mist into the place it had been, closed the gateway, and released the princess' face.

She blinked, frowning, and touched her temples. "It felt . . . strange. As though something moved inside my head. Then there was a sense of loss. But you didn't *do* anything."

"No?" I asked. "What is the memory you chose?"

Snow Tiger gave me a blank look, then unrolled the scroll she carried, reading the bold characters to herself by moonlight. "Do you know what is written here?"

I nodded. "Yes, my lady. You wrote of the first time you disarmed your tutor, the first time he praised you. It made you happy and proud."

"You." She took a sharp breath. "You are a bit frightening at times, Moirin of the Maghuin Dhonn."

It didn't comfort me. "I don't mean to be. I'm just . . . me. And it only works if you give your consent," I added. "Old Nemed was very, very clear on that point."

"So you said." Sensing my discomfort, the princess touched my arm gently. "Forgive me. I misspoke. It is your gifts that are unnerving, Moirin. Not you. You, I have come to trust wholly."

"Thank you." It made me feel better.

"You are welcome." She studied the scroll in her hands a second time, then gave herself a shake. "Come. We'll have to wake my father."

EIGHTY-SEVEN

I repeated the demonstration on the Emperor himself.

It was profoundly unnerving. I hadn't expected it, although I should have. This was a matter of the utmost gravity. As much as he respected his daughter, the Son of Heaven would not place his trust in my gift on her word alone.

Like her, he chose a memory and committed it to paper. Generals and counselors watched with somber, doubting eyes. The Emperor was careful not to let me see what he wrote, not trusting in my alleged illiteracy.

I felt very young, very foreign, and very out of place.

"I will need . . ." My voice cracked with nerves. I cleared my throat. "Celestial Majesty, I will need to lay my hands on you."

"Then do so."

Reminding myself that I was a child of the Maghuin Dhonn, a rulerless folk awed by no one, I took his face in my hands and bade him to hold the memory in his thoughts and offer it freely.

I leaned close, close enough to feel his breath against my face.

Like his daughter, the Emperor had chosen a joyous memory, one of climbing the palace wall to steal peaches from a garden in the women's quarters. The happy sense of mischief in it made me smile ruefully. He offered it without hesitation, his gaze steady and unwavering, eyes only inches from mine.

I called the magic, breathed in his memory, and took it away.

I blew mist in the place where it had been.

Emperor Zhu shuddered slightly when I released him. He turned to one of his counselors, reaching out his hand for the scroll, then read what was written on it. His face was expressionless.

"Peaches," I said. "A memory of stealing peaches as a boy."

He tapped the scroll against his palm. "I chose a memory no one else could possibly know. That I remember. Committing it to paper, I remember. And yet . . ." His brows knit in perplexity. "I have no memory of stealing peaches."

I was silent.

"What is the purpose of this gift among your people?" the Emperor asked. "It is a dire weapon."

I took a deep breath. "When we come of age, we are taken to a sacred place, Celestial Majesty. A place with a doorway onto the spirit world. Beyond the doorway, the Maghuin Dhonn Herself accepts or rejects us as Her own."

A muscle in his face twitched. "Your bear-goddess."

"Yes," I said simply. "Those whom She rejects have their memories of it taken. It is done that the place might stay hidden. And they offer it freely because it is a memory too painful to endure."

He tapped the scroll again, deep in thought. "And you believe *this* is what you were sent to do?"

"I don't—" I halted. My *diadh-anam* flared inside me, casting out doubt. Somewhere, Bao felt it, too. I remembered the Maghuin Dhonn's deep, sorrowful gaze on me. "Yes, Celestial Majesty. I do. It is not a weapon. It is a gift intended to protect the sacred places of the earth. And I know it is strange, so very strange, that a foreign deity would send Her child so very far to do this thing, but . . . if you saw Her, you would understand. You would not find it strange after all. All the strength and glory of the oldest places on earth are in Her."

"Like the dragon," Snow Tiger said softly.

I cast a grateful glance at her. "Yes. As different as earth and sky, and as alike as parts of the whole. My people have been stewards of such places and their ancient magic from time out of mind. I believe I was sent to help stem the tide that threatens it. We have used our gifts unwisely in the past. I do not believe I do so now."

"All ways lead to the Way," the Emperor murmured, and my throat tightened to hear Master Lo's familiar words spoken. His gaze sharpened.

"There are over six hundred soldiers awaiting death, and hundreds more alchemists, engineers, and smiths yet to be discovered. Are you capable of a task of such magnitude?"

"I hope so, Celestial Majesty," I said. "I very, very much hope so."

Emperor Zhu gave a decisive nod. "So do I."

Word of the reprieve went out at dawn, followed by a great roar of cheering from the camp. Amazing to me, not a one of the condemned soldiers had protested against their fate, reckoning it just under the Mandate of Heaven against which they had rebelled unwittingly.

But they were grateful to be spared.

Thus, the process began.

It took place in the gardens where I could draw strength from the earth, from the trees, and flowering shrubs, from the lake and the mountain reflected in it, from the open sky overhead. One by one, the soldiers were escorted into the garden.

Many of them were young, scarce more than boys. Operating the weapons of the Divine Thunder was a dangerous job, one given to the rawest of recruits. They were half-dazed at their good fortune, scarce comprehending what was being asked of them, awed by the presence of Snow Tiger, who stayed firmly by my side.

Once they understood, they offered their memories freely.

They were terrible memories, memories of bronze and blood and fire-powder, torches and acrid smoke, ear-splitting thunder, misfires, and blasted limbs. I breathed them in and sent them away, summoning the magic again and again, breathing the cool mist of forgetfulness in place of a thousand terrible memories.

I could not erase *everything*. Some memory of the horror would linger, a poisonous seed that might one day bear fruit again. Thousands of others had witnessed it, too many to eliminate in any manner. But I could take away enough that no one would remember how those deadly weapons functioned, and mayhap the horror that lingered would serve to remind them that such knowledge should never be sought, lest another such dreadful war arise.

Stone and sea, it drained me!

But Master Lo had been right; I was using my gift as it was intended, and I could feel that the strength that went out of me seeped back into the world around me, where I could draw on it again. I was not spilling myself on barren ground.

In between every ten soldiers, I paused to meditate, breathing the Five Styles and restoring myself.

At the end of the first day, I had swallowed the memories of more than a hundred soldiers. I was tired beyond words, too tired to think, and my head was full of blood, war, smoke, and thunder. I ate because the princess insisted on it, then fell into a sleep like death.

For a mercy, I did not dream. I don't think I could have borne it if I had dreamed.

The next day, it began all over again.

I didn't count the number of days it took or the number of men whose memories I breathed in and swallowed. It took as long as it took, one day blurring into the next, one anxious young face after another blurring into an endless stream of humanity. Each soldier to come forward was given a reward, some small sum of money. In the end, I think it was more than seven hundred. In the early days, a few with no direct experience with the weapons put themselves forward, trying to offer memories that didn't exist. I shook my head and sent them way, and word spread that it was no use trying to fool me.

Blood, war, smoke, and thunder.

Over and over, I swallowed it.

If it hadn't been for Snow Tiger, I'm not sure I could have endured it. She never left my side, reminding me to rest when I forgot, badgering me to eat when I didn't want to.

"Like it or not, I have become *your* necessary inconvenience," she said calmly when I protested that I was too tired. "At least for a time."

"Do you still think of me thusly?" I asked wearily.

"No, Moirin. Not for a long while. I told you so before." The princess regarded me. "Do you know what rumor says? It says that you dazzle their wits with your strange, foreign beauty and jade-green eyes, dazzling them until they forget."

"Oh?" Even in the depths of exhaustion, I had to own it cheered me a bit. I was not wholly immune to D'Angeline vanity. "Would that it were so easy."

She smiled. "I know. Now eat."

So it went, day after day, until the endless stream slowed to a trickle, then ran dry. There would be others, countless others, but not from the poor soldiers of Lord Jiang's army.

That was when Bao came.

I felt him drawing nearer, felt the twinned flame of my *diadh-anam* approaching. I always knew in what direction to find him. But my wits were clouded with memories of blood, smoke, and thunder, and I was tired enough that I didn't realize how close he was until he was there in the garden. The Imperial guards escorting him didn't realize he was anything more than one last straggler, having seen so many men in the past days.

My heart leapt.

My *diadh-anam* blazed.

"Moirin." Bao's voice was husky. A faint shimmer of darkness yet clung to him, and he held the broken halves of his staff in one hand.

"Bao." I blinked away tears.

Snow Tiger gave me an inquiring look. I tilted my head, and she understood. We had come to understand one another very well, she and I. Without a word spoke between us, she quietly ordered the dismissal of the guards and attendants in the garden, withdrawing after them to leave us alone.

I sat cross-legged on the grass.

Bao sat opposite me.

"Master Lo—" I began.

"Don't." He held up one hand. "Moirin . . . I know it was his doing, and not yours. I needed time to understand it. But this . . ." He laid his hand over his heart. "I don't know how to live with it. And I have yet to find an answer."

I rubbed my stinging eyes. "What are you saying?"

"I'm not sure myself." He looked away. "Everything I have done in my life, good and bad, I have chosen." His upper lip curled. "Ever since I said yes to Brother Thunder and agreed to be his peach-bottom boy. Even that, I chose, because I wanted so badly to learn. But this I did not choose."

"Neither did I!"

He looked back at me. "I know. Master Lo Feng chose it for us. And if . . . if I had been given the choice, I would have chosen it. Not his death, never that, but you. I would have chosen you."

I couldn't seem to halt my tears. "So why—?"

"What would you have chosen?" Bao asked softly. "Do you even know?"

"No," I admitted, sniffling. "Bao, I don't even know what choice you would have offered me!"

His gaze was steady. "I know you would not wish to stay in Ch'in, even though I think you have come to love it a little bit. It is not your home. Me, I have no home. No mother, no father. If you had wished it, I would have asked Master Lo for his blessing to leave his service and go with you." He smiled sadly. "You may be a sorceress capable of breathing night into day, swallowing men's memories, and coaxing plants to grow, but you are also a girl quick to give her heart away, and sometimes it may be to a noble dragon, but sometimes it is to an ambitious bully eager to use you. I would have protected you, Moirin."

"And I would have said yes!" I cried. "Bao, I *do* love you. I don't know if it's enough to last through eternity, but I wanted to find out! Why does what happened change everything?"

He fidgeted with his broken staff. "I don't know. But it does."

I wiped at my tears. "Are you punishing me for Master Lo's death?"

"No!" he said quickly. "No. And I would never leave you if I didn't believe you would be well cared for. You are an Imperial favorite, Moirin. If you wish for a greatship to carry you home, the Emperor will give it to you."

I felt his half of my *diadh-anam* pulsing inside his breast, calling to mine. "I don't understand."

Bao looked away again. "And I don't know if I can explain. What Master Lo did bound us together. I am yoked to your destiny. And . . . I need to know that I can bear to live without you before I can accept it."

"I don't understand," I repeated helplessly.

"When I was dead . . ." he began, then halted. "When I was dead, I stood before the God of Places. Before he could begin to review my deeds, the Maiden of Gentle Aspect came for me. She held a lantern like a star in one hand, and she was smiling like the sun." He bowed his head. "I have done good things and bad things, but I died a true hero's death. I would have been spared judgment and punishment."

I didn't speak, having no idea in the world what to say.

Bao lifted his head and touched his hand to his chest again. "Now I don't even know what I am, Moirin. There is a flame that burns inside me and yearns for you. I dream of bears. What *am* I?"

"Yourself," I whispered.

He shook his head. "I do not know how to be this self. I need to learn." He gave me a sidelong look. "And I need to find a way to believe, somehow, that you would have chosen me for myself, not because Master Lo Feng's sacrifice bound you to me."

Grief and weariness broke over me like a wave, tinged with anger. "How am I to prove it to you? What is done cannot be undone, Bao."

"I don't know." He rose with lithe grace, the broken halves of his staff in one hand. "Moirin, I'm sorry. I don't want to hurt you. But I have to go away."

"You already went away," I said tiredly, hauling myself upright.

"Farther away and longer." Bao's haunted gaze met mine. "I will know where to find you. No matter where in the world you go, I will always know."

I put out my hand. "Give me your staff." He hesitated, then obeyed. I fit the broken halves together, leaned my brow against the splintered, battered bamboo, and called the magic with the last reserves of my strength, breathing it into the wood and willing it to be whole.

The staff shivered and twisted in my hands, momentarily alive.

Bao's eyes widened.

I handed it back to him, whole. "I *don't* understand, but I do know that there is no arguing with you, my stubborn peasant-boy with the strange, infuriating, and rebellious sense of pride. So take this with my love and my blessing, and when you are ready to make *us* whole, come find me."

"I will try," he said in a hoarse whisper. "Before all the gods, I swear I will try. But I cannot promise it."

I swayed on my feet. For a moment, I thought he would reach out to steady me, that he would cup my face in his hands as I had done to so many men in the past days, that he would kiss me. And my twinned *diadh-anam* shone so brightly, so gloriously, at the prospect, that I knew Bao would never leave if he did.

Bao knew it, too.

With a visible effort, he took a step backward. "I'm sorry," he repeated, offering a ragged, graceless bow. "I have to do this."

I watched him walk away, carrying with him half the divine spark that was my birthright as a child of the Maghuin Dhonn with him. And then I sank to the grass, covered my face with my hands, and wept.

EIGHTY-EIGHT

It was the princess and the dragon who got me through the worst of my grief.

Snow Tiger was gentle and kind and careful with me, but she was firm, too, refusing to let me wallow in sorrow.

And the dragon . . .

He came two days after Bao's departure, the day before we were scheduled to leave for Shuntian. He came in silvery-white glory, arrowing through the skies, descending to settle into the rapidly cleared town square to the eternal delight of the villagers.

I went to him.

"Treasured friend." The dragon's voice was a deep rumble. "I grieve to see you in sorrow."

I smiled at him through tears. "And I rejoice to see you in splendor."

He arched his neck, preening. "Yes." I laughed. The dragon extended one clawed foreleg. "I made you a promise. Will you come with me to the slopes of White Jade Mountain to plant the bulbs you have carried so far? I will watch over them, forever and always, thinking of you." He paused, then lowered his immense voice. "Where is the princess? I would like it if *she* came, too."

"So would I," I agreed.

Ah, gods! It was a poignant, painful, and glorious thing. For the second time in our lives, Snow Tiger and I rode in a dragon's claw. He cast himself like a spear into the skies, corkscrewing through the air, carrying us tenderly. I clutched my worn canvas satchel, trying to hear the snowdrops' song, hoping they were still alive. The princess leaned against the dragon's palm, her face more peaceful than I had seen it in days.

Up and up and up, we soared.

The air was thin in the heights, gaspingly thin, but oh, so pure. The dragon settled gently on peaks where no mortal foot had tread, opening his claw.

I smelled dirt beneath the snow and dug, unearthing soil. "Here?"

His opalescent eyes gleamed. "It is a good place."

The princess and I dug together, making the hole wider and deeper, getting dirt beneath our nails. The dragon watched and rumbled his approval.

I rummaged in the depths of my satchel and found the jar with three snowdrop bulbs nestled within it.

I breathed on them.

They answered. Faint; oh, so faint. But alive.

Tears stung my eyes. I laid the bulbs in the hole we had dug, thinking of Master Lo Feng, who had wanted so badly to bring them to Ch'in. Thinking of Terre d'Ange and my first intoxicating taste of *joie*, of the pageantry of the Longest Night and the beautiful licentiousness of Cereus House, the adepts of the Night Court indulging in every pleasure.

Jehanne, her eyes sparkling with delight . . .

And later, on the ship.

Bao . . .

"Very tonic, Master Lo," I whispered. "Very tonic, indeed." With loving care, I covered the bulbs with soil.

"They will thrive," the dragon assured me. "And perhaps here on these sacred slopes, they will grow even stronger." His long jowls parted in a smile. "Perhaps one day they will play a role in someone else's story."

I wiped my eyes. "I hope it is a beautiful one with a happy ending."

"So do I," Snow Tiger murmured.

And then the dragon carried us back to the village. He flew low over the battlefield where the Imperial armies were preparing to break camp. Everywhere, men turned their faces to the sky, lit with joy for the sheer beauty and majesty of the dragon in flight.

In the village square, we bade farewell to the dragon for the last time. I put my arms around his sinuous neck, pressing my cheek to the smooth, silvery scales.

"Be well, treasured friend," I whispered. "Guard your pearl carefully."

I will. He spoke in my thoughts, pouring all his incomprehensibly vast affection into me. *Do not fear, Moirin. All will be well in time.*

"Thank you," I said, adding, "What does time mean to a dragon?"

The dragon only laughed deep in his chest.

I withdrew to let the princess say her farewell to him in privacy. Whatever was said, their voices were inaudible—a feat I hadn't reckoned the dragon capable of achieving. She stood for a moment in the tender embrace of his coils, then walked away toward where I was waiting with Ten Tigers Dai and an escort of patient guards.

The dragon launched himself in glory, undulating against the blue sky. We stood and watched his gleaming figure dwindle, watched until he had settled himself atop the distant peaks of White Jade Mountain, blending into the snow-covered landscape.

Snow Tiger sighed. I reached out to take her hand, squeezing it. She returned the pressure gratefully. "He is where he belongs."

"Aye," I agreed. "Home."

Home.

It was a lovely word that made my heart ache. I wasn't sure what it meant to me anymore. What was home? The cave in Alba where I had grown up, warmed by my mother's reassuring presence? The City of Elua, where I had found my serene, wonderful father and an unexpected place of honor as the Queen's companion?

I didn't know.

None of it seemed to fit so long as one infuriating peasant-boy was wandering around Ch'in with half my *diadh-anam* inside him. And while I didn't know what time meant to a dragon, I had a feeling it was going to be a very long time before I was able to figure out what home meant to me.

"Try not to think about it." Reading my silence, the princess gave me a quick glance. "We have a long journey to Shuntian, and there will be much for you to do along the way."

"I know." I had agreed to serve as the Imperial swallower-of-memories for as long as was necessary. "It's all right. Bao's travelling in the same direction, more or less."

"Do you know where he's bound?"

I shook my head. "I don't think he knows himself, my lady. Away from me. That's all that matters."

"He'll be back," Ten Tigers Dai said unexpectedly. He flushed under my gaze. "He will, I am sure of it."

I hoped he was right. "We'll see."

On the morrow, we departed. Everything was so very different on this journey, it seemed strange and unreal to me. I had crossed war-torn Ch'in in disguise with a quartet of stick-fighters, a sage, and a dragon-possessed princess. Now I was part of the Imperial entourage travelling in peacetime.

Kang was gone, recovering at the monastery. Tortoise was gone, torn apart by the Divine Thunder. Master Lo was gone, sacrificing himself that his magpie might live. Bao . . . Bao was gone, wandering somewhere ahead of us, his lead growing thanks to our slow progress. The dragon was gone, left behind to happily dream of clouds and rain atop his beloved White Jade Mountain.

That was good, at least.

I reminded myself of it every time I felt alone and lost. Much that was different was good. In the eyes of the world, Snow Tiger had fled Shuntian as a demon-haunted abomination, feared and reviled. Now she was a heroine. The tales stretched before us, tales of how she had fought to protect the commonfolk, slaying an entire company of Lord Jiang's men. Tales of how she had descended from the sky in a dragon's claw and put an end to a war.

The people loved her for it. Everywhere we went, we were cheered, and the princess more than anyone. Time and again, I saw the Emperor's face soften, beaming with a father's pride. No one doubted anymore that he had lost the Mandate of Heaven, and no one questioned his choice of heir.

They did not know how dark the memories she carried were, nor how much she still ached at the dragon's absence. I knew. More than ever, I sympathized with her sense of loss. And all the cheers in the world could not erase the memory of blood-soaked horror. Still, they helped, and I was glad to see it. I was glad to see her unbend her dignity to smile in genuine gladness and gratitude, glad to see the healing sword-cut on her face fade from an angry red to a faint pink as we travelled.

Like her memories, it would never be gone altogether, but it was better. And she was learning to live with it.

Everywhere that there was rumor of Lord Jiang or Black Sleeve's followers laboring on the weapons of the Divine Thunder, we made camp and took quarters. Again and again, the offer went out: In return for offering their memories freely, men would be rewarded with Imperial favor and money.

Once again, I kept no count of the memories I swallowed. We visited smithies and workshops. Most of the time, the alchemists, engineers, and laborers who had built the weapons came forward of their own accord. They brought intricate sketches of the weapons, formulas for fire-powder recorded on paper. Those we burned.

I breathed in their memories and swallowed them. Memories of complicated formulas of sulfur, charcoal, and saltpeter, memories of acrid bronze fumes, memories of complicated spiral grooves.

They did not all come forward willingly. Some were betrayed by folk eager to bask in Heaven's favor. Those were dragged from their hiding places and offered a choice between surrender and execution.

I hated those.

But I did it, I did it all. And all the while, my *diadh-anam* shone steadily inside me, an unerring compass promising that I had not chosen unwisely.

Calling insistently to its other half, too.

I learned to ignore the call as best I could, concentrating on the task at hand, using the lessons Master Lo had taught me. I wondered if Bao was doing the same.

The bulk of the Imperial army dispersed, sent to the various posts from which they had been summoned. With the core that remained, we travelled up the river in ships drawn by teams of oxen, stopping along the way to root out more of Lord Jiang and Black Sleeve's accomplices. Traces of their memories remained inside me, tingeing my thoughts with the taste of smoke and metal.

I wished I could be rid of it.

It sparked an uncomfortable thought in me. When this was over, I would be the last person in the world with detailed knowledge of how the weapons of the Divine Thunder were built and wielded. Gods knew, I would take it to my grave. But I did not know if the Emperor trusted me enough to believe it.

I kept my fear to myself, but it made me uncomfortable and withdrawn, and Snow Tiger noticed it. She didn't press me, but she watched me with such a look of troubled concern that I broke down and confessed my fear to her.

"No, of course not!" The princess' eyes widened with horror. "My father would never do such a thing to you."

"He would have done it to six hundred soldiers," I reminded her.

"Six hundred soldiers who took up arms against the Throne of Heaven. Six hundred soldiers who were not sent by strange gods to the aid of Ch'in." Her expression turned fierce. "Even if the thought crossed his mind, I would not allow it. I will not let anyone harm you, Moirin."

It made me smile, hearing an echo of the dragon's words in her voice. She recognized it and smiled too, a little sadly.

"I suspect *he* would come roaring all the way from White Jade Mountain if anyone in Ch'in raised a hand to you," she said. "So do not think it."

I believed her.

Although it seemed as though our journey and my immense, impossible task would never end, in time it did. We crossed into territory that had never left Imperial control, and there were no more rumors of accomplices. I was content to watch the river unfurl beneath us, the green landscape slide past. Bao was right, I had come to love this country.

I wished he would come back.

But he didn't.

EIGHTY-NINE

We returned to Shuntian in triumph.

There was a week's worth of celebrating, of parades and fêtes and displays of pageantry beyond my imagining. The streets were thronged with revelers. Even in the Celestial City, the mood of orderly decorum gave way to one of joy.

If Bao had been there, I would have loved every minute of it. Even in his absence, I took pleasure in it.

Out of curiosity, I went to the quarters that we had rented with Master Lo, now occupied by a nice young family. The wife told me that Bao had been there some weeks earlier. He had retrieved the snowdrop bulbs that Master Lo had reluctantly left behind to dry.

For some reason, that gave me a pang of hurt and jealousy. I wondered what in the world he meant to do with them.

Nothing, mayhap. Mayhap they were just one last souvenir of his beloved mentor, whom I had helped to die.

When I thought of it that way, I could better understand why Bao needed to be away from me. But it didn't lessen the yearning of my *diadh-anam* inside me.

I knew where he was, of course. I always knew. He was somewhere northwest of Shuntian, no longer on the move. Whatever he was doing, my stubborn peasant-boy had decided to stay put for a while. So I stayed where I was, and waited for him to come to me. Like me, he knew perfectly well where I was.

Apart from Bao's absence, it was a pleasant time. I was an Imperial favorite, the noble heir's attendant, the jade-eyed witch who had become Ch'in's lucky talisman. Emperor Zhu showered me with gifts. I had beautiful robes of embroidered silk to wear, strings of pearls, the finest jade jewelry.

And although I wasn't serving as a royal companion in the D'Angeline way, Snow Tiger liked having me near her. She took it on herself to further civilize me, teaching me the rudiments of Ch'in writing, laughing at my feeble attempts to memorize and replicate even a handful of the myriad characters. I didn't mind. She read poetry aloud to me, tracing the characters with one finger, showing me how the beauty and grace of the brushstrokes enhanced the beauty of the poem's words and images.

Mostly, we understood one another. Having proven his mettle, Ten Tigers Dai had been granted the very special privilege of being allowed to serve as her personal bodyguard and keep his manhood. When the sight of him hovering protectively behind her, staff in hand, made me melancholy, the princess understood.

When any one of the thousand dragon effigies twined around columns or perched atop the tip-tilted rooftop corners caught her eye and made her ache with loss, I understood.

I understood the fear that came at night, too.

It happened less, but it still happened. When it did, it would wake me from even the soundest of sleep, and I would rise from my bed in an adjoining chamber and go to her. Sometimes she would send me away with a slight shake of her head, choosing to battle the blood-soaked memories that haunted her on her own. Other times, I stayed and held her, willing the warmth of my body to keep the memories at bay; and I daresay it comforted me as much as it did her.

I had been in Shuntian for almost a month when I sensed that Bao was on the move once more, the twinned flame of my *diadh-anam* moving away.

It hurt.

"Stupid boy!" I muttered, my eyes stinging. "Where do you think you're going?"

"Perhaps he *is* going somewhere," Snow Tiger said with calm logic. "Could you point out his direction on a map?"

I shrugged, feeling helpless. "Mayhap." She ordered a copy of the most recently wrought map of the Celestial Empire fetched from the archives, and we pored over it together. Once she had it oriented so that I understood where I was in relation to the insistent call of my *diadh-anam*, I pointed. "There. That way."

The princess looked up at me. "He's heading for Tatar country."

"Why . . ." I swallowed. "Oh. His father."

Her brows furrowed. "I thought he was an orphan."

"Not really." I touched the fine-grained paper, remembering words Master Lo had spoken long ago. "Through no fault of his own, Bao is a child of violence."

The princess remembered, too. "Yes. When we acquired the horses, he spoke of his cursed rapist of a father being a Tatar." The delicate furrow etched between her brows deepened. "Why would he seek to find him?"

"I don't know," I murmured. "But it's the first thing I set out to do when the Maghuin Dhonn Herself laid this destiny on me. I didn't know what else to do. Mayhap Bao doesn't, either."

We exchanged a glance.

Snow Tiger sat on her heels, her expression grave and serious. "You *do* have a choice in this matter, Moirin."

Such simple words—and yet they opened a door in my thoughts.

I did not have to wait.

I could follow him.

My *diadh-anam* flared wildly in agreement, making it hard to breathe. I laughed, unexpectedly unfettered and joyful. "I do, don't I?"

"Yes." There was a shadow of sorrow in the princess' smile. "And I will see to it that you are given every assistance."

"No." I shook my head. "No. I think . . . I think that if Bao is ever to believe I chose this on my own, I must do it on my own. I cannot hunt him down with the Imperial army at my back. I must go alone."

She inclined her head. "As you wish."

I frowned. "It is not that I am ungrateful, my lady."

"I know." Snow Tiger lifted her head, meeting my gaze with an effort. "It is only that . . . that before you go, I would ask one thing from you. It has been in my thoughts that this day would come. And . . . I do not know if it is wrong of me to ask it. Because of this matter with Shangun Bao, because you are not sworn to her service as you have told me your father was, but . . ." She steeled herself, her spine straightening, her eyes soft and vulnerable. "You are her child nonetheless. I would ask for the blessing of your D'Angeline goddess of desire."

I stared at her, my lips parted.

If the princess had not blushed, I would not have been certain of what she was asking of me. But she did, a tide of blood rising to kiss her throat with crimson, flushing her cheeks, even the tips of her ears. It was so unexpected, and so utterly, utterly charming, all I could do was stare at her with surprised delight.

"I should not have asked, should I?" She scowled. "Forgive me, I do not know the protocol for such a thing. It is only that . . . I do not think anyone in the world needs her blessing as much as I do. And . . . what the dragon did when first we met, I know he intended well, but it was *not* helpful." Her voice faltered, then continued, resolute and determined. "And yet you understand in part because of it. So I thought, although it is against custom, after all, it is a little late to worry about that, and you are the one person I trust . . . Moirin, would you please say something? Why are you smiling like that?"

There was a fluttering burst in my belly like a thousand doves taking flight at once. I did not have to consult my *diadh-anam*. This was not the business of the Maghuin Dhonn. This was Naamah's business.

The bright lady approved—oh, so very much.

"Yes," I said softly. "The answer to the question you ask is yes, my lady. And I am smiling because it makes me happy."

"Truly?" She smiled in profound relief.

"Truly," I assured her. "Well and truly, I promise you."

The following day, as I made my preparations to travel, it lay between us unspoken. Every time I thought about it, I smiled. Every time I smiled, the princess blushed.

If there had been aught I had desired for the journey, she would have given it to me, but I had to trust my instincts. The matter lay between Bao and me. It would be best if I left quietly, without fanfare. I didn't like being alone, but one can be alone in the midst of strangers. I had grown up in considerable solitude, and I could take care of myself.

And the dragon had promised I would always find love on my path.

So I sorted through the many gifts I had been given, setting aside the gorgeous robes stiff with embroidery and packing a couple of the more sensible garments. Most of the jewelry I kept, hidden in the bottom of my pack next to the crystal vial of Jehanne's perfume and a purse of D'Angeline coins. I kept a belt knife that Snow Tiger had given me, a slender blade with an ivory hilt carved in the shape of a dragon. I had the yew-wood bow that my uncle Mabon had made for me.

I had a horse, a virtual twin of the valiant chestnut that had carried me across the battlefield. The Emperor had made me a gift of him. Now I accepted the gift of a pack-horse and supplies.

There was one last gift of jewelry I accepted, too—a jade medallion strung on a silk cord. It bore the image of the Imperial dragon carved on one side and the Emperor's seal etched into the other. It signified that I was under the protection of the Son of Heaven and to be afforded every courtesy.

"It will not help you on the far side of the Great Wall," Snow Tiger reminded me.

"I know." I hesitated. "Are the Tatars truly so fearsome?"

She frowned in thought. "They are a wild folk. Nomads. But there have been enlightened rulers among them in the past. I don't know how you will find them."

"I come from a fairly wild folk myself, my lady."

"True."

It seemed like there should have been more to do to prepare for such an undertaking, but by the end of the day, I was finished.

There was only one thing left to do, and that was ask for Naamah's blessing.

NINETY

The princess was nervous, so nervous.

After dismissing all her attendants, bidding them not to disturb us until summoned, she quivered with restless uncertainty, watching me light sticks of incense and offer a prayer to Naamah.

"Do you think she will hear so far away?" she asked me.

"I do not think far means anything more to the gods than time means to a dragon." I watched the fragrant smoke coil. "And the dragon himself told me that although the gods do not always answer, they are always listening."

"Oh." She sat stiffly on the bed.

I sat beside her, close, but not touching her. Strange though it might seem, I wished I could talk to my father. I was sure of Naamah's approval, but I wasn't sure how to proceed with this very brave, deeply wounded young woman. For all that I understood it, her anxiousness wasn't making this easy for me. From an awkward beginning of forced intimacy, we had navigated a difficult path to genuine friendship, and I was not certain how to go beyond it without doing harm. "We need not do this if you don't wish, my lady."

"I do wish it." Snow Tiger gave me a fleeting glance. "Only . . . if I change my mind, will you forgive me?"

"Yes, my beautiful girl." It had been one of Jehanne's endearments for me, and it came unbidden to my lips. The princess ducked her head, flushing a bit with pleasure, and I knew it was the right thing to say. She was a motherless child raised as a warrior, and there had been no one in her life to speak sweet words to her save in praise of her skill with a blade. "I will understand, I promise. Are you changing it now?"

She shook her head, darting another shy glance at me. "No."

I lifted her chin gently, brushing a kiss on her unscarred cheek, then on her temple, then on the curve of her jaw. The kiss of drifting petals, the D'Angelines call it; they are all mad for flower imagery, especially in describing acts of love. I let her feel the warmth of my breath against her skin, and kissed the outer corner of her lips.

Something stirred in her gaze. She turned her face toward me, wondering where the next kiss would fall.

But it was not right, not quite.

There was desire in her, but there was tension, too. Fear, too much fear. For her, the memory of pleasure was coupled inextricably with the memory of helplessness and terror. I shifted, tucking my legs beneath me and kneeling. I had offered a prayer to Naamah, but I had not *truly* prayed.

Now I did.

I closed my eyes and thought about how Naamah had offered herself in love and desire. I thought about my father, and how generously he gave of himself. I thought about Naamah's effigy in the temple, and her tranquil, beautiful face.

My ancestress.

And I thought about the first time I had sensed Naamah's presence in my life when I was but a child, the first time Oengus had visited, and my mother had gone with him out into the night. The first time I had felt the sensation like doves fluttering in my belly. I had been frightened and called upon my *diadh-anam*, but it had been the bright lady who answered. I remembered her kind laughter, the sense of terrible beauty, and lips pressed to my brow in a bright, shining kiss.

"Lady, I am yours tonight," I whispered. "Help me."

She answered.

I felt her love and compassion showering down upon me, flowing through me, warming me. I opened my eyes, and took Snow Tiger's hands in mine. I opened my mouth and let the goddess speak through me.

"Tonight I belong to you and to Naamah, my lady." There was a ringing echo behind my words. "And in her name, I swear to you, you have naught to fear from your own desires. Not now, nor ever again."

The mantle of Naamah's grace settled upon us both, as gentle and mighty as a dragon descending from the skies, as warm and golden as sunlight, as tender as a kiss.

I felt the princess' fears melt away before it.

She laughed, a short, wondering sound. Fear was banished, the memory of helplessness was banished.

Her dark eyes sparkled to life, filled with determination.

Freeing her hands from my grasp, she cradled my head and kissed me—kissed me for the first time entirely of her own volition. And ah, gods! It felt wonderful. I wrapped my arms around her waist and tugged her down with me onto the bed, tangling our limbs together. She let out a startled squeak, and I laughed.

"Laughter is acceptable?" Snow Tiger's intent eyes gazed into mine.

I slid one hand along the curve of her spine. "Yes, my beautiful girl. Always. And tonight everything is acceptable."

She smiled. "Good."

When Jehanne had spoken to me of the pleasures of untutored ardor, I hadn't truly understood. How could I? I was too young and inexperienced. Tonight I understood. It was a gift that Snow Tiger offered me, a gift dangling from a fragile thread of trust forged under the unlikeliest of circumstances. I let her do what she wished, reveling in it. I drank in her kisses and caresses, returning them in kind, pleasure rolling over me like a river.

I felt the exact moment when she faltered—not scared, only uncertain of how to express her desire.

Smooth and sure, I took control back from her. I undressed her; I undressed us both, peeling away the bedamned robes that separated us. Like a good attendant, I hung them carefully on the stand.

"Everything?" she asked me.

"Everything," I confirmed, my hands gliding over her breasts. They were shallow, but lovely. I dipped my head to capture one nipple between my lips.

Her back arched.

When at last I moved one hand lower, parting her thighs, Snow Tiger tensed. I listened to Naamah and traced a lazy circle with one fingertip.

"This is called Naamah's Pearl," I whispered, capturing her hand and making her feel it, letting her regain a sense of control through understanding. "Do you see? It is the seat of a woman's pleasure."

"I see!" she gasped.

I kissed a path down her body, feeling her taut belly quiver beneath my lips.

"You're not—"

I spread her thighs gently, teasing her nether-lips apart with the tip of my tongue, circling her pearl. I teased and coaxed her with the utmost delicacy, until she groaned and sank her hands into my hair, surrendering wholly to the sensation, her hips rising toward my mouth. I smiled, and with an inexorable gentleness that was the very opposite of the dragon-lashed storm of that other encounter so very long ago, I brought her to climax, delighting in the feel of her shuddering beneath me.

In the aftermath, she looked sweet and flushed, at once bright-eyed and languid. She kissed me, tasting her juices on my lips, pulled back to consider it, and kissed me again. "It pleases you to do that?"

"Aye, it does."

"Hmm." She stroked my bare skin, cupped one breast. I shivered with pleasure, my nipple hardening, and watched the awareness of her own power to bestow pleasure dawning in the princess' eyes. "Maybe I am more like your licentious D'Angelines than I thought."

She was.

Naamah's blessing had freed her to be tender and ardent and loving, and she was all of these things, more than I ever could have reckoned, so much so that by the end, I wasn't sure which of us the goddess had blessed more. There was an unexpected capacity for playfulness in her that charmed me beyond words. I wondered if she had even known it existed, and prayed I wouldn't be the only person in the world to experience it.

"I will miss you, Moirin," Snow Tiger said afterward. "Very much."

"Ohh . . ." The call of my *diadh-anam* was fainter than it had been since Bao first left. "I could stay awhile longer." It seemed like a very good idea.

"No." She shook her head. "The dragon said there was time for grace. This, tonight, was grace. More would be indulgence."

I opened my mouth to protest.

"And no." She pressed a finger to my lips. "Before you say it, no, I am not punishing myself. I do not think I am undeserving of indulgence. And it is not because it is against custom." She smiled. "I suspect I would even be forgiven it, at least for a time. People would say I am only purging an excess of yang energy left behind by the dragon."

"Why, then?"

Her expression turned grave. "It is too easy to accept the comfort you offer. Too easy to become dependent on it. I have a duty that lies elsewhere. You have a destiny to follow."

I toyed with her hair, heartily sick and tired of my everlasting destiny. "A week is a very short time," I said. "A week could not possibly be reckoned much of an indulgence." Inspiration struck me. "Besides, do you not wish to be certain you are capable of love-making without a goddess in attendance?"

The princess narrowed her eyes at me. "That is a shameless threat wholly without merit, isn't it?"

I laughed. "Aye."

"I love you very much despite it." Her smile returned. "And maybe a little bit because of it. Fine. One week."

The simple declaration took me by surprise. Even Jehanne had not told me she loved me until I asked her, and Bao . . . Bao had *died* with the words unspoken, and gone away without ever saying it. I had not known the words mattered so much to me. My heart expanded in my chest and throat tightened unexpectedly, tears filling my eyes.

Snow Tiger's brows quirked. "What is it? I thought you would be happy."

"I am happy," I assured her. "And I also love you very much, my beautiful girl."

One week.

It fled more swiftly than any week I had ever known, the days filled with poetry and music, the nights with pleasure. And although I did not need to invoke Naamah's blessing again, I felt it hovering over us. It brought me no end of joy to see Snow Tiger give herself fearlessly over to pleasure, sighing my name against my skin over and over. I lavished affection on her, and she accepted it with gladness. She had been right; if the multitude of servants and attendants in the palace suspected anything, they kept it to themselves and did not gossip, glad to see their noble mistress happy and at ease, no matter what the cause. Somewhere in the distance, I thought I sensed the dragon's shimmering approval.

And I thought about how very strange was the path my life had taken that I could find myself loving such very, very different people.

Jehanne and Snow Tiger, as unalike as two women could possibly be. My fickle, vain, impossibly charming Queen, my unlikely rescuer. My relentlessly noble, impossibly valiant princess, to whom I had once been an unwelcome necessary inconvenience.

Cillian, my first lover, my oldest grief.

I thought about Raphael de Mereliot, whom I had thought I loved. The healer with the golden touch. I had been so sure he was my destiny. Even now, my *diadh-anam* yet flickered at the thought of him.

There was a destiny there . . . but I no longer believed it was a good one.

Bao.

For him, my *diadh-anam* blazed. Stubborn, infuriating Bao with his thorny sense of pride.

I missed him.

It never went away, not altogether. The ache of his absence was like a shadow on my soul. But I had chosen this respite, and I was glad of it. Every time the princess smiled at me with unreserved sweetness, I was glad of it. Every time she said my name with a certain lilt in her voice, I was glad of it. And I understood a little better Bao's need to find a way to *choose* a destiny thrust upon him unasked and unwanted, a destiny that had denied him a hero's death and stolen his mentor's life.

One week.

It was tempting to stay longer. I might have if the princess had let me. Winter was approaching fast enough that I could convince myself it would be wiser to stay in the Celestial City, wiser to wait for spring.

That Bao, wherever he was bound, would be forced to stay put. I suggested it hopefully to Snow Tiger.

"No, Moirin," my princess said firmly. "It is time for you to go."

She was right, of course.

I sighed. "You sent me away the first time, too."

"This is different." Our eyes met in a familiar silence, in the void left where the dragon had been. It was still strange to me not to see his silvery coils reflected in her pupils—and for her, too. "This time I am sorry to do it."

So I went.

True to my wishes, I took my leave with no fanfare. I repacked my things, replenished the supplies I would carry. Snow Tiger escorted me quietly to the gates of the Celestial City. Unlike Jehanne, she did not kiss me farewell. This was Ch'in, not Terre d'Ange. Instead, she gave me a small, private smile that was just as good as a kiss, filled with extraordinary tenderness.

Imperial guardsmen opened the gates.

I rode through them, leading my pack-horse.

I glanced behind me once. Slender and upright, my princess watched me ride away, Ten Tigers Dai hovering like a faithful shadow behind her, his staff planted firmly, ready to defend her against anything. He was in love with her, of course. I hadn't told her. She would discover it for herself when she was ready. I hoped he liked poetry.

Mayhap there was a story there.

If so, I hoped it was a beautiful one with a happy ending.

The gates closed behind me.

I consulted the unfailing compass of my *diadh-anam*. I turned my face northwest, took up the reins, and set out to find the errant half of my soul.